THE SERPENT'S CURSE

THE SERPENT'S CURSE

BOOK THREE IN THE LAST MAGICIAN SERIES

BY LISA MAXWELL

MARGARET K. McELDERRY BOOKS

NEW YORK   LONDON   TORONTO   SYDNEY   NEW DELHI

MARGARET K. McELDERRY BOOKS

An imprint of Simon & Schuster Children's Publishing Division

1230 Avenue of the Americas, New York, New York 10020

For information about special discounts for bulk purchases, please contact Simon & Schuster Special Sales at 1-866-506-1949 or business@simonandschuster.com.

The Simon & Schuster Speakers Bureau can bring authors to your live event. For more information or to book an event, contact the Simon & Schuster Speakers Bureau at 1-866-248-3049 or visit our website at www.simonspeakers.com.

Jacket designed by Russell Gordon

Interior designed by Brad Mead and Mike Rosamilia

The text for this book was set in Bembo Std.

Manufactured in the United States of America

First Edition

2 4 6 8 10 9 7 5 3 1

Library of Congress Cataloging-in-Publication Data

Names: Maxwell, Lisa, 1979- author.

Title: The serpent's curse / Lisa Maxwell.

Description: First edition. | New York : Margaret K. McElderry Books, [2021] | Series: The last magician ; 3 | Summary: "Esta and Harte race through time and across the country to steal back the remaining elemental stones needed to bind the book's power, stop the Order, and save the future of the Mageus"—Provided by publisher.

Identifiers: LCCN 2020025262 (print) | LCCN 2020025263 (ebook) | ISBN 9781481494489 (hardcover) | ISBN 9781481494502 (ebook)

Subjects: CYAC: Magic—Fiction. | Time travel—Fiction. | Demoniac possession—Fiction. | Gangs—Fiction. | New York (N.Y.)—History—20th century—Fiction.

Classification: LCC PZ7.M44656 Ser 2021 (print) | LCC PZ7.M44656 (ebook) | DDC [Fic]—dc23

LC record available at https://lccn.loc.gov/2020025262

LC ebook record available at https://lccn.loc.gov/2020025263

For Sarah,
whose fingerprints are on every page.
Thank you for making this story
immeasurably better.

〜

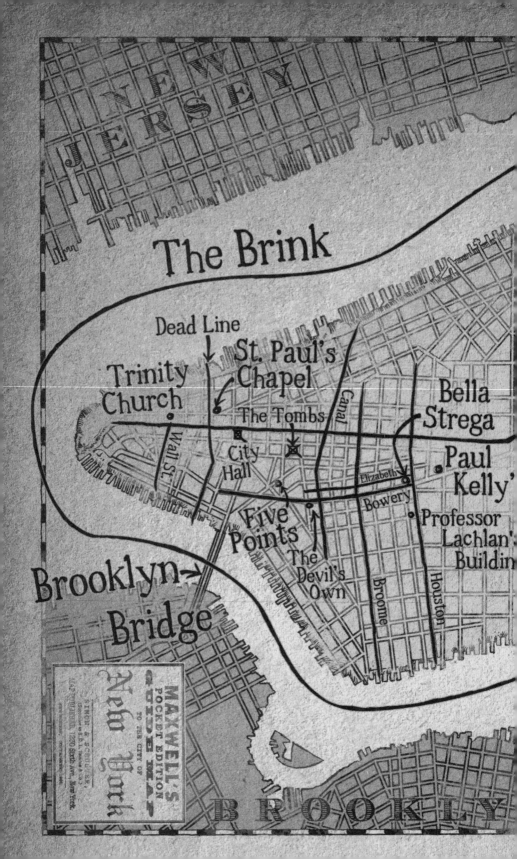

HUDSON RIVER

Wallack's
Theatre

ymarket

Broadway

CENTRAL
PARK

←Satan's
Circus

J. P. Morgan
Mansion

Khafre
Hall

Park

on
ing

Third

3 4th

42nd

59

74th

BLACKWELL'S ISLAND

EAST RIVER

QUEENS

MAINE

WISCONSIN

MICHIGAN

NEW YORK

Chicago

PENNSYLVANIA

OHIO

NEW YORK CITY

NEW JERSEY

INDIANA

ILLINOIS

WEST VIRGINIA

Atlantic Ocean

St. Louis

VIRGINIA

KENTUCKY

OURI

NORTH CAROLINA

TENNESSEE

NSAS

SOUTH CAROLINA

MISSISSIPPI

ALABAMA

GEORGIA

na

LOUISIANA

FLORIDA

Gulf of Mexico

BROWN'S

RAILROAD

MAP OF THE

UNITED STATES

1904

Compiled from Latest Official Sources, showing carefully
selected list of Cities in readable type for quick reference.

PUBLISHED BY SIMON & SCHUSTER

THE SERPENT

1902—New York

The Serpent waited, concealed in the shadows of the city. His attention was focused on the bunching and shifting of the Aether around him . . . and on the estate just across Fifth Avenue from where he stood. The mansion, like its neighbors, glowed with electric light, an island of impossible luxury in the midst of a city that teemed with poverty and violence. But it was no safe haven, not even for the powerful men inside.

Despite all that had happened, the leaders of the Order still believed themselves to be inviolable. It did not matter that Khafre Hall was now a pile of ashes or that their artifacts and the Book of Mysteries had been taken from them. The Order of Ortus Aurea had continued on as though their greatest humiliation and defeat had been nothing more than a temporary embarrassment.

Let them parade around in their silken finery, the Serpent thought. Let them put on their airs and believe in the illusion of their superiority. No amount of wealth would protect them from what was coming—a new world, where those with the old magic would no longer be held back and beaten down. A world where *true* magic would be the key to power and where *he* would wield more than anyone.

As the Serpent waited, the Aether shifted around him again. Invisible to most, the Aether was the very quintessence of existence. To the Serpent, the world had a pulse. Soon his plans would begin to coalesce, and then *he* would be the one to make it race. To make it dance like a puppet on a string.

1

Certain as his victory seemed, though, the Serpent tempered his anticipation. After all, nearly two years before, he'd stood in that very place, expecting a victory that had never arrived.

The Aether lurched like an electric charge had sped through it, and the Serpent knew that the game was changing. If all went well, soon the cane he leaned against would be more than a crutch. Soon he would have the ring, and the cane would become a true weapon, just as it had once been for another. Once the power contained within the gorgon's head was fully unlocked, those who wore the mark would be his to command, and with them under his control, he would begin to rebuild the world anew.

By the time the door to the mansion opened to release a flood of people, the vibrations of the Aether had been whipped into a frenzy, and with it, the Serpent's certainty grew. Dressed in silks and satins and the dark wool of fine tuxedos and top hats, the rich poured screaming from the mansion like rats from a sinking ship.

The Serpent wasn't surprised. Humans were basically animals, stupid and instinctual. Easily led with the right incentives. No amount of money changed that. Let them scurry and flee—it would do them no good in the end. He had already made his plans, had already positioned his pieces on the board, and now he had only to wait. Soon one of the Order's artifacts would belong to him, and with it, *true* control over the Devil's Own . . . and then so much more.

THE GIRL WITH THE KNIFE

1902—New York

J. P. Morgan's ballroom was a riot of noise and violence. Viola Vaccarelli watched as the people around her erupted into panic. Jack Grew had tried to set a trap for her brother, but the moment Jack had given the word for the police to arrest him, Paolo's Five Pointers had revealed themselves and started to attack. As gunfire erupted in the ballroom, the members of the Order, along with their wives and rich friends, seemed suddenly to realize that their gala had turned deadly and that no amount of money would stop their blood from spilling. Tuxedoed men and silk-clad women toppled chairs and one another as they fled, but Viola cared for none of it. All she could see was the blood on her blade.

Jianyu's blood.

She had not been aiming for him. There had been a girl—one of Morgan's maids—with skin dark as any of the Turkish peddlers her father used to complain about back in the old country. The girl had been going for the ring. Viola had been sure of it.

Viola had not stopped to consider who the girl might be or whether she even understood the artifact's true value. She had simply pulled Libitina from its hidden sheath in a practiced fluid motion, as she'd done a hundred times before. Drawing back her arm, Viola had sent the knife flying. Then, out of nothing and nowhere, Jianyu had appeared, directly in the path between the girl and the blade.

She had named the knife for the goddess of funerals because it never missed. Because her blade always struck deadly and true. The ballroom had continued to roar around her, but Viola's eyes were fixed on Jianyu's shoulder, where Libitina was sheathed to the hilt in the flesh and muscle and bone of a man she had once considered a friend.

The brown-skinned girl had gone ashen with the sight, but Jianyu had paid her no attention. His eyes had been steady on Viola, despite the pain that had shadowed them. His mouth had formed careful words, but Viola heard only the roar of the room, the blood pounding behind her eyes, and her own shallow breathing.

Still, Jianyu's gaze had never wavered. His expression had creased with determination as he'd pulled Libitina from his shoulder. Blood had soaked the material of his tunic in response, and his hand had trembled as he held the dagger out to Viola. An offering. A truce. But all Viola could see was the blade, still sticky with his blood. It was a lurid stain on the shining metal and another dark mark on her soul.

Viola knew too well the weight of a soul. As Dolph Saunders' assassin, she'd taken so many lives. She'd accepted those black marks, one after another, in the hope that one day others like her would not have to struggle as she had. She'd made peace with her own certain damnation—had only hoped that it might have meaning. Now, staring at Jianyu's blood, Viola understood that she'd been a fool to ever hope for redemption.

Shame and guilt wrapped around her like a noose, but before her ears could clear, before she could understand Jianyu's words, his legs wobbled beneath him, and a man with skin as dark brown as the girl's scooped him up. Jianyu, who had always held himself with a determined strength, who had always seemed somehow apart from the rest of Dolph's gang, did not fight this man, and Viola understood immediately that they were friends—Jianyu, the girl, and this man. She realized in that instant the depth of her mistake.

Before Viola could say a word or take a step toward them, Jianyu's head lolled back. His body went slack in the man's arms, and his hand, which had been holding Libitina, went limp. Viola's dagger fell to the floor, and the brown-skinned girl scooped the blade from the ground. She did not offer it, as Jianyu had, but instead lifted the knife in warning as she met Viola's eyes with a silent challenge. Judgment and anger and fear all burned at once in her dark eyes—and rightfully so.

Because Viola knew what the knife could do, she held steady. Even in the hands of a Sundren, a mere nick of the blade could be deadly.

Which is why I need to make them understand. She could fix this—all of it. The misunderstanding. Jianyu. The blood on the blade. Her curse was her gift as well. But Viola saw Jianyu's limp hand swinging listlessly—*lifelessly*—and felt a familiar heaviness pressing her down. For what she had done once again. For what she *was*.

When they began to back away, taking Jianyu with them, Viola could not seem to make her feet move or her mouth speak, even as the words waited on her tongue. Urgent. Necessary. The room was still rollicking, and Viola knew that she needed to go—with them, away, it did not matter. She could not stay there, and yet she seemed to be rooted in place.

Then a movement in the corner of her vision drew her attention back to her original destination, where a great stone beast sat upon a woman's chest. It looked like something from a nightmare, roughly hewn from rock or perhaps from clay, but the beast moved as though it were alive. It shifted, puffing itself up in warning to any that might approach. Guarding its treasure.

The ring.

Viola had only agreed to accompany her brother to the Order's gala because Nibsy Lorcan had told her that an artifact would be here. The last time she'd seen the ring was in the depths of the Order's Mysterium. Then, it had been on Krzysztof Zeranski's finger. The Order had taken the man, along with other powerful Mageus, and had bespelled him. They had been draining his affinity—killing Krzysztof and the others—with false magic, presumably to restore the power in the artifacts. Then, Viola had allowed Darrigan to get the better of her and slip away with the ring, but now Viola knew she had a second chance.

The ring was within her reach again, there upon the dead woman's hand. It was so close, this item that Dolph Saunders had desperately wanted. This artifact that Dolph had believed could help to free them all. Dolph had been her mentor and her friend. He'd given Viola a home and a purpose. He'd given her hope, too, that the world could be different.

But he'd lied.

Viola understood that now. She had seen the truth for herself, written in Dolph's own hand. He might have scooped Viola from the gutter and saved her from a life of misery under her brother's thumb, but she learned in the end that Dolph Saunders was a man of secrets. He'd done terrible things alongside the good.

Viola turned back to Jianyu, but the man carrying him had already disappeared into the crowd, and Viola felt a sharp pang of something too close to longing. She could simply walk away from all of this—from the danger swirling around her, from her brother with his anger and threats, and especially from the mad path that Dolph Saunders had set them all upon. She could leave the ring and follow Jianyu and his new friends, whoever they were. She could make right her mistake.

It's already too late. She had seen Jianyu's hand swinging lifelessly. She had no power over death.

Then the great beast shifted again, drawing Viola's attention back to the ring that glinted on the finger of the woman who lay dead beneath the heavy creature. The monstrous thing adjusted itself over the woman's lifeless body with a menacing lurch, and Viola was reminded that it was not only Dolph Saunders who had been after the Order's artifacts. Nibsy Lorcan had killed for his chance to possess them, and the Order would kill to retrieve them as well. Perhaps it already had. Perhaps this great stone beast was their work. Whatever Dolph Saunders might have been playing at, whatever his secrets or lies, Viola knew that neither Nibsy Lorcan nor the Order could be allowed to have the ring.

Viola had no idea where the couple was taking Jianyu, and with each passing second it was growing more impossible to follow, but the ring was *here*. She could not leave it. Letting her affinity unfurl a little, she sensed the lives of each person in the room. Their heartbeats surrounded her, but she felt nothing from the creature.

Because *this* was not life, she realized. The beast was nothing more than manipulation of matter, and Viola's affinity was for the blood of the living. It had no power over this creature.

Perhaps with her knife she could slay it. . . .

But Libitina was gone. It had disappeared into the crowd, along with Jianyu.

All around Viola, women still screamed and fainted, and men continued to run for cover as Paolo's scagnozzi stirred the confusion with their own violent glee. She ignored all of them. She moved slowly, cautiously slinking on satin slippers toward the dais where the woman lay. Viola knew the beast watched her. Still, she inched steadily closer. When she was little more than an arm's length away, the creature squared its shoulders in warning.

Viola didn't allow herself to hesitate or second-guess. She lunged for the woman, grabbed hold of her limp hand, and started to tug at the ring. But when Viola's fingers brushed against the cool smoothness of the ring's gemstone, suddenly the sound of blood became riotous in her ears. Her affinity flared, stirred by the power in the stone, and for a moment she felt the pulse of life in the room. Every beating heart. And she knew she could end them all.

But the beast was already moving toward Viola, and before she could move away, the force of its weight knocked into her. Her hand lost contact with the stone, and the clamoring rush of blood went silent.

The creature lurched again, and Viola thought her bones would crack beneath its weight as it shifted to press a broad clawed paw squarely on her throat. With the pressure, Viola could not draw breath, and she knew that with one more movement, the creature would snap her neck in two. Still, she reached for the woman's hand, careful not to touch the stone this time.

With the beast's weight crushing her, Viola's vision was starting to blur as she tugged at the ring until . . . *there*. Just as darkness pulled her under, the ring slipped free.

ANTICIPATION

1902—New York

Watching his gala dissolve into madness, Jack Grew felt the Book tremble against his chest. As gunfire rang throughout his uncle's ballroom, the most powerful men in New York revealed their cowardice. The leaders of the Order had lorded their power over him for so long. They'd thought him a failure—an *embarrassment*—but now they screamed like women as their fear exposed their truest selves.

The old men who led the Order were weak. *Impotent.* They had allowed their wealth and position to blind them to the truth—their days of power were nearing an end. Jack had seen their faces while he commanded the stage. All the demonstrations he'd performed upon that stage were mere parlor tricks compared to the power that was still undiscovered within the pages of the Book. Still, the old men of the Order had been shocked. They'd been awed by what they'd seen, and perhaps most gratifying of all, they'd been *afraid.* And that was *before* Paul Kelly and his men had turned the gala into a melee.

Jack's lips twitched as the Order debased themselves in front of common criminals. So much for their power. So much for the Order's great might. But the amusement of the moment could last for only so long. Across the room, Jack's beast waited, as did his prize.

The clay golem that Jack had formed with his own two hands and brought to life with knowledge he'd gleaned from the Book sat atop the broken and lifeless body of Evelyn DeMure. The harlot had tried to manipulate him with her siren's song, but in the end, her feral magic was no match for the gifts the Book had bestowed upon him. Her end was only the beginning for Jack. Her death would bring into being the world he would build, a world where every maggot who lurked in the shadows would finally be dealt with. Once he had the ring, he'd rebuild his machine, and there would be nowhere for them to hide.

Another shot rang out, but Jack barely heard it. The familiar bitterness of morphine lay on his tongue, emboldening him, and the power of the Book urged him on. Why should he bother to cower? What bullet could touch him now?

The Book trembled like a second heartbeat in the breast pocket of his jacket, and his blood answered, churning in anticipation. But then Jack saw that someone had reached Evelyn before him. A girl in purple, whose bright satin stood out amid the sea of dark suits. She was tugging at Evelyn's hand, trying to remove the ring.

With her cheap gown and swarthy skin, she certainly wasn't one of the fair porcelain dolls of society ballrooms. *She came with Paul Kelly*, Jack realized, remembering the girl from earlier in the evening. He'd dismissed her then as nothing but a trollop from the Bowery, but now he saw the determination in her dark features. Clearly, this girl knew what the ring was. The Book shuddered again, and Jack understood— she was one of *them*.

Ignoring the chaos around him, he stepped down from the small stage where he'd been presiding over the evening's events and pushed his way through the churning crowd. The Book beat an erratic tattoo against his chest as he clambered over toppled chairs, determined to reach Evelyn's body before Kelly's whore could take his victory. He was nearly there when another volley of shots rang out, and from nowhere, Jack found himself dragged down, pushed over, with the air knocked from his lungs.

"Get off, you damn—" Jack was already bringing his arm back to swing at his attacker.

"Now, just hold on there, Mr. Grew. It's not safe to—"

Jack stopped midswing, realizing it wasn't one of Kelly's men. It was instead one of the police who had been present to deal with Kelly. "This isn't necessary," he told the man through gritted teeth as he struggled against his would-be savior. "I'm perfectly fine."

"You need to stay down." The man pressed Jack to the floor again as more shots were exchanged.

He couldn't move the officer, but Jack wasn't without resources. His connection to the golem was stark and bright, and even pinned as he was, Jack's lips moved in a silent incantation. To protect the artifact. *To kill.* Against his chest, the Book felt like a brand.

Only when the gunshots ceased completely did the officer finally move and help Jack to his feet. From the corner of the room, Jack caught a flash of violet and saw the girl being carried away, limp and still, by one of Kelly's men.

He didn't bother to go after them. Instead, he went for the dais. There lay Evelyn, broken as a painted doll. Her lips were still a bright, unnatural red, and the rouge on her cheeks looked luridly pink against the pallor of her lifeless skin. Her hand was outstretched, but the ring was gone.

AN UNFAMILIAR COUNTRY

1904—Texas

Esta Filosik stood on the open platform at the back of a train heading into the West. The wind tore at short strands of her hair, whipping them against her cheek as she took in the view. There was a wild beauty to the land, but the stark openness of the seemingly endless sky unnerved her. Despite the warmth in the air, a chill had sunk deep into her bones. It felt suspiciously like regret.

Harte was gone.

When she'd discovered his absence a little while ago, she hadn't even been surprised. Not *really*. His desertion felt strangely familiar. Almost expected. Maybe a part of her had been waiting for him to leave for weeks now, but it didn't hurt any less to know that she'd been right.

Not that she would ever admit *that*. Not even to herself.

It didn't seem to matter that he had a good reason to put distance between them. Back in New York, Harte had tried to warn her that the power that had once been within the Book of Mysteries was dangerous. In St. Louis, he'd tried to explain that it was growing stronger and becoming harder for him to control. But the night before, when that ancient power had overwhelmed him in the Festival Hall, Esta had finally understood. Harte's usual stormy eyes had gone black, and his expression had become so foreign that Esta had known instantly it wasn't Harte looking back at her.

And when she'd tried to help him—when she'd *touched* him? A shudder ran through her at the memory of the power she'd felt tearing at her.

No. Not a power. A person. *Seshat.*

Once, the ancient goddess had tried to save the old magic, but Seshat had been betrayed and trapped in the pages of the Ars Arcana. Now, after being imprisoned for so many years, she was furious and probably more than a little unhinged. To get her revenge, Seshat would destroy the world itself, and she would use Esta to do it.

So yes, maybe Harte had been right to leave, to put space between them until they had a way to control the goddess's power. But he should have discussed it with her. They could have made a plan. *Together.* Like the partners they were supposed to be. And he *certainly* shouldn't have taken the Key. It was, without a doubt, the bigger betrayal.

Esta wasn't *exactly* sure how time might unravel if she never returned to the city and gave her younger self the cuff with Ishtar's Key, as Professor Lachlan said she must. One thing was certain, though—Esta was undeniably connected to that small girl she had once been. She now wore the evidence of this link on her wrist, where a scar had appeared only days before.

Despite being new to Esta, the silvery letters looked like they'd been carved into her skin long ago, a single word in the Latin she'd learned as a child—the Latin that Professor Lachlan had taught her. *Redi.*

He'd used the imperative. It was a demand that she return to him.

The scar's sudden appearance was proof that however twisted and tangled time might be, the person Esta was now and the young girl Nibsy held captive were one and the same, as Nibsy and Professor Lachlan were one and the same. It was a sign—a warning—that Esta had no choice but to return the Key to her younger self and put her own life on its proper course. If she didn't, her present would become impossible. The person she was would cease to be.

Maybe that would be better.

Esta felt suddenly numb with a mixture of grief and exhaustion. Again and again she had tried to right the wrongs of history. She had tried to create a better future for those with the old magic, but she had failed—

No, Esta thought darkly. *I've made things even worse.*

When she and Harte had left New York weeks before, they'd only meant to find the artifacts before Nibsy could, but Esta had mistakenly brought them forward to 1904 and had destroyed a train in the process. Because of that mistake, the Devil's Thief and the Antistasi had been born. History had been set on a different path: the old magic had been deemed illegal, and *so many* had suffered because of it. And that was before they'd attacked the Society's ball—and the president. Esta could only imagine the ways history might continue to change because of what she'd done.

She should have listened to Harte and focused on collecting the stones. Instead, Esta had let her anger blind her, and she'd helped the Antistasi deploy a serum that turned out to be deadly. Worse, Jack Grew had still managed to slip away, taking the Book—and all of the secrets it held—with him. Without the Book, there was little chance of finding a way to use the stones to stop Seshat without Esta giving up her life.

But even sacrificing her life wasn't enough to right the wrongs she had created. Esta was willing to give up everything to stop Seshat here and now, but even if Harte could take the Key back to New York for her and give it to her younger self, the world was likely already changing in ways Esta couldn't predict and didn't want to think about.

She took a step toward the edge of the platform, ignoring how the wind lashed at her. Below, the ground rushed by in a blur of rock and brush. Maybe it would be better if she *didn't* return the stone. After all, without her meddling, the Book and its terrible power would have disappeared, as it had once before, and Seshat would never have been a threat. The world would be safe.

Safe. Esta looked out at the far-off horizon and tried to imagine that world, but she found she couldn't. Hadn't she learned long ago that safety was nothing but an illusion?

Her death was no solution. She *knew* that. If she never returned the Key, if history did unwind itself, the old magic would die, as Seshat had feared so long ago. Esta had grown up in that world, in a time far in the future, where magic was nothing but a fairy tale. And before magic faded away? There would be a century of fear and pain for those Mageus unlucky enough to have been born with a connection to the old magic. Removing herself from the equation wouldn't stop the Order or any of the Brotherhoods. It wouldn't end their hate or their violence or the power they held over the city she loved. It would simply leave the innocent as unprotected as they'd ever been. And Harte Darrigan would be gone as well, lost to history and memory, his life ended on a cold and lonely bridge.

It was that final thought that felt most impossible of all.

Esta's fingers brushed at the bracelet at her wrist. The cheap strand of beads was the only thing Harte had left her, but he'd used his affinity to make it something more. As soon as Esta touched it, she felt Harte there, like he was standing right beside her. His voice echoed softly through her mind, explaining where he would go, what he planned to do, and when his words died away, Esta thought she could almost feel the warm brush of lips against the column of her throat: a promise and a plea all at once.

To control Seshat and stop the ancient power from unmaking the world, they needed the other lost artifacts, but with Seshat's power growing, Harte's time was running out. The Dragon's Eye waited for him on a distant shore, but the Pharaoh's Heart was closer. It was where they would have traveled together if everything hadn't gone wrong in St. Louis. But with the threat of Seshat's power, they couldn't afford to waste time traveling together.

Find the dagger. Then meet me at the bridge. Together they would go back to the city and collect the final artifact.

It wasn't *exactly* a command. Harte hadn't used his affinity to take away Esta's will, as he could have. He'd left her behind, trusting that she would be able to do what he asked of her. Trusting that she'd be willing.

Or maybe he didn't trust her *completely*. . . . He'd taken her cuff, after all.

The land flew by around her, wide and open, a world filled with possibilities that were not for her. Would never be for her. Esta would do what Harte had asked. She would find the dagger and then meet him at the bridge, but she would not allow herself to forget where her path would inevitably lead. She would use her affinity to stop Seshat, and in doing so, she would lose her life. Once Seshat was no longer a threat, it would be left to Harte to take the Key to the small girl Esta had been and stop time from unwinding. There was nothing Esta could do about the tragedy she'd caused in St. Louis. There was no way she could see to take the stones back to 1902 without crossing them with themselves and losing them again. But she *could* still stop Seshat from unmaking the world. Perhaps with Seshat's power under control, Harte and the others they'd left in the city could fight the Order and create a different future for magic. Perhaps that could be enough.

Esta reached for the bracelet once more, the beads cool against her fingertips. Again Harte's voice came to her. She couldn't stop herself from closing her eyes as his words brushed against her and his presence surrounded her again. Nor could she stop her throat from going tight at the feel of his lips against her skin, but when she opened her eyes, she was alone in the middle of a wide sweep of unfamiliar country.

She tore the bracelet from her wrist, letting the tiny glass beads scatter like seeds in the wind. Esta wouldn't let herself rely on the comforting presence of Harte's voice, nor could she afford the distraction of his kiss. Both were only reminders of a future that could never be.

But first the dagger.

The air smelled faintly of the coal smoke expelled by the train, and the morning sky was a bright cornflower blue overhead. The train didn't seem to be slowing anytime soon, but that didn't mean that Esta couldn't get off. Far off in the distance, the jagged teeth of a town broke the endless stretch of the horizon. It was an opportunity.

Esta let her affinity flare until she could sense time hanging around her, but she'd barely started to reach for the seconds when she saw something else in the corner of her vision. A shadow lurked there, and the darkness had her drawing back and releasing her hold on time.

She'd seen darkness like that before. It had happened the first time, weeks ago, on the train out of New Jersey, and then again in St. Louis. Each time, destruction had followed. But every time it had happened before, Esta had been touching Harte; their connection had allowed Seshat's power to amplify her own. That couldn't be what was happening, though. Harte was gone, and Seshat's power with him.

Wasn't it?

Esta shook off the unease that had turned the warm summer wind suddenly cold against her skin. She took a deep breath to center herself, letting the rhythm of the train steady her, but before she could reach for her affinity again, she noticed that a small puff of smoke had appeared on the horizon. It was enough to make her pause.

Not smoke, Esta realized. It was a cloud of dust thrown up by a group of horses galloping toward the train. Even from that distance, she could tell they carried riders.

Esta took an instinctive step back from the railing, pulling herself out of sight. She didn't know who the riders were, but her instincts were screaming that their appearance was no coincidence.

The Order had found her.

A WHISPERING CERTAINTY

1904—St. Louis

It was not yet six in the morning—an ungodly hour, to Jack Grew's thinking—when he found himself walking through the empty midway of the world's fair. Dark clouds hung heavy above, mirroring the mood of the whole city. As far as Jack was concerned, the gloom of the early morning suited him. His overcoat warded off the dampness of the day, and within a hidden inner pocket, the weight of the Book was a comfort, a ballast stone to keep him steady on his course. Within his mind, a new consciousness was taking form, a whispering certainty that he would prevail.

The grounds of the Exposition would not be open to the public today, not after the embarrassment at the ball that had happened the night before. The highest-ranking members of the Veiled Prophet Society—and consequently, all of St. Louis—had retreated to their individual mansions and boardrooms to lick their wounds and hide their fear, leaving the people of the city to fend for themselves.

Jack wasn't exactly surprised. The men who held power in the Society weren't any different from those who led the Order. Who could the men of the Veiled Prophet Society ever hope to be if they would not even reveal their faces?

Nothing. No one.

Luckily, Roosevelt was fine. The president had been removed from the Festival Hall moments before the attack, right before everything had erupted. Before leaving town late last night, Roosevelt had commended

Jack on his bravery, thanked him for his assistance and his loyalty, and given him a new position.

So, yes, perhaps Harte Darrigan and the girl had managed to slip through Jack's fingers, but the chaos they'd unleashed had worked in Jack's favor. Because of their actions, Jack had more authority than ever before. Because of their recklessness, the entire country understood exactly how dangerous feral magic was. The yellow journalists would sensationalize the events to sell their tawdry rags, and the fear and hate that was already spreading like a wildfire through the land would become the forge that could bring Jack's ultimate goals to fruition.

At the sound of steadily approaching footsteps, Jack turned to find Hendricks—one of the Jefferson Guard who had helped him in the previous weeks—approaching. *Right on time.*

Jack didn't bother calling out a greeting or lifting a hand in welcome. Instead, he kept his hands tucked into his jacket pockets, where his fingers brushed against the artifact he carried.

He'd found the piece years before, but after the events of the Conclave, he'd used the pages of the Ars Arcana to secret it away. To protect it. For the last two years, however, the Book had refused to return the artifact, stripping Jack of the power he might have otherwise wielded . . . until the night before. Now the familiar coolness of the stone in the artifact sent a thrill of anticipation through his blood, and the same whispering certainty rose within him again.

Hendricks' gaze shifted restlessly, as though he expected an attack. "Sir," he said in greeting. "Everything is ready. Just as you've required."

"Good," Jack said, ignoring the outstretched hand and withholding the praise he knew Hendricks craved. "Let's be on with it, then."

The two men made their way past the enormous sepulchral buildings, all quiet in the morning's gloom, until they came to a tower at least twenty stories high, as tall as the skyscrapers that were already starting to transform the skyline of Manhattan. The building at the base of the tower housed a mixture of working machinery and displays about the wonders of wireless telegraphy. Jack had already seen the exhibit—and the one in the Palace of Electricity, where the ever-present crackle of high-voltage electricity had signaled that the De Forest wireless machine was at work. He'd already watched the operators send messages to and from this very tower, through the air—as if by magic.

Jack wasn't as ignorant as the people whose eyes had goggled in wonder, though. He knew that it wasn't magic but *science* that accomplished the task, and he also knew that scientific thinking applied to the occult arts could reap great rewards.

Years before, Jack had worked in secret to create a machine that could cleanse the world of dangerous, feral magic. He had hoped to reveal his masterpiece at the Conclave. He had imagined his machine in the Wardenclyffe Tower, the wireless installation that J. P. Morgan had been financing for Tesla out on Long Island. Jack had planned to use the machine to lead the Order into the future. Now he had bigger dreams.

Here was evidence that Tesla's project had not been a waste of resources, as J. P. Morgan had eventually come to believe. Here, disguised as a novelty, was evidence that Jack's plan might one day be possible.

"How many know that we're here this morning?" Jack asked as the elevator began rising through the steel-framed tower. All around, the fairgrounds lay quiet and empty. Beyond, St. Louis looked as ragged and uninspiring as it did from the ground. It was nothing compared to New York, and thanks to the Society's inability to protect the fair—and to stop Esta and Darrigan from stealing the necklace—it never would be.

Hendricks' expression was like flint. "The bare minimum required, as you requested. They're all trustworthy."

"You're sure?" Jack asked, eyeing Hendricks. "This project is of the utmost importance, and secrecy is a necessity."

Hendricks glanced at Jack, a question in his eyes.

"By order of President Roosevelt himself, of course," Jack said easily. It wasn't a complete lie. Roosevelt *had* ordered him to take charge of the investigation into the incident at the ball, and the president had created the new cabinet position that granted Jack the power to do just that. "You know, I could use a good man like you on my staff."

"*You* could?" Hendricks asked, his brow wrinkling.

"On behalf of the president, of course," Jack amended humbly.

"Of course," Hendricks echoed. "It would be an honor to serve." He stood a little taller.

Even with his freshly starched uniform, Hendricks couldn't hide his softness. He was no soldier, honed for battle, but maybe he and the Guard could be useful nonetheless. The men who ran the Order and the Society were a minority too small to really wield power . . . unless the more insignificant members of the population yielded it voluntarily. With Hendricks, Jack might well be able to take control of the entire Jefferson Guard.

"The president will be honored by your commitment," Jack said solemnly as the elevator reached the top of the tower. "As am I."

Hendricks nodded and puffed out his chest even more.

The elevator shuddered to a stop, and the doors opened to reveal the observation platform. Windows encased the space. To the east, the Mississippi curved, muddy and dark, bisecting the country. To the west, endless possibility.

Hendricks made the introductions to the men who were waiting at the top and operating the tower. One sat at a long table that was cluttered with machinery. His concentration remained on the controls, as the other explained how the tower received signals.

"How far can you reach?" Jack asked, studying the machine, his mind whirling.

"So far we've managed to get messages from as far as Springfield, Illinois. A distance of over two hundred miles, sir," the operator told him.

Two hundred miles. It was twice what he had hoped to reach with the Wardenclyffe Tower. "I'd like to see the transformer," Jack said, wondering how they'd contained the enormous amount of electricity. It had been the singular problem of his original machine: the abundance of power it harvested could not be contained safely. Though the comforting weight of the artifact in his pocket reminded him that perhaps he already had an answer to that particular problem.

"Just through there, sir," the man told Jack, pointing to a partitioned area with only a small pane of glass to peer through.

Jack went closer and examined it. As he watched, the room lit with a dazzling brilliancy, and a muffled whoosh of sound carried through the heavy door.

"Open it," Jack told them.

"I'm not sure that's the best idea," the operator said hesitantly.

"I didn't ask if it was a good idea," Jack said, keeping his voice calm and even. "I asked you to open it."

"But the amount of voltage necessary to receive a message is quite dangerous," the operator hedged.

"I'm willing to assume that danger." Jack glanced at the man.

The operator blinked, clearly torn about what he should do, but eventually he relented. As he worked on unlocking the door of the partition, Jack took a vial from his pocket and placed a cube of morphine beneath his tongue, allowing the bitterness to flood his mouth slowly, so he could savor it. Just as he would savor this.

"Hendricks, you're free to wait outside if you'd like," Jack told the Guard, not bothering to look in his direction. He could sense Hendricks' hesitancy, but to the man's credit, he stayed.

Silence descended upon the observation tower as they all stood stock-still and waited for a message to arrive.

The flash of blinding light came without warning. The roar of a cannon surrounded him, as the hairs on the nape of Jack's neck lifted with the residual voltage that sifted through the air. The other men raised their hands to ward off the light, but Jack stared into the brightness, relishing the power that the tower managed to conduct. He gripped the artifact in his pocket, felt the coolness of the stone beneath his fingertips, the way it seemed to shudder and tremble at the power flooding through the room.

It seemed to Jack that the stone understood what it was meant for.

When the moment was over, Jack thanked the operator and indicated that he could reseal the transmitter behind the partition. The man was obviously relieved, and Hendricks did not bother to hide his nervous sigh. But none spoke against Jack. Not so long as he was the president's man.

They were nothing more than sheep. Expendable, stupid animals more concerned with their own meager lives than anything of real importance. Let them believe they were serving the president. It wasn't a lie, exactly, but the Guard—and the technology held within this tower—were just the beginning of Jack's plans.

SURROUNDED

1904—Texas

E sta watched the riders in the distance for another few seconds, and when it was clear that they were definitely heading toward the train, she made her decision. Even if she'd been willing to dismiss the shadow as a trick of her eyes—and she wasn't sure she should—she couldn't simply pull her affinity around herself and run, not if it meant leaving behind the two Antistasi who'd helped her escape from St. Louis. Instead, she went back into the car, rushing down the narrow corridor toward the berth she'd been sharing with North and Maggie. Before she could even grasp the handle, though, the door slid open to reveal more than six feet of irritated cowboy.

Jericho Northwood's mismatched eyes widened in surprise at the sight of her standing there, but then they narrowed. "Where do you think—"

The train lurched with a sudden burst of braking that made the car sway, but Esta didn't lose her footing. She pushed past North, tugging him inside the small Pullman berth and securing the door behind him. "We have a problem," she said, brushing off his clear irritation.

"You're damned right we have a problem," North blustered as Maggie crossed her arms over her chest. "We woke up and found the two of you gone, right along with our necklace."

"That's the least of our worries right now," Esta said, not bothering to correct him. The necklace was never going to be his, but she figured pointing out that fact wouldn't help. Instead, she moved past Maggie to peer out from a crack in the drapes that covered the windows. The train had slowed enough that the riders had come up to escort it into town. Most of the men wore the silver stars of law enforcement on their dark lapels. All of them carried guns.

"Where's Ben?" Maggie asked, using the name Harte had gone by in St. Louis. When Esta turned back, the other girl was peering through the thick lenses of her silver-rimmed spectacles, waiting for the answer—completely oblivious to the danger they were currently in.

"Gone," Esta told them.

"Gone *where*?" North demanded, stepping toward her.

"I don't know," she lied. It wasn't like she planned on taking the two Antistasi with her, anyway.

"Like hell," North said. "There's no way Ben went off without telling you where he was headed."

"That's what I would've thought too." Esta let her real disappointment and frustration infuse her tone. Even knowing he'd probably been right to go, she felt Harte's absence like a fresh bruise.

"But the necklace—" Maggie started.

"It's gone. He took my cuff as well," Esta told them, hoping that the bit of truth she was offering would be enough to distract them from their suspicion. She couldn't fight them and deal with the riders, too.

"You can't really expect us to believe you don't know where Ben went," North said.

"It won't matter what you believe if we can't figure out how to get out of the trouble we are currently in." Esta pulled the curtain back a little.

"What is all that?" Maggie moved toward the window, her brows bunching in confusion as she peered through the split in the curtain.

The riders had come up alongside the train now. Some of the marshals rode with their eyes forward, but others looked to the train cars, clearly searching for something.

Esta let the curtains fall back across the window to obscure their view.

"That ain't no welcoming committee," North told them, his voice dark.

Maggie's eyes were wide behind the lenses of her glasses. "But how could they have known we'd be here? No one saw us leave St. Louis."

"Maybe someone on the train recognized us," Esta said. It wasn't like they would have been easy to miss, with her and Harte barely conscious. "It wouldn't take much for someone to telegraph a message to the authorities."

North cursed under his breath. A moment ago, he'd been confident. Now he looked worried—scared, even—and he had good reason to be. The news of the attack they'd launched on the Veiled Prophets' ball would have spread quickly. Any news of the Devil's Thief would have, but an attack on the richest men in St. Louis—on *the president himself*? An attack like that wouldn't go unanswered.

"Where are we?" Esta asked North.

"We were heading toward Dallas, so we should be deep into Texas by now," North said.

"Texas?" That wasn't anywhere close to the dagger.

"It was the first train we could catch. I figured it would be far enough away from the mess we left in St. Louis. Plenty of wide-open spaces and people who usually mind their own business," North said. There was a challenge in his tone, daring her to contradict him. "It wasn't like you were in any shape to come up with something better."

"I didn't say I was." Esta barely remembered how Maggie and North had managed to get them away from the Festival Hall. "I'm grateful for all you did to get us out of St. Louis last night."

North snorted his contempt. "So grateful you and your partner decided to hightail it out of here without so much as a word."

"*I'm* still here," Esta reminded him, letting a chill settle over her words. *For now.*

Maggie stepped forward. "We don't have time for arguing. We'll sort everything out later—*after* we get out of this mess."

"There isn't any way out of this," North told Maggie. "Once this train stops, we'll be surrounded. Hell, we're *already* surrounded." He rubbed his hand over the coppery stubble on his jaw, his expression tight.

"There's always a way," Esta said, considering their options. "Give me a minute to think."

"Think all you want, but it won't help any," North said, trying to sound like he was in control of the situation, but there was a note in his voice that betrayed his fear. He swallowed hard, his throat working as his mismatched eyes met hers. "I've seen what happens with crowds like that. You can't reason with them, and you can't outrun them."

"After what we did . . ." Maggie's voice trailed off like she was remembering everything that had happened the night before. She grasped North's arm to steady herself. "When they find us—"

Esta understood Maggie's fear. Maggie had seen firsthand what had happened to the people they'd doused with Ruth's serum in St. Louis. She'd watched their magic awaken, and then she'd watched them die. She had every reason to be worried.

"There's no reason for them to find us," Esta said. They were still Mageus, weren't they? The two of them were *Antistasi*, for goodness' sake, and wasn't she the Devil's Thief? Maybe Esta didn't have her cuff, but they weren't powerless. They weren't without options. "You have your watch, don't you?" Esta asked North.

"What about it?" he said with a frown.

North's watch didn't tell time; it *changed* it. In St. Louis, they'd used his watch to try to undo the damage they'd done. It had all been too little and too late, but it didn't have to be too late now.

"Use it," Esta told North. "Take us forward, once this has all cleared out."

"That's not how the watch works." His mouth pressed itself into a flat line. "We're on a moving train. Even if we weren't, I can't go farther ahead than I've already been. I wouldn't know where I might land."

"You can't see where you'll end up when you use that thing?" Esta asked. It was a limit that Ishtar's Key didn't have. When Esta slipped through time with the cuff, she could see where she was going. She could find the right moment in the layers of years, like picking out a single word on the page of a book.

For a second Esta considered leaving, like she'd intended to before she'd seen the riders. Maybe North's watch couldn't save them, but there wasn't anything stopping Esta from pulling the seconds slow and slipping away. Maybe if she wasn't with them, North and Maggie would have a fighting chance. After all, Jack had only seen her and Harte in St. Louis. Without the necklace, there would be no proof that the two Antistasi had been involved in anything at all. Maybe without her they would be okay. But "maybe" wasn't enough for Esta to bet on.

If they had been seen together on the train, North and Maggie would still be targets. Esta couldn't walk away. She owed them too much—for standing against Ruth, for being willing to leave the Antistasi, for trying to help save the ball from Ruth's serum, and maybe most of all for saving Harte when Esta had been pulled under by Seshat's terrible power, help-less to do anything at all.

If North couldn't use his watch, there was only one way Esta could see to get out of the mess they were in. It meant breaking the rule that she lived by.

Never show them what you are. Never show them what you can do.

Professor Lachlan's words came back to Esta then, unwanted and unwelcome but true just the same. She hadn't even shown the truth of her affinity to Harte until that day on the bridge, when it had been a choice between revealing what she could do or letting a bullet take his life. There wasn't any bullet speeding toward them this time—not literally—but the danger was every bit as real.

The memory of the shadow she'd seen moments before rose, but Esta pushed it aside. It was only nerves or exhaustion. Nothing more. Seshat's power was in Harte, and Harte wasn't there.

Esta straightened her shoulders. "I can get us out," she told them. She only hoped they would all live long enough for her to regret what she was about to do.

THE COLD WITHIN

1904—A Train Heading West

Harte Darrigan leaned his head against the frame of the train's window and watched the continent pass by. He took every bit of it in—the long sweep of boundless plains that eventually climbed into mountainous terrain and then finally leveled itself out in the west. Once, he would have betrayed anyone and given up anything to have this view. Now, he knew that whatever possibility those wide-open spaces might hold, they were not for him. Maybe they never had been.

The bench seat beneath him was hard and nothing like the comfort of the Pullman berth he'd woken in the night before. Harte had been shaken from the soundness of sleep by the terrible dream he'd been having. In it, he'd been standing over a pit of vipers. He'd started to back away but had stopped short when he'd noticed something trapped within the writhing snakes: an arm. Then he'd realized the arm was Esta's. He hadn't thought or hesitated. He'd jumped into the pit with only one thought in his mind—to save her—but the snakes had quickly wrapped around him and began to pull him under as well.

When he woke, it had taken Harte a moment to realize that it wasn't a serpent wrapped around him but Esta's arms. Even once he understood that he was safe—that *she* was safe—his heart had continued to race. It was only as he focused on Esta—the warmth of her arms, the closeness of her face tucked into the crook of his neck—that Harte had started to breathe again. Esta had smelled lightly of sweat and the smoke from Maggie's devices, but beneath the grime of what they'd been through was an essence that was so undeniably *her*. For a moment Harte had simply lain there, willing away the vividness of the dream, but the second he'd started to truly relax into Esta's warmth, Seshat had lurched, rattling at the thin boundary that kept the ancient goddess from overtaking him completely.

Maybe he should have thrown himself from the speeding train and ended the danger Seshat posed right then and there, but Harte knew he couldn't, not yet. Not as long as the artifacts were out there, unprotected in the world, where Nibsy might retrieve them, and especially not when Jack Grew had the Book. Or rather, Harte remembered, the thing that lived *inside* Jack had it. *Thoth*. The very being that had trapped Seshat thousands of years ago in an attempt to take magic for himself was inside Jack now, pulling his strings in ways that Harte didn't yet understand.

It was Harte's own fault that the Book had ended up in Jack's hands—in *Thoth's* hands—and it was his responsibility to fix that mistake. But the danger Seshat posed to Esta was too real to ignore. Harte had known he couldn't stay. He couldn't risk losing her, not like that.

He had untangled himself from Esta's arms, and as the train slowed, pulling into some unknown station, he'd slipped the beaded bracelet onto Esta's wrist and touched her cheek softly, letting his affinity flare, just a little. He'd barely made contact when Seshat surged again, and it had taken everything Harte had to pull his magic back. His affinity had suddenly felt like something raw and untamed. Like something *apart* from himself that he could not completely control. He'd drawn back his hand, but not quickly enough. Esta had flinched in her sleep, pulling away from his touch.

Harte hadn't dared to touch her again. Even though Seshat seemed to recede, he could sense her anger at being denied once more.

He shook off the memory as the train sped along and told himself that leaving Esta had been the only way to protect her. He told himself that it would be faster this way. He would retrieve the Dragon's Eye for her, and then he'd meet her at the bridge. They would each find one of the missing stones, and then they'd find each other. Harte only hoped that Esta would come to understand, and that she wouldn't kill him when she found him.

It wasn't like she wouldn't have a good reason. The weight of her cuff tucked into his inside jacket pocket felt far heavier than the small piece of jewelry should have, as though his guilt was adding to its burden. It was, perhaps, the worst of all his betrayals.

He still didn't know why he'd taken it. Or maybe he simply didn't want to admit that he needed to know that she *would* come for him—even if it was only in wrath and fury. Because he couldn't bear to let her go, even if he would never deserve her.

Turning away from the window, Harte pulled his jacket around himself to ward off the chill. If there was any such thing as freedom—and he heartily doubted that there was—he knew now that it wasn't in the landscape that passed outside the train's windows. It was certainly nothing like the dream he'd once had to get out of Manhattan.

Now he had a different goal.

It wasn't a dream, exactly, because that word—"dream"—was for people who had a future in front of them, and Harte knew that he was already living on borrowed time.

Find the stones. Take back the Book. Save the girl. He repeated the words to himself like a mantra.

What makes you believe she's yours to save? The woman's voice echoing in his mind was low and soft with a breathiness that made him think of torn paper.

She's not mine. She never would be. But that didn't mean Harte wouldn't do everything in his power to save her just the same.

Seshat had been quiet since Harte had left Esta on the other train, but she laughed now, long and with a mocking edge that didn't seem quite sane. He pushed open the window, desperate for air as he tried to shove Seshat back into the cage of his own soul. It was July, but the mountain breeze coming in through the open window had a bite of coolness to it. Or perhaps the cold was within him, deep down in his bones, where he'd never be able to shake it free.

A REVELATION

1904—Texas

Two years had passed since Jericho Northwood had been in Texas, but it might as well have been yesterday for how familiar the sun and heat felt on his face. North had barely managed to get out of the state with his life, and this time wasn't turning out to be much different. Except now they had Esta. North's own eyes told him that what was happening—what Esta was doing—was real. But there was a part of him still struggling to believe what he was seeing.

Everything had all happened so fast. One second, at Maggie's urging—and against his better judgment—North had taken Esta by the hand, like she'd wanted. The next second, it was like he'd lost his hearing. It wasn't simply quiet, though. Everything had gone completely *silent*, like his ears had plum stopped working. But the second North opened his mouth, he could hear *himself* talking, so he'd known it wasn't his ears. It was everything else.

"What the—"

"We need to go," Esta said, her voice shaking a little as she cut off his question.

"Are you okay?" Maggie asked Esta.

North could see why Maggie was concerned—everything about Esta looked strung tight as a bow. Her jaw was clenched, she was holding her body like someone about to be slapped, and the color had all but drained from her face.

Esta gave a small nod. "I'm fine," she said in a strained voice that didn't sound fine at all. "But we have to move."

Before North could argue, Maggie was already reaching for the door. When she opened it and they stepped out into the corridor, North couldn't stop the curse that came out. "What did you do to him?"

The porter was standing at a berth two doors down, his hand poised to knock. Frozen like a statue. The man's face was lined, and there were tired circles beneath his eyes from his all-night shift. His dark-brown skin shone with sweat from the heat of the corridor, but though he was looking right at them, he didn't seem to be seeing them.

"I didn't do anything *to* him," Esta explained through gritted teeth. "I slowed things down *around* him."

"Time," Maggie said, without even a bit of fear. She sounded more curious than surprised. "You can manipulate time."

Esta's expression was still tight as she nodded. "We have to keep moving."

As they passed the porter, Maggie took something from her pocket and tossed it at him. A moment later, a violet-colored haze began to swirl around the man's head.

"What's that?" North asked. "Something new?"

"New-ish. It's a confounding solution," Maggie explained. "It won't hurt him," she added quickly. The color deepened on her cheeks, like she was embarrassed—maybe even a little ashamed—of the concoction. Or maybe she was embarrassed because she'd been caught trying to keep this one from him.

Maggie knew how he felt about some of her formulations. It was one thing to use a bit of smoke to get away from the Jefferson Guard or the Society, but when you started messing with people's minds—with their free will? Well, North didn't quite know what he thought of that. "What, exactly, does it do?"

Even with her furious blushing, at least Maggie had the courage not to look away from him as she explained. "The solution will confuse his memories for a few days. He won't be able to give anyone information about what happened or what he saw. Not for a while, at least. It will buy us some more time."

"Can you two talk about this later?" Esta asked, looking even more pale than she had a moment before. She gave a nod to indicate that they should keep moving, and from the look she was wearing, North decided not to argue.

Outside the train, nearly two dozen riders, maybe more, were frozen on horseback, exactly like the porter had been. They looked like statues made of flesh and blood, defying the very laws of nature. Some of them were staring toward the train, and others had their mouths open, like they were caught in midshout. All of them were wearing a kind of angry determination North had seen in the eyes of Sundren too many times before.

Suddenly he understood the full significance of what Maggie had already realized. *Esta could manipulate time.* And she didn't need any watch to do it.

Maybe that revelation shouldn't have come as such a shock to him, but North had always thought the pocket watch his father had given him made him somehow exceptional. Now he understood that the watch—and his own affinity right along with it—wasn't much more than a parlor trick compared to what Esta Filosik could do. He'd been around a lot of Mageus during his time with the Antistasi in St. Louis, but North had never seen anything like this. Like *her.*

The Devil's Thief.

He'd helped Mother Ruth and the Antistasi use the legend of the Thief to undertake all manner of deeds as they fought against the Veiled Prophet Society, but North had never really imagined that there could be anything to the stories. He'd thought it was all a bunch of horseshit to pretend that any single person could be *that* powerful. Now he found himself thinking—and hoping—that he'd been wrong. Esta had better be every bit as powerful as all the papers believed, because if she let go of time now, they would be exposed.

They maybe could've tried to make it to the town, but who knew what was waiting for them there—probably more of the same marshals, since that was the direction the riders seemed to have come from. In the near distance, though, a cluster of wooden towers sprang up from the otherwise desolate landscape and gave them another option. They looked like oil rigs.

"If we can get over there," he told them, pointing toward the oil fields, "maybe we can lie low and figure out what to do next."

"Then let's go." Esta nodded for North to lead the way.

They took off together, with the two girls following North in an awkward, loping run. Each step drew them closer to safety, and North started to think that maybe they could get out of the mess they were in after all.

They were about fifty yards from the train when North felt Esta jerk him back, her grasp tightening like a vise around his hand. He looked back to find out what had happened, but what he saw didn't make any sense. Esta had stopped short, her expression twisting like she was in pain, but it was hard to look at her for very long. North could see her clearly enough when he didn't stare straight at her, but he couldn't quite *focus* on her. Beyond Esta, the world had gone all blurry-like. He couldn't make out much of anything at all, including Maggie.

North didn't have time even to begin processing what he was seeing before Esta's hand went suddenly slack. Her grip had been so steady, so determined, that the last thing he'd expected was for Esta to let go of him, so he wasn't prepared when her hand slipped from his and her legs collapsed beneath her. The second Esta released him, everything lurched into chaos. North was already moving, acting on instinct to scoop Esta into his arms before she hit the ground. Around them, the noise of the world felt suddenly deafening with the heavy roar of the train and the thunderous beats of the horses' hooves.

A shout went up, and North knew they'd been spotted. The shot ricocheting off the ground next to them a moment later confirmed it. With one look at Maggie's terrified expression, he began to shift his grip on Esta so that he could reach for his watch.

"Put me down," Esta demanded, wriggling to get free from his hold. From how feebly she was pushing at him, he wasn't sure she could walk on her own, but North let go. Sure enough, her legs wobbled a bit, and he had to catch her with one arm.

Maggie held out her hand to Esta. "We need more time."

But Esta didn't reach for Maggie's hand again, like North had expected. Esta's eyes were wide and her face had drained of all its color. She was shaking her head. "We need to go—the watch."

"What do you think I'm trying to do?" North ground out as he flipped open the cover. His hands shook as he adjusted the dial. "Grab hold of me," he told them.

Another volley of shots rang out, the clear report of them echoing through the hot Texas sky as he closed the watch's face. The world flashed white, the way it always did, but as the day shifted into the coolness of night, North felt an invisible fist punch him in the gut, knocking the air from him. He stumbled, leaning into Esta. His legs felt like they were going out from under him. Esta swayed under his weight, and they both went down.

At first North didn't feel any pain at all. He tried to sit upright, but he couldn't bring the air back into his lungs.

"Jericho—" Maggie's voice was shaking.

When Esta let out the kind of curse most women don't know, much less say, North knew it was bad. He wanted to tell them that he was fine, but all that came out was a ragged groan as pain erupted, hot and searing, through his side.

With the two girls panicking, North's mind was having trouble making sense of what had happened. The world was quiet now, dark as he'd intended. He'd taken them backward a few hours, and now above him, the Texas sky was swept with the brightness of stars he'd once marveled at. They lit the otherwise depthless night, but even the wonder of the stars couldn't take away the aching pain.

With his free hand, North reached for the source of that pain, grasping his side. He couldn't understand, at first, why his shirt should be wet. Then he looked down at his fingers and saw them coated with the dark stain of his own blood.

NO SUCH THING AS TOO LATE

1904—Texas

Esta staggered under North's weight, struggling to keep them both upright, as the reality of what had just happened slammed into her. From almost the moment she'd pulled time slow, the shadow of Seshat's power had been there, and the longer she'd held the seconds, the more intense it had become. By the time they'd run from the train, darkness had been swirling thick above her, like a storm threatening to break. And then it *had* broken, whole and complete, crashing over her until the world went dark. She didn't remember anything else until she'd come to, slung over North's shoulder like some kind of damsel who needed saving.

She'd dismissed the shadow she'd seen earlier, because she hadn't wanted to think there was any way Seshat's power could still affect her without Harte being close by. But Esta hadn't survived for so long by ignoring the truth when it was staring her in the face. Something had changed.

There wasn't time for her to consider what it meant, not when they were so exposed and not with the cowboy examining the blood on his fingertips like he didn't know who it belonged to. All the while, the dark spot on his light shirt continued to grow.

My fault. Esta had lost her grip on time, and they'd been seen. There was no escaping that fact. North had been shot because she'd failed to do what she'd promised.

"No," Maggie said, covering North's wound with her hands, trying to stop the bleeding. "No, no, no . . ."

"Can you walk?" Esta asked North, ignoring Maggie's growing panic. Even if the posse was gone and the night seemed quiet, they would be safer out of sight.

North's jaw tightened as he met Esta's eyes and nodded. Gently, he brushed Maggie's hands away. "I'm fine," he said, trying to straighten. He groaned when he moved, wincing with pain, but he managed to stay upright.

Clearly, he wasn't fine, but Esta wasn't about to argue if North was able—or at least willing—to walk on his own. North was tall, with a thin, rangy build, but he was solid beneath his clothing. She could help take some of his weight—and she did—but Esta doubted that even together she and Maggie would be able to carry him. The faster they found cover the better.

Esta suspected that North had taken them back a few hours, to the night before the train arrived, but she didn't know when the news of their impending arrival might have been sent to the marshals in town. There was no telling who might be watching for them. Before, she might have wrapped them in the cloak of her own affinity, but now she didn't dare risk using her magic again. Not until she understood why Seshat's darkness could touch her apart from Harte. After all, Esta knew too well what the darkness could do.

Trains derailed.

Elevator cables snapped.

Holes big enough to swallow horses split the ground.

It was more than bad luck. Seshat's ability to pull apart the Aether around them and unmake the order of existence was like Esta's own power, but stronger. Infinitely more potent.

"How far back did you take us?" she asked North.

"About six hours," he said with another pained groan.

It wasn't much time. Not nearly enough to get clear of the danger the marshals posed, even if North hadn't been injured.

"We need to get going," Esta told the two of them, hoping that her voice didn't give away her worry.

Thankfully, Esta didn't have to do more than support North's weight as they made their way toward the oil fields, where the enormous rigs stood like sentries against the night. The fields were two, maybe three hundred yards away, but they might as well have been in another country, especially since North seemed to be moving more slowly with each step.

Finally, they reached the edges of the oil fields and found an abandoned rig that had a small shed leaning close to its base. Inside, it smelled of dust and mold and a hint of something mechanical, but it was clear no one had been there for a while. The roof was only partially clinging to the walls, and moonlight streamed in from above, lighting the small space. Esta tried to help ease North down, but his legs went out from under him and he crumpled to the ground instead.

Maggie knelt next to him and started pulling away his jacket and shirt to see the wound beneath, but she went still when she exposed the small, jagged hole in his abdomen. She looked up at Esta with horror. "He needs a doctor."

Esta took one glance at the wound, ragged and still oozing blood, and knew the truth—a wound like that? A doctor wouldn't be able to help. Even if a doctor cleaned and bandaged him, the bullet would still be inside of North, and Esta knew that a shot to the gut like that one wouldn't heal. Without modern medicine, it would be a painful infection that would take North, rather than the loss of blood.

"No doctors," North said.

"Hush," Maggie whispered. "We'll find someone to get the bullet out of you and stitch you up and you'll be fine. We're going to take care of you."

North's eyes were steady on Esta, and she knew he understood. But she certainly wasn't going to be the one to tell Maggie, so she settled for the other reason. "He's right," Esta said. "You saw that posse. They rode out nearly at dawn. Chances are they're already expecting us. Finding a doctor would only bring them faster."

"I'd rather be in jail than know I could've tried to save him and didn't," Maggie told Esta.

Esta saw the determination in Maggie's eyes, but she knew the truth. "Why do you think we'd even make it to jail?" Esta asked softly.

"No doctor," North said again through gritted teeth. "No one's gonna be able to help me anyway."

"You don't know that," Maggie argued.

"I do," North said, grimacing again. He was looking worse now, paler, and his breathing seemed more ragged. "You two need to go while you can. It's not much, but six hours should give you a little room to get ahead of the marshals."

"We're not going anywhere," said Maggie, her voice cracking as she met Esta's gaze. "I won't leave him like this."

"Six hours won't make enough of a difference anyway," Esta agreed, her mind already furiously racing.

"You can't stay here," North told them.

"I won't just sit here and watch you die," Maggie said, stubborn as ever. "And I'm not leaving you behind." She glared at Esta, daring her to contradict this.

"We're not going to leave anyone behind," Esta told Maggie, pacing a little as she tried to think of some way out of the mess they were in. Absently, her fingers went to the scar at her wrist, and as she traced over the words, she had an idea. "We could use your formulations," she told Maggie.

"I don't have anything to heal a wound like that," Maggie said, stone-faced.

"Not to heal the wound," Esta said. "But maybe with a big enough distraction, we can get out of here and save North all at once."

"No," North told them. "You two need to go. It's too late for me."

"You of all people should know there's no such thing as too late," Esta told him. "But if we're lucky, maybe we'll be right on time."

IMPOSSIBLE CHOICES

1902—New York

With a strangled gasp, Viola jerked upright. Her eyes were wide open, but she saw nothing but inky blackness. The dream she'd been having lingered. She could still hear the roar of the crowded ballroom, still feel the beast's rough weight as it pressed the air from her lungs. Her mouth was dry with panic, and there was a dull roaring in her ears. Within her chest, her heartbeat felt unsteady, and for a long moment Viola did not remember where she was.

As the dream faded, the preceding days came back to her. Viola's eyes began to adjust, and soon she could make out the familiar slant of the low ceiling above her bed, the shape of the worn furniture, and the cold bare walls of the attic room closing her in. The air was warm and stuffy, but she rubbed her arms where gooseflesh still rose on her skin. Even without a window, Viola knew that it was nowhere near dawn. She also knew that she would find no more rest that night. If she closed her eyes again, she would only see Jianyu—the blood creeping across his shoulder, his lifeless hand dropping her knife—and she would feel the beast pressing down on her throat. She would dream of her bones cracking beneath the pressure of its grip and of her failure, as she had every night since the gala.

Instead of staying abed, Viola dressed quickly and, without lighting the lamp, pulled her hair back into a simple knot. Then she stepped soundlessly across the rough attic floorboards, making sure to miss the ones that would creak and alert her brother that she was stirring before a respectable hour. It would not do to rouse his suspicions, not now, when so much was at stake.

Paolo, he still watched her too closely—they all did—despite his claims that her actions at the gala had proven her loyalty to the family and to him. Since he'd rescued her from the beast's grip, Viola had continued to make sure that Paolo could find nothing of concern in her actions, even if that meant she had to remain small and meek. It did not matter that the weight of the role she played grew heavier with each passing day. She could not walk away from her brother or her mother or any of this—not until she knew for sure what had happened to the ring.

Though Viola remembered nothing after the great stone beast had crushed her beneath its weight, she was convinced that Paul or one of his men must have taken the artifact. When she'd come to in a carriage rattling toward the Bowery, her brother across from her and John Torrio's arms pinning her to him, no one had spoken of the artifact. Torrio's fingers had been rubbing against the underside of her breast, where her brother would not see, as the two gloated over their victory, and she knew it had not been the time to ask.

Viola shook off the memory of Torrio's wandering hands with a shudder and then headed downstairs. In the kitchen, the iron stove was waiting for her. It was a reminder of the tediousness sure to be found in the day ahead. Silently, she cursed it—and her own luck at being stuck once more under her brother's thumb. Viola was not made for chopping onions and baking bread. She knew that she had no talent for any of the domestic chores Paolo and their mother expected of her, but she would bide her time and do what she must to appease them . . . at least for a little while longer.

Again, her thoughts drifted to the night of the gala, but to her shame it wasn't Jianyu she thought of now, but Ruby Reynolds. The blond heiress had said dangerous things to Viola that night. But then, Ruby was rich enough to be brave and stupid all at once. In the quiet shadows of the kitchen, Viola could not stop herself from remembering how Ruby had looked that evening, draped in little more than a cloud of silk. Ruby had been dressed as Circe, the witch who turned men to swine, but with a mouthful of impossible words and a single kiss, the silly slip of a girl had done far worse to Viola.

Lifting her fingers to her lips, Viola stopped short of touching them. She forced herself to lower her hand. It did no good to think of things that could not be. Could *never* be. Pretty promises and the soft press of skin had simply given her a taste of a world that could never be hers. It had given her hope, the most dangerous of spells, but in the end Ruby's kiss had changed nothing at all.

Cursing softly, Viola slipped out the back door as noiselessly as she'd done everything else since waking. She muttered every vulgar word she could think of as she made her way to the outhouses behind the cafe, but by the time she was finished with her business there, she'd fallen silent. Not even the phrases that would make a sailor blush gave her any real satisfaction.

When Viola stepped back out into the cleaner night air, she knew she was not alone. She walked steadily toward the building, waiting for the intruder to show himself, and when she was nearly to the kitchen door, she paused.

"I know you're there," she said, her voice soft in the night. She missed the reassuring weight of Libitina—or any knife, really. Like a fool, she'd ventured out unarmed. In the distance, a dog howled, but no other sound reached her ear. "Whoever you are, show yourself. Only a coward hides in the shadows."

Viola waited, listening to the city rustling itself awake, a constant hum of life all around her. Just as she thought that maybe she'd been wrong, a man stepped from the alley that ran behind the row of buildings. He seemed enormous, with impossibly broad shoulders, dark, flashing eyes, and even darker skin.

Viola stepped back and instinctively drew on her affinity until the man was on his knees, but then she saw what he was holding in his hand—

Libitina.

She released her hold on his life at once, and the man slowly stumbled back to his feet, his free hand rubbing at his chest. "Where did you get that?" she asked, moving toward him. She realized that he wasn't so large as she had imagined him to be. He was simply a man, no taller than her brother or any other in the Bowery. His skin was not made of the darkness of night, but was instead a warm deep brown.

The man flinched, raising his hands in surrender, and she realized he was not a stranger. It was the same man she had seen at the gala, the one who had carried Jianyu away.

"He told me you would come if I showed you this," the man said, his eyes still wary as he held the knife to her, handle first. "Jianyu. He told us that you would believe me."

"Who are you?" Viola didn't reach for the blade, even as her palms itched to feel its weight.

"My name's Johnson. Abel Johnson," the man said again. His voice had gone tight with a fear that Viola recognized too well, but still this Abel Johnson offered her the knife—*Libitina*—once more. "Jianyu sent me to get you."

She was already reaching for her blade when she paused, the man's words—the significance of them—finally registering. Her heart felt suddenly lodged in her throat. "He's alive?"

"Only just," the man said, releasing the knife to Viola's keeping. "We've tried everything. Doctors and praying and every home remedy my mother ever knew, but nothing closes up the wound you gave him. He's been bleeding for days now." The man's jaw was clenched, but Viola could not tell whether it was fear or the usual male pride that he now held between his teeth. "He said that you would come, that you could do something about it. We have to go now. He doesn't have much time."

Viola felt herself torn in two. She could save Jianyu. She had thought him dead, already past healing, yet if his heart still beat, she could help him. But if she left now, she could not return. And if she did not return, she might never discover where her brother was keeping the ring.

"If you come with me now—"

Viola was shaking her head. "I can't."

"You can't come or you can't help him?" Abel asked, tucking his hands in his pockets.

"You don't understand. My brother—"

"I know all about your brother," Abel said, his mouth twisting as though he'd tasted something foul. "He's a dangerous man, and the men he surrounds himself with aren't much better. But Jianyu seemed to think that you were stronger than him."

Viola glanced back to the door. In a matter of an hour the sun would be up, and with it some of Paul's men. If she were discovered missing, and especially if anyone discovered who she had gone off with . . . "It's not so simple. Paul, he knows where the ring is."

Understanding flashed through Abel's expression. "Paul Kelly has it?"

"He must," Viola told him. "Right now he trusts me. If I leave without an excuse, he'll grow suspicious, and I won't be able to find out where it might be."

Abel Johnson looked like a man fighting with himself. "This ring— everyone keeps saying it's so important. But do you really believe it's worth a man's life? Your *friend's* life?"

Pressing her lips together, Viola met his eyes. "Jianyu knows how important the ring is. He wouldn't risk a chance to retrieve it for anything. Not even for his life."

Abel let out a frustrated breath. "Look, I don't pretend to know anything about this magic mumbo jumbo you all are involved in. It doesn't have anything at all to do with me. But Jianyu saved my sister's life twice now, so ring or not, I'm not leaving until you agree to come."

Viola wasn't sure what she should do. If Abel Johnson didn't leave, he'd get himself into trouble with Paul, and for what? Niente. It would only put them all in danger and make the ring even more difficult to locate. It certainly wouldn't save Jianyu.

She glanced back at the building. Her brother was an early riser. Soon he'd be stirring, and he'd expect her to be there. "There's no time for me to return before Paolo realizes I'm gone, but once the sun is up, I could make an excuse."

"I don't know if Jianyu has that long left," Abel told her. His expression was serious, and Viola could not tell if the look he wore was the truth or simply a bluff.

Guilt twisted her stomach, but she lifted her chin. Jianyu's life was in her hands, but she could not lose her chance to find the Delphi's Tear—to *protect* it from Nibsy, the Order, and even from her brother. Jianyu would not want that. He would understand. None of them were worthy of the power it contained. If any one of them had control of an artifact as powerful as the ring? Viola knew well the suffering that would follow. She could not allow that to happen.

"Come back at noon. Paul goes out after his lunch to check on his businesses around town. I should be able to slip away for a while then. Wait at the corner of Great Jones Street," she told him as she forced down her guilt. "If I can, I'll meet you there."

"That's not good enough," Abel said, his hands fisted at his sides.

"It has to be." Then Viola turned away from him, ignoring his protests as she walked toward the kitchen entrance of the Little Naples Cafe.

She did not look back as she closed the door behind her and leaned against it, pressing her back against the heavy wooden panel. She knew that every second that passed until noon would be a trial. If the ring weren't so important, if the others after it weren't so dangerous, her choice would have been easier.

When are choices ever easy? she thought darkly, and before she could stop herself, Viola was thinking of another choice—perhaps another mistake. What might have happened the night of the gala if she hadn't turned Ruby down? What if Viola had simply accepted the gift of Ruby's kiss, if the two of them had left the gala together, right then and there, for some impossible future? She would not have thrown her blade. She would not have hit Jianyu. She would not be in this position, stuck between the anvil and the hammer.

Viola lifted her fingers to her lips, and this time she touched them. But she could no longer feel the imprint of Ruby's mouth upon hers. Even the memory of it was beginning to turn hazy. Perhaps her refusal that night had been a mistake, but what other choice could she have made? Perhaps her refusal now was a mistake as well. She let her legs fold beneath her and began counting the minutes until Abel's return.

THE MOMENT APPROACHING

1904—Texas

The early-morning sun beat down from a crystalline sky as Esta finished placing the last vial of incendiary, and then, brushing her hands on her pants, she made her way back to where Maggie was waiting with North. He looked worse than before, his skin nearly gray and his breathing shallow.

"Is everything ready?" Maggie asked, looking up from where she sat cradling North.

"I think so," Esta said, glancing out to where she'd laid the charges.

"You really think this will work?" Maggie asked, her voice like glass.

Turning back, Esta saw Maggie sitting there, her skirts covered in the dust from the ground, her arms filled with North and her eyes filled with fear. "It has to."

Esta wasn't sure that Maggie heard, though. The other girl's attention was on North, and Esta wondered if the look on Maggie's face was the same one she herself had worn the day Harte nearly tumbled from the bridge, or the night before, when Jack Grew was choking the life out of him. She allowed herself a moment to wonder where Harte was, whether he'd made it off the train as he'd planned and was safely away, or if he too was trapped.

She wanted to believe that she would know if something had happened to him. She wanted to believe that maybe the fact that Seshat's power was still connected to her meant that Harte was as well, but Esta had never been one to spin fairy tales. And anyway, wanting a thing didn't make it so.

Far off in the distance, the keening whine of the train's whistle sounded. A few minutes later, it came into view, and the time for wondering was over.

Esta jogged to the place where the fuses she'd laid earlier all came together and ducked behind a row of scrubby bushes. She ignored the prickling brambles as she checked the position of the sun and wished she had a watch of her own. So much of the plan was dependent upon everything happening at exactly the right time, and yet she would have to rely only on instinct, hoping that she remembered and reacted when necessary.

The train was coming closer now, and when Esta turned, she saw that the posse was coming as well. A sense of déjà vu swept through her as she saw the horses at full gallop. Then she noticed that a small group of them had steered their mounts to the center of the tracks. The engineer must have seen the horses, because Esta heard the wailing screech of the brakes and the hiss of steam being released from the boiler as the train struggled to slow in time.

She remembered then how the train had swayed with the sudden braking, and she continued to watch the scene, waiting. Right now, the other versions of themselves should be leaving the Pullman berth. Soon they would make their way out of the train, as they had the first time. With the way Esta had used her affinity earlier, she wouldn't be able to see when her past self exited the train with Maggie and North. She wouldn't be able to tell when it was approaching—the moment she would lose hold of time and North would be shot. But if she could distract the posse right when it happened, if the men on horseback turned away instead of aiming for North, maybe she could rewrite what had happened.

She could only hope that there would be some sign of when to act once the train came to a stop. Because if she acted too late, all their plans would be for nothing. If North was shot as he was before, nothing would have changed.

As the horses' thundering hooves grew closer, Esta thought she saw the flicker of something—a wavering of her vision in the spot where they might have once stood a little ways off from the train. Her instincts told her that it was as good a sign as she'd ever get. She touched the scar at her wrist and hoped that her theories were right.

The igniter Maggie had given her was a strange contraption made from a glass vial that cracked in two to create a small explosion. It was easy enough to use, and Esta quickly activated the formula inside and set it on the fuses before pulling back under cover when the horses galloped past her.

A moment later, the entire landscape erupted as Maggie's incendiaries exploded, their flames consuming the small clutches of brush and shrubs where they'd been placed all along the landscape. The Flash and Bangs erupted next, like fireworks at close range. One by one they exploded at random intervals, drawing the riders' attention in multiple directions at once. The horses reared up, shying away from the noisy confusion despite their riders' commands. As Esta watched, the strange multicolored flames from the incendiaries that had set fire to the brush began to produce an ethereal fog. It wasn't the cloying smoke of a normal fire, but instead glowed a strange lavender as it swirled into the sky, a cyclone of power and flame that blocked the riders' way. It blocked their view as well. A few tried to shoot, but their leader held up a hand to stay them.

Esta waited, trying to remain calm, but she didn't know what was coming. If her theory was right, if they had been able to save North, then her present should become impossible. If time worked the way that Professor Lachlan had explained, her present self—the one crouching in the bushes and hoping—should no longer be. But what that meant, Esta didn't exactly know. . . .

As she continued to watch, the landscape around her fuzzed in and out of focus, and suddenly Esta felt a bolt of utter dread. She could sense time hanging around her, but the seconds had become erratic and unstable. The landscape flickered, and time felt suddenly dangerous. *Hungry.* She could almost feel the seconds turning toward her. Coming for her. She could sense their desire to devour her—to tear her from the world—but when she reached for her affinity, desperate to stop whatever was happening, Esta could no longer grasp the seconds. Her affinity slipped through her fingers like sand.

As the world around her shifted, she had the sudden, awful thought that she'd miscalculated. She'd wondered what would happen if she didn't return the cuff to her younger self. She'd wondered what it would feel like to disappear—whether it would hurt to be unmade or whether it would be soft, like sinking into darkness. She thought maybe it would be like forgetting—like nothing at all.

Now Esta understood. Now she knew how truly terrible it was to feel time pulling her—and everything she was—apart. Ripping her from existence.

Esta's mind raced for some solution, some way out of the trap she'd set for herself, but before she could do anything, she felt herself being unanchored from the present moment, torn away, torn back through the layers of time and place. Until she wasn't anything at all.

THE COVER OF NIGHT

1904—San Francisco

When Harte Darrigan finally disembarked from the train in California, he was still across the bay from the city he was trying to reach. He followed the line of railroad passengers to the long ferry boats and climbed aboard, the whole time trying not to look too overwhelmed by the sights around him. He'd lived his entire life on an island, but he'd never ventured close to the water's edge if he could help it. In California, though, there was no trace of the cold power that kept Mageus away from the shores of Manhattan. Harte felt only the briny dampness of the sea air and the strange coolness of the summer day as the wind ruffled his hair. He'd watched the continent unfold itself for the last few days, and now he'd reached its end.

Fog cloaked the sea as the ferry carried Harte onward, but as they drew closer to the opposite shore, San Francisco finally came into view. It was something to take it all in, the hills that flared up around the bustling docks, barely visible through the misty fog. Beyond the jut of land where the city sat, the bay emptied out into an endless sea, one that led to a world far wider and stranger than even Harte could imagine. Somehow, this view of San Francisco almost felt like enough to make up for the life he would never have.

Then the wind shifted, and suddenly Harte smelled himself instead of the sea—the days-old sweat and sourness rising up from his body and the other passengers' cigar smoke that had permeated his clothes on the train. His skin felt sticky, and his hair was a heavy, unwashed cap against his scalp. For a moment he had the ridiculous thought that he would give nearly anything to be back in New York, in his own apartment, sinking into the steaming water of the pristine porcelain tub he'd worked so long and so hard to call his own. But that life was gone now, and the apartment right along with it. There was no going back, not when he carried within his skin a power that could destroy the world itself.

As the ferry shuddered to a stop, Harte pulled his jacket closed to ward off the chill he felt and began to follow the other passengers once again. He told himself that it definitely wasn't stalling to clean up before he continued on. It wouldn't do to show up looking like a tramp when he went to retrieve the Dragon's Eye, the fanciful golden headpiece with an amber stone that seemed to glow from within. It would be hard enough to explain who he was and why he was there—*how* he was there—to a woman he'd never met. She probably hadn't even known Harte existed until the Dragon's Eye had arrived on her doorstep two years before.

It was early in the evening and the sun was already starting to set by the time Harte finally left the cheap boardinghouse and began to make his way up Market Street and into the heart of the city. The area near the docks was filled with squat rows of wooden buildings that housed saloons and worn-out hotels, along with cluttered shops that catered to travelers and sailors. But as Harte traveled away from the water, the city changed. The tumbled wooden structures near the water became well-made buildings of stone and brick that housed banks and offices. Instead of the workmen that had crowded the docks, filling the air with their raucous banter and all-too-human smells, the sidewalks in the business district were filled with men in suits who walked silently on, wearing serious, harried expressions.

Once, Harte might have relished every sight. Once, he might even have wished to be one of those men. Now, though, his only thought was for what came next—finding the Dragon's Eye. Meeting Esta. Defeating Seshat.

As though I would allow you to . . . Or didn't you learn your lesson, back on the train?

Harte shook off Seshat's voice and kept his pace steady and determined, but days with barely any sleep had taken their toll, and his steps felt as heavy as the artifacts weighing down his pockets. It didn't help that he knew that each step drew him closer to facing the past he'd been running from for so long.

When Harte turned onto California Street, he paused, confused by the grinding, growling whir he heard, until he realized it came from the cables that ran beneath the paved road. They sounded like some slumbering dragon waiting to rouse itself. Manhattan didn't have anything like the odd, open trollies that traversed the steep hills of this city. The thought of using one was briefly tempting, but Harte knew he needed to save his last few coins for the trip back to the bridge. Instead, he continued his hike, trying to prepare himself for what might come.

With his affinity, retrieving the headpiece shouldn't be difficult. A simple touch, skin to skin, and he could have it easily—and the person he was visiting would never even remember losing it. Nor would they remember him. Now, though, Harte wasn't sure that would be the wisest move. After he'd left Esta, he'd thought to use his affinity to board the next train, but when he'd tried, Seshat had lurched within him, making his magic feel like something apart from him, uncontrollable and dangerous. Harte had barely pulled back in time to stop her from doing whatever she'd planned, and after, he hadn't risked using his affinity again. Instead, he'd made the rest of the trip with nothing but his own cunning and what little money he had left.

It was clear that Seshat didn't like the other two artifacts he carried, and he imagined that the ancient goddess would do everything she could to prevent him from retrieving a third. Harte decided that it would be safer to depend on his wits and whatever was left of his charm. He would keep his affinity tucked away and use it only as a last resort.

Eventually you will need to rely on what you are, Seshat purred. *And when you do, I will be waiting.*

Harte shook off her voice. He didn't want to consider that Seshat might be right, especially since he didn't have much confidence in his charms. Maybe he would have had more if he'd known anything about the person who had the Dragon's Eye other than her name—Maria Lowe—and the address on Dawson Place, where she lived. He'd memorized both years ago, when he was still a boy and his mother had still been living with the man who had fathered him. That was before Molly O'Doherty had tossed Harte out into the streets, even though he was still a child. It was before Harte had taken up with Dolph Saunders and the Devil's Own and then, later, with Paul Kelly's gang. In those days, he'd still been Benedict O'Doherty, a name he'd only recently resurrected. He hadn't yet fashioned himself into Harte Darrigan or pulled himself out of the Bowery through sheer determination.

Harte still didn't want to look too closely at where the impulse to send the headpiece to the woman had come from. After everything that had happened at Khafre Hall—and with Seshat's voice newly echoing in his mind—he hadn't exactly been thinking straight when he sent the Order's artifacts out into the world. He'd only had the impulse that he needed to get them out of the city, because he knew that Nibsy Lorcan could never be allowed to retrieve them.

Back then, the country had seemed impossibly large to Harte. He'd thought that by separating the artifacts, by sending them out into the far corners of that enormous world, it would be impossible for *any* single person to bring them back together and harness their power. He'd been wrong, of course. Even if Nibsy Lorcan might not find the artifacts for decades, Harte's experience in St. Louis had shown him how easily they could fall into the wrong hands. Julian hadn't been able to resist wearing the necklace that contained the Djinni's Star, and the Society had found it. Harte had seen the discarded newspapers that littered the trains as he'd traveled; he already knew that Julian had paid the price for his naive stupidity. He only hoped that Maria Lowe had not been so unlucky.

Harte increased his pace, but walking faster couldn't turn back the years or undo the mistakes he'd made along the way. Already the sky was growing darker and the city was beginning to come alive. Now that evening was falling over the streets, there was something about San Francisco that reminded Harte of New York. The two cities were nothing alike, but beneath the cover of night, they weren't so very different. He'd come thousands of miles only to find himself in the same place he'd started—a crowded, filthy cluster of buildings filled with work-weary souls who only wanted to make it to the next day. A trap dressed up like a dream.

The thought made Harte walk faster, not that he could ever outpace the memory of the boy he'd been. He was so deep in the darkness of his thoughts—so determined that whatever mistakes he'd made in the past, he would find the headpiece and make this one mistake right—that he almost didn't notice the fencing. Or the men who guarded it.

Harte pulled up short just before he crossed Kearny Street. On the other side of the intersection stood a trio of men. Each held a billy club as they watched the pedestrians with sharp eyes. They weren't police, or at least they weren't wearing the uniform of police, but behind them, a barricade of wood and barbed wire blocked the intersection. In the deep recesses of his mind, he heard Seshat laugh.

EXILED

1902—New York

Ruby Reynolds barely cared that she was crumpling the sheet of paper in her hand as she stormed into the Barclays' library and slammed the door behind her. Theo didn't so much as look up as she propped her hands on his desk.

"Your sister said you were in here working," Ruby told him.

Theo continued annotating the notebook he'd been writing in, the words pouring from the tip of his pen in a slow, steady stream as ink transformed itself into his eminently readable hand. She knew that she was interrupting his studies, but she couldn't stop herself.

"Aren't you going to ask me why I've come?" Ruby demanded, her irritation growing by the second.

"I assumed you would tell me whether I asked or not," Theo told her with a small, impertinent smile.

"They've all refused me." Ruby threw herself into the nearby armchair. "It's now official. Every single reputable paper in town has rejected me. I just received the *Sun*'s rejection this afternoon. They publish the absolute rubbish that Sam Watson spouts on a regular basis, but they rejected my article about the gala outright. Can you imagine?"

"Not at all, darling. You're only going after the most powerful men in the city."

Ruby knew that Theo was her greatest supporter—had been since they were children—but his words still rankled. "Who are they to deny the people of this city the truth?" She felt her indignation rise once more.

60

"Who indeed?" He finished the line he was writing and set the pen on the table before looking up at her.

"They're a bunch of cowards. All of them," Ruby said, still stewing with anger. "And I told the editor, Mr. Bartleby, so myself."

Theo frowned at that piece of information. "You did *what?*"

"I marched straight into the *Sun's* office and demanded to see the editor. They told me I had to have an appointment," she muttered. "An *appointment*, if you can believe that!"

"What a novel idea," Theo mused.

"This isn't a joke to me, Theo." Ruby felt her shoulders sink right along with her spirits.

"I never said it was, darling," Theo said. "I'm merely imagining you storming into the offices of the *Sun* like an avenging Valkyrie. Did you finally manage to see Mr. Bartleby?"

Ruby deflated a little more. "No. He refused to meet with me, but I stood my ground. I told them exactly what I thought of their editorial choices."

"You didn't." His mouth kicked up a little.

"Do *not* mock me, Barclay." Then her temper faltered a little. "I couldn't bear it if you thought I was a joke too."

Theo's expression softened. "I would never think that of you. But you had to expect this would happen," he said, his smile fading. "I read your piece. It was wonderfully brave and honest, but the Order's reach is long."

Ruby let out a tired breath. The members of the Order might be some of the wealthiest and most powerful men in the city, but she had truly believed that publishers would want the truth. At the very least, she'd expected that Hearst and Pulitzer and all the rest would have craved the sales the headlines would have inspired. But one after another had slammed the door in her face.

"I'm not going to give up," she said, pulling her wits about her.

"That's my girl—"

"I'm going to try the *Spectacle*," she told him, glancing up to see what his reaction would be.

Theo's mouth fell open a little. "That's a terrible idea, Ruby."

She twisted her hands in her lap. "What choice do I have?"

"The *Spectacle* is nothing more than a gossip rag," Theo said as though Ruby needed to be reminded. "If they do accept your piece, you'll never be taken seriously again."

He was right, of course. Only the desperate or the stupid believed anything in the *Spectacle*, and once R. A. Reynolds was associated with it, her career would be over before it had even truly begun.

"Maybe I think it's worth the risk," she told him, trying to sound confident and failing miserably.

Theo's expression shifted, and his voice was softer when he spoke. "There are other ways to reach her, darling."

"I don't know what you're talking about," Ruby said, straightening a little.

"Ruby, when have you ever been able to hide anything from me?" Theo asked.

"This isn't about Viola," Ruby lied.

"Of course it is," Theo argued, coming around the desk so he could crouch in front of her. "I've read the piece. It more than stands on its own merit, but it's clear you wrote it for *her*."

Ruby lifted her chin, refusing to admit anything. "People should know the truth about the old magic," she said, her voice trembling more than she would have liked.

Hadn't Ruby recently discovered that for herself? Magic hadn't destroyed her family—that had been her father's fault, with his careless disregard for anything or anyone but himself. And magic hadn't destroyed whatever it was that Ruby might have been building with Viola. That had been all her *own* fault.

Theo took Ruby's hands in his. His grip was warm and steady, as always, like Theo himself. "Let me take you home," he said, pulling her to her feet. "You need time for this defeat to settle before you do something you'll regret. R. A. Reynolds has started to build a name for herself in this city. You can't throw it all away on the *Spectacle*. Not even for Viola Vaccarelli."

Ruby wanted to argue, but Theo was right. "Can we take the long way? I can't bear to deal with my family quite yet."

Outside, the heat of early summer was beginning to simmer. Even so, they took a route that meandered through the park, walking until Ruby's feet ached and the tightness in her chest had almost started to ease.

"Better?" Theo asked as they approached the front steps to her family's town house.

"A little," she admitted.

"It will all work out," Theo assured her.

She looked up at him, handsome as he ever was, and felt a rush of affection. Their whole lives, she'd felt that same affection, but it was nothing compared to the warmth she felt every time she remembered her lips on Viola's.

Ruby pushed that memory down where it belonged. "Would you like to come in?" she asked, forcing a brightness to her voice she didn't feel. But when Theo hesitated, she gave herself a shake. "Of course, you have your studies to get back to—"

"I have a few minutes," he said, his expression filled with something too close to pity for Ruby's liking. Still, she didn't send him on his way.

When she opened the door, it was clear that something was happening. Voices were coming from the front parlor, and the chattering of women could only mean that her sisters had assembled—*all* of her sisters. Ruby glanced at Theo, as if to tell him that he should go before it was too late. Heavens knew that once her mother and sisters started clucking about something, they wouldn't soon stop. But Theo, the dear, simply offered her his arm.

"Mother?" Ruby asked, stepping away from Theo a little when she saw who was assembled in the parlor. Two of her sisters had brought their husbands, and her uncle Archibald—her father's brother—was also there. "What is all of this? Has something happened?"

Her mother glanced at Ruby's older sister, Clara, who was the one to answer. "We've called the family to a meeting."

"Clearly," Ruby said, her unease growing. "But you seem to have forgotten my invitation."

"It was rather a last-minute decision," Clara said primly. "Still, we've made quite a lot of progress without you. We have your trip nearly planned."

Ruby understood the words coming from her sister's mouth, but they made little sense. She glanced up at Theo, who seemed equally as confused. "What trip?"

"We've decided that you will be accompanying Eleanor and Henry to the Continent this summer," Ruby's mother said, finally finding her voice.

"I've already been to the Continent. Just last spring," Ruby reminded them. "I've no wish to go again so soon."

"You have a trousseau to complete," her mother said, dismissing this concern. "You've put it off long enough."

"My trousseau can wait," Ruby told them. "I have work to do here, important work."

Clara's expression went stony, and her tone hardened. "Your *work* is exactly the problem."

Ruby blinked. "My work is not a *problem*." She knew that her family merely indulged her dreams to be a journalist, but they had never spoken outright against her vocation before.

Eleanor stepped forward, giving Clara a warning look. "You have to admit that what happened at the gala was quite . . . unsettling."

"Unsettling?" Clara said with her usual haughty laugh. "It was more than unsettling. It was downright improper. It's bad enough that you embarrassed the family at the Order's gala with your indecent display, but it's quite another thing to continue in your attempt to publicize that embarrassment for the entire world to see."

"Embarrassed?" Ruby couldn't make her mouth work to say anything else.

Her mother sighed. "You're no longer a girl, Ruby. And you cannot continue carrying on with such complete impropriety."

"I don't know what you could possibly mean." Ruby's head was still spinning when her uncle stepped forward.

"I received a call from Mr. Bartleby of the *Sun* a few hours ago," Uncle Archibald said. "It seems that you paid him a visit today. From what I understand, you made quite the spectacle of yourself this morning." He narrowed his eyes in her direction. "This cannot go on, my girl. Your family has been through enough."

"The *Constantina* departs on Thursday," Clara said.

"I won't be on it," Ruby told them, lifting her chin in a show of defiance.

"I'm afraid you have no choice in the matter," Ruby's mother said. "Your dear friend Emily Howald and her mother have graciously offered to host you at their London town house after you make your tour of the Paris dressmakers. You'll stay through the summer, of course. Possibly into the fall."

This was not a pleasure trip, Ruby realized suddenly. She was being exiled. When she spoke again, her voice sounded as hollow as she felt. "You would send me away for so long?"

"I would and I am," her mother said. "The summer will give you ample time to amass a respectable trousseau before the wedding."

"We've not even set a date yet," Ruby said, glancing at Theo, who looked every bit as taken off guard as she did.

"That is another problem that we have allowed to go on far too long. You'll be married when you return," her mother said. "It's all been arranged."

"You cannot simply *arrange* our lives, Mother," Ruby said, the panic rising hot and fast in her throat. "Shouldn't Theo and I have any say in the matter?"

"He's had his say. He has asked for your hand, and you consented. The family has given you ample time to set a date." Her mother's expression went carefully blank. "Perhaps I've not been as firm as I should have been with you, but I can no longer stand by while you ruin the chances of your younger sisters with your wild, reckless behavior."

"I hardly think—"

"That is the entire problem, my girl. You *don't* think. Do you know what I was told this morning?" her mother said, her tone turning suddenly icy. "Right now, at this very moment, all of society is atwitter with the rumor that *you* were seen kissing someone at the gala."

Ruby's stomach twisted as she pasted on a bright smile. "Surely Theo and I—"

"It was *not* Theo," her mother said. "Millicent St. Clair is being quite vocal about what she saw behind the curtains—particularly *who* it was that you were with." Her mother sank back into her chair, apparently too overwrought to remain upright.

Suddenly the air went out of the room. "Millicent St. Clair is nothing but a jealous harpy," Ruby said, but even she could hear the trembling in her voice. Someone had seen her kiss Viola.

"Of course she is," her mother said. "But the truth doesn't matter when gossip is involved."

"Mr. Bartleby had been doing his best to convince the other publishers to quash these rumors as a personal favor to me and to our family," Uncle Archibald said. "But after your performance in his offices today, he has reached the end of his patience."

Ruby's stomach turned with the understanding of what her uncle was saying. If that particular rumor found its way into the gossip columns, it would impact more than only herself. Her entire family—her two younger sisters especially—would be affected as well.

"I allowed you to put off setting a date for the wedding because of your father's *situation*," her mother said softly. "I had believed that we all needed time to heal. But this is too much, Ruby. I cannot allow you to ruin your younger sisters' chances at a good match. Not when they are so close to their debuts." Her mother put down the handkerchief she'd been crumpling into a ball with her fingers. "You'll go with Eleanor and her husband, as we have arranged. You will spend the summer in Europe while this whole mess blows over, and when you return, you will be married. With any luck, society will have put this vicious rumor to rest once and for all by then."

"That is assuming, of course, Barclay will still have you," Archibald said, lifting a brow in Theo's direction.

Ruby looked around the room, at the many pairs of eyes that were united in this against her. Theo seemed as shocked as she was.

You can throw me over, she wanted to say. But of course Theo would do no such thing.

"I've no wish to sever my engagement with Ruby. I'll have the notices sent to the papers immediately," he told them.

"Theo—"

He ignored the protest in Ruby's voice as he took her hand and placed a soft kiss upon her knuckles. Though he smiled at her, there was a sadness in his eyes that nearly broke her heart.

THE WHITE WOMAN

1902—New York

The pot on the stove was burning, but Viola didn't notice until it started to smoke. Not that she cared about the food inside. Her brother could eat his lunch burnt and bitter as far as she was concerned, but she removed it from the fire anyway. It wouldn't do to make Paul angry. Not when she'd already risked so much to keep his suspicions at bay.

Viola ladled some of the bitter greens and half-burned potatoes into two bowls, then added some thick slices of bread to the side. She took a moment to prepare the mask she wore around her family, and then she carried the tray into the dining room, where her brother and Torrio waited. She'd already made her excuses about leaving for the market. As soon as they were served, she could go, but she couldn't allow them to realize she was in a hurry, or they'd have questions.

"We'll need a third," Paolo told her, barely glancing up as he poked unhappily at the food she placed in front of him.

"You have another guest?" Viola asked, frowning. "Mama or—"

"If it were any of your business, I would have already explained," her brother said, glaring up at her in warning. He set the fork down and took a cigarette out of his silver case, his eyes steady on her while he lit it.

"Of course," she told him, letting her gaze drop. Not in deference, though he would certainly read it that way. No, Viola only lowered her eyes so her brother wouldn't see the hate burning in them. It was a trick that had served her well since she'd come to him for protection after the fiasco that was Khafre Hall.

Viola retreated to the kitchen, her cheeks burning in anger and shame all at once, silently cursing Paolo—and herself—as she violently scooped out another serving. Paul might have taken her from the grip of the demon at the gala, he might have commended her for attacking Jianyu, but that hadn't changed anything between the two of them.

When she returned to the front of the house with the third bowl, Viola's steps halted. Her brother's guest had arrived.

"Hello, Viola." Nibsy Lorcan's mouth curved in a small, satisfied smile as he took his place at the table with Paul. "I see you're still safe and well in your family's keeping."

At first Viola couldn't do more than stare in shocked confusion. After Mooch, one of the Devil's Own, had attacked Tammany's firehouse, she'd thought her brother had realized what a snake Nibsy Lorcan could be. "This one, *he's* your guest?" she asked, her words coming before she could think better of them.

One glance at Paolo, though, and Viola understood that something was happening here, some bigger game she'd not been made aware of. Her brother's expression narrowed ever so slightly—a warning. "Mr. Lorcan and I have business to discuss," Paul said, taking a final drag on his cigarette before stubbing it out.

Nibsy glanced over his spectacles. "You should join us," he said easily. "You might be interested in what I have to say as well. After all, we are old friends." He met her eyes, his gaze steady, as though reminding her of the last time they'd met—when he'd returned Libitina to her and revealed what Dolph had done to Leena.

"Viola has other things to attend to, I'm sure," Paul told Nibsy, cutting another meaningful look in her direction.

He wanted her to go, which made Viola want to stay all the more, but she didn't need to glance at the clock to know that the minutes, which had crept by all morning, were now racing toward the time when Abel would be waiting for her. Still, Nibsy Lorcan was dining with Paul, and Paul hadn't yet killed him. Something was happening.

"I thought you were on your way to the market," Paul said, raising his brows in question—another challenge. It only confirmed her suspicions.

As much as Viola wanted to stay and listen to their conversation, the clock would not wait. Abel, Jianyu, and the blood on her hands would not wait.

"I was just leaving," she said tightly as she placed the bowl in front of Nibsy. Then, still torn, she left her brother and Nibsy Lorcan to whatever business they had between them.

Outside, the summer day had turned hazy and humid. Viola glanced down the street toward the end of the block, where she'd expected Abel to be waiting, but there was no sign of him. As she began to feel the fear—the *relief*—that perhaps Abel hadn't come after all, he stepped from around the corner and glanced her way. Even from that distance, she could see his impatience.

"Something's happening," Viola said as soon as she was close enough. She motioned him to step around the corner and into a blind alleyway. When they were out of view of Paul's place, she tried to explain. "Nibsy Lorcan just arrived—"

"I don't know who that is," Abel said, interrupting her. "And I don't particularly care. You need to come now. Jianyu hasn't woken up all morning."

Viola froze. "He's worse?"

"This morning, not long after I left to find you, he closed his eyes and that was that." Abel's jaw went tight. "His skin feels like it's growing cooler."

Viola was shaking her head. Nibsy Lorcan was up to something—so was her brother—but she knew she could not stay to discover what it was. She could not have Jianyu's death added to the black marks against her soul.

"I can't go back to my sister again without you," Abel said. "I have a carriage waiting on the next block over. *Please.*" He started to offer her his hand—or maybe he meant to take her arm—but then his eyes shifted to something behind her, and he took a step back instead.

Viola turned, expecting Paul or one of his boys to be there, following her. Instead, she found Theo Barclay squaring his shoulders with suspicion and something strangely close to anger gleaming in his eye. Next to him, dressed in the most ridiculous mint-green frock of lace and chiffon, was Ruby Reynolds.

At the sight of her, Viola felt like her feet had been nailed to the ground and her tongue had been cut from her mouth. For a moment she could do nothing but stare at Ruby, there like some sort of apparition, with her cheeks flushed a becoming rose-petal pink and her eyes bright with some emotion Viola could not interpret.

"Are you okay, Miss Vaccarelli?" Theo's voice was tight, and his words were unusually clipped. Ruby clasped her hands silently next to him.

"Theo?" It took Viola a moment to realize she wasn't imagining them. Why had they come? "I'm fine," she said, realizing that she was staring and that Theo was wearing a look that indicated he viewed Abel as a threat. "Really, Theo. I'm okay."

"You don't look fine," Theo said, glowering at Abel. "Is he bothering you?"

She let out an impatient huff. "He's not bothering me. What are you doing here? I've told you it's not safe," she said, trying to draw Theo's attention back to herself.

"Ruby insisted we come," Theo said, glancing at the girl next to him.

"I needed to speak with you," Ruby said, stepping forward. Her voice was soft and breathy, as it always was, but there was that same thread of steel in it that had piqued Viola's interest in the weeks before.

Viola backed away. "I have nothing more to say."

"I'm leaving for Paris on Thursday with my sister. This was my only chance to come," Ruby told her.

"Paris?" Viola said, still not sure why either of them were there.

"I'm being exiled," Ruby said, her voice suddenly heavy with fury.

Viola frowned, not understanding.

"She'll be out of the city for a while—a few months," Theo explained. "Her family thought it best if she . . ." He shook his head. "It doesn't matter."

"Why would you bring her here?" Viola demanded.

Theo looked abashed. "She was quite insistent—"

"I threatened to come on my own if he didn't," Ruby clarified. "I couldn't leave without knowing—" She glanced at where Abel stood, waiting a few paces beyond Viola. "Could we could go somewhere more private to speak? Ferrara's, perhaps, or . . ."

"We have to go," Abel reminded Viola. "Jianyu can't wait."

Viola glanced at Abel and knew from the unease shadowing his voice that this was no lie or bluff. Still, she turned back to Ruby. "I'm sorry, but I have to go."

The color drained from Ruby's cheeks, but she didn't argue.

"With him?" Theo frowned at Abel. "Do you really think that's wise?"

"Yes," Viola said, but Theo's expression still remained creased with doubt. "Mr. Johnson is a friend."

"But we came all this way—"

"There is nothing to talk about," Viola said, her heart firmly in her throat and her eyes burning with unshed tears. "Good-bye, Theo. Good-bye, Miss Reynolds." She stepped around the two and started walking toward where she hoped Abel's carriage would be waiting.

She hadn't gone more than three paces, when someone grabbed her arm. Viola turned on her heel, expecting it to be Theo, but it was Ruby whose fingers were wrapped around her wrist. Suddenly the day felt too warm—her *skin* felt too warm. Suddenly Viola couldn't breathe.

"I know what you must think of me," Ruby said, pausing as though to steady her voice. "But please—" Her voice broke, and Viola realized that Ruby was pressing a folded piece of paper into her hand. "This is for you. Whatever you may think of me, read it? Please?"

Viola stood shocked and frozen. It would be so easy to reach for Ruby, to return the gentle pressure she felt as Ruby gripped her hand. Instead,

Viola pulled away—turned away—and as her heart ached, she walked on.

Abel had caught up to her a few seconds later. At first he didn't speak, but Viola could feel his interest. "He's not happy you're going with me," Abel said finally, tossing a glance behind them as they rounded a corner. "Neither of them is."

Viola felt strangely numb. The paper was still crumpled in her fist, the day was too warm, and yet she felt nothing at all. Nothing but an aching regret in the space where her heart had once beat steady and sure.

"You don't think he'll cause trouble, do you?" Abel asked.

Viola realized then that Abel was speaking to her and that he sounded strangely nervous. "Who? Theo?" She glanced up at Abel, who looked uncomfortable. "Why would he?"

"He seemed . . . concerned." Abel frowned.

"He's a man." Viola gave him an impatient look. "Isn't this what you men do? Interfere with the lives of women who aren't asking for your help?"

"I think he might be more concerned about the color of my skin." Abel's voice had a strange dullness to it. "And the color of yours."

Viola turned to him, understanding dawning, but she dismissed it with a wave of her hand. "I'm nothing to Theo Barclay. He's one of them—a rich boy, born con la camicia. And what am I? No one. An immigrant. An Italiana. And with the old magic as well."

"I don't think he sees it like that," Abel said.

"You know what they call us, don't you? Verme. Dagos. Filthy Guineas," Viola told him, snapping the words out. "No better than—" She stopped, her stomach twisting.

Abel's gaze was steady, as though he knew what she'd been about to say. "You sure look like a white woman to me. And whether you realize it or not, you become one to him the second we're together."

They stood there for a long moment, neither one looking away. Neither one willing to budge, even as the air grew tense between them.

"This was a bad idea," Abel said, finally glancing away. "I told Cela, but she wouldn't hear a word I was saying. We never should've gotten wrapped up in this. We have enough troubles without adding magic and white people to them."

Viola studied him. "I don't want to add to your troubles, Mr. Johnson."

"Maybe not, but tell me," Abel said. "What happens when this is all over? Where does that leave Cela or me—or any of us? Especially with your friends eyeing me like something the dog dragged out of the trash?"

Viola could only stare at him, because she had no answer— she had not even thought it a question until now. "I don't know," she told him, the raw honesty of that single statement making her feel suddenly exposed— suddenly too stupid for words. "I thought you said Jianyu couldn't wait?" she asked, shoving aside the uncomfortable emotion that had settled in the space below her rib cage.

Abel gave her an unreadable look before he climbed inside the hack. Viola could see Theo and Ruby over Abel's shoulder. Ruby had turned to him, but Theo was still watching with a look of concern on his face. Then the door closed and they were off, leaving behind Theo Barclay and Ruby Reynolds, as well as any chance Viola might have had to find out what Nibsy Lorcan and her brother were up to.

DÉJÀ VU

1904—Texas

E sta awoke slumped over North's shoulder. The darkness that had overtaken her as they ran from the train was still shadowing her vision. At first she didn't know where she was.

Then she remembered—the train, the posse, and then . . . nothing but Seshat's power.

"What the hell?" North's voice sounded strangled, but she couldn't see what had put that emotion there. Actually, Esta couldn't see anything but his backside.

"Put me down," she demanded, trying to wriggle free of his hold, and he complied, letting her slide to the ground. She barely managed to catch herself on unsteady legs before she turned to see what the other two were looking at.

In the direction of the town, a cyclone was growing, but from the way it glowed with an eerie light, it didn't look like anything natural. It was a monster of a thing, a towering column of heat and light that wove itself along the ground between them and the men on horseback. Strange colors flashed within as it tracked back and forth, blocking the riders' path. In the distance, Esta heard explosions sounding, like firecrackers.

"Where did that come from?" she asked, her head still swirling. It was so enormous that, even from where they stood, she could feel the telltale warmth of magic in the air, soft and compelling. She knew in an instant that whoever had created the cyclone had used an affinity.

"I don't know," Maggie told her. "You fell and then, out of nowhere, fires started erupting. They looked like . . ." She shook her head, frowning. "I don't know how it's possible, but they looked like my incendiaries." Maggie glanced at North. "Do you think there are other Mageus here? Maybe even other Antistasi?"

"It's possible," North told Maggie. But he didn't sound like he thought it was likely.

Esta had the strangest premonition then, like a shiver of dread running down her spine. Something had happened that she couldn't quite remember. She was sure of it. "We need to go," she said, trying to shake off her unease. "Who knows how long that thing will keep those marshals occupied."

North took the lead as they started running for the oil fields, which had been their original destination, but Esta still felt off-kilter. Her vision remained tinged with the shadows that had darkened it before she passed out. With the posse occupied by the strange cyclone, they made good time, but when they finally reached the towers, they realized that the fields that had looked deserted from a distance were actually crawling with laborers.

Skirting around the edges of the area, the three of them moved from the shelter of one tower to another. Eventually they reached a place where they couldn't go any farther. Cutting through the center of the sprawling oil fields was another set of tracks, which held a line of massive tanker cars ready to transport the raw petroleum. There were men, too, lots of them. Beyond their hiding place, dozens of workers checked the pipes that were loading the tankers and prepped the shipment for travel. The engine stood waiting, its massive boilers releasing steam in a slow, lazy hiss.

The three of them pulled back, retreating to the shelter of an old, abandoned shed. Esta's skin crawled when they entered it. Something about the place felt . . . wrong, but it was also weirdly familiar in a way she couldn't explain.

"We're stuck," Maggie said. "There's no easy way around all those men."

"Even if there were, we don't know what's on the other side," Esta agreed.

"We could try for the town," North suggested. "Maybe we could blend in, lie low for a while."

Esta knew that would never work. "Once those marshals realize we're not on the train, they're going to start searching," she said. "In town or here, it doesn't matter. If they knew we were on that train, it means that someone recognized us. We're not going to be able to blend in."

"I could take us back," North said, reaching for his watch. "Maybe we could jump another train and get farther down the road, ahead of them."

Something in Esta recoiled at that idea, but she couldn't have said why. "No," she told him, going on nothing but instinct. "How much time could we possibly buy? Six hours, maybe twelve. The authorities already know we're headed in this direction. A few extra hours isn't going to help if we're spotted again—not when a telegram takes only a few seconds. They're going to keep hunting for us, and eventually they'll close in."

"We got off the train, didn't we?" North asked, frowning. "We can't just give up now. We have to keep going."

"Maybe there's someone here who'd be willing to help," Maggie said, biting at her lip. "Those fires didn't start themselves, and they didn't seem to be on the side of the riders."

"Maggie's right," North said. "Maybe there are Mageus here who could hide us. We might find ourselves some allies, maybe even a few Antistasi."

"Considering the way we left things with Ruth, any Antistasi we find might also be enemies," Esta reminded them. There was something about that strange cyclone of flame that just felt wrong to her, something that told her there was more to it than she understood. Not that she'd convince the two of them on a hunch. She went for logic instead. "Think about it," she pressed. "By now plenty of people know what we did in St. Louis. Just because there might be Mageus here doesn't mean they're necessarily friendly. Or maybe . . ." A thought occurred to her that seemed too ridiculous to be true.

"What?" North pressed.

Time was such a tricky thing, twisting and unpredictable, but Esta had never had to account for someone else who could manipulate it before. "You said those fires looked like your formulas, didn't you, Maggie?"

Maggie nodded. "Yes . . ."

"Is it possible that we *already* went back?" Esta asked. The two of them only stared at her, so she explained. "Maybe we're the ones who rescued *ourselves*."

North was still frowning, but he wasn't disagreeing. His hand went to the pocket in his vest, where his watch waited. "It's not impossible," he admitted. "But even if that's the case, it doesn't help us to get out of here now. There's nowhere to go and too many damn witnesses."

Esta considered the men working the oil fields nearby, and an idea began to form. "Maybe we can use them to our advantage." She turned to Maggie. "Maybe we can use one of your formulations or devices."

"Of course," Maggie said, frowning. "But if we do that, they're going to know for sure that we're here."

"That's the point," Esta told her as she considered the waiting engine below. There was one thing necessary for a truly great trick—Harte had taught her that. *Misdirection.* "Those marshals wouldn't have been riding out to meet the train if they didn't already think we were on it, and thanks to whoever made that giant inferno of a cyclone, they know that *someone* has the old magic. So let's confirm their suspicions. And then let's disappear."

"Disappear?" Maggie said doubtfully.

"We'll need a distraction," Esta told her. "Something big enough for them not to notice us getting away. Something that will ensure they won't come looking for us later." She met their eyes, held their gaze. "I think it's time to kill the Devil's Thief."

A PARTNERSHIP OF SORTS

1902—New York

James Lorcan took another bite of the half-burned sludge from the bowl in front of him, but his awareness was still on Viola's departure, and on the way the Aether moved in response. His stomach turning at the taste of the food, he set the fork down and picked at the bread. Its flavor was familiar—a hearty rye with a hint of sweetness that had once been served in the kitchens of the Bella Strega. Despite her clear lack of talent for cooking, Viola, it seemed, had learned something from Tilly after all.

Which wasn't surprising. Dolph's assassin might be as sharp and unyielding as the blades she favored, but she'd always had a soft spot for Tilly Malkov. James hadn't missed the way Viola's eyes had followed the other girl around the kitchen in the Strega.

Kelly flashed a look at Torrio. "Follow her."

Torrio's mouth half fell open. "But I thought—"

"I don't pay you to think," Kelly said. "My sister is up to something, and I want to know what it is."

Torrio glanced at James, disgust clear on his face, but James was careful not to look too directly at him. There was no sense giving anything away here, in front of Paul Kelly.

"You don't think I should be here?" Torrio asked. "I thought we had business with—"

"*I* have business," Kelly said, cutting him off. "You have my sister to attend to."

"I ain't a nursemaid," Torrio told him, crossing his arms. Kelly slid a deadly look in Torrio's direction, but Torrio didn't so much as flinch. He returned the glare and allowed his lips to twitch with amusement. "And anyway . . . you sure you want me *tending* to Viola?"

Tension crackled across the table between the two Five Pointers. "I realize you *aren't* a nursemaid," Kelly said, keeping his voice dangerously even. "And I'm sure that *you* know how important my sister is to me. I send you because I trust you, Johnny. Don't tell me that trust is misplaced?"

Torrio's jaw was tight, and James sensed the Aether around him tremble. He kept his expression placid, watching the drama play out and making a note of this weakness as he planned all the while. Paul Kelly was a thorn in James' side, a danger as long as he held any real power in the Bowery. The trick would be to neutralize the danger of the Five Pointers in general, and even better if he could do so in a way that was *productive*.

With a violent thrust, Torrio was on his feet. He tore the napkin from where he'd tucked it into his shirtfront and stormed off. His anger would be useful, James thought . . . as long as it could be properly harnessed.

Once Torrio was gone and James knew for sure they were alone, he placed the bread on the table and dusted the crumbs from his fingers. "It's good to have people you can depend on," he said easily, keeping all trace of mockery from his voice.

Kelly glared at him. "What about you, Lorcan? Do *you* have people you can depend on?" he asked. "Or haven't you managed to take the Devil's Own in hand?"

It was a point of contention between them. Kelly would have happily taken the Strega and all who were loyal to Dolph by force, but James had managed to persuade Kelly of the benefits of coaxing the gang to his side first. It bought James time and provided access to—and protection from—the Five Pointers that he wouldn't have otherwise had. But James Lorcan knew Kelly's patience was running out. He'd have to figure out a way to take care of the threat Kelly posed soon.

"Without Saunders, the loyalty of the Devil's Own is already beginning to wane, as I predicted. The desperate and fearful forget quickly," he told Kelly. It was true—mostly. As soon as he had the ring, it would be true in fact. Not that Kelly needed that information. "They'll be ready for you."

"Good." Kelly's eyes gleamed, clearly satisfied with this news.

Of course James had no intention of *ever* handing over the Bella Strega *or* the Devil's Own. Once the artifacts were his, Kelly would be no more than a fly to be swatted. And the Five Pointers? They'd make a fine addition to James' own numbers.

Paul Kelly gave him a knowing sort of look. "I'm sure it helps that you've seen no problems from Tammany. . . ."

Since Dolph's team had robbed the Order, Tammany's patrols had been ever present in the Bowery. Buildings had burned, beer halls had been destroyed. Any business that had even a pretense of association with the old magic had become a target. But Kelly had kept his end of their bargain—at least in that regard. The Bella Strega stood intact, untouched by Tammany's men.

"None," James admitted. "Although I'd point out that we've both benefited from our little arrangement," he said easily. "I trust you managed to enjoy yourself at the Order's gala."

He could tell by the slight tic in Kelly's jaw that his remark had hit its target. After all, without the warning that James had provided, Kelly and his men would have been sitting ducks, unprepared for Jack Grew's betrayal.

The ensuing fight should have provided the cover Logan Sullivan needed to retrieve the ring. Logan, who could find any magical object, had been a gift from James' future self, but so far the boy had failed to live up to his potential. The ring should have been easily obtained from the gala, but Logan had still managed to return empty-handed. Somewhere in the confusion, the artifact had disappeared, and since then, Logan hadn't been able to find any hint of it in the city. But then, Paul Kelly wasn't confined to the city, unlike James and every other Mageus.

"I didn't bring you here to talk about the gala," Kelly said, brushing the topic aside with a wave of his hand.

"Why *did* you call me here?" James asked. "I must admit I was surprised when I got your message."

It was a lie, of course. James had known almost immediately after Logan had returned from the gala empty-handed that he and Kelly would cross paths again—sooner rather than later. After all, they had an agreement. A partnership, of sorts. For now Kelly was useful. His men could go where James couldn't. They had the ability to move outside the city and search for the artifacts that Darrigan had managed to snatch right out of James' grasp, and James had something Kelly wanted—the Bella Strega and, with it, the Devil's Own. But Kelly's thirst for expanding his criminal empire made him vulnerable, and James had every intention of turning that against him when the time was right.

James considered Kelly. "Unless your little summons means that you have news for me?"

Kelly didn't rush to answer at first. Instead, he took another bite of greens and chewed without so much as grimacing. It was a tactic that James understood was meant to unnerve him, but he had no intention of filling the emptiness with unnecessary chatter. He simply waited as Kelly gracefully dabbed at his lips with the napkin from his lap.

Only after Kelly folded the napkin and set it aside did he finally speak. "I'm sure you're aware that the Order had some difficulties back in March," Kelly said with a sardonic lift of his heavy brows—a reminder of exactly how much he knew about the Khafre Hall job. "Word is that they've been looking for a new location to establish their headquarters."

"Oh?" James said, trying to cover his surprise. "They aren't simply going to rebuild Khafre Hall?"

The journal Logan brought him had made it clear—the Order wouldn't build a new headquarters in time for the Conclave. They would go into that gathering scattered and unorganized, weak enough that the Conclave would turn out to be a failure. They would not consolidate their power. They would not take control of the Brotherhoods, and because of that failure, the Order would never be the same. After, the journal had assured him, the Order and the other Brotherhoods would remain secretive organizations that worked in the shadows, always at odds with one another. They would still be a danger to Mageus, but after the failure of the Conclave, they would not be the threat they might have otherwise been.

"No," Kelly said. "Word is that something changed after Morgan's big gala."

A lot of things had changed after the gala—including the notebook Logan had brought him. After the gala, James found that his once clear, familiar handwriting seemed to have come alive, the letters flickering like a candle about to gutter, shifting into new arrangements that he could make neither heads nor tails of. When he first received the journal, he'd thought it would be the key to his victory, but after the gala—after Logan's failure to retrieve the ring—it had become all but worthless. Now he wondered if this was the reason.

"What do you think the cause for this change is?" James wondered.

"I can't be sure, but they have more confidence now," Kelly told him.

"You think they've retrieved an artifact," James realized.

Kelly squinted a little at James. "I don't know for sure, but I suspect that might be the case. So does Tammany. The Inner Circle is anxious to get into a new location, and soon."

If the Order had managed to retrieve one of their artifacts, if they suddenly had plans for a new headquarters, it meant that something had occurred that *hadn't* before. The entire future had been thrown into question. "How soon?"

Kelly took a cigarette from the gleaming case, rolling it a little between his thick fingers before placing it between his lips. "From what I hear, the Order already has a location picked out—the Fuller Building."

James frowned. The Fuller Building seemed an odd selection. While Khafre Hall had been a stately piece of old New York architecture, steeped in tradition and secrecy, the Fuller Building was a new landmark. Located across from Madison Square Park, it was an ostentatious thing, a blade of a building that the entire city had watched rise in a surprisingly short amount of time. With its strange, spindly skeleton of steel, everyone was sure that it would fall before it was finished. It was also one of the more exciting pieces of architecture in the city. It would be an enormous structure—if it stood. It would also be a landmark, James realized.

He supposed it made a sort of sense, especially if the Order had managed to retrieve the ring at the gala. The new skyscraper was a testament to science and demonstrated man's ability to rise up above the rabble of the streets, and it was situated in the beating heart of the modern city. Selecting the Fuller Building was tantamount to a declaration—the Order was not content to remain in the past. They were staking a new place, and they were declaring their continued importance.

"The building will be opening by the end of next month, won't it?" James asked.

Kelly lit the cigarette and took a long drag, letting the smoke enwreathe his head like some sort of demon. "Rumor has it, the Order will be moving what was left of their treasures into their new headquarters in a matter of weeks."

James frowned. "I hadn't realized they had much left after the fire." His mind was already whirling with the implications. Dolph had been so focused on the Book and the artifacts, could he have missed that the Order had something else of value?

"They have a couple of wagonloads, apparently," Kelly told him. "From what I've been able to learn, they've been storing them somewhere in Brooklyn—outside the Brink. Originally, they were going to rebuild Khafre Hall, but what happened at the gala made them anxious to move into their new headquarters and reestablish themselves as a force to be reckoned with in the city *now*, before their Conclave at the end of the year."

"That would be unfortunate for both of us," James said. "But perhaps it's also an opportunity?"

"I agree," Kelly told him. "Which is why I called you here. I want the Devil's Own on board."

"Certainly your Five Pointers can take care of a few wagons of goods," James said, the implication clear.

"You don't bring a knife to a gunfight, Lorcan, and the Order has weapons far beyond what my boys are equipped to handle."

James understood now. "You're afraid of their magic."

"I'm not afraid," Kelly said, his tone unyielding. "But I'll admit I don't have the specific skill set that you and your people do."

James knew this was the real reason Kelly wanted control over the Strega and Devil's Own. Kelly might have despised his sister—he despised everyone with the old magic—but he wasn't above using Viola or any other Mageus for his own means.

"Think of this as another way to solidify our partnership," Kelly said when James didn't immediately agree. "A show of continued good faith. After all, it would be a terrible shame if the Strega started having the same problems as some of the other saloons in the area."

James saw the threat for what it was, and he found that he had little interest in being Kelly's pawn. Still, he understood the opportunity that the situation presented.

"Of course," James said, pretending deference. "It does seem like it would be in *both* of our interests to make sure the Order can't regain a footing in the city."

James was glad suddenly that he hadn't simply allowed the Order to remove the threat of Paul Kelly at the gala. He'd wanted to, but the Aether had whispered otherwise, and once again his intuition had proven correct. Kelly, it seemed, could still be useful. When the time came, James would pit his two greatest enemies against each other and watch as they destroyed each other instead of him.

As he listened to the information Kelly offered, James' mind was already whirling with possibilities. The Aether bunched and shifted around him. He would retrieve the artifact he'd lost and take care of the problem Paul Kelly posed all at once. He'd help Kelly rob the Order, all right. Then he'd help the damned Five Pointer right into a noose.

MISDIRECTION

1904—*Texas*

North had done his damnedest to argue against Esta's plan, not only because it seemed like they were taking unnecessary risks, but also because it provided the Thief an opportunity to leave them in the dust, like her partner had. She assured them she wasn't interested in running, but North had a feeling that Esta could lie better than most. Still, it wasn't like he had a better idea, so there he was, right where he hadn't wanted to be, watching the train yard from a spot on an outcropping a little way off.

"It'll be okay," Maggie whispered from her place next to him. She could always read the direction of his thoughts too easily. "She's not going anywhere."

North grunted his disagreement.

From their vantage point, North could see the men going about their business, unaware of what was about to happen, and he didn't exactly envy them. Esta was below as well, inching toward the tracks. She'd wrapped some fabric they'd found in an empty shed around her waist as a makeshift skirt and covered her head with another strip of bright fabric to make it look like there was more hair beneath. She might have looked a mess, but Esta still moved with the kind of easy confidence that made you believe she could do practically anything. Which was exactly what North was worried about.

Together, they watched as Esta slunk around the edges of the train yard. When no one was looking, she climbed into the engine compartment.

None of the men seemed aware of what was happening. No one seemed to notice the girl pressing a gun against the engineer's spine, so they couldn't have seen her use Maggie's confounding solution on the poor guy. No one even looked up, not until the train's engines started humming and the wheels squealed as it began to move down the track. They paid attention then, because some of the tanker cars were still hooked to the pipes that fed them, and as the train pulled away, black liquid poured out onto the ground.

Before the train could pick up too much speed, North saw Esta push the engineer from the train. He rolled to his side, and some of the workers ran to him. As the engine continued away, the workers launched into action. Some were trying to stop the flood of crude oil that poured from the pipeline, but others were running after the train and trying to catch hold of one of the rails so they could climb up into the engine compartment. The sound of gunshots rang through the air, and North pulled Maggie back to protect her from any stray bullets.

"We need to go," he told her.

But Maggie shook him off. "We need to be sure." She turned back to the scene playing out before them.

A moment later, Esta emerged again from the back of the engine, the barrel of a pistol aimed toward the nearest tower.

One, two, three shots erupted from the pistol North had loaned to her, each echoing with the telltale puff of smoke from the firing. But nothing happened.

"Come on," Maggie whispered.

When the fourth puff of white smoke erupted from the gun, the tower exploded in a burst of blue flame. Two others followed in rapid succession, the sun-dried wooden frames burning so hot and so fast, North had to turn his face away. When he looked back again, flames were licking up into the sky. Blue and purple, green and orange and red, the inferno flickered with energy, like electricity gone feral. Like *magic*.

The crowd of men below were no longer focused only on the train.

Almost as one, they turned in horror. Some fled, while others started working to put out the fires before they could spread, but it was already too late. The buckets of water didn't touch the strange flames.

The explosions had done their job, just like Esta had thought they would. The posse of men who'd been investigating the other train arrived a few minutes later, charging in on mounts that became immediately skittish at the sight of the strange flames. The horses pranced uneasily beneath their riders, tossing their heads like they could shake away the heat.

A pair of men broke through the posse's ranks and came to the front. From the way they sat their horses and surveyed the destruction with a kind of stillness, North figured they must be the ones in charge. One of the men listened as the others in the yard all tried to talk at once, pointing and shouting in the direction the train was going, but the other man pushed back his hat and looked to the burning oil towers.

Beneath the brim of the hat, the sun revealed a face North hadn't seen in at least two years. A face he would never forget. *Jot Gunter.*

The man owned the ranch North had worked on years before, back in Crabapple, Texas. When Gunter had discovered the mark on North's wrist, he'd ordered North beaten, tossed from the ranch, and left for dead. Even from that distance, the rancher was easy to recognize, and North could tell that Gunter hadn't changed one bit. Same heavy white mustache. Same beady eyes. His presence there in the oil fields of Corsicana, Texas, though, was a variable North couldn't have predicted.

"We have to go. *Now*," he said again, this time taking Maggie by the hand and forcibly tugging her along.

"But Esta—"

"This whole crazy plan was her idea," North reminded Maggie. "She knows where to meet us." They needed to get away while they could.

As they went, North kept his eye on the engine picking up steam in the distance. But there was no sign of any change, no sign of Esta.

North wasn't sure what had worried him more—that Esta might run off on them, or that she might not be able to get free of the charging engine. The last time she'd used her affinity, it hadn't gone well. She wouldn't tell them what, exactly, had happened, and he hadn't been sure how smart it was for them to depend on her magic again.

When he'd brought up the issue earlier, she and Maggie had assured him that it would be fine. Esta would only have to hold on to time for a few seconds, long enough to make it off the train without breaking her neck. With luck, everyone else would believe that the Devil's Thief was still on the locomotive, while the three of them headed the other way. *Misdirection*, Esta had called it, but North suddenly had a sinking suspicion that the crowd wasn't the only audience she'd had in mind.

In the distance, the train was going faster. The smoke spewing from its smokestacks turned from a light gray to a darker, dangerous cloud of sooty black. Esta had accomplished what she'd planned to do, and now it was up to him and Maggie to get away from the crowd while they had the chance. North tugged Maggie on, and this time she came willingly, but as they reached the far edges of the oil fields, North felt the earth begin to rumble beneath his feet.

At first he didn't think much of it, but then he realized it was more than the train he was feeling. The vibrations under his boots were getting stronger even as the train was pulling farther away. It felt like the earth itself was about to split open.

"What's happening?" Maggie asked, her hand tightening around his as she tried to keep her footing. "My incendiaries wouldn't cause this."

"I don't know, but we need to keep moving."

He'd barely gotten the words out when the earth beneath the engine broke open into a long, jagged gash that swallowed the train whole. The chasm continued to travel in multiple directions from the place where the train disappeared, and moments later the locomotive itself exploded. Even from that distance, the force of the earth shaking nearly rocked them off their feet. Instinctively, North wrapped himself around Maggie, threw them both to the ground, and covered her with his body.

When the rumbling finally stopped and North allowed himself to look up, the dark iron body of the locomotive was gone. They could see nothing but a column of flames that rose from the broken ground, pouring black, sooty smoke into the sky that blotted out the blue. North cursed long and low as he looked over the terrible scene. He sensed Maggie trembling, and he understood what she was feeling. Something had gone terribly wrong.

When Maggie turned to him, her eyes were wide and her face had drained of color. "I didn't think—it wasn't supposed to explode yet. Not until it was farther down the track. Do you think Esta made it off before—" Maggie's voice broke. Her expression was so pained that his heart nearly cracked in two.

In the distance, fingers of fire reached high into the sky, and behind them, the oil fields looked like hell come to earth as another of the towers went up in flames. North and Maggie were stuck in the middle, lost in a thick haze that burned North's eyes and throat.

"I'm sure Esta's fine," he told Maggie, hoping he sounded more confident than he felt.

The riders had already gotten their horses under control. Half were stuck on the far side of the chasm, and some had tumbled into the split in the earth, but the remainder began to gallop toward the wreckage.

"Come on." North pulled Maggie gently along. "We need to get moving if we want to get to the meeting place on time."

"What if she doesn't show up, Jericho?" Maggie asked. "What if she got off the train too late? What if you were right to worry about her affinity and she's—"

"Esta Filosik has more lives than a cat," North said, even as his own stomach churned. "If she doesn't show up where she's supposed to, we can always go back and get her." His thumb rubbed across the worn metal cover of his pocket watch. Because, for Jericho Northwood, there was no such thing as too late.

II

ON DAWSON PLACE

1904—San Francisco

Harte Darrigan pulled back into the empty doorway of a closed shop, out of view from the eagle-eyed guards at the barricade's entrance across the street. He wasn't sure what the men were looking for or why they were blocking the intersection. On the train, he'd read about the raids that were happening all over the country in retaliation for the Antistasi's attack in St. Louis. The barricade could be related to those actions.

Whatever the case, the address Harte was looking for was somewhere beyond that fencing. He supposed he could go around, but the barbed wire wasn't just across the one intersection. Blocks in either direction were cordoned off from the rest of the city. It was already growing late, and he didn't want to waste time on a detour, especially when there was no telling how far the blockade stretched.

As Harte tried to figure out how he could get past the guards without being seen or recognized, a pair of men approached the entrance. They were laughing and talking, their pale cheeks already bright pink from a night of drinking. After they spoke briefly with the guards, the gate was pulled back to allow them to pass.

So there was a way through.

After a few minutes more, it became clear who the guards were letting pass—men. That wasn't a surprise, though. Harte hadn't seen many women out on the streets since he'd arrived. San Francisco seemed like a city populated almost entirely by men. From the looks of it, the police were admitting a steady stream, mostly made up of white day laborers and sailors. If only he knew for sure what the sentries were looking for.

Harte noticed a driver leaning against a horse cart about halfway down the block. The man was smoking a thin cigar and reading a rumpled newspaper as he waited for his next fare. As Harte approached, the driver glanced up over the newsprint.

"You need a ride?" the man asked, as if to determine whether Harte was worth his time.

Harte shook his head. "Not at the moment. I have a question you might be able to answer."

The driver frowned and returned to reading with an annoyed snap of his paper. "That depends on what you want to know."

"What's going on over there?" Harte asked, tilting his head toward the barricade.

"Quarantine." A single, gruffly spoken word that didn't explain anything. "They have all of Chinatown cordoned off."

"Quarantine?" Harte repeated, relieved that it didn't have anything to do with Mageus or the Antistasi. "Why is there a quarantine?"

The man glanced up. "Plague, if you can believe that," he said with a grunt. "We haven't had a case of it in this town for three years, and now the Committee's saying they found multiple cases just this week."

"The Committee?" Harte asked.

"Vigilance Committee," the driver said, looking vaguely annoyed at the stream of questions. "Used to be the mayor who would determine quarantine, but now the Committee's got the bigger say. So maybe it's the plague, or maybe they're trying to root out some of the maggots that make trouble from time to time. What with the recent events, I'd expect it to be the latter." The man glanced up over his paper briefly. "Not that I'm complaining, mind you. No use taking any chances. If you ask me, the Committee'd be smarter to burn the whole damn Chinese quarter down."

Harte watched another man approach the checkpoint and then get ushered through. "People are still going in," he observed, an unspoken question in his tone.

"Quarantine don't stop people from their own stupidity." The driver turned the page without looking up. "If sailors who've been stuck on a boat for months don't care about their manhood falling off from some pox or another, a little thing like the plague ain't gonna scare them off either."

The idea that the actual *plague* was here seemed to be a bit far-fetched, but Harte knew how people could be, especially when it came to Chinese immigrants. He'd seen how they'd been treated in New York, and he couldn't imagine things were any better here in California. Not that he was going to risk pointing this fact out to the driver.

The man glanced up, clearly at the end of his patience. "Look, do you need a ride or not?"

"No," Harte said. "I was only—"

"If you don't need a ride, then shove off," the man said, jerking his thumb over his shoulder. "You're scaring away actual customers."

Harte thanked the man for his time before walking a bit farther down the sidewalk, toward the next intersection, where another entrance was guarded by another pair of armed men. Harte felt Seshat pacing like a caged tiger, but he wasn't sure what was making her so nervous—that he was getting closer to retrieving the artifact or the risk he might be taking by breaching the quarantine.

Plague or not, the Dragon's Eye was beyond the barricade. Maybe he could go around, but it would take more time and it was already getting late. Besides, he had no idea how far Chinatown stretched, and he didn't want to waste time figuring it out. Even now Esta might have the dagger. She might already be on her way to meet him at the bridge, and he would not leave her waiting. The faster he reached his destination, the better. He looked down the stretch of the street, considered the seemingly endless checkpoints, and decided to go through.

Harte approached the checkpoint like he belonged there, and his show of confidence seemed to work. The guard gave him only the briefest of glances before letting him pass. On the other side, the streets changed. The buildings were the same Italianate style as those throughout the city, but they dripped with red banners, hand-painted with the elegant, curling scrollwork of Chinese characters. Most were also canopied by wooden balconies that clung precariously to the walls of the buildings.

The sights and smells reminded Harte of Mott Street in New York, where dried shrimp would be piled in baskets along the sidewalk and roasted duck hung in the windows of the stalls. He found himself briefly, uncharacteristically homesick. But New York felt like a lifetime ago, and Harte couldn't afford to dwell on the past.

Pulling out the map he'd purchased earlier, he double-checked his direction and located the quickest route to the street name that he'd memorized as a boy. Then he set out, determined.

He wouldn't have discovered that such a place even existed if his father hadn't been so drunk that day. Usually, Samuel Lowe didn't return to the cramped two-room apartment that he shared with Harte's mother until late at night, when he was thoroughly drunk and ready for a fight. One day, though, Harte had come home to find the man who had fathered him sprawled out on the floor in the middle of the afternoon. His father had looked lifeless as he lay there in a puddle of his own vomit, and Harte's first thought had been, *It's over.* Then a snorting snore told Harte that his father wasn't dead, only unconscious.

It would have been safer to retreat and pretend he'd never seen that particular scene. But he *had* seen it. Harte had also noticed the loose papers on the table and the stack of letters tied with twine. The sheets were already soaking up the amber-colored whiskey that had spilled.

Harte had been barely twelve then, but he'd known what would happen if his father woke and found the papers soaked and damaged—Samuel Lowe never accepted responsibility for any of his misfortunes. Instead, he would take his frustration out on whoever happened to be closest. If Harte had left, he knew that person would have been his mother, and her bruises had barely started to heal from the last time.

Careful not to wake his father, Harte had taken the sopping papers and tried to shake the liquid from them before the ink smeared. He hadn't intended to look at the uneven scrawl on the damp pages, but the word "California" had shimmered up from the front of an envelope, drawing his attention as surely as a fairy tale.

When he was younger, Harte had never given any thought to who Samuel Lowe had been before he'd arrived in New York and started drinking himself into nightly stupors. Harte had spent so much energy avoiding his father's fists that it had never occurred to him that his father could possibly be the kind of person anyone would want to write letters to. He hadn't been able to stop himself from skimming over the contents, and the next thing he knew, he'd untied the other stack and was reading the correspondence in earnest.

As he read, Harte had discovered that his father had family in California, a mother he'd been sending money to. The more Harte read, the more his blood turned to fire. Samuel Lowe had never seen Molly O'Doherty as anything but a convenience. He'd used Harte's mother for the money she brought home each night, but he'd never planned to stay with her. It was all there, stark on the page. Molly O'Doherty had worked herself into exhaustion because she believed that Samuel Lowe loved her, never knowing that she was actually paying for his escape.

Harte had been so engrossed that he hadn't noticed when his father had started to stir. The old man's face had been blotchy with rage as he demanded the letters back. His father's demands always came with a raised fist, and that time had been no exception. But Harte had refused to take one more beating. Instead of cowering, he'd demanded answers. Of course, his old man had refused to give him any.

Maybe he should have simply taken the letters and left. Harte could have shown his mother the proof of his father's betrayal. But he was young and brash and filled with an anger that made it difficult to see straight. Instead, he'd used his affinity and issued a command, ordering

Samuel Lowe to leave the city and to forget that anyone was waiting for him in California.

It was only later that Harte understood the consequences of that decision. Instead of understanding—instead of *thanking* Harte for saving her—his mother had recoiled. She'd called Harte a liar and went after the man she loved. That choice ended up destroying her, leaving her a shell of who she'd once been.

For years Harte had carried the guilt of what he'd done. He knew that his choices that day proved beyond a doubt that he was truly his father's son—reckless and careless and undeserving. Once he was older, though, he had come to understand that the impact of those choices went far beyond what he'd done to his mother. Maria Lowe had been an innocent as well. She couldn't have known that the money her son sent belonged to someone else. She might even have been dependent on those funds, and she had likely imagined spending her old age with a son who would tend to her needs. Maybe that was why when Harte had been faced with the question of what to do with the stones, he'd sent the Dragon's Eye to her, hoping that it was enough to repay one more debt.

That was before Harte had understood that the artifacts were nothing but liabilities. Now he could only hope that the grandmother he'd never intended to claim still had the crown and that no one else had gotten to it—or to her—first.

After a few blocks, Harte passed through the barricade on the other side of the quarter and continued on a little farther before he finally arrived at the address that had loomed for so long in his imagination. Dawson Place was a small dead-end street that he would have missed if he hadn't been looking for it. Standing in front of the door, he was surprised at how plain and unremarkable it was. As a child, he'd imagined everything in California to be nothing short of fantastical, but this was simply a door—and a rather meager one at that. Still, his palms were damp from nerves, and he found himself wishing that Esta were standing next to him.

At first Harte couldn't even bring himself to knock. More than two years had passed for whoever waited behind the door. Two years when anything could have happened. *The Dragon's Eye might not even be here.*

He felt Seshat's amusement taunting him, but he brushed it aside. The crown *had* to be there. If it wasn't, maybe Maria Lowe could tell him where it had gone, and he would find it one way or another. Esta would be waiting for him soon enough, and Harte would not arrive without the artifact he'd promised her.

Once he knocked, Harte heard an immediate rustling from inside, and a moment later the door opened to reveal a small woman. Her hair was a dark, burnished blond shot through with ashy gray. It was pulled straight back from a round face, and her skin was smooth and unlined, except near the corners of her wide-set eyes. She looked younger than he'd expected, but he still hoped she was the woman he was seeking. Even though her expression was wary, Harte found himself searching for some trace of himself in her features.

"I'm looking for someone," he said to her, finally remembering that he was here for the Dragon's Eye and not to claim a family that didn't know he existed. "Are you Maria?"

The woman shook her head, frowning, and started to close the door, but Harte placed his foot in the jamb and tried again. "Maria Lowe," he repeated, this time more slowly. "Is she here? Do you know her?"

"There's no one here by that name." The woman again tried to push the door shut, this time with more force, but there was something in her expression that made Harte persist.

"If you aren't Maria, can you tell me where I could find her? She has something of mine," he said, his voice unsteady with the urgency he felt. "Something I sent her. A headpiece. Like a crown." With his foot still in the door, he motioned around the crown of her head. "With a large amber stone in it."

The woman's eyes widened.

She knew. Harte was sure of it.

It would only take a brush of skin against skin to find out, and it just might be worth risking whatever Seshat might do to retrieve the artifact. Harte reached for the woman, determined to use his affinity no matter the cost, but before he could touch her, he heard the sound of a pistol being cocked, and a voice came from the alleyway behind him.

"Don't even think about laying your hands on her."

Harte froze. His body reacted before his mind could catch up, steeling itself for the blow that it expected to feel.

"Put your hands up where I can see them," the man said. "And step back, or I will not regret putting a bullet in you."

Harte raised his hands so the man would know he meant no harm as he turned, slowly, his brain struggling to accept the truth. *It can't be.*

"Hello, Samuel," Harte said. He'd never called this man "Father" before, and he wasn't about to start now.

"Who are you?" The man narrowed his eyes and adjusted the gun, but Harte didn't miss the flash of unease in his father's eyes.

Harte's first thought was that the man before him was far too small to be the same terror he remembered from his childhood. But *of course* he would seem smaller. Harte had grown since then. It was more than the height that threw him off, though. There was something essentially changed about his father. Samuel Lowe was wearing a dark gray suit, nothing as precisely tailored as Harte had once bought himself, but well-made nonetheless. His eyes were sharper and clearer than Harte had ever seen them, and his skin was lined but not sallow or puffed from too much cheap gin. If Harte had met this man on the street, he might not have realized who he was.

"You *are* Samuel Lowe?" he pressed. "The same Samuel Lowe who once lived in New York with Molly O'Doherty."

"I don't know anyone by that name." He was still aiming the gun at Harte, but uncertainty flared in his expression. "Who *are* you?"

If Harte had any doubts about who this was, they evaporated. Even so many years later, his body still remembered the fear that tone used to inspire.

But Harte wasn't a child any longer. He was a few inches taller than his father, his body lean and strong from years of discipline and training, and he'd survived in a world that was bent on destroying him for too long to fear much of anything now. Instead of cowering, as he might have before, he straightened a little, jutting out his chin in an unmistakable challenge.

"You know exactly who I am," Harte said flatly, tossing the words out like a dropped gauntlet. "Or don't you recognize your own son?"

CORSICANA

J ack Grew wiped the sweat from his brow as he directed his horse to follow along behind the sheriff of Corsicana, Texas. Once he'd received news that Esta had been spotted, Jack had taken the first train he could get out of St. Louis, but he'd still been too late. The Devil's Thief had evaded him again. Darrigan as well. And they'd left a trail of destruction in their wake.

Some of the men who had witnessed the events of the day before were with him. Riding behind Jack were Jot Gunter and other members of the Ranchers' Syndicate. Gunter was like many of the Syndicate's members: old, rich, and entirely too convinced of his own importance. But then, the ranchers in the Syndicate thought far too highly of them- selves in general. They might own large swaths of the country, land where oil had been discovered a few years back, but they were still upstarts. Parvenus. Without breeding or history. The horses they rode had finer pedigrees than the men themselves, and the fact that the men seemed so proud of their backwater dump of a town only proved how pointless they were.

The last time Jack had seen Gunter was in New York at the Conclave, back in 1902. Gunter had been one of the representatives from the Syndicate. Like the men from the other Brotherhoods, he'd come to gloat. The members of the other Brotherhoods had believed the Order had been dealt a blow when Khafre Hall had burned, but they'd found out differently that cold December night two years before. Thanks to Jack, the Order had prevailed and would continue to lead the Brotherhoods through the new century.

Not that Jack would remind these men of this. He could pretend that they hadn't once been adversaries now that he had won. After all, it was always good to have allies, especially when they were weak men who could be controlled.

A quarter mile from the town itself was the site of the engine's explosion. There, the ground was scarred and split. Deep gashes spread from a larger chasm in the dusty earth, which was being guarded by a group of men with guns at the ready. As they got closer, a pair of men on horseback with bronze stars on their lapels rode out to meet the group. Other men, both on horseback and on foot, stood watch, probably to keep away the scavengers and newspapermen who swarmed around tragedies like vultures.

Federal marshals. Jack should know—he'd given the order for them to be there. The last thing anyone needed was for the locals to muck up the investigation.

Gunter and the mayor exchanged some words with the pair of marshals. Gunter made a show of puffing himself up as he spoke, but the two lawmen listened with uninterested silence, their faces shadowed by the broad brims of their hats. They simply shook their heads. Impatient with their lack of cooperation, the sheriff nudged his horse forward and tried to speak with the men. That didn't make any difference either. The two marshals only frowned at him as they exchanged words in low, hard tones, and the sheriff grew more agitated by the second.

Jack could feel the sweat rolling down his back as he allowed the sheriff and Syndicate men a little more time to display their own ineptitude. Then, growing bored, he urged his horse forward.

"Good afternoon, gentlemen," Jack drawled, giving the marshals a status they didn't quite deserve. "I've come to survey the site on behalf of Mr. Roosevelt."

The marshals recognized him immediately. To the sheriff's irritation—

and Jack's immense satisfaction—they moved quickly, so the group could pass. This time it was Jack who took the lead out toward the crevasse that had been torn into the earth by the explosion of the train.

The wreckage was still in place, but the engine itself was hardly recognizable, a twisted shell of metal and soot that might have at one time resembled a locomotive. But the destroyed engine wasn't what truly interested Jack. The deep hole that had been ripped into the ground and the gaping pit carved in the earth where the remains of the train lay were far more interesting. The medallion that Jack had taken from Hendricks and now wore on his own lapel began singing its high, dissonant warning call. Its blue glow indicated feral magic was nearby, and beneath his jacket, the Book seemed to almost shudder against his chest.

Jack had seen the same sort of scar carved into the earth before. It had been over two years now—the day Esta Filosik and Harte Darrigan destroyed a different train and escaped from his clutches. That day had set him on this new path in his life.

One look at the wreckage confirmed what Jack had suspected. Esta Filosik had been there. Probably Darrigan had as well. But whatever the sheriff of Corsicana or the men from the Syndicate thought, the wreckage didn't mean that the Thief was dead. Jack knew exactly how slippery Esta and Darrigan could be, and he wouldn't believe they were gone until he saw their bodies for himself.

ON THE HOOK

1904—Somewhere in the West

Esta surfaced slowly, the remnants of a strangely vivid dream clinging to her. The heat of a desert landscape still brushed against her skin, and her mouth felt dry, as if she'd actually spent the night running through blistering sand, trying to escape whatever beast slithered beneath. Her body was sore, and her head ached as the room swayed around her. It took her a moment to remember what had happened, and even then, it came back to her in disjointed bursts.

Slowly Esta realized that the motion of the room wasn't in her head. She was on a train, and from the rough, hard floor beneath her cheek, it wasn't a Pullman berth. The noise was deafening, and the air was stuffy and hot. At first she couldn't bring herself to do much more than lie with her cheek pressed to the floor, breathing in the dust and feeling the jarring vibrations of the track. When she finally opened her eyes, a shadow seemed to hang over her vision. She blinked, willing away the darkness, and tried to remember how she'd gotten there.

"Looks like Sleeping Beauty's coming to."

North. Esta rubbed at her eyes and forced herself to sit up.

She didn't know how North and Maggie had gotten her onto this train, and when she started to ask, the words wouldn't come. Her mouth felt like every bit of moisture had been drained from it, and all that came out was a hacking cough.

Maggie offered Esta some water and helped hold the canteen to her mouth so she could drink.

Esta only meant to take a swallow, just enough to be able to speak, but the water was like heaven, and she ended up nearly draining it. When she was done, she wiped her mouth with the back of her hand. "Where are we?"

"Not in Texas anymore," North said, like it was the only piece of information that mattered. When he finally spoke again, he didn't sound happy. "That was some show you put on back there. Causing an earthquake wasn't part of the plan."

"An earthquake?" Esta repeated, not bothering to hide her shock. "What are you talking about?" She remembered being on the locomotive now, remembered feeling a hesitancy that wasn't like her. But she'd pushed herself onward, believing that if the darkness rose again, she could simply release her hold on time before it could take her. But after that—

"You don't remember?" Maggie asked, her eyes soft with concern behind the lenses of her glasses.

"Everything happened so fast. . . ."

The darkness had come. Seshat's darkness. Esta struggled to remember more, and it came to her little by little, in flashes of memory. This time there hadn't been the slow seeping, like ink dropped in water. Instead, almost from the moment she'd pulled time slow, the blackness had rushed around her like a flood. She was only supposed to hold on to the seconds long enough to get off the train and out of sight, but too quickly she had been submerged beneath a different power. Esta had barely been able to push back the shadows, as her magic had turned into something wild and unhinged. The seconds had suddenly felt *alive*, and even as she'd climbed down from the engine and started to run from the train, she'd felt that time itself might turn on her. The darkness had pulsed and billowed, chasing her from the train like a phantom haunting her.

Hunting her.

It came back to her then, how the earth had started to quake. The ground had rippled beneath her as she'd sprinted away from the overheating engine, but before Esta could release her hold on time, darkness had pulled her under.

"The train . . . It *did* explode, though?" Esta asked. It was essential that the authorities believed the Thief was dead.

"Yes, but . . ." Maggie pressed her lips together and glanced at North.

"What happened back there was more than the boiler overheating," North said. "The ground shook clear out where we were, and the earth cracked as easy as an egg. Swallowed men and horses whole. It was a hell of a lot more than what you told us you had planned." His eyes narrowed. "Then you didn't show up like you were supposed to."

North wasn't exactly wrong to be suspicious. Esta *had* planned to use the distraction of the train exploding to slip away from the two Antistasi. She had a dagger to find, and once the Thief was presumed dead, they would have been safer without her.

"But you came back for me," Esta said. "Why risk that? Without the Thief, the two of you could have gone on and started over. You would have been safe."

"You and your partner still owe us a necklace," North told her.

"It wasn't only about the necklace." Maggie shot North a sharp look. "We couldn't leave you there," she said gently, touching Esta's arm. "You were willing to risk everything in St. Louis to help us try to stop the serum from deploying. I told you before, you're one of us now. The Antistasi take care of our own."

Esta wasn't sure how much she believed Maggie's explanation. North's statement about the necklace felt more like the truth. Still, without Maggie and North, the posse of marshals certainly would have found her, collapsed and unconscious somewhere between the train and safety. She owed them her life . . . again.

"You really don't have any idea what happened?" Maggie asked.

The two Antistasi were staring at her expectantly, and Esta knew she had a decision to make. Since finding Harte gone, every time she'd tried to use her affinity, she'd been surprised by a power she could not control. One thing was clear—if Seshat's power was somehow still affecting her, she might need the Antistasi's help more than she originally thought.

"I honestly don't know what happened back there," Esta said, using this truth as an anchor for the lies that were sure to come. "But I think it's tied to what happened back in St. Louis." She glanced up at them, trying to gauge their willingness to believe her. "Or maybe it began even before that."

Esta started slowly, picking her way through the minefield of her story, giving them enough of the truth to make her lies and omissions believable. She couldn't tell them about Harte or the other stones, but maybe she could tell them enough to ensure their continued help.

"The stories are true," she told them. "Two years ago, I did manage to break into the Order's vaults. We were trying to steal their most prized possessions, but instead, we unleashed something we weren't expecting. . . ." Esta told them about Seshat, about the power of the ancient goddess and how she had possessed Harte. And she told them about the threat that Seshat's power posed to the world itself.

"Maybe Ben thought leaving us was for the best," Esta said with a stiff shrug. "He must have believed he could use the stones to take care of the danger Seshat posed on his own. But maybe something more happened that night. Maybe part of Seshat's power is connected to *me* now."

She explained to them about the darkness that had appeared as they ran from the train, about how she'd lost hold of the seconds and woke up over North's shoulder. She told them, too, about the shadows that had pulled her under before the explosion. By the time Esta was finished speaking, Maggie's rapt and serious expression told Esta that she was on the hook. But North's mouth was still twisted with suspicion.

"That sure is some story you spun there," he said, not giving an inch.

"It's not a story," Esta assured him. *Not completely.* "You know what I can do with time. If I only wanted to distract you, I would have been long gone, not passed out cold waiting for the marshals and the rest of their posse to find me."

"She has a point," Maggie told him.

"You don't actually believe this story she's spinning?" North said to Maggie.

"I don't know what I believe." Maggie seemed to be measuring each of her words carefully. "But I know this much: Something *did* happen back in the Festival Hall. I was there. I *felt* it," she said before turning to Esta. "You're *sure* you don't have any idea where Ben went?"

"No," Esta lied. She paused, pretending to be nervous, and when she spoke again, she made her voice as soft as a secret. "But I do know where we might be able to find another artifact."

Maggie's expression brightened immediately, but North's brows bunched together, like he still didn't want to believe her. Still, Esta could sense the yearning behind his doubt, and she knew he was more interested than he wanted to be.

"You're telling us that you've known all along where *another* of the lost artifacts might be?" North asked.

"Possibly," Esta said. "Ben and I had a backup in case the necklace turned out to be a fake or in case we couldn't get it away from the Society. There's a dagger called the Pharaoh's Heart that holds a stone every bit as powerful as the Djinni's Star." She allowed the moment to settle around them, giving them the space to start believing that such a treasure could be theirs. "If you help me retrieve it, we can perform the ritual to break whatever connection I have with Seshat before she can do any more damage. Once we do that, the Pharaoh's Heart would be yours. I know it's not the necklace. . . ." She bit her lip a little, like she was sorry about this fact.

Maggie looked ready to accept, but North spoke first.

"You'd up and *give* this artifact to us?" He waved his hand dismissively. "Just like that?"

"The Antistasi need it more than I do," Esta said, telling them the exact thing she knew they wanted to hear. "And anyway . . ." She looked to Maggie now and spoke the words she knew would sink the hook. "Aren't we all on the same side?"

"Yes, of course," Maggie said, giving Esta a small, relieved smile. Then suddenly the pleasure drained from her expression. "But if you're telling us the truth about this Seshat creature and her possible connection to you, we have a bigger problem right now." She lifted her eyes to the ceiling of the boxcar as it rattled down the track before meeting Esta's gaze again. "If you weren't in control of *whatever* it was that happened back there in Texas, what makes you think you could stop it from happening again?"

Her meaning was clear to Esta. "You think I'd do something to this train while we're on it?"

Maggie shook her head. "I'm not saying you'd do it on purpose, but you have to admit, you don't have the best record. First the train in New Jersey and then the one in Texas. . . ."

"But if I don't use my affinity—"

"What makes you think you'll have a choice?" Maggie asked. "I *did* see Ben back in the Festival Hall. He had his hands around your neck. I believe you when you say that it wasn't him in control, but what will you do if this Seshat creature does the same to *you*?"

Esta's stomach twisted. She wanted to argue that it wasn't possible, but she couldn't make herself form the words to lie.

Maggie took Esta's hand. "If Seshat is as powerful as you say she is, what would stop her from using your affinity against you?" Her voice went even softer, like she was afraid Seshat herself might hear. "What if Seshat makes good on her threats before we can find the other artifact?"

Esta felt the train rumbling beneath her. The cadence of the wheels meeting the track was so much steadier than she felt. Maggie was right. Harte hadn't been in control back in St. Louis. If Seshat's power was still somehow affecting Esta's affinity, they had no idea what they were dealing with.

"You're right," Esta said softly. "I shouldn't be here. I'm a danger to both of you—to everyone." She wasn't sure why this clear way out of her entanglement with the Antistasi should feel so unsettling. And so depressing.

"Maybe you don't have to be," Maggie said, pulling a small leather pouch from her skirts.

"What do you mean?" Esta asked, frowning.

"Seshat wants your affinity, right?" Maggie asked, and Esta reluctantly nodded. "She can only use you through your magic."

"As far as we know," Esta admitted.

"It's a problem I might be able to take care of." Maggie took a small white pill from the leather pouch and held it up between her fingertips.

Esta knew all about Maggie's concoctions. She'd experienced some of the more potent ones back in St. Louis when she'd had her first run-in with the Antistasi, and she'd seen for herself what Maggie's serum was capable of. "What, *exactly*, is that?"

"It's sort of an oral version of Quellant," Maggie explained. "Unlike the fog we used back in St. Louis, this tablet can mute an affinity without leaving the person completely unconscious. It's also a lot more potent—it'll last close to twelve hours instead of the usual two." She held it out to Esta. "It stands to reason that if you can't reach your affinity, Seshat won't be able to either."

"You want to take my magic from me," Esta realized. Her body felt suddenly cold. She remembered what it was like to have her affinity stripped away by the Quellant back in St. Louis, especially the strange emptiness she'd felt.

"No," Maggie said, shaking her head. "I'm asking you to consider giving it up. Temporarily, at least. It would only be until we get the artifact."

Maggie's explanation seemed completely reasonable, but everything in Esta was screaming for her not to take the pill. The idea of willingly relinquishing her link to the old magic made her recoil. To give up the power that was so much a part of her—even for a short time . . .

But Maggie could be right about the danger Esta might pose to them. Esta had felt Seshat's furious determination back in St. Louis, and she had no other explanation for her inability to control her affinity now. If Seshat took her over the way she'd taken over Harte . . .

Reluctantly, Esta accepted the pill from Maggie. It was small and unimpressive, but she could feel the warm energy that spoke of old magic coming from within. Every instinct she had was screaming for her not to place it in her mouth, not to put herself at such a disadvantage. But she remembered the darkness, uncontrollable and absolute, as she'd run from that train. If Seshat actually did have a connection to her, it might happen again.

No. It would *happen again.* There was no denying that Seshat would keep trying. The ancient power wouldn't stop, not until they stopped her.

Still, Esta couldn't bring herself to do it. She was already starting to hand the tablet back, when another thought occurred to her—one that tipped the scales. If the Quellant could *truly* hold back Seshat's power, then perhaps it was an answer to a problem Esta had believed to be hopeless. Maybe with the Quellant, she and Harte could keep Seshat controlled enough to return to 1902 *together*.

It wouldn't do anything to protect the stones. If they returned to 1902 with the artifacts, they would likely lose the ones they currently had. But if they *could* return to the time they should have been in, Julian would never have given the necklace to the Society. The Devil's Thief never needed to exist. The Antistasi wouldn't have stoked the hatred of the Occult Brotherhoods with their violent deeds, the Defense Against Magic Act would not have been ratified, and the attack at the Festival Hall never would have happened. The serum wouldn't have been deployed— it might never be invented. Even if they couldn't find a way to bring the artifacts with them, she and Harte could fix the mistakes they'd made. They could start fresh.

They could have more time.

Going back wouldn't give Esta a future. She understood that. Seshat would still need to be dealt with, and if they couldn't retrieve the Book—if the Book didn't hold the answers they needed—Esta would willingly give her affinity and herself to control the ancient being. She would stop Seshat from taking her revenge on the world and save Harte from what that power would do to him. She would give him a future.

As she placed the pill in her mouth, Esta told herself that it was worth the risk. It was only temporary, and besides, she didn't need her affinity to steal the Pharaoh's Heart—and she still needed the dagger, especially if the Quellant didn't work. When she crushed the bitter pill between her teeth, she felt her affinity draw away from her almost immediately. Where her magic had once been, Esta felt only a strange, indescribable hollowness, but little else. There was no way to tell if it was enough to block Seshat's connection to her. There might never be, she realized. Not unless it didn't work. As the train rattled on, Esta could only hope that she'd made the right decision and that she hadn't just managed to hook herself.

FURY AND GRIEF

1902—New York

Cela Johnson didn't have any magic, and she hadn't ever particularly wanted any. But as she'd watched Jianyu grow paler and weaker over the past few days, the wound in his shoulder steadily seeping even as it had started to turn with infection, she had to admit that having *something* more than hot water and a few old herbs at her disposal might have been helpful. *Especially* when there wasn't anything natural about the wound itself.

She was fussing with the bandage and trying to ignore the way Jianyu's breathing had grown shallower since Abel had gone to get Viola a little while before. The house was mostly quiet now. A few of Abel's friends were in the kitchen, working on an article for the *New York Age*. The paper belonged to Timothy Thomas Fortune, the man who'd lent them the use of his house after their own had been burned to the ground by men from the railroad who'd wanted Abel to stop his organizing. But Cela couldn't hear the others from where she was in an upstairs bedroom. It might as well have been only her and Jianyu in that big old house, all alone.

Taking another blanket from the shelf, Cela layered it over Jianyu, knowing full well it wouldn't do a thing for the way his fingers had been growing colder. Still, if he was in there, she hoped that this bit of comfort might help.

"Just hold on a little longer, now," she murmured, tucking the blanket around his too-still body. "You said this friend of yours can help, and she's on her way."

Or she'd better be. Still, Cela couldn't help but think that they should've already been back.

A few minutes later, she felt her nerves unwind a bit at the sound of the door opening in the hallway below. The familiar rhythm of Abel's steps sounded on the stairs, and Cela turned from her vigil to see her brother standing in the doorway. Standing behind him was the white girl from the gala—the one who'd tried to kill her and who had created all this trouble in the first place. She wasn't overly tall, and Cela supposed there were those who might consider her pretty, but the uneven stitching of her hem and the rough material of her shirt made it clear she was as poor as everyone else.

Abel had been against getting mixed up with Jianyu from the start. Nothing good could come of messing with magic, he'd said, and he'd been right, like he usually was. But after all Cela had been through, she also knew that trouble had a way of following you just as soon as you tried to walk away from it.

"Is he—" Abel's voice was soft, and Cela could hear the worry in it. For all his blustering, he cared what happened to Jianyu as much as she did.

"He's still with us, but only just," Cela whispered, not quite stepping aside even as she could see the girl—Viola, Jianyu had called her—try to peer around her. From her deep olive skin and thick dark-brown hair, she looked to be one of the Italians who'd been filling the area around Mulberry Street since a few years before Cela was born.

Cela shifted her gaze to study the girl. At the gala, Cela had only seen a lady dressed in silken finery, but she'd known even then from the cut of the ready-made gown that the girl wasn't one of the Order's women. Now, Viola was dressed in a simple, serviceable navy skirt, her hair pulled back from a heart-shaped face. Her eyes were a strange shade of violet, but they were sharp, and a certain intelligence lurked behind them. If she attacked again, Cela was certain Jianyu wouldn't survive it.

"Even after what you did, he told us to send for you."

"We're friends," the girl said, her voice carrying the cadence of another land.

Cela only frowned, crossing her arms.

"Or we were once." The girl stepped forward, her face dappled in the shadows thrown by the lamp in the corner. "I didn't mean to hurt him."

"No," Cela said, still feeling a kind of prickly coolness. "You meant to hurt *me*."

Viola shook her head, but to Cela's surprise, it wasn't a denial that came out of her mouth. "I didn't know you were with him. I was trying to save the ring. I thought you were trying to steal it."

"Of *course* you did. You took one look at me and thought theft was the only possibility, but I can't steal something that belonged to me in the first place," Cela said, her words tart. When Viola's expression flashed with the disbelief and judgment Cela recognized too well, she gave Viola a cold smile in return. "Harte Darrigan gave that ring to me as payment for taking care of his mother. Not that I should have to explain myself to you."

"Darrigan?" The girl's eyes flashed. "You knew the magician?"

"I worked in the theater with Darrigan," Cela said. "Though I should have known better than to agree to help him, or to take anything he offered."

"That ring wasn't his to give," Viola said, her voice suddenly turning dangerous, and Cela was reminded that this girl was no innocent. At the gala, she'd let her knife fly, straight and true, with an intent to kill and an aim deadly enough to make good.

But Cela Johnson wouldn't let Viola see her nerves. "What Darrigan did or didn't have any right to doesn't matter now," Cela said, changing the subject. "Jianyu doesn't have much longer, and that's because of you. Can you help him or not?"

Viola's jaw went tight, like she was getting ready to argue, but when Cela stepped to the side, revealing Jianyu in the bed behind her, the girl's expression went slack with something that looked too similar to Cela's own grief. The way Viola took a halting step toward the bed, she could have been sleepwalking.

"Can you *help* him?" Cela repeated, placing herself between Jianyu and Viola. Her arms were crossed over her chest, but she was ready—to do what, she didn't know. But ready just the same. "Because I won't let you hurt him again."

Cela wasn't exactly sure where the nerve to speak so forcefully to a white girl had come from . . . but then Viola Vaccarelli wasn't *really* a white girl, was she? Maybe out in the wide world, Viola could pull on the protection of whiteness if she was standing next to Cela herself. But alone on the streets? She was a lowly immigrant. Not even a citizen. And here? In Mr. Fortune's house? Viola was only as important as what she could do for Jianyu.

"Cela," Abel warned gently from the doorway. He'd told her about what had happened earlier, the way his chest had ached like it was on fire and he'd thought his heart would explode. Viola had made it clear that she didn't need knives to kill.

Viola's only response to Cela's pointless threat was a quiet shake of her head. "I won't hurt him. I can help."

Cela didn't move away as Viola stepped toward the bed. She wasn't about to stand by if this little bit of a girl decided to finish the job she'd started at the gala.

"I thought I had killed him," Viola murmured as she knelt next to the bed. "I would have tried to find you sooner, but I thought it was too late." Pulling back the covers, she took one of Jianyu's hands in her own, shuddering a little, probably at the coolness of his skin. Then she glanced up at Cela, her strange plum-colored eyes brimming. "Thank you. For being his friend when I was not. For saving him."

Cela only nodded, glancing briefly over to where Abel stood in the doorway, as watchful as she felt. "I haven't saved him yet."

"You brought me here," Viola said. "It's not too late." Her lips pressed tightly together as she closed her eyes, her face tense with concentration.

Cela waited, but nothing seemed to happen. The minutes ticked by as the silence in the room spun itself around them. The city buzzed outside the open window, but it might as well have been another world altogether, because inside the room, they were all caught in a moment of dangerous hope. Viola's forehead wrinkled, her expression creased from some unseen exertion, her skin now damp with sweat. The hand that clutched Jianyu's trembled slightly.

Cela glanced up at Abel, who looked every bit as unsure as she felt.

It was taking too long. Certainly, something as powerful and dangerous as the old magic could have worked by now. Something was wrong.

Cela didn't know what she'd intended when she took a step toward the bed, but before she could touch the girl or pull her away from Jianyu, Viola gasped. Her eyes flew open as she released her hold on Jianyu and tumbled over, barely catching herself before she slumped to the floor.

"What is it?" Cela asked, stepping toward Jianyu. She took his hand and noticed that it felt warmer, but that could have been from Viola's grasp. He still wasn't moving. She squeezed Jianyu's hand slightly and touched his cheek to wake him. But nothing. Jianyu didn't so much as stir.

"Is he okay?" Abel asked from somewhere close behind her.

Cela didn't answer her brother. *Couldn't.* She turned on Viola, her throat tight with fury and grief all at once. "You said you could help him."

But Viola didn't respond. When she looked up at Cela, she was wearing an expression that could have been carved from stone, her eyes wide with something that might have been shock . . . or fear.

NOT COMPLETELY,
NOT ENOUGH

1902—New York

Viola felt the fury in Cela's voice as soundly as a slap across her face, and she welcomed it. Her hands were flat against the worn rag rug next to the bed, and her entire body trembled with the exertion to stay upright. But she wouldn't allow herself to grovel before these strangers. Instead, she pulled herself upright, back to her knees, and leaned against the bed. Jianyu's color looked a little better, and his breathing *had* improved. She took his hand again and felt that his skin was warmer now, but it wasn't enough.

She hadn't been enough.

Viola had allowed her affinity to unspool until she'd found the too-slow and too-unsteady beating of Jianyu's heart. He'd lost so much blood since the gala, and she found the reason—the tear made by her blade had not healed. It had continued to bleed, and because of that, Jianyu was still very far gone.

But not completely, she'd reminded herself. She'd bought him some more time.

She'd been barely aware of the two in the room—brother and sister, she'd finally realized. Not a couple, as she'd first assumed. It was an understandable mistake, considering that she herself had never seen that sort of easy affection between siblings before. Not in her own family, at least.

There had been no time for self-pity, though. No time to think of Paolo, his hatred or his fear. Instead, Viola had thrown herself into the work of saving her friend, pressing all of her affinity, all that she was, into

Jianyu's wound. She'd used her magic as it had always been intended to be used. For life, not death.

Viola was not—had never been—a gentle creature, but in this work, she was careful and soft. In this work, she sank herself more completely than perhaps ever before, until she and her affinity had become one. Until she'd felt overheated, slick with sweat from the exertion. Until the shame she'd carried for so long seemed to evaporate in the warmth building within her.

But it wasn't enough.

No matter how much of her affinity she'd channeled into Jianyu, his wound would not be healed. The flesh remained stubbornly insistent, fighting against her magic. She had done what she could, knitting together the tissue and bone, only to have them unravel again and again. So she'd changed direction and worked on the blood itself, urged it on until all that had been lost was replenished. Blood still seeped from the wound, but at least Jianyu was no longer in immediate danger of death. It had taken every bit of her strength.

"You said you could help him," Cela said again, her voice as wild as the fear in her eyes, as the panic Viola felt already churning within herself.

Viola looked up at Cela, accepting her judgment.

"He told us that you could *save* him," Cela demanded.

Viola was shaking her head, because she couldn't explain it. She didn't have words to counter the distrust in Cela's expression—distrust that she had more than earned.

Cela took a step toward Viola. "I don't know what you're playing at—"

Abel pulled his sister back, his hands steady on her shoulder. "I think what my sister is trying to say is that he doesn't look any better."

Viola glanced back at the bed, where Jianyu remained unmoving. His breathing looked steadier now, though, his color less faded. "He *is* better," she said softly.

"But not completely," Cela countered.

She turned back to them. "No. The wound wouldn't be healed." She tried to explain how her affinity worked, how she'd tried to knit the wound together and how it had resisted her.

"How is that possible?" Cela asked, her voice fraying a little at the edges. "You made the wound. Your knife did this. *You* should be able to *fix* it."

"Cela . . ." Abel's voice was a warning. He looked distinctly uneasy as he pulled his sister back gently.

Because he was afraid of her. Viola had given him a good enough reason to be.

Viola turned back to Jianyu and pulled herself to unsteady feet. She could feel their frustration, their suspicions, and she could not blame them. Placing Jianyu's hands back across his abdomen, she tucked the blankets around him gently.

The movement must have disturbed him, because his eyes fluttered open suddenly. Unfocused, they stared toward the ceiling until she leaned over him, hope caught in her throat, and then he looked at her.

Jianyu tried to speak, but his voice was a scuffed thing, rough and barely there. His brows pulled together, ever so slightly, but Viola couldn't tell if it was confusion or anger or pain that knitted them.

"I'm sorry," she whispered, hating the catch in her own throat and the way her eyes burned with tears. "I can't—" His mouth moved a little, but she shook her head. "You must rest," she said, pulling her hand back. She was suddenly afraid to touch him, because touching him meant facing her own failure.

His eyes were on her, still glassy and unfocused, when another unintelligible husk of a whisper came out. But she was already backing away.

Cela had gone to Jianyu's side and was already leaning over the bed and speaking in urgent, hushed tones as she held his hand. But Jianyu's eyes were following Viola.

"You can't just up and leave," Abel said.

Viola met his gaze and wondered what she would do if he tried to stop her.

"Vee—" Jianyu's mouth formed the first syllable of her name. From across the room, his eyes met hers, and she knew that he saw her standing there. Knew that he understood what she had done, and what she had failed to do.

She should have stepped toward him. She should have tried again, but Viola felt the weight of Cela's judgment and the unease in Abel's posture. She felt their distrust heavy in the room and knew that there was nothing more she could do for Jianyu, so she turned and she ran.

Outside, the early-summer heat was already starting to make the city air feel too close and too heavy, but Viola barely felt it. She was already overheated and chilled all at once, and the shift beneath her skirts was damp with her own sweat. She turned to look around the neighborhood, trying to figure out where she was in the city. She knew which direction she needed to go. South. Toward the Bowery.

THE BULLDOGGER

sta arrived in Colorado with Maggie and North two days after the mess in Texas. She'd taken dose after dose of the Quellant, but she still wasn't used to the gnawing emptiness where her connection to the old magic should have been. She doubted she ever would be. As unpleasant as the constant ache from her missing affinity was, at least nothing else had happened. The train had remained steady on its tracks, and no shadows had threatened the edges of her vision. And if Esta wanted to crawl out of her own skin from being so separated from such an essential part of herself? It was a small price to pay for the assurance that Seshat could not touch her.

Before they'd boarded a train for Denver, Esta had checked the headlines and found that the ruse in Texas seemed to have worked. The Devil's Thief was presumed dead, but any relief Esta might have felt was quickly erased by the sight of Julian Eltinge's picture looking up at her from the second page. Julian was among those who were already showing strange symptoms from being exposed to the serum in St. Louis. Esta knew what would eventually happen to those poor souls. First a connection to the old magic would awaken, and then a few days later they would die. They would not have easy deaths.

Esta tried not to think about Julian, with his whip-smart humor and sharp intelligence, suffering like that. He'd been nothing short of heroic at the parade, despite being cornered into a terrible situation, and the idea that he'd been doused with the serum gnawed at her. She couldn't stop herself from wondering what terrible affinity the serum might awaken in him, or whether he would have anyone at all to comfort him at the end. And as the train climbed into the mountains, she discovered the bitter taste of true regret.

When they finally arrived in Denver, Esta was completely on edge, but the sky that greeted them was wide and blue, and the mountain air didn't have the heavy blanket of humidity that had made Texas feel so oppressive. The Colorado air was thin, but she forced herself to focus on what lay ahead instead of the path of destruction she'd left behind.

The three of them had spent their time aboard the train planning, and as soon as they arrived, they headed directly for the edge of town, where the Curtis Brothers' Wild West Show—and with any luck, the Pharaoh's Heart—waited.

Even without her affinity, Esta was confident that she could retrieve the dagger quickly, but when they crested the hill and saw the Curtis Brothers' Wild West Show sprawling in the fields below, some of her confidence waned. This wasn't a simple rodeo. Instead, the grounds stretched over multiple acres, with an enormous tent of billowing white canvas holding court at the center and a large encampment of other tents sprawled around it.

"How will we ever find the dagger in all that?" Maggie asked, voicing Esta's own worry as they looked out over the grounds.

"One of those will belong to Bill Pickett," Esta said, pointing to the village of smaller tents clustered beyond the big top. "Once I figure out who he is, finding the dagger should be easy enough."

"You mean, once *we* figure it out," North corrected, eyeing her. He was still suspicious, and rightly so.

"Of course," she said easily. "But it will go faster if we split up."

"Like hell," North told her.

"It'll be safer, too," she added. "There's less chance of anyone recognizing us if we're not together. In case they're still looking for us."

"The Thief is dead," Maggie reminded her. "The headlines all said so."

"Just because the authorities *say* the Thief died in the crash doesn't mean the Order or any of the Brotherhoods have stopped looking," Esta argued. "The faster we get the dagger and the less we're seen together, the better."

"I don't like this," North grumbled. "You going off on your own is exactly the sort of thing you'd want to do if you were fixing to run."

Esta's patience was fraying. "I've taken the Quellant, haven't I? Besides, you have your watch. I can't outrun that."

It was a problem Esta had been considering, especially since her own affinity was out of reach at the moment. She didn't want to take the watch from North—it had been a gift from his late father—but she couldn't see any way around it. When the time was right, when she had the dagger in hand, she'd make sure they couldn't stop her from leaving.

North's eyes narrowed at her, like he could almost sense the path of her thoughts.

Esta let out a frustrated breath when she realized North was set on digging in his heels. They were wasting time arguing. "Look, you're welcome to come along with me. I'm sure Maggie can handle herself down there without you."

Her words had the desired effect. North might have hated to let Esta out of his sight, but he wasn't about to leave Maggie unprotected.

They split up, approaching the grounds of the show from opposite directions. Esta cut through a field that held horse-drawn wagons waiting for their drivers. It was peppered by the occasional motorcar, the past and future colliding. A little farther on, she passed corrals that held cattle and horses. There were people *everywhere*. Families and groups watched the ranch hands work. Couples wandered arm in arm, taking in the sights. Small children draped themselves over the fences to watch horses graze with a kind of bright-eyed excitement that Esta herself had never felt about much of anything, except maybe lifting a fat wallet or a diamond stickpin.

Or besting Harte.

Esta's chest felt suddenly tight at the thought. She almost wished she hadn't been so impulsive on the train and that the string of beads was still on her wrist. Surrounded by so many people, she felt strangely apart from them. The lies and omissions even kept her at arm's length from North and Maggie. It might have been nice to have Harte's voice in her ear right then, a sign that she wasn't truly alone.

A breeze kicked up, and Esta's nose wrinkled at the strange combination of fried food and popped corn and sawdust that assaulted her. But it was the scent of the animals that swept away all thoughts of Harte as another memory rose unexpectedly, as stark and clear as the sky above. The grief it brought with it nearly made her stumble.

Esta had grown up in the shadows of skyscrapers and spent her childhood navigating narrow canyons of brick and glass, breathing air laden with exhaust and the other smells of city life. But the scent of horses brought her back to the days when Dakari had taken her to see the tired-looking ponies that waited to cart tourists around Central Park. She would wander along, looking at the horses, while Dakari visited with old friends from when he was one of the drivers—back when he'd first come to the city, before the Professor had found him.

She'd been young then—no more than seven or eight—but the memory was so clear, it might as well have happened last week. Esta had never thanked Dakari properly for those trips. She'd never really thanked him for anything, she realized. Now it was too late.

The memory of the last time she'd seen him rose then, replacing that other, happier memory of those days near Central Park. When Esta had returned to her own time, when she'd discovered the truth about everything, she'd tried to fight. But Professor Lachlan had called Dakari into the library, and Dakari had come, unaware that he was about to be killed to teach Esta a lesson—another sacrificed pawn in Nibsy's deadly game. She drew in another deep breath, willing the scent of the horses to shove away the bloody image of Dakari's last moments. She refused to let *that* serve as her memory of the man who had been her trainer and healer, and also her friend.

The horses in the field nearby were nothing like the ponies from her youth, though. These beasts were tall and athletic, with well-muscled flanks and coats that gleamed in the midday sun. The horses of her childhood had always looked tired as they'd waited on the side of the busy street, silently resigned to their fates, chewing on grain from dirty plastic buckets amid the blaring traffic and noise. They didn't run or buck. With the blinders they wore, they couldn't even see much of the world around them. They simply followed the path set for them, driven on by the person who provided them food and water and a safe place to sleep. Maybe even then she had known that those horses' lives weren't so very different from her own, Esta thought ruefully, shoving the memory aside.

As she moved with the crowd toward the big top, she put her thoughts of the past behind her, right where they belonged. She needed to focus on the task at hand—finding the dagger and then figuring out a way to untangle herself from the two Antistasi, so she could get to Harte.

If she had hoped that getting the dagger from Pickett would be easy, that hope died at the sight of the two men standing on either side of the entrance to the big top. Each wore a serious expression on his face and the silver star of the US marshals pinned to his chest. *They could be looking for anyone. . . .* But Esta pulled the brim of her hat down anyway. Picking up her pace, she joined the tail end of a group entering the big top and made sure to keep her eyes ahead of her as she passed.

Once inside the enormous tent, Esta didn't bother to find a seat in the bleachers. There was an area to the left of the entrance, where men in cowboy hats and worn jeans leaned against the railing to watch the show. It was a standing room, and the men who filled it didn't look like the type to sit still long. They watched the horses and riders with a kind of critical squint, smoking hand-rolled cigarettes and commenting on the mounts each performer rode. A few who had positioned themselves closest to the arena's entrance hooted and hollered whenever a female rider went past or shouted slurs at the brown-skinned men who wore cavalry uniforms. The performers either didn't hear or pretended that they didn't care. They kept their shoulders back and their eyes forward as they kicked their horses into action and entered the arena to the cheers of the crowd.

Two men held court in the center of the arena. They looked like inverted images of each other—one fair and blond and the other with ruddier skin and dark hair—with horses to match. They were dressed in fringed leather that could have belonged in a Vegas show, and they took turns using a large, cone-shaped megaphone to announce each new act that rode into the arena. Esta figured they must be the Curtis brothers.

It quickly became apparent that, even with the clear skill of the riders, the Curtis brothers' version of the Wild West was about as authentic as Harte's old act as an expert in the mystical arts. She wondered briefly how it must feel for the buffalo soldiers to parade around for the same people who would keep them from sharing a table at a restaurant in town, or how the Lakota must feel about displaying their traditions in the same arena as the painted clowns who distracted the bulls. Esta wondered why any of them did it—if there was some benefit from being part of the Curtis brothers' entourage, or if the men and women were there in the ring because it was the lesser of the evils they could have chosen from. Maybe they thought they could change their fate.

Esta knew otherwise. In the end, history would march on toward a future where people would still be pushed down, kept away, and discarded. Maybe once she'd hoped that by destroying the Brink, she could change the future, but with everything that had happened, she wasn't so sure anymore. Fear and hatred and ignorance seemed so . . . *inevitable*.

Yet the future *had* changed, she reminded herself. The problem was that it had changed for the worse. She needed to concentrate on the job in front of her—finding the artifacts and containing Seshat's power—so there could be a future to worry about at all.

On posters at the train station, Pickett had been billed as a "bulldogger," whatever that meant. Esta didn't really care as long as the cowboy still had the dagger and didn't put up too much of a fight handing it over. With any luck, they'd never have to actually meet. Nothing good could come from that—especially not for Pickett himself. But for a long while, there was no sign of the cowboy. The show felt endless. Rider after rider, act after act, and Esta wondered if Pickett would ever make an appearance.

Nearly an hour in, the fairer of the two Curtis brothers announced the next act—a sharpshooter. At his signal, a woman rode into the arena, her horse kicking up dirt and dust. Esta couldn't help but be transfixed by the drama that filled the ring. In this time, before microphones and loudspeakers and in an arena filled with the chattering noise of a crowd, the woman relied on a sort of pantomime to create her act, flirting with the audience as she accomplished ever-more impressive feats by hitting impossible targets. Somehow Esta wasn't surprised to feel the warmth of magic sifting through the air whenever the woman took aim. Mageus had hidden among the theater folk back in New York. Why wouldn't they hide in plain sight here as well?

After the sharpshooter left the arena to thunderous applause, Esta's patience was finally rewarded.

"Ladies and gentlemen," the fairer of the brothers called. "We have a real treat for you today. Direct from the plains of Texas comes the dusky demon himself, a man who can subdue even the strongest steer with nothing but his force of will—Bill the Bulldogger Pickett!"

Pickett tore into the arena, a blur of speed on horseback, before he came to a dead stop mere inches from the Curtis brother who had announced him.

Esta had expected a giant of a man, a showman decked out in fringe and beadwork like the rest of the performers, but Pickett was dressed simply in the clothes of a working ranch hand: dark pants and a lighter shirt, with a hat that looked well loved and faded from days under the sun. She couldn't see much of his face beneath the brim, but his dark-brown skin had reddish undertones, and a heavy mustache shadowed his upper lip.

Pickett didn't turn when the men in the gallery around Esta whistled and shouted slurs. Under his command, his horse didn't so much as flinch when a bottle lobbed from the crowd shattered on the ground before him. Beneath the broad brim of his hat, his expression was placid, uninterested. Like he knew exactly who he was, even if everyone else was a fool. While the Curtis brothers droned on about Pickett's achievements, he busied himself with tying a rope into a lasso.

Esta admired confidence like that, and as she watched Pickett work—methodically, carefully—she thought she understood why Harte had entrusted the Pharaoh's Heart to this particular man. There was something steady about him. Something that set him apart from the others she'd seen prancing around the arena that day.

Once the Curtis brothers retreated, the mood in the arena changed again. The drums rolled once more, and at the sound of a rim shot, a steer was released into the ring. Pickett was off, faster than anything Esta could have expected. Faster than anyone she'd seen yet that day. In a matter of seconds, he chased the animal down and tossed a rope around its horns in one try, jumped from his horse and wrestled it to the ground in a single, fluid motion, and finished by tying up the animal's four legs. The entire process couldn't have even taken a whole minute, and then Pickett was back up on his horse, tearing around the arena again in a victory lap, while a couple of other men wrangled the steer away.

The audience cheered, whooping and hooting their approval, but the cheers were peppered with the same slurs from before. The men standing near Esta seemed more disgusted by Pickett's expertise than impressed, but Pickett continued to ignore them as he circled the ring, waving his hat but not letting so much as a smile curl beneath the heavy mustache. As he passed the standing gallery, Esta saw that Pickett's eyes were sharp, probably on the lookout for any others who might mean to cause him trouble.

Another drumroll rose, and another steer was released into the arena. Pickett kicked his horse into a gallop until he was next to the animal, but this time, instead of using the rope, which was still on the other animal, he swung himself out of his own saddle and leapt five, maybe six feet, onto the steer's back. The animal was more than twice Pickett's size, but that didn't seem to bother him. He grabbed it by the horns and then slid off so he could dig his boot heels into the ground to slow the beast. He twisted the horns until the steer's nose was pointing upward, and then he did something—Esta couldn't quite tell what it was, but she thought he might have latched onto the animal with his *mouth*—and a moment later Pickett's hands were in the air. He waved them in a victory wave as he was dragged along. The steer took maybe three or four more steps before, unbelievably, *impossibly*, it stumbled to its knees and went down. The bull writhed beneath Pickett's hold until, finally, it seemed to give up and remained there on the ground, completely subdued.

Esta searched for the feel of magic sifting through the air once more, but of course there wasn't any of the telltale warmth. Pickett never would have gotten out of Manhattan if he'd had the old magic. This was something else—talent, perhaps. Mastery, definitely. All born of a lifetime of work.

The crowd was strangely silent for a second before the arena exploded in shouts and cheers. As he stood and waved his hat to the crowd, Pickett looked even smaller than he had atop his horse. Next to the steer, he seemed utterly human.

It was the strangest and perhaps most impressive thing Esta had ever witnessed. Even once Pickett had released it, the steer remained on the ground, as shocked by what had happened as everyone else.

Esta was so taken by the display in the ring that she almost didn't notice the movement of the two men to her right. A pair of other performers were dragging the stunned animal out of the arena and Pickett was taking his final bow, but at the edge of the standing room, a group of marshals weren't watching the show. They had already started moving into the crowded standing-room area, and soon they were joined by others. Even if they weren't looking for her specifically, Esta realized they'd find her easily enough with the way they'd surrounded the crowd of men.

With her affinity, it would have been simple to slip away unseen, but the Quellant was still thick in her blood. Her affinity was out of reach.

The Thief is dead, Esta reminded herself. The marshals could be looking for anyone, but she wasn't going to take a chance of being accidentally found. Considering her options, she decided on the most expedient and gave the man in front of her a violent shove, which caused him to topple into the man next to him.

The effect was immediate. In a matter of seconds, the standing room erupted into angry shouting, and Esta ducked away from the heat of the growing brawl and slipped out the back of the big top as the marshals rushed in.

THE MARK OF THE ANTISTASI

1904—Texas

Jack Grew rolled the whiskey around in his cup and studied the way it sloshed from side to side. Watery and sharp, it had definitely been cut with something else, but the drink was doing its job, at least. The tension of the day had started to ease after the first biting swallow, but it wasn't gone. And it wasn't going fast enough.

The amber liquid stared back at him, mocking. The porter who'd first reported seeing Esta on the train had been no help. The man had been bewitched so resolutely that what came out of his mouth was nothing but rubbish. Which meant that Jack was stuck. He couldn't leave Corsicana without answers—not when the trail had gone cold. There was nothing to do but wait until the haze of whatever spell the porter was under lifted.

He stared down into his cup, and it hit him suddenly that the color of the whiskey reminded him of something . . . *Esta's eyes.* They'd been the most unsettling shade of gold, much like whiskey. For a short time, she'd made him believe that she wanted him. Even after all he'd lost in Greece, even after all he should have learned there, Jack had let himself be swayed once more by a set of round hips and a pretty pair of long lashes batting in his direction. The memory of it was almost enough to turn his stomach.

Jack lifted the tumbler, ready to throw it against the wall. He wanted to watch the glass shatter, the amber liquid splatter and slide down the wall. He wanted to imagine it was Esta he was destroying. But he stopped himself. What was the use of wasting a perfectly good drink, especially one that he'd already paid for? Instead of tossing the glass, Jack took one of the cubes of morphine—how was it that there were only three left?—and dissolved it in the whiskey, watching as the amber-colored liquid turned cloudy. Just as Esta's lovely eyes would when he finally finished her.

He was on his third drink and feeling *almost* calm again, when the saloon doors opened in a burst of noise. Jack turned to find Hendricks there, panting heavily with a shit-eating grin on his face.

"The spell is lifting."

Finally. Jack tossed a couple of coins on the countertop and followed without a word.

Back at Corsicana's jail, Gunter and a couple of other men from the Syndicate had already arrived. They all tipped their hats to Jack, a greeting that was becoming a familiar sign of their mutual respect.

"I hear things are changing?" Jack said, speaking to Gunter more than the others.

"Whatever they did to him, it's wearing off," Gunter said, nodding toward the barred cell.

"And?" Jack pressed.

"It's still slow going," Gunter told him with a frown. "But we expect that as the spell wanes, it'll work faster."

Behind the iron bars, the porter was sitting on the narrow cot, his elbows on his knees and his hands pressed on either side of his head. Next to him, a deputy held a heavy billy club, while the sheriff leaned lazily against the wall and asked another question.

"I told you," he said, sounding like a scared animal. "I don't remember."

The sheriff gave a nod, and the deputy jammed the club into the man's side. The porter let out another moan and tried to curl away from the attack, but he didn't drop his arms. They'd likely beat the sense out of him before the spell lifted.

Jack stepped toward them, but Jot Gunter snagged the sleeve of his coat. Jack looked down at the man's hand and then at the man himself.

"Have patience," Gunter said. "The sheriff is working on it. These things are delicate."

"Are they?" Jack asked, jerking away from Gunter and walking into the cell.

"If I may?" He glared at the sheriff, who shrugged and stepped out of the cell.

Once the man was gone, Jack spoke in a low, soothing voice, introducing himself to their prisoner. "Hello, George. My name is Jack Grew. I work for the president."

"My name isn't George," the man said, lifting his chin. "It's Johnson. Abel Johnson."

"Mr. Johnson," Jack acknowledged, pretending he cared. "We were told that you were the one who spotted the Thief on the train last night."

"I already told these men everything I remember," the porter said. His uniform was rumpled and stained. One sleeve had been ripped from his coat.

"If there's anything at all, any detail," Jack said softly, and then waited.

"Like I said—"

"Your record with the railroad is an interesting one," Jack said, his voice more clipped now. "You've been involved in labor strikes in the past, and you have a record of instigating unrest among the other porters."

"That was years ago," the man said, his eyes shifting away. Guilty. Nervous. Like he knew he'd been caught.

Jack repressed a satisfied smile. "I can understand you might be sympathetic to the Thief's cause, but—"

"I'm *not*," the porter said, his voice like a lash. He looked up then, one eye swollen shut. *The sheriff's work, no doubt.* "I don't have any sympathy at all for the Devil's Thief, and not for the rest of them either. My sister died because she got wrapped up with their kind." He grimaced. "I know they did something to my head. I can't put two thoughts together. When I try, everything gets all confused."

"So the Thief wasn't alone?" Jack asked, glancing up at the sheriff with satisfaction. "Can you describe the others? Even the smallest detail could help."

The man's face crumpled. "She was dressed in men's clothing, like the notices said she would be. And there was another woman too, I think. One wearing spectacles. And a man with them."

It didn't seem possible that a lead this promising might not pan out. "Did he have dark hair, nearly black?"

"No," the man said. "He had orangey hair poking out from beneath his hat and a tattoo of something on his wrist. A snake, maybe. But I can't remember anything else."

Not Darrigan.

Jot Gunter was already stepping toward the bars. "This man . . . did you happen to get a look at the color of his eyes?"

The porter held his head. "They might have been brown . . . or maybe green? Both feel right, but I don't see how that can be."

"Oh, it can be," Gunter said.

Jack turned to Gunter. "You know the man he's describing?"

Gunter looked far too pleased with himself. "I do. He's a maggot that should have been dead years ago—a ranch hand who once worked for me. He's a rather distinctive fella, actually—he has one green eye, one brown. And the mark of the Antistasi on his wrist."

A WRONG TURN

Once free of the crowd, Esta caught sight of Pickett moving away from the big top. He'd dismounted and was leading his horse toward a corral. After handing off his mount, he headed toward the village of tents. She tossed one more glance over her shoulder, to be sure she wasn't being followed, and then went in that direction as well.

Luckily, most of the other performers were still in the arena. Even without using her affinity, it wasn't difficult to follow Pickett through the grounds. Finally, he stopped at a cluster of smaller tents located at the back edge of the encampment. They were a little more faded and worn than some of the ones closer to the main big top. Outside, a couple of buffalo soldiers sat talking. Pickett greeted the pair before disappearing into his own tent for a few minutes. When he came out again, he was wearing fresh clothes—the jacket a bit more elaborate than the one he'd been wearing before. He joined up with the war veterans, and together they made their way back toward the main tent.

Esta waited a little longer to be sure no one was around before she slipped inside Pickett's tent. The cramped space held only a narrow folding cot for a bed, a small chest, and a table with clothes draped over the chair that stood nearby. It wouldn't take long to find out if the dagger was there. She started with the bed, but nothing was concealed under or within the thin mattress, so she moved on.

Her stomach sank when she saw the lock that secured the lid of the steamer trunk. It seemed too old and too simple to be the kind of lock that protected anything important. If the Pharaoh's Heart wasn't in the tent, it meant that Pickett was either carrying it with him . . . or it could already be gone.

Esta refused to think about that second option. Making short work of the lock, she started going through the contents of the trunk. Mostly it contained some clothing and papers, but the bottom seemed higher than it should have been. When she pushed aside the rest of the contents, she found that the floor of the trunk was actually a thin piece of wood that had been placed like a false bottom. Carefully, she pried it up, and when she saw what waited beneath, she felt the smallest spark of hope. A metal box was hidden there. It was secured with a combination lock—and it was about the same size as the dagger.

Her mouth was dry and her hands were shaking a little, but Esta examined the lock. She could have just taken the whole thing, but Bill Pickett was more likely to notice the missing box faster than he would notice if its contents went missing. It might take a little longer to open the box, but if Pickett didn't realize it was empty, she would have more time to get farther down the road.

Leaning her ear close, Esta began to rotate the tumbler to find the combination. She relaxed into the simple normalcy of the task. The first two numbers were easy enough, and she was well on her way to the third, when she realized that something was happening. Outside the tent, she heard voices. *Just a little farther . . .* and *there.* The final number snapped into place, but a new noise outside the tent stilled her hand. There was nowhere to hide, and without her affinity, Esta had no way to escape without being seen.

"Esta?" a familiar voice whispered from outside, and a second later Jericho Northwood stepped into the tent.

She let out the breath she'd been holding. "What are you doing here?"

North's expression was unreadable as he glanced down at the box she was holding. "Is that the dagger?"

"I don't know. I haven't gotten this open yet," she told him, scowling.

"Well, bring it with you. We have to go," North told her.

"I can't just take it," Esta explained.

"You're a thief, aren't you?" He peeked out from the flap of the tent without looking back at her.

"Yeah," Esta shot back. "But I don't usually tip off my mark by doing something as dumb as leaving a mess like this." She gestured to the contents of the trunk she'd piled on the ground to get to the box.

"You're going to have to," North said flatly, stepping toward her. "We have trouble."

"The marsh—"

Before she could finish the word, North held a finger to his lips. Then she heard it too. *Voices.* Men's voices, right outside the opening of the tent.

"Take the left side there, and I'll take the right," one man said, his voice a rough bark.

"It's some kind of raid," North whispered. "We saw a group of marshals arrive not long after we split up, but we couldn't find you in the crowd."

"They're looking for us," she said, certain.

North frowned like he didn't want to agree. "You saw the headlines, same as I did. But I don't think we should take any chances."

"Where's Maggie?" Esta whispered.

"Safe." He was already pulling his watch from his pocket. Despite the calmness in his voice, Esta didn't miss the way North's hands shook.

"I'll take this one," the first man said, closer now.

North was already extending his other hand to Esta as his thumb moved the dial of the watch. She reached for his hand without argument, but before she could take hold, an explosion sounded nearby. Both of them jumped, North nearly dropping his watch.

Outside the tent, the men started shouting as another explosion echoed. And then they were gone, off to deal with whatever had just happened.

Esta and North exchanged silent, uneasy looks, as though speaking might chase away this bit of luck that had managed to find them. In the distance, an alarm started to sound, the heavy metallic noise calling out its warning. Then the tent flap rustled, and Esta tensed again, but it was Maggie who'd stepped through the split in the canvas, her cheeks flushed pink.

"Mags?" North stepped toward Maggie. "What are you doing here? I told you to wait back outside the gate."

"You're lucky I didn't listen," Maggie said. "If I had, those men—"

Realization struck. "Tell me that explosion wasn't you," Esta said. "Tell me it wasn't an incendiary like back in Texas."

"It was a Flash and Bang," Maggie admitted, not quite meeting her eyes. "What else was I supposed to do? Let them find you in here?"

"You did fine," North told her, the new tremor in his voice betraying the truth. "But Esta's right. They're going to realize that wasn't any regular explosion soon enough. We have to get out of here. *Now.* And we're taking *that* with us." North grabbed the box before Esta could stop him. "We need to be gone before they *really* start looking for us. This way," North said, leading them toward the back side of the fairgrounds—away from the explosion Maggie had caused.

They made it past two more tents and were rounding the edge of a third, nearly to the back border of the encampment, when a woman stepped out, blocking their path. It was the sharpshooter Esta had seen in the show earlier.

"Y'all are an *awful* long way from the big top," the woman said, her voice carrying with it the cadence of the South.

This close, Esta realized that the woman wasn't as old as she'd seemed in the arena—she was maybe twenty, if that. Her plain dark hair was cut into a heavy fringe that framed her plain round face, and her nose was freckled beneath tight-set eyes of a cloudy blue. The sharpshooter wasn't exactly pretty and she wasn't exactly tall, but she certainly moved with an easy confidence that Esta might have admired if she hadn't been standing in the way of their escape.

"We must have taken a wrong turn when we were leaving the show," North said, stepping to shield Maggie.

"A wrong turn isn't all y'all seem to have taken." The woman's eyes were sharp on the box in North's hands. "That there don't look like it belongs to you."

A SERPENT MADE OF BONE

1904—Denver

N orth moved to block the woman's view of Maggie and Esta as he placed his hand in his pocket, ready to use his watch. It wouldn't take much to avoid this whole situation. A minute or two and they could miss the woman completely and slip out the back of the grounds.

The sharpshooter drew out one of her pistols and leveled it in his direction. "Keep your hands where I can see them. I don't want to shoot you," the woman said when North didn't immediately comply. "But I will. You should know right now that I never miss."

In the distance, an alarm was being sounded again, and North could smell smoke heavy in the air. Reluctantly, he took his hand from his pocket. He hadn't even managed to get the cover of the watch opened, and the body of the timepiece felt suddenly heavy, a useless weight in his pocket.

"Give it here," the woman said, holding out her free hand for the box.

North didn't make any move to comply. If the dagger was inside, he couldn't give it up. They'd already lost the necklace because he'd been stupid enough to fall asleep when he should have been keeping watch. He wouldn't be the cause of another powerful artifact slipping right out of the Antistasi's hands.

The woman raised the gun again, pulling back the hammer this time. "Whatever's in there ain't nothing to die over. Hand it over, and I'll let you go on your way. We can pretend all this never happened."

"You expect me to believe you're going to let us go?" North asked with a huff of disbelief.

"Don't do it, Jericho," Maggie said as she came up next to him. He tried to move back in front of her, but Maggie was too focused on the box in his hand.

"Y'all don't have much of a choice in the matter." Then the sharp-shooter shifted the gun, aiming it at Maggie. "Like I said . . . I *never* miss."

North sensed Esta behind him, but he couldn't tell what she was doing—and he didn't dare take his eyes off this new danger to look. All he knew was that she'd been quiet so far, and he hoped she'd *stay* quiet and not do anything stupid. The last thing they needed was for someone to recognize her.

"You can't give it to her, Jericho," Maggie pleaded again. "She's not really going to shoot me."

"You willin' to bet your life on that?" the sharpshooter asked, her voice easy as the summer breeze.

North glanced between the gun and Maggie, who was shaking her head. Silently pleading for him not to hand it over. But he knew that the woman wasn't making an empty threat. "Mags, we don't have a choice."

He sensed Esta moving as he started to slowly offer the box, but he ignored her and Maggie both as he eased the box toward the woman's outstretched hands. The second he saw victory flash in the sharpshooter's eyes, North made his move, flinging the box toward her head with a vio-lent shove. She did exactly what he'd hoped and lowered her gun in an attempt to catch the unwieldy package before it hit her flat in the face.

It gave him the opening he needed to lunge for her, pushing her down and pinning the hand holding the gun to the ground. He ripped the gun out of her hand and tossed it aside. Then he covered her mouth with his hand to keep her from making a racket that might give them away.

"Get the box," he told Maggie, who was already scurrying forward to retrieve it from where it had landed.

Esta went for the gun without having to be told.

Beneath him, the woman fought like a wildcat, and for a second North had the unpleasant realization that he had no idea what to do next. Even if she had cornered them and blocked their escape, he couldn't bring himself to knock out a female. But if he let her up, she was sure to alert the marshals, especially now that he'd attacked her. And he certainly didn't want to take her with them.

"Do you have anything for her?" he asked Maggie. "Quellant or—"

But the woman had gone completely still, her blue eyes wide as she stared at his wrist.

Inwardly, North cursed. He knew exactly what she was seeing. The edge of his shirt cuff had crept up his arm during the struggle, revealing the dark edge of his tattoo. Suddenly he felt a sharp pain in the palm of his hand, and he jerked away, looking at the red welts of teeth marks there with disgust, but the woman didn't scream as he'd expected her to.

"You're Antistasi," the woman said. It wasn't a question, and to North's surprise, it also didn't sound like an accusation. The woman looked up at Maggie. "You're the ones who set off the explosions." Understanding shifted quickly to concern. "You need to get out of here. If they find you—"

"That's what we were trying to do before you got in our way," North said, bristling with unease at the implication that this woman knew what they were.

Another shout sounded nearby. The group of men who were searching the tents were getting closer.

"If you get off me, I can help." The sharpshooter seemed younger and less battle-worn than she had a few minutes before. Not that it made North trust her.

"If I get off you, you're liable to turn on us," North said.

"Why would I do that, when we're on the same side?" Again the girl's eyes tracked to where Maggie and Esta stood behind him, and recognition lit her expression. "I wouldn't do anything that could help them catch the Thief."

"I don't know what you're—"

"Esta Filosik." The sharpshooter was ignoring North and speaking directly to Esta now. "I didn't recognize you at first, but now I ain't sure how I missed it. When the news came from Texas about your death, we all hoped it wasn't true. We knew it *had* to be a mistake, but then no one heard anything after."

There was a question in her statement, but Esta, thankfully, didn't respond. She met the woman's excited chatter with a long, cold silence. She seemed to be measuring the moment, the same as North was.

"You said 'we'?" North asked, still suspicious.

The woman's gaze returned to him. "Y'all didn't really think Mother Ruth's little band of Antistasi were the only ones interested in the Thief, did you? A lot of people paid attention to what happened in St. Louis. You must be Jericho Northwood." The sharpshooter's gaze flicked back to Maggie. "And Margaret Feltz, Ruth's baby sister. I'm surprised she let you go at all."

"I was never her prisoner." Maggie was at his side now.

"But you were most certainly her weapon," the woman said. "Everyone knows that. It was your affinity that kept Ruth in power."

North glanced up at Maggie, but he couldn't tell what was running through her pretty head. Maggie had been loyal to Ruth. She'd believed in her sister's vision and in the serum she created, but when that serum had turned out to be dangerous, when Ruth had refused to be swayed, Maggie had been brave enough to leave everything she'd ever known— and her only family—to do what she believed was right. And, somehow, this woman knew all about it.

"Who *are* you?" North asked, his instincts prickling. She knew too much about them for his liking.

"Cordelia Smith," the woman said. "I work here at the show, but I'm like y'all."

"What's that supposed to mean?" North demanded.

Esta came closer, still holding the pistol. "She's Mageus. I felt her affinity back in the arena."

"I'm *Antistasi*," the sharpshooter corrected. "Check my leg. You'll find your proof of my loyalty there."

"Go on," North said after a moment, refusing to let the woman's flirting throw him off. "Check her."

He kept focused on Cordelia Smith as Maggie pushed the woman's skirts high enough to check her leg.

"Higher," she said with a saucy curve of her lips, never breaking her gaze with North. "My left thigh."

North ignored the way his cheeks felt like embers and forced himself not to so much as blink. Whatever game this woman was playing, he wasn't interested.

"Let her up, Jericho," Maggie said, her voice soft but determined.

Making sure to keep his hold on the woman beneath him, he glanced back to see Maggie crouched over the woman's legs. Cordelia's skirt had been lifted to reveal long, slender legs covered in silk stockings, but above her garters, a tattoo wound itself around her thigh. A snake. Not a living serpent, like his, but an ouroboros just the same, its fanged skull devouring the delicate bones of its tail.

"She's not lying," Maggie said.

The sharpshooter only smiled at him, like a satisfied cat.

"It could still be a trap," North argued. He couldn't help but wonder why Cordelia had chosen to mark herself with death instead of the living serpent that was at the center of all the stories he'd heard as a child.

"Let her up, Jericho. If this were a trap, we'd already be caught," Maggie told him, lowering the woman's skirts. "She's not the one with the gun right now, anyway."

Another shout went up, closer still. The smell of smoke was thicker now, and North wondered what exactly Maggie had set on fire.

"Jericho . . ." Maggie's tone was firm, and she had that determined look she got sometimes when she wasn't going to be swayed. "If she says she can get us out of this mess, I don't think we have much choice but to give her a chance."

North didn't like the idea of letting the woman go, but he knew it was going to happen eventually. It wasn't like he could sit on her indefinitely, even if there weren't marshals searching the grounds. "Fine." Slowly he let go of Cordelia's arms, keeping himself ready for her counterattack, and when it didn't come, he rose from where he'd pinned her to the ground.

As the sharpshooter stood and readjusted her skirts, North backed away, edging closer to Maggie. He was already reaching in his pocket for his watch, in case he needed it, but Cordelia didn't attack or shout for help or try to run. She simply brushed herself off. She was still looking at the box, though, and—Antistasi or not—her expression was transparent enough that North could tell she was too interested for his liking.

"My gun," she said, holding out her hand to Esta.

"You said you could get us out of here," North said, stepping between the two. "You can have it back once we're safe. Until then, if you try anything at all, I won't be the least bit sad if she has to use it."

THE TRAITOR

1902—New York

The Bella Strega was crowded, the air filled with the usual cheap tobacco smoke and the scent of ale. Along with those common scents was the familiar warmth of the old magic. For James Lorcan, that warm energy signaled something more. It was a power that was filled with *possibility*. With the right tools, it could be molded and shaped. With the right choices, it was a power that he could someday *control*.

So far, though, *someday* remained elusive. The Aether moved in strange currents around him, teasing James with the promise of victory but holding it *just* out of reach. It was a curse to sense the future coming but be unable to see it clearly. Still, each day his plans grew more sure and the tenuous grasp he had on the Devil's Own grew stronger. Each day Dolph's people trusted him a little more, *depended* on him a little more, but James knew implicitly that nothing was guaranteed. Not yet. Not until he had the ring and could unlock the power in Dolph's cane. Then, and only then, would his control over the Devil's Own be absolute.

Seated near the rear of the saloon, his back against a wall, James watched his kingdom. He considered his options as he tried to read the message in the Aether.

"You really think the Order has the ring?" Logan asked. He was sitting to James' left, nervously picking at his nails as his eyes shifted uneasily around the room.

Clearly, Logan was still unsure about his new environment, but at least he was smart enough to keep his voice low. He'd have to be a complete fool not to see the way the others glared at him. They saw him as an interloper who'd taken an undeserved spot at James' side. Even now James sensed Werner watching them from across the barroom. He could practically feel Werner's annoyance. It couldn't be helped, though. Logan's ability to track objects would, no doubt, be useful, but James understood that the new boy could be dangerous, too, if his loyalty ever shifted. Better to keep him close, even if it caused those in the Strega to wonder. Better to make him believe that he had a home here, a friend.

"Paul Kelly's contacts at Tammany have all but confirmed it," James told Logan, tracing a circular stain on the table. "Considering that you've found no sign of the artifact in the city, it only makes sense that someone's taken it through the Brink and beyond our reach."

"It could be a setup, though," Logan said, frowning. "Kelly could have taken it just as well as the Order. This might be a trap to get rid of you and take the Strega without a fight."

"I've considered that," James told Logan, trying to keep the irritation out of his voice. Of *course* he'd considered it, but the Aether didn't lie. He had to play Kelly's games . . . at least for now. "No doubt Kelly will play dirty and try to turn the tables on us at some point, but I don't think his belief about what the Order is planning is a complete lie."

"What does the journal say?" Logan whispered.

"It remains as unreadable as ever." But with the new information from Paul Kelly, James found that the change in the journal no longer worried him. Instead, it *emboldened* him. Perhaps the future was no longer his to read, but that only meant that it was changeable. The future, it seemed, was his to *make*.

"There's no doubt that Kelly is up to something," James assured Logan. "Maybe he wants us to take the fall for what happened at Morgan's gala, or maybe this is all a distraction so he can take the ring for himself."

"But you won't let that happen," Logan said with smug satisfaction.

James couldn't help but smile softly at Logan's sureness. He'd been wary about Logan in the beginning, but Logan had proven himself—or at least, he'd proven his loyalty. Ever since his failure to retrieve the ring, he'd been *that* much more committed, and James was more than happy to use that commitment. It was so much easier than doling out threats.

"No," he told Logan. "That isn't going to happen. The stupid dago will get what he has coming to him."

The Aether in the barroom trembled suddenly. In the vibrations, James sensed a warning of approaching danger—but also something that felt like possibility. He barely had time to register the change before the doors of the Strega burst open with a violent crash. Everyone except the most inebriated turned to see what was happening, and the noise of the saloon died to a strangled whisper as they all realized who had entered. The smile that had been playing about James' mouth only broadened.

Viola had come home.

The customers parted as Dolph's assassin stalked toward the back of the barroom to the table where James sat, her dark skirts swishing around her legs and her violet eyes burning with fury. Werner, who'd been behind the bar, started to move, but James stayed him by lifting a hand.

"She's the girl from the gala," Logan said, his voice low and urgent. "The one who was going after the ring. I thought the beast crushed her."

"Such a shame it didn't," James told him, his words dripping with disdain.

He'd known all along that Viola was loyal to Dolph, but her little performance on the bridge a few weeks before had changed things. When she'd attacked James in defense of Esta, she'd made herself his enemy. He'd just as soon see her dead, except every instinct he had screamed that he couldn't take her out of the equation. *Not yet.* Now that she'd appeared in the Strega, the Aether was rearranging itself, suggesting a new way forward that he had not previously considered.

James himself didn't stand to greet the intruder. He simply leaned forward a little in his seat, as Dolph might have done, and tightened his grip on the gorgon-shaped topper of the cane he held. He could almost sense the power trapped within the silver. It was a reminder that everything that surrounded him—the bar, the people, and the power that came with them—was his now. *Not* Dolph Saunders'.

Without slowing her steps, Viola took her knife from her skirts and launched it at him. The air seemed to drain from the room as the blade sailed toward him and landed at the edge of the table, right in the center of the ring he'd been tracing earlier. But James didn't so much as flinch. Viola hadn't come to kill.

Not this time, at least. Not any other, if he had his way.

"Bastardo," Viola growled when she finally stood in front of him. She leaned down, her hands gripping the edge of the table until her knuckles flashed white. The stiletto knife was sunk into the table between them. "What have you done to my blade?"

"Hello, Viola," James said easily. "How delightful to see you've finally returned to us. You've made quite the entrance."

"I'll make more than that in a minute." She bared her teeth at him.

"You seem to be upset," James said, pretending surprise. "Strange, considering that *you're* the one who attacked me on the bridge." His gaze was steady, and he spoke only to her, but he made sure that his voice was loud enough for anyone nearby who happened to be listening to hear. "You remember the bridge, don't you? The day that you allowed Harte Darrigan to escape after he betrayed us all."

"You would have killed Esta," Viola reminded him through clenched teeth.

James leaned forward. "Esta would have deserved it." He did not stop the ice from flowing through his words. "She chose that traitor of a magician over us."

"It doesn't matter anymore." Viola's eyes narrowed. "Esta is gone and Darrigan is dead, Nibsy. As you will be if you don't tell me what you've done to my knife."

"Dead?" James let his mouth curve. "Certainly you've heard the reports by now, Viola. It's been in all the papers—Darrigan and Esta were seen *outside* the city. Alive and well. They betrayed us, and then she left with him *and* the treasures Dolph wanted so badly and you risked so much for." He watched the slight widening of her eyes, the way her breath caught. He enjoyed it, that moment of her distress. "Ah . . . So you *hadn't* heard."

Viola only stared, but James could see the indecision flickering in her expression. "I don't care about Esta or the damned magician. I want to know what you did to my knife."

"I kept it safe, and then I returned it to you," James said. "After I pulled it from my own leg, of course."

"No," Viola said, shaking her head. "You gave me Libitina after you let Mooch be taken by my brother, and like a fool I accepted it without looking for the trick. As though we were friends."

"We *were* friends once," he reminded her, ignoring the rustling unease that had gone through the Strega at her announcement about Mooch. There had been questions about what had happened to the boy ever since he'd helped James by setting one of Tammany's fire stations ablaze. James had pretended as much confusion—and dismay—as anyone, but now he barely cared if the whole barroom knew the truth. Now he cared only for the direction the Aether pushed him . . . *toward* Viola.

"I see exactly what your friendship is worth," Viola sneered. "Tell me, Nibsy, have you even tried to free Mooch from the Tombs?"

James only stared at her, feeling the world around him rearrange itself. Trying to discern the correct path, the correct words. "You can't really believe I would leave one of our own? I'm doing all I can. Mooch is a *friend*."

The barroom eased back into its rhythm, apparently pleased enough with that answer.

"You were a friend to Dolph as well," Viola charged. "Now here you sit, in *his* seat, presiding over *his* home. Tell me, Nibsy, what have you done to avenge his murder?"

"What would you have me do?" he asked, pretending innocence. "You know the position we're all in now. You know how dangerous everything is because of *your* failure to retrieve the Book. You were the one who handed it to Darrigan, along with the artifacts, if I remember correctly. Not me."

Viola laughed, an ugly, hollow sound that had the people closest to them shuffling nervously back. "You were always slippery as a snake," she told him, her voice dangerous now. "Dolph trusted you, and this is how you repay him?"

"At least I'm here." James didn't so much as blink. "When the Bowery went mad, when Tammany's patrols started burning the homes of the innocent, what did *you* do? You *disappeared*." He paused then, because he knew that those around him were listening. "How is your brother doing, Viola? There are plenty here who've been marked by Kelly's men. I'm sure they'd like to know what it's like living under his protection."

"Perhaps you should tell them yourself," she huffed. "After all, you dined with him earlier, didn't you?"

"Business," James said with a cold smile. "I keep my friends close and my enemies closer, the same as Dolph did. All for the Devil's Own, Viola. *All* for the Devil's Own—"

He felt the sharpness of pain in his chest, but it was light enough that he knew she was only toying with him. If she'd wanted him dead, she could have killed him three times over by now. But then, if she'd wanted him dead, he would have known.

"Careful, Viola. My boys have orders should anything happen to me." The pain intensified so that his voice became strained. *Good. Let her dig her own grave.* "It would be a shame if something happened to your dear mother. Pasqualina, I believe her name is? She came by your brother's cafe after you left today. A lovely woman."

"My brother would kill you before her blood hit the ground," Viola snarled, but the threat had worked. The pain in his chest eased. "Tell me what you did to my knife," she demanded. "Why can't I heal the cut it made when you are just fine?" She gestured to him.

"You call this *fine*?" James asked, pretending to be more shocked than he was. He made a show of pulling himself to his feet, of leaning against the cane. Viola was a small woman, and even hunched against the cane, he was taller. "Because of what you did, I'll never walk on my own again."

"I could have killed you instead," Viola told him. "I should have."

"But you didn't *want* to," James told her, letting the sheer irony of it hang in the air between them. "I wonder why that is, Viola. Unless you knew even then, on the bridge, that I was right about Darrigan, and right about everything else as well."

Viola shook her head. But James knew that she could not dismiss the words that were already working into her mind, worming their way into her sureness. "Tell me what you did to Libitina. Why won't the wound heal?"

James could see the frantic fear in her eyes and he *savored* it. "You think I had something to do with *that*?"

"Who else?" she demanded.

"Have I had a hand in the others you've killed?" he asked. "You were Dolph's assassin, weren't you? How many did you use your blade on? How many have died by your hand, Viola?"

Her mouth was drawn tight, and James could see the guilt in her eyes, the *shame* of what she believed herself to be. It was a weakness that she hadn't yet accepted the choices she'd made or the power she held. It was a weakness that she still foolishly worried about a god who would never answer her cries. It was also a vulnerability that he could exploit.

"Who was it that you wanted dead this time?" James pressed, considering the question seriously for himself. Feeling the Aether bunch and shift. "Why try to save this poor soul now?"

Viola lifted her chin, her eyes narrowing. "It's none of your concern who I save."

James didn't agree. To his estimation, and based upon the way the Aether moved, the person Viola wanted to save had *everything* to do with him. The vibrations around him were moving in harmony now, urging him onward. *This* was what he needed—Viola's involvement *and* the involvement of the person she wanted to save.

Jianyu. The moment the name came to his mind, James knew he was right. Now he understood. He needed their affinities and their commitment to getting the ring. Could *use* them.

James had no idea what had caused Viola to cut Jianyu with her knife, but it was clear they were now aligned. He needed them both. Or rather, his plan did. But he couldn't make saving Jianyu too easy for her. *No.* That would raise her suspicions. Viola needed to hate him, and so James would gladly give her reason to. He would use that hatred to his own benefit, and then he would crush her and Jianyu both and take the victory that should have always been his.

A NEW ALLIANCE

1902—New York

Viola drew herself upright, refusing to let Nibsy see the way his words had affected her. "Tell me what you did to my knife, Nibsy." She let her affinity unfurl again, a small jolt this time. A clear reminder of what she could do. And what she was willing to risk.

"Do you truly not know?" Nibsy said. It looked as though he was trying to laugh, but all that came out was a weak cough. "Your knife. Libitina, you call it. It's not some random blade. It's the same as this cane, the same as any number of items floating through this city—it's been *changed* by magic. It's not natural magic, of course, but that sort of thing never really bothered Dolph, did it?" He eyed Viola, daring her to disagree.

But Viola couldn't. She knew about the cane, about what power it had over the marks they all wore when Dolph wielded it, and thanks to Nibsy, now she understood how the cane had been made. How Dolph had *taken* from Leena, had made an unwilling sacrifice of her power.

"I know this already," she said. "But you haven't explained why I can't heal the cut it made." She tried not to dwell too much on the fact that her knife had an origin like Dolph's cane.

"Viola . . ." Nibsy shook his head as though disappointed in her. "Dolph gave you a blade that could help you to kill because he knew you were too . . ." He waved a hand. "Let's be frank. Dolph knew you were too *weak* to use your affinity as it was meant to be used, and so he gave you the knife instead. Have you never wondered why your blade is so deadly? *Why you never miss?* It's ritual magic, Viola, crafted to work with what you *are*. It calls to blood, just as your magic does. If you intended to kill someone with that blade, they'll die. If someone is dying from your blade, that's not something I did. That, my old friend, is all your *own* doing. And it *always* has been."

Viola watched numbly as Nibsy took the knife from the tabletop in front of him. It was sunk inches deep, like the table was made of bread instead of wood. Then he placed it flat in front of him, the handle facing Viola.

At first all she could do was stare at it.

She'd known. *Of course* she'd known that the blade wasn't normal. It had a certain weight that seemed far heavier than its steel and an ability to do what no other could. But Viola had convinced herself that the lives Libitina took had nothing to do with her affinity. She'd believed that she could separate herself—what she was—from the things she did. As though that made any difference at all.

She'd been lying to herself. Willfully blind. *Because* this *is what I am. What I've always been.* Viola stared at Libitina, perhaps seeing it truly for the first time. Even now, even accepting what the knife was, her hands ached to hold the comforting weight once more.

"Nothing you can do with your affinity will save the person you've tried to kill, Viola." Nibsy gave her a rueful look. "False magic can only be broken by false magic. You know that."

"Tell me how to fix this." It took all of her effort to keep her voice from shaking. She glanced up from the blade, looking at him with fire in her eyes.

Nibsy's expression was unreadable. "Are we friends again, Viola? Because from your little display, I would have said you still consider me an enemy." He paused, letting the challenge filter through the nearly silent room. "I find that I have *very* few reasons to help an enemy."

Viola felt her temper spike. He was toying with her. Cat and mouse in front of an audience thirsty for blood—for *her* blood. But she would not give him the satisfaction. In the end, she would be the one to kill the snake.

She swiped the knife from the table and had it at Nibsy's throat before he could blink. Around her, the room contracted, and she sensed the boys she'd once seen as allies coming for her.

"Call them off, Nibsy." She nudged the point of the blade against his delicate skin. "You know what this can do, and I find that I have very few reasons to keep you alive if you won't help me. How do I fix this? I know you have the answer."

Nibsy raised his hand to stay the Devil's Own, but his gaze never left hers. "Dolph was hardly a fool," he told her, his eyes glinting over the rims of his lenses. "He would never have given you a weapon that strong unless he had some assurance that he could protect himself should you ever turn on him. Dolph knew how to reverse the effects of the knife," Nibsy said. "I'm sure he left instructions behind, along with the rest of his books and his things. You've seen for yourself how carefully he recorded the details of his work. . . ."

Viola ignored the amusement in Nibsy's tone as she thought of the sheet of paper he'd given to her just a few weeks before. A trick wrapped up in the truth. Viola had read over those notes countless times since then, hoping that she could find some sign that Dolph Saunders had not betrayed the one person he loved more than any other for something as small and as petty as power.

"You will give them to me now." Viola again increased the pressure of the knife against his throat. "Or I will take them myself."

Nibsy only laughed. Then he lowered his voice, so only the two of them could hear. "You can't fight them all, you know. Kill me if you must. Make me into a martyr." Nibsy's eyes shone with satisfaction. "You'll never make it out of this room. They're mine now, Viola. The Devil's Own, the Strega, and everything Dolph built. So have a care."

Her chest ached with the truth of his words. If she killed him, the people surrounding them in the barroom would not let her escape, and she could not kill them all—*would not* kill them all, even if she could. They were no more than pawns in Nibsy's game, the same as herself. But games were not something Viola had time for. Not when Jianyu was still so close to death. She'd done what she could, but his wound would continue to bleed. Unless she solved the problem, his death would be on her soul as well.

"Besides," Nibsy told her, "it's not only the instructions you need, Viola. Even if you killed me, even if you managed to find Dolph's notes and escape with your life, you'll need something more to reverse the effects of your knife." He took the blade of Libitina between his fingers delicately and moved it away from his own throat. "You need an object that contains false magic as powerful as that in your knife. A seal, perhaps, like the one we took from the Metropolitan, might do the trick. It's a pity it was lost that night, or you might already have the answer you need." He looked up at her over the rims of his spectacles. "It *was* lost?"

"Yes," Viola lied, her instincts screaming. "Along with the rest."

"Pity." He paused, the hesitation making her temper start to crack. "There's one place, of course, one organization rather, that might have another such piece."

"You mean the Order." She shook her head. "We took their treasures already. I watched the building burn myself."

"True, Khafre Hall burned, but you can't really imagine that the Order lost everything? After all, the Mysterium was far below ground level and well protected, physically and magically."

Viola disagreed. After all, she'd seen the walls of Khafre Hall crumble. She'd barely escaped them herself. If there was anything left, certainly it had been lost in the collapse.

"The Order still continues to persist," Nibsy pressed. "You were at their gala, so you know that they aren't completely powerless, and the entire city knows that their plans for the Conclave continue. That doesn't sound like an organization that has lost everything." He paused, picking at some dirt beneath his nails, but Viola knew he was baiting her. "I hear they have plans for a new headquarters. They'll be moving what was left of Khafre Hall there soon."

She lowered her knife, her mind spinning with the implications. "Why are you telling me this?"

Nibsy held her gaze. "Because the Order is still a threat."

"So am I," she growled, knowing there was something more Nibsy wasn't saying, some trick or trap he was setting for her.

"I've always appreciated that, Viola. Even if the rest of them didn't."

She huffed her disbelief.

"You don't think I understand?" Nibsy asked, far too innocently. "I know how they looked at you, what they must have thought was between you and Dolph—"

"Nothing was between us but friendship," she said.

"As you insist . . ." Nibsy merely shrugged. "You think I don't know what it's like to have the Devil's Own suspect that you don't *truly* belong." He adjusted his grip on the cane—*on Dolph's cane.* "I know all too well. I can only imagine what it must be like for you now, though, to be under the thumb of your brother, a man who could not see your promise if it bit him on the nose. It doesn't have to be this way, Viola."

She was shaking her head, denying everything he said even as his words wrapped around her mind. "You know nothing."

"I know that your brother is planning on attacking the Order," Nibsy said, and when Viola couldn't stop her eyes from widening, his mouth twitched. "So Paul hasn't told you."

Of course he hadn't told her. Paolo never told Viola anything but what he wanted for dinner or how much of an embarrassment she was to him and to their family.

"Why would he do something so stupid?" she asked, trying to dismiss this tale even as her instincts jangled that it smacked of the truth. Paul might have saved her from the gala, but Viola had suspected that her brother still didn't trust her. Now she knew for sure.

"Jack Grew tried to kill him," Nibsy said with a shrug. "That alone makes it personal. But your brother's not a stupid man, Viola. Right now he enjoys the protection of Tammany, but he knows how inhospitable the city could become for him and his Five Pointers if the Order is able to rebuild their power. If the Order takes power away from Tammany, he would be at risk. He's asked me to help him destroy them."

"What should I care if he goes after the Order? Why should you?" Viola asked. She couldn't be drawn into his games. Not when she couldn't trust a word he said. "If Paolo wants to go after rich men, he's un idiota. One who will deserve whatever he gets."

"I have to admit, it wouldn't break my heart if the Order took care of Paul Kelly," Nibsy said. "But I'm afraid I can't stand by and not get involved. Not when your brother believes that the Order retrieved the ring at the gala."

"You don't mean . . ." She frowned. "Paul, he doesn't have it?" She'd assumed her brother or one of his men had taken it when the great stone beast had nearly killed her. Everything she'd done—every order she'd followed and meal she cooked for him—was because she'd been trying to figure out what Paul had done with the ring. But if Nibsy was to be believed, it had been for nothing.

"No," Nibsy said. "I don't believe he does."

Viola's thoughts were swirling, careening. "What do you want from me, Nibsy?" she asked, barely leashing her impatience.

"I want you to help me get the ring back," Nibsy said. "I don't trust Kelly to simply hand it over, as he's promised. I expect that he'll try to get rid of me instead. If he does, what will happen to the Strega? What will happen to the Devil's Own?"

Viola knew exactly what would happen—her brother would take everything Dolph Saunders had built. He would bend the Devil's Own until they broke, like he did to everything he touched.

"What do you think I can do?" Viola asked, wary.

"You can give me information," Nibsy told her. "I need to know what he's planning and what he's withholding. You can help me protect the Devil's Own from your brother's control."

Viola considered his proposal.

"I need your help, Viola," Nibsy said, looking somehow younger than he had a few minutes ago. Suddenly he wasn't the conniving snake that had greeted her but the boy she'd once known. "I know what you think of me. I know you don't trust my motives, but the Order cannot be allowed to keep the artifact. And your brother must not get the ring instead. An item like that holds power, even for Sundren. Think of what he would do with it."

It was far too easy to picture it. Even false magic in Paul's hands would be a nightmare, for Viola and for the entire city. "You are asking me to betray my family—my own *blood*."

"What has your blood ever done for you?" Nibsy asked. "They tossed you out and treated you like some scullery maid when you're more powerful by far. Because they have never understood you, and they will never accept you. Not like we do. Come back to the Devil's Own, Viola. If you're willing to put our past differences aside and start anew, we can end the Order once and for all. We can hit them now, before they're able to regroup for their Conclave. We can retrieve the artifact, like Dolph wanted us to, and in the process, you can save whoever it is you've hurt this time. Agree to pledge yourself to the Devil's Own once again, and I will hand over Dolph's notes. Help me, and I will help you as well."

Nibsy extended his hand across the table, but Viola did not take it. Nibsy Lorcan was a rat, and she'd be a fool to trust him. And yet, what was her alternative? She couldn't attack the Order alone, and she would never depend upon Paul to help her.

Viola did not sheath her knife as she considered the offer.

"We can begin to put Darrigan's betrayal to rights," Nibsy urged, his hand still extended. "We can avenge Dolph as well by driving Paul Kelly and his Five Pointers from the Bowery. I plan to go after the ring either way, but it would be easier together. If we were on the same side, we would have a real chance." He paused, a dramatic beat during which the entire room seemed to hold its collective breath. "It's what Dolph would have wanted."

It *was* what Dolph would have wanted, but Viola knew that Nibsy's words were all tricks and lies. She would be a fool to believe them without question. If she agreed to betray her brother, Nibsy would surely turn on her, like a viper turns to attack an intruder in its den. She *knew* that. But Jianyu's life was in the balance, the ring was within reach, and her teeth were every bit as sharp as Nibsy Lorcan's. If she was cunning, she would not have to battle Nibsy alone.

THE SUMMONS

1902—New York

Jack Grew strode into his uncle's mansion feeling every minute of sleep he'd lost since the gala. The ring had been there in the ballroom the night of the gala. He'd seen it sparkling on Evelyn's finger as she primped and teased him before the event. It had been there when she died as well, crushed beneath the great beast, and then . . . it was gone. In the weeks that had passed, there had been no sign of the artifact, no sign of the girl in the purple satin or what had become of her. And with Tammany still protecting Paul Kelly, Jack had no way to get to either of them. But the truth was clear—

He would find them *and* the ring, and when he did, he would make them all pay.

For now, though, Jack had other worries. He still wasn't sure why he'd been summoned to his uncle's home without warning or explanation. The Order had been quiet, and its members had been guarded after the gala. The event had been a success, of course, even with the mishap at the end. The papers had all marveled at the demonstrations, as Jack's aunt Fanny had hoped they would when the blasted event was arranged.

And yet, after all of the press they'd received, there had been only silence on the part of the Order. No one from the Inner Circle had congratulated Jack on his victory. No one had thanked him for the service he'd provided. Especially not his uncle. It was strange, then, for Jack to suddenly find himself so abruptly summoned. And so urgently.

The messenger had tracked him down earlier that morning. Jack had been on his way out and had planned to spend the day in his warehouse by the docks, trying to make sense of the pile of metal that had once been his machine. He was beginning to understand why it hadn't worked before. The stones he'd been using to focus the machine's power—expensive and precious as they might have been—weren't strong enough. He needed a stone imbued with a different type of power—a stone like the one in the ring.

The Delphi's Tear might have evaded him for now, but it was only a matter of time, Jack reasoned, before the artifact revealed itself to him. Or before the Book showed him another way.

Jack handed his hat to the maid who answered the door. He barely spared her a glance as he brushed past, ignoring the maid's sputtering protests, and made his own way back into the mansion, where his uncle's office lay in burnished silence.

If he'd expected a quiet family meeting, Jack was immediately disabused of that notion the second he turned into the west hall and heard low voices coming from Morgan's office. His steps faltered a little.

Jack allowed his hand to dip into his jacket pocket so that he could caress the cracked and worn leather of the Book's cover. It was a reminder to himself that he would ultimately prevail. Then Jack took one of the morphine cubes from the vial he always carried and let the bitterness of the drug drain away the slight pounding behind his eyes.

In the office, Jack found three men: his uncle, the High Princept, and another older man he didn't recognize. Each was richer and more pointless than the last. They stopped their conversation when he entered. When the maid came stumbling in directly behind Jack, apologizing and trying to explain how she had tried to stop him, Morgan himself glowered so darkly that Jack knew the girl would be working her fingers raw in the laundry before the end of the day.

"Your messenger told me that you required my presence," Jack said, ignoring the drama his unexpected entrance had created. "He said it was urgent and insisted that I come immediately, despite my being otherwise occupied."

Morgan harrumphed, his bulbous nose twitching with disdain. "Drinking and whoring does not constitute an occupation."

Jack fought the urge to sneer at his uncle. So this wasn't to be a commendation after all. He hadn't supposed it would be, but Morgan's words galled him nonetheless.

Still, he would not allow these men to goad him. "I would have thought I'd more than demonstrated my ability to *occupy* myself with something other than wine and women, Uncle," he said dryly.

"You did indeed." The High Princept stepped forward, placing himself between Morgan and Jack to defuse the situation. "It was an impressive display to be sure, my boy. Quite impressive."

"Except for certain complications," Morgan grumbled.

"Complications?" Jack lifted a single brow as he tried to read the tenor of the room. "It's true that the ending was somewhat . . . disorderly, but I'm sure you have ample funds to repair the damage to the ballroom. I imagine Aunt Fanny is beside herself, considering the opportunity she now has—"

"You killed a girl," Morgan said, throwing the fact like a gauntlet at his feet.

"She was a chorus girl. A common harlot," Jack told them, brushing away the issue.

"That may be, but Evelyn DeMure was a well-known performer in the city—unfortunately, one the public seems to have a certain amount of sympathy for," the Princept said. "There are a great many who are outraged by her death and who blame the Order."

"They're all fools, then. She was nothing but a maggot, one who would have used her feral powers to destroy the Order," Jack reminded them. "She was a siren, a threat. Now she is not."

"Have you no shame?" his uncle demanded.

"Why should I be ashamed when I am guilty of nothing?" Jack asked, his temper flaring. "Have I been charged with anything? *No.* The girl's death was deemed an accident."

"But the question remains—what kind of accident was it?" the Princept wondered.

Jack's instincts suddenly prickled. "I fail to understand your meaning."

"When did you learn that the girl had possession of the Delphi's Tear?" the High Princept asked, his gaze steady. Deadly calm.

Realization suddenly hit. They knew. Which meant that it wasn't Kelly's girl, nor Kelly himself, who'd managed to slip away with the ring. These men had it. The Delphi's Tear was back in the hands of the Order.

"I'm not certain what you mean," Jack hedged, weighing the moment—and his options—carefully.

"Let's cut through the bullshit," Morgan said, his mouth drawn into a flat, uncompromising line. "You're a constant disappointment, but despite what others have said, you're not an idiot. I don't give a fig about what the public thinks about the death of some showgirl, but I do care about loyalty, boy. And you've displayed an appalling lack of it. At some point, you knew that DeMure had one of the Order's most prized possessions, and still you kept that information from us."

"The question we've been asking ourselves is *when* you knew," the Princept said, his wizened old face not betraying any emotion.

"You think I *hid* this from you—that I was trying to take the artifact for my own?" Jack asked, changing tactics by pretending to be shocked.

"Why else keep it a secret?" Morgan blustered. "Why not tell the Inner Circle immediately, so the situation could be dealt with quickly and quietly—and most importantly, out of the public's view."

"Think carefully about your answer, boy," the Princept warned. "Your membership with our hallowed organization depends upon it."

His membership? Jack wanted to laugh in their faces. He wanted to *dare* them to revoke his membership, when he alone held the key to their future, but he knew that it would be a mistake. Without access to the Order, without the benefit of their trust, he might never be able to retrieve the ring from them. Certainly, there was no sense in making his task any more difficult.

"I admit that I had heard a rumor Evelyn had a ring resembling one of the lost artifacts," he started, choosing his words, careful to sound contrite and nervous. "But I didn't know for sure."

"You should have told us immediately," Morgan said.

"You of all people should understand my hesitance, Uncle." Jack bowed his head and tried to hide his fury behind a mask of remorse and humility. "After the mistakes I made in the past? I knew I couldn't afford another. I knew that retrieving one of the lost artifacts would be only one step toward atoning, but I was reluctant to give you false hope. I certainly never intended to keep the ring for my own," he lied. "Had I retrieved it, I would have given it to the Order immediately."

"How are we to believe you?" Morgan asked.

"Believe whatever you will," Jack told them, clenching his teeth to keep his anger from showing. "Revealing Evelyn's duplicity was to be a victory, but not for myself. It was to be a gift to the Inner Circle, to the Order itself, a grand moment when a maggot who had fooled so many would finally be held accountable for her crimes publicly, exposed for all the city—and the world—to see. After all, the gala was not for my benefit alone. Was it not meant to show the entire city that the Order had not been weakened by the fires of Khafre Hall? Apprehending Evelyn DeMure would have helped with that." Jack drew himself up, squared his shoulders. "But then Paul Kelly ruined everything. By the time I got to Evelyn, she was dead, and there was no sign of the ring."

"Still you didn't tell us, even after?" the Princept pressed.

"I didn't know for sure that she'd ever actually had it," Jack lied. "I thought that my instincts had proven false, and I was grateful that I hadn't exposed my mistakes once again." He glanced up, pretending an epiphany. "But how did you know? Unless—*did* she have it? Is the artifact back in the Order's possession once more?"

"It is," the Princept boasted, unable to hide his satisfaction.

"I'm glad to hear that," Jack said. It wasn't a complete lie. Now that he knew for sure where the Delphi's Tear was, he could set his sights on obtaining it. "I'm only happy to have helped, however small a role I might have played."

Morgan was clearly frustrated. "Your *role* in this could have ruined everything. Do you know what would have happened if the ring had fallen into the wrong hands?"

"But it didn't," Jack pressed, tired of being chastised like some misbehaving schoolboy. "The Order retrieved it, as I'd hoped they would."

"Enough." The Princept raised his hand to silence them both. "The Order currently stands at a great precipice," he said. "However, now that we have one of the lost artifacts back in our possession, our position is not quite so dire as it once was."

"Our situation is *still* tenuous," Morgan argued. "The Conclave at the end of the year was supposed to demonstrate our strengths—to the other Brotherhoods, to the entire country. The Brink was to be reconsecrated. *Expanded.* Instead, we've found ourselves far behind in our preparations. We may have retrieved the ring, but the rest of our most important artifacts remain missing. Khafre Hall still lies in ashes."

"Your new headquarters will make everyone forget that Khafre Hall ever burned," the third man said, breaking his silence. He had the kind of satisfied confidence that made Jack's teeth hurt.

"I don't believe we've been introduced," Jack said dully. "You are?"

"Harry Black." The man didn't bother to extend his hand.

Jack glanced at Morgan, wondering if he was supposed to know who this was. Wondering, suddenly, why this stranger was even here.

"Black is president of the Fuller Company," the Princept explained. "He's one of our newer initiates."

"I was at the gala, and I was impressed with what I saw," Black said, eyeing Jack. "*Very* impressed."

"He's offered the Order the top floors of his company's newest building for our headquarters," the Princept said, his mustache twitching.

"Which building is that?" Jack asked, though he had a feeling he already knew.

"The skyscraper being built on Fifth Avenue, across from Madison Square Park," Black said.

"The one that people have been taking bets on to see how far the debris will fall when it topples?" Jack said, incredulous. "What have the papers taken to calling it? The Flatiron?"

Black glared at him. "Only uneducated fools believe that the structure won't stand for an eternity. Steel construction is the future. With it, the city can grow to untold heights. The new building will be one of the tallest in the city when it's complete in a few weeks. Where better to house the Order? 'As above, so below,' after all."

"Certainly this won't be permanent. Khafre Hall will be rebuilt," Jack said. How could it not be? The old structure had been constructed on a site selected for its location over the confluence of two subterranean rivers. It was believed to be a powerful locus for elemental energy, water and earth coming together as they did. "The location alone—"

Morgan closed a ledger that had been open on his desk, closing the topic of conversation as well. "We didn't call you here today to hear your opinions. The matter has already been decided."

"Perhaps the location of Khafre Hall was important in the past," the Princept explained, "but the new headquarters has certain advantages that Khafre Hall does not." He glanced at Black.

"The building itself has been designed with principles of the occult arts in mind: the sacred triangle, the alignment of its sides with the sigil in the park and with the path of the stars." Black was clearly proud of this particular fact. "Even the height of the building will serve as a testament to the Order's power. Khafre Hall was the past—and a glorious past it was—but the new headquarters will serve the Order long into the future."

"We'll move into the building in a matter of weeks," the Princept explained. "During that time, the artifact will be installed in the new Mysterium, along with the rest of what was left from Khafre Hall. The building will be dedicated and warded with protections on the city's solstice. Which is why we asked you here today."

"This is a terrible idea," Morgan muttered.

"The boy has answered our questions," the Princept said, turning to Morgan. "I'm more than satisfied, and you know we could use his talent."

"I'd be happy to serve you and the Order in any way I can," Jack said, ignoring his uncle, who had clearly been overruled. He tried to hide his amusement at the situation, forced himself to appear humble and gracious.

"For now, the question of your membership to the Order will be set aside," the Princept said. "As I imagine you are aware, we had planned to use occasion of the Conclave to bolster the power of the Brink, as we must every century to maintain its power. But this centennial was to be different. This year, we were to do more than simply reconsecrate. We had planned to use the occasion of the Conclave to *build* on the work of those who came before us."

"The rumors were true, then?" Jack asked, knowing already that they were. It was no secret that the Inner Circle believed that the Brink could be made stronger, wider, but he hadn't known for sure that they'd managed it. "You found a way to expand the Brink?"

The High Princept nodded, a satisfied glimmer in his eyes. "Before the events of Khafre Hall, we'd already managed to bolster the power of the artifacts in preparation. With all five stones, we could have expanded the Brink's power and pushed out its reach. Ellis Island and the maggots who evade our inspectors there would no longer have been a problem. But now, with only one artifact in our possession, we must do what we can simply to *preserve* the Brink. Everything depends upon it."

"*Can* you perform the reconsecration ritual with a single stone?" Jack wondered.

"Thanks to the work we did before they were stolen, we believe we can," the Princept said. "But you can see why it is more essential than ever to protect that artifact at all costs. After your display at the gala, we believe you can be of help. It is essential that our new headquarters is impervious to any attack. If you're able to bring your considerable talents to aid us in the coming weeks, I believe we can put this whole unfortunate question of loyalty to rest. In fact, if all goes well, there will be a place for you in the Inner Circle."

"But if you screw this up," his uncle said, glaring. "If you think to betray our trust again—"

"You'll find no fault in my commitment to our cause," Jack told them with a small bow. "I will do all I can to ensure the safety of the artifact and our new headquarters."

They were the right words. The Princept's eyes glimmered with satisfaction.

By the time the three old goats finally dismissed him, the morphine had all but worn off. Jack could feel the ache building behind his eyes again, but he barely noticed. When he'd entered his uncle's mansion, he'd worried he might never find the ring, but he'd left with the Order's hopes—perhaps its very future—sitting in the palm of his hand. And if all went well, soon the artifact would be his.

BLOOD WILL TELL

1904—San Francisco

Maybe Harte Darrigan should have felt some satisfaction as he watched Samuel Lowe's expression shift from anger to confusion and then to disbelief. Instead, he felt nothing at all.

"Benedict?" the older man said, lowering his gun.

Harte had imagined this moment often enough—when he was a homeless urchin, struggling to survive alone in the New York streets, and later when he was a successful headliner on one of the biggest stages in the city. Even with the guilt he'd carried, Harte had wondered what it would be like to look his father in the eye and force the man to acknowledge him. He had imagined his old man discovering that Harte had survived—had *thrived*—without him. *In spite* of him.

"I don't go by that name anymore." Harte continued to glare at the man who had fathered him, but he felt only a dull emptiness where triumph should have been.

Samuel Lowe never should have been able to make it back to California, but he had. Worse, the years seemed to have been kind to him. True, his father had more gray at his temples, and lines now carved deep valleys across his forehead, but he looked healthier than Harte had ever seen him. From the clothes his father wore, he certainly wasn't destitute. On the smallest finger of his right hand, a gold ring glinted in the streetlight, yet another testament to his father's elevated station in life. While Harte had lived with the ever-present guilt of what he'd done to his mother, he'd never spared a second thought for his father. He'd assumed that Samuel Lowe would die drunk in a ditch somewhere. Harte had never considered that his father might have gone on to live his life without consequences.

The woman still standing in the doorway said something in a language that Harte could not understand—German, perhaps—but she no longer interested him. He took a step toward his father. He didn't care what Seshat might do to this man. Harte would finish what he'd started years before. But the movement of a small boy peeking out from behind his father's coat stopped him dead.

The child was dressed neatly in short pants with a well-fitting brown jacket over a clean white shirt. His dark-blond hair framed a round face, and there was a small scar that cut across the corner of his upper lip, but he had the same gray eyes Harte saw every time he looked in the mirror. Eyes he'd inherited from his father.

Harte wasn't sure how old the boy was—maybe seven? Perhaps a little younger?

His father—*their father*—stepped in front of the child, blocking him from Harte's view before he could decide. He bent down and said something close to the child's ear that Harte couldn't hear, then lifted his hand. Harte instinctively tensed, his muscles ready to protect the child—to protect *his brother*. But before Harte could take a step, his father's palm simply patted the boy on the back and pushed him along.

The child darted past Harte, toward the woman still waiting at the door behind him, but he pulled up short before he reached her. He turned back to Harte and examined him once more with a serious look on his face.

"Sammie," Harte's father warned. He said something in German—a language that Harte had never before heard his father use—that made the boy frown.

The sternness in Samuel Lowe's voice was like a slap to the face, bringing Harte back to himself, and the boy's eyes widened before he finally disappeared into the warmly lit interior of the home. The woman stared at Harte a beat longer with suspicion—and a warning—in her eyes. *A mother's eyes.* She likely wasn't Maria Lowe, then.

Whoever she was, the woman knew something about the Dragon's Eye, which meant that Harte's father probably also knew about the artifact. If that was the case—especially if Samuel Lowe had the Dragon's Eye—it would be much more difficult to get it back than Harte had anticipated.

Harte felt Seshat's pleasure at this discovery. *You could have your victory, and instead you hold back,* she whispered. *You could have everything you desire, but you will never defeat me. Your softness will be your undoing.* In the distant recesses of his mind, he sensed her satisfied amusement, but Harte shoved Seshat's taunting aside.

His father was saying something to the woman in short, clipped tones, and her mouth curved downward as she continued to examine Harte. She clearly wasn't happy, but eventually she pulled the door shut, closing off the light that had been spilling into the alley and leaving Harte alone with a ghost from his past.

"How are you even here?" his father demanded, turning on him. The gun wasn't raised, but it was still in his hand.

Harte didn't answer, and he refused to let any emotion show.

"You're supposed to be dead," his father said.

"I'd hoped the same about you," Harte said, keeping his tone bland.

His father's face creased with irritation, and Harte didn't miss the way his fist clenched. "You dare come here to my home and disrespect me after what you—" The sound of shouting nearby had Samuel Lowe pausing. His gaze slid beyond Harte, to the mouth of the alley. "It's the Committee's watchman. I won't let you ruin me again. You will go," his father ordered, a command that brought Harte back to his childhood.

"I'm afraid you lost the right to make demands of me a long time ago," Harte said, failing to keep his voice measured as he crossed his arms over his chest.

His father frowned, his nostrils flaring slightly in a strangely familiar sign of agitation. But there was something else in Samuel Lowe's eyes—something that looked gratifyingly like fear.

Harte allowed the corner of his mouth to curve. "I'm not going anywhere until I get what I—"

His father held up a hand to silence Harte when another shout sounded nearby. "We can't stay here arguing in the streets."

"I don't want to stay here at all," Harte told him, ignoring his own worry. He couldn't be caught there, but neither could he leave without the Dragon's Eye. "I'm perfectly happy to go—as soon as I get what I've come for."

"I don't owe you *anything*," his father sneered. "Not my time, not my wealth."

"I don't want either of those things," Harte told him, and he found that it was true. Maybe as a boy, he'd wished for his father's attention, but now Samuel Lowe was just a man like any other. A stranger. "Two years ago, I sent a package to Maria Lowe. Your mother. I've come to retrieve it."

Samuel Lowe's expression shuttered. "My mother is dead," he said flatly and without any emotion at all.

Harte frowned. "Her death doesn't change anything," he said. "I need the item I sent her—a headpiece made of gold that holds an amber stone."

"I don't know what you're talking about." His father feigned confusion, but Harte could tell he was lying. Samuel Lowe knew the Dragon's Eye. It was there, clear in the panic that colored his expression.

"That would be a problem for you," Harte told him. "There are men who want the crown, and when they come for it, you won't be able to protect yourself or the son you've claimed. Better you give it to me now, so I can draw them away. The piece isn't worth what keeping it will cost you."

"I think I'll take my chances," Samuel Lowe said, lifting his chin.

"I don't think you understand," Harte told him. "You don't have a choice. You can either give me what I've come for, or I will destroy this new life you've built for yourself piece by piece. I will destroy you, too, just as you destroyed my mother."

"And what about my son?" Samuel Lowe asked. "Would you leave him destitute and fatherless? Unprotected?"

Harte hesitated, thinking of the boy with the gray eyes so like his own, and that hesitation was enough.

Samuel Lowe's mouth twisted mockingly. "No . . . You won't hurt him," he said. "You don't have it in you."

Seshat laughed her dry, papery laugh, as though she agreed.

But Harte was sick of both of them. "Are you so sure?" He clenched his fists at his sides. "Blood will tell, after all, and it's your blood that runs in my veins."

His father blanched, but the second the words were out, Harte felt a wave of revulsion wash over him. He'd just threatened a child's life—his own *brother's* life—to get what he wanted. Could he really do it, if the moment arrived?

His father looked wary, and Harte hoped that the threat alone would be enough.

"You should go," his father said again, as another echoing shout sounded in the distance. "The Committee has eyes and ears everywhere, and you wouldn't want their watchmen to find you. Especially considering what you are. They make it their personal job to clean the city of filth like yours."

"If they take me, I'll be sure to direct them back to you," Harte said, without flinching. "You're better off to let me in."

Color climbed into the old man's cheeks, but he didn't take the bait.

"The woman who answered the door," Harte said. "She doesn't know about your life before, does she?" From the way his father's eyes shifted to the side, Harte knew he was right. "I bet you hadn't told her anything about New York. And the boy—I'd wager that he didn't know about me either."

His father's expression went tight, but Harte couldn't quite read the emotion. There was definitely anger there, but there was something more, something that couldn't possibly be regret clouding his father's eyes. After all, the man he'd known hadn't been capable of remorse.

"You can make all of this go away," Harte said again, more gently this time. "Simply give me what I came for, and I'll disappear. You'll never hear from me again, and you can go on pretending that I don't exist. It will be like this never happened."

Suddenly Samuel Lowe looked older and more exhausted. "It's not that easy," he told Harte, shaking his head.

It never is, Harte thought.

"I won't discuss this here. Not in the open. We'll go to a place not far from here, where it's safe. To talk." This time the old man didn't wait to see if Harte would follow. He simply started walking away, toward the streets beyond the narrow alley.

Why don't you take him now? Seshat whispered, taunting. *It would be so easy for you to reach out and take what is yours. What keeps you from it, other than weakness?*

What did keep him from reaching out and using his affinity against his father? It *would* be easy to command him to hand over the crown. . . . But Harte knew that if Seshat was urging him on, she was up to something. She would never allow him to retrieve the Dragon's Eye so easily, and now that he knew about the existence of his brother, there was more than one life at stake.

Weak, Seshat whispered, mocking. *It is the reason you cannot hope to win.*

Harte hesitated only a moment before, cursing to himself, he followed his father back into the heart of Chinatown.

CARELESS VIOLENCE

1904—San Francisco

I
t was growing late, but as Harte followed after his father, the sidewalks
were still teeming with a mixture of Chinese men in traditional wear
with queues down their backs and groups of white men in more
Western-style clothing, who were clearly there for whatever amusement
they could find.

The presence of those outsiders felt somehow different than in New
York, where the rich from uptown would often go slumming on Mott
Street to gawk at the Chinese people who were only trying to go about
their day. Here the other white men didn't seem so much observers as
participants, and the air was filled with the kind of electric anticipation
that can happen only at night, when the world turns toward the shadows
and revels in its baser instincts. The air was filled with the scent of grilled
meats and heavy spices, garlic and liquor, all mixing together with the
familiar smells of the city that Harte loved and hated at the same time.

They wound their way through the crowded streets and then exited
the other side of Chinatown through the barricade. A few blocks away,
they turned off the larger boulevard to find a stretch of blocks tucked
away from the main thoroughfare. There, saloons and beer halls lined
both sides of the streets. Women in various states of deshabille stood near
some of the doorways, calling to the men who passed.

Harte's father paid little attention to the women as he walked, but
eventually he stopped at a building with a large restaurant on the first
floor. The doors were wide open to the night air, and Harte's stomach

rumbled at the heavy scent of food. Inside, the noise of the streets gave way to the chatter of diners and the clinking of glasses. Waiters stood at the ready along the walls as a mixture of men dined in the main room. There were no women, at least not any that Harte could see.

His father lifted two fingers to get the attention of the waiter standing closest to the door, who clearly recognized him. After a quick exchange of words, they were shown to a table at the back of the restaurant. It was quieter there, but it wasn't exactly private. There were still other diners and waiters at tables nearby.

"Sit." His father took one of the seats on the other side of the table, clearly placing himself out of Harte's reach, as he had on their walk.

Harte could have argued, but creating a scene would not help him find the Dragon's Eye, so he took the seat across from his father. At first neither of them spoke. Harte understood that it was a test—impatience would be seen as a sign of weakness, so he kept silent. He refused to appear weak. Not before this man. *Not ever again.*

Deep within his skin, Seshat only laughed. It was the same papery thin laugh that set Harte's nerves on edge. But he shoved her down and focused on the man across from him . . . and on what would come next.

A little while into the uncomfortable silence, a waiter appeared with a tray of crabs and prawns along with an assortment of other side dishes. As the covers were removed from each plate, the fragrance of butter and garlic filled the air, reminding Harte that he hadn't eaten since he'd been on the train, hours before. Even then, he hadn't allowed himself to buy more than a stale sandwich and a mealy apple each day of his journey.

Samuel Lowe pointed at the tray of food. "It's been a hell of a long day, and I'm not dealing with you or your idiotic demands on an empty stomach, boy. You might as well eat."

"I'm not hungry," Harte said, despite the answering growl of his own stomach. After all that had happened between them, after all this man had done to Harte's mother, it seemed somehow wrong to break bread together like it was nothing.

　　　　　　　　　　　　　　　　　　　LISA MAXWELL

On the other side of the broad table, Samuel Lowe ignored Harte's refusal. Even before the waiters were done serving, he'd started wielding an assortment of silver instruments to crack claws and withdraw the glistening meat from the various sea creatures on the table in front of them. The way his father worked with fluid, almost elegant movements made the gold ring on his finger flash. It also made Harte's stomach twist. The motion was familiar, but not because he remembered it from his childhood. It was familiar because it reminded Harte of *himself.* He used the same flick of his wrist as a distraction onstage during sleight-of-hand tricks.

Seeing this tiny echo of himself in his father's movements made Harte wonder again if all the stories he'd told himself about being something more than his father's son had ever been true. He'd betrayed so many people and hurt so many others. Not for the first time that night, Harte considered whether his intentions had ever mattered. Maybe the destruction he'd left in his wake—his mother, Julian, Esta, even Dolph—was evidence of the one thing he'd never wanted to accept: that his father's careless violence flowed in his own veins. That there was no escape from what he *was.*

Be glad if it gives you strength, Seshat hissed. *The world will drag you down and tear you apart for sport, but only if you allow it to. I do not understand your hesitation. Why do you fight what you are? Why not use it to your favor?*

Harte went still. Never before had her voice seemed so clear, so utterly logical to him.

I feel your hatred for this man, she urged. *Still you hold back. You could so easily make him pay for the pain he's caused you. Show him what you are. Make him understand how powerless he truly is . . . I will help you destroy him. You have only to promise me the girl.*

Never. Harte tried to shake Seshat's temptation from his mind. It would be so easy to do what she said, to use his affinity to destroy the life his father had built for himself. He could pay Samuel Lowe back for every black eye and every bruise the man had ever given him and for every time he'd ever touched Harte's mother.

Maybe once that decision would have been easier. After all, there was a time Harte had done *exactly* that, and his decision had left a trail of pain and tragedy in its wake. But Harte Darrigan wasn't the boy that Benedict O'Doherty had been. He'd made himself into something new—and he'd done it in spite of everything he'd come from and *despite* everything Samuel Lowe might have bequeathed to him in blood. Harte had to believe that his reluctance to take his revenge wasn't softness, as Seshat might think. He had to believe it was something else.

"I didn't come here to eat," Harte told his father, taking control of the situation. "And I don't have time for a pleasant visit. I only want the crown. Don't pretend you don't know what I'm talking about."

His father glanced up with a look of satisfaction as he dipped a prawn into a cup of melted butter and then, his fingertips slick and glistening, popped it whole into his mouth, but Harte didn't care that he'd lost this particular pissing contest. He'd stopped caring about this man's approval years before. All that mattered was retrieving the Dragon's Eye. *For Esta.*

His father wiped his mouth with the back of his wrist. "The fact of the matter is that I don't have the item you're looking for."

Harte had been watching for the lie, but as his father spoke, he found only truth. "But you must know where it is?"

"It's gone," his father told him with a wave of his hands. "When my mother died, I found the headpiece among her things. I didn't know why she had it, but I could tell immediately that it was valuable. About a year ago, I sold it to William Cooke and took the profit to buy my shop."

"Did you buy that piece of gold as well?" Harte asked, gesturing to the ring that glinted on his father's finger. He was close enough to see it more clearly now—its surface was etched with the image of an open eye that held a piece of onyx as a pupil.

His father's hand fisted, and without so much as blinking, he covered the ring with his other hand.

"I'll need an introduction to this William Cooke," Harte said. "If he doesn't still have the crown, he'll know where it went next."

His father shook his head. "You have no idea what you're asking."

"I'm a quick study," Harte told him.

His father couldn't hide his irritation, but then he relented and began to explain. "Cooke is a high-ranking official in the Vigilance Committee. He didn't keep the piece for himself. He used it to gain the highest-ranking office in the organization. They have the crown now, so you can just forget about getting it back. I won't allow you to go mucking around in things you can't understand. You could destroy everything I've built here, and I'm not about to let that happen after all I've been through to get where I am."

"I don't particularly care what you went through," Harte said. "As far as I'm concerned, you can keep your life and whatever it is you think you've built, as long as I get what I've come for."

Samuel Lowe considered him, and the calm intensity of the older man's stare made Harte suddenly uneasy. This man looked like his father, but the man Harte had known had been predictable in his violence—it had been a saving grace to be able to read Samuel Lowe's moods by the look in his eyes. But Harte couldn't tell what *this* man was thinking, and that felt more dangerous than his father's fists had ever been.

"You're very much your mother's son," Samuel Lowe said finally, but his tone made it clear that his words were not meant as a compliment.

"That's true enough," Harte agreed easily.

"You take pride in it?" his father asked. "Being the bastard of a whore. An *abomination*."

"In case you've forgotten, I'm *your* bastard as well," Harte said, clenching his teeth around the word.

Before his father could answer that charge, a waiter arrived with a pitcher of water, and an uneasy silence descended over the table while it was being poured. Harte's and his father's eyes remained locked, and after the waiter left, his father spoke again. "It's clear you don't even care about the hell you put me through."

"I certainly wouldn't hold your breath waiting for an apology," Harte said coldly.

"I would never expect one from the likes of you," his father said. "You know, I understood what you'd done the second you touched me that day." It confirmed Harte's suspicions about why he'd been keeping the distance between them. "I knew exactly what was happening, how you'd cursed me. I didn't want to leave New York. I wasn't ready yet, but I couldn't stop myself. Because of your evil spell, I was ranting like a madman when I crossed the bridge out of the city. The compulsion to keep moving didn't stop until I reached Brooklyn, but by then I'd already caught the notice of an officer, who thought I was drunk."

"You were," Harte reminded him. "In case you've forgotten, you'd passed out in your own vomit, a glass of liquor still in your hand."

His father ignored this fact. "They put me in jail rather than into a sanitarium, and they left me there for weeks."

"If you ask me, they should've left you longer," Harte said, unable to dredge up any sympathy at all.

His father glared at him. "You have no idea what I suffered in that place, how terrible it was to come off the drink with no help and no comfort. But by the time I was sober, I realized I was no longer compelled to return to your mother's side as I had been for years."

"My mother didn't compel you to stay and torture us."

"Didn't she?" Samuel gave a dry, ugly laugh. "Go on and tell yourself stories about what a saint she was, but Molly O'Doherty was nothing but a common bit of trash."

Harte's fists clenched. "Watch yourself, old man."

But his father ignored the not-so-veiled threat. "Once your mother had her claws in me, I couldn't break away. Only the liquor helped make any of it livable. But as soon as I crossed the bridge, I was free, well and truly—from the evils of drink and from the abomination that was your mother."

"You're lying," Harte spat, unwilling to believe that anything that came from this man's mouth could be the truth.

"In the end, my suffering proved the strength of my soul," his father said, lifting his chin as he ignored Harte's accusation. "My trials forged me, cleansed me of my sins, and made me into a new man. A man *worthy* of claiming a new life. Eventually I was released, and I returned here to take up the life that was waiting for me."

Harte still wasn't sure how that could be possible. He'd ordered his father away from California, ordered him to forget this life. . . . Unless Samuel Lowe *wasn't* lying about what Harte's mother had done. If that was the case, maybe there was something about the Brink that had broken through the compulsion Harte had tried to force upon his father, just as it had broken through whatever his mother's affinity might have done.

"My prosperity is evidence of my righteousness," his father went on, unaware of Harte's thoughts. "As I continue on the path, I continue to be rewarded—with my store, which prospers more every year. With a place in my city, and with a strong son who carries my name."

I'm your son. Harte shook off the thought. He'd never wanted to claim this man's name before, and he wasn't about to start now.

"I won't let you upset the life I've built here," his father continued.

"I'm only here for the Dragon's Eye," Harte reminded him. "Tell me where I can find it, and I'll leave you to your righteousness and your rewards."

"I told you. It's impossible." His father leaned forward, and there was panic in his eyes. "The Committee isn't a bunch of unorganized brutes, like the gang bosses you grew up around."

"You're afraid of them," Harte realized, not missing the way his father flinched at the accusation.

"My soul is blameless, my conscience clear," Samuel Lowe said, avoiding the question. "But I can't help you. I won't."

Harte kept his voice easy, but he made sure there was a note of menace in it as well. "I don't think you quite understand. I'm not asking."

Show him what you are, Seshat taunted, endlessly tempting. *Make him see you now as he never has before.*

It would be easy enough there, even with the prying eyes of the other diners, to reach across the table. It would be worth the risk to take his father by the hand—or by the *throat*.

The violence of the image shook Harte back to himself, and he looked at his outstretched hand, trying to remember when he'd raised it. His father had jerked back and was already reaching for his gun, when a commotion erupted on the other side of the restaurant—a clatter of dishes and metal serving plates. A waiter appeared suddenly, whispering an urgent rush of words to his father that Harte couldn't quite make out. His father's expression hardened as he nodded to the waiter.

Then Samuel Lowe turned to Harte. "We have to go. *Now.*"

A noise came from the front of the restaurant, and the waiter gestured urgently for them to follow. But Harte wasn't going to allow himself to be distracted. Not when he was so close.

"I'm not going anywhere," he said, crossing his arms and leaning back in his chair. "Not until I have what's mine."

"The Committee's watchmen are here. They're searching the restaurant," his father said, getting to his feet.

"What are they searching for?" Harte asked. He stood and prepared to block the old man's way if necessary.

"The same thing they're always searching for," his father said as he tried to skirt around Harte. "The Committee's main purpose is to eliminate the threat of creatures like you. If we stay here, you're likely to be swept up in the raid."

"Why would you help me?" Harte asked, suspicious. "Why not let them take me away? It would eliminate a problem for you."

"I can't risk being connected to you," his father said, and there was enough disgust in his expression that Harte believed him. "If they knew I didn't turn you in immediately, I'd be ruined."

The explanation contained enough of the truth that Harte stood and followed his father through the back of the restaurant toward a rear exit from the dining room, but before his father could disappear through it, Harte caught the older man's arm. "We're not done with our conversation."

"No," his father said, tearing his arm away. "We're nowhere near done."

The exit led to a passageway that ran behind the main dining room and through the kitchen. Around them, the cooks and waiters were in a panic, but their waiter led them through the confusion, toward a small door in the floor at the rear of the building. The waiter opened it, revealing a staircase that went down beneath the building, and then waved them through.

"Where are we going?" Harte asked, eyeing the dark space below.

"The tunnels. They connect various buildings in the city, if you know the right people. This one ends a couple of blocks from here. Far enough away to be safe." His father motioned that Harte should go first. When he didn't immediately move, his father raised one eyebrow, a challenge. "Unless you'd rather stay and deal with the watchmen on your own."

A crash came from the other side of the kitchen, followed by angry voices that signaled the watchmen were getting closer. There was no other exit that Harte could see. His only real choice was to accept the help his father was offering.

It was a mistake.

Harte was only three steps down into the gloom when he felt a sharp blow to the back of his skull. A blunt shove pushed him from behind and sent him tumbling down the steep steps. Harte tried to catch himself, but stars exploded across his vision, and he couldn't tell if the darkness that surrounded him came from the blow to his head or the lightless tunnels beneath.

COMPLICATIONS

1904—Denver

To Esta's relief, Cordelia Smith kept her word. The sharpshooter knew her way around the grounds and managed to avoid the marshals as she led them back toward the main entrance, but she didn't leave them once they were free from the show's grounds. Instead, Cordelia insisted on accompanying them into the city, where she took them to a small, barely furnished apartment. It was a safe house that she said was sometimes used by Antistasi who needed a place to lie low or meet with locals when traveling through the area. Clearly, no one had used it in a while, though. Dust covered everything, and the air had a kind of closed-up, musty smell.

Once they were inside and the door was secured, North placed the box they'd taken from Pickett on a rickety wooden table. Maggie went to open a window.

"Whatever's in there must be really something," Cordelia said, eyeing the box with too much interest for Esta's liking. "Especially considering the risk y'all took to get it."

Esta exchanged an uneasy glance with North and Maggie, who didn't look any more certain about Cordelia than she felt.

"Well?" Cordelia pressed. "Are you gonna open it or what?"

"We will," North said, clearly hedging. "But there's no rush."

Understanding, and then anger, flashed in Cordelia's eyes. "I think I have a right to know what y'all are up to, considering that you got me wrapped up in it as well."

"We didn't exactly ask for your help," Esta reminded her, which earned her a sharp look from Maggie.

"But y'all needed it, didn't you?" Cordelia asked. "Without me, you'd've been caught up back there in the middle of the raid."

Esta wasn't in any mood to admit that Cordelia was right. Maybe with the Quellant thick in her blood, she wouldn't have been able to slip past the marshals unseen, but she would have found another way out. She *always* found a way.

"We appreciate all you've done for us," North said before Esta had the chance to argue the point any further.

"But you still ain't gonna tell me what you're up to?" Cordelia paused, considering them. "It makes me think maybe the rumors I've been hearing were right."

"What rumors?" Maggie said.

"There's plenty that think you betrayed more than Ruth when y'all left St. Louis." Cordelia eyed Maggie, her expression suddenly suspicious. "And then after that train exploded? Seems like y'all should have contacted *someone*. Instead, you let everyone think the Thief was dead. Makes a body think maybe you've got something to hide."

"We didn't know who might be sympathetic to Ruth," North explained. "You said yourself that you couldn't believe she let Maggie go. We couldn't risk any of Ruth's followers coming after us."

Cordelia's expression shifted. "There's other rumors too, you know. Rumors that Ruth stole the real necklace from the Society, and that when y'all left St. Louis, you took the Djinni's Star right out of Ruth's grasp."

Maggie glanced at North, looking every bit as guilty as if she'd taken the necklace herself.

"It's true, isn't it?" Cordelia asked, excitement brightening her watery blue eyes.

North and Maggie exchanged an uneasy glance, but Esta decided to take control of the situation before the two of them could make things worse.

"We couldn't exactly let Ruth keep it, could we?" Esta asked, like this was obvious. Denying it would only make the sharpshooter more suspicious. The best she could hope for at this point was to keep Cordelia on their side and buy a little more time. Clearly, the other girl was loyal to the Antistasi. If Esta could make Cordelia believe that she, too, was loyal to the Antistasi's cause, the sharpshooter might be less of an obstacle. She might even be a help. "After what happened with the serum, we couldn't risk Ruth using the artifact against anyone else—other Antistasi, for instance. Could we?"

Cordelia turned to Maggie. "So when y'all left St. Louis, you were choosing the Antistasi over your sister?"

"My loyalty to the Antistasi didn't begin when I left St. Louis," Maggie told Cordelia, and Esta was surprised to see there wasn't even a hint of prevarication in her words.

Cordelia considered this for a long, uncomfortable moment before her expression cleared. "Well, where's it at?" she asked. "I'd sure like to take a look at it."

Which was, of course, impossible. The Djinni's Star was with Harte, traveling toward the other side of the continent. Not that any of them needed to know about that.

But North and Maggie looked uneasy, and Esta had the sense that the two Antistasi didn't want this woman to know they'd lost the necklace. Maggie opened her mouth and closed it again, like a fish gulping for air.

"We can't show you right now," Esta said, stepping in to save Maggie from another poorly told lie.

"Why not?" The suspicion returned to Cordelia's expression. "Y'all ain't fixin' to keep it for yourself, are you?"

"Of course not," Maggie said too quickly.

"Then it won't hurt to let me have a peek, as a show of good faith."

"We would," Esta told Cordelia, trying to draw the sharpshooter's attention away from Maggie, who apparently couldn't lie to save her soul. "Of *course* we would. But we don't have the necklace with us at the moment. You said yourself what a risk it was we were taking today," Esta reminded her. "You don't think we'd take the chance of putting something as important as the Djinni's Star in that kind of danger, do you?"

Cordelia frowned. She didn't want to agree with this logic, but she also couldn't find any fault in it. "Where is it?"

"Somewhere safe," Esta said. "We wouldn't want it to fall into the wrong hands, would we?"

"And that box there?" Cordelia said. "What was so important that y'all were willing to die for it?"

"Something that could help the Antistasi," Maggie offered.

Cordelia's brows drew together thoughtfully, and then realization seemed to strike. "You're talking about another artifact."

"Why would you think that?" Maggie said, unable to hide the anxious tremor in her voice.

But Cordelia only crossed her arms and stared at them. "That settles it. I'm not going anywhere until you show me what it is you took."

"Go on," North told Esta. "Open it."

"And try to be quick about it," Cordelia said, like she'd already guessed Esta's plan to delay. "I have another show this evening, and I don't need people noticing that I've gone missing."

"These things take time," Esta told them. She made a show of leaning her ear close to the lock and slowly working the tumbler.

A lock like this actually *didn't* take that much time—and she already had the combination—but none of the Antistasi watching her knew that. Esta wasn't in any hurry to box herself into a corner, though. Once the dagger was in play, things would become more complicated. Especially without her affinity to rely on.

"We should just break the damn thing open," North said, after a long few minutes of silence had ticked by while Esta pretended to listen to the lock.

"And risk damaging what's inside?" Esta asked.

North grumbled but didn't press any further. Still, with each turn of the tumbler, Esta could sense the impatience in the room swelling. But there was nothing she could think to do that would help her avoid opening the lock. She'd taken the Quellant, so there was no way to stop time, and even if she could, it wouldn't do her any good. As long as North had that watch of his, he could bring her right back. If that happened, Esta would have lost whatever trust she'd built with them.

"Almost—" Esta said, trying to stall as her mind continued to race. There had to be a way. . . .

She twisted the tumbler again, blinking, as she tried to focus on the numbers, but her vision was doing odd things. It looked like there were two of the box, two of the lock. Two of every number. Esta willed her vision to clear. "I've almost got it," she said, annoyed with the tremor in her voice.

Suddenly, the room wouldn't hold steady. One second everything was fine, and the next second, the room had shifted, transformed, before flickering back, and Esta went still, frozen by the strangeness of what she was seeing.

North and Cordelia and Maggie were all looking at her expectantly, but then her vision flickered again, and they were gone. It felt like all the layers of time that had ever been, all the layers that might ever be, were rising up around her. Even though she'd taken the Quellant, and even though her cuff, the one that held Ishtar's Key, was hundreds of miles away, Esta felt like she did right before she slipped through to a different time. Except now, time felt like a separate living thing. Time flexed and rose around her, pulsing with a strange energy. Unsteady. Unwieldy. And it felt *hungry*.

The three Antistasi were there again suddenly, and then, just as quickly, they weren't. Esta tried to keep herself upright as the room around her shifted and changed. She was standing in an empty room—and then her vision shifted again, and the room was filled with strangers dressed in clothes from her own time—then another shift, and the room changed again as reality faded in and out, like an old TV set blinking through a bad connection. The net of time that held the world in place—the very Aether that ordered reality—seemed to contract around her. It pressed in on her. Like it wanted to *devour* her.

The scar on Esta's wrist burned, and the word there felt like it had been freshly sliced into her skin. Then all at once, everything went still. The room stopped flickering, and the present moment seemed as ordinary and stable as ever.

"Well?" North demanded, apparently oblivious to what Esta had just experienced. One glance around the room told her that the others hadn't sensed anything at all.

"I'm working on it," Esta told him, her words sounding strangled even to herself. It took real concentration to keep her hands steady enough to move the tumbler into place, lining up the last number in the sequence that would open the lock.

What the hell was that? It had seemed like reality itself had splintered, like the seconds were trying to consume her. It had felt like time was trying to devour her whole, until she was . . . nothing. Esta rubbed absently at the scar on her arm as she opened the lock. The raised ridges of the Latin command ached beneath her touch.

She'd taken the Quellant. She had relinquished her affinity to protect herself—and everyone else—from Seshat, but Esta had the sense that whatever had happened *wasn't* Seshat. There had been no shadows, no darkness. Whatever that was felt more like time itself had tried to pull her under—like time had tried to *erase* her. Like Professor Lachlan had warned it would.

But why now? What changed? Esta had assumed that as long as the Key could be returned to her younger self, all would be well. Now, with the Quellant, she might even be able to go back to where time had splintered into a new future. She could still send her younger self forward. She should be okay, as long as that was all still a possibility.

Unless something has happened to Ishtar's Key.

The thought made Esta's breath catch. Harte knew how important the cuff was to her. He would never willingly let anything happen to it. She *knew* that. But maybe he hadn't been willing—

No. She wouldn't let herself think about that possibility. Harte was too smart and had survived too long to get caught now. The Key couldn't be lost. Maybe it was taking them too long to return it. Maybe time was simply running out of patience.

North clearly was. He grabbed the box from Esta when she didn't immediately open it, and she was still too unnerved to bother with fighting him.

Maggie moved closer to him. "Well?" she asked, her voice almost trembling, as North stared at the contents of the box.

After a few frozen seconds, North tossed the box on the table so violently that the coins and papers it held threatened to escape. "It's not here." Then he turned on Esta. "You told us it would be here. You promised that Pickett had the dagger."

"The dagger?" Cordelia asked, her eyes going wide. "You're talking about the Pharaoh's Heart."

North was still too busy glaring at Esta to answer.

"Y'all *are* going after the other artifacts," Cordelia said, excitement coloring her voice. "You're going to make the Sundren pay."

"No one is going to make anyone pay," Maggie said, sounding a little taken aback. "We're only here for the dagger. Or we were . . ."

Cordelia's excitement shifted to confusion. "But why would y'all ever think Bill Pickett would have an artifact?"

"Because that's what *she* told us," North said.

"He's a simple cowpoke," Cordelia told North. "He ain't even Mageus, or I would've already recruited him."

"He *has* to have it." Esta forced herself to ignore the trembling in her limbs and the burning of the scar as she stepped closer to look through the box herself. Harte had sent her to Denver to retrieve the dagger. If it wasn't there, she didn't know what she would do next. But North was right. Inside was nothing but a pile of coins and some papers with scribbled IOUs.

"It must be somewhere else, then," Esta told them.

"You already searched Pickett's tent," North reminded her.

"So maybe it's not in his tent," Esta said, trying to keep her voice steady. "Maybe Pickett keeps the dagger on him."

"Or maybe he never had it in the first place," North said, his eyes narrowing with suspicion. "Maybe this was all a bunch of *misdirection*, like that crazy tale you told us on the train about ancient goddesses and the end of the world. I knew we shouldn't have trusted her," he told Maggie.

"The fact that my tale was so *crazy* should tell you that it's true. Why would I make something like that up when I could have left you in the dust? Pickett has the knife," Esta snapped. "I wasn't lying about that before, and I'm not lying now. We have to go back. We have to look again."

"You'd be nuts to go back there right now," Cordelia said. "Artifact or not, there'll be marshals crawling all over back there for hours. Syndicate, too."

"The *Syndicate's* here?" Maggie asked, glancing nervously at North.

"Who do y'all think was in charge of that raid today?" Cordelia frowned like this was something they should have already known. "They've been gathering up people suspected of illegal magic ever since what happened in St. Louis. All the Brotherhoods have."

"Do you two have experience with this Syndicate?" Esta asked. It was clear the Syndicate was another of the Brotherhoods, but that didn't account for the severity of Maggie's and North's reaction.

"They helped run me out of Texas a couple of years back," North said, apparently not wanting to tell the entire story. He was still looking at Maggie. "I didn't want to worry you before, but . . ." His mouth pressed into a hard line before he spoke again. "I saw Jot Gunter back in Texas."

At this news, the color drained from Maggie's face. "You're sure?"

North rubbed at the back of his neck. "He was with the men at the oil fields."

They traded a meaningful glance, and Esta understood that there was some bigger story there—something that they were not saying.

"How do y'all know Jot Gunter?" Cordelia asked, her thick brows bunching. "He's one of the Syndicate's highest-ranking members."

"We go way back," North said darkly. "But I'd rather not run into him again anytime soon if I can help it."

"Jericho, they're definitely going to realize that my explosions today were the same as the ones I set off in Texas, and when they do . . ." Maggie raised her hand to cover her mouth, as though she could hold back the truth of what she'd done.

"It doesn't matter," Esta told them. Jot Gunter or the Syndicate or whoever was in her way—none of it mattered. She didn't know why time had wavered around her, but the warning had been clear enough: Her time was running out. "We have to go back. Bill Pickett has the dagger, and I'm not leaving until I get it."

A TRUTH TOO TERRIBLE

1904—Denver

Maggie hadn't missed the way Esta had said "I" rather than "we," and she wondered, not for the first time, if Esta would leave them as Ben had, empty-handed and without explanation. True, Esta had taken the Quellant, but Maggie had seen her in action over the past couple of weeks, and she didn't believe that something as simple as a missing affinity would stop the Thief if she set her mind to something.

And yet . . . Esta didn't look quite right. For all the confidence in her voice, she looked almost green and her hands were trembling. Maybe the emptiness of the box had shaken her badly, or maybe Esta had been shocked by the news about the Syndicate being in Denver. Whatever the case, Maggie couldn't worry too much about Esta's state. Not when they still didn't have an artifact in their possession.

When Esta had told them about the dagger, Maggie had thought that maybe fate had given her a way to correct the mistakes she'd made. Maybe the necklace was gone, but with the possibility of collecting the Pharaoh's Heart, she still had hope. Now she wasn't so sure. The dagger hadn't been in the box, and they were still empty-handed.

"Esta's right," Maggie told the others. "Bill Pickett's the only lead we have. Even if the Syndicate *is* here, we need to put all of our focus into figuring out whether Pickett still has the dagger, and if he doesn't, we need to find out if he knows where it is."

Jericho clearly didn't feel the same. "I don't know, Mags—"

"We need the Pharaoh's Heart, Jericho," Maggie said, cutting him off before he could give her all the good reasons they shouldn't. They'd lost everything else. They couldn't lose this, too. Especially not with the Antistasi sharpshooter looking at them with suspicion.

Jericho didn't respond at first, and Maggie could see in his expression that he still wasn't sure. For a moment she worried that he might refuse.

"You promised," she reminded him gently. "When we left St. Louis, you told me you understood how important this was. You told me I could depend on you."

He let out a ragged, frustrated breath. "You can. You *know* that."

Somehow, though, Jericho's reluctant acceptance didn't feel like the victory it should have been.

"I've never seen Pickett with anything that could be mistaken for a lost artifact," Cordelia said.

"That doesn't necessarily mean Pickett doesn't have it," Esta said. "If he's smart, he wouldn't have shown it off."

"A piece *that* valuable? I'd expect he'd keep it somewhere safer than his tent," Cordelia said. "Might could be that he left it back with his family in Texas."

"I'm not going back to Texas," Jericho said with a frown. "I just managed to get out of that state alive for the second time. I'm not interested in trying for a third."

"Not unless we have to," Maggie promised. Then she glanced at Esta. "The first thing we need to figure out is whether Pickett has the dagger with him here in Denver. Then we can go from there." She turned to Cordelia. Maggie was still unsettled about Cordelia implying she hadn't been faithful to the Antistasi's cause, but she figured the best way to neutralize the threat Cordelia might pose was to include her. "Cordelia, you know your way around the show. . . . How well do you know Bill Pickett?"

"Not well enough to go asking about some priceless lost artifact," Cordelia said, arching a single brow. "Besides, even if Pickett is sympathetic to our cause, I can't imagine he'd tell me a thing, not with the marshals prowling around today."

Cordelia was right. With all that had happened, and with how quickly the news had spread about the theft of the Djinni's Star and the attack on the world's fair, it wasn't likely that Bill Pickett would admit that he was in possession of one of the Order's other lost artifacts. Not willingly.

The weight of the leather pouch Maggie had carried with her from St. Louis suddenly felt heavier than it had a moment before. If they could get close enough, there *was* a way to ensure that Pickett revealed everything, but using the concoction she had in mind meant divulging secrets she'd never intended to reveal. At least not like this.

"Maybe there's a way you could earn his trust?" Maggie said hopefully.

"It would take time we don't have," Esta said, dismissing the idea. "With those explosions you set off, someone is bound to start piecing things together. It's not going to be hard to figure out no one died in the train explosion back in Texas. Once they do, they're going to know to look for us. The faster we get the dagger and get out of town, the better."

Esta was right. It had been a mistake to use the Flash and Bangs, and now Maggie had to deal with the consequences. As much as she wasn't keen on revealing this *particular* secret, the artifact they were seeking was too important for Maggie to put her own personal worries before her duty to the Antistasi . . . especially considering that she was mostly responsible for the mess they were in. She wouldn't allow herself to fail again, even if it meant Jericho might never look at her the same.

"I *might* have a formulation that could help with Pickett," Maggie said slowly, knowing that what she was about to reveal would change everything.

North turned to her, clearly surprised. "You do?"

She hesitated, staring at a snag in her skirts because she couldn't meet Jericho's eyes. She knew what his reaction was going to be. "If we can give it to Pickett, he won't have any choice but to tell us the truth about the dagger."

"What, like a truth serum?" Esta asked, getting to the point far more quickly than Maggie would have liked.

"Something like that," she admitted.

"You've been busier than I realized," Jericho said with a low whistle. "First the confounding solution you used on that porter, and now this? How many new formulations have you been working on, anyway?"

Maggie could have let the omission lie, but she couldn't bear one more thing between them. Better to tell him now than have him discover she'd withheld the truth from him twice. "It's not new," she told Jericho, finally risking a glance in his direction.

She must have looked as guilty as she felt, because understanding registered in Jericho's expression immediately.

"You never told me you had anything like that," he said, an unspoken question looming behind his words.

Maggie knew how he felt about some of the formulations Ruth had directed her to make. Oh, he was fine with the ones that flashed and banged, the ones that they needed for protection against their enemies, but he'd been uncomfortable all along with the idea of the serum, and with any formulation that took away a person's free will.

"I haven't used it in a long time," Maggie told him. That, at least, was the truth.

Jericho looked a little sick. "Well, as long as you've never used it on me."

Maggie didn't respond. She couldn't bring herself to lie, but the truth seemed impossible to tell.

Jericho frowned at her silence. "You *haven't* used it on me, have you?" he asked pointedly. "Maggie?"

Maggie's cheeks heated. "It was a long time ago," she said softly, like that was any excuse at all.

The color drained from Jericho's face, leaving his freckles stark against his pale skin. "When?" he asked, his voice sounding strangely hollow.

"You have to understand . . . We didn't know you yet," she tried to explain.

"When did you use it on me, Maggie?" Jericho asked.

"When you first arrived in St. Louis." She stared at the ground, because she couldn't bear to face him. "Ruth never trusted newcomers, so she usually used it whenever someone wanted to join us. We never gave a full dose, only enough to loosen a newcomer's tongue but not so much that they'd realize what was happening. You were no exception, but I had a feeling you were going to be different. I knew it was a mistake as soon as I gave it to you."

For a long stretch of seconds, the room filled with the kind of silence that chafed. "You never told me. Even after all this time we've known each other?"

"I didn't know how." She glanced up then, and the look on his face was even worse than she'd imagined it might be.

"All those nights we sat up late, talking about all sorts of things. I thought we were—" Jericho let out a dark laugh. His eyes, usually so warm and soft, glinted with anger. "You let me prattle on like a fool, and all the while you already knew everything there was to know about me."

"It's not like that," Maggie said, stepping toward Jericho, reaching for him. But he pulled back, and she let her arm drop to her side. "The minute Ruth started asking you questions, I *left*. Don't you remember? I left because I didn't want to hear what you told her. I didn't want to take your secrets from you."

"You sure didn't stop your sister from taking them, though," North charged.

Esta and Cordelia were silent, but Maggie could feel their attention on her. This whole scene was bad enough, but somehow having these two witnesses made her shame burn that much hotter.

"You're right," Maggie admitted. There was no way around it, and no reason to pretend now. "I let Ruth pressure me, like I always did, but I knew the minute I met you that things were going to be different. I had the sense that you were going to change everything for me. I couldn't stop Ruth—" She paused, shaking her head. "No . . . I didn't even try. But making that mistake changed something in me."

"You left me alone with her," Jericho charged.

Maggie took his anger, without argument or complaint. "I left, because I didn't want to take anything else from you. I wanted you to *give* me your story, free and clear. I wanted to deserve it."

"I thought you did," North said, and somehow the way his voice had gone soft and hollow tore through her.

"I'm sorry, Jericho," Maggie told him, taking another step closer. "I was a different person then, but that's not an excuse. I've never stopped being sorry—"

"If you were so sorry, you would have told me," he said.

That made Maggie press her lips together. There was no excuse for what she'd done, but there was even less of an excuse for keeping the secret for so long. Still, she had to make him understand. "I can't go back and undo it. I wish I'd been brave enough to trust you. But I need you to know that making that mistake made me realize that Ruth wasn't perfect or infallible. And I never let her do it again. *Ever.* Not to you, not to anyone." She glanced at Esta, who was frowning thoughtfully at her. "Not even when it would have been easier."

"You're willing to do it now, though," Jericho pointed out. "You've kept it all this time, and now you're willing to take the choice from a man who's done nothing to you."

"If there were any other way . . ." *If getting the dagger weren't so important.* Maggie met his eyes then, her shoulders a little straighter. "I can't take back my past, Jericho. But with the dagger, we might have a real chance to make a different future for ourselves. For everyone with the old magic. So, *yes.* I'm willing to use the truth tablets again to make that future—for you. For *us.*"

"Whatever happened in the past, Maggie's right—we need to focus on what we can do now," Esta said softly. "I don't love the idea of drugging someone, but the sooner we know if Pickett still has the dagger,

LISA MAXWELL

the sooner we can either retrieve it from him or get on with finding it. I don't see any other way. Not with multiple Brotherhoods closing in."

Maggie was thankful for the support, but it didn't stop North from turning away from her. It was like he couldn't even look at her.

"Cordelia," Esta said. "What are the chances you could slip Pickett the formulation?"

Cordelia frowned. "We work together, but not *together*, you know? People mostly keep to their own, and it might draw attention if I'm cozying up to a man I've never shown any interest in before. Especially a man like Pickett." She let out a sigh. "Honestly, that alone might cause Pickett trouble with some of the others. Not everyone in the show was happy when the Curtises added him to the bill, mostly because of the color of his skin. A lot of the cowboys didn't like being upstaged by someone they see as beneath them."

"Then that won't work. We don't want to cause Pickett any more trouble than we absolutely have to," Esta said. "Is there anyone else that could help? Another of the Antistasi you might trust?"

"I can do it," Jericho said, his voice flat and dull as an old penny.

"Jericho—" Maggie started, but the look he shot in her direction had her going silent.

"There are too many people involved as it is. If Cordelia can get me onto the grounds, maybe get me a position in the show, I can get close to Pickett. I know my way around a horse well enough."

"But the Syndicate is there." Maggie's stomach dropped. Jot Gunter had almost killed North once before. If they found him now . . .

"I can handle myself around the Syndicate," Jericho told her. "At least with them, I know exactly what I'm dealing with."

Maggie felt his words land hard, and the look he gave her was worse than a fist to her gut.

"It might be tricky with the raid, but then, maybe that'll help. There's sure to be some positions open. I could introduce you to the manager and try to get you set up today?" Cordelia offered.

"Sounds fine to me," North said, grabbing his hat from the table as he ignored Maggie's fragile silence. It was almost like he couldn't wait to get free of her.

"What about us?" Maggie asked.

"It'll be safer for y'all to stay here," Cordelia told her flatly.

"But—" Maggie protested.

"No way. We're coming with you," Esta insisted.

"The grounds were crawling with federal marshals when we left," Cordelia reminded them. "With all that happened earlier, we can't risk someone recognizing you as easily as I did. And you"—Cordelia looked directly at Maggie—"what do *you* know about cattle?"

Maggie shook her head. "Nothing," she admitted. But she didn't want to let Jericho go off without the two of them patching things up.

"It's bad enough Pickett has probably already realized someone's robbed him," Cordelia told her. "We can't chance you sticking out like a sore thumb and drawing attention."

"Cordelia's right," Jericho told them, but he didn't look at Maggie when he spoke. "It'll be safer for both of you to stay here." His words felt like a door closing, and she didn't have the key.

"Then it's settled," Cordelia said, clearly satisfied. "The two of you will stay here, and I'll take Jericho back to the showgrounds with me and get him introduced to Aldo."

"I'll need the formulation," Jericho said.

"You think you can give it to him today?" Esta asked, clearly surprised.

"Probably not," he admitted. "But I might get lucky, and I want to be ready. No sense wasting any more time going back and forth. The sooner I'm done with all this, the better."

"Of course," Maggie said, forcing her voice to stay calm. She refused to let a single tear break free as she dug through the small pouch. Finally, she found what she was looking for.

Jericho reached for the tablets, but Cordelia held out her hand. "It'll be safer for me to hold on to them . . . in case they search you."

Maggie frowned. She trusted Jericho to hold the tablets. He had a sense of right and wrong that wouldn't allow him to abuse them, but Cordelia? Antistasi or not, it could be disastrous if she gave the tablets to the wrong person.

"You never know what to expect with the Syndicate," Cordelia said. "I'm a known performer. They're not likely to look at me. But if they search him . . ."

"I can handle myself just fine," Jericho said.

Maggie couldn't take that risk. "You only need one, but you'll have to dissolve it in something," she told them as she handed the tablets to Cordelia. "It'll have a bitterness to it, so alcohol is best if you can find some. To hide the taste."

"They were in the beer, weren't they?" Jericho asked.

Maggie turned to him, confused.

"When you gave it to me," he clarified. "You put them in the beer that first night."

She couldn't lie to him, wouldn't ever again. But she also couldn't bring herself to say the words, so she only nodded.

Disappointment flashed across Jericho's expression—or maybe it was something closer to hurt. He let out a resigned breath that made it seem like he was deflating, and then he gave Cordelia a nod. "Let's get this over with," he said, opening the door to escort the sharpshooter out. "I'll be back as soon as I can," he told Maggie, but he didn't give her cheek a kiss as he usually did before he left.

"Are you okay?" Esta asked when Maggie didn't do anything but stare blankly at the closed door. Now that Jericho was gone, the tears that had been threatening all along would not come.

The question shook Maggie back to the moment. "I'm fine," she said, swallowing hard past the knot of regret in her throat.

"You don't seem fine," Esta told her.

"Well, I am," Maggie said. "Or I will be once North and Cordelia come back with news of the Pharaoh's Heart." She told herself it would be enough. It *had* to be enough. Especially if retrieving it had cost her everything else.

Esta was frowning, her dark brows pulled together thoughtfully. "I'm still not sure how I feel about Cordelia knowing all of our business."

Me neither. "She's Antistasi," Maggie said instead. It meant that she was an ally, but it could also be a problem. If Cordelia found out that they had managed to lose the necklace, the entire network would know. From the sound of things, people had already started to doubt her loyalty, which was also a problem. Maggie couldn't afford anyone to know that she'd failed to keep hold of the artifact. Not until she had a replacement for it.

"I'm still not sure I like her," Esta grumbled.

"I'm not either," Maggie admitted, giving Esta a resigned shrug. "But it looks like we're stuck with her. If she can help us get the dagger—"

"As long as she *does* help," Esta said. "All that talk of making Sundren pay . . ."

Maggie hadn't liked that bit either. "If Cordelia tries anything, Jericho will take care of it. Even if he *is* furious with me right now."

Esta held her gaze. "If he loves you half as much as he pretends to, he'll get over it."

"I'm not sure that he will," Maggie said, remembering the way Jericho had looked away from her. She knew how much his pride meant to him.

"Then he's not the man you thought he was," Esta said.

Maggie frowned. "Jericho deserved better than what I did to him."

"Maybe he did." Esta shrugged. "But sometimes the choices life hands to us aren't that simple. *People* aren't that simple. Look at your sister."

"What about my sister?" Maggie asked, suddenly wary.

"The serum was a mistake, and you left because you had to. But that doesn't mean you hate Ruth. It doesn't mean you can't forgive her."

"No," Maggie said, meaning it. "I could never hate her." Ruth had been like a mother to her. Whatever mistakes Ruth might have made, she was family, and Maggie would do almost anything to protect her— *had* done almost anything. Now she worried about the choices she'd made, because Maggie understood that choosing to protect Ruth might very well cost her Jericho in the end.

THE OUROBOROS

1902—New York

I t was early afternoon, and the barroom two floors below James Lorcan's flat was probably already filling with those who needed something to make their day easier. A glass of Nitewein to blunt the edge of unused magic. A few moments of quiet solitude among their own, surrounded by the familiar warmth of power. No doubt the boy, Logan, was waiting uneasily for him to appear, but for now James craved solitude. The Aether had been trembling, anxious and unsteady, ever since Paul Kelly had revealed that the Order had retrieved the ring, but James hadn't been able to find the solution that would make it stop.

Unlike the saloon, the apartment was quiet. It had once been Dolph Saunders', and with its damask chaise and lace curtains, the rooms still held the mark of Leena's more feminine touch, which made it comfortable as well. But the apartment was so much more than a place to lay his head or calm his nerves—it was also the key to his eventual victory. The shelves lining the wall contained all of Dolph's research—all of his secrets.

It had been those books that had originally drawn James to Dolph a few years before. On the surface, the gang leader had seemed like any of the other players on the deadly game board that was the Bowery, but when James had seen that shelf of books—*real books*, bound in leather and smelling of the wisdom of centuries—he'd known immediately that Saunders was something different. Perhaps even something useful.

Compared to James' own father, Dolph Saunders was nothing, of course. A common criminal at best. Yet, unlike Niall Lorcan, Saunders had somehow managed to amass an entire *shelf* of books. The unfairness of it had almost been too much to bear.

When James was younger, his family had only one book—not the Bible, as so many of his countrymen might have owned, but a well-used volume of *Le Morte d'Arthur*. Ragged though it was, the volume was a prized enough possession to warrant a spot in his family's meager luggage when they came to this terrible new world. It was a story of heroes and traitors, of magic and those who would discount its power.

His father had believed in Arthur, the boy king who could unite a country and lead a people, just as he believed in a better world for his family and for all Mageus. Niall Lorcan had brought his family to America so that he could help build such a world. James, on the other hand, had always felt a certain secret kinship with Merlin, the sorcerer who could prophesy the future. Merlin, who should have been the hero all along.

James had been a child when his father had crossed the wrong ward boss. In retaliation, they'd arrested his father and burned his family's home—his mother and sisters still inside—leaving James orphaned and alone in a city that didn't care if he ended up dead.

Perhaps if James hadn't been so tired from his endless hours on the factory floor, his concentration only on the danger the machine press posed to his small fingers, he might have sensed the reason that the Aether had rippled and bunched that day. If he'd been paying more attention, James might have understood the danger that was approaching. Perhaps he would have fought the foreman, who'd held him over that extra hour, and he too would have been in the family's apartment when it caught fire.

They told James later that the wooden tenement where his family had lived in two cramped rooms had burned like a torch, too hot and too fast for anyone to escape. To his neighbors, it was simply another random tragedy, too common perhaps, but unavoidable in a city that cared little for the lives of the poor. James had known differently, though. With the combination of affinities his family had been keeping secret, they should have been able to get out of the burning building. To die like they had? They must have been trapped somehow, locked in or blocked from escaping. James couldn't help but think that it would have taken more than locks to hold his family back—possibly even magic.

Not that anyone cared to listen to him. Instead, every one of his neighbors turned away—Mageus and Sundren alike—afraid to see the truth of what was happening all around them. Afraid to disturb the fragile equilibrium that kept their own families safe.

In the end, he'd been left alone to watch the building smolder for days, and as the charred beams turned to ash, James Lorcan had transformed as well. He'd vowed to himself that he would never again be taken off guard. He would never allow himself to be as weak as his father had been, believing in fairy tales and heroes and the lie of righteousness. When he'd walked away from the ashes of his former life, James had promised himself that he would determine his own fate. He'd decided there and then that he would change the world. And he would never again be at someone else's mercy—neither Mageus nor Sundren.

James had been patient. He'd carefully plotted and planned, and now the shelf of leather and vellum—and all of the wisdom contained in Dolph's volumes—was his. He ran his fingers over the spines, caressing them with the reverence a lesser man might reserve for gemstones or gold. James understood exactly how precious those books were and what a victory it had been to take them from Dolph, perhaps even a greater victory than taking the Devil's Own. After all, the riffraff Dolph had surrounded himself with was expendable. The Bowery teemed with other Mageus just like them—desperate and easily led. But these books? The knowledge they contained? Irreplaceable.

Selecting one of the volumes from the shelf, James brought it to the desk and opened it. It was a small ledger, filled with handwritten notes in various languages, sketches of alchemical recipes, and collected scraps from other sources. He turned to one of the inked illustrations. James had been drawn to this particular page again and again over the last few weeks—ever since he'd seen the newspaper accounts of Esta's and Darrigan's supposed deaths, ever since he'd realized they were still out there in the world, still within his grasp. The figure on the page was the image of a snake eating its own tail. Wrought in brilliant ink, the gilded highlights made the snake seem like it was moving each time the page shifted.

James could tell that the image was important by the care that had been taken with it. He ran his fingers over the serpent, wondering what, exactly, it had signified for Dolph. In general, the ouroboros was an ancient symbol that represented the beginning and end of time. Chaos and order. Magic and its opposite. But Dolph had placed enormous importance on this ancient symbol. He'd adopted the symbol as the mark for his gang, doubling it to include two interlocking snakes—one living, one no more than a skeleton. Life and death, Dolph used to say. Two sides of the same coin. Inscribed into the skin of any who pledged Dolph Saunders loyalty, the mark stood as a signal to others in the Bowery, but it also served as a guarantee that they would not betray the gang.

No . . . the marks had been a guarantee that the Devil's Own would not betray *Dolph Saunders.*

Dolph had infused the gorgon's silver head with Leena's ability to nullify nearby power, and combined with Dolph's own particular ability to borrow the affinities of any Mageus he touched, the cane had been a uniquely devastating tool. While Dolph had lived, that smiling Medusa had the ability to tear the affinity from any who wore the mark—and in doing so, destroy its bearer. But the power in the cane was larger than Dolph Saunders, and the possibilities it held had not ended with his pathetic life. Like the snake in the image, forever devouring its tail, the magic within the silver gorgon head continued on—infinite. Like all magical objects, that power could be *used.* James had only to figure out a way to access it completely, and to align its power with his own.

He had been working tirelessly ever since he'd moved into Dolph's rooms, but the only thing he'd managed was to make his own mark tingle with awareness. Once, he'd managed to make Werner look almost unsettled. But to *use* the power in the cane? To direct it as easily, as *effortlessly* as Dolph had? He would need something more to amplify his affinity. He needed the ring.

It wasn't lost on James that had Logan not failed so spectacularly at the gala, he might already have complete, unbreakable control over the Devil's Own. As it was, there was still unease within their ranks. Everyone had been nervous since Dolph had been killed. Everyone had been on edge with the constant threat of Tammany's patrols and the Five Pointers' presence in the Bowery, but Viola's appearance the day before had only made things worse. She'd been an unwelcome reminder of the past, and the news she'd brought about Mooch's imprisonment was still filtering through his ranks.

If she'd only accepted his offer of a new partnership. Instead, she'd told James that she needed time—to consider, to think. She'd walked out that night without any promise to return.

Viola's departure might have meant that she was plotting against him, but it didn't matter. The movement of the Aether assured him that whatever Viola might attempt to do, she was only setting her own trap. All he needed to do was watch and wait. The answers would come to him soon enough.

Suddenly James felt the Aether tremble. He paused. Something was happening. Some new part of the game had begun.

He closed the notebook and placed it back on the shelf. It would be best to get back down to the Strega, to make his presence felt before his meeting with Kelly. Best to shore up his authority now, before he went.

At first everything seemed as it should in the saloon. Men and women curled around their drinks, and warm magic filtered through the air. The Aether still trembled uneasily, but it did not immediately reveal the danger.

Then James realized the change—near the bar, a boy with a shock of red hair was talking to Werner. The last he'd seen the boy, Mooch had been unconscious on the street. He should have still been in the Tombs—or better, dead—not here in the Strega where he could tell the others how James had left him behind, ripe for the picking by Tammany's patrols. Mooch was a problem James would have to consider, but for the moment, the Aether gave him no answers.

Soon that would change, James thought as he gripped the cane's head and felt the power vibrating within it. Soon his plans would fall into place. He would no longer be forced to feel his way through darkness, and the Devil's Own—Mooch included—would be his to command. But for that future to arrive, James needed the ring, which meant he needed to keep Paul Kelly on the hook. He glanced at the clock and realized that, for now, the problem of Mooch would have to wait. Paul Kelly would not.

THE HEART OF THE MATTER

1902—New York

Viola waited behind a pushcart parked near the corner of Elizabeth Street, watching for the sign that was supposed to come from the back door of the Bella Strega. Next to her, looking every bit out of place, was Theo Barclay, who had refused to leave after he'd helped her free Mooch from the Tombs.

It had been a mistake to bring him into this. Viola knew that to the pit of her soul, but she hadn't known what else to do. When she'd returned to Paul's after confronting Nibsy, only to find Theo waiting for her at the corner, Viola had taken it as a sign. Ruby had sent him, or so he'd claimed. She'd wanted to make sure that Viola was safe and well, as if an assassin needed a soft schoolboy to keep her safe. But after failing to heal Jianyu, after confronting Nibsy, Viola hadn't had the strength to push him away. The next thing she'd known, she was in his carriage, telling him far more than she'd intended to, and he was agreeing to far more than was safe.

"Do you think your friend did what you've asked?" Theo wondered, examining a bin of candy that the peddler was selling. The man who owned the cart was eyeing them both, but Theo especially, with his well-cut suit and fair hair.

"If you're not going to buy that, you should leave it be," Viola told him, purposely ignoring his question. "And I wouldn't exactly call Mooch my friend."

The truth was that Viola felt like expecting Mooch to uphold his promise was like chasing butterflies. He was as hardened by the streets and his experience as any of the Devil's Own, and the Bella Strega—even with Nibsy Lorcan at its head—represented safety in a dangerous city. Mooch would be a fool to risk his place, his *home*, even for the favor Theo had done by getting him out of the Tombs.

Theo placed a couple of coins into the peddler's outstretched hand in exchange for a paper sack of the candy, and Viola pulled him onward. He offered her a piece, but she waved him off.

"I still don't know how you convinced the judge to let him go," she said, shaking her head in disbelief.

"Judge Harris knows my father," Theo said with a shrug. "Besides, there wasn't any real evidence against him. It was all circumstantial."

As if that ever matters, Viola thought.

"It's been too long," she said, growing more impatient. They'd already looked at all the carts, and if they went through the vendors again, it would certainly draw attention. If the firebrand of a boy was going to help them, he would have opened the back door of the Strega by now.

"Let's give it a minute more," Theo said, popping one of the hard candies into his mouth. "These are quite good. . . ." He sounded mystified.

"Confetti," Viola said, absently wondering how anyone so rich could have gone through life without tasting such a common bit of sweetness. "Let's go before—"

The door of the Strega opened, and Mooch appeared, his red hair gleaming in the summer sun. Theo pocketed the candy and started to move.

"No," Viola said, stopping him. "You are not coming with me. Not in there."

He blinked at her with the frown of a man unaccustomed to not getting his way. "Of course I am."

"No," she told him, shaking her head. "The Strega isn't simply some saloon filled with your common ubriaconi. Mooch, he can burn a house down around you, and others are more deadly still. They're not friends, not anymore, and I won't risk your life."

"I'm not sure that's your decision to make," Theo said, visibly bristling.

Mooch was growing impatient, but Viola would not give in. "I will not be the one to tell Ruby what became of you if this goes poorly. If not for me, please, go. For her. Ruby will need someone to come home to."

Theo's jaw tensed, but finally he relented. "I'll expect a full report."

"Bene," Viola said. "Whatever you want. But you must go. *Now.*"

She didn't wait for Theo's agreement this time, but turned and made her way toward the impatient boy waiting at the back entrance of the Strega.

"What took so long?" she asked Mooch. The meeting her brother had set up with Nibsy should have started already.

"You told me to wait until it was clear," Mooch said with a cocky shrug. "Nibsy didn't leave like you said he would. Not right away, at least."

"He's gone now?" she asked.

"Went out the front a few minutes ago."

Viola frowned. If Nibsy was late for his meeting with Paolo, her brother would be in a wretched mood later. But there was nothing she could do for that, and there was no time for her to worry about things she could not change.

"Thank you," she told Mooch, meeting his eyes and trying to soften her expression. "I wasn't sure if you'd—"

"I owed you one favor for getting me out of there. No one else came," Mooch said with a shrug, but his voice was empty of emotion, hollow as Theo said his expression had been when they'd brought him into the courtroom. Then Mooch's mouth went tight. "But don't think this means I've forgotten what you did to Nibs on that bridge. You took that damn lying thief's side over the Devil's Own, and you made sure that Nibsy'll never walk good again. This don't make us friends. It only makes us even."

"Of course," Viola told him, hiding her frustration. She didn't regret her actions on the bridge, but there was no way to convince Mooch—or any of the Devil's Own—that she'd been right to protect Esta. Not when Nibsy was whispering his lies into their ears.

It might have been less trouble to just kill him, but Viola understood that his death wouldn't be enough. *Make me a martyr,* Nibsy had taunted, and he'd been right. To break his control over the Devil's Own, Viola knew she had to expose Nibsy for what he was first, or else the vacuum of his death would destroy everything Dolph had tried to build.

"My loyalty is to Dolph—and to what he stood for," she told Mooch, lowering her voice. "I'm not your enemy, Mooch. I never was."

"Yeah, well . . . that remains to be seen." Mooch frowned, as though he was suddenly unsure about what he'd promised to do. But he relented a second later, stepping aside to let her in.

Viola hadn't been inside the private quarters in the back of the Bella Strega since the day when everything had fallen apart on the bridge. She'd assumed then that nothing could be worse than what had happened after Khafre Hall, when they'd realized all had been lost—the Book, the artifacts, and their leader. But a few days later, she'd lost even more. She'd lost her home. Her purpose.

Stepping into the back rooms of the building was like stepping back into a different part of her life. The Elizabeth Street entrance opened into a small vestibule, where the aromas of the kitchen had seeped into the wood. The air from outside brought with it the sharpness of the trash that littered the alley, and the mixture of the two was a scent as familiar to Viola as her mother's rose water. There was something missing, though. Something was off. Then she realized—she hadn't been greeted by the warm smell of bread baking, as she had been when Dolph sat in the barroom, holding court, and Tilly stood at the great iron stove making the food that knitted them together.

"You'd better get on with it," Mooch said. "The place is crawling with the boys, and I can't keep them occupied all by myself."

With a sure nod, Viola took the narrow staircase up two floors to the hallway she'd once called home. She didn't bother to enter the room that had been hers. There was no time, and she had no desire to feel more loss than that which already creased her heart. Instead, she went to the end of the hall, where Dolph and Leena—and then later, Dolph alone—had made a home.

The door was locked, a marked change from when the rooms had belonged to Dolph. He had never feared intrusion, not when his gang wore a mark that could unmake them. Viola doubted that anyone would have dared cross his sanctuary without an invitation, even without the marks. It simply wasn't done. The Devil's Own was a gang, yes. A rowdy, dangerous bunch. But Dolph Saunders had given them a place to build a home for themselves, and there was a certain honor among thieves.

A pin from her hair made short work of the lock, and Viola let herself into the quiet of the flat. Once inside the apartment, she paused, allowing the past to wash over her. She'd been Leena's friend before Dolph's, and together they'd spent hours in these rooms. How many times had she sat in that chair by the window, learning her letters or talking strategy? How often had the rooms been a haven, free of judgment and shame, filled with something that had felt like hope?

Dolph should still be here. Dolph, who had lied to her . . . or at least, who had hidden the truth about too many things. About his cane and how it came by the awful power it held. About Libitina.

Why had he not explained how the blade worked and let Viola make her choice?

She knew already the answer. It had been a trick, yes. One that perhaps a true friend should not have played, but then, Viola had not really *wanted* to know. She'd accepted the knife without question, used its deadly blade without considering, because she'd wanted to believe that an acquired skill was somehow different from the heart of a thing. Viola had wanted to imagine that she could refuse that essential part of what she was—and what she felt drawn to do with her affinity. Healing and death, two sides of life itself. One impossible without the other.

The truth was that her friend had deceived her. The truth was also that he had done her a kindness. Dolph had allowed her to *be*, without judgment, what she was made to be. If Libitina was only so deadly because

Viola was actually channeling her own magic through the knife, then it meant that Dolph had given her a way to use her affinity without wrestling with the shame of it. He had given her a way out of the torture that would have come from holding herself back, from denying her magic.

How many Mageus had Viola watched suffer as they tried to hide what they were? How many turned to Nitewein or worse to dull the ache of unused affinities? *Too many.* She'd seen them in the Strega and in the streets, desperate and aching. She'd thought she was different somehow—stronger—and she'd pitied them, not knowing how close she'd come to being in their shoes.

Viola looked around the apartment and realized that nothing had changed—not really—but even so, the rooms were different now. The feel of the space was colder, despite the warm breeze that came in through the lace curtains. The oil painting they'd stolen from Morgan's collection still hung on the wall over the bookshelf, and Viola took a moment to trace the strange design on the book Newton held, remembering the night Dolph had told her why the Ars Arcana was so important. Something about that painting sparked another memory. . . .

There had been something carved into the cover of the Ars Arcana, hadn't there? But Viola couldn't remember whether it had been this design or some other, not with whatever Harte Darrigan had done to her that night.

She would never know for sure. The Book was gone now, along with Esta and the Magician.

Viola turned away from the painting and the questions she had no answers to and focused on what she *could* find instead. Running her finger across the spines of the books on the shelf, she dismissed some immediately. Voltaire and Kierkegaard wouldn't have the answers she needed. There was the book they had taken from the Metropolitan, an ancient-looking thing that had once belonged to Newton himself, but the answers she was looking for wouldn't be there, either. Finally, she came across a simple volume, bound with stitched cloth instead of leather, and she pulled it from the shelf. Thumbing through it, she could not stop the emotion of seeing Dolph's familiar script from crashing over her— the warmth of the memories and the disappointment as well.

As she flipped through the pages, Viola realized there was too much there: notations about the Brink, notes about the stones and the Book, and pages filled with crude sketches done in scratches of ink. There were notes written in English and Italian, German and French. As she searched for what she needed, Viola heard voices in the hallway, and panic slid down her spine, but . . . *there.* A sketch of a familiar shape. It was clearly Libitina, with her thin, sharp blade and ornate handle, sketched onto the page. But Viola could not read the words. They were written in a language she did not know, as though Dolph had been purposely cautious and intended to keep this knowledge from her.

Viola shook off her disappointment as she tucked the notebook into her skirts. It was a risk, maybe even a mistake, but she could not be sure how many of the pages she needed, and she could not leave without the knowledge she'd come for.

The voices were closer now, just outside the door, and even if they weren't heading for Dolph's apartment, Viola knew that she could not leave the way she'd come. Without hesitating, she went for the window. The gauzy curtains fluttered in the breeze when she opened the window wider. She pulled herself over the sill to the fire escape, then pushed the window back to where it had been before, and began the climb down. She did not look behind her to see if she'd been spotted, and her heart did not stop racing until she was on the ground and far away from the one place that had ever felt like home.

TIME'S FANGED JAWS

1904—Denver

North and Cordelia didn't come back that first night—Esta hadn't really expected them to, but she could tell that Maggie had hoped. They waited up until late, and she helped as Maggie tried to keep herself busy by making more of the Quellant. By the time they finally finished, the city outside their window was quiet, but the thoughts running through Esta's mind were too loud to let her sleep.

She wondered if Harte had made it to California yet, and she hoped he was having better luck than she was. She still regretted getting rid of the bracelet he'd left her. Even traveling with the two Antistasi, she felt alone, but it was never worse than in the middle of the night, when the world was quiet and endless with sleep. In those deep hours, she would have welcomed the sound of Harte's voice in her ear, the feel of his lips against her skin. She should have appreciated the bracelet for the gift it was. Once they met up, it was likely they wouldn't have much time. At least with the bracelet, she could have had the illusion of him.

The sky was already lightening when Esta finally drifted off, but her dreams were not easy. She found herself in a desert where dangerous magic swirled through the air. Beneath the sand, a monstrous serpent slid along, chasing her across an endless stretch of emptiness. Ahead, silhouetted against the blazing sky, she saw Harte standing with his back to her. Her heart leapt at the sight of him, and in response, the serpentine monster changed course, aiming instead for him.

Esta shouted, but Harte didn't turn. She started to run, but she knew she would never reach him in time. When she reached for her affinity, her magic lay cold and dead, and in the end, the serpent rose from the sand and lunged for Harte, its fanged jaws wide. As the serpent's teeth clamped shut, Esta woke with a start, the scar on her wrist burning again.

Despite the warm breeze coming in through the window, she felt chilled. Across the room, Maggie snored softly, but Esta didn't even try to sleep again.

They spent the rest of the next two days keeping themselves busy while they waited for news that never came. Esta watched and helped Maggie when she could, but the days dragged on, and they both grew more impatient and anxious for word from North and Cordelia.

"I think you've killed it," Esta said. She couldn't take listening to the sound of the pestle grinding against the marble mortar anymore. It was the afternoon of the third day, and she'd been watching out the window, jealous of everyone who was free to go about their business in the streets below as she tried to distract herself, but now she turned back to look at Maggie.

"What?" Maggie paused and looked up over her glasses.

The room finally descended into blessed silence. Maggie's hair had been threatening to fall from its loosely pinned bun all morning, and now a long piece did fall in front of her face. Maggie pushed it back, blinking a little, like she'd been so preoccupied with her work that she'd forgotten about Esta completely.

"Whatever you're grinding up in there—it's dead," Esta said, trying to keep her voice pleasant and not as frayed as her nerves felt. "Completely and utterly. You can't do anything else to it."

Maggie glanced down and gave a small curse that might have been amusing in any other situation. "I overdid it," she said. "And it was the last of my camphor. I won't be able to make any more of the Quellant until I get more." She cursed again.

"So let's go get some," Esta suggested. She wasn't used to sitting still for so long, and being trapped inside the dingy apartment was doing nothing for her nerves. "I'm sure there's a pharmacy or a shop or *something* in this town."

Maggie chewed on her lip, considering Esta's proposal, but eventually she shook her head. "I'll start on something else instead. If Jericho happens to come back today, I don't want to miss him."

"I'm sure North would wait for you," Esta told Maggie. She actually *wasn't* sure, considering how angry he'd been about the truth tablets.

But Maggie ended the conversation by returning to her work.

A breeze stirred through the window, but it did nothing for the close stuffiness of the small apartment. "Or we could go to *them*," Esta offered. "We can head out to the show and see if they've learned anything or made any progress. Getting out of this apartment might be what we both need." After all, she couldn't steal the dagger from a distance, and she definitely didn't trust that Cordelia wouldn't take it for the Antistasi.

"We already agreed that it's safer for us to stay here," Maggie reminded Esta, but the yearning was clear in Maggie's expression.

"Did we?" Esta asked, her patience ragged. "Because I don't remember having much say in the matter."

"With those incendiaries I set off, they're probably already looking for you—for all of us," Maggie said. "Jericho and Cordelia were right to leave us here."

Esta let out a long, resigned breath. "Maybe, but I hate that we have no idea what's happening out there." And that fact, along with the gnawing absence of her affinity, was driving Esta mad.

"I trust Jericho," Maggie said, like he was the only variable.

"Sure . . . but do you trust Cordelia?" Esta pressed.

"She's Antistasi," Maggie said, and it sounded an awful lot like she was trying to convince herself.

"Maybe . . ." Esta frowned. "But it feels like we're putting a lot of faith in someone we don't really know."

"You saw that tattoo on Cordelia's leg." Maggie pushed her glasses back up on her nose. "It covered most of her thigh. Putting herself through that would have taken a real commitment to the Antistasi's cause."

"Ruth was committed too. Look how that turned out," Esta said, before she could think better of it.

She realized her misstep immediately when Maggie's brows drew together.

"I didn't mean—" Esta stopped, knowing from Maggie's expression that she needed a different approach. "I'm sorry," she said, backtracking. "It's not like you were the only one who was blind to Ruth's faults. I was right there with you, and I should have known better."

Maggie's expression softened a little. "It's not like she was *your* sister."

"No, she wasn't," Esta admitted, thanking her lucky stars for that fact. "But I knew someone a lot like her once. It's just . . . well, you'd think I would have learned by now."

Maggie was staring at Esta now, pestle still raised. Her expression had shifted from anger to interest. "What happened?"

"Nothing," Esta said, pretending to brush aside Maggie's interest. "It doesn't matter."

"You might try trusting me, you know," Maggie said. "After all we've been through at this point . . ."

Esta didn't immediately answer. She knew it would be better if Maggie had to work a little for the information. It would land better, hook her more completely.

Maggie frowned at her. "Never mind. Forget that I even asked. Clearly you're not ever going to trust me, no matter how many times I save your life."

Esta could have made up some lie or changed the subject, but she had the sense that she was being presented with an opportunity. Harte was hundreds of miles away, and she was without both her cuff and her affinity. Now that Cordelia had entered the picture, Esta was starting to understand that the Antistasi's influence might reach farther than she'd expected. She might need an ally, and Maggie seemed the most likely candidate.

LISA MAXWELL

"No," Esta said, the portrait of contriteness. "You're right. You *do* deserve to know. But it's hard for me to talk about my past."

"You don't have to," Maggie told her with a resigned sigh. "But it's not like we have anywhere to go."

Esta knew instinctively that the moment in front of her was delicate. Maggie was right there, ripe for the con, but any lie she told could be too easily unraveled. If she truly wanted Maggie on her side—if she wanted to *keep* her there—Esta knew she had to give Maggie something true.

Too bad the truth was a secret she often kept even from herself.

Esta studied the yellowed lace covering the windows for a long stretch of seconds, considering where she should start.

"I told you about what we did in New York—how we broke into Khafre Hall and stole the artifacts—but I didn't tell you about before that." She paused, gathering her courage. It felt monumental to reveal so much, even if she had a strategic reason for doing it. "Before I was the Devil's Thief, I was just *a* thief," she began, her voice shaking more than she'd expected. "It's what I was raised to be—nothing more and nothing less—and I was fine with my situation because I believed in the person I was following. In fact, I never questioned him. If he was hard on me, I dismissed it as his right." Esta shrugged, remembering the times Professor Lachlan had berated her for her impulsiveness, the small failures that he never let her forget. "After all, he'd raised me. I was willing to lie, steal, and betray whoever he asked me to, all because I wanted to prove myself worthy of the life he'd given me."

"That's completely understandable," Maggie said softly. "I didn't know my mother. Ruth was the only family I ever really had, and I understood exactly what she'd sacrificed to raise me. It's one of the reasons I didn't leave after what she did to Jericho. That, and what she was working toward seemed bigger than my own petty concerns."

Esta turned back to Maggie and wondered for the first time if maybe she wasn't as alone in this as she'd suspected. "It was the same for me," she admitted. "I wanted to earn my place, but maybe even more, I wanted the dream he offered," she told Maggie, meeting her eyes now. "He told me that I could help him destroy the Brink—that together we could save the old magic. I was so committed to that cause, I didn't see the truth." Esta took a breath before she forced herself to go on. "I found out eventually that the dream I'd committed myself to wasn't even possible. All his talk of bringing down the Brink and saving magic? It was a lie. He'd only ever wanted power for himself. And in the end, a lot of people got hurt because I realized that too late." Dakari and Dolph, and so many others she'd betrayed.

"The Antistasi's cause isn't a lie, Esta," Maggie said as ardently as a true believer. "I have to believe that making the world safe for those like us is possible."

"I hope you're right," Esta said honestly. "I want that every bit as much as you do. But I hope your commitment to that cause doesn't blind you to the danger Cordelia might pose." She held Maggie's gaze. "Or to the Antistasi's faults."

Maggie frowned, considering Esta carefully, and Esta couldn't tell what she was thinking. She wondered if she'd gone too far.

"This person you're talking about—the one you were following," Maggie ventured. "It's Harte, isn't it?"

At first Esta didn't realize what Maggie had just said. But then understanding struck fast and hard. "What did you call him?" The words seemed stuck in her throat.

Maggie hadn't said "Ben," the name Harte had given the Antistasi in St. Louis. She'd said "Harte," which meant that she knew.

"Were you ever going to tell us who Ben really was?" Maggie asked, her expression unreadable.

Maggie's mouth was still moving, but suddenly Esta could no longer hear her. All of the sound in the room drained away. At first it felt like shock, but when Esta shook her head, trying to dislodge the silence, it didn't work.

Then Esta's vision flickered.

The world around her began fuzzing in and out of focus, and again it reminded her of the picture on one of those old TVs, and she understood instantly that this was more than simple panic. Whatever had happened to her before was happening again.

But so much worse.

Maggie must have already realized that something was wrong. She was moving across the space between them, holding out her hand to Esta. She hadn't taken more than three steps before Esta's vision flickered again, and then Maggie was gone.

The room looked suddenly different. It was the same apartment, but a family was gathered around a table eating together. Another flicker and she saw an empty room. Then a room with three men playing cards. Then Maggie. And then Esta could see everything at once, the different versions of the room layered one on top of another, superimposed. It felt like all of the possible realities were vying for prominence.

Esta felt the seconds sliding around her, slithering across her skin like the serpent from her dream. The scar on her wrist was burning as she tried to grasp hold of the present, where Maggie was still trying to reach her, but reality blurred and flickered, and then time opened its fanged jaws and swallowed her whole.

GONE

1904—San Francisco

In the moment before sleep gave way to waking, when the world was still obscured by the haze of dreams and the shadows of night, Harte Darrigan thought he was back on his couch in New York. At first he thought it was still weeks before, when he'd been forced to sleep in his parlor because Esta had taken over his bed. Before everything came rushing back to him, he could imagine her there, sleeping a few feet away behind his closed bedroom door, her scent on his sheets in the home he had made for himself from nothing more than determination and a dream for something more.

Then Harte felt a sharp, burning itch on his leg, and when he went to reach for it, he found that he couldn't. His arms had been pinned behind his back and secured at his wrists. He opened his eyes, not to his apartment, but to darkness as the scent of dust and dampness burned away the rest of the dream. All the events of the past few weeks and days and hours came rushing back in a dizzying, horrible flood.

The headpiece. His father. *Esta.* She would be waiting for him.

The thought of her had Harte sitting up with a sudden lurch that made his head spin again. His ears were ringing, and his stomach flipped at the movement, but he swallowed down any nausea. He wouldn't be sick. He *wouldn't.*

How long has it been?

Now that his eyes had adjusted to the dim light, Harte saw he was in some kind of cellar. Across the way, a door was fitted so poorly that light came in around the edges and kept the room from being pitch-black. It was cold like a cellar too, and Harte started to shiver.

As he waited for the room to stop spinning, he used the toe of one foot to rub the back of his ankle, trying to satisfy the aching itch that had woken him. The spot was tender to the touch, and he felt more pain than satisfaction when he scratched it. He tried not to think about the vermin that had been crawling all over him while he'd been unconscious, but he'd spent enough time sleeping on the streets or in flea-infested boardinghouses to know when he'd been bitten by something. Even though it hurt, he couldn't stop himself from scratching, but at least the pain of the bite was distracting him a little from the more persistent ache throbbing through his head.

His father, or whoever had hit him back at the restaurant, had done a thorough job of it. His eyes still weren't quite focusing correctly, but Harte could almost begin to make out the features of the room. One wall was lined with shelving that contained boxes and glass bottles. On the other was a row of large burlap sacks filled with dry goods. Harte realized then that the uneven pallet he was currently sitting on was a pile of those sacks, which had been emptied and stacked along the third wall. His father had mentioned that he owned a store—maybe he'd brought Harte there?

In the corner, Harte could hear something scratching and rustling—a rat, probably. Maybe a couple of them. But otherwise, the room was silent as a grave. The wide, rough floorboards that made up the ceiling above were quiet. If anyone was up there, he couldn't tell. He didn't plan on sticking around to find out.

With effort, he managed to get to his feet. He took one step and then two, and just as he thought he might be able to make it to the door, the room tilted again. Harte felt his legs going out from under him, and then the floor gave way and he collapsed. Since his hands were still tied behind him, he couldn't catch himself, and he landed hard, rattling his already-throbbing head again.

The earthen floor felt cool and damp against his cheek, and Harte couldn't do much more than breathe in the scent of dirt as he tried to keep his stomach from revolting.

He needed to get out of the ropes. It should have been easy enough— already he could tell that they weren't tied with any kind of expertise. He writhed a little, twisting his hands and shoulders to work at them, but every movement made his head spin and his stomach rebel. The only thing that helped was to close his eyes and hold perfectly still. His head was pounding so sharply within his skull that Harte was sure he could actually see his heartbeat.

It was a long time later when he realized that his position on the floor should have been more uncomfortable. The necklace with the Djinni's Star and Esta's cuff had been secured beneath his shirt. He'd wrapped the two artifacts close to his skin with a length of material, because he wanted to make sure that no one could lift them from his pockets—and because Seshat seemed to retreat when they were close to his body. They should have been poking into him—uncomfortable lumps between his body and the hard, earthen ground. But they weren't.

Harte sensed Seshat laughing then, a low rumble of mockery. *I told you,* she said. *You were soft and let an old man get the best of you. How could you ever expect to stop* me*?*

Harte rolled to one side and then the other, pressing his torso against the floor in a desperate bid to find some sign that the artifacts had simply shifted. But the movement made him dizzy, and panic made his vision blur and darken around the edges, and as he slipped back into unconsciousness, Harte knew that no amount of wishing or anything else would change the fact that the two stones that had been in his possession were gone.

THE TRIALS OF OTHERS

1904—Denver

Once he was officially hired, North immediately threw himself into his new position with the Curtis Brothers' Show. He mucked stalls, brushed down horses, and lifted bale after bale of hay. By the end of that first night, his muscles ached something fierce. As long as he was working, he wasn't thinking, which was fine by him. Because if he started thinking, he'd have to make a decision—whether to forgive Maggie for what she'd done to him. Or for keeping it from him for so long. Whether he even could.

He didn't go back to town that first night or the next. Instead, he finished each day by collapsing into his assigned bunk and letting himself be pulled into a dreamless sleep. Then he rose early the following morning to start all over again. He'd figure things out with Maggie soon enough, he reasoned. It wasn't like he had anything to tell her yet, anyway. Three days in, and he'd only managed to see Bill Pickett from a distance. Cordelia had been right—the bulldogger kept to his own work and minded his business.

But then, everyone around the grounds was keeping to themselves. A few of the hands had been arrested during the raid, and no one was much interested in getting to know the newcomer who'd taken their place. North's experience in the mess tent had been the worst part, at first. There, men sat in small groups arranged by position and race, their backs turned and their heads down to ward off any intrusion.

Pretending not to notice the unspoken boundaries between the various groups, North sat directly in the space left between a couple of sullen-looking white cowboys and a couple of older gentlemen with skin even darker brown than Pickett's.

The older men turned out to be soldiers, veterans of the 10th Cavalry, who'd mostly served after the Civil War and out in the western territories, where they'd worked to maintain the peace by fighting against some of the same Lakota they now shared the arena with each afternoon. At first the men were pleasant if distant, but after a bit they warmed up enough to start regaling North with stories of their days in the cavalry. The stories grew more fantastic as each man tried to outdo the one who'd spoken before. Their good-natured competition wasn't exactly a chore to listen to, and North's enjoyment of—and growing respect for—the men wasn't an act, even if he was still angling for an introduction to Bill Pickett.

North felt a certain camaraderie with a sergeant named George, an older man with a long, narrow face capped by heavy brows. His brown eyes were speckled with amber, deep-set over a hooked nose, and his droll mouth drooped a little on one side when he talked. It was the result of a fever, he explained, after the army's hospital wouldn't admit him for treatment even with his many years of service. George didn't say it outright, but North understood—it was because of the color of his skin.

George looked far older than his fifty-odd years, but when he talked, his eyes lit with humor, and North could almost see the younger man George must once have been: the man who'd been born on a plantation and had run away and taken his freedom for himself when he wasn't more than twelve. George had taught himself to read so he could take up command of his own battalion instead of taking orders from the white sergeants who refused to see him and his men as their equals. He'd joined the Curtis Brothers' Show after his wife, Letty, had died a few years before. After she'd passed, George couldn't bring himself to stay in the house they'd shared. Too many memories, he'd told North.

North could appreciate the way George talked about his Letty, like she had been and still was the one and only light in his life. That kind of sentiment North understood deep to his core—it was exactly how he'd felt about Maggie, almost from the moment he'd met her. It was how he *still* felt about her, he realized, *despite everything*. And he found himself telling George about Maggie in turn.

Listening to their stories got North to thinking, though. He'd never known many people of color before—not in Chicago or Texas or even in St. Louis. It wasn't that he'd ever had any poor feelings about a person because of their skin, though he knew plenty who did. It was more that he simply hadn't thought to step outside his own steady path. Even on Gunter's ranch, he'd stuck to the group of Anglo cowhands and hadn't bothered much with the vaqueros unless he was working with them. He'd certainly never socialized with them.

Talking to George and his friends, though, and taking their easy company for the gift it was, North started to think that maybe he'd spent too much of his life only worrying about himself—and about the magic that flowed in his veins. He'd been so focused on how the world saw those with the old magic, he'd never considered that there were a lot of other folks with trials of their own.

The next morning, North was leading one of the horses in from the field to saddle it for the show, when he realized that his body hadn't felt so well used and sore from a good, solid day's work in a long, long time. The jobs he'd done in St. Louis for Mother Ruth and her Antistasi were often dangerous, but they'd never been all that physically taxing. Now North was starting to remember what it felt like to use his body the way it was intended. His skin was tender from the sun, and he knew he smelled of horse and sweat, but he felt happier than he had in years.

He patted the side of the horse he was leading, a pretty dappled Appaloosa mare the color of caramel. Out in the field, she'd rolled herself in a nice patch of mud, and while it might have made *her* feel better, it meant more work for North. He'd have to get her light, speckled hindquarters clean before the evening's show.

The sun was already low in the sky as North looped the mecate reins through his belt and started to fill a bucket of water from the pump. The mare seemed biddable and good-natured, from what he could tell. Maybe that was why he let himself get distracted by someone watching him from the edge of the corral. North thought he saw something on the man's lapel glinting in the sun. It wasn't the silver star of a marshal, but a round medallion that looked like a type he'd seen too many times before.

But that couldn't be right. There was no reason for the Society to be so far from St. Louis, way out in the mountains of Colorado.

North was so busy trying to get a look at the man without really looking that he wasn't paying attention to the mare like he should have been. Without warning or reason, the horse spooked, and before North knew what was happening, the animal's body was slamming into him. Nearly a thousand pounds of horseflesh pushed him into the fence as her hind leg kicked out.

He managed to dodge the worst of it. The hoof only caught the back of his thigh as he tumbled to the ground. But then the mare reared up, screaming her disapproval, and North knew he was in trouble. He barely had time to turn away, and he only had his arms to shield himself from the pummeling that was about to happen as the horse rose above him. Before her hooves could do any damage, though, someone else was there, standing between him and the Appaloosa. At first North only saw the shadow of a man silhouetted against the bright sun. He'd turned away from North as he walked the horse back, clicking and cooing at her until she stopped huffing her fear and finally calmed down.

North was still trying to catch his breath when the man turned. For a second he was too stunned to believe it could be Bill Pickett standing over him. It took Pickett extending a hand to him before North managed to pull himself together.

Pickett's grip was strong and sure, and the other cowboy hoisted North up to his feet like he weighed nothing at all.

"You okay there?" Pickett asked, squinting a little. He offered North the leading rope again.

"I think I'll live," North said, taking the rope. "Probably'll have a bruise on my leg to show off tomorrow, but it could have been a lot worse. 'Specially if you hadn't been there."

Pickett's brows went up in what looked to be amusement, and the heavy mustache over his mouth twitched. "Worse? You would've been *dead* if I hadn't been here. Can't get much worse than that."

Pickett was maybe in his early thirties, a decade or more older than North. His tightly curling dark-brown hair was clipped close to his head beneath his hat, and he carried himself with the confidence and self-possession of a man who knew what he was about. North had heard someone comment that Pickett's mother had been Choctaw. It hadn't been a compliment, but now North wondered if maybe they were right. Pickett's dark russet skin looked like it was permanently being warmed by the sun.

Then he decided it didn't matter. "Seems like I owe you my life, then," he told Pickett. "You didn't have to put yourself at risk like that."

"Yeah, well . . . I wasn't in any real danger. From the way you were walking when I saw you leading the mare in from the fields, I figured no one had warned you that she spooks easy around people she don't know." Pickett patted the horse's nose affectionately. "Steady as anything for Jimmy when he's riding her, but anyone else? She acts like she's still barely green broke."

"Well, you have my thanks," North told Pickett as he held out his hand. "I'm Jeric—" He stumbled a bit, tripping on his own tongue to keep himself from saying his actual name instead of the one Cordelia had given to the show's manager.

Pickett's brows went up again, until they were completely hidden by the brim of his hat. "Don't you know your own name?"

"Sorry. Must still be a little spooked myself," North said, trying to play off the slip with humor. "I'm Jerry. Jerry Robertson."

"One of the new ones," Pickett said with a tone that seemed more resigned than anything else. "You from here in Denver, then?"

"No, sir," North told him.

"No?" Pickett looked surprised.

"Originally, I'm from back east. Near around Chicago. But I've been traveling out around these parts for a while, looking for work here and there," he said.

"Well, watch yourself around this pretty girl," Pickett told him. "Last thing you want is to get your head kicked in."

The whole exchange lasted a couple of minutes, and before North could even consider what to do with the opportunity, Pickett was on his way. North turned back to the Appaloosa, more than a little shaken. The man on the other side of the fence was gone, but North realized suddenly where he'd seen the man before. It had been in St. Louis. The man had been wearing the uniform of the Jefferson Guard at the hotel the night the Antistasi had rescued the Thief.

If he was right, it meant that the Society was here, and if that was the case, there was a good chance that they'd been followed all the way from St. Louis.

It was hell to wait until his shift was over, but leaving sooner would only draw attention. As soon as North was done in the barn, though, he walked right past the mess tent toward the exit to the grounds. He hadn't gotten far when he ran into Cordelia.

"Where are you headed?" she asked, her dark brows bunching like caterpillars as she frowned. He could see the suspicion in her eyes and in the tightness around her mouth.

"We have a problem," he told her, explaining what he'd seen and who he thought the ruddy-faced man was. "It was probably the explosions Maggie set off. They would have been a dead giveaway to anyone familiar with her work in St. Louis." *And in Texas.*

Cordelia's frown deepened. "What about Pickett?"

"Pickett can wait. I *told* you—I need to talk to Maggie," North said, moving to go around the sharpshooter. He'd already waited too long. "I need to warn her."

Cordelia stepped in front of him. "*You* need to get the dagger from Pickett."

"You don't understand," North said. "The Jefferson Guard are the Society's own private police force. If they're here, it means they know we're here too."

"Then it's even more important that we get the dagger before they find you," Cordelia said.

"But Maggie—"

"Is safe right now," Cordelia told him. "I was headed into town anyway. I'll take care of warning the others." She pulled something from her pocket—one of the white tablets Maggie had given her—and placed it in his hand. All North could do was stare at it. Pickett had saved his life. Could he really do what he'd promised?

"Go on," Cordelia said, shooing North on when he didn't move immediately. "If you're right about what you saw, the sooner you find the dagger and get out of town, the better."

FRIENDS IN HIGH PLACES

1904—Denver

S*he's gone.*

It was all Maggie could seem to think as she stared in shock at the place where Esta had been sitting a few minutes before. If Maggie hadn't seen it for herself, she never would have believed it. Esta had flickered, looking oddly like a moving picture Maggie had seen once at a traveling dime museum. Then Esta's whole body had gone nearly transparent. Maggie had been able to see straight through the silhouette of her, to the room beyond. One second Esta had been there, whole and real, and the next she was gone.

No . . . No, no, no . . . First the necklace and now the Thief?

Maggie never should have pushed. She shouldn't have questioned Esta or revealed what she knew about Harte Darrigan. She should have kept playing along, but Esta had seemed so sincere talking about her childhood that Maggie had thought maybe they could finally trust each other. She hadn't been able to stop herself from asking, and because Maggie had pushed too far, Esta had run, the same as Maggie had feared from the very beginning.

Except . . . that wasn't *possible*. Esta had taken a dose of the Quellant earlier that morning. She shouldn't have been able to use her affinity to evade them. And yet . . .

Maggie stared at the spot where Esta had been and willed her back, but though the minutes ticked by, Esta never returned. Instead, a little while later the door to the apartment opened without warning, and Cordelia entered.

The sharpshooter took one look around, and her expression hardened. "Where's Esta?"

"Gone," Maggie said, realizing how completely insipid she sounded the second the word was out of her mouth. She knew exactly how bad it looked that Esta wasn't there.

"You let her go out alone?" Cordelia asked.

Maggie was shaking her head. "I didn't *let* her do anything."

"Well, she's clearly not *here*."

Maggie didn't know how to explain other than to say, "She disappeared."

"Disappeared?" It was clear Cordelia either didn't understand or didn't believe her.

"Like a ghost. One second Esta was sitting right there. We were talking, and . . ." Maggie didn't want to admit that maybe she'd been the cause. "It was like she'd never been there at all."

"She can't be gone," Cordelia said, sounding suddenly every bit as worried as Maggie felt. "Losing the Thief would be a terrible mess for the Antistasi"—her eyes narrowed—"and for you."

Something in Cordelia's tone struck a chord of warning in Maggie. "What's that supposed to mean?"

"It means that you ain't the only one with friends in high places, Margaret," Cordelia said, not quite answering her question.

Panic buzzed through Maggie like a swarm of angry bees. She couldn't get herself to think clearly. She had to *think*.

"I gave her the Quellant," she said as much to herself as to Cordelia. That fact alone should have *meant* something, but Esta had still managed to get away from her. Fear was starting to claw at Maggie now. "She shouldn't have been able to go anywhere."

A knock came at the door, and Maggie had a rush of hope that Esta had returned. But it wasn't Esta. Jericho walked in, and for a second the buzzing stopped, the fear receded, and everything fell away—everything but Jericho Northwood.

He came back. All Maggie could do was take in every inch of him, grateful and happy that Jericho was there despite what she'd done to him. She could only hope it meant that maybe he'd started to forgive her, but before Maggie could say even a word of welcome, Cordelia piped up.

"What are *you* doing here?" Cordelia sounded more angry than surprised. "I thought we agreed that you'd stay where you were."

"Maybe you agreed, but I told you I needed to talk to Maggie," he said, stepping past Cordelia without even looking at her, but he'd only partially closed the distance between them when he stopped short. "Where's Esta?"

"Gone," Cordelia said, her nostrils flaring. "She managed to slip away from Margaret."

"She *disappeared*," Maggie corrected.

Jericho frowned. "Weren't you still giving her the Quellant?"

"She took a dose this morning," Maggie assured him. Then another thought struck her. The idea had been rustling in the back of her brain for some time, but it had grown louder when she saw Esta vanish. Now she could no longer ignore it. "You don't think the whole story Esta told us about Seshat could have actually had some truth to it, do you?"

"No," Jericho said. "Of course not." But he didn't look as sure as he was trying to sound.

Maggie could sense Cordelia's unspoken questions, but she couldn't worry about them. Not right then. She couldn't let go of the idea that maybe Esta hadn't been lying, as they'd originally suspected. The story she'd told them in that boxcar as they were leaving Texas had seemed ridiculous. Neither of them had *really* believed her, but Maggie had been happy to use Esta's tale to her own advantage. Now she couldn't help but worry that maybe she'd been wrong. "Still, if the story about that ancient goddess was real—"

"It's *not*," North told her. "We're still here, aren't we? The world hasn't ended like she claimed it would."

He had a point. They *were* all still there, whole and real. The world was still spinning on, seemingly untouched. If Seshat was real, the goddess certainly hadn't followed through on her threat.

"Maybe this is all for the best," North said, looking almost thoughtful. Almost relieved.

"I don't know what either of you is going on about, but there ain't no way this could *possibly* be for the best," Cordelia said. "The Antistasi need Esta Filosik. She's necessary to our cause."

But Jericho wasn't looking at Cordelia or paying her any attention. His gaze was on Maggie, and there was a light in his eyes that made her stomach flip a little. "Maybe Esta doesn't have to be necessary to *our* plans," he said softly. "To yours and mine."

"What are you talking about?" Maggie asked, not quite understanding. The Antistasi's plans *were* their plans. *Weren't they?*

Jericho came over to take Maggie's hands in his. She could feel how rough they'd already become. "I've been doing a lot of thinking over the last few days, Mags. Maybe we should let this whole business go. The Antistasi. Esta Filosik. We could leave it all behind. We could start a life somewhere before we run out of chances."

Maggie's whole body suddenly felt cold. "Even if Esta's gone, we still have a chance to get one of the artifacts."

"One of them?" Cordelia asked. "But y'all said you have the necklace."

Maggie exchanged a nervous glance with Jericho.

"You said you had the Djinni's Star," Cordelia repeated. "Y'all told me the necklace was safe."

"We did have it," Jericho told Cordelia. "But her partner took the necklace and ran off as we were leaving St. Louis."

"Y'all are telling me you lost the artifact *and* the Thief?" Cordelia said, her expression unreadable. "That's the real reason y'all disappeared after the train explosion, ain't it? You were hiding your failure. I bet you wouldn't have even bothered to return to the Antistasi if I hadn't found you."

"Of course we would have!" Maggie exclaimed. Her stomach churned at the way Cordelia was staring at her, but she had to stay calm. She had to figure this out. "I thought if we could get the dagger, it would make up for losing the necklace," she explained. "We hoped it would be enough." She turned back to Jericho. "Which is why we *have* to get the Pharaoh's Heart. We can't give up now. Not when there's still a chance that we could help the Antistasi to change things—*really* change things—for Mageus in this country."

North pushed back a piece of hair that had fallen into her face. The motion was so gentle, and the look on his face was tender enough to make Maggie want to cry. "If the Antistasi haven't changed anything in a thousand years, what makes you think that *we're* the ones who can finally get the job done?"

Because I have to, Maggie thought, the buzzing panic swarming through her again now.

"Who else will do it, Jericho?" she asked instead.

"Let Cordelia here take over," he said. "Let's get out of here. You and me. Right now."

Jericho didn't understand. How could he, when she hadn't told him everything?

Maggie's head was shaking already, as though her body knew what the answer had to be. "You found me because of the Antistasi. Who am I if I'm not this?" she asked him. "Who am I if I walk away without even trying to make it right?"

Jericho let out a ragged breath, and she could sense his growing frustration. "I found Ruth's organization because I was young and hotheaded, but you have to know by now that I only ever really stayed for you, Mags. Maybe Esta disappearing is the sign we needed. Let's go somewhere new and start a life together. We could stop running and fighting and just *be*. We don't have to stop helping people. *You* could help a lot of people with those formulas of yours, if you wanted to. We could build a little home and maybe even have us a couple of kids. We could be *happy*."

Maggie could practically see them already, the children the two of them might have one day. Carrot-colored hair and freckles and impish, dimpled smiles. She could see them running and playing in this fairy tale he was building for her out of nothing but his words, and her heart clenched. Because she wanted it so *desperately*.

But it could never be hers if she walked away from this.

"And what then?" Maggie asked, her voice hollow as she turned the dream against him. "If these children you're imagining are born with the old magic, will we teach them to hide themselves away, as we were taught? Will we teach them to push down whatever affinity they might have and tell them that the old magic is a secret no one can know?"

North's expression softened. "I don't know, Mags. I don't have all the answers, but we're not the only ones with hardships in this world. There are plenty of Sundren who carry their own burdens through life, and they don't let those problems stop them from loving and living."

Maggie was aware of Cordelia standing nearby, watching and listening to every word they said. The sharpshooter had contacts in the network, but Maggie was only truly worried about one.

You're not the only one with friends in high places. Cordelia's words ricocheted through her brain, stirring up fear. Hardening her resolve.

Maggie wished she could set her responsibilities aside and step into Jericho's arms, but her burdens weren't so easy to set down, not when they were shaped like the lives of the people she loved. For her, stepping away from the path she'd been on her whole life would be more like walking off a cliff.

"I can't give up now," Maggie whispered, almost wishing that it wasn't true.

"It's not giving up to reach out and claim a life for ourselves, Mags," North said, squeezing her hand gently. In his eyes was the hope for a future she'd never thought to imagine.

She might have said yes. The word was pressing at her mouth, willing her to let it out, but before she could, a noise drew her attention. A moaning sound that soon solidified into a girl.

Esta was back.

A SIMPLE TRICK

1904—San Francisco

The next time Harte woke, there was no delay between returning to consciousness and remembering everything that had happened. The pain in his head, the ache in his shoulder, and the maddening, burning itch on his ankle reminded him immediately of where he was—and of the reality of his situation. His failures washed over him in an icy flood of shame. He'd been outmaneuvered by his sham of a father, and the artifacts in his possession, the necklace and the cuff—*Esta's cuff*—were gone.

Because you are weak, Seshat whispered. *I warned you, and still you allowed a powerless rat to best you.* Her voice was threaded with the same mockery that Harte was so used to. But there was a trembling energy to her words, except, *no*—the trembling was coming from *him*. His limbs were shaking a little, and the chill in the air made him feel almost feverish.

Maybe he *was* feverish. His body ached, and despite being unconscious for so long, he wanted nothing more than to close his eyes again.

Foolish boy, Seshat hissed. *You would accept your failure so easily? You are too soft and far too pitiful to be worthy of the girl or the power she holds within her.*

That was probably true, but Harte wasn't ready to accept it. Certainly, he wasn't going to lie there and wait for whatever his father had planned for him. But he felt so incredibly *awful*.

Get up, Seshat urged. *Or you will die here, and the girl—and every possibility she contains—will be lost.*

The tremulous energy in Seshat's voice struck a nerve. *If I die, what happens to you?*

Seshat didn't respond.

Harte realized then what emotion had colored Seshat's words—*fear*. It was so uncharacteristic of her usual rage and fury that it was almost enough to distract him from trying to figure out whether his shaking was from exhaustion or fever. He and Seshat had been locked in a battle of wills ever since the moment he'd touched the Ars Arcana and she'd used his affinity to channel herself into him. If Seshat was well and truly afraid now, it meant that Harte was in more trouble than he'd realized.

A single word floated through his mind—*plague*.

Before the wave of panic that thought brought with it could overwhelm him, Harte realized suddenly that he wasn't alone. He could hear breathing close by that didn't belong to him. It was either the biggest rat he'd ever seen—and there had been plenty of those in New York—or . . . He rolled over to his other side and found a small face framed by a cap of close-cropped dark-blond hair sitting on the floor next to him. Curious and too-familiar gray eyes sat above a button nose. They widened, and the child scrambled to his feet when he saw Harte looking at him.

It was the same child who had been with Harte's father. *My brother.* All thoughts of sickness were replaced with the strange and unsettling realization that he was not completely without connections in the world. Whether he would claim them, though, was a different matter altogether.

With some effort, Harte rocked himself upright. As he tried to make the room stop spinning—and tried to keep from heaving up the contents of his stomach—the boy backed up a little more. The child didn't shout or call for anyone, though. His eyes were still curious, but also wary now.

As he sat up, Harte realized his head felt a bit clearer. His ankle still itched and burned, and now when he scratched at it with his toe, the bites there ached sharply. It wasn't the first time he'd dealt with vermin, though, and he knew there was little he could do until the irritation ran its course. Still, they hurt more than most bites he'd had before—his entire leg ached—and he hoped that they hadn't become infected. Or maybe he hoped that they were infected, since that would be a lot easier to deal with than the plague that had quarantined Chinatown.

Seshat remained quiet, still withdrawn and far away, but Harte knew she was watching . . . and waiting. He wasn't sure how much time had passed since he'd last awoken. There were no windows in the cellar, so he couldn't even tell what time of day it was. It could have been the next morning or days later. Esta might already have found the dagger. She might be traveling back toward the bridge, or she might have already arrived. Maybe she was waiting there for him, wondering if he had deserted her again. If she thought he'd truly betrayed her, she might not wait long.

No . . . she would wait, because he had her cuff.

Or, he'd *had* it. Harte needed to get it back, which meant that he needed to get out of that dank basement, even if he'd rather curl up and go to sleep.

Harte's arms were still tied behind him, and his shoulders ached from being in that position for so long. With the small boy's eyes upon him, he tested the ropes again and found they hadn't been secured any better than they had been before. It wouldn't be hard to free himself, but the boy posed a problem. With the child there, Harte would have a witness to his escape. Possibly, the kid might even sound an alarm if Harte tried to leave.

"Where am I?" he asked the boy as he considered his options.

The boy didn't respond. He just stared at Harte without any indication that he'd understood.

"Do you speak English?" Harte asked, searching his brother's face for some indication that the child comprehended. "Can you understand me?"

The boy's brows drew together a little, but still he didn't respond. He just kept staring.

It was possible that the boy *didn't* know English. His father had spoken something that sounded like German to him before. It was likely that his brother had no idea what Harte was saying. At least he hadn't yet made any move to alert someone that Harte had awoken.

"Can you tell me where I am?" he asked the boy, trying again. "Is this your father's store?"

Nothing.

Harte tested the ropes again. They'd grown a bit looser from his earlier movements, and he could be out of them without much trouble. He *needed* to get out of them—and out of that cellar. He felt sore and tired and, well, he felt outright *sick*. But he pushed the thoughts of plague out of his mind. He had a feeling that the longer he stayed trapped in that dank cellar, the less chance he'd have of escaping successfully. Besides, he'd worked through illnesses before. He'd survived New York winters on the street; he would survive this as well. He had to. He had a promise to keep. But first he needed to get free.

"Would you like to see a magic trick?" Harte asked, trying to stop shivering long enough to give the boy a conspiratorial smile.

The boy's expression shifted then, a slight widening of the eyes. A spark of interest warred with the caution and curiosity that were already there.

He understands, Harte realized, grateful for this small mercy.

"I bet you *would* like to see a magic trick," he told the child, brushing away any misgiving he might have had about using the boy. "I'm a magician, you know. Did your father tell you that?"

The boy didn't speak, but he shook his head ever so slightly. His small, bright eyes burned with interest.

"I'm a rather famous one, actually." Harte was already working the ropes on his wrists, making small, refined movements that would have been imperceptible to the boy. "Have you ever seen a magician?"

"Magic is an a-a-bomb-bli-nation," the boy said, parsing out the difficult word slowly and carefully. His small voice was clear as a bell and uninflected with any emotion at all. The words came like they were something he'd memorized without understanding the meaning.

"Abomination," Harte said softly, not missing the way the boy flinched at the gentle correction. He'd heard the echo of his father's intonation in the boy's voice, and he understood what that flinch likely meant. But Harte wouldn't let himself be distracted. There was nothing he could do for this child. He was no hero—had never wanted to be. He was a liar. A bastard and a con, and he would not let himself forget that again. "That's an impressive word for such a small fellow. Do you know what that means?" Harte continued working the ropes—he nearly had it now.

"It is against the path of rightless—" He paused, his young eyes widening a little in something that looked like fear before he corrected himself. *"Righteousness,"* the boy finished. He looked relieved to have gotten the word out.

Harte would have bet enough money to fill his porcelain tub that the child had no idea what he was saying. "I see," he told the boy, careful to keep his voice gentle. "Well, I know some people see things that way. Perhaps your father does?" He paused, noting that the boy looked a bit more nervous. "But not everyone feels the same, you know. I, for one, happen to believe that magic isn't an abomination at all. Magic can be beautiful or exciting, and sometimes, magic is nothing more than a skill that comes from a lot of practice," he told the boy, and with a flourish, Harte drew the rope from behind his back with his now-freed hands.

The boy's eyes were as wide as saucers now, and he started to scurry back, clearly afraid. But he didn't yell or sound any alarm.

"Wait!" Harte said, putting his hands up to show he was harmless and offering the rope to the boy. "It's okay. Go ahead and have a look. No abomination there. It's only a simple trick I learned when I wasn't that much older than you." He offered the rope again. "Go on."

Fear warred with desire in the boy's expression, and Harte rubbed at his arms as he waited, trying to dispel the chill that had sunk into his bones. His skin was tender and his muscles ached when he touched them, but he couldn't worry about what that might mean. Infection or worse, it didn't matter. For now he needed to focus on the boy, to draw him in and earn his trust.

Finally, the boy inched forward and snatched the rope from his hands.

"See?" Harte said gently, hating himself a little for what he was about to do. "It's nothing more than a regular old rope."

The boy continued studying the length of rope with a serious little frown.

Now that his arms were free, Harte turned to the ropes around his ankles. As he'd expected, there was a series of angry red welts on his calf—flea bites, from the way they were clustered. They didn't look particularly infected, but his entire leg ached. If they were infected, it might explain the way he felt. He *hoped* that explained the way he felt.

"Would you like to see another trick?" he asked, trying to ignore the burning itch and the way his body ached.

The boy considered this question seriously, but to Harte's relief, the boy eventually nodded.

"My name's Harte," he said softly, tentative as he began the introductions. "Harte Darrigan. What's your name?"

The boy stared at him for a long, thoughtful moment. Then his small face screwed up with determination, and he spoke, his voice barely more than a whisper. "Sammie."

"It's nice to meet you, Sammie," Harte said, and once the words were spoken, he felt the truth of them. He was somehow almost happy to know this child, a brother he'd never thought to want.

A brother who could never know him.

Use him, Seshat whispered. *The faster you are free, the faster you can find the girl.*

Harte tried to brush off her words, but Seshat had a point. He hadn't traveled to California to find a family. He'd come for the lost artifact that held the Dragon's Eye. He *would* find it, and he would only stay long enough to retrieve Esta's cuff. He would use this boy if that was required, and he wouldn't allow himself to give in to sentimentality. He would not hesitate. *Not again.*

He felt Seshat stirring in his depths, still far off from the boundary between them, but now there was a shivering anticipation to her waiting.

The boy simply stared at him with the look Harte had seen countless times in the eyes of children he'd grown up with on the streets, children who had learned young that adults couldn't be trusted. Children who would never know a childhood free from the terror of living unprotected. It was a look Harte had probably worn too often himself. But there was nothing he could do for this boy, he reminded himself. He knew how his father—*their* father—would react when he learned that Harte had escaped. This child would pay the price. Harte couldn't take a child with him, and he certainly couldn't change the kind of man their father was. The most he could offer was a bit of happiness.

"Are you ready to see another trick?" he asked.

When the boy nodded eagerly, Harte gave Sammie—his *brother*—a few minutes of wonder. He offered a few simple tricks and illusions that could never make up for the nest of hornets Harte was about to overturn in his life. By the time he'd run through the tricks he could pull together from the supplies in the room, Sammie had become transformed. His serious little face was bright now, his gray eyes smiling in a way that Harte's maybe never had. Not even when he was young.

Harte took an elaborate bow, making it into a ridiculous gesture that had his hands nearly brushing the ceiling of the cramped and musty cellar. His brother applauded, and Harte hated himself even more than he had a moment before. He had the sudden thought that there must be another way. Maybe he *could* take the boy with him—

The sound of footsteps and voices above him drew Harte's attention, and he realized how stupid a thought that had been. He'd wasted enough time, and he needed to remember what was truly important—and what he still had to accomplish. It was time to go talk to his father.

REVELATIONS

1904—Denver

W hen Esta finally came back to herself, it wasn't quick, and it wasn't easy. She had to fight to regain her body, wrestling it away from the pull of time, until she emerged from the Aether—*through* the Aether—wrung out and feeling completely untethered to the world around her.

At first she felt as if she were viewing the world through a fog. She could see Maggie and Cordelia and North in the room, but she didn't know them. They were nothing to her, and she, herself, was also nothing. But eventually the fog began to lift. Esta started to feel her body again— the ache of her muscles, the burning of her scar—and soon everything else came back to her as well. She remembered then who she was and what she was meant to do. Even then, fear vibrated through her body, and the scar on her wrist burned.

The aching scar seemed the surest sign that whatever had just happened was connected to her link with her younger self. The way time itself seemed to have devoured her—along with the fact that her affinity was still deadened by the Quellant—made Esta think, once again, that it hadn't been Seshat's doing. It felt more like a sign that her time to return her cuff might be running out.

Or maybe something happened to Harte.

She dismissed that thought immediately. Harte was too smart and too experienced to get himself into trouble he couldn't get out of. He was fine—so was her cuff. *He had to be.*

Maggie helped her to sit up, but Esta was only tangentially aware that it was trembling and not the world itself. It took a while for the quivering to die down enough to accept the cup of water Cordelia brought over. Maggie helped, but when Esta tried to drink, the water tasted bitter and her mouth felt like it was filled with sand. She could barely choke the liquid down.

"What happened?" Maggie asked.

"I don't know," Esta told them. "I was here, and then I . . . I wasn't." She explained what it had felt like, the way the room had shifted and reality had flickered and how time itself felt like it would swallow her whole. "How long was I gone?"

"Nearly an hour," Maggie told her. "We thought you'd left for good."

"We assumed you ran," North said, glaring at her.

"No." Esta was shaking her head. "It wasn't me. I didn't do anything to make that happen."

"But you will run," Cordelia said, the flatness of her voice sending a shiver of unease up Esta's spine. "The minute you have the dagger, you'll leave. You'll take it, like your partner took the necklace. Won't you?"

Esta meant to say *no*. But that wasn't what came out when she opened her mouth. "Of *course*," she blurted, the words tumbling out like they'd been *pulled* from her. Shocked, she clasped her hand over her mouth to stop herself from saying anything else.

North looked every bit as taken aback by her outburst as Esta felt, but his surprise quickly turned to irritation. "I knew it," he huffed, turning to Maggie. "Didn't I tell you? She's not even trying to hide it now."

Maggie's eyes had gone wide. "Esta? You said you'd give us the dagger. You *promised*."

"I lied." Esta was shaking her head to deny the words even as she spoke them, but there was a warmth flooding through her, a strange compulsion that made her want to tell them whatever they asked. "You gave me something," she realized, and then she turned on Maggie. "You used the truth tablets on me?"

"No," Maggie told her, frowning.

Cordelia took the glass that Esta had just drunk from and dumped the contents onto the floor. "We don't have time for any more games."

"Cordelia?" Maggie still looked like she was having trouble catching up. "What have you done?"

"What *you* should have done the second you lost the necklace," she told Maggie. "Clearly, she's bamboozled you into thinking she's on your side, but it's past time we have some answers."

North shifted a little, like he was suddenly uneasy, but he didn't say a word against what Cordelia had done.

So much for his lofty principles. Apparently they only applied when *he* was the one being drugged.

Esta was trying to school her features, but she was failing. No amount of training or self-possession was helping her to fight the effects of the drug she'd been given. How many tablets had Cordelia given her? How long had Maggie said the truth serum lasted? Esta couldn't be sure, but she knew her best chance was to delay. Maybe if she could hold out long enough, she'd be able to fight it.

"Does Pickett really have the Pharaoh's Heart?" Cordelia asked. "Or is this all nothing but a ruse to waste our time?"

"He has it," Esta said through gritted teeth. The more she tried to withhold, the more she felt compelled to speak. "Or he did."

"How do you know?" Cordelia demanded.

Again Esta tried to keep back the words, but Maggie's formulation was too strong. "Harte told me. He sent the dagger to Pickett himself."

Cordelia's eyes widened. "Does he know where the other artifacts are as well?"

Esta closed her eyes against the pain that was building in her head, the ache in her throat. She could handle a little pain, but she couldn't fight Maggie's formulation. "Yes." She looked up to Maggie, silently pleading with her to understand—to stop this—but Maggie only turned away from her.

"Do *you* know where the other artifacts are?" Cordelia asked.

Esta shook her head, but the word *yes* slipped from her lips, and when Cordelia pressed her for more information, she could not stop herself from answering. In the end, Esta told them everything she'd been trying so hard to hide: where Harte was going, what he was doing, and where they planned to meet. She might not have known every detail, but she knew enough to be dangerous. By the time Cordelia was done interrogating her, Esta's chest was heaving, and she felt like she'd been running for miles.

Maggie and North both looked overwhelmed, but Cordelia looked extremely pleased with herself.

Esta glared at the sharpshooter. She was furious, but anger was only part of what she felt. Fear also coursed through her, because she understood exactly how much she'd given away—and she had no way to warn Harte that he might be in danger.

"I knew you were hiding something," Maggie said softly. "But I thought you understood. Any one of those artifacts could have helped so many people—so many Mageus all over this country."

"One artifact alone wouldn't have done anything," Esta told Maggie, feeling too wrung out to bother trying to stop her words now.

"But you know where the others are," Maggie pressed. "The Antistasi could have used them."

"The Antistasi won't even exist if Seshat gets her way. Nothing will," Esta reminded them.

"You truly believe Seshat's real," Maggie said, frowning, like she had not considered that an actual possibility. "She's not just a story you made up to play on our sympathy?"

"I *did* use her to play on your sympathy," Esta admitted. "But that doesn't mean she's not as real as I am. Seshat's not some figment of my imagination or some delusion. She was betrayed by Thoth and trapped in the Book of Mysteries eons ago, and now she's in Harte—I didn't lie about that back on the train, and I'm not lying about it now. You were there in the Festival Hall, Maggie. You *saw*—" Esta didn't finish. She didn't want to remember the vacant, alien expression on Harte's face, or how close she'd come to losing him and to being lost herself. Then another thought occurred to her. "Why would you give me the Quellant if you didn't believe I was telling the truth about Seshat trying to use my power?"

"What if you do manage to get the five artifacts?" Maggie asked, ignoring the question. But she didn't have to answer, because Esta understood. Esta had let her fear lead her, and she'd been conned. "If you do manage to use the stones to control Seshat's power," Maggie pressed, "would you hand over the artifacts and give that power to the Antistasi?"

Esta hesitated, trying to choke back the truth, but in the end a single word escaped. "No," she whispered.

"I'm not exactly surprised," North grumbled.

"Why, Esta?" Maggie asked, looking more hurt and confused. "With that sort of power, the Antistasi could put an end to the Brotherhoods once and for all."

"Ending the Brotherhoods was never supposed to be the Antistasi's job," Esta said, fighting against every word that broke free, trying to choose the words that would work in her favor. "I have to try to make things right."

"If you gave Seshat's power to the Antistasi, you *could*," Maggie said.

"It's not that simple." Esta was shaking her head, but the words came anyway. "We didn't attack some random Sundren in St. Louis. We attacked the leaders of the Veiled Prophet Society, and more than that, we attacked the president of the United States. No one is going to forget that. Because of the serum, people who didn't give Mageus a second thought will be more aware of us than ever now. Regular people—*Sundren*—who never thought about the old magic before are going to be afraid now."

She paused, trying to figure out how to explain without making things worse. "This isn't about the Brotherhoods anymore, Maggie. Because we couldn't stop the serum from deploying, we have changed things in ways we can't even begin to predict. I have to try to fix that."

"But all that's done," Maggie told her. "It's over. We can't go back—"

"Maybe *you* can't," Esta said, clenching her jaw, but the serum was still thick in her blood, and there was little she could do to stop herself.

"You can?" North was frowning.

"With my cuff, yes," she admitted.

"How far can you go?" North asked, looking distinctly uneasy.

She met his gaze. "A lot farther than your watch."

Maggie's eyes widened. "Could you stop the parade?" She sounded interested despite herself.

"Much farther," Esta said.

"Why would you *need* to go farther than that?" Maggie asked. "If you could stop the parade, you could stop the serum from deploying."

"It's not enough," she told them.

"Seems like more than enough, if you ask me," North said.

"Because you don't understand . . . The Devil's Thief never should have existed," Esta told them. It was too much effort to hold back, so she decided to use the truth serum for her own purposes. She told them about the train leaving New Jersey back in 1902, the damage she'd done because of Seshat's power, and the way she'd been unable to control slipping through time. "Don't you see? If the Thief hadn't been created, there wouldn't be a Defense Against Magic Act. The Act shouldn't exist. Without the Thief, things were different. The *world* was different. It wasn't perfect, but it was easier. For a while, I didn't think I *could* go back—not with Harte. I didn't think it was possible with the way Seshat's power affected my affinity, but the Quellant changed all that. I think it's enough to block Seshat's power, and if I'm right, then I *have* to go back. I have to take Harte and the artifacts and try to put history back on the course it should have taken."

And if the stones disappear? It was possible they might not find an answer for the problem of the artifacts crossing with themselves when she slipped them back through time . . . but Esta would deal with that worry later. It was more important that they *could* go back. They could stop *this* future from becoming.

As silence descended on the room, Esta thought that maybe, just *maybe*, Maggie would understand. That she would agree.

"But without the Thief, there wouldn't be any Antistasi," Cordelia said, her voice cold with the truth of the matter.

Maggie's expression was suddenly unreadable. She was staring at Esta, as though seeing her for the first time.

"Where, exactly, would that leave us?" North asked, breaking his silence.

"I don't know. Wherever you should have been," Esta told him. "Not fighting a war you can't win."

"Maybe I'm already right where I'm supposed to be." North took a step closer to Maggie, as if to protect her. "Maybe I don't need you messing with that."

"You don't understand," Esta told him.

"I understand enough," he drawled. "You're not only talking about fixing what happened with the serum in St. Louis. You're talking about messing around with time itself. You could destroy our very *lives*."

"We've *already* destroyed lives," Esta said. "Plenty of them. Or have you forgotten the people in St. Louis who died from the serum? Have you forgotten *all* of the innocent people who have been caught up in the Antistasi's actions over the last couple of years? Is your life worth so much more than any of theirs?"

None of them looked ready to concede the point, and Esta understood their reluctance. Going back meant the possibility of saving some, but there was no way to predict how many other lives might be changed—or *how* they might be changed. Weighing one set of lives against another was an impossible arithmetic, one Esta didn't feel worthy to calculate.

But the Antistasi had no idea how different *this* version of 1904 was from the one that had once been—the one that was *supposed* to have been. Nothing she could say would give them a true sense of what life without the Defense Against Magic Act was like. More importantly, none of them—Esta included—could really know how different the future might *still* be because of what they'd done in St. Louis.

"You would risk destroying everything we worked for?" Cordelia said. "All of the progress we've made against the Brotherhoods? All that the Antistasi have become—you would endanger it?"

"Possibly," Esta admitted.

"What makes you think we would let you?" North asked as he drew out a pistol and leveled it directly at her chest.

THERE'S ALWAYS A CHOICE

1904—Denver

Maggie looked at the pistol in North's hand with a strange sense of detachment. She had known all along that Esta had been lying about who Ben—*Harte*—really was, even before they'd left St. Louis. She'd suspected that the two had been hiding their true motives as well, but her orders had been to bring them both to the Antistasi's side. Maggie had worried, of course, about whether she'd been doing enough, but now she saw how tenuous her control over the situation had been all along.

"Put down the gun, Jericho," she said, taking a slow, careful step toward him. He looked more afraid than angry, but fear could make people do things they normally wouldn't.

"I won't let her undo all that we have." The pistol shook, unsteady in his hand.

"You don't want to do this." Maggie kept her voice soft as she took another step. "We aren't killers."

"You heard what she said," Jericho told her. "She'd undo our lives if we let her."

"It's not going to come to that," Maggie said gently, sidling closer. "Put the gun down, Jericho. *Please.*" But he didn't respond to her request.

"Killing me won't save you, anyway," Esta told him. She looked drained, but her voice was steady.

"It sure might be worth a try," Jericho said.

Esta shook her head. "You don't understand. If you kill me now, it won't help. You won't get to keep this version of the present."

"You can't know that," Jericho said.

"I told you about the man who raised me," Esta said, looking to Maggie now. "But I didn't tell you everything. The man who trained me didn't only lie about what he wanted. He lied about *everything*. He killed my parents to get to me when I was a baby. I was born in 1899. But he sent me forward when I was a toddler, and I lived most of my life a hundred years from now, in the twenty-first century. I only came back to 1902 recently, a few months ago. But by coming back, I've changed things."

Maggie could tell that Esta was choosing her words, still fighting against the pull of the truth serum, but the tale Esta wove for them was nothing short of astounding. If Maggie didn't know what North was capable of with his watch, and if she didn't have so much faith in her own truth serum, she might not have accepted a word Esta was saying. To believe that Esta came from some time far beyond their own seemed too incredible to countenance. But Maggie knew that events could be changed. She'd seen North do it more than once. She didn't doubt her own abilities either. It hadn't been long enough for the effects of the truth tablets to wear off, which meant that this time—no matter how impossible her story seemed—Esta wasn't lying.

"If I don't take Ishtar's Key back to the girl in New York, time will unspool," Esta explained. "The world will go back to how it was before I stole the artifacts from the Order and before the Thief destroyed the train. This version of the present won't exist, and neither will the Antistasi—at least not as you are right now."

North turned to Maggie, to Cordelia, like he was looking for some sign that this was another trick. "That can't be right."

"She can't lie right now," Maggie reminded him, wishing it were otherwise.

"Put down that gun, Jericho," Cordelia commanded. She took out a small revolver of her own and pointed it at him.

The gun was still in Jericho's hand when he turned to Cordelia. "Don't tell me you're on her side too. I can't believe you'd sit here and let her destroy everything the Antistasi have done—everything that we are?"

"It doesn't matter what you believe or what you think," Cordelia told him. "The Thief is essential. *You* are not."

Panic skittered through Maggie. She didn't think that Cordelia was making an empty threat. "*Please*, Jericho."

He turned to her, his expression shadowed. "You want me to stand by and help her rearrange our lives? She'll destroy everything we have."

"I don't think even Esta Filosik has that kind of power," Maggie told him, the words coming before she could stop them, but they felt right somehow.

"She sure thinks she does," Jericho said, glaring at Cordelia.

"You showed up in St. Louis wearing a snake around your wrist and carrying the Antistasi's name in your mouth," Maggie reminded him. "You of all people should know that the Antistasi are older and bigger than any one group of us. They existed long before the Thief, and they'll exist long after, whatever changes Esta *thinks* she can make."

"Margaret's right," Cordelia said. "Fate itself brought the Antistasi into being, and it will preserve us, whatever time—or this Thief—might have in store." Her expression glowed with a kind of beatific fervor.

"Please, Jericho," Maggie said again, pleading. "The Antistasi can survive this. They're so much larger than one moment."

"I wasn't talking about the Antistasi," he said softly. The pistol in his hand lowered a little, and the sadness in his eyes made Maggie's throat go tight.

Too late, she realized his true meaning, and she stood, unable to move. Unable to speak. Stuck between two impossible choices.

"Let's just *go*, Maggie," Jericho pleaded as he lowered the gun completely. "Let Cordelia stay and deal with Esta if she wants, but if *this* life might disappear like it never was, why not enjoy what we have now? However long we might have left together." He held out his hand to her.

"I wish I could," Maggie whispered. She did not bother to stop the tear that broke free.

Jericho's eyes shuttered. "But you won't."

"I have to see this through," she told him, dashing at the wetness on her cheeks. Her throat was tight with everything she could not say, and her heart felt like lead. "You promised once that you would help me, Jericho. I'm asking you now to keep that promise."

Jericho stared at her for a long moment, and Maggie worried that he would refuse. Cordelia still hadn't lowered her gun, and Maggie wasn't sure that the sharpshooter was in any mood to be forgiving. For the first time in a long time, Maggie could not tell what Jericho Northwood was thinking.

"This is really what you want, Mags?" Jericho asked.

Maggie only knew it was what had to be. "Please . . ." She wasn't exactly sure what it was she was asking for.

Her plea hung in the air, and the silence that followed opened a chasm between them. In that moment, Maggie sensed that Jericho would turn from her, and after all she'd done to him—all her lies and evasions—it would be what she deserved. All she could do was stand there and hope, because she knew if Jericho turned away from her now, he would not come back. It would signal the end of something, and until that moment, she hadn't quite understood how much she needed the dream of a future with them together.

"In that case, I suppose I should be getting back," Jericho said finally. His voice rang as hollow as Maggie felt. "It appears I have a promise to keep." He tucked away his pistol and gave Esta another cold, appraising look. But he wouldn't look at Maggie, no matter how much she wanted him to.

Maggie didn't feel like she had any right to ask Jericho for anything more, so she didn't make any other plea. He left without another word between them, and she could not stop herself from flinching as the door closed behind him. With his leaving, something important had changed between them, and Maggie suspected that she would live to regret the choice she had made.

Cordelia stepped forward, but Maggie barely seemed to notice until the sharpshooter spoke. "You made the right choice, Margaret."

"Did I?" Maggie asked, still staring at the closed door. She wished there was a way she could go after him and take it all back. "Because I'm not so sure."

"You put your commitment to our cause—to the Antistasi—before your own personal gain," Cordelia said. "It is what we all gotta do. We all make sacrifices for the greater good."

But Maggie didn't see Cordelia making any such sacrifice. All she could think about was the way the light had gone from Jericho's eyes when she'd turned him down for the final time. She'd never forgive herself for being the one who'd dimmed it.

Cordelia turned to Esta. "Once we have the dagger, you'll take us to the other artifacts. I'm sure you understand what a waste of time and energy it would be for you to try to run."

Esta stared at her without replying, but even Maggie could read the defiance in her expression.

"We already know where y'all are going and what your plans are," Cordelia reminded Esta. "If you try to leave, there ain't no train you could take that's faster than the telegram I'll send to the network. Antistasi all across this country'll be waiting for you and searching for your magician friend. Something just might happen before you could reach him."

Esta's eyes lit with fury. "If you do anything—"

"What?" Cordelia gave her a small, amused smile. "You ain't in any position to make threats right now. I get that Ruth's actions made you suspicious, but Ruth Feltz ain't the Antistasi. We're not your enemy, Esta. Help us, and there ain't no reason Harte Darrigan needs to come to any harm."

Esta didn't immediately respond, but Maggie thought she likely understood exactly how stuck she was. "It doesn't seem like I have much choice," Esta said finally.

"There's always a choice," Cordelia told her, looking eminently pleased with herself. "But you gotta make the right one."

"If I help you?" Esta asked, her voice tight. "If I commit myself to the Antistasi's cause?"

"Once we have the artifacts, we'll be unstoppable. We can end the Brotherhoods' power once and for all. All the Sundren who've forced us into the shadows will live to regret their hatred."

No, Maggie thought as confusion flashed through her. *That isn't right. Revenge wasn't what any of the Antistasi's work had been about. . . . Was it?*

"We don't want to treat you like an enemy," Cordelia told Esta. "Not when you could be our ally." Then she turned to Maggie with a serious look. "I guess I should be getting back. If nothing else, we need to find the dagger, and soon. Especially if Jericho was right about seeing some kind of guard from St. Louis at the show."

"What?" Maggie's head whipped around. "You don't mean Jefferson Guard?"

"May could be that's what he called them," Cordelia said. "It happened earlier today. It must have slipped his mind to tell you, considering everything else that's happened." She finally tucked the small pistol away.

"If there are Guardsmen in Denver, it means the Society knows we're here," Maggie said. Suddenly nothing seemed as important as getting to Jericho. She turned to her table and started collecting as many of the devices and formulations as she could. She might need them all to get him out of there safely.

"What're you doing?" Cordelia asked.

"I just pushed Jericho out the door and straight into a trap," Maggie said, counting the incendiaries as she filled her pouch. "I'm coming with you."

"*I'll* take care of Jericho," Cordelia said.

Maggie looked up. "No, I have to—"

"I know my way around the show. No one will notice me. You, on the other hand . . ." Cordelia looked her up and down, and Maggie felt

LISA MAXWELL

her cheeks warm with the implication that the sharpshooter found her wanting. "You'd only draw attention and make things even more dangerous for him."

"But—"

"No. You'll stay here and make sure Esta doesn't forget where her loyalties should lie," Cordelia decided. "*If* you think you can handle that much."

"I can handle it," Maggie said through clenched teeth.

"Good." Cordelia adjusted her hat in the hazy mirror. "You know, Margaret, for a second there, I really thought you might accept Jericho's offer to up and leave. I thought maybe you'd forgotten what you have at stake in all of this."

Something in Cordelia's voice sent a trickle of foreboding down Maggie's spine. "What is that supposed to mean?"

"Nothing much," Cordelia said. "But I'd watch yourself, if I were you. The Professor has already started to wonder if his trust in you has been misplaced."

"The *professor*?" Esta sat up a little straighter. "What professor?"

Maggie ignored Esta. "I didn't realize you were in contact with him," Maggie told Cordelia, trying to remain calm. But the room swam a little as she realized what that meant. What the Professor might already know.

"He ain't too happy with your recent silence," Cordelia said, looking far too satisfied with herself. "Don't worry, though. I've assured him that all's well." She gave a small shrug. "Of course, that was before I learned that y'all had lost the necklace. If I were you? I wouldn't give me any other reason to doubt your loyalty—not unless you'd like him knowing. Now, if you'll pardon me, I need to be getting back. We wouldn't want to let Jericho go off unsupervised. He might start thinking about leaving again or doing something else you'd regret."

HIS FATHER'S SON

1904—San Francisco

Harte ignored the ache in his head and in his leg as he considered what to do with the boy—his brother—and how to get out of the basement storeroom. He had to get back the artifacts that had been taken from him, and to do that, he had to find his father. Maybe the boy could help with that.

Squatting down until he was eye level with the child, Harte leaned in as though he had a secret. "You know, I could do a really wonderful trick if I had more space," he said, hating himself for the duplicity. But it would be far easier to have the child show him the way out than to risk taking a wrong turn in the building. For now the child seemed to like him. He'd use that—even if the boy ended up hating him later. "Would you like to see another one?"

The child nodded, his expression bright and hopeful.

"Do you know where we might find a little more room?" Harte asked. "This cellar's awfully cramped. There's no way an elephant would fit in here."

"An elephant?" the boy breathed.

Harte ignored the pang of guilt he felt and leaned in a little to sink the hook. "I think I might manage to conjure one up, *if* I had the room for it." He paused, pretending to think. "We would need to get outside, but I don't know the way. . . ."

"I do!" The boy took Harte's hand and began tugging him out into a corridor that was little more than a dirt-packed tunnel lined with dry goods and supplies. There was no real light there, except the daylight that spilled from the open doorway at the top of a steep set of steps.

At the foot of the steps, Harte had to pause to catch his breath. If he'd been denying his situation before, the fact that he felt winded and tired from walking such a short distance forced him to realize the truth. He was sick. He could have happily climbed back onto that filthy makeshift pallet and rested, but he knew implicitly that this was his one chance at freedom.

Sammie put his finger to his mouth to quiet Harte, who hadn't said a word since they'd stepped out of the storage room.

"Is your father up there?" Harte whispered, straining his ears for some sign of what might be waiting for him above as he gathered his strength. His whole body felt hot and cold at the same time, and his muscles ached.

The boy nodded, and his expression was suddenly shadowed. "In his shop." His small, feathery brows drew together in an expression of worry. "I wasn't supposed to talk to you. He'll be angry when he finds out. Especially about the"—Sammie paused, clearly still nervous—"about the *magic*."

"He never has to know," Harte told the boy solemnly. "If you don't tell him, neither will I." He made a cross over his heart and held up a hand in an oath.

The boy looked doubtful, but interest seemed to win over caution.

At the top of the steps, Harte found himself in a short hallway that connected the store at the front of the building to the exit at the rear. Sammie motioned that Harte should follow him toward the back of the building, where the exit waited. Harte started to follow, but voices from the store drew his attention.

Hearing his father's voice made Harte pause, but when his father began to laugh, it flipped a switch of sorts. Before Harte even realized what he was doing, his feet were carrying him toward the storefront and the source of his father's voice. The boy tried to tug Harte back, whispering urgently that it was the wrong direction, but Harte wasn't listening.

He didn't bother with stealth. He simply stepped into the main room of the store like he owned it.

Immediately, Harte was surrounded by the scent of dry goods and dust. The walls were lined with wooden shelves that held glass jars filled with flour and sugar. One wall was taken up by a large cabinet that held a variety of tools and bolts of fabric.

This was no doubt his father's store, and from the look of things—the gleaming glass and wood in the shop, the shelves stocked with all manner of expensive inventory—the old man had a well-established business. A *thriving* business. This realization only stoked the fire of Harte's anger that much more. He felt like he was looking through a haze, though the blurring of his vision might also have been from the fever. Even with his entire body aching, he took another brazen step into the shop, daring the two men at the counter to ignore his presence.

At first Samuel Lowe didn't realize that he and his customer were no longer alone. He was weighing out some dark sugar on a large scale, and it was only when the customer he was helping lifted his gaze toward the rear of the shop that his father looked as well. When he saw Harte standing there, his face drained of color.

His father's shock lasted for only a moment. As soon as he saw Sammie standing behind Harte, Samuel Lowe's nostrils flared and his eyes narrowed. But Harte was no longer a child, and the instinctive, reflexive fear that sparked within him drained away quickly. He moved squarely into the center of the shop, daring his father to ignore him.

To Harte's surprise, his father did just that. Samuel Lowe turned back to the customer, an older man with silvery hair, and continued to wrap up the contents of the scale. His father took his time as he finished securing the parcel before handing it over, then waved the customer off without taking payment. Once the customer was gone, he finally returned his attention to Harte, and his expression had transformed into something more familiar—a mask of barely leashed rage.

Harte had seen that expression on his father's face too many times as a child. Then, he had never known what would be the right move—to run and hide, or to stand and protect his mother. Now, he didn't so much as blink. He doubted there was anything this man could threaten to take from him that Harte hadn't already given up, tossed away, or lost for himself.

"You shouldn't be here," his father said, but he wasn't addressing Harte. His gaze had focused on the spot behind Harte, where Sammie stood. "You were to wait in my office, practicing your figures."

"Don't blame the boy," Harte said, putting a protective arm around the child. "If someone hadn't done such an abysmal job of tying the ropes, I'd probably still be secured in that cellar you put me in. Was it one of your lackeys at the restaurant who tied me up? Or was that particular incompetence all yours?"

His father didn't answer, but Harte saw when the barb hit its mark. "It was for your own good." A line Harte had heard far too many times as a child. "If the Committee found you—"

"Nothing you ever did to me or my mother was for our good. Last night wasn't any different," Harte said, cutting the old man off.

"Last night?" His father looked confused. "The raid on the restaurant happened two days ago." The coldness in his father's eyes gave Harte the uncomfortable feeling that he wasn't lying.

Two days? He'd lost two days.

"You should be grateful I didn't let the watchmen take you," he sneered.

"Somehow, I doubt that," Harte said. He took a moment to look around the shop. "What was your plan, anyway?" he wondered. "I'm surprised you didn't already dispose of me."

His father clenched his jaw. "Merchant ships are always in need of new crew, and there was one about to leave. But then you came down with the fever."

"How very caring of you to let me recover before sending me anyway," Harte mocked, even as he felt his skin ache. The very mention of the fever seemed to have reminded his body of how terrible he felt.

"They don't take sickness on board." His father ground the words between his teeth. "I couldn't risk anyone tracing you back to me. The Vigilance Committee has the whole city on edge with talk of the plague, but at least right now they're focused on blaming the Chinese. I wasn't about to give them the opportunity to quarantine this building. It would ruin me."

"So you were planning to keep me down there indefinitely?"

"You would improve or you wouldn't," he said with a shrug.

"Well, I'm afraid you won't be able to ship me off now," Harte said, trying not to look half as awful as he felt. "I'm not going anywhere without the Dragon's Eye, and I'm *definitely* not leaving without the other items you stole from me."

"I stole nothing," the old man said. "Those items do not belong to you. They simply confirmed what I have known since you were a boy—you were never going to be anything more than a common criminal. When I figure out who you've taken them from, I'm sure I'll be handsomely rewarded for their return."

"You will return what belongs to me, and you will hand over the Dragon's Eye, or I will take *everything* from you." Harte put his hand on the boy's shoulder and felt an echo of Seshat's satisfaction when his father's eyes widened.

"If you think I'd let you—"

"Try me." Harte felt the boy trembling now, the birdlike bones of his shoulder fragile beneath his hand. "Or . . . you could help me retrieve the item I came for. Help me, and for your son's sake, I will let you keep your pathetic life and all you've built."

"Even if I believed your lies, I can't help you. The Committee won't give up the crown."

"I wasn't planning on asking for it."

"I won't help you steal it either," Samuel Lowe said. "If that piece goes missing, and they trace what you've done back to me, I'll lose everything anyway."

"What if I can keep you safe?" Harte asked. "I can make sure the Committee won't ever touch you. Your pathetic little life can continue on as it is now."

His father's expression flashed with understanding, and Harte could see the hatred warring with indecision. "You can't make such assurances. . . ."

"You of all people know that I can," Harte told him. Even though he wanted nothing more than to destroy Samuel Lowe, Harte would keep his word. Harte would leave his father untouched if it meant protecting the boy. "You know what I'm capable of. Help me, and I can make sure you keep the life you've built here. Or don't, and I will gladly tear it apart. Either way, I *will* get what I came here for."

Harte saw the exact moment when his father relented. "Fine. I'll take you to the crown, and then you'll see how impossible it is."

"You'll also give back the belongings you took from me," Harte added.

"After," his father said.

"No—" Harte began to argue, but his father held up a hand.

"Once I'm assured that you haven't done anything foolish to put me at risk, we'll discuss those other pieces. Until then, I'll keep them as insurance against you double-crossing me," his father said. "This is my offer. Take it or leave it."

Harte considered his options. Perhaps it was another trap, but accepting his father's terms would get him one step closer to retrieving the Dragon's Eye. Even if it was a trap, Harte had some insurance of his own.

He put his hand on the boy's shoulder. "Fine," he agreed. He would win one way or the other.

"Leave my son," Samuel Lowe commanded, eyeing Harte's grip on the boy. "He's not to be a part of this."

"I'm afraid he's already a part of this, and I find that I require some insurance of my own." Harte glanced down at the boy, and when he noticed the fear in the child's too-familiar gray eyes, he knew himself for what he truly was. A bastard. An abomination.

Truly his father's son.

And if Harte felt his resolve softening as he looked at the boy? If he felt the beginnings of regret for what would happen to the child once he was gone? He would not give in. He *couldn't*. This time, he would not allow himself to lose sight of what was most important: Retrieving the artifacts. Finding Jack and the Book. Giving Esta a chance at a different future.

Even with the small victory of his father's agreement, though, Harte still worried. He didn't like how quiet Seshat had become. He was used to her mockery and to her constantly testing the boundary between them. He'd expected it, especially as he drew closer to obtaining the artifacts that could end her, but instead, she remained silent.

With every passing second, Harte's legs felt heavier, and he was having more trouble holding back the shivering that threatened to rack his body. He'd grown so weak over the past couple of days of confinement. It would have been easy enough for Seshat to rise up and breach his defenses. But she hadn't. Because Seshat knew she had to allow this—to allow *him*—to find the stones. Because his promise to Esta was the only thing keeping Harte from curling up somewhere, from *giving* up and letting whatever this illness was take him—and Seshat along with him.

Harte did not mistake Seshat's silence for acquiescence, though. He didn't trust it. Instead, he reminded himself—and Seshat—that he needed the artifacts. Without them, he would not return to Esta . . . and that was the thing they *both* desired most of all.

THE PROFESSOR

Only once before had Esta ever been in a situation that had seemed impossible to escape. She'd been lashed to a chair in Professor Lachlan's penthouse library, adorned with the five artifacts, and everything she'd once believed about her life had been crumbling around her. Maybe the Antistasi in Denver hadn't tied her to a chair, but she still felt every bit as trapped. Her free will had been obliterated by Maggie's formulation, and there was nothing Esta could do to take the information back now that she'd given it to them. Worse, she could not let go of one word Cordelia had said before she'd left.

"Who is the Professor, Maggie?"

Maggie turned to Esta. "What?"

"Cordelia said that there was a professor you've been in contact with," Esta pressed. "Who is he?"

For a second it looked like Maggie would try to lie to her, but then she relented. "I don't know who he is, exactly. I don't think he's actually a professor." She frowned. "Not like you're *actually* a thief. It's what everyone calls him because he knows so much about the old magic."

"He's in New York, isn't he?" Esta asked, knowing already what the answer would be.

"Yes, but . . ." Maggie looked suddenly more alarmed. "You know of him?"

Esta ran her finger along the scar on the inside of her wrist once more. Its sudden appearance had told her that Nibsy still planned on using her, but she hadn't considered that Nibsy could be involved with the Antistasi.

But I should have.

"What does he have on you?" Esta asked, instead of answering Maggie's question.

Immediately, Maggie's eyes widened and fear darkened her expression. "I don't know what you mean."

"Yes, you do." Esta took a step toward Maggie. "He's holding something over you, something so big that you decided to stay here with Cordelia and me instead of going off with North like I *know* you wanted to."

"I didn't—" Maggie's voice broke, betraying her once more.

"You *did,*" Esta said, looking almost sympathetic. "It was right there, plain as day on your face, how much you *wanted* to say yes to him. But you didn't. You let Cordelia threaten you. Why?"

Maggie was shaking her head. "I can't . . . I'm not supposed to—not even Jericho knows about it."

"But Cordelia does," Esta pressed. "You didn't know that, though. Did you?"

Maggie looked completely miserable. She lifted her eyes to Esta, but still didn't explain.

"If Cordelia is working with this professor of yours, Maggie, you're in bigger trouble than you think."

"You can't know—"

"I *do* know. The man I told you about, the one who raised me?" Esta said, interrupting. "We called him Professor Lachlan. I would bet everything that they're the same person." Maggie was still shaking her head to deny it, but Esta wouldn't allow her to. "Think about it, Maggie. Two people who call themselves Professor, who both have deep knowledge about the old magic, and who both happen to live in Manhattan? You know I'm not lying about this," she pressed, using her situation to her advantage. "Cordelia made sure of that."

Maggie stared at her for a long, terrible moment before her face crumpled.

"Whatever he's holding over you, there has to be a way around it," Esta promised.

"There's not," Maggie whispered. "I thought I was helping, but I've made everything worse. You couldn't possibly understand."

"I *do* understand, Maggie," Esta said gently. "I know exactly how persuasive he is. He makes you feel important, like you're the only one who can help him, the only one capable of doing whatever he needs done. But he was only ever using you. It's what he does. He manipulates people, and when he's done with them, he discards them." She thought of Dolph, cold on the bar top, and Dakari falling lifeless and bloodied to the floor. But Esta pushed those memories away because she had to focus on *this* moment and especially on making Maggie understand. "He'll discard you, and he'll discard North as well." She took another step toward Maggie. "You don't have to let him, though. I can help you. We can do this—"

"I can't," Maggie moaned, cutting her off. "If I don't do what I've promised and bring you and the artifacts to New York, he'll kill Ruth and everyone else we left back in St. Louis."

"How?" Esta challenged. "He's trapped behind the Brink."

"But the Antistasi aren't," Maggie told her. "They're *his*."

"What do you mean?" Esta asked, trying to make sense of Maggie's fear. "The Antistasi are ancient—you said that yourself."

"The stories are, yes, but the network Cordelia's been talking about? *He's* the one who organized it," Maggie explained. "Maybe once the Antistasi were a loose organization, but that hasn't been the case for a couple of years now. The whole network is loyal to him. The Professor doesn't need to be anywhere close to St. Louis to hurt the people I care about there. He has plenty of others who will gladly follow his orders."

"Was Ruth following his orders too?"

"For a while," Maggie admitted. "But she grew tired of the arrangement.

She thought there was a better way to fight the Brotherhoods, so she cut him out. I was worried about her plan to break away from the larger network, so I agreed to be his eyes—his *spy*. I thought I was helping her." Maggie paused, clearly gathering her thoughts. "When you arrived in St. Louis, the Professor promised he would forgive Ruth *and* her followers if I could bring you to our side. I sent him a message when we left St. Louis to let him know I was with you and that we had two of the artifacts. But after Harte took the stones, I didn't tell him they were gone. I thought I could get the dagger instead. I hoped it would be enough to replace what I'd lost. When Cordelia tells him—"

"We can stop her before that happens," Esta said.

"It's probably already too late," Maggie said, sounding deflated and resigned. "Cordelia probably went straight to the telegraph office. He might already know—" Her voice broke, and she buried her face in her hands.

"Maybe, but I don't think so. Cordelia wouldn't put herself at risk by telling the Professor anything before she has the dagger in hand," Esta said. "What if she failed to retrieve it? She'd be in the same position you're in right now."

"I don't know," Maggie said.

"Fine. What if it *is* already too late?" Esta asked. "If that's the case, we don't have anything else to lose. But if I'm right? We still have time, Maggie. We can get ahead of this."

Maggie didn't answer immediately. She turned away and went to the window, looking out over the city streets instead of at Esta.

"Help me," Esta pleaded. "I wasn't lying about Seshat, Maggie. If I can't bring the artifacts together, if I can't control her power, then Seshat *will* destroy the world. She almost succeeded back in St. Louis. If we can stop Cordelia from alerting the network, we can get the stones. Help me, and I'll do whatever I can to make sure the Professor can't hurt you or anyone you love. I promise."

Esta waited a moment, but Maggie didn't respond. *"Maggie?"*

"Something's happening." She waved Esta over. "I *know* that guy. I saw him in St. Louis. He was there that night of the ball, in the Festival Hall."

Beneath the window was a long line of carriages and police wagons. With them were a half dozen of the Jefferson Guard and a group of marshals.

And watching over them all was Jack Grew.

As though he sensed them watching, Jack went very still and then turned to look up at their window. Esta pulled Maggie out of sight and motioned for her to be quiet. She eased the curtains back again, just enough to take another look. The last time she'd seen Jack had been in the Festival Hall. He'd been attacking Harte. Or, rather, the thing inside of him had been attacking the power inside of Harte. *Thoth.*

If Jack was there, it meant trouble. *Big trouble.* But it also meant a second chance, Esta thought suddenly. If Jack was in Denver, then so was the Book, and that meant there was a possibility she could leave Denver with both the Book *and* the Pharaoh's Heart in her possession. It would take finesse—and it would take convincing Maggie to abandon her commitment to the Antistasi and join her.

"If Jack Grew is here, he knows the Thief isn't dead," Esta said. Then she looked Maggie straight in the eye. "I know you care about your sister, and I know you don't want to believe anything I told you today, but if Jack Grew and the Jefferson Guard are here, things are worse than we suspected. They're here for us. Whatever threat the Professor might be holding over you, North is definitely in danger right now. We *have* to get to the show before they do," Esta said, telling Maggie the one thing she knew the other girl needed to hear. Luckily, it also happened to be true.

A WICKED BIT OF MAGIC

1902—New York

Cela Johnson had been trying to take in the dart of a dress for the last thirty minutes. It should have been an easy enough job, simple compared to the intricate beadwork on the costumes she'd once worked on at Wallack's. *Before all this.* But *before* felt like a lifetime ago. Considering how she'd up and taken off without notice, Cela knew she'd never work there—or in any of the white theaters—again.

The needle slipped and pierced her thumb, and Cela hissed in a breath, sucking at the wound for a second or two and tasting the copper of her own blood. She was never clumsy with a needle and thread, but it had been nearly impossible to concentrate ever since that Italian girl had come sweeping in—and then right back out—without saving Jianyu, as they all had hoped she would.

Though Cela had to admit that he did look a little better since Viola had used her magic on him. His color wasn't so ashen and his skin wasn't as cool to the touch, but Jianyu still wouldn't wake. Viola hadn't said that she would return, and there'd been no sign of her for days. And Cela had so many questions. . . .

Neither Cela nor Abel were quite sure what they should be doing about the ring Jianyu had been looking for. Somehow it didn't seem quite their business, and yet Cela couldn't shake the notion that she was supposed to keep looking for it. She was already involved, after all, even if she still couldn't remember why she'd agreed to take Darrigan's mother. She'd accepted the ring as payment, and she'd done so without questioning how a stage magician—even one as popular as Harte Darrigan—could have afforded such a thing.

Jianyu was only hurt now because Cela had accepted the ring and he'd been sent to watch out for her. But for Cela it was more than a simple case of what was owed. Before Abel had come back from the dead, Jianyu had become a friend. He'd trusted her with the truth of the ring when he could have lied about its power, and she'd promised him that she would help him find it in return. Cela Johnson wasn't going to back out now. Hadn't her Nan always said a promise spoken had to be kept? Well, she'd spoken all right. She just didn't know what she was supposed to do next, and she especially didn't know what she was supposed to do if Jianyu never woke up.

Outside the open window, a carriage rattled by, but instead of proceeding down the road, it came to a stop a little ways beyond the house. There wasn't anything special about the sound of it, but something stirred in Cela. She put aside the mending she'd been trying to do and went to the window, but the carriage had stopped beyond her view.

Rubbing at the back of her neck, Cela gave herself a moment to stretch. The room was too warm, and the scent of sickness was thick in the air, but she didn't trust leaving Jianyu alone, even if he wasn't in any shape to go moving on his own. If he woke, she wanted to be there. If he didn't wake, well, she wanted to be there for that as well.

A moment later she heard voices from below, soft and urgent, and then footsteps sounded on the stairs. Cela stepped in front of the bed, even though she couldn't have done much more than poke at the intruder with her needle, but the door opened to reveal Viola. The girl was dressed every bit as plainly as she'd been the first time she visited, but now her eyes were ringed with dark circles, like maybe she hadn't slept since she'd failed to save Jianyu either. When she stepped into the doorway, a white man filled the space she'd just vacated. He had hair the color of straw, slicked back in waves around his broad forehead, and was wearing a casual day suit tailored so precisely it practically screamed money. And money usually meant problems.

Cela nodded toward the stranger in the doorway. "Who is he?"

"Theo Barclay, miss. I'm a friend of Viola's." The man held his hat in his hands, and his mouth formed something that looked like it was trying to be a smile, but his expression remained tight and guarded. He looked every bit as uncomfortable as Cela felt with him crowding into the room.

"Why would you bring him here?" Cela asked Viola. Abel was out for the day, but he'd have a fit if he knew she'd brought a stranger to Mr. Fortune's house when they were supposed to be lying low.

"I tried to leave him behind, but you know how men get when they decide you need their help." Viola let out a frustrated sigh and gave Cela a long-suffering look, one that Cela sympathized with despite herself. "It's even worse when they have money."

Cela wasn't sure what Viola was going on about, but she had a feeling that this man's appearance couldn't mean anything good. "I thought we'd never see you again after the way you tore out of here last time. It's been two days without so much as a word." She didn't bother to stop herself from scowling.

Viola's eyes shifted toward the floor. "I'm sorry." It looked like she was swallowing her own tongue as she tried to force out the words.

"Why did you come back, anyway?" Cela demanded, her hands crossed over her chest. "It's clear you can't do him any good."

"Maybe not before," Viola said. "But now I think I can."

"What's changed?" Cela asked, trying to ignore the hope that made her feel light-headed.

"This," Viola said, pulling a small object from her skirts. She held it up for Cela to see. It was about the size of a thin cigar, halfway smoked, and seemed to be made of clay or stone. Or maybe some kind of dark-red rock.

"What is it?" Cela eyed the object, trying to figure out how it could help anything.

The white man's eyes lit up. "Where did you get—"

"Where is not important," Viola said, cutting him off with her words and a look. "What is important is this—Libitina, she's not a normal knife." Viola's full mouth pinched tight, but then she explained that the knife's blade was a wicked bit of magic—false magic, she called it, though it seemed to Cela true enough if it could cause a man's death so easily. "I was trying to heal him with my affinity, but it won't work alone. We need false magic to break false magic."

"And what about this one?" Cela glanced at the man who was blocking the doorway. "Is he some kind of wizard or something to help with your 'false magic'?"

"No," Theo Barclay said with an uneasy smile. It was the sort of wobbly smile men who hadn't grown into themselves still used on their mothers. "I'm a student, actually. Art history."

Cela couldn't stop her brows from rising. "That sounds . . ." She was about to say *pointless*, but nothing good came from speaking ugly, so she simply shook her head instead. "If you think there's something you can do, then you best get to it," she said reluctantly. She wouldn't let herself hope. Not yet.

Viola started toward the bed, but Cela suddenly had a wave of apprehension and stopped her. "You're sure this won't hurt him?"

"It shouldn't." But Viola's strange violet eyes looked unsure. She glanced up at the white man again, like she needed the confirmation.

"I've done the translations twice," he said. "It will work."

This was another gamble, Cela realized. Another shot in the dark. She hesitated a moment longer, torn and frustrated at her own powerlessness, before she finally relented and let Viola pass. It wasn't as if there was anything more she or any of Abel's friends could do for Jianyu. If Viola thought she could help, then who was Cela to stand in her way?

"You ever done this before?" Cela asked as Viola approached the bed.

"Once," Viola told her, but she didn't elaborate. "Help me get his shirt off?"

They worked together to carefully remove the shirt until Jianyu's bare chest was open to their view. When Cela removed the bandage, she saw that the wound in his shoulder hadn't changed. It was still raw and angry, still seeping blood after so many days. Behind her, Cela could sense Theo Barclay inching closer, but she tried to put him out of her mind—she only hoped he was gone before Abel returned. And that he wouldn't cause any trouble for them later.

At first Viola didn't move. She stood, staring at Jianyu. But if just looking at him could fix him, he would've been well already.

"Now what?" Cela asked, prodding Viola.

Viola glanced at her. "Now we try . . ."

The object was the shape of a cylinder, and now that she was closer, Cela could see that its surface was carved with a series of strange markings. When Viola rolled the object through the dark blood oozing from Jianyu's wound, it acted like a stamp and created a lurid trail of scarlet inscriptions across his shoulder and down over his chest.

Cela thought she had understood what it meant that Jianyu was Mageus. She'd been with him when he'd cloaked them both in his magic to escape a Bowery saloon. Back in Evelyn's apartment, she'd been caught in a siren's spell. But this was different. A strange energy filled the room, lifting the hairs on the nape of Cela's neck. Theo Barclay didn't seem as shaken as she felt, though. He was watching Viola work with bright interest, but Cela felt only deep unease. She steadied herself as Viola traced the small amulet in strange looping patterns over Jianyu's chest, and as Cela watched, the bloody runes began to glow.

PLANS TO MAKE

1902—New York

Coming back to life was not at all like waking up. There was no gentle stirring or warm satisfaction to be found in the comfort of a safe bed. Coming back to life was like surfacing through concrete. It was like being trapped in the maze of Diyu, lost between the levels of torments, unable to find the way back.

Jianyu's chest burned as though he were being flayed alive. His limbs felt like fire was running through his veins, but he was not yet at the surface. Darkness surrounded him, strangled him, even as he struggled against it. But soon the pain was nothing but noise. Soon, even through the terrible weight of it, he could begin to feel something other than the absolute certainty of death.

His eyes opened, but at first he could not see. It took minutes, maybe hours, for the world to come back to him, dim and blurred. He heard voices. Felt the pain recede as worried hands touched his skin. A pair of eyes appeared above him, and he found that he knew them.

"Viola?" Jianyu tried to form the shape of her name, but his mouth was still missing.

He had asked for Viola, had told Cela and Abel that she alone might be able to help him, but he had not been sure that she would come. Not when she had no idea of anything that had happened—not about how Dolph had been murdered or why Darrigan had done what he did. If she was here . . . If she had saved him, then truly, they might still have a chance.

"He needs water." Another voice, soft and sure. *Cela.* In the darkness between life and death, he had heard her voice coming to him from a distance, but he had not been sure whether it was real or a dream. He would likely never be able to repay her for all that she had done.

Jianyu felt something wet and cool against his face, liquid trickling down over his chin, and then his body seemed to understand what needed to be done. Suddenly he was swallowing. Gulping down the bright, cool liquid like it was the source of life itself, until he realized his body's mistake—or perhaps his body realized his—and he began coughing it back up. He barely cared that the two women leapt to fuss over him, like he was a very old or very incompetent fool of a man. His embarrassment at their fussing did not matter. He was not *dead*.

Perhaps he had wondered once or twice before what the future could possibly hold for him, trapped as he was in this country—on this island— so far from his homeland. He had wondered when he realized the truth of the Brink, and when a group of men had held him down and cut his queue, making it certain he could never return home. Often Jianyu had questioned whether the constant struggle of simply existing was worth the seemingly endless exhaustion, the endless battle. He had continued on, but he had wondered many times before what it was all for.

Jianyu had found the answer to that question as soon as he realized how desperate his injury was. As he had grown weaker, the wound constantly seeping with his blood and his life, and then later, when he fought against the ceaseless undertow that pulled him toward nothingness, Jianyu had understood that the struggle had always been worth it. Always, even in its darkest moments.

He was not *dead*. He had somehow survived, and these two women— Viola and Cela, who were so different from one another, so different from Jianyu himself—were the reason. He allowed them to cluck and fuss because he understood they needed to. He could only be grateful.

A while later, when he was dry and clothed and propped back up in the bed, Viola explained how they had solved the problem of the wound her knife had made, and Jianyu finally told her everything about what had happened in those days after the bridge. Eventually, they came to other things that needed to be said. Difficult things that belonged only between the two of them.

The atmosphere in the small room shifted, and Cela seemed to understand. She excused herself, pulling Theo Barclay out of the room along with her, so Jianyu could speak with Viola alone.

"When I told them to send for you, I was not sure that you would come," Jianyu admitted, forcing himself to meet Viola's eyes.

Viola frowned. "Why would you think something so stupid?"

"You were so angry at the gala, and I had not the time to explain." He paused, knowing these were excuses. "I also wondered if you had ever forgiven me . . . for Tilly."

Viola stiffened slightly. "What happened to Tilly wasn't your fault," she told him.

"The others were never so sure. I heard what they whispered about me, even after Dolph gave me his support," Jianyu told her, remembering those dark days after the Bella Strega's cook had been struck down by some unseen power. He had never felt as if he truly belonged to the Devil's Own, but after Tilly . . . it had felt even more impossible. He had stayed only for Dolph, because of Dolph.

"The others were fools," Viola told him, taking his hand in hers.

"Perhaps, but there were days after when you looked at me with fire in your eyes. There were days I wondered if the moment would come when my heart would seize in my chest." Jianyu squeezed her hand gently. "I know what Tilly meant to you. We all did."

Viola's gaze broke away to study their intertwined hands, and her throat worked like someone who was holding back tears. "I wouldn't have harmed you—I never blamed you."

Jianyu accepted her words, allowed the relief of them to wash over him before he spoke again. "And I do not lay any blame on you for what happened at the gala."

"I nearly killed you," Viola said, looking back up at him.

"Nearly is a great distance when it comes to dying," Jianyu reminded her. "You saved me. Now there is truly nothing to forgive."

"Tell that to the one downstairs," Viola told him, nodding toward the door. "She has knives in her eyes every bit as sharp as the one I carry."

"Both of you must lay them down," Jianyu said, feeling suddenly tired.

Viola gave an indelicate snort that reminded Jianyu of so many days sitting around the kitchen table at the Bella Strega, talking like friends— almost like family.

"Lay down your knives, Viola," Jianyu repeated. "Dolph Saunders believed that the only way to win against the Order, the only way to free the old magic, was to do so together." The memory of his old friend sent a wave of sadness through him. "You went back to the Strega?" he asked. "To get the information that saved me?"

"A few days ago, yes." Viola frowned.

"How did you find it to be?"

"Not the same, of course." Her expression darkened. "Nibsy sits at Dolph's table, and the Devil's Own look to him now."

"It is all as he planned," Jianyu told her. He'd seen it for himself when he'd been taken to the Strega as a prisoner by Mock Duck a few weeks before the gala.

"I still can't believe the little snake could have done all of this on his own," Viola said. "I still say that if Darrigan hadn't—"

"Dolph trusted Darrigan," Jianyu reminded her. "*Especially* at the end. Dolph's trust is enough for me, and so it should be enough for you as well."

Viola snorted her disagreement. "You trust too easily. So did Dolph, it seems. Now Darrigan is gone, and the artifacts with him."

Jianyu pushed away the blanket and swung his legs over the side of the bed. With each passing minute, he felt a little stronger. A little more like himself. He had wasted far too much time lying on his back. When he thought about all that had happened, all that had been lost and betrayed, fury coursed through him. He accepted the heat of his anger, let it buoy him. Gathering his strength, he placed his feet upon the rough rug and tested his strength.

"It was the only way," Jianyu said. "He and Esta will find the artifacts, and they shall return to us. Then we will end Nibsy together."

With some effort he pulled himself up, wobbling a little on his unsteady legs. Viola was there in an instant, offering her arm. Jianyu took it gladly, but only for a moment. Only long enough to regain his balance.

"Will we also end the Devil's Own?" Viola wondered, frowning at him. "They follow Nibsy because they believe him. They don't understand any of this."

"The Devil's Own follow Nibsy because he fills a need, *not* because they believe in him or in the world he wishes to build. They do not have the same loyalty to him as they once had to Dolph. We can use that knowledge to our advantage when the time comes." He would use his fury then as well.

"You need to rest," Viola said.

"I have rested enough," he told her. "The Order will not wait, and we have plans to make."

COMPLICIT

1904—San Francisco

As Harte followed his father through the city, he tried to formulate a plan even as he struggled to hide how awful he felt. He wasn't sure where they were, or how far from the restaurant his father's shop was, but Harte realized quickly that he was weaker than he'd first suspected, and there was a particular pain in his left thigh that shot through his hip, growing worse with every step he took. The summer breeze felt like ice against his too-tender skin, and his heart was racing unevenly in his chest. He knew that the illness was something more than a simple infection, but he pushed that worry aside to save his strength as he followed his father through the unfamiliar streets.

At first, every time his father nodded silently to someone they passed, Harte tensed, but after a few blocks, he realized that his father's reputation seemed to matter to him far too much to risk drawing attention. Besides, Harte had hold of Sammie for a reason. If he felt guilty for using the boy—his own brother—as a hostage? He pushed that guilt down deep.

They stopped at the corner of Jackson Street and Montgomery, an area defined by wide thoroughfares lined with low, two- or three-story brick buildings. Many had iron shutters thrown open to bring in the summer breezes. These were not the same tumbledown wooden structures near the docks. Nor were they surrounded by the busy open-air market stalls or rickety-looking balconies of Chinatown. This, Harte could tell, was a place where men of means did business. Neat awnings capped a few of the shops, and signs were painted in ornately curling letters to declare their proprietors.

Harte's father came to a stop in front of a large brick building. It was a bank—Lucas, Turner, & Co.—and at three stories, it was taller than some of the others that surrounded it. The first floor was made from large, light-colored stone blocks. The two floors above were brick. Wooden fire escapes ringed the top two floors, and over the arched doorway, a bronze medallion depicted Lady Justice holding her scales aloft. But she was not blindfolded. Her eyes were open, and they seemed to stare down in judgment of the people on the sidewalk below.

"The Committee's offices are on the second floor," his father said, turning to Harte. "They keep the crown in their temple on the top floor, under lock and key. It's impossible to get into if you're not a member. You'd have to get through the bank's security and then make it past the men who work in the offices above. By then, the men inside would stop you before you could even hope to open the chamber on the top floor. So you see, *impossible*. You can let the boy go now. You won't be getting the crown."

Sammie looked up at Harte with a question in his eyes—and now the fear that Harte had inspired back at the shop had grown more complete.

I'm not going to hurt you, Harte wanted to tell the child, but he couldn't make that promise. He'd already hurt the boy by using him as a pawn. He'd promised his brother magic, but in the end he would betray him, just as he'd betrayed everyone else. Harte told himself that this was how it had to be. He could not turn back, not now. He had made a promise to Esta that he would die to keep, but even Harte Darrigan couldn't convince himself that he wouldn't have regrets in the end.

"Maybe it would be impossible if I were here alone," Harte said, hardening his resolve. "But I'm not. I have you—a member—to help me."

His father blanched, confirming what Harte suspected. "You don't know—"

"But I do. Maybe if you hadn't been wearing that ring, I wouldn't have put it together, but of course you wouldn't be able to resist showing everyone the mark of your status. You didn't simply sell Cooke the crown for cash. You got yourself into their little club. It's why you were so worried that the Committee might find out you didn't turn me in immediately."

Samuel Lowe's nostrils flared slightly, the only sign that anything Harte said had struck a nerve.

"You want your son back? I want the Dragon's Eye," Harte told him. "Take me to the crown, and I'll consider handing him over."

"You'll *consider*—"

"You still have items that belong to me," Harte reminded him. "It seems only fair that I keep something of yours until mine are returned."

"Father?" The boy's voice was a question and a plea all at once.

"Enough, Sammie," his father said, snapping at the child.

Harte felt the child flinch at the sharpness of their father's tone. He bent down so that he was eye level with Sammie. "Would you like to see another trick? Perhaps I could make something disappear?" he asked, infusing mischief into his tone.

The boy looked wary, but he screwed up enough courage to jut out his stubborn little chin as he met Harte's eyes. "I *want* to see the elephant."

Harte had to choke back a laugh at the boy's insistence. "Yes, well . . ." He glanced up at the sky, which was shrouded with the same clouds that had greeted his arrival to the city, and transformed his expression into regretful disappointment. "I'm afraid it doesn't look like elephant weather today after all. Perhaps a different trick? One that your father might help us with?"

"No," Samuel Lowe said, trying to imbue his voice with its usual authority and failing to hide the tremor of fear vibrating through it.

"No?" Harte asked, a warning in his voice. "You agreed—"

"I will show you where the crown is kept, but you will make no move to retrieve it," his father said. "Not now. Not when I or my son could be considered complicit. You will give me your word. Or I will make certain that you *never* see the other items again."

Harte didn't let the threat sway him. "You're not in any position to make threats," he told his father as he stepped closer to the boy, ignoring the pang of guilt he felt. "Enough with the stalling. I'm going in one way or the other. I can either make a scene and bring you down with me, or you can help me and make this easier for everyone."

Samuel Lowe seemed to know when he'd been outmaneuvered. "You will keep your mouth shut and remain silent once we're inside. Don't draw any attention to yourself. You're an outsider here," he told Harte. "This city is nothing like the streets you grew up running wild in."

Harte doubted there was much difference. Already, he saw the similarities—secret organizations that required loyalty and gave protection for a price, residents who were afraid to cross the wrong lines. And the Vigilance Committee, a group of men who seemed as determined to root out the old magic as any of the other Brotherhoods.

He followed his father through the arched doorway and was instantly surrounded by the opulence of the bank's lobby. The walls were polished wood that gleamed in the dim light, and the floors were inlaid with marble. A high counter ran along the back side of the room, where three men dressed in crisp dark suits sat behind brass bars, working steadily.

One of the men glanced up as Harte's father approached. The two spoke in low whispers, and Harte had to stop himself from gripping the boy's shoulders too tightly. He tried to steady himself, preparing for the betrayal that was likely to come as he waited in the stuffy quiet. It felt like being inside a tomb.

The clerk kept tossing glances in Harte's direction. When the clerk's brows drew together, Harte had the sinking feeling that he'd let himself walk into a trap, but after a moment the two seemed to have come to some understanding. The clerk gave a small nod finally, and his father directed Harte to a door just left of the counter. Still unsure, Harte followed, gently tugging the boy along with him for protection.

On the other side of the doorway, a steep staircase led upward. With his leg throbbing and his entire body aching, the climb felt impossible, but Harte did what he could to keep pace. He didn't want his father to know how winded he was or how dizzy he felt when he looked up the seemingly endless stretch of steps. *Esta will be waiting,* he reminded himself as he lifted his foot to the next step.

When they reached the third floor, they came to a heavy brass door inscribed with an unusual design. The etchings in the metal reminded him of some of the alchemical symbols he'd learned in the preparation of his stage act, but he didn't recognize any specifically. His father withdrew a brass key from his vest pocket and used it to unlock the door.

Beyond the door, a darkened antechamber led into a larger space. It looked like some kind of temple.

If Harte had thought that the lobby was beautiful, this room made it seem downright plain. The chamber was a large, octagonal space capped with a high, peaked ceiling. Beneath the ceiling, a line of transom windows let in daylight, and the floor was wood, patterned in the shape of the same opened eye that Harte had seen on the ring Samuel Lowe wore. The center of the eye was inlaid with precious stones, bright blue lapis lazuli and onyx. Gilded columns surrounded the room, and they were carved into human shapes, like sentinels. Harte thought he recognized the image of Washington in one, possibly Jefferson in another, but the rest were unfamiliar to him. The chamber was like stepping into another world, and in the center of that world, atop a carved altar of granite and gold, was the Dragon's Eye.

Harte moved toward the altar, pulling the boy along with him, but his father stepped in front of him, blocking his path to the crown. "You gave me your word."

The absurdity of this statement snapped the temper Harte had been holding back. "You don't deserve my word," he said, glaring at his father. "You stole everything from my mother. You don't deserve to keep this life. You don't deserve your reputation—or your son."

The boy whimpered, clearly misunderstanding Harte's meaning, but Harte ignored him.

"You understand *nothing.*" His father shook his head, disgust clear in his eyes. "You cannot take this piece. It would ruin me. It would destroy all I've built here—and anyone who depends upon me."

"I don't particularly care," Harte told him, but his conscience had already been tugging at him, and his father's words only served to make it worse.

"Do you have any idea how difficult it was for me to get a real start in this town? New money isn't taken seriously. Even though I gave Cooke everything by selling this crown to him, I'm still pushed aside and kept from my true potential," his father told him.

"You think you're the only one who has had to build a life from nothing?" Harte asked, incredulous. "You're not the only one who has people depending on him."

"It's not the same thing," his father sneered. "You're unnatural. An abomination, and anyone who depends on you is a fool who deserves what he gets."

That was probably true enough . . . but it wouldn't keep Harte from his objective.

Harte leaned down, eye level now with Sammie. "I think it's time for our magic trick," he told the child. "Are you ready?"

"Ben—" his father warned.

"That isn't my name," Harte said, never looking up at his father. His eyes were on the boy. "Do you know that magic tricks have certain requirements?"

The boy shook his head.

"I'll tell you the one thing that no trick can work without." Harte paused for a second, because everything depended on what would happen next—and also because he'd always liked a bit of drama. He lowered his voice. "The most important part of any magic trick is the *misdirection*. Do you know what that is?"

"Don't listen to him, son," Samuel Lowe commanded.

But the boy—his *brother*—was already drawn in, entranced. His eyes had grown wide with wonder, and again Harte felt the shame of what he was about to do—but he could not turn back now. He would not allow himself to soften.

"Would you like me to show you?" Harte asked, and when the boy nodded, he began to count. "One . . . two . . ."

On the count of "three," he released the boy, giving him a gentle push straight toward his father. It worked exactly as he'd planned. As Samuel Lowe caught the child, Harte gathered all of his remaining strength and sprinted for the crown.

It was in his hands in an instant, and because he could—because Sammie was still watching with bright, inquisitive eyes—Harte made the Dragon's Eye disappear with a flourish, tucking it securely into his jacket. He barely had time to see the smile light Sammie's serious little expression before he ran for the door, but it took every last bit of his strength to keep upright as he tried not to tumble down the steps to the floors below.

A PROMISE KEPT

1904—Denver

Jericho Northwood knew that playing with time came with consequences. He'd seen that for himself. Sometimes the consequences weren't all that noticeable, but other times they were—like when he saved a man's life in Oklahoma only to have that same man try to kill him a year later. Jot Gunter should be dead, but because North had been naive enough to save him, the rancher had lived to become an enemy.

What Esta was talking about doing, though, was a lot more than the handful of hours North's watch could give him. If she was truly able to go back years, she could change a whole lot of things. The effects of her meddling could ripple out in ways none of them could predict. North might have liked to think of his concerns as noble, but in truth, there were parts of his life that Jericho Northwood didn't want changed.

But he'd made Maggie a promise. If she wanted him to get the dagger from Pickett, then that was exactly what he'd do. As for after? He still wasn't sure.

Pickett's tent was on the far end of the performers' encampment, which suited North just fine. It meant fewer people would notice his visit and there was less of a chance that someone would interrupt. He snagged the half pint of whiskey he'd kept in his bunk, and when he was sure no one was looking, he put in the tablet Cordelia had given him earlier, so it would have time to dissolve. Then he gave the bottle a shake to be sure. He'd probably only get one chance at this.

If Pickett was surprised by North's visit, he didn't show it. The cowboy offered North a seat and welcomed his offer of a swig of whiskey. North told Pickett that it was a thank-you for saving his life. If he had any misgivings at all, he focused on Maggie instead.

After Pickett was done, North lifted the bottle to his own mouth and pretended to drink. By the time he'd lowered it and wiped his mouth with the back of his hand, the change in Pickett's expression told North the drug was working.

North allowed Pickett to talk for a few minutes about pointless things—horses and the weather. When their conversation turned to how Pickett felt every time he had to enter the arena to catcalls and slurs, how every performance he had to prove that he was more than the names they called him, North knew the other cowboy was ready.

Still, North wasn't completely without feeling. He'd seen the effect the formulation had on Esta. Taking a man's self-control was about the lowest thing a person could do. *You promised,* North told himself as he leaned forward and propped his elbows on the table between them.

"So I hear tell that you have a piece that's pretty impressive to see. . . ."

North left Pickett's tent not long after, with his legs feeling unsteady beneath him. He probably should've stayed with Pickett until the drug wore off completely, but he had to get to Maggie. It didn't matter that he'd left angry and hurt, not with what he'd just learned. He had to warn her.

North was so focused on getting back to his girl that he didn't even hear the person shouting his name at first. Even once he realized that one voice was louder than the rest of the usual background buzz of the grounds, it didn't register that the voice was calling for him, especially since the name they were calling wasn't the one he'd been born with. But then it clicked. For a moment North considered ignoring whoever it was. But the voice was getting louder and more insistent, which meant whoever wanted him wasn't giving up. When he glanced over his shoulder, North saw Aldo, the manager of the grounds, scurrying after him, waving for him to stop.

North had the sudden, uncanny sense that he needed to get out of there, but the grounds manager was one of the few people he couldn't easily ignore, and the person with Aldo was definitely one of the others: Clem Curtis, one of the brothers who owned the show. North cursed silently to himself, but he slowed his steps to get the meeting over with.

"Mr. Aldo," North said, lifting a finger to the brim of his hat and trying not to look half as impatient and frustrated—or nervous—as he felt.

Aldo was a broad-shouldered man whose paunch had won the battle against the waistband of his trousers years ago. His light hair curled around the base of his neck, and sandy stubble shadowed his jawline. North hadn't liked Aldo when he'd been forced to ingratiate himself with the man to get hired, and he liked him even less now.

"Something I can help you gentlemen with?" North asked, trying to appear indifferent at their interruption.

"Mr. Curtis here wanted to meet you," Aldo said.

"Me?" North asked, confused. He tried to make his surprise appear as interest, but mostly he felt uneasy. He would have preferred to remain unnoticed. "Can't imagine why," he said, falling into an affable, aw-shucks persona that he hoped would get him by.

"I've been hearing good things about you, Robertson," Curtis said, using North's assumed identity. "Aldo here says you've made quite a mark for yourself as a hard worker since you started."

"It's only been a couple of days now," North said, feigning humility.

In actuality, he was getting more nervous with each passing second. There was no reason for anyone to have noticed him. He hadn't been working any harder than anyone else—he'd made sure of it, so as not to stick out.

Tucking his hands into his pockets, he lifted his shoulders, clearly embarrassed by the attention. He used the movement to mask what he was really doing—maneuvering his pocket watch, flipping open the glass face . . . in case.

"But you've done well," Curtis said. "I probably don't need to tell you how hard it is to find good workers these days. I thought maybe you'd want to stay on with us permanently."

"Oh, I don't know," North said, not yet sure whether to feel relieved. His thumb hesitated over the dial of the watch. "That's a fine offer, but I'd have to consider—"

"What's there to consider?" the Curtis brother asked. "You don't already have another job lined up, do you?"

"Not exactly," North told him.

"A wife to support?"

"Mr. Robertson here isn't married," Aldo confirmed, looping his thumbs through his suspenders as he rocked on his heels. "He already assured me of that."

"Then what's holding you back?" Curtis asked.

"I can't think of anything at all," North admitted. There was a part of him that could almost imagine the life Curtis was proposing—traveling from place to place. Seeing the country while he spent his days with the horses he loved. Living out in the fresh, clean country air . . .

But it was an impossible dream. North was already on a path, and it didn't lead out into the wide world. It led to Maggie, which meant it would be guided by principles he'd already committed himself to long ago, maybe even before he could have possibly understood what they were.

Curtis didn't need to know that, either, though.

"I guess I'd be a fool not to accept," North told the men. It didn't matter that he wasn't planning on following through.

"Then it's settled." Curtis extended his hand. "I'll have Aldo draw up a contract, and we'll make it official."

It took everything North had to return Curtis' smile. He'd never have a life like the one Curtis proposed, one where all a man had to do was shake a hand, make a deal, earn a living doing what he loved. Without questions. Without fear. The best North could hope for was to keep fighting for the life he might have one day with Maggie, if he was lucky enough. He took Curtis' hand, shaking on the deal he'd never keep.

He wasn't really surprised at how tightly Curtis grasped his hand. There were a lot of men who thought they could prove themselves through the strength of their handshake. North was surprised, though, when Curtis' other hand whipped out to latch onto his wrist. Before North could stop him or pull away, Curtis was ripping back the sleeve, exposing the dark snake inked into the skin of his wrist. He tried to fight free, but Aldo already had a pistol out and was aiming it directly at him.

"Good work, Aldo," Curtis said as a trio of other men came seemingly out of nowhere to take North by the arms. They pulled his hands from his pockets and wrenched them behind his back. In the process North's watch slipped from his fingers and landed on the ground as the men restrained him.

He looked at Aldo, pleading silently, but the other man turned away.

"I think we have the fella you were looking for," Curtis said.

"Nice work, Curtis." The voice was familiar . . . but North couldn't place why at first. Then Jot Gunter was there in front of him, shaking Clem Curtis' hand like they were old friends. He noticed the watch on the ground, and with a smile tugging up the edges of his heavy mustache, he crushed it beneath the heel of his boot.

No. No. No. No. No—

But it was too late. The watch was beyond his reach.

"He's been going by the name Jerry Robertson," Curtis told the men. "I noticed him around the other day, and when I heard about the Syndicate looking for a redheaded cowboy with two different-colored eyes, I had a feeling this might be the one."

Gunter came a little closer and examined North with squinted eyes. North refused to blink, but he couldn't help noticing that Gunter had a silver medallion on his lapel. It looked familiar—like the ones the Jefferson Guard wore back in St. Louis to detect illegal magic in the area.

"I believe it's him all right," Gunter said. "Jericho Northwood. You're supposed to be dead."

North let the pain and anger of losing his father's watch chase away the fear, and he gave his old boss a cold look. "Sorry to disappoint, Mr. Gunter, but it appears I'm a hard man to kill."

Gunter only stared at him. "We'll see about that." Then he turned to Clem Curtis. "Good work finding him for us."

"It was an honor to be of service," Aldo said, inserting himself between the two men.

Gunter glanced at the grounds manager and then dismissed him in the next breath as he returned his attention to Curtis. "The Syndicate won't forget this. We take care of our own."

The blond Curtis brother puffed up beneath the praise.

"Does anyone else know of this situation?" Gunter asked.

"Only a few people I trust implicitly," Curtis assured him. "Like you requested."

"Good," Gunter said. "And the arrangements for this evening's performance?"

"Your men will have complete access to the grounds," Aldo assured him.

Gunter gave Aldo a dismissive glance. "The president's man will be here this evening to supervise the raid personally. I trust we won't have any trouble."

"Of course not," Curtis told Gunter. "What would you like us to do with this one?"

"The secretary is set to arrive any minute now. I expect he'll want to interview this maggot for himself. I'll let him decide what's to be done with him after," Gunter said with a satisfied smile.

North struggled against the hold the other two men had on him, but it wasn't any use. They were too strong, and he was too outmanned.

Curtis glanced at the men holding North. "Take him over to the supply tent and keep him contained there. No one talks to him until the secretary arrives."

SIGILLUM

Viola paused on the small landing outside Jianyu's door, not quite sure what she was supposed to do next. From the way he'd pushed her out of the room, she doubted he wanted her to wait. He wanted to dress himself, and she had the sense that he needed to be left alone, to walk on his own power down the stairs. She'd been around enough men to know that they usually preferred not to test their weaknesses with an audience.

She realized suddenly that she still had the seal in her hand. Even once the bloody printed runes had started to glow, even once Jianyu woke and began looking more like himself, Viola had kept it tight in her fist, as though releasing it might somehow break the strange power it held. The small stone cylinder still felt oddly cool against her palm—a mark of the corrupted ritual magic it contained.

Thank the heavens it worked.

Viola hadn't been completely sure that it would. She'd hoped, of course, because she hadn't wanted to go back to Nibsy Lorcan, but knowing such things wasn't Viola's strength—it had been Dolph's.

Her old friend hadn't been like the other Bowery bosses, who attacked first and considered later. They'd taken the seal and many other objects from J. P. Morgan at the Metropolitan because Dolph had known that this small, unassuming object would be needed to steal the Book. He made a study of such things, because for Dolph Saunders, *knowing* had been the most important part of the battle.

But Dolph hadn't known about Nibsy, Viola thought, as a wave of grief and fury rose within her. If Jianyu's story was to be believed—and she had no reason to doubt it—not even Dolph Saunders had seen Nibsy's betrayal coming. He'd trusted the boy, and he'd paid the price. They all had.

Viola examined the stone seal, the markings on it still darkened by Jianyu's blood, and then she tucked it away as she said a silent prayer of thanks that she had kept it. She said one more prayer for Jianyu's continued health, and then she made her way down the stairs.

In the kitchen, Viola found that Theo had not yet left, as she had expected him to. He was sitting at the small table, studying the volume she'd taken from Dolph's apartment earlier that day—Dolph's notebook. Viola still couldn't believe Theo was there at all, much less that he'd waited so long. He *shouldn't* be there. It was a sweet sort of torture to be near him, to both feel closer to Ruby through his presence and to be reminded of what she could never have.

Cela was sitting next to Theo, peering over at the notebook as he turned the pages. Her hands were wrapped around a cup of something warm and steaming. At the sound of Viola's entrance, she looked up and stood all at once, a small burst of panic breaking out in her expression. "Is he—"

"He's up," Viola said. "He'll be down soon."

"I should go help him," Cela said, already moving in the direction of the stairs.

Viola caught her arm gently, felt her flinch at the touch. "He's well now, Cela. Let him be strong enough for this."

Cela looked like she disagreed, but she relented. "You want some coffee?" she asked, pulling away from Viola. "I put some on already."

"Please," Viola said gratefully.

She went to the table and took a seat near Theo. "You find anything interesting?"

Cela offered her the cup of steaming coffee before returning to her own seat on the other side of Theo.

"This journal is remarkable," Theo told her, frowning. "The collection of languages here alone—French, German, Spanish, even Latin. It's astounding that these are all in the same hand." He glanced up at her. "It doesn't seem possible that your friend could have written all of this on his own."

"Dolph Saunders had many talents," Viola said tightly, trying not to bristle at Theo's presumptions. She took a sip of the coffee to keep herself from saying anything else. It was burnt and bitter, but the bite of it settled something inside her.

Theo turned another page. "From the looks of it, he was brilliant," Theo said, sounding more than a little surprised by this.

"And why wouldn't he be?" Viola asked, this time unable to keep the reproach from her tone.

"I don't know," Theo said, frowning. "He lived in the Bowery and owned a saloon. I hadn't expected a scholar."

"Dolph Saunders lived in the Bowery because he was unwilling to hide what he was." Viola's heart clenched with the memory of her old friend. "He chose to live among the people who needed him." Outside the law. Outside of safety.

"I would have liked to meet him," Theo told her, and she had the sense that this was more than simple politeness.

"He was a complicated man," Viola admitted, wondering if any of them—including Leena—had ever really known Dolph.

"Most of them are," Cela said, sharing a knowing look with Viola, and for the moment, some of the tension between the two of them eased. "Or at least, a lot of them like to *believe* they are."

Viola could not stop her mouth from curving in agreement.

"Methodical, too," Theo told her, seemingly unaware of the small joke they'd made at his expense. "The amount of detail in some of these notes is astounding."

Something on one of the pages caught her eye. "I know this," she murmured, touching a finger to the illustration before he could turn to the next page.

"You've seen this before?" Theo frowned up at her, looking surprised.

"Sì." Viola had seen that same strange design earlier that day in Dolph's apartment. It had been part of the painting they'd stolen from Morgan's collection, depicted clearly—though maybe in not so much detail as this—on the cover of the book Newton held beneath the tree, under a sky with two moons.

"It's some kind of sigil," Theo told her, studying the illustration. "They're fairly common in ancient art, but this is one of the most intricate I've ever seen. You're sure *this* is the one you've seen?"

"Yes," Viola murmured. "In a painting . . ." *And somewhere else?* Again, it seemed strangely familiar, and she wondered if her memory of the Book of Mysteries—hazy as it might be—had any truth to it. "In the painting, it wasn't so clear as this one," she told them.

It *was* intricate. Looking at the diagram was enough to make Viola's eyes hurt. It felt impossible to follow the lines of the various shapes as they wove into one another, interlocking and then doubling back. They seemed to have no beginning, no end. They seemed almost alive on the page.

"What's a sigil, anyway?" Cela asked, sipping her coffee and peering over to look at the page. "I've never heard of such a thing."

"Traditionally, a sigil is nothing more than a symbol, usually something like a small diagram," Theo explained. "It comes from the Latin 'sigillum,' or 'seal.'"

"It doesn't look like the seal you all used to help Jianyu, though," Cela said.

"No," Theo agreed. "Sigils are more like written emblems than objects. I've seen some before in old illuminated manuscripts—especially medieval ones—but nothing like this." He squinted as though he was also having trouble focusing on the pattern. "Often, they're meant to represent the true name of an angel or a demon."

Viola was frowning now. "Why would anyone want such a thing?"

"Because names have power," Cela said softly. Her eyes were focused on the page, thoughtful now. "Naming is a way of claiming, isn't it?

Claiming yourself, claiming what you are. Names are powerful things, even without any magic attached."

"Exactly," Theo said. "If you knew the name of a demon or an angel—the true name of it—you could control it. Or so groups like the Order would believe."

"Che pazzo," Viola said, crossing herself. Only a madman would want such a thing.

"The Order really believes they can control a demon?" Cela sounded uneasy about this idea, and for once Viola agreed with her completely.

"Maybe not an *actual* demon." Theo's mouth curved a bit, though Viola couldn't begin to see what was amusing about any of this. "Over the centuries, people have used the word 'demon' to describe pretty much anything they couldn't explain or control . . . including those with magic."

Unease made Viola pause. "Someone could use this . . . this *sigil*," she said, the word tasting heavy on her tongue, "and they could control a person's magic?"

"Possibly," Theo said, frowning. "Though I only know the theory behind these as pieces of art. I'm less familiar with their actual use."

Hadn't the notes Nibsy gave her weeks ago indicated something similar? Dolph had taken part of Leena's magic and placed it into the head of his cane to use it. To control it. He'd taken a part of *her* to control for his own. It seemed to Viola the worst sort of betrayal, and she would not have believed it of her friend if she'd not seen the evidence written out in his own hand.

Dolph's cane and Viola's blade were only two examples of ordinary objects infused with power. She'd heard tales of many more, but Viola had never understood where those objects came from. Was this strange diagram what was needed to take the magic from a person? And if so, how did it work?

"What does that say?" Viola asked, pointing to the strange markings on the page near the sigil.

"I'm not sure," Theo admitted. "I've never seen this particular language before. It could be some kind of cuneiform, or some kind of code? I'm not exactly a student of languages."

"Dolph was," Viola said, more to herself than to any of them. She couldn't help but wonder why her old friend had chosen to inscribe this page with such strange figures when he could have used any one of his other tongues. *Unless he didn't want anyone else to be able to read what he wrote.*

Perhaps Dolph had known about the coming betrayal, but the question remained: What, exactly, had Dolph Saunders been trying to hide about this image? And why had he felt the need to hide it so thoroughly?

They would never know, Viola realized. Dolph was gone, and with him the answers to this puzzle.

"There are more notes on the back," Theo said. "It seems as though someone—possibly your friend—had the same idea. There are some notes here about the plan for an experiment, but . . . the next page seems to be missing." He flipped the page over to show Viola the place where one or more pages had been torn from the binding of the notebook.

"Sounds like nothing but a bunch of trouble, if you ask me," Cela said. "Whoever wants to go stirring up demons is nothing but a fool. Some things aren't meant to be messed with." She took her mug of coffee to the sink, done with the conversation.

Viola, though, could not take her eyes from the place where pages were missing from the book, or from the writing on the back of the page that held the strange illustration. Familiar writing, and this was in English. She took a piece of paper that she'd tucked for safety in Libitina's sheath and slowly, carefully unfolded it. On the surface was Dolph's hand, clear as day, describing what he'd done to Leena, or at least describing the aftermath of his efforts.

It was the same size—the same type of paper—and when she held it up to examine it, Theo's brows drew together.

"Nibsy gave this to me," she told him, answering his unspoken question. "Before the gala. He wanted to show me proof that Dolph wasn't who I believed him to be. He wanted to turn me against him."

A movement in the doorway drew Viola's attention.

Jianyu was standing there, a frown on his narrow face. "That is what Nibsy Lorcan wanted from everyone."

A DEVIL'S BARGAIN

1902—New York

C ela turned at the sound of Jianyu's voice to find him standing in the doorway, looking nearly like himself, if only a little thinner. She stepped toward him immediately, almost reflexively, but then she stopped herself. Suddenly she wasn't sure if she was *supposed* to go to him. She'd been taking care of him for days now, but Jianyu hadn't exactly had a choice about it. He hadn't been in any position to accept or reject her help.

Now he moved into the kitchen slowly, but he was holding himself upright in a way that had Cela hesitating. As much as Cela didn't want to admit it, maybe Viola had been right to stop her from going up to him a few minutes before—it was clear he needed this moment. It was there in his eyes, the quiet satisfaction—the *relief*—he must have felt in no longer being unable. This wasn't the same man Cela had tended to in the bed upstairs, but the Jianyu she had known from before. The one who had thrown himself in front of a knife to save her life. The one who had pulled a blade from his own shoulder without so much as wincing at the pain of it.

"Where is Abel?" Jianyu asked, taking a seat next to Theo Barclay at the table.

"He's out with his friend Joshua, working on some project or another for the union they're trying to get established," Cela told him. "He should be arriving anytime now, and he'll be glad to see that you're up and about."

Jianyu's shoulders relaxed a little as Cela placed a mug of the coffee she'd made in front of him. When he hesitated, staring down at the dark liquid, Cela realized that she didn't know if Jianyu even *liked* coffee.

She started to reach for the mug. "I could boil some water for tea—"

He put his hand on her arm to stop her. "Thank you." For a long moment they just kind of looked at each other.

It felt like his thank-you was for more than the coffee. He didn't say anything, but Cela felt it nonetheless. *Thank you for not leaving me. Thank you for caring for me. Thank you . . .* It was all there.

Or maybe it wasn't. Maybe she was spinning stories in her head.

Jianyu's hand was larger than she remembered it being—*he* was larger and more solid than she'd remembered him being as well. Somehow, over the past week or so, the idea of him seemed to have shrunk in her mind as he lay sick and unmoving in that bed. Now she remembered again how tall he was, how his slenderness belied his strength.

Now Jianyu's skin felt warm against hers, and with his hand steady on her arm, Cela realized that she had not expected him to wake again. Not *really.* She certainly hadn't expected that he'd recover so quickly.

Magic, she reminded herself. It was easy to forget the truth of that when she was with him—with all of them, really. They didn't seem any different from Abel or herself—or anyone else—until they did something strange and uncanny that made the hair on her neck rise to know that there was power she didn't really understand at work in the world.

Then again, there were a lot of things Cela Johnson didn't understand about the world. Who would have guessed that the strange gathering taking place in this house's too-small kitchen would have even been possible? The Italian girl with her glittering eyes and sharp tongue, Theo Barclay, whose suit declared that he was every inch Fifth Avenue, and then Jianyu with his short-cropped hair, and herself. None of them would have ever met if not for Harte Darrigan and the blasted ring. Their worlds should have remained separate, as neatly divided as the streets of the city were, each with their small enclaves and communities. Each keeping to themselves, because *that* was how you were supposed to keep yourself and the ones you loved safe and secure. So many different worlds were colliding in that tiny room, and not a single one of those worlds was safe *or* secure, and Cela couldn't help but wonder what would come of it.

"We need to discuss what will happen next," Jianyu said, almost as though he'd been thinking the same thing. He pulled back his hand and lifted the chipped mug of coffee. He didn't ask for any cream or sugar, just took a small sip, black as it was.

It had to be bitter—probably burnt, too, considering that it had been on the stove for too long now. But Jianyu's eyes fluttered closed for a second and he smiled, the barest curve of his lips. It was a private, inward-type smile, the sort of smile that told Cela that he maybe felt the same way about coming back, like maybe he hadn't really believed it would happen either, but now that it had, he was grateful.

"Thank you," he said again, and again Cela felt those two little words held a whole lot more than what he was saying. Then he set the chipped mug back onto the tabletop, and she wondered if the moment had even happened or if she'd only been imagining that something new was building between them.

"The only thing that *needs* to happen next is for you to rest," Cela told him, her voice sounding too tart, even to herself. "Everything else can wait until you're stronger."

"Do I look so weak?" Jianyu asked, lifting his brows in a challenge.

Cela frowned. "You look . . ." He looked fine, she admitted to herself. He looked healthy and whole and better than he had in days. She let out a sigh, already knowing she was going to lose this particular battle. "Not even an hour ago, you were two steps away from death. You need to rest."

"I have already rested more than enough for an entire lifetime," Jianyu said, dismissing her concern. "The Order cannot wait, not if they truly have the Delphi's Tear in their possession." He looked to Viola.

"Nibsy believes they have it," she confirmed. "My brother must believe it too. I can't see any other reason he would be willing to include Nibsy Lorcan in whatever it is he's planning."

"You're going off the word of people that none of you even trust," Cela said, her instincts prickling. Jianyu was barely well and already he was going to toss himself into danger, and for what? For the girl who hadn't thought twice about skewering him with a knife. "This Nibsy person could be lying, for all you know. So could Paul Kelly. Either one of them could be setting you up."

"It is possible, but the fact remains that neither can be permitted to take possession of the ring," Jianyu told her—told all of them—and there was such a strength and sureness in his voice that even Cela, who would have rather seen him climb back into bed, couldn't argue with it. "We must retrieve it from the Order before they can use it to reestablish their power. Darrigan and Esta will return to us, and we must not be empty-handed."

"What, exactly, do you think you're going to do?" Cela asked, with no small amount of disbelief and more than a little worry. "Even if you *can* turn yourself into a ghost, I was at that gala. I saw what the Order's capable of."

"I agree," Theo said. "I know those men—too well, in some ways. They have money and power that make them nearly untouchable."

"We touched them before," Viola challenged. "We burned Khafre Hall to the ground and took their most precious treasures."

"You sure didn't manage to hold on to them long, though," Cela said, earning herself a sharp look from Viola.

Viola's eyes flashed, but Cela didn't care, exactly. Viola's confidence irritated her in ways she couldn't explain. Maybe it was the absolute sureness in her voice and the way she carried herself, like the world couldn't touch her. Or maybe it was that she seemed to assume all was forgiven for what had happened at the gala. As though Viola's healing Jianyu should've been enough to forgive her from nearly taking his life in the first place.

Maybe it *should* have been enough. But for Cela, who had sat by Jianyu's bed for days, who had fretted over his cooling skin and sluggish breathing, it didn't *feel* like enough. The only problem was that Cela wasn't exactly sure what *would* be.

"Cela is right. Before, we were more than two," Jianyu reminded Viola. "When we went to Khafre Hall, we had an entire team we trusted, and a leader to guide us. We can't hope to retrieve the ring as we are now. We still do not know when or where or how the ring may appear again, but clearly Nibsy and your brother know something more. We should use them as we can."

"My brother has told me nothing," Viola said stiffly, like she was almost embarrassed by this fact. "I doubt he will be any help at all."

"But Nibsy Lorcan might be," Jianyu offered.

"No," Viola said, shaking her head. "Better we kill that snake now before he can cause any more trouble."

"Funny how that seems to be your answer to everything," Cela said dryly, cutting her eyes in Viola's direction. Cela always tried to give people the benefit of the doubt. She knew too well what it was like to be judged for what she looked like instead of who she was, but Viola wasn't making the best case against the common idea that Italians couldn't be trusted with their tempers. "Throw your knife. Slice someone open. It's always the same with you."

"Cela," Jianyu said gently, but Cela could hear the reproach in his tone.

"You really forgive her so easily?" Cela asked, her throat suddenly tight. "You nearly *died*." She was more than a little mortified to hear how her voice broke.

"There is nothing to forgive," Jianyu told her. His dark eyes held such a soft sureness, a clear conviction, that Cela realized he really *wasn't* angry at Viola. More, she saw that he wanted *her* not to be angry as well.

Maybe he was right, but Cela was finding it awful hard to forgive Viola when she understood the truth of the matter—that knife hadn't been intended for Jianyu. It had been intended for *her*, and Cela doubted that Viola would've cared if *she'd* have been the one to die.

"Don't you ever get tired of being so . . ." Cela let her hand wave vaguely. "You're so damn unflappable all the time. Don't you *ever* get angry? Don't you ever just want to *scream?*"

Jianyu's mouth turned down. "Always. I am always angry." But he didn't say anything more. He didn't bother to explain, only met her eyes, willing her to understand.

Then, all at once, she did. Of course he couldn't rage and spout off. *Of course.* Jianyu was too visible in this city, just as she often was—even more so. Anger was a dangerous luxury when you had no one to stand with you, no safe place to fall.

"I didn't mean—" Cela stopped short, not knowing what she could possibly say.

"Cela's right," Jianyu said to Viola, mercifully changing the subject. "We cannot trust Nibsy, but neither can we simply remove him."

"Maybe *you* can't," Viola told him, but her gaze cut to Cela—a clear challenge. "For me, it wouldn't be so hard."

"Patience, Viola," Jianyu said. "Death is always easy. It is what comes after that is difficult. Think . . . what would happen to the Devil's Own without Nibsy's leadership? Would they follow you? Certainly they will not follow *me*. You may have forgiven me for what happened to Tilly, but for many of Dolph's numbers, it only proved that I never belonged."

Cela heard the note of something larger than sadness in his voice, and she thought that maybe she understood what had put it there. After all, she knew what it felt like to not belong where you were *supposed* to belong. She'd been reminded of that during the short stay with her aunt, and she thanked her lucky stars that Abel had come back, because he was maybe the one place where she felt she always belonged.

Here, too, she thought suddenly. She shouldn't feel that way at all, not with the strange mix of people all sitting around this table—especially not with Viola still staring daggers into her heart—but for some reason Cela felt more comfortable sitting next to Jianyu, talking through this strange business of magic, than she maybe had even with her own family at times.

Cela took Jianyu's hand before she realized what she was doing. It seemed natural somehow to reach for his hand. She told herself that it was because she still couldn't believe he was really sitting there, whole and healthy. She felt the need to touch him, if only to make sure the moment was real.

A flash of surprise and a question lit Jianyu's eyes, but then his fingers tightened around hers, and Cela realized that touching him—that reaching for him so easily—had been a mistake. She'd touched him a thousand times while he was sick without even thinking about it. But this? The small squeeze of his hand, the warmth of his skin against hers, and the sure strength of him made her too aware of things she hadn't realized she felt. Dangerous things that she had no business feeling.

She had to force herself not to pull away. She had to work hard to sit there and pretend that everything was exactly the same as it had been before.

"If we remove Nibsy now, the Devil's Own will fracture and crumble," Jianyu said, finally turning back to Viola. "You know this is true. The various powers in the Bowery will come for what is left, scavengers on the carcass of all Dolph built. We cannot allow that to happen."

Jianyu released Cela's hand then, and she felt relieved and bereft all at once. She pulled her hand back from the table, tucked it into the skirts that pooled in her lap, and ignored the way her heart felt like it might fly clean out of her chest.

"I know." Viola sighed. "I hate it, but you're not wrong. Even Mooch, even with what we did to help him, he doesn't trust me. He won't trust you, either."

"Nibsy has already offered you a new partnership," Jianyu told Viola. "It is a way back in."

"No," Viola said, all fire and vinegar. "He offered me a devil's bargain, not a partnership."

"Devil's bargain or not, I believe you must accept his offer," Jianyu said. "Allow Nibsy to believe that you are with him once more. Feed him enough information to keep him happy, and when the time is right, we shall pull back his mask and reveal him for what he truly is."

"It's too dangerous," Theo said, drawing their attention to him. He'd been so quietly watchful, and Jianyu's hand around hers had been such a distraction, that Cela had almost forgotten he was sitting right there.

"I can handle Nibsy Lorcan," Viola said, sounding suddenly insulted, where a moment before she'd been making the same argument herself.

"I'm sure you can handle damn near anything," Theo told her. "But you'd all be foolish to depend on this Nibsy fellow's information—or your brother's for that matter, Viola. If you do, you'll always be working blind, three steps behind the others. You need someone on the inside of the Order, someone who could make sure that you know more than either of them."

Jianyu tilted his head, clearly taking Theo's measure. "Where do you propose we find such a person?"

Cela knew what Theo Barclay would say even before the words were out of his mouth, because of course he would volunteer. Putting himself in such unnecessary danger was exactly the sort of thing someone would volunteer for when the world had never touched them and when they had no idea how much there was to lose.

"I can help," Theo said. "I know people. With the right incentives, it wouldn't be that difficult for me to find a contact in the Order—maybe even earn their trust."

"No," Viola said. "Assolutamente *no*. You're not getting involved with this."

"He's *already* involved," Cela pointed out. Her heart was still unsteady in her chest, and her skin felt too hot, because she understood that they were all tied up in this inextricably.

Whether they wanted to be or not.

THE EVENING SHOW

1904—Denver

The sound of the sirens clanging in the distance spurred Esta on as she and Maggie rushed toward the Curtis Brothers' Show. Jack Grew was in Denver. That was bad enough, but maybe even worse was the fact that Nibsy had been aware all along that she and Harte were in St. Louis. He'd been pulling strings that Esta hadn't even known existed. He was *still* pulling those strings, and if they didn't get to Cordelia first, Nibsy would send his network of Antistasi after the artifacts, and there was no way for Esta to warn Harte.

As awful as those developments were, the knowledge that Jack was in Denver urged Esta onward. The Book would *certainly* be with him, because there was no way Jack—or the thing that lived inside of him—would ever let the Ars Arcana out of sight. If Esta had any hope of finding a way of controlling Seshat's power without giving up her own life, it would be in the Book of Mysteries. If she could get it back from Jack, maybe she could begin to imagine a future for herself after all.

Esta pushed herself and Maggie along with her, nearly jogging the entire way to the show's grounds, but the thin mountain air made it hard to breathe. By the time they reached the edge of town, where the city fell away to the fields and mountains beyond, Esta's head was spinning.

"There are so many people," Maggie said, looking more than a little overwhelmed by the view of the crowded grounds. The evening show was clearly more popular than the afternoon.

"North was going after Pickett, so let's start with the performers' encampment," Esta told her.

Once they were on the grounds, it was easy enough for Esta to pretend confidence and blend in with the crowd that had come to watch the show, but Maggie couldn't help but look guilty. *No . . .* Maggie looked *scared*, which amounted to the same thing. While everyone else around them was smiling and appeared excited, Maggie's unease stood out like a beacon.

Esta was still wearing men's clothing, so she looped Maggie's arm through hers to escort her and offer some more support. "Relax," she murmured, pretending to be interested in the crowds and excitement. "We're going to find him. But you need to breathe."

They continued through the crowd, but as they went, Esta noticed a number of men trying to blend in among the families and couples. They were way too serious-looking for being out for a pleasant evening at the show, and if the men weren't actual marshals, they certainly moved like them.

"We need to keep moving," Esta said, pulling Maggie along steadily through the crowd.

They'd gone only a little farther, though, when Maggie stopped short. "Look at the medallions those men are wearing on their coats," she murmured. "To the left of the tent there."

Esta glanced at the trio of cowboys that Maggie had nodded toward. They all wore broad hats and the work clothes that were common for ranch hands around Denver. They also wore matching silver medallions on their jackets.

"Those men are wearing the Jefferson Guard's badges," Maggie said. "The ones they used to detect illegal magic at the fair."

"They aren't dressed like the Guard, though," Esta told her.

"Maybe they don't want to be recognized," Maggie said.

"Or maybe they're not Guard at all." Esta studied the men. "Didn't Cordelia say that more men from the Syndicate arrived today? It's possible that the Brotherhoods are working together now, maybe even sharing resources."

"That doesn't make sense," Maggie said. "The whole point of the Society wanting the necklace—the whole point of their stupid ball—was to make a show of their supremacy and put the other Brotherhoods in their place."

"I told you before, the attack on the Society likely changed things," Esta told her, considering the men. "If the two groups are working together, it means that what we did in St. Louis didn't weaken the Brotherhoods."

"You're saying that we made things worse by attacking the ball," Maggie whispered, horrified. "Our actions brought the Brotherhoods together."

"It looks like it. But we can deal with all that later," Esta said, trying to draw Maggie's attention back to the situation in front of them. "Right now we need to find North before anyone else does."

The walk to Pickett's tent seemed endless, but Esta knew they couldn't rush, not unless they wanted to draw attention. Once they were past the public areas, they picked up their pace a little, until they finally made it to the back of the encampment, where Pickett's tent was located.

When they were close, Esta heard voices coming from within and pulled Maggie back behind a nearby tent.

"What is it?" Maggie asked.

"Pickett has a visitor."

"Jericho?" Maggie asked.

Esta shook her head. "It doesn't sound like him."

She'd no sooner realized why the voice seemed so familiar when the flap of Pickett's tent opened and Jack Grew walked out. He had another man with him, the ruddy-faced blond Esta had seen that first day patrolling the show. Neither of them looked happy.

Esta cursed softly. If Jack was visiting Pickett, it meant there was a good chance he knew about the Pharaoh's Heart. Esta could only hope that if Jack had actually *found* the dagger, he would look more pleased with himself.

"Can I help you?" a voice said from behind them.

Esta and Maggie turned to find one of the buffalo soldiers standing there with a rifle slung over his shoulder. The older man's curling hair was graying around the temples of his long face, and he wore his mouth screwed up into a serious scowl.

"No, thank you," Esta said, pulling an air of confidence around her and wishing she'd thought to change into a skirt. Two women might have seemed less like a threat. "We're fine."

"You're not supposed to be here," the man said. "This here area's for performers only. Not for spectators."

"We were looking for someone," Maggie said. "A friend of ours."

His eyes were still suspicious as he turned his attention on Maggie. "Were you, now?"

"My . . . Uh . . ." She paused, like she suddenly didn't know what to call North. "My fiancé," she said finally. "He's new here, and I wanted to surprise him. My . . ." She glanced at Esta. "My brother and I wanted to say a quick hello before the show."

As lies went, it wasn't as bad as it could've been, but the man looked at Maggie, letting the silence grow uncomfortable between them. Then his expression shifted. "You don't by any chance go by the name of Margaret Jane?"

Maggie's eyes widened, and her cheeks went a little more pink. "My friends call me Maggie," she said, the words slow and careful.

"You're Jerry's girl, aren't you?"

"*Yes*," she said, her voice coming in a rush. "Yes, I am."

The older man's expression softened. "I've heard a lot about you," he told Maggie. "He told us all about how pretty you were . . . and how smart. I'm George."

Maggie shook the soldier's outstretched hand, still looking a little shell-shocked by this turn of events, but Esta wasn't letting her guard down, no matter how friendly this man seemed.

"You don't by any chance know where we could find Jerry?" Esta asked, getting to the point.

George frowned, his entire expression darkening with something that looked like regret. "I'm afraid he's gone. They took him 'bout an hour ago."

"*Who* took him?" Esta asked as Maggie went deathly still beside her.

"Aldo, the grounds manager, and Clem Curtis himself, along with a couple of other fellas I didn't recognize," George told them, shaking his head. "I'm sorry, miss. I hate to be the bearer of bad news. You know, I liked Jerry right from the start. He seemed like a good man."

"He is," Maggie whispered. "The *best* man."

"That might be," George said, "but he must have done something awful wrong to have those men acting like they were."

"He existed," Esta said darkly, realizing exactly how difficult things had become.

George met her eyes, and she saw by his expression that he understood. After a long pause he gave a small nod, like he'd come to some decision. "Let me show you where they put him."

THE END OF THE LINE

Ｎorth swallowed down the blood that was pooling in his mouth as he tested his front incisor with his tongue. It was loose all right, but maybe if he let it be, it wouldn't fall out. Clem Curtis' men had done a number on him before they tied him up and dumped him in one of the supply tents to wait for whoever it was that would be interrogating him next. His left eye was swelling shut already, and from the feel of it, they'd split his lip as well.

As far as North could see, there wasn't a clear way out of the mess he'd found himself in. No one knew where he was, and he doubted anyone would find him in time. So when he heard voices outside the tent, he thought the knocks to his head had him imagining things. But his chest felt tight with panic when he understood it *wasn't* his imagination after all.

No. Maggie can't be here.

North struggled against the ropes, but Maggie and Esta had already stepped into the tent before he'd managed to do anything but make his wrists raw. Still, even with his fear and panic scooping his heart plum out of his chest, the sight of Maggie standing there, her hair falling from its pins and worry shadowing her face, made North feel like he could finally breathe again. She might have turned him down earlier, but she'd come for him now—and that fact made him both the happiest man who'd ever walked the earth and also unbearably afraid.

"What the hell are you doing here?" he asked, panic sharpening his tone more than he intended, as Maggie knelt in front of him and lifted her hands to his face.

"Oh, Jericho." From the horror in her expression, he must have looked even worse than he felt. "What did they do to you?"

It didn't matter what they'd done to him; he couldn't let them touch her. "You have to go," he told her, trying to pull his head away from the gentle touch of her hands. "And you gotta go *now*. It isn't safe here. Jot Gunter's here, and the Jefferson Guard is too."

"It's worse than that," Esta said, already working on his ropes while Maggie pulled some salve from her pouch. "They're working together— the Guard and the Syndicate. We saw men wearing the Guard's medallions just now on the grounds."

North batted away Maggie's fussing. "Even more reason for you to get out of here right now."

"I'm not going anywhere without you," Maggie told him, her voice shot through with steel.

North tried to focus on her with the eye that wasn't swelling shut. All he wanted to do was look at her, because whatever danger they might be in—whatever might happen next—she'd come back for him. That *had* to mean something. "I shouldn't be glad that you're here. . . ."

Maggie's eyes softened a little. "I never should've let you walk out that door."

Something loosened in North's chest. "I never should've asked you to choose."

"There are things I have to tell you—"

"You can tell me later," North told Maggie. "Right now you have to get out of here. When they dumped me here, they were talking about some kind of raid. You have to leave before you get caught up in it. Esta, you have to take her and—"

"We're not leaving without you," Esta said. "But you're right. We *do* have to get moving. George is working on distracting your guards, but he's not going to be able to hold their attention for long. Can you walk?"

"George?" North was trying to keep up. "How could you possibly know George?"

"He found us when we were outside Pickett's tent," Maggie explained. "When he told us they'd taken you—" Her voice broke before she could finish.

"Mags?" North reached up to cup her face gently with his hands. "Come on, sweetheart. Don't you go crying over me. I'm fine." He'd be a lot better when she was safe.

She lifted her glasses enough so that she could wipe the tears from her eyes; then, with a sniff, she looked at him, serious as she'd ever been. "I didn't mean it, you know. I want that life you were talking about. I want to find a place where we can start over. I want all of it, and I'd do anything to have it—"

"It's okay, Mags," he said. "We're going to figure this out."

"Did you manage to give Pickett the serum?" Esta asked as she worked on the ropes.

North met Maggie's eyes and saw hope burning there so bright it nearly blinded him. How was he supposed to tell her?

"Well?" Esta asked when he didn't immediately answer. "Is the dagger here, or—"

"It's gone," North said, the frustration of the discovery still churning in his belly. "Pickett hasn't had the piece for more than a year." He tossed the ropes off his legs and tried to get to his feet, but his right ankle screamed under his weight.

"Did he say what he did with it?" Maggie asked. She glanced at Esta with some silent meaning that North didn't understand.

"He sold it a while back. . . ." North explained what he'd learned from the cowboy. Pickett hadn't wanted to part with the piece, but he wasn't given much of a choice when he'd been approached by a young white businessman from out east. The way Pickett told it, he was given the choice to sell the dagger to the guy for a pittance, or the guy would have him arrested for stealing it.

Pickett had known his word wouldn't mean anything against the easterner's, considering the colors of their respective skins. He'd wanted to do right by the old friend who'd sent it to him for safekeeping, but he hadn't been able to see how spending his life in prison was going to help anyone.

"Did Pickett get the guy's name?" Esta asked.

North frowned. "Some New Yorker. John or Jack something."

"Jack?" Esta asked, her voice going oddly hollow. "Tell me it wasn't Jack Grew."

"That might be it," North said.

"Jack Grew isn't 'some New Yorker,'" Esta told them. "He's the one in St. Louis who attacked Harte. He also happens to be here. In Denver—we saw him coming out of Pickett's tent a few minutes ago."

Every inch of North's body felt like it had been battered and bruised, but his mind was clear and his determination steady. "If this Jack Grew character is here, then we can get the dagger from him."

But Maggie shook her head. "No, Jericho."

"*Yes*, Mags. Don't you see? We have another shot at getting an artifact, just like you wanted," he said. Now that she'd come back for him, there wasn't anything he wouldn't do to keep her. "Let me do this—for you."

"Jericho, *look* at you." Maggie's voice broke again, and she pressed her lips together, pausing to collect herself before she went on. "None of this ever would have happened if I'd listened to you earlier. You and I could be on a train to somewhere safe, a place where no one knows us and no one is looking for us. You were right. We could have gone off and spent whatever time we had together. Instead, we're here, with you beaten and bruised near to death. When I think about what could've happened—" Her voice broke.

The tears were welling in her eyes, and all North wanted was to make them stop.

"What if I hadn't run into George?" Maggie asked. "You might have disappeared tonight, and I would never have known what happened to you. And for what? *Nothing.* Because I'm chasing a dream that isn't even mine. It hasn't been mine for some time." She wiped her eyes and looked straight at him. "When you walked into my life, that was it for me, Jericho Northwood. The only dream I'm going to chase now is the life I can build with you."

"That's all fine and good, but what about Cordelia?" Esta said, shattering the perfection of the moment into a million pieces.

"What *about* Cordelia?" North asked. The sharp-mouthed sharpshooter wasn't his concern, not when all he wanted to do was take what Maggie was offering and never look back. "Cordelia's a smart girl who can shoot better than anyone I've ever seen."

"Which is unfortunate for you," Cordelia said as she stepped into the tent, her gun already drawn. "Margaret . . ." There was a gleam in her eye that North didn't like the look of. "I thought we went over this. You know what will happen to your sister if you leave."

"What does Ruth have to do with any of this?" North asked through clenched teeth. He'd seen the glimmering possibility of a future with Maggie, and he'd be damned if this woman would brush it away like some desert mirage by reminding Maggie about her sister.

"Maggie has responsibilities. She's made promises to the Antistasi," Cordelia said, her voice deadly even and calm. "She can't walk away . . . not without facing the *consequences.* It ain't just your lives at stake here. If she walks away—"

"I know," Maggie said, cutting Cordelia off. "But my sister made her choices. I've done what I could to protect her, but I can't do that forever."

Cordelia's expression hardened, and panic sparked in her eyes. "You can't walk away from the Antistasi, Margaret."

"I'm not walking away," Maggie told the sharpshooter as she tightened her grip on North. "I'm walking toward something else. Something more important."

North wasn't exactly sure what they were going on about, but as far as he was concerned, the discussion was over. They needed to get out of that tent and away from the showgrounds while they still could—*if* they still could.

"Maggie's done more than anyone could have asked. She's given up everything for the Antistasi—her home, her sister. If she's ready to walk away, you're not going to stop her." North ignored the pain in his leg as he put an arm around Maggie. "We're leaving. *Now.* Considering the situation out there, I'd suggest you do the same. You can go on and get whatever artifacts you want, and we wish you the best, but this is the end of the line for us."

He turned away from Cordelia, leaning into Maggie for support more than he would've liked.

"Well, at least y'all got that much right," Cordelia said, and as she spoke, North heard the hammer of her pistol click into place.

SURROUNDED

1904—Denver

The moment that Cordelia cocked her pistol, Esta knew things had become more complicated. It was clear that the sharpshooter didn't have any intention of letting them go, but there was more than pure fury in Cordelia's eyes. Fear was there too.

"You don't have to do this, Cordelia," Esta said, trying to draw her attention in a new direction. "Whatever the Professor has on you, we can help. *I* can help you fight him."

Cordelia only stared at her. Then the sharpshooter's mouth twisted into a sneer. "He told me you'd say that. He warned me that you would try to win me over with false promises, but it ain't gonna work. I won't let your lies turn my head."

"They're not lies, Cordelia. The Professor doesn't care about you. He doesn't even care about the Antistasi," Esta said. "You're nothing but a means to an end for him. He's using you to get to me."

Cordelia aimed the pistol at Esta. Her eyes had gone wide and more than a little wild. "That's where you're wrong. The Professor ain't *using* me. He *chose* me because he trusts me, and I will not betray that trust. We are so close to a different future. So close to freeing the old magic, like he promised." She was shaking her head. "I can't go back—I *won't* go back—to hiding myself away and living in fear of people who ain't got any kind of real power."

"You can't kill me," Esta reminded Cordelia, trying to ignore the way her heart skipped at seeing the gun's barrel pointed directly at her. "You

327

might want to, but you know what will happen if you do. You know I wasn't lying."

"You're right." Cordelia's mouth went flat, but her eyes were more furious than ever.

Esta saw what was coming even before Cordelia swung the gun toward Maggie and North. She didn't have her affinity to reach for, so she couldn't pull the seconds slow or move the bullet out of its path. She only had herself. Before she considered what the consequences might be, Esta leapt at Cordelia, hitting the sharpshooter at the same moment the gun went off. The sound of it firing rang in Esta's ears as she pushed Cordelia to the ground and knocked the pistol from her hand.

Cordelia blinked, but her surprise lasted only a heartbeat, before she pushed Esta away and scrambled for the gun. Esta wasn't about to let Cordelia get it, though. She lunged, and in a matter of seconds, she'd straddled the sharpshooter, pinning Cordelia to the ground.

But then Esta heard North make a keening, wailing sound like some kind of wounded animal on the other side of the tent, and Cordelia began to laugh.

"I told y'all before," she said. "I never, *ever* miss."

Esta looked back to see that Maggie's eyes were wide and her face had drained of color. She was clutching her hands to her side, and North's hands were pressed over them as well, but blood was already seeping from beneath their fingers. For a moment all Esta could do was stare numbly, while Cordelia's unhinged laughter continued to vibrate beneath her. Then suddenly Cordelia wrenched herself to the side, throwing Esta off-balance.

Cordelia was on Esta before she'd even hit the ground. The sharp-shooter's hands grabbed Esta's neck and started to squeeze, even as Esta tried to fight her off.

"That's enough," a voice said, accompanied by the second click of a pistol being primed. "Get off her now."

Cordelia went still at the sound of the voice, which was enough for

Esta to throw her off. She looked up to find George standing over them with Cordelia's gun in his hand.

"What in the Sam Hill is going on in here?" he asked. He took in the scene, and his mouth opened in a kind of disbelief when he saw Maggie bleeding in the corner of the tent. Then he looked back to Cordelia, and understanding dawned. "You did this?" he asked her.

Cordelia started to cackle.

"Hand me that rope," Esta said. They didn't have time for long explanations, and she doubted Cordelia was in any mind to give them anyway. "We need to get her secured before she can hurt anyone else."

On the other side of the tent, North was still cradling Maggie as he tried to stop the bleeding. "Maggie . . . Stay with me, honey," he pleaded. "Come on now, darlin'. Just keep looking here in my eyes. Right here, Mags . . ."

As George finished securing Cordelia's arms, Esta went over to help North with Maggie. He was cradling her in his arms, and Esta suddenly had the strangest sense that this scene had already played out. Maybe not quite like this, but . . . She shook away the thought. North was trying to get Maggie to focus on him, but she kept blinking and staring off, like she was seeing something in the distance.

"You can go back," Esta told him, feeling the full horror of what had happened. "A minute or two is all you'd need to fix this. You can use your watch—"

North was shaking his head. "It's gone. Gunter destroyed it when they got me earlier."

George had finished securing Cordelia and crouched next to them. "Let me?" he asked. When neither of them moved, he gently took North's and Maggie's hands away from the wound in her side. "It looks like the bullet went clean through. Maybe with a doctor—"

"Too much of a risk," Maggie said. "They'll realize—" She gasped in pain.

"The doctor I have in mind won't care," George said. "And she won't talk."

"Is she Mageus?" Esta asked.

"No, but Dr. Ford would be understanding," George said. "You'd be able to trust her."

"No, Jericho—" Maggie gasped.

"If there's a chance of saving Maggie, we should take it," Esta told North. "But we need to go now. Someone will have heard that shot, and with so many people swarming around looking for us—"

"Leave me and go," Maggie said, each word coming with visible effort. "While you can."

"No." North shook his head again. "I'm not going anywhere without you." He was already arranging her skirts so he could lift her in his arms.

But Esta had gone to check the flap of the tent, and what she saw outside made her stomach sink. "It doesn't look like we're going anywhere," she said. "We're surrounded."

THE HANDS THAT
HELD HIM DOWN

1904—San Francisco

Harte struggled to stay on his feet as he took the steps down from the temple two at a time. The weight of the Dragon's Eye was secure within the inner pocket of his coat, and deep within him, Seshat was rioting, pressing at the boundary between them. He couldn't tell if she was trying to stop him or urging him on, so he ignored her. He had enough to worry about with the feverish haze that coated his vision and the ache in his upper thigh that made each step feel like he was being stabbed. When he got to the second-floor landing, he paused long enough to catch his breath and to consider his options. The clerks in the bank lobby below would probably already know what happened. It was possible that his father might have even warned them. There was no way he was going to be able to walk out the front door.

Then Harte remembered the fire escape he'd seen from the street below.

Instead of continuing down the staircase, he went down the hall cutting through the middle of the building. Taking a chance, he opened one of the doors to find a small office with a pair of surprised clerks sitting behind desks piled high with stacks of papers and ledgers. The room was plain, nothing like the grandeur of the temple above, but there was a portrait of Lady Justice, her eyes wide and accusing, hanging on the wall behind them that told Harte these must be more of the Committee's offices. The men glanced up when Harte burst in, but his attention was on the open window on the other side of the room.

He pulled on his most charming smile. "Pardon the interruption, gentlemen. I need to do a routine check. I'll be out of your hair in a few minutes."

He was nearly through the window when the door opened again and another pair of men burst through, yelling orders at two office workers. Their surprise turned to action, and the closer of the two clerks lunged for Harte, catching him by his coat.

The man cocked his arm, ready to swing, but Harte had grown up in the streets and new how to fight fast and dirty. He blocked the blow and then shoved the man, pushing him into the others. As they stumbled back, Harte was out the window and onto the fire escape, which creaked under his weight. He'd almost made it to the ladder when he was pulled backward again. His head spun with the motion, and this time he didn't manage to dodge. Instead, he took the blow straight to his temple. The instant the fist connected with the side of his face, Harte's vision flickered.

Then came another blow, and another before Harte could fend them off. He felt the crunch of his nose breaking, followed by the warmth of blood running down his face. The coppery tang of it on his lips shook him into action. He finally managed to fend off the next fist, but before Harte could regain his balance completely, the man had bent him backward over the railing of the fire escape, holding him by the throat. The structure creaked under the pressure of their combined weight, but Harte couldn't do much to fight the man off—especially not with the world tilting and his vision blurring.

Inside of him, Seshat had gone strangely, uncomfortably quiet. Harte reached for his affinity, but his body was so weary and weak, and his mind so unsteady from the combination of fever and the battering he'd taken, that he could barely grasp the edges of his magic.

Help me, he pleaded, desperate for air. *Do something.*

Why should I help you, when you have done nothing but fight me? Even now you plan to use that stone to destroy me, Seshat told him, her voice a hollow whisper.

I wouldn't—

LISA MAXWELL

I know your heart, boy.

Harte's vision was beginning to go dark around the edges. *If they kill me, you die as well.*

Seshat rustled at that, clearly amused. *You were willing to die to destroy me before,* she taunted. *Why should this be any different?*

Because it *was.* True, Harte had been willing to give up his life if it meant saving Esta—he still was willing, if it came to that—but to die at the hands of these men? For *nothing?*

No. Not like this. Harte wanted to live. Even with the fever raging and shaking his limbs, he wanted to see tomorrow. He wanted to take the Book back from Jack and force its pages to give up their secrets. He wanted to find another path—another way. Most of all, he wanted to see Esta again.

Pulling on all of his remaining strength, Harte tried again to break free of the man's arms.

"You're not going anywhere," the man growled. He leaned in close, and Harte could smell the sourness of his breath. "You didn't really think the Vigilance Committee would allow you to walk away with a treasure as priceless as the Dragon's Eye?"

"If they didn't want it stolen," Harte rasped, writhing and trying to jerk away as he choked out the words, "they . . . shouldn't have left . . . it . . . unguarded."

The man only laughed—at Harte's words and at his unsuccessful attempt to free himself. "Who said it was unguarded? You walked right into our trap, just like we expected you to."

"Trap?" Harte realized his mistake. It made a sickening sort of sense now—the long conversation his father had with the man at the entrance, the ease with which they gained access to the temple, and the way the crown wasn't even in a case.

"You really think we'd keep something like that unprotected?" The man laughed again. "It was only on display because we were hoping to catch the Devil's Thief."

"Sorry to disappoint." Harte could barely choke out the words, but he refused to let the man know that he and Esta were connected. "But you have the wrong person."

"You don't disappoint," the man said, giving Harte another hard jerk that had his vision swimming. "Not completely, Mr. Darrigan."

Harte went suddenly still. They knew his name. He doubted that his father would have told them—he wouldn't have risked it. But still, they knew who he was. They'd been expecting him.

"Secretary Grew should be just as happy with you when he arrives."

Secretary Grew? There was only one person that could be.

Within his skin, Harte felt Seshat shudder. Still, he could not grasp his affinity. He was too exhausted, too feverish, and too unsteady to pull his magic around him. He needed help, and there was only one place he could turn.

Help me, he pleaded again.

He could sense Seshat there, watching and waiting. But she did not reply.

Harte understood that she was toying with him. *You heard him. Once Jack arrives, we'll be his prisoners. You know I won't be able to fight him. I won't be able to stop Thoth from taking your power. Not as weak as I am.*

Seshat remained silent as Harte continued to writhe against his captor's grip.

Thoth will finally have his victory, Harte told Seshat as he struggled to focus on his affinity, but again his magic slipped through his fingers. *He will take your power and use it for his own. He will destroy you.*

Isn't that what you would do as well? Seshat asked. *What makes you any different?*

Harte couldn't disagree, and he knew there wasn't a lie he could tell that Seshat wouldn't see right through, not when she lived inside his skin. Not when she knew his every whim and desire. *Because I don't want it for myself. Help me,* he pleaded. *For Esta.*

The girl. She is the only way. With her, I can unmake the world and destroy

Thoth once and for all. Seshat's voice came to him then, clear and close to the surface. *Will you promise not to stand in my way?*

You know I won't promise you that, Harte told her. *I will do anything to keep you from harming her. You know that. But help me now, and together we can destroy Thoth. Help me now, and I swear to you, I will do anything in my power to make him pay.*

Harte felt the skin of the man's palms against his tender neck. Everything ached. Every particle in his being hurt, but he didn't care. He focused everything he was on gathering his affinity . . . only to feel it slip away. Water between his fingers. Again.

Seshat remained silent. Distant.

Harte felt as though he were drowning and Seshat was standing on the shore, close enough to help but refusing to touch even a toe to the water. His vision was already starting to go dark at the edges, and his lungs were burning, and he knew—*knew*—that he had failed.

Harte knew that when Jack arrived, there would be no way to stop him from finally claiming Seshat. Thoth would have everything he'd ever wanted—all of the power he'd schemed and lied and betrayed for. Thoth would win, and the world would be remade under his control.

Suddenly Harte felt the goddess lurch, rousing herself unexpectedly. Her power rose alongside the familiar warmth of his own magic, and before his vision went completely dark, he used what was left of his strength to shove his affinity toward the man holding his neck. *Commanding* him.

The man holding him screamed. He released Harte and grabbed at his own head like he was trying to hold himself together. It was enough to let Harte drag in a deep breath, enough for the darkness in his vision to start to lift. He took a moment to get his legs steady beneath him. The man was still screaming and writhing, and the whites of his eyes had been all but obliterated by a swirling darkness. Harte backed away, horrified at what Seshat had done—what *his own* affinity had done. The man let out one more manic scream before turning to attack the others.

Harte swayed a little, gripping the railing for balance. He wasn't sure whether he could make it down the ladder, not with the way he currently felt, but he knew implicitly that if he didn't try now, he wouldn't get another chance. He wiped the blood that was still dribbling from his nose with the back of his sleeve and moved toward the fire escape again.

The world was still swimming, his limbs were trembling, and his balance was unstable, but somehow Harte managed to shimmy down the rickety ladder to the sidewalk below. When he was nearly there, his foot missed a rail and he stumbled, gripping the rungs so hard to keep from falling that he knew he'd have to pry splinters from his palms later. It didn't matter. Not when he was so close to being free.

Harte's feet hit the pavement, and he pulled himself upright, steadying himself on the side of the building for a moment. He'd barely started to move again, though, when the front door of the building opened, bringing with it the noisy clang of an alarm bell and a group of men. Behind him, another group had come out of the building next door, and Harte found himself surrounded. He turned in a slow circle, the horizon tilting and pitching as he tried to stay on his feet. His body shook from the exertion and from the fever, but he managed to keep himself upright.

There were twelve, maybe fifteen, people surrounding him now, but they were mostly soft-looking men dressed in rumpled, ill-fitting suits. Bank clerks and merchants, from the looks of them. If his vision hadn't still been blurry and his stomach hadn't been threatening to turn itself out onto the sidewalk, Harte might have considered fighting his way out. But that wasn't an option, not even with Seshat prowling within his skin, her power buoying him up and urging him on. He'd have to try running.

Then Harte heard the whimper.

It was such an insignificant noise, but he knew immediately what the sound was. He turned back to the entrance of the bank to find a man holding the boy—his *brother*—by the child's hair. The blade of a dagger was poised at the boy's throat, but Harte's father—*their* father—was standing off to the side with his arms crossed, doing nothing to free his son.

"You have something that belongs to us," the man said, pushing the boy forward. The knife never left the boy's throat.

"You'd let them kill your own son?" Harte asked Samuel Lowe, fear making him shudder more than even the fever could.

He already knew the answer. Of *course* his father would sacrifice the boy, especially if it meant saving his own reputation and the comfortable life he'd built.

Samuel Lowe only glared at him.

"He's a *child*," Harte said, his head still swimming from the blows. "He's *your* child."

"My wife is still young enough to bear me more sons," his father replied, with a cold sureness to his voice. "This one is a disappointment anyway—he proved that when he allowed you to escape." Sam Lowe's expression was deadly in its sincerity.

"The Dragon's Eye," the other man ordered as he pressed the knife against the pale skin of the boy's throat. "You will give us back the crown, or the boy will die."

Sammie whimpered again. A line of blood trickled from the knife's blade, and the boy began to cry in earnest. His eyes were locked with Harte's, and they shone with fear and the too-mature understanding of this betrayal.

Run, Seshat commanded, her whispering urging him on. *Why do you stand here like a lamb at the slaughter? Go while you can!*

His father stepped forward. "Why put the boy through this? You won't allow him to die. You're too weak. You always have been."

Harte had the crown secured in his jacket. With Seshat's help, he knew he could likely make it far enough to disappear into the city. He knew where his father lived; he might even be able to find the other artifacts before the fever took him completely. He could send them to Esta. He could keep his promises.

He should leave now, while he could. Even if it meant letting the boy die. After all, what was a single life measured against the many lives that could be helped by the artifacts?

Everything.

But the voice that came to Harte with such startling clarity was not Seshat's. It was the voice he'd stopped listening to years before. His own.

Go! Seshat commanded. *You cannot allow your weakness to destroy us both.*

She was right. If Harte stayed, if he gave up the Dragon's Eye, he might not escape again. Esta would never know what happened to him, and her cuff would be lost. If he left now, the boy might die but Harte could avoid Jack finding him. He could keep Thoth from claiming Seshat. The world would have a chance. *Esta* would have a chance. It would be so easy to add this boy's life to the scrap heap of his past. He only had to walk away.

But he couldn't. He never should have left the boy behind with their father. He'd convinced himself that there was nothing he could do for the kid—for his own brother—because *he* was no better than his father. After all, everything he'd accomplished in his life had been built from scheming and lies, grift and larceny—all qualities he'd believed he'd inherited from the man who had refused to claim him. He was his father's son, wasn't he? Whatever success he might have found had always felt tainted with that truth. It was why Harte pushed everyone away, including Esta.

But the boy was *also* his father's son, and the child was an innocent. As Harte had once been. Suddenly he saw the truth that he'd been denying for too long. The blood in his veins meant *nothing.* The rot at the center of his life had always been his father, but the choices Harte had made through the years, those were his own. They always had been.

With a flourish of his hands that had the men tensing to attack, Harte produced the crown, seemingly out of thin air. He saw Sammie's wonder—and his relief. The small body seemed to shudder at the sight of the Dragon's Eye, as though he understood that he'd somehow been given a reprieve.

Harte ignored the swirling spots in his vision and the way his muscles quaked with exhaustion as he held the crown over his head, making sure that everyone who had surrounded him could see it. Even in the overcast day, the gold seemed to glow, and the stone in the center of the headpiece shone with a peculiar light.

Seshat rattled the bars of her cage as she understood what he meant to do.

His father smiled cruelly, elbowing the man next to him. "I told you he would give in, with the right pressure."

Harte didn't pay any attention to the man who'd fathered him. Not his father, just a man, and a meager excuse for one at that. His attention was on the boy. On his *brother*. Blood dampened the collar of the boy's shirt, and fear was stark in his expression, but Harte would not allow the child to be harmed. He would give his brother a chance at a different life.

"It will be okay," he told Sammie, who had started crying. "I won't let them hurt you." It was a promise he would go to any length to keep.

"Put the crown on the ground in front of you and step back," the man holding Sammie said. "Carefully now."

Harte lowered the crown, struggling against the fury of Seshat's rage and his own weakened body to keep himself from toppling over. Before he placed it on the ground, he spoke directly to the boy. "I'm sorry," he told Sammie. "You didn't deserve any of this. You don't deserve his fists or his anger. They come from *his* failings. *Not* yours. Remember that. Whatever happens, I want you to remember that you're a thousand times better than he'll ever be."

Harte had barely gotten the final word out when he was tackled from behind. The crown fell from his hands, and before he could fight his way free, he was pinned to the ground, his face pressed into the dirty street with a boot to the back. He looked up to see his brother staring at him, his eyes wide. Sammie was still being held in place, but the man had lowered the knife from his throat.

"I think I can manage one more trick," Harte said, barely able to get out the words. "Would you like to see it?"

The boy's chin trembled, but he nodded ever so slightly.

"Remember what I told you," Harte said, and he managed to hold on to consciousness long enough to gather the strength he needed to grab tight to his affinity and push it into the hands that held him down.

FATED

1904—Denver

Esta took one more look before she eased the canvas back over the tent's entrance. All around the tent, people had gathered, Guard and Syndicate alike. Among the crowd Esta spotted the glint of the marshal's stars and silvery medallions that glowed an eerie blue in the twilight.

"It was Cordelia's shot," she realized. "It must have triggered the Guard's medallions."

"We have to get her to a doctor." North adjusted Maggie in his arms.

"There's no way out," Esta said. "It's as bad as when we were trapped on the train."

"You got us out of that mess," North said, his voice rising with his desperation.

"I had my affinity then," she reminded him. "With the Quellant—"

Maggie was trying to say something, but the pain was twisting her words.

"Shhh, sweetheart," North crooned. "We're going to figure this out."

But Maggie was shaking her head. "She can do it. . . ." She met Esta's eyes. "There's an antidote. In my pouch."

North dug into Maggie's pouch and came up with a red tablet that looked similar in size and shape to the Quellant that Esta had been taking ever since Texas and offered it to her. She felt the warmth of its energy wash over her palm, but she didn't raise it to her lips.

"Go on," North said, frowning. "Maggie's running out of time. We all are."

George was eyeing them with an uneasy curiosity, but Esta couldn't be concerned with him.

"What about Seshat?" she asked.

"What about her?" North growled.

"You know what happened before, in Corsicana and with the train. You still might not believe I'm telling the truth about her, but I know I am."

"Wasn't Seshat," Maggie said, coughing the words with some effort.

"You don't know that—"

"I *do*." Maggie gasped, like a bolt of pain had shot through her, but then she recovered herself. Her eyes were serious as she looked at Esta. "My fault," Maggie whispered. "Not Seshat. *Tell her*," she directed North.

"She gave you something when we left St. Louis," North explained. "Some new concoction she was working on. To disrupt affinities."

"More in Texas," Maggie said, grimacing. "Before the explosion . . ."

"I don't understand," Esta said.

"Leaving St. Louis, we didn't know exactly what side you were on, and we didn't know what you could do. Maggie gave you something to make your magic unstable, so you wouldn't be tempted to use it against us," North said. "The darkness you saw back in Texas—that wasn't from any ancient creature. It was because of Maggie."

"I know what I saw," Esta argued. The darkness, the way the earth shattered from her affinity. It had to have been Seshat.

"It's the same," Maggie said, struggling with the words. "Always *you*."

"Seshat used my affinity—she amplified it," Esta said as understanding dawned on her. "That's what your formula did as well?"

"Unstable," Maggie rasped, closing her eyes against the pain.

"And the Quellant?" Esta demanded.

"Used your fear," Maggie told her softly.

"Why have me take it at all? You could have just stopped drugging me."

"Because I knew what you could do," Maggie admitted, grimacing. "The Professor warned me. Before we left St. Louis . . . I knew."

"Maggie used your worry to get you to agree to the Quellant," North explained. "Her new formulation seemed too risky, considering what happened in Texas, but we knew for sure that the Quellant would stop you from leaving us in the dust like your partner did. Or at least it would give us a fighting chance."

"You really are Ruth's sister, ain't yeh?" Cordelia asked Maggie. Then she started laughing again.

But Esta was impressed despite herself. For all Maggie's failures with lying, she'd managed to keep this secret. Still, if what they were saying was true, Esta had been a fool. She could have used her affinity all along, but she'd been trapped by her own fear instead. Well, she certainly wasn't going to be trapped by it any longer.

For a moment she considered leaving. After what North and Maggie had done to her, they almost deserved to be caught there by the Brotherhoods. *But George doesn't.* He was an innocent in all of this, a bystander who'd tried to help—who was still trying to help. And if the Syndicate found him here with the other three? Esta doubted they'd believe in George's innocence.

Esta took the antidote from North and crushed it between her teeth. The effect was almost immediate. Her affinity flooded back to her, warm and real and secure, and Esta could have wept from the relief of it. But she didn't have time for relief. They still had to get through the mob that had surrounded them.

It took a second to get everyone situated, so that each one of them had some grip on her. "Whatever you do, don't let go," she said as she pulled the seconds slow. She waited, but there was no darkness, no shadow over her vision. There was only the absolute rightness of having such an essential part of herself back, the exhilaration of flexing her affinity and letting it unfurl.

When they left the tent, Esta heard George's sharp intake of breath as he saw the crowd outside nearly frozen in time. He let out a curse—or maybe it was a prayer—but Esta kept her grip tight on his wrist so he couldn't slip out of her control.

"It's fine," she said. "We need to get past the perimeter."

To her left, she saw a familiar blond head of hair: Jack Grew was there, talking to a man with a white mustache. One of the Jefferson Guard was at his side, as the rest of the crowd waited for his orders. Esta made herself a promise that she'd come back for Jack and the Book, once the others were safe.

The group moved as quickly as they could, a many-headed hydra maneuvering through the crowd that had surrounded the tent. Finally, they made it through the grounds to the field where wagons and horses stood right alongside motorcars.

"Do any of you know how to drive one of those?" Esta asked, pointing to the cars, and when no one answered, she settled for a wagon with a pair of horses.

She had to release her hold on time so they could set Maggie in the back of the wagon. As George climbed into the driver's seat, Esta helped North make Maggie comfortable. Maggie looked bad, and North looked completely shell-shocked, but Esta hoped that everything would work out. They'd find the doctor for Maggie, and with any luck, she would survive. But Esta couldn't go with them. Not while Jack Grew was so close—and with him, the Book of Mysteries.

Esta started to back out of the wagon's bed, but North grabbed her by the wrist. "Where do you think you're going?"

"If Jack Grew is here, so is the dagger," she told him, starting to pull away. "And Harte will be waiting for me."

North was shaking his head as his grip on her wrist tightened. "No," he said. "You're coming with us. No way am I letting you run off to destroy our lives."

"I have to go," Esta told him, trying to keep her voice steady and calm. "You *know* that. If I don't find Harte before the Professor does, if I can't retrieve the cuff, you lose everything anyway."

He was still shaking his head, still holding on to her like it was the only thing that mattered.

"Let her go," Maggie whispered.

"It's going to be okay," North soothed. "Don't you concern yourself with any of this, Mags. You focus on staying awake until we can get you to this Dr. Ford, and I'll worry about Esta."

"No, Jericho. You have to let her go." Maggie coughed, a wet, groaning cough. "It's the only way."

"The only way for what? If I let her go, she'll go back and change everything," North said, his eyes burning with a kind of unholy fire. "I only just got you back."

Maggie was shaking her head, or she was trying to, but the effort of it seemed nearly too much for her. "There's nothing that could keep me from you, Jericho Northwood. Call it what you want. Fate. Destiny. Some things are meant. *We're* meant. Time can't unmake what we are. Even if this bullet is the end of me."

"It's not gonna be," North said, clutching Esta more tightly to him.

"Might," Maggie whispered, her eyes fluttering closed.

"She'll have a better chance to survive this if you get her to George's doctor," Esta told him. "You don't need me for that."

"I can't let you go," North said, turning his grief on her. It wasn't anger in his expression now, but pain and sorrow and fear.

"Yes," Esta said. "You can. Go on and release my wrist and take care of your girl."

North seemed frozen with indecision. "She's the best part of my life. I can't let you take her from me."

"I'm not going to take her from you, but that bullet might," Esta told him. "Maggie's right. Nothing is going to stop the two of you." If that wasn't the truth, Esta would do whatever she could to *make* it the truth. "Let me go, North. You're wasting time. We all are."

North stared at Esta, his eyes brimming. Still, he didn't release her.

"What if she doesn't make it?" Esta asked. "If I go back, this never has to happen. Maggie never has to be here. She never has to get wrapped up with me. She could *live*. She could spend her whole life safe and sound in St. Louis."

"Without me . . . ," North whispered.

"You'd risk her life to keep her?" Esta asked softly.

North seemed torn between the different ways he could lose her, stuck in his indecision.

"If I make it back, like I'm planning to, I'll do everything I can to make sure the two of you find each other," Esta promised. "But I don't think I'll need to. I think Maggie's right. I think there are some things that time itself doesn't have any power over." At least, she hoped there were.

North looked like a man being split in two. "I'm betting my whole world on you keeping your word," he said, before he finally released her.

"I will do *everything* in my power to keep it," Esta told him. One way or another, she would make this right. "Now get going before they realize we're gone."

Esta watched the wagon drive off into the night, heading in the direction of town. She didn't know what would happen to Maggie. The wound had looked bad, but Esta's concerns now had to be on Jack and on retrieving the Book that could change her fate. She pulled time around herself, familiar and comfortable as her own skin, and started back.

Slipping through the crowd was easy enough, especially with her affinity clear and steady. No darkness tinged her vision, and the knowledge that it had never been Seshat was both a comfort and a source of bitterness. She'd wasted so much time with fear and hesitation—for *nothing*. She wouldn't waste another second.

Jack wasn't there with the rest of the crowd, but from the tableau of people all looking in the direction of the supply tent where they'd found North, Esta had a feeling where he would be. She wasn't wrong. Inside the tent, she found Jack and two other men. Cordelia was slumped against the pole where they'd tied her, but her face had been bloodied. She looked to be unconscious, but Esta wasn't interested in wasting time on the sharpshooter now. Her focus was only on Jack.

The days that had passed since she'd seen him in St. Louis had clearly taken their toll. He had his hand in the air, his finger pointed toward one of the Curtis brothers, and his face had turned a dangerous shade of red. The way his jacket tugged to one side made it painfully obvious that Jack was concealing something there—at least, it was obvious to a thief.

She was so close. *So close.* It was a simple matter of easing up next to Jack, of dipping her fingers into his inside jacket pocket—careful not to touch any part of him—and . . . *yes.*

Esta's fingers brushed the worn leather of the Ars Arcana, and she carefully started to pull the small volume from Jack's pocket. Little by little, she worked it free, and then, after what felt like an eternity, she had it. The Book dangled from her fingertips, and Esta could barely breathe from the relief of it all. But when she adjusted for a more secure hold of the Book, Jack's hand grabbed her wrist. His fingers felt like iron, and for a second Esta didn't quite understand what was happening. The world was still silent, still suspended in time. . . .

But Jack was not.

FROM THE DEPTHS

1904—San Francisco

B y the time Harte had been deposited into a windowless cell, the
fever had him well in its clutches. He didn't regret the choice he'd
made, even if Seshat continued to rail at him. Maybe he *could* have
saved himself, but he'd used his last bit of strength to try to save his
brother instead.

Seshat rattled the bars of her cage, raging at his stupidity and weakness,
but Harte couldn't remain conscious. Even with the goddess screaming
within him, a dark and empty sleep pulled Harte under. He'd already
broken too many promises anyway.

He surfaced a while later, confused and lost. Something had happened. *Esta.* She'd changed the illusion, switched out her gown for a
costume that barely covered her in a sprinkling of stars.

No . . . that wasn't right.

A brightness appeared. It disappeared and then came back once again,
each time bringing with it pain that throbbed with each beat of his heart.

Voices. He couldn't make sense of what they were saying.

The crown. He reached for where he'd placed it in his coat but found it
gone. He'd been in the chamber of a heart, a cold fire . . . and the crown
had been there.

No . . . Something happened.

His thoughts were jumbled, unclear. Gray eyes and dark-blond hair.
The boy.

Where was the Dragon's Eye?

It's gone, you fool. You gave it up for the boy, Seshat said, her voice the only steady thing in his world. *You doomed us both to save him.*

Gone. She was right. The crown was gone. Harte remembered now. He'd given it up for a chance that the boy could escape. *His brother.*

You could have escaped, and instead you let them take you. It was an accusation, but there was a question in Seshat's voice as well. It felt like she was trying to understand the puzzle before her. *You had the crown. You had everything you needed, and you let it all go. For a* child.

For my brother, Harte agreed.

He will grow to hate you and all that you are, she told him. *They always do. Even the ones we trust.*

Maybe he will. His heart broke a little at the thought. He would deserve at least part of Sammie's hate for how he'd used the boy. But Harte hoped it would be otherwise. He'd done what he could to try to make it right.

Now they will take everything you have and destroy everything you love. For a meaningless child. Confusion and frustration colored her words.

Not meaningless. Sammie was innocent, as Harte had once been. He would have the chance at a life that Harte had never had. *I didn't have a choice,* he said, a truth that could not be denied. It had been the right thing to do. He knew that still. *The only thing I could do.*

It was the last thing he thought before sleep pulled him under once more.

The seconds ticked by like hours. Hours passed like seconds. The cuffs that bound his wrists and the locked chain that attached his ankles to a bolt in the wall would have been easy enough to break out of, but the room wouldn't stop spinning, and the pain throbbing through his body felt like too much. He was so incredibly weak. All he could do was allow his eyes to close, allow the darkness to pull him down. . . .

Wake up. Seshat's voice was louder now. Urgent.

Harte stirred a little, wondering how long he'd been out, when an unexpected brightness seared his eyes. The blinding light pulled him from the depths, making his head swirl again.

People were close by. With him in the cell. Unseen hands touching him. If only he could remember where he was . . . or why he was there, pinned to a rough blanket and secured hand and foot.

Harte lay perfectly still, feigning sleep or unconsciousness as he tried to remember. It was easy enough, since it hurt too much to move. Body and soul, *everything* hurt too much.

The hands went away, but the voices did not, and a moment later Harte felt himself being hoisted upright, propped against a hard surface. Someone grasped his face, shaking him, smacking his cheeks until he couldn't stand the pain of it any longer and opened his eyes.

A man stood there. Dark hair. Dark eyes set into a blur of a face. Harte couldn't tell who it was. His eyes wouldn't focus. Even propped against the wall, his body felt heavy, dense. Weak.

"You will eat," the face said.

A gloved hand pulled down Harte's jaw. A spoon was placed at his lips. The salt of beef broth flooded his dry mouth.

Harte choked and sputtered. His throat was so raw it had forgotten how to swallow. He turned his head, closing his eyes to refuse more, but his captors were insistent. Again the hand, the spoon. Again the wash of salt and blandness of the beef. Over and over, until Harte stopped fighting it and simply closed his useless eyes and allowed it to happen.

In the end, the front of his shirt was soaked with broth, and they left him damp, smelling of old meat. The thin broth felt heavy in his stomach, and Harte felt nauseous again, but he knew that if he was sick, there was a good chance he would have to sit in his own filth. So he forced himself to take steady breaths and managed to keep the food down. He felt exhausted and aching, and oddly . . . better. But when he felt Seshat curling inside of him, when he remembered that Jack Grew might already be on his way to California, he wondered if *better* was really what he wanted to be.

Sometime later, the door of his cell opened and a group of people entered. Two men held him down, even though he didn't have the strength to move, as an older man entered.

"See what you can do to keep him alive," a voice said. "Secretary

Grew arrives in two days. He only has to last until then."

The older man took the order in silence. Moving forward, he pressed at the underside of Harte's wrists, moving his fingers and varying the pressure as though palpitating to sense something beneath his skin. The man's hands were gloved, like the hands of those who had fed him, but Harte was too weak to reach for his affinity anyway. And after what had happened on the fire escape, he didn't trust Seshat to help.

A moment later the others were cutting away Harte's shirt. It was stiff from the broth, and as they pulled it off, it felt like they were peeling away his skin as well.

Harte barely cared about the pain. Jack Grew was coming—soon—and with him Thoth. At that thought, Seshat lurched inside of Harte. He could feel her anger and panic and, again, her fear. It reminded him, suddenly, of a desert night beneath a star-swept sky that Seshat had shown him once. He'd felt the fear that had coursed through her when she'd realized what Thoth's intentions were. He felt that same fear, that same desperation now.

The man began to mark Harte's body with a brush dipped in dark ink. He drew strange figures at various points: his wrists, his breastbone, down the center of his abdomen. The man's expression was serious as he worked, and Seshat remained quiet, almost thoughtful, as Harte tried to struggle away from the hold the two younger men had on him, but he was too weak.

The doctor ignored Harte's protests and concentrated instead on positioning small clear crystals over the various inked figures. When the last was in place, Harte felt a sharp jolt, a burst of cold energy that coursed through his body, followed by a dull throbbing that wasn't exactly painful even if it wasn't pleasant.

He felt Seshat pacing, felt her interest in what was happening to him. But she remained silent.

Finally, the doctor seemed satisfied. "He should last for a few days more now."

The other men seemed relieved.

As the older man retrieved his crystals and wiped the ink from Harte's skin, the dull throbbing eased, and in its absence, Harte thought that perhaps he felt a tiny bit better. His leg still throbbed with pain, but he was no longer shivering *quite* as much from the fever.

Harte remained perfectly still, completely docile as the men left, locking the cell behind them. He knew as soon as they were gone that he had to get out of there. Even if he had plague, even if he couldn't make it to Esta, he could not lie there and wait for Jack Grew—or Thoth—to take Seshat's power for their own. He wasn't cured, not completely, but he could move now. He could *try*. He would do what he could to give Esta the weapons she needed in the fight that lay ahead, even if he didn't live to see her victory.

Harte's body still ached, and his skin felt like it was on fire. He still felt *so* weak, but he would not simply allow himself to wait around for Jack Grew and the creature that lived inside of him. Once the men left him, Harte pulled himself upright. His head still spun, but deep within his skin, he felt Seshat urging him on. He ignored her anticipation as he started working at the lock of his cuffs.

TIME AND ITS OPPOSITE

1904—Denver

Before Esta had time to react to the fact that Jack Grew was not constrained by her affinity, he'd already plucked the Book from her hand. The world remained silent and still around her, but somehow Jack wasn't stuck in the hold of time as he should have been. Instinctively, Esta wrenched her arm around to break Jack's hold, but his fingers were unbelievably strong as they dug deeper into her skin. He gave a violent jerk of her arm, pulling her closer. His eyes were wild with anger, and Esta knew that it wasn't only Jack looking at her. There was something far more ancient there, lurking in the darkness of his expanding pupils.

"Thoth," Esta whispered.

Jack's mouth curved into what might have been a smile, but his eyes were so dead and vacant that it looked more like something was manipulating him from within. "Yes?" said the thing inside of Jack.

It wasn't Jack's voice that came from his mouth. It was that same otherworldly voice Esta had heard in the Festival Hall when Jack had Harte pinned to the ground and was trying to tear Seshat's power out of him.

"Let me go," Esta growled, trying to rip herself away from his grip and again failing.

"Did you think I wouldn't protect what is mine?" Thoth asked.

"The Book doesn't belong to you," Esta spat. "You stole it, just like you stole every bit of power you've ever pretended to have." She lifted her shoulder as she twisted, and this time it was enough of a distraction for her to wrench away.

The world remained frozen, held in the net of time and magic, but Jack was still free.

"That is a rather odd accusation coming from a thief," Jack mocked. When Esta didn't respond to his taunting, he began to circle slowly around her. "Isn't that what you are, Miss Filosik? A common criminal who pretends to be something more."

She wouldn't let his words distract her from her purpose—as long as the Book was within reach, it could still be hers. If she only knew where he was hiding the dagger . . .

"I've never pretended to be anything I'm not," Esta said, matching Jack step for step as he continued to circle her.

"But you do," he whispered, pausing as he considered her. "I've seen what you are, girl. I've seen everything you've ever been and everything you will never be. You may pretend to be some kind of savior, but in truth, you are nothing. An abomination." Jack moved then, faster than Esta had expected, and grabbed her arm. With a finger that felt like ice, he traced the word carved into her wrist, like he understood what it implied. "You are an *impossibility*, Esta Filosik. You believe that your life is your own, but you live on borrowed minutes. Soon time will take what it's owed. Time *always* takes what it is owed. Like a devouring serpent, it will claim you for its own, and you will not even be a memory. But I could save you from the jaws of time and help you become something more. You only need to give me what I want. Give me the key to controlling Seshat."

Esta ripped her hand away from him then, but she knew it was only because he allowed it. "Never."

"I see you, girl, even if you refuse to see yourself." Jack tilted his head, his lips pulling up as the two of them circled each other. "We're not so different, you and I."

"I am *nothing* like you," Esta told him.

"No?" Jack purred, unmoved by her emotion. "Do you not borrow power to become more than you are? Or do you truly believe that your use of Ishtar's Key—and the life it contains—is so innocent?"

Esta lifted her chin, ignoring the echo of unease at Thoth's words. She'd worried about that very thing ever since the Professor had told her how the stones were created, but she wouldn't allow Thoth to distract her now.

Jack—or the thing inside him—seemed amused. "It wasn't meant as a judgment, girl. Whatever people are careless enough to lose can be taken, and whatever can be taken can be made our own. Lives included."

"And power?" Esta pressed, her mind racing. She would not leave until she had the Book.

"*Especially* power," Thoth said, glowing from within Jack's eyes.

"Even if it destroys the people you take it from?" she asked. Esta wasn't sure how she was going to get out of this, but she knew she had to keep Thoth talking. As long as he was going on about himself, he wasn't trying to kill her, and as long as Jack was still standing there, she could try to get the Book.

"If a person isn't strong enough to protect what's theirs, they deserve to be destroyed," Thoth whispered. "So many are born with power they are unworthy of."

She turned a little more, keeping him squarely in front of her. "Like Seshat?"

Jack's eyes went darker still. "*Exactly* like Seshat. If she had been stronger, she would have protected herself . . . and her power."

"She didn't think she needed to," Esta said. "She considered you a friend—she trusted you."

"Which only proves my point. From the beginning, Seshat was far too weak. Far too *soft*. She relied on sentiment instead of strength," Thoth hissed. "She had the ability to touch the very strands of creation. She could have had endless power at her disposal, and instead, she allowed everything to slip through her fingers."

"So you betrayed her."

Jack's eyes narrowed, and the amusement drained from his expression.

"I gave Seshat every chance—I gave her a *choice*. I showed her the unfairness of the world. I showed her how those born without an affinity must suffer the capriciousness of fate in silent resignation. She could have helped me. Together we could have taken the beating heart of magic and made it our own. Instead, she refused to wield the power within these pages as it was meant to be used."

"She disagreed with you, so you destroyed her," Esta challenged.

"I did what was *required*." Jack grimaced as though struggling to control the muscles in his face. "Seshat tried to keep me from my fate, but she failed, as she was always destined to fail. She attempted to save the heart of magic by creating the Book, but it was *I* who transformed the Book into something more. Every page bears the mark of *my* work. Over eons I have collected the rituals and spells within those pages. Over centuries I have worked to fill each and every page with the very secrets of magic. Soon it will be complete."

Esta pretended to be unaffected by his claims. "But it's still nothing without Seshat, isn't it?"

An ancient laugh came from deep within Jack. "Even without her, it is so much more than a simple tome. With it, I have already gone far beyond the bounds of what anyone else has yet imagined."

"Maybe," Esta said. "But without Seshat's power, you're just Sundren. A ghost within a man. You're pretending to be more than you are, because you still need her power."

"That power belongs to *me*," Thoth growled, contorting the skin and muscles of Jack's face as he leaned toward her.

Esta held her ground. "How could Seshat's power *possibly* belong to you?"

"Did I not encourage her?" he snarled, closer now to her face. Nearly close enough for her to reach the Book. "It was I who gave her the idea of placing the last bit of pure magic in these pages. Because even then, I knew that one day I would be able to wield it. You see, girl, everything Seshat did, everything she created, was because of *me*."

Esta doubted that was true. "Without Seshat, the Book is nothing but some paper and vellum bound in a ratty old cover."

"Is it?" Thoth laughed from somewhere deep inside of Jack. With a flourish, he tossed it into the air, where it hung, suspended in the Aether.

Energy snaked around Esta, hot and cold alike, and the Book began to rotate and turn in midair, opening as it did so. Light poured from the surface of its pages as the Ars Arcana floated above Jack's outstretched hand. As Esta watched, something began to emerge from the opened pages—a hilt and then a bloodred stone.

"You recognize this dagger, don't you?" Jack had moved closer to her, and she felt Thoth's energy flowing through him, licking at her, like he was trying to taste her power. "You've been searching for it."

The Pharaoh's Heart. It was so close—an arm's length away—protruding from the pages of the Book.

Esta tried to understand what she was seeing. The dagger was rising from the pages like they were some sort of a portal.

"Any stage magician could do the same," Esta challenged, pretending to be unmoved. But she had the sense that she needed to understand what she was seeing. "It's a nice illusion, but that's all it is."

Jack pulled the dagger completely from the Book, and in a flash he had the tip of the knife poised at her throat. "Does *this* feel like an illusion?"

The blade pressed against her skin, so close to where it had once cut her before. She felt her affinity tremble as it sensed the icy, echoing power of the stone in the dagger's hilt, but she pretended indifference. "It doesn't seem any different than pulling a rabbit from a hat," she told him, schooling her features so he wouldn't see her fear.

"A rabbit from a hat?" Jack—or Thoth—seemed almost amused by her challenge. "A moment ago this dagger did not *exist*." His eyes flashed, the darkness growing in them.

"That isn't possible," Esta told him. "Things are or they aren't."

"Perhaps it's not possible for someone like you." Jack scoffed. "But then, magic this powerful demands a more sophisticated mind, one capable of understanding—of wielding it."

"One like yours?" she asked, not bothering to hide the scorn in her voice.

"Exactly," Thoth said, every bit as obtuse as Jack himself. "Do you know what magic is, child?"

"It's the possibility within chaos," Esta told him, remembering the words Seshat had used.

"Yes," the creature inside of Jack hissed close to her ear, seemingly impressed despite himself. "But do you *truly* understand? Chaos is ancient and endless. Timeless and eternal. In chaos, the power of the old magic was forged. It is the very *antithesis* of the order imposed by time." Jack smiled—or maybe it was Thoth. She could no longer tell them apart. "Do you not see? Seshat created this Book to save a piece of pure magic within these pages. She understood that the old magic and time could not coexist, because time is the *antithesis* of magic—the *destroyer* of magic—and so she used her affinity to take a piece of the old magic, breaking it from the whole, and use its power to create an object *outside* the ravages of time."

"That's impossible," Esta said, refusing to believe him. It was a trick, a lie. He was only trying to distract her.

"Is it? You of all people should know that with time, the old magic will fade, and eventually, those who once held an affinity for it will become ordinary—*weak* as any Sundren has ever been. Look at the Order. Look at what they have become over the centuries," Thoth said.

He wasn't wrong. Professor Lachlan had told Esta the same: once, the Order had themselves been Mageus. When they came to the New World, they noticed their affinities were waning, and they created the Brink to *protect* the strength of their power. But the Brink had been wrong from the start. Instead of providing protection, it had become a trap, and over time their affinities faded . . . and they forgot what they had once been. As time passed, their power became dependent on the magic they could steal through ritual.

"Seshat came to understand the truth of this paradox too late," Thoth continued. "She created writing because she thought to protect the old magic. Instead, she created a *new* type of magic, *ritual* magic. But Seshat hated that this new magic made power accessible to those souls cursed by the accident of birth to have no affinity for the old magic. She hated that unworthy Sundren could now claim what *she* wanted only for herself."

"No, she hated what *you* did with ritual magic," Esta charged, remembering the visions Seshat had revealed to her in the Festival Hall. "She understood you were perverting its possibilities for your own greed and gain. She wanted to protect that power from *you*, because she knew that you only cared about accruing more power for yourself."

"Perhaps she did," Thoth admitted. "But to keep that power from me, she had to keep it from time itself."

Still holding on to her, Jack whipped the knife from her throat and stabbed the blade into the Book, which was still hovering in the air. But it didn't tear the paper. It simply sank into the surface, and as it disappeared, the energy that had been coming from it faded. When he snapped his fingers, the Book clapped shut and fell into his hands.

"No, Esta Filosik. This is no simple illusion. The power locked within these pages is far stronger than you could possibly imagine. Because of the piece of pure magic within it, the Book can *transform* time, and once I finally unlock the beating heart of magic contained in these pages, I will be able to *use* that power. I will remake the world anew," he said, and the darkness in his eyes lit suddenly with strange lightning.

The idea was horrific. If Thoth could unlock and control the pure piece of magic, he could transform time itself. There would be no place to hide, no way to avoid his tyranny. But Esta could sense that there was something she was missing, something essential that Thoth wasn't saying. "But you still need Seshat to grasp that piece of pure magic, don't you? You need something more than you have right now to control it. If you didn't, you'd have taken that power for your own already."

Something shifted in Jack's expression. Annoyance, maybe.

"It's too much for you, isn't it?" Esta taunted. "You're not as strong as she was. You're not strong enough to control the beating heart of magic on your own."

"Thanks to your magician, I won't have to," Thoth said. "Seshat sealed her doom when she chose the boy to carry her power. He's allowed himself to become sloppy and weak. I recently received news from California, and it seems he's gotten himself captured by some of my associates. Soon he—and Seshat's power with him—will be mine."

Thoth's words landed like a blow, and before Esta could recover herself, Jack had moved—almost inhumanly fast—to capture her again. His arms were like a vise around her.

"You're lying," Esta said.

"Am I?" Thoth whispered. "As soon as I'm finished here, I'll board a train to California. Harte Darrigan and the bitch who lives within his skin will both be mine. But I could spare his life if you agree to help me."

"Never." Esta kept struggling.

"Why fight me, girl? Are you so eager to die?" Thoth asked. "I see your heart. I know your plans. You hope to control the goddess by giving everything you have—everything you are—to stop her from taking her revenge." The darkness in Jack's eyes seemed to swell then. "Give your power to *me* instead, and you can live. Give your affinity over willingly, like so many have before you. You need not die. With your affinity, I could control Seshat's power. With your magic, I could remove Seshat from the magician without destroying the boy who holds your heart. The world will spin on. I've no desire to destroy it, as Seshat does."

"No," she charged. "You want to control it."

Jack shrugged. "Would that not be better than ending it?" Esta could see Thoth's amusement in Jack's eyes.

Her mind raced. "But what of me? Won't time take what it's owed?"

"You've seen for yourself what the Book can do, what I can do with the Book," Thoth said.

"You could take me outside of time?" Esta asked.

"Or the child who will become you." Thoth shrugged. "Either way, you could live beyond the reach of time, and your magician with you. But make no mistake . . . I plan on taking your affinity either way. Fight me now, and I will destroy you and all that you hold dear."

"You expect me to trust you?" Esta asked, considering her options. His offer might have been more tempting if he hadn't also just revealed something important: She and Harte had assumed Seshat *was* the power within the Book, but Thoth's words confirmed that Seshat had succeeded in placing a piece of pure magic in those pages. If she and Harte could harness it, there was no telling what they might be able to do, all the people they might be able to save.

It felt more important than ever to get the Book. And to get it here and now, before Thoth could get away.

"Trust or not, it matters little," Thoth said. "One way or another, your affinity will belong to me, and so will Seshat's. I will no longer be beholden to the tedium of time. My power will truly be limitless."

"But not really," Esta told him. "There's only so much you can do without a body. After all, you needed Jack to get this far. Such a *glorious* specimen of manhood you've selected to do your bidding."

Jack's face twisted. "His weakness served my purposes, but soon I will be beyond the need for anything so pedestrian as a body."

"Maybe," she said. "But there's one thing you forgot when you hitched your entire plan for world domination to Jack Grew."

"I've forgotten *nothing*," Thoth sneered.

"The funny thing about bodies—especially male bodies—" Esta brought her knee up sharp, right between Jack's legs, and ancient demigod or not, Jack crumpled at the impact. "They have a certain weakness."

She didn't stay to gloat. Snatching the Book from where it hovered in midair, and with time still pulled around her, she started to run, but she'd barely reached the opening of the tent when her vision flickered.

No. This can't be happening. Not now.

But as she moved, she felt time turning on her. The present moment was there, and then it wasn't, as the world around her flashed, cycling through the layers of time. Past. Present. And future. All at once. All terribly imminent. She felt herself start to fade, felt the Book fall through her fingers. She grabbed for it again, but it was like she was nothing but a shade, grasping for the reality she was no longer a part of.

PROMISES KEPT

1904—San Francisco

Harte Darrigan had once made a vow to himself that he would never again be tainted by the muck and filth of the streets. He'd spent too many nights curled in doorways with newspapers for warmth, fighting off rats and men alike. Now, though, standing across from the same door he'd approached when he'd first arrived in California, he felt so exhausted and worn down that he could have happily sunk right into whatever the slippery substance was under his feet. But he had the feeling that if he gave in to that longing to rest, he might never get up again.

He hadn't *truly* realized how weak he'd become until he'd made the decision to move. It still seemed incredible that he'd managed to get out of the hovel the Committee had kept him in at all. It was another mark of how bad he must have looked—they hadn't bothered really guarding him. As Harte freed himself and began navigating the streets of San Francisco, he realized that he was in serious trouble. With each new bout of feverish shivering, the mantle of dread he wore felt heavier.

He understood that he would not be able to make it back to the bridge, as he'd promised. He knew that he would never see Esta again, but Harte was determined to make right his biggest mistake. He would retrieve her cuff and return it to her—he would *try*.

What had he ever been thinking to take it from her in the first place?

He *hadn't* been thinking. He'd been desperate. Harte saw now that he hadn't been brave enough to stay after what had happened in St. Louis.

He'd been too afraid that Esta would turn away from him, disgusted by what lived inside his skin. He'd been a fool, and now it was too late.

Harte could only hope that Samuel Lowe hadn't had a chance to sell Ishtar's Key yet. Maybe he wouldn't be able to make it to their meeting at the bridge, but if the cuff was still somewhere in his father's home, Harte would find it. He could send it to Cela Johnson. Cela could leave the city. She could find Esta and explain. Harte had already asked far too much of the seamstress, but he would ask her for this one last thing as well. He would do everything he could to make sure that Esta knew he hadn't betrayed her on purpose.

Harte leaned against the damp brick of the building and watched the door across the alley for what felt like ages, until night fell over the city and lights glowed from within the windows around him. But no lights came on in his father's house. It remained dark and quiet, with no sign of anyone inside.

It was possible that the woman and the boy had left. Harte knew that his father wouldn't return. He'd made sure of it when he'd used the last of his strength to push his affinity into the men who'd wrestled him to the ground outside the bank. He could have used the opportunity to escape, but instead, he'd chosen to make the men believe they'd seen proof of his father's treachery. He'd ordered them to put Samuel Lowe on the first merchant ship they could find. It was the most he could do for the boy— one last trick to make the monster in Sammie's life disappear for good. He hoped it would be enough to give the kid a chance at a real future, a chance Harte had never had.

He closed his eyes and gathered his strength. In the darkness behind his eyelids, he could almost see the familiar lines of Esta's face, and in response, he felt Seshat stir with interest.

You can't have her, Harte said. *Neither of us can. But help me now, and we can both give her what she needs to defeat Thoth. Help me now, and we can end your enemy. You can have your revenge, even if neither of us lives to see it.*

He felt Seshat's frustration at his words, but he also sensed her resignation. Harte didn't wait for her agreement. Instead, he started across the street and let himself into the darkened house.

The light from a streetlamp poured in through the small windows, casting an eerie pall over the home. It was a small space that held a living area and kitchen all together, but it was neat and tidy, with matched pieces of well-made furniture. On one wall was a large wardrobe cabinet flanked by a couple of low couches. In the opposite corner, a stove stood cold and waiting. It clearly hadn't been used in some time, but the air still held the smell of spices and oil.

Confident that no one seemed to be home, Harte leaned against the nearby table, but breathing only caused him to erupt into a fit of coughing, which shook his body and sent jolts of pain through him. He gripped one of the chairs, hunching over as he tried to brace himself. Finally, when the fit had passed, he gathered what little strength he had and turned back to his business. He had to find Esta's cuff.

He started with the wardrobe on the far side of the room. It was a large piece, solid and well made. Behind the closed doors, Harte found a combination of shelves and drawers. He started to open one of the drawers but stopped short. If it hadn't been so deathly quiet in the house, he might not have heard the noise, but in the muffled silence, the sound of a gun being cocked might as well have been as loud as a cannon. Harte froze.

"Your hands. Put them where I can see." It was a woman's voice, soft and accented, but confident just the same.

He turned slowly, raising his hands so that he could show he was no threat. On the other side of the room was the woman who had answered the door so many days before. His father's wife. She had seemed surprised then—maybe even afraid. Now she wore an expression both fierce and unwavering.

"Who are you?" she demanded. "Who sent you?"

"No one," he told her.

She shook her head. "I know what you are," she said, continuing to aim the gun at the center of his chest. "Committee rat. You've been sniffing around my home for days. I already told the other that I don't have what you're looking for."

"No," Harte said, feeling more light-headed than he had a moment before. "Not Committee."

"Then who sent you?" she demanded. Harte had no doubt that she would shoot if she didn't get the answer she wanted. "What do you want?"

"Please . . ." Harte stepped into the beam of light. "I'm not from the Committee. No one sent me. I only want the items your husband took from me—a necklace and a cuff," he told her, making a circular motion around his upper arm that had her leveling her gun at him again. "They weren't mine. I need to return them to their owner."

A blur darted from the back room, and it was all Harte could do to keep from falling over from the impact. *Sammie.* The woman put down the gun immediately and issued an urgent command to the child clinging to Harte's legs. But the boy argued back, refusing to let go.

"*You're* the one who gave yourself up for my son?" the woman said, surprise coloring her expression.

"It was the least I could do. I was the one who put him in danger in the first place," Harte said, gently pushing the child away from him.

"No," she said. "That was his father." The woman's expression shifted to concern, as though she'd finally taken stock of Harte. "You don't look well."

"I'm not," Harte admitted, swaying a little. "Which is why it's even more important that I retrieve what I came for. I need to return the pieces, and I don't know how much time I—"

"They're gone," she told him, her expression closed off.

"Gone." The word came out in a rush, and Harte felt like he'd been sucker punched.

"I'm sorry." The woman did not seem sorry.

"They can't be gone." He'd been having trouble staying upright before, but now the devastation of this information threatened to push him over completely.

"I had to. My husband's creditors would have taken the house if I hadn't paid them. It was the only way to save him, to save us from—"

A loud banging erupted on the other side of the door, followed by shouted commands that had the woman's eyes widening.

"Were you followed?" she demanded in a hushed whisper.

Harte shook his head, but in all honesty, he couldn't have known.

The woman seemed to sense this. She spoke to the child, who nodded obediently, before she looked back at Harte. "Go with Sammie and remain silent." Then she tucked the gun into the folds of her gown and shouted something to the people on the other side of the door.

"But—" Harte shook his head. Even as he wobbled on his feet, it seemed wrong to leave her to defend him.

"Go," she commanded. "You cannot be found here. Do you understand?"

The fear in her eyes told Harte everything he needed to know. He'd put this family in danger once again. This time he didn't argue when the boy took him by the hand and led him through a doorway to a bedroom. There Sammie pulled back the rug and opened a hatch in the floor to reveal a set of earthen steps leading down into a compartment that looked like a root cellar. There were blankets and pillows piled on the floor, along with a couple of carved wooden toys.

"Have you been staying down there?" Harte asked.

The boy nodded. "My father owed many people many debts, so my mother makes me hide when they come. She's been afraid for me ever since the Committee's men brought news that my father had been sent away."

"He's gone, then?" Harte asked, trying to keep himself awake.

"On a ship. He won't be returning," the boy said.

"Does that make you sad?" Harte asked, wondering if he'd made the wrong decision again.

"It should, but my father . . ." Sammie paused.

"It's okay," he told the boy. "You know it wasn't your fault?"

But Sammie only frowned, clearly unsure. Then his brows drew together. "It was you, wasn't it? This was your trick?"

Harte nodded, because he couldn't lie to the kid. "Does that make you angry with me?"

Sammie considered the question. "I don't think so. It will be harder for Mother with him gone, but she is strong, and she is smart." His eyes widened. "Your hand feels like fire."

"It's nothing," Harte said, pulling away from the boy's grasp. "I just need to rest for a while." His body suddenly felt every bit of the energy he'd exerted in escaping, in making it this far. "But there's something I need you to do for me—"

From the front of the house came a loud, clattering noise—Sammie's mother shouted something in German, which was followed by a crash.

The boy's eyes went wide, bright with fear and anger as he urged Harte toward the hideaway. *"Hurry."*

Without further argument, Harte stumbled down the handful of steps. His legs gave out before he reached the bottom, and he collapsed into the softness of the quilts as the boy began to replace the trapdoor that covered the hideaway.

"Wait," Harte told him, which made the boy pause. "I need you to do something for me. . . ."

Or that was what he'd intended to say, but his vision went dark, and the words felt cumbersome on his tongue.

There was something he had to tell the boy, something he needed the child to do for him. He had to get a message to Esta, but Harte was too exhausted for words, so he reached out his hand to the boy, pleading silently for Sammie to take hold. He tried to focus on his affinity, but the darkness was pulling him down again, and he didn't know how much longer he could fight it.

Why do you continue to lie to yourself? Seshat asked, suddenly closer now than she had been for days.

If we want to defeat Thoth, I need to make him understand. Harte was reaching for the boy, and his brother was leaning down to him, taking his hand, but Harte had so little strength left. His affinity felt so far from him. *Esta needs her cuff. He could send it to her. Or a message*, he thought frantically. There had to be a way to tell her. *Help me.*

I already have.

Seshat's power surged then, hot and sudden and so much stronger than Harte had expected. He felt his brother flinch and saw Sammie's eyes go wide with confusion. With an expression too much like pain.

No. This wasn't what he had intended at all. . . .

She will come for you, Seshat whispered as the power coursed through him. *You knew that. You made sure of it when you took her cuff. And when she finally arrives, you will be too weak to fight me. When she comes for you, she will be mine.*

THE RIGHT INCENTIVE

J ack Grew crumpled to the ground, cupping his groin as pain radiated up through him and turned his stomach inside out. The world spun. The dingy walls of the tent tilted and swam, and all he could do was roll to his side and try not to retch as he watched Esta Filosik scoop up the Book of Mysteries from where he'd dropped it and begin to run.

Groaning, Jack gritted his teeth, willed himself up, but every movement was agony. His stomach churned, and the throbbing pain between his legs stole his breath.

But Esta didn't get far. She hadn't even made it to the opening of the tent when her steps faltered and then, right before his eyes, she disappeared. One moment she was there, destroying everything, and then it was like she was a ghost of a girl . . . and then, nothing at all.

The Book fell to the ground, its pages splayed open and the inscriptions upon the vellum glowing as though it understood how close it had come to being lost. The second she was gone, the silence that had plugged Jack's ears while they'd argued drained away, and a great roaring took its place. With it came the continued cackling laugh of the girl they'd found tied to the tent post in their prisoner's place.

"What the hell are you doing down there on the ground?" Clem Curtis asked, blinking in confusion at Jack's position on the ground. "What's wrong? You're breathin' all funny-like."

"I'm fine," Jack said, the wheeze in his voice betraying the lie as he tried to pull himself up.

"You don't look fine," Clem said, offering a hand, which Jack ignored. "You look practically apoplectic."

A moment before, Jack had been railing at the clown for losing the Antistasi cowboy who'd been slinking around the grounds of the Curtis Brothers' Show. They'd been so close to getting answers, and the Curtises had let the damn maggot get away. But Clem Curtis hadn't been privy to everything that had happened—*because Esta Filosik can control time.* Jack would have laughed at the idea of it, but his stones were screaming.

Get up.

Jack ignored Clem's question and listened instead to that voice inside him, that stronger part of himself that had guided him for years now. The voice had rarely been wrong, and so Jack obeyed. Forcing himself to his knees, despite the shooting pain that pulsed through his entire lower half every time he moved, he began the torturous crawl toward the Book.

Faster. Before Curtis realizes . . . Jack reached for the Book and felt an answering pulse of victory when his fingers wrapped around it. Ignoring the pain in his balls, he secured the Book of Mysteries inside his coat.

"Secretary Grew?" Curtis took a step toward him. "Are you going to explain what the hell is happening here?"

"It was an attack, or don't you remember?" Jack said, squeezing the words out through the pain as he pulled out his morphine tablets, placing two on his tongue. Then adding a third for good measure.

Clem looked around the tent, his expression suddenly anxious. "What attack?"

"The maggots got away," Jack sneered, pulling himself up to his feet. The world still swam every time he moved, and his balls felt like they'd been pushed up inside his body, but the quick-acting morphine had cut through some of the sharpest pain. "Tell your men to block every exit. No one gets off these grounds until I find the Antistasi bastards who are responsible."

The girl they'd found tied to the tent post had been cackling the whole time, a strange, unhinged laugh that sounded like something inside her was broken. Now she laughed harder.

"What is so goddamn funny?" Jack demanded, his temper finally fraying beyond any hope of control.

The girl went silent, pressing her lips together as hysterical mania lit her eyes. "You'll never catch them," she said before she cackled again. "The Antistasi will get to the Thief long before you do."

Jack glared at her, measuring her words. "You know Esta, don't you?" he asked. "You're one of them."

She only smiled at him, the wild smile of a woman gone mad.

He felt the weight of the Book and the dagger anchoring him.

"Who is this?" he asked Clem.

"Cordelia Smith," Clem told him. "She's our sharpshooter in the show."

"Did you know she's Mageus?" Jack asked.

Clem Curtis blustered and made excuses, but Jack's focus was on the sharpshooter, an ordinary-looking girl no one would miss.

"You are Mageus, aren't you, Cordelia? Feral magic runs in your veins," Jack said, feeling suddenly better about the situation. "Antistasi, too, from the sound of it."

The girl spat at him, but he was far enough away that she didn't even come close to hitting his shoes.

"I'll take her with me for questioning," Jack said, disgusted. "Perhaps with the right incentives, she can give us what we need to stop this plague of violence."

"I'll give you nothing." She bared her teeth like a feral cat.

"I think you'll find I can be quite *persuasive*," Jack told her, ignoring the hysterics. There was something about her that appealed to him—not her looks or her body, of course. But something inside of her that made him take notice.

Now that the Book had returned the Pharaoh's Heart, Jack had everything he needed to follow the instructions that Newton himself had left in the pages of the Book. With the ritual, he could create another artifact—a stone finally worthy of powering the machine he'd long dreamed of building. All he needed was a maggot with enough power worth harvesting.

Jack took the girl by the chin and couldn't help smiling when she jerked away and then tried to bite him. Cordelia Smith had a strength within her that might one day be useful.

"It doesn't matter what you do to me," Cordelia told him. "The Antistasi cannot be stopped. We are endless as a snake devouring its own tail. Infinite as time itself."

Jack only smiled. "Perhaps we should see how infinite *you* are?"

A RESCUE

1904—Denver

O nce again, Esta felt herself returning long before she fully became a part of the world around her. First came the feel of the ground beneath her, the uneven and hard-packed earth that served as a floor for the tent. Then came the scent of smoke, which burned her throat and her nose until finally she could feel her body, her *self*, as something real and whole.

She pushed herself up from the ground, trying to make sense of the scene around her as she coughed. A moment ago she'd been certain of her victory, but now she remembered—Jack had been there. Thoth as well, and he'd told her about the Book before time had *unmade* her.

Time will take what it's owed, Thoth had told Esta. He'd called her an abomination, and now she wondered if there was any merit to his words. Maybe the two lives she led—the young girl back in New York and the girl she was now—couldn't coexist any more than copies of the stones could. Or maybe the reason time had tried to pull her apart again was even worse. Hadn't Jack told her that Harte had been captured in California? If that was true, maybe something had happened to Ishtar's Key. If Harte had lost the cuff, she wouldn't be able to take it back to the girl. It might explain the previous episodes—if Ishtar's Key was gone, her very present couldn't exist.

But she hadn't disappeared completely, which meant that there must still be a chance to retrieve Ishtar's Key—and with it, a chance to save

Harte. There might well come a day when time would not release her from its grip. A day when the darkness would win, and she would be unmade. But that day had not yet arrived.

Esta pulled herself upright. She didn't know how long she'd been gone this time. Seconds or minutes . . . or *more*? However long it had been, she didn't need to search the tent to know that Jack was gone, and with him, the Book. But she thought of Harte and what might be happening to him on the other side of the continent, and it was enough to shake her from her self-pity and to focus.

She pulled herself the rest of the way to her feet and staggered out of the tent into the cooler air of the summer night. At first she couldn't understand what she was seeing. All around her, the grounds of the Curtis Brothers' Wild West Show had devolved into confusion. She barely had time to jump out of the way of a trio of horses as they thundered by, nearly trampling her in the process. Another cowboy on horseback followed, already swinging a rope.

A pair of strong hands caught her from behind, and she turned to find the older man who'd helped them earlier. "This way, and keep your head down," George ordered as he pulled her through the chaos by the hand. "We gotta get you out of here."

"What's going on?" Esta asked, still feeling a little adrift, like she wasn't completely part of the world quite yet.

"All hell's breaking loose—that's what's going on," he said as though she should have figured that much out for herself. "A bunch of Antistasi troublemakers set half the horses loose, and the Syndicate's men are trying to round them all up—horses and men alike."

"I thought you went with North and Maggie," Esta said, following George without any argument.

"I got them all set up with Doc Ford a couple of hours ago. She'll take good care of the girl, but Jerry sent me back for you."

"Hours?" It had been more than a few minutes, then. "Why did he send you back?" she asked, suddenly uneasy.

"He said you might need a ride to the station."

"I do," Esta said, relaxing a little when she realized this was a rescue and not an attack.

George helped her into the wagon he had waiting for them at the far edge of the grounds, and they kept off the main roads as he drove her back to town. Once they saw the outskirts, where the streetlights glowed up ahead of them, he pulled the cart over.

"This is where we part ways," he told her. "I went around to the south, so if anyone's watching for people coming from the show, they shouldn't be looking in this direction. But it'll be safer for both of us if you go on foot from here." He pulled a familiar leather pouch from the underside of the driver's seat and offered it to her.

"Where'd you get this?"

"Miss Maggie sent it along for you," George explained. "She said you might need it."

Esta took the offered pouch, still heavy with the formulations that she'd helped Maggie prepare over the last few days. It contained a veritable arsenal that would surely come in handy in the days ahead— especially with whatever she would have to face in San Francisco.

"Thank you," she told him. "For everything."

"It wasn't much," George said. "Anyone would have done the same."

"No," she said, shaking her head. "That isn't even a little bit true. Could you do me one last favor, though?"

George raised his brows in a silent question.

"Check on Bill Pickett for me? Keep an eye out for him if you can. I have a feeling that the people who were after us might go for him next."

"You don't have anything to worry about when it comes to Bill. We'll make certain to keep an eye out."

Esta gave George a sure nod, wishing that she could give him some-thing else—one of Maggie's concoctions or some protection or assur-ance beyond that. She was leaving him, Pickett, and everyone whose lives they'd touched in as much danger as they'd left Julian back in St. Louis. But there was nothing she could do except turn toward the city of Denver and the train that would carry her across the country to her magician. Esta picked up her pace, hoping that time wouldn't take her before she could reach him.

OUTMANEUVERED

1902—New York

Viola Vaccarelli barely trusted herself to speak as she walked alongside Theo, back to his carriage. She wasn't exactly sure how she'd lost the argument against him helping with the Order, but she had. Even Jianyu and Cela had agreed that if she wasn't willing to use Nibsy, they needed a way to get more information than what she might glean from her brother. And she *wasn't* willing to risk working with Nibsy. Viola knew her refusal to work with the little snake had confused them all—Viola included. But how could she explain to them why she was so afraid to take Nibsy's bargain when she couldn't even explain it to herself?

They thought her reluctance was because she hated Nibsy—and she did. But they did not understand that she could not give Nibsy what he wanted—information against Paul. Information that would likely destroy her brother. It didn't matter that Paolo could take care of himself or that he did not deserve her protection. Viola would have gladly destroyed Paul herself if it hadn't been for what that action would do to their mother.

Pasqualina Vaccarelli loved her son like she loved her saints. In her eyes, *Paolino* could do no wrong, and if he *had* done wrong, Viola's mother would never willingly admit it. Losing Paolo might well kill their mother. And if it didn't kill her? If Pasqualina ever found out that Viola had been involved in orchestrating Paolo's downfall? Certainly that would turn any love her mother might yet hold for Viola to hatred.

She wasn't sure why it mattered. Viola could not even explain to herself why she still cared, when her family had never been particularly kind or loving to her. They had never accepted her, not for the magic that lived beneath her skin nor for her headstrong temper nor for her unwillingness to find a nice boy and settle for the life she was *supposed* to want. They'd never looked at her with the clear affection that Abel had shown Cela, but they were still her family, weren't they? They were her blood, and she could not quite bring herself to betray them . . . not completely.

And if her mother had made life difficult for Viola, wasn't that only a mother's right? Pasqualina could not help having a daughter who refused to be meek and subservient, who would not take a man and settle down to a proper life. She could not help having a daughter born with the old magic, one who used that power to break the Lord's commandments with such impunity. Perhaps Pasqualina Vaccarelli had never shown Viola the patience that she reserved only for Paolo, but she *had* tried to show Viola what was right. That was surely a sign of her mother's love . . . *wasn't it?*

When they reached the carriage, Theo opened the door and offered Viola his hand, as he always did. Ever the gentleman, even if Viola was nothing like a lady. From the expression he wore, Theo was far too pleased with himself and far too sure as well.

Viola hated that he was right. Theo *could* gain access to the Order easier than any of them. He could verify the information from both Nibsy and Paul, and he could give her and Jianyu the upper hand, so that they could be the ones to retrieve the ring. But Viola could not accept the possibility that Theo might be hurt for helping her—not when he belonged to Ruby.

He was one more worry she had to add to her pile. One more life in her keeping.

"I still say that you don't need to do this," she told Theo, when they were finally secure in the carriage and on their way back to the Bowery.

"I believe it's already been decided," Theo said pleasantly. Always *pleasantly*. It was impossible to argue with him.

"You saw what happened at the gala," she said. "You understand what the Order is capable of. If they discover you're against them, your money and family name won't protect you."

"Perhaps," he admitted. "But I don't plan for them to find out."

She threw her hands up in exasperation. "No one *plans* for things to go wrong, Theo," Viola told him. "It's not worth risking yourself to help us. We have been living under the threat of the Order since we arrived in this city. Jianyu and I can handle ourselves."

"I'm not doing this for Jianyu," Theo told her. "I'm helping *you*, Viola. I'm helping my friend."

Her stomach twisted. "I am not worth your life."

"I don't think that's quite true," Theo said. "Neither does Ruby, or she wouldn't have made me promise to look after you. Blame her if you'd like, but I never break my promises."

Viola choked on a laugh. "I was sent to *kill* Ruby, or don't either of you remember how we met?"

"But you *didn't* kill her—or me," Theo pointed out.

That fact was irrelevant. "Every day you make me think that decision was a mistake," she muttered.

"Maybe it was," Theo agreed. "But it doesn't change the fact that you *did* spare us, and in sparing us, I believe you became stuck with us."

"What is one life spared when so many others were not so lucky?" He started to speak, to argue with her, but Viola shook her head and held up her hand to stop him. "*No.* You need to understand, Theo. Ruby, she has ideas—"

Viola's throat went tight suddenly as she remembered Ruby's ideas— how she had leaned in the night of the gala and kissed her. *Kissed* her.

Why did you do that? Viola had asked.

Because I saw you . . . and I wanted to.

As though anything could ever be so easy or simple. As though the press of lips, the stirring of breath didn't have to be worried over or fret-ted about or *earned*. As though it could just simply *be*. Without shame, without reservation.

What about Theo? Viola had asked.

He wouldn't care.

"Ruby always has ideas," Theo said with a sigh. "She doesn't always think them through, but she's also not often wrong."

He was looking at Viola with an unsettling softness in his expression. His light eyes and his pleasant face and his golden hair had no place in Viola's world, but Theo Barclay was looking at her like he understood something about her that even Viola did not have words for.

"She's wrong this time," Viola told him, wishing it were otherwise. "I need for you to *think*. I need for you to understand. Don't tell yourself stories about me, about my hidden goodness. I was *made* to be what I am. Every heart I stopped from beating was a choice. *My* choice. And I do not regret those choices."

Theo was still looking at her with an unreadable expression. "You didn't kill Ruby," he said finally. "You didn't allow me to die. You risked quite a lot to save Jianyu today, and it's clear from the way you speak of your friend Dolph that you would have gladly given your life if it could have saved his as well."

"It's not enough," Viola told him, feeling the truth of those words as clearly as she felt her own affinity. "One bit of good doesn't erase the rest."

"Maybe not," Theo agreed, his eyes soft with pity. "Maybe you are an assassin, by birth and by choice, but you are also my friend, Viola. You are *Ruby's* friend as well." He shrugged. "In my estimation, that's more than enough reason to help you, but in case you've forgotten, I have a stake in this too. Jack Grew was the one who ordered Ruby's death. For that reason alone, I will do whatever I can to help you bring down the Order, and Jack right along with it."

"Theo . . ." Viola sharpened her voice in warning.

"You might have saved me once before, Viola, but aside from that one unfortunate incident, I've done rather well at taking care of myself—and Ruby, too, for that matter. In fact, with her gone this summer, I won't have to constantly extricate her from problems of her own creation, and I would very much hate to find myself *bored*." He gave a mock shudder.

Viola realized then that there would be no talking Theo out of this. He had no affinity, no way to protect himself from the Order's magic or power. He had nothing at stake in this fight, but he was committed all the same.

"This is a terrible idea," she told him.

"Most amusing things are," Theo said, flashing an uneven smile as he patted her leg.

"The Order won't hesitate to make you disappear if they feel you're a threat," she told him. "They've had too much practice."

"I'll be fine," Theo said, looking far too pleased with himself. "You know, I believe this is the most excitement I've had in my life since Ruby decided to dress in men's clothing and infiltrate a Knights of Labor meeting. She practically caused a riot when her hair fell out of her hat and they discovered she was actually a woman." He laughed softly at the memory, his eyes gazing off into a past that Viola could not see.

Whatever Ruby might have said that night at the gala, Viola had the sense that Theo Barclay very much cared.

"You love her," she realized, her heart clenching a little at the thought.

"Of course." Theo gave her a small, sad smile. "Who wouldn't love Ruby Reynolds?" He winked before opening the carriage door, effectively ending their conversation.

Viola hadn't even noticed that they'd stopped, but now she saw that they'd arrived at the corner Theo usually dropped her at—one that was a safe enough distance from Paolo's building. After she'd alighted, she turned back to him. "I wish I could talk you out of this."

"I know," he told her. With a small, impertinent shrug, he closed the carriage door.

As she watched his carriage rattle away, Viola felt a sudden, inexplicable wave of sadness rush over her. *Who, indeed, wouldn't love Ruby Reynolds?*

She could not help but think of the moment at the gala when Ruby's lips had touched hers. It had been completely unexpected, but along with the shock of it, she'd had the strange sense of the world being right in a way it never had before. It was as though every bit of her life that hadn't *quite* fit together had rotated solo un pó, the pieces locking together in a way that finally made sense. Her affinity had never made her feel like that. Neither had her family or the hours she'd spent on her knees in church. But for the space of a heartbeat, the slice of a single moment, Viola had glimpsed a possibility that she had never imagined could be hers.

She'd immediately rejected it, of course. It was too unbelievably terrifying to think about what *real* happiness might look like—might *feel* like. It was too dangerous to even consider. She had the memory, though, and if it was all that she would ever have, Viola would take that memory and carry it with her—that perfect moment of happiness that was shaped precisely like Ruby's mouth.

The clanging of a nearby shop closing its shutters for the evening shook her back to herself. She didn't have time for dreams. There was too much work still ahead, too many lives she had to keep safe, and Paolo would be waiting for his supper.

A TWISTED KNOT

James Lorcan sat in the quiet of his rooms considering the telegram. Two years ago, he'd taken inspiration from one of Dolph's books to wrestle the loose, unorganized pockets of resistance into a network that was a true adversary to the Brotherhoods' power. For two years now, he'd plotted and planned and waited, certain that his patience would be rewarded. Certain the Antistasi would deliver Esta and Darrigan to him.

He turned the telegram over in his hand, but he knew that there was no secret message to be found in the ordinary sheet of paper. It simply confirmed what he'd suspected when he'd felt the Aether shudder the day before: Cordelia Smith was as good as dead. She'd been taken by Jack Grew and the Brotherhoods, and her capture had shaken the Antistasi's network. Badly. His contacts across the country were nervous.

The Antistasi were the least of James' worries, though. As their leader, James knew that the network could be brought in line easily enough once he took care of Ruth Feltz. Her death would send a message, and after he'd installed his own people in St. Louis, the Middle West would be back under his control. The bigger problem was Esta Filosik, and what he was going to do about her.

James took the notebook from his jacket pocket. He'd stopped worrying about the unreadable words years ago. What he needed wasn't on those pages anyway. He carefully pried loose the back cover and removed the small slip of paper he'd found months after everything had collapsed around him at the Conclave. It was impossibly old and impossibly fragile, but he understood that it was also the key to bringing Esta back to him, and with her, the artifacts and the Book.

If Cordelia had been captured, and if the Brotherhoods weren't crowing about apprehending the Devil's Thief, it meant that Esta had escaped. Already, she would be on her way to California, undoubtedly to find Darrigan and the other stones. He tested the Aether, considered his options. With his network in disarray, it would be more difficult to bring them to heel. Too much could go wrong, as it had already. No . . . a different tack was necessary. It was time, James thought, to remind Esta of what was at stake.

As he walked toward Orchard Street, the Bowery smelled of the coal smoke from the elevated trains and the sour rot of the vegetables and trash in the gutters. He'd been paying the rent on an apartment at the top floor of the building for more than three years now—ever since Leena had died on the bridge that night and Dolph had not. Three years of continuing to conceal Leena's darkest and most powerful secret. It was two years longer than he should have, based on what the notebook had originally told him. The timeline had changed, yet the girl was still there . . . and Esta was still alive.

Time was a twisted knot, as dangerous and impossible to untangle as a ball of snakes. Anyone who tried to pry it apart was liable to find time's venomous teeth sunk deep into their wrist. But James Lorcan believed himself up for the task.

The matron who lived on the top floor was an old woman with rheumy eyes and a voice like a rusted gate. She opened the door immediately at his knock, used to his oddly timed visits. He paid handsomely enough that she did not question him, never scolded or tried to turn him away, not even when he came in the dead of night.

She knew better.

"Where is she?" James asked.

The woman pointed toward the back bedroom. "She's napping, though."

"I don't care if she's spinning straw into gold," he said, brushing past the old lady and into the apartment.

He'd done what he could in the year after Leena's death to make the girl comfortable. Now the child must be close to seven, and each time James paid her a call, she reminded him more and more of who she would one day become—the viper who would betray him.

If only he could kill the child now, or rather, let the city do what it would with her. It would have been far easier than raising her. But before it had become worthless, the notebook had taught James that taking the girl's life would mean losing everything else. His only chance at regaining the destiny that had so far eluded him was through Leena's daughter. He hoped that with a firm enough hand, he could still mold the child into what she should have been if not for that damned magician. Either way, he would use her as he could.

The girl entered the room a moment later, holding tightly to the old woman's hand.

"Come here, child," he said.

The girl shrank from him, the same as she had each time since the night he'd first marked her two years before. James didn't blame the child for the fear in her golden eyes. It was another indication of how smart she was and how cunning she would become.

"We're going to play a little game," he told her, and held out his hand.

"Please, sir. No . . ." Her voice was no more than the mewing whine of a kitten, but he had no pity for her. Kittens grew into cats with claws, feral and dangerous if left unattended.

"Now, Carina," he said sternly, and she finally complied, slipping her trembling hand into his, even as her small mouth was pressed tight.

The mark on the underside of her wrist had long since scarred over into the shiny pink of new skin. The girl trembled in his grasp as James traced over the letters with his finger, and he wondered how close the connection was between this child and the girl she would become. Could Esta see his warnings? Could she feel the touch of his finger through the miles and the years? More importantly, would she understand?

He had not brought Viola's knife, but James doubted the make of the blade was what mattered. Tears were running down the apples of the girl's cheeks even before he touched the small pocketknife to her skin, and by the time it drew blood, she was crying in earnest.

James ignored the girl's tears.

As long as Esta Filosik was still in play, nothing was ever over. *Nothing* was ever too late.

PART

III

NEW ALLIANCES

1904—San Francisco

The air was oppressive with the fog that was coming in off the bay when Jack Grew arrived in San Francisco. He'd left Denver immediately after dealing with the maggot sharpshooter. Her affinity had been a welcome addition to the collection of power held within the Book. He had not bothered to stop and confer with Gunter or any of the others before he left. He brought Hendricks with him, but that was only because Jack had happened to see the Guardsman as he was leaving the grounds of the Curtis Brothers' Show.

Denver had been a fiasco, but at least it hadn't been a complete catastrophe. In Jack's pocket, the Book's power still throbbed in time with his own heart. Esta Filosik might have slipped away from him, but he knew exactly where she was heading, and he had allies already waiting.

When the ferry finally docked, Jack was met by one of the leaders of the Vigilance Committee. William Cooke was in his thirties—a decade older than Jack, but still young enough not to be part of the old guard. Jack remembered Cooke from the Conclave two years before. He'd been an attendee then—a junior delegate from the Vigilance Committee. Even then, Jack could sense a hunger in the other man, and in the time between, Cooke had apparently managed to rise through the ranks of his organization with impressive speed. He could be a rival for power unless Jack neutralized that threat right now.

Cooke seemed unaware of the direction of Jack's thoughts as he welcomed Jack on behalf of the entire organization to their "fair city" with a haughtiness that made Jack want to punch him. "Fair" was stretching things, in Jack's estimation. He'd traveled any number of places with the president, and even more on Roosevelt's behalf, but he'd never been this far west. Now he saw that he'd been missing nothing. The shores of San Francisco teemed with working-class miscreants, and the buildings along the waterfront were no better than shacks. Years before, New York had already made improvements in even its poorest neighborhoods that far surpassed these streets.

But he didn't tell Cooke any of this. There was no sense upsetting the man before he proved himself useful.

"I trust you've made the necessary arrangements," Jack said, lifting a handkerchief to his nose to ward off the smell as Cooke led him through the docks.

"After I received your telegram, the Committee doubled the watchmen's patrols."

"And the Thief?" Jack asked.

"So far there's been no sign of her," Cooke admitted.

"You've kept all of this quiet?" Jack asked. "We wouldn't want our quarry to get word that we're searching for her. If she has allies in this city, they might warn her off."

"We've kept everything in-house, like you wanted," Cooke assured him.

"There haven't been questions about the increased patrols?" Jack wondered.

Cooke shook his head, clearly self-satisfied with the job he'd done. "We're already dealing with a bit of an issue in Chinatown right now—a possible outbreak of plague." He shrugged. "It's been easy enough to explain the increased patrols throughout the city as being related to that. There's enough negative sentiment about the Chinese in the city that nobody has questioned our methods. If anything, the citizens approve of keeping a tighter watch on the foreigners, and they've welcomed the increased surveillance. They don't care who else we might be watching for."

Good. "President Roosevelt sends his heartfelt appreciation for all you and your men have done to help protect our great nation," Jack said solemnly. It wasn't *exactly* a lie. He was sure Roosevelt would have appreciated Cooke's assistance if he'd had any notion that Jack was still tracking the Thief. But while the president had been upset by the events at the world's fair, he didn't understand the true threat that feral magic posed to the country. Roosevelt cared about assimilation of the immigrants who brought the feral magic to the country, but he didn't understand that maggots with that sort of wild, dangerous power could never be truly American. Simply forcing a maggot to speak English would never be enough, not unless or until the power they carried was neutralized.

Cooke preened all the more. "Myself and my city are gratified to be of service to the president."

"You have my personal appreciation as well," Jack added. "I know that in the past our respective Brotherhoods have been at odds, but the events of the last few weeks have illustrated how important our mutual cooperation will be in this new century. I'm glad that men like yourself—modern men of action and intelligence—have the foresight to understand that our shared enemy requires new alliances."

"Alliances?" Cooke glanced at him.

"Unity against a common enemy," Jack clarified. He looked to Hendricks. "The medallions."

Hendricks gave a sure, obedient nod, removed a small linen pouch from his bag, and offered it to Cooke, who took it with some confusion.

"The Veiled Prophet Society and their Jefferson Guard offer you a token of our shared Brotherhood," Jack explained. "It is time to put our differences aside. It is time to act as one."

Cooke opened the pouch and removed one of the medallions to examine it. "What is this?"

"This is a device that the Jefferson Guard developed back in St. Louis. The Veiled Prophet Society uses them to detect feral magic," Hendricks explained. "And now . . . so shall the Vigilance Committee."

Cooke seemed suddenly more interested. "The Society sent this?" He frowned, turning the medallion over.

"As I said, we're stronger together against a common enemy. The Society believes this. I hope that the Vigilance Committee will come to believe it as well. Withholding from one another only weakens us all. Distribute them to your men with my compliments and thanks," Jack told Cooke. "They'll offer some protection against the Thief's feral magic and against any maggots who might think to help her. We can't let the Thief get away from us," he warned. "For the good of the country."

"For the good of the country," Cooke agreed.

They finally pushed through the crowds at the docks, and Cooke led them to an open-air carriage. The hills of San Francisco were barely visible through the murk of the cloudy day.

He would need to spend time with Cooke and the rest of the Vigilance Committee later, once this was all over, Jack thought. With Cooke under his influence, the Committee would likely be valuable allies in the future, but for now Jack was only interested in one thing—obtaining the artifact that was waiting for him, and making the damn magician sorry for ever crossing him.

"Now," Jack said. "About the other issue you wanted to discuss with me . . ." He took another cube of morphine and let it fortify him for what was to come.

A PREMONITION

The journey to California took Esta three interminable days. As the train cut through the country, she didn't know how much of a head start Jack might have had from Denver. She had no way of knowing if she'd be in time to reach Harte before anyone else could, but a new scar had appeared on her wrist. Considering that the scar had appeared somewhere in the middle of the Rocky Mountains, Esta figured Nibsy also knew that she'd managed to escape his reach in Denver. If he knew that, it was also likely that Cordelia had already notified Nibsy and the rest of the network about where Harte had been heading.

The scar formed a single word—*clavis*—but beneath that word there was a line of strange markings. Esta understood what the word meant—"key." It was Nibsy's way of ordering her to return with the cuff, but the markings were a puzzle. They seemed oddly familiar, but she couldn't remember where she might have seen them before, and she didn't know what they signified.

Even if Esta had any intention of bowing to Nibsy Lorcan's demands—and she definitely didn't—she didn't have Ishtar's Key. Until she found Harte, she *wouldn't* have Ishtar's Key, and she had a feeling that her arrival in California wouldn't go as easily as she hoped. After all, they'd left the sharpshooter behind, basically tied up like a gift for the Brotherhoods. If the Brotherhoods had Cordelia, it was possible that they already knew everything that Nibsy knew. They might have already found Harte. They might already be waiting for Esta as well. Even if she managed to slip past all of that danger and find Harte, Cordelia knew their final destination, which meant that the Brotherhoods probably would as well. If they could manage to make it out of San Francisco, returning to Manhattan to retrieve the final artifact had now become more dangerous.

Of course, none of that would matter if Esta couldn't reach Harte. From the way time had pulled her under, she now knew for sure that *nothing* would matter if she couldn't retrieve her cuff.

By the time Esta boarded the Pacific Railroad's ferry into San Francisco, she was both bone-tired and completely on edge. Each night she had tried to sleep on the train, but her dreams had taken her to the same tormented desert landscape, and every morning she awoke with the sand serpent rising, its fanged jaws wide to devour her. Surfacing from those dreams felt too much like coming back to herself after time had pulled her under in Denver. But the dreams also reminded her of Thoth's mocking threat: *You live on borrowed minutes. Time will take what it's owed.*

Esta no longer doubted that time itself had become a danger, like the serpent in her dreams, but as the train carried her onward, she realized that Thoth had given her an unexpected gift by revealing what the Book could do. The memory of Jack withdrawing the dagger from the pages of the Book had stuck with Esta as she'd run from Denver. She'd turned that image over in her mind instead of watching the landscape pass outside the train, and in the end she came to believe it was the solution that she had only dared to hope for.

The Ars Arcana was infused with a piece of pure magic. Seshat herself had revealed how she'd placed it there in those brittle pages an eon ago, but until Esta had watched Jack pull the dagger from the Book, she hadn't realized what that truly meant. Thoth's actions—his bragging—had demonstrated it more clearly than words could have possibly conveyed. The Book itself was a container of sorts. Its very pages could be used to take objects *out of time.* If she and Harte could get the Book, they could use it like Thoth had. They could place the artifacts outside of time and return back to 1902 without losing them.

And they *could* get the Book. Jack had told Esta that he was heading to California, hadn't he? They would be in the same city. She would have another chance to take the Ars Arcana from him—as long as she found Harte before Jack did.

Esta hadn't had any trouble at the station back in Oakland, but now that the ferry had finally shuddered to a stop, its engines rumbling beneath the steel decks as it came to rest next to the docks, she wondered if her luck would hold. The day was slightly overcast, but there was none of the famous fog she'd expected of the city. Even from that distance, she could see San Francisco huddled on the shore of the bay. It wasn't the city she was used to seeing in movies and pictures. There was no Coit Tower, no skyscrapers. Beyond the jut of land, the mouth of the bay lay wide open, devoid of the iconic Golden Gate Bridge, which wouldn't be built for decades to come.

As the other passengers began to move toward the exits, Esta wondered what she would find once she disembarked. Harte could already be gone. If she was wrong about what the episodes in Denver meant, he might not be in danger at all. He might already be traveling back to New York to find her. Even now he might be expecting her arrival, and when she didn't come . . .

He would wait for me, Esta thought. If this trip to California turned out to be nothing but a wild-goose chase, she could be back to the bridge in a few days. Harte wouldn't give up on her so quickly.

Esta tucked her coat around her and pulled the stolen hat farther down over her forehead as she followed the crush of people eager to leave the ship. She didn't check her pocket, where she'd secured Maggie's pouch, even though she wanted to. She wasn't green enough to make herself a mark for pickpockets who might be casing the crowd.

As the travelers from the ferry began to filter into a line down the gangplank, Esta searched the dock for any sign of trouble. She'd almost relaxed when the glint of metal on a dark lapel caught her eye. A pair of men were waiting not far from the exit to the ferry's dock, and they were both wearing medallions that looked too similar to the Jefferson Guard's to be a coincidence. Esta didn't know to which Brotherhood the men owed their allegiance, but it didn't really matter. If these men had medallions from the Society, it meant that the Brotherhoods' influence had already reached farther than she'd realized, all the way across the continent. Worse, it meant that they were expecting trouble—they were likely expecting *her*.

Esta hadn't thought the trip to California would be easy, but these two men definitely complicated things. Stuck in the line of passengers on the narrow path of the gangplank, though, there was little she could do without drawing attention. If she used her affinity to get past the men, it would trigger the medallions. She'd be past the danger, but the medallions would alert the men to the magic she'd used. If these men were waiting for her specifically, as she suspected they were, it would only confirm her arrival. She couldn't afford for the Brotherhoods to realize she'd arrived. Her affinity was always an option if push came to shove, but if she could avoid the men's notice without using it, she would.

But maybe these two men could help her. Esta had no idea where to find Harte. She'd boarded a train to California knowing only that she had no other choice. Thoth had told her that Harte had been captured by some associates of his. If the men were linked to the Brotherhoods, perhaps they could lead her to Harte.

Esta trailed behind a group of businessmen down the gangplank, and once they'd reached the dock, she kept close to the group, hoping that anyone who saw her would assume she was one of them. Once she was past the men with the medallions, she could get herself into a better position. They wouldn't wait at the docks forever, and when they left, she could follow them.

She was nearly past the men when a small boy appeared seemingly out of nowhere to tug on her jacket. She looked down at him, imagining him at first to be some kind of urchin trying to con travelers out of a few coins. His eyes were wide with an expression that looked strangely like surprise, considering he was the one who had approached her. There was something familiar about him, but she didn't have time to figure out what it was.

"I don't have anything," she said, pulling away. But the words were no sooner out of her mouth than Esta's vision blurred, and the boy flickered. He was there and then he wasn't. It happened so quickly that she might have dismissed it as a trick of her tired eyes, except that she knew it wasn't really the boy flickering. It was happening. Again.

Esta drew in an uneasy breath and held it, as though if she remained still for long enough, time would forget her debt. But her pulse was already racing, her skin clammy and damp with a cold sweat, and she felt the same panic she'd felt when she was chased by the sand serpent in her dreams, trying to outrun the impossible.

The world steadied a second later, but Esta didn't lie to herself about what had just happened. She understood and accepted the warning for what it was, and she knew she couldn't predict when time might open its jaws—like the serpent in her dream—and pull her under. She had the unmistakable premonition that there would be no waking from that if it happened again.

The boy was tugging at her again, but she jerked away once more and tried to push through the crowd to escape him.

"Miss Esta?" His small, high voice carried over the din of the crowded docks, but Esta didn't allow herself to turn back, not even when it registered what he had called her.

The scene in front of her flickered again. She saw the docks all around her and the shoreline beyond, cluttered with haphazard shack-like structures and teeming with people, and then they were gone. The city around it—past, present, and future—glimmered and flickered like a double-exposed image, unsteady and unmoored from her own moment in time.

Vaguely Esta was aware of someone shouting her name as the scene solidified again into the San Francisco of 1904. She turned, feeling like she was stuck in a dream as she watched the men with the medallions grab the boy. He was writhing and kicking as he tried to get away from them, and he was still shouting for her.

She didn't know how he knew her name, and she didn't care to wait around to figure it out. The men hadn't seen her yet. They were too busy wrestling the kid, and Esta knew that she should use the distraction to her advantage. She turned to go, but the second she turned away from the men and the boy, the world flickered again. And she knew—the boy was important. She didn't know who he was or how that could be, but she reached for her affinity anyway, pulling the seconds slow as she turned back. With each step she took toward him, her vision became clearer. The world became more stable and steady.

When she touched the boy and brought him into her net of time, he gasped and tried to pull away. Esta held tightly to his wrist as she dragged him away from the men and toward the mess of the city that lay beyond the docks. She didn't stop until they'd traveled far past the ramshackle buildings near the water and were well into the city proper. It was the San Francisco from before the earthquake that would level it. With the stink of the sewers and the trash heaped in the streets, it felt like an untamed outpost of humanity, and it made even Old New York seem practically clean and modern by comparison.

Finally, when Esta thought they were far enough away, she released her hold on the seconds. This time the boy didn't try to pull away again, but looked up at her, his eyes wide with something that might have been wonder. Or maybe it was fear, which would have made him smarter. He couldn't have been more than seven or eight. He had a tousled head of dark-blond hair, and beneath his button nose, his mouth was pressed in a flat line. But there was no fear in his expression.

"Who sent you?" she asked, trying to decide if the boy was a threat.

He simply stared at her, not answering. Perhaps he didn't know English?

"How did you know my name?" she demanded.

The child didn't move, but Esta knew he understood. Keen intelligence sparked in his eyes, but it looked like he was trying to figure out a difficult puzzle.

"How did you know who I was?" she pressed. After all, she was dressed in men's clothing. She didn't look like a "Miss" at all.

Again she had the thought that there was something about him that seemed familiar. Something that made her pause. "Did Harte send you?"

The boy's eyes widened as he nodded, and that was when Esta realized that his eyes were the same perfectly stormy gray as Harte's.

"Where is he?" she asked, her stomach turning at the shadow that crossed the boy's expression. "What's happened to him?"

But the child only shook his head. "You have to come with me."

TRUE POWER

When James Lorcan received yet another summons from Paul Kelly on a random Wednesday afternoon, he took his time about answering it. He knew that Kelly was only calling the meeting—a last-minute and unplanned meeting at that—to prove that he could. It was another volley in their battle of wills, and in return, James made sure to keep Kelly waiting, because James knew that *he* could.

Kelly might believe that he was the more powerful of the two of them—certainly, an argument could be made that Kelly's Five Pointers were the wildest and most dangerous of the gangs in the Bowery—but James knew otherwise. He understood that true power moved best in invisible currents, like electricity . . . or like magic. Those who knew how to wield it, to hold it firmly in the palm of their hand, didn't always require muscle and brawn. Often, they simply required a bit of patience—something Paul Kelly did not have.

Once he'd arrived at the Little Naples Cafe, James didn't miss that Kelly did not so much as offer him a glass of water. He didn't ask for one either, despite the growing warmth of the day. Instead, he waited for Kelly to finish the sandwich he'd been eating when James arrived and pretended that he hadn't been pulled away from his own business.

Kelly finished finally, dabbed at his mouth delicately with his napkin, and then pushed the plate aside. "I have news."

James inclined his head. "I figured as much."

"Things are moving faster than we expected," Kelly told him.

"How *much* faster?" James asked, allowing his affinity to unfurl a little to detect the way the Aether moved in response to this news. He might be working with Kelly, but James didn't trust the gangster. He had no plans to allow Kelly to obtain the upper hand in their dealings.

"We originally thought the plans were to move the goods during the summer solstice," Kelly said.

"They're not?" The solstice had made sense. Sundren, like those in the Order, often believed the movement of the planets and stars had important meaning, but then, maybe they did for false magic. "Why the change?"

"Not a change, exactly," Kelly said. "A misunderstanding. The Order *is* making their move on a solstice, but it's not the one on the calendar. It's a day they're calling the *Manhattan* Solstice, whatever that means."

"When?" James asked, because it was the only question that truly mattered.

"Not in late June, like we've been planning," Kelly said, looking almost annoyed. "They're planning on making the move on the twenty-eighth of May."

"That's only four days from now," James said. He had been operating under the assumption that he still had time to prepare. He'd planned to bring Viola to heel and align his forces *just so*.

"There's more," Kelly said.

There's always more, James thought with no little frustration. He didn't allow any of the concern he might have been feeling to show, though. Not in front of Kelly, where any display of weakness could be a weapon turned against him.

"Tell me," James said easily, as though they had not lost *weeks* of preparation.

"They're not bringing the goods across the bridge, like we originally thought." Kelly took out one of his small cigarettes and didn't bother to offer James one before he lit it. "They're bringing everything in by boat."

James tightened his grip on the gorgon's head. "You're sure?"

"Positive," Kelly said. "After the mess at Khafre Hall, the Order has decided that bringing the goods over the bridge would leave them too vulnerable. But by boat?" Kelly took a long drag on his cigarette, the tip glowing as he squinted through the smoke. "There are a lot of docks in the city. Word is, the Order figures that this plan will make it harder to predict where the boat will arrive."

"They're expecting an attack," James said, unsurprised. The Order would have been stupid not to expect some difficulty, especially after Khafre Hall.

"It seems that way," Kelly agreed.

It doesn't matter, James reminded himself, adjusting his grip on his cane. Beneath his hand, the sharp outlines of the serpents that formed the gorgon's hair pressed into his palm. The cool energy beneath the silvery surface was a balm to any anxiety he might feel. It was a reminder of the possibility that lay ahead. He'd been working diligently on accessing the magic held within the cane, and already he could sense the power there beginning to answer his call. Once he had the ring, he would have everything he needed to unlock that power completely.

"This change," James said. "It doesn't give us much time to plan."

Kelly shrugged. "It doesn't give *you* much time. My boys are ready to disable the Death Avenue train and lead the wagons right where we want them, but if we can't get our hands on the goods, the risk is all for nothing. Have you made any progress figuring out what the protections might be?"

They'd learned already that the Order was planning on using some kind of ritual to protect the wagon carrying their treasures, but James hadn't been able to quite figure out what it might entail. Maybe if Dolph's journal hadn't gone missing, he would have already had the answer.

Still, the information Kelly was providing might be of use, even if the new timeline was nothing short of a disaster. The Manhattan Solstice sounded like some kind of a fantasy that only the rich could devise, but

James had enough experience under his belt not to discount anything when it came to the Order. "I'll figure it out."

"I trust you'll let me know what you discover?" Kelly said.

"Of course," James lied, inclining his head. Once he figured out what the Order had planned, he'd tell Kelly just enough to let *that* particular problem take care of itself.

Outside the cafe, the streets were half in shadow, an effect of the slant of the sun and the tightly crowded buildings. There was still plenty of daylight left, but James didn't have any interest in lingering too long in Kelly's territory. Luckily, the man he needed to talk to was already waiting for him.

John Torrio was at the corner, talking with another of Kelly's lackeys, Razor Riley. The two had been more than helpful in manipulating Harte Darrigan into helping with the job at Khafre Hall, but James knew that Torrio was already chafing under Kelly's control. It was one thing to be taken in, trained, and groomed by one of the most powerful criminals in the city. It was another to remain his lackey when you'd outgrown that particular role.

James himself understood that feeling. It had been difficult to take orders from Dolph in those final few weeks, when James had known how close he was to his own victory. It had taken patience and fortitude to continue pretending, to hide what he was planning from Dolph, but his effort had paid off. Unlike James, Torrio was every bit as impatient and fiery as his boss. It was a convenient weakness that James had every intention of exploiting.

He gave Torrio a small nod of acknowledgment, but continued on, walking in the direction of the Strega. It took a few blocks for Torrio to finally come up beside him.

"You have news about Viola?" James asked, not pausing as the two strolled side by side.

Dolph's journal had gone missing the day after Viola had charged into the Strega, and James knew she'd been the one to take it. The loss hadn't bothered him, not when the Aether suggested that the theft had been necessary. The journal was nothing more than a pawn to be sacrificed in order to move his game forward, and besides, James had already read over Dolph's nearly obsessive notes enough to no longer need them. But he still needed to understand *exactly* what Viola was up to, and the Aether didn't reveal those sorts of details.

"I got the information you asked for . . . if you have what *you* promised." Torrio jerked his head toward one of the basement bars that populated the area.

James decided it wasn't worth arguing about the meeting place. Not when their timeline had been cut so much shorter, and not when he needed Torrio on his side.

The saloon was like most of the basement bars in the city—dark and stuffy, smelling of sweat and stale lager. It was also the type of place where no one paid attention, and if they did, they certainly didn't talk.

"Your boss might not be smart enough to see that the world is far bigger than New York City, but I'm certainly glad that you are." James pulled the thin packet from inside his vest and held it out. Torrio grabbed for it, but James held firm. "Now, about Viola . . ."

"She's still spending her days up in Harlem," Torrio told him.

"With the same group as before?" James asked. He hadn't quite understood how Viola had come to know the person who owned the house—a colored man who operated a small newspaper in the city—but she'd been sneaking off from her brother's watch to meet people there fairly regularly.

Not people, James thought. *Sundren.* The same Sundren he'd seen with Jianyu at Evelyn DeMure's apartment before the gala. It wasn't a coincidence. It meant that he'd been right. With the missing journal and Viola's continued meetings, it indicated that Jianyu was likely in play now as well . . . and that it was past time for them to be brought to heel.

"That isn't news," James said, impatient. He still held firmly to the envelope. "Is there anything else?"

Torrio's eyes narrowed a little. "Maybe. If your information there is good." He nodded to the envelope.

"You won't know unless you share what you have on Viola," James told him, pulling the envelope back and moving to tuck it away again.

"There's nothing new about Viola," Torrio said. "But that toff she goes around with has been doing some interesting things lately. Seems he's been spending his days with Morgan and some of the Order types."

"Has he?" James asked, suddenly more interested. It began to make sense now why the Aether had insisted that Viola was so essential. If she had a link to the Order, that was likely a connection James could use to his favor. "You still haven't told Kelly anything about his sister's other activities?"

Torrio shook his head. "Not a word, like you insisted."

"Maybe it's time we let your boss know about where his dear little sister is going when he's not paying attention. Don't let him know anything about the toff, but I think it might be a good thing for Kelly to doubt his sister a little more." With the right pressure, Viola would be back where he'd wanted her—Jianyu as well. Both of them would be firmly under his control, and with a little luck, her connection to the Order would come with her.

James released the packet, handing it over to Torrio. "It's all there," he said when Torrio started to open it.

Torrio turned the envelope over like he wanted to pry inside of it. "It doesn't look like much."

"Looks can be deceiving." Then he gave Torrio a pat on the shoulder and headed out.

He had work to do and only four days to do it. Four days to bring Viola to heel, four days to discover what corrupt magic the Order might use, and four days to plan. The Aether bunched again, shifting with a shivering awareness of his certain victory. Four days, and the ring, along with all the power it contained, would be his.

THE TUNNELS

Esta followed the boy through the streets of the city, leaving the confusion of the docks behind them. She wanted to ask him a million questions, but mostly, she didn't want to scare him into running, especially if he could provide some clue to Harte's whereabouts. Instead, she kept her affinity close, ready and waiting for her to grasp the seconds at a moment's notice, and she held a vial of incendiary laced with Quellant tucked in her fist, cool against her palm, because she knew that a pair of gray eyes meant very little. There were too many who might have known she would arrive in the city, and young as the boy seemed, Esta knew she might well be walking right into a trap.

The boy led her through the maze of the city, up roads that climbed so steeply that horses and wagons didn't even bother and along trolley routes that cut through the wild tumble of streets. She almost didn't realize that they were skirting Chinatown until she saw the signs painted with the Chinese characters hanging from the buildings beyond what looked like a barricade. But the boy didn't try to enter through the checkpoints, which was fine with Esta. Especially since the men guarding the entrances all had medallions glinting on their lapels.

"What's happening there?" she asked the boy.

"The Vigilance Committee." He glanced up at her, his small brow furrowed with determination. "Don't worry. We won't go that way."

He led her instead to a side street that turned into another alley. At the end of it, he opened a gate into a courtyard behind what appeared to be a restaurant. The bins of trash overflowed with rotten food that buzzed with flies and other vermin, but the boy didn't seem fazed, even when a rat scurried almost directly over his foot. He continued to the back of the courtyard, where he pulled open one of the wooden doors of a coal cellar.

"I'm not going down there," Esta told him, the darkness in the shaft below making her skin crawl. But the boy went first, disappearing into the shadows below, and Esta's only choices were to lose him completely or follow.

She followed. He'd already taken a candle from his pocket by the time she reached the bottom, where he waited, and a few seconds later he had it lit. That single flame was the only illumination they had as they traversed a series of tunnels that seemed to have been carved from the earth below the city. It wasn't long before Esta's boots were completely soaked from the layer of muck they had to walk through. From the smell of the place—earthy and rank at the same time—she didn't want to think too closely about what the mud might contain. She concerned herself instead with not slipping as she struggled to keep up with the sure-footed boy.

After a few minutes, though, Esta started to think she'd made a serious miscalculation. She'd been trying to memorize the twists and turns the boy had taken, but she soon lost track. Water trickled somewhere nearby, and the sounds of creatures scurrying and scratching followed them, but otherwise the tunnels were quiet. If this was a trap, if the tunnels opened into an ambush and she died here, it would be like she'd walked into her own grave. Still, despite the danger she might have been in, Esta felt stronger and steadier the farther she walked. Even in the darkened tunnel, her vision remained clear and focused. As far as she was concerned, that was even more confirmation that following the boy was the right decision.

Finally, the boy pushed aside a wooden board that exposed another branch of the tunnel. Once they were through, he replaced the board, then led her a little farther still, until they came to a short ladder. It didn't look overly sturdy, but the boy scaled it easily and rapped a short, staccato rhythm on the wooden ceiling above. A moment later, a panel moved aside, and a woman's face appeared. From the color of her hair and the shape of her nose, it was clear that she was the boy's mother and that she'd been expecting them.

The boy scrambled up through the opening, and Esta followed. As her eyes adjusted to the brightness, she found herself in a storage room lined with shelves of dry goods and ceramic jars. The woman stepped back to allow Esta through, then secured the door to the tunnel behind her, barring it with a length of wood as she scolded her son sharply in German, clearly assuming Esta wouldn't understand.

"I told you how dangerous it is for us now," the woman told him. "I told you to stay in your room. Every day I tell you the same, why can't you listen like a good boy would?"

The boy somehow looked even younger and smaller under his mother's reprimands. "I tried to stay, but I couldn't stop myself," he complained, tears making his eyes look damp and glassy. "I had to go."

"Lies on top of disobedience?"

"Not lies," the boy said, suddenly looking more stubborn. "See! This is the lady I had to find. This is Miss Esta."

The woman's eyes cut in Esta's direction. "You're not a man," she said in English.

"No," Esta agreed. "I'm not. My name's Esta. Esta Filosik."

"I know who you are," the woman said, but there was no heat and no fear in her voice.

"I'm looking for a friend of mine. Harte Darrigan. He's here, isn't he?"

The woman considered the question. Then she let out a long, tired-sounding breath. "I knew that one would be trouble."

Relief flashed through Esta. "Then you *do* know him? Do you know where he is?"

The woman nodded before turning back to the boy and instructing her son to finish setting the locks and the alarms. Finally, she gestured for Esta to come with her and led the way into the apartment proper.

"I didn't believe Sammie when he told me that he had to find someone—a lady from far away named Miss Esta," the woman said. When she spoke, her voice was soft, and her English had the sharp accent of her native German. "Sammie is usually such a good boy, but for the last few days, he has driven me mad with his disobedience. He kept trying to tell me, but I didn't believe that you could possibly exist, but now . . ." She closed her eyes, as though blinking would be enough to wake her from this awful dream, but when she finally opened them again, Esta could see the fear in her expression. "You have to understand. . . . My husband has been sent away. My child is all I have left."

"I'm not here to hurt either of you," Esta said softly. "I'm just looking for my friend. I think something might have happened to him. I'm hoping that your son finding me means that you can help me find him?"

The woman studied her, and Esta had the sense that it was not a matter of whether the woman could help her, but whether she *would*.

"Please," Esta said. "Do you have any idea what happened to him?"

At first the woman only sighed, like she had finally resigned herself to a fate she did not want. "Two days ago, your friend broke into my home, like a common thief, and I nearly shot him, thinking he was from the Committee. But then Sammie explained what your friend had done for him. He's sick, very sick," the woman told Esta, motioning that she should follow her toward a doorway at the back of the living area. "He practically collapsed at my feet that night. I've done what I could for him, to make him comfortable."

"Thank you . . ."

"Patience," the woman said. "Patience Lowe."

"Thank you, Patience. For helping him."

Patience shook her head sadly. "I couldn't call a doctor, not with the Committee's quarantine. But it would not have mattered. The sickness he has, it's not one that people recover from."

The woman stepped aside and waved Esta into the room beyond. There was a low platform bed and a large oak wardrobe in the corner. Harte wasn't there.

Before Esta could ask, Patience brushed past her into the room and rolled back the rug. Then she pulled up a panel of the wood flooring to reveal an indentation beneath. But nothing the woman had told her—or could have told her—prepared Esta for what she found below.

TO TOUCH HER ONCE MORE

1904—San Francisco

I t wasn't the feverish chills that racked Harte's body, making every bone ache clear to the marrow, or even the pervading stench of vomit and sweat and sickness that he hated the most. Those things were awful, but Harte could have suffered them well enough. But the way his skin was so alive with pain that it felt like it was crawling with vermin every time he moved? *That* was true torture.

Not that he could have lifted his arm to scratch at his skin, even if he wanted to. Harte had become far too weak to bother with moving, and besides, there was barely room for him to fit head to toe in the makeshift cellar where Sammie and his mother had placed him. The hole where they'd hidden him smelled of dirt, a dark, damp scent that surrounded and overwhelmed. The walls had been dug from the earth, and the space, about the size of a small root cellar, clearly hadn't been part of the original building's plan.

The boy's mother had checked in on Harte often. Sometimes she would speak to him as she tried to spoon water past his cracked lips. She talked as she tried to help him, telling him about herself and explaining that her husband had created the hideaway. He'd dug it out by hand a few years before for when he needed to hide from the various people he owed money. The path of righteousness had apparently taken Samuel Lowe through the back room of more than one saloon, where he'd lost large sums of money playing cards with the wrong kind of people. Her husband's absence hadn't stopped his creditors from coming to the house, demanding their debts be repaid by a wife who had nothing to offer. It was one of many reasons Harte had to continue to remain hidden.

Sometimes, in the darkness of his burrow, Harte thought he could hear Seshat speaking to him. Once he even dreamed of her, dressed in blinding white, her eyes a black fire. Other times he dreamed of Esta. She would come to him, her soft mouth and devil's eyes sparking with anger and humor all at once. But Harte could never seem to reach her. He would've given damn near anything to touch her again and to tell her how sorry he was for being a fool by leaving her as he had.

In the darkness, Harte's other regrets came to him as well, one by one, along with the ghosts of all the people he had betrayed. His mother. Dolph Saunders. *Esta.* Countless others that he'd thrown aside for his own ends. Their faces rose up in the darkness, silent in their judgment, before fading away and leaving Harte alone once more.

The boy—his brother—never returned, though. Not after that first day when the child had led him to this hovel. He was likely afraid now. Harte hoped he was safe—he couldn't forget the way Seshat's power had surged through him, and he worried about the boy's absence and what it might mean. He also couldn't forget the threat Seshat had made about what she would do if Esta did finally find him.

Harte began to hope that death would take him—and the angry goddess inside his skin—before Esta could arrive. He came to realize that Seshat was right. Esta would never simply accept it if Harte didn't meet her at the bridge, as he'd promised. She might well come for him, even if it was only to make him pay for his betrayal. But Harte knew that if she did, he would not be able to hold the goddess back.

But perhaps he would not have to worry about that eventuality. He knew, the same way a wounded animal knows to find a quiet place to lie down for the last time, that he didn't have much longer. There was an ache in his inner thigh where a tumorlike growth had swelled hot and evil beneath the skin. It was so painful now that he couldn't even move his leg. His fever felt like a brand against his skin, and eventually even Seshat had abandoned him. She, too, had pulled inward, far beneath his surface, as though she had started to understand that her time was growing as short as his own. Trapped as she was inside of him, there was at least *some* consolation in the fact that Seshat's danger would pass when he did.

Harte only hoped that someone would remember him after he was gone. That someone could tell Esta what had become of him.

Esta.

In the darkness behind his eyes he could see her—the tilt of her full mouth when she smirked at him. The cut of her chin, sharp as her words. Her eyes, the color of whiskey and sunlight. The feel of her skin, softer than anything he'd ever held. And the scent of her. Clean and unsullied, like hope itself. From the very beginning, the very moment he'd seen her so many weeks ago in the Haymarket's ballroom, she'd called to him like a beacon. And he'd walked away. Again and again, he'd tossed her aside. Because he was too weak to trust. Too scared to stay.

If he concentrated, Harte could almost hear her voice. The deep, rough timbre. The irritation that colored it. Calling him.

He opened his eyes and could almost see her there, a dark vision above him, surrounded by brightness—Esta. *Like some saving, avenging angel.*

No. Not an angel. Esta couldn't be dead, and Harte's life certainly hadn't been pure enough for heaven.

But she seemed so *real*.

It was nothing but the delirium brought on by the pain and the fever. Or maybe he was dead already, and hell was nothing more and nothing less than this, being inches away from the girl he loved—

He *loved*? How ridiculous to discover that now, when it was far too late. When he would never be able to tell her. How painfully appropriate to fade away taunted by his greatest regret.

Harte tried to lift his hand, because maybe if he could only touch the angel looming above, it would be enough to pull him through to the other side and end this misery. But lifting his arm felt like trying to push through leaden waves. Still, the apparition floated above him, and he had the sense that if he could reach her, then maybe Esta would know how sorry he was for everything. If he could just touch her once more . . .

JAGGED HOPE

1904—San Francisco

When Patience Lowe opened the trapdoor in the floor, the smell from below rose in a noxious wave, sick and stagnant and strong enough to make Esta gag. Below, a figure lay curled on his side.

At first Esta couldn't believe what she was seeing. Harte Darrigan, with his meticulous cleanliness. Harte, who hated to be dirty in any way. It was unthinkable that the wretch curled below could really be him. But it was. The space where he was lying was nothing more than a hole that had been clawed out of the earth, like the burrow of a rat beneath the city streets. It made Esta's chest hurt to see his skin slick with feverish sweat and his ragged clothes crusted over with his own sickness.

She couldn't tell at first if he was even breathing, but then Harte's eyes cracked open and his head turned toward the light. He seemed to be seeking out something other than the darkness he'd been buried in. His skin was sallow and grayish, and there were dark hollows beneath his eyes. His lips were cracked and scabbed over from bleeding, and the smell that wafted up to her carried with it the unmistakable reek of infection and death.

It was clear he wasn't seeing her. Not really. The whites of Harte's eyes were yellow and tinged with a feverish pink as he stared up, not quite focusing. His mouth was moving, like he wanted to speak, but all that came out was an indecipherable rattling. He tried to raise his hand like he was reaching for her, but the motion seemed labored, and he allowed his arm to fall back to rest on his abdomen again, his eyes closing from the effort.

"He needs help," she told Patience. "A doctor or—"

"No," the woman said, shaking her head. "There's no medicine that can help him now. The fever is too great. All we can do is wait."

Esta's temper spiked as the woman stood by. "How could you just leave him like this? It's like you put him in a grave to die."

"What else could I do?" Patience asked. "If I called for a doctor, they would have reported his illness to the Vigilance Committee, which is where he'd escaped from. Surely the Committee would have realized who he was. They would have taken everything I had left—my home, my child—and they would have used his illness as an excuse. They would have made an example of me, as they are making an example of the Chinese people in this city. My neighbors excuse the Committee's tactics—their patrols and their quarantine barricades—because it's happening to Chinatown and not to them. Because they already hate the Chinese people who live there. But most fool themselves into believing sickness can be held back with barbed wire. They are so terrified of the plague escaping those confines, they'll excuse any cruelty the Committee commits. Especially with my husband gone, there would have been no one to protect us."

"Plague?" Esta asked in disbelief. As in, *the* plague? Patience *had* to be overstating things.

"There has been news of cases in town recently," the boy's mother confirmed. "Because people fear catching the sickness, no one will speak against the Committee, no matter how terrible their tactics. What would you have had me do? The Committee has ruled this town with an iron fist, using the threat of magic to establish their power, for years now. How would you have me fight that power?"

Esta wasn't sure. It should have been enough that this woman had taken Harte in, had cared for him as much as she could, despite the apparent risk.

"His fever grows worse," Patience told her. "It will not be long now."

"I won't stand here and watch him die," Esta said. "People don't die of fevers—"

Except that they did. She *knew* that. In 1904, before modern medicine had given the world the miracle of antibiotics, a person could die from so much less than Harte was suffering from. It was astounding that he'd held on so long, considering the state he was in. In another time, he wouldn't have suffered so needlessly. In another age, he didn't need to die.

He doesn't *need to die. . . .* Not if she could get him to that other time.

Esta pulled the edge of her jacket up over her face, to ward off the smell, before she lowered herself down to where Harte lay. His skin felt like fire, and his limbs felt almost delicate as she moved them, checking for some sign of her cuff.

"Did he have anything with him?" Esta asked the woman. "A package or . . . *anything?*"

Patience shook her head. "He didn't have anything with him when he arrived."

Harte's hair was a tangled mess, and his clothes were filthy. Esta touched him, trying to wake him so she could speak to him, but he didn't stir. His breathing worried her even more than his lack of consciousness. The breaths he took were shallow and ragged, and there was a wet-sounding rattle in his chest. Esta had heard a sound like that before—back in New York, when she stood vigil with Viola and Dolph as Tilly took her final breaths.

No. She refused—*refused*—to accept this.

"It has to be here," she said, more to herself than to anyone else.

Harte knew what Ishtar's Key meant to her—to both of them. There was no way he would have taken her cuff and then lost it. The Harte she knew might be heavy-handed. He might be stupid and stubborn and predictably pigheaded, but he wasn't careless. She ignored the stench of him as well as the way he moaned as she tried to move him onto his side, to search beneath him.

But she didn't find anything. No cuff, no necklace. *Nothing.*

I'm still here, she reminded herself. If the Key were gone, she would be as well.

When Esta looked up again, Patience was shaking her head, and there was something that made Esta wonder if she knew more than she was saying.

"He should have had a silver cuff with him," Esta explained, making a circular motion around her own arm, where the cuff had once sat. "A bracelet that held a dark stone, and he should have been carrying a necklace as well. A *beautiful* necklace, with a bright-blue stone that looks like stars are trapped within it. But the cuff is what's really important. If I have the cuff, I can help him. I can take him away from here, and you and your son would no longer be in danger from someone discovering him."

The woman's eyes had widened slightly. She looked suddenly unsure, maybe even guilty.

"*Please,*" Esta pleaded. "If you know what I'm talking about at all, if you saw anything like the pieces I described, you have to help me. I can pay you for them. I can give you whatever you want. I can *save* him if I have that cuff."

The woman didn't respond or react.

"If you do have the pieces I'm talking about, you can't keep them. There are people looking for them—dangerous people," Esta told her, trying another approach. "If you're worried about this Committee, they're nothing compared to the people who will be coming for you."

Patience hesitated a moment longer. When she finally spoke again, she made her voice no more than a whisper, like she was afraid the walls themselves might overhear. "My husband brought home pieces like you describe some days ago. But they're gone. I gave them to satisfy my husband's debts when his creditors came demanding payment," she said. "What could I do?"

Esta's stomach sank. "Tell me you didn't give away the cuff. *Tell me.*"

"I didn't have a choice," Patience explained, her voice filled with remorse. Then the woman's expression shifted. "You can't imagine what it is to live my life. Do you know that my father lost me in a card game? To be rid of his responsibility, he forced me to marry a man I would never have chosen. Now all I have is my child and this house. Our only chance to survive is to keep my husband's shop. Unlike you, I cannot pull on trousers and jaunt off and leave my responsibilities—my son—behind."

"I know," Esta told her softly. "You're right. I don't have a child to protect or a husband to find."

"I don't want to find my husband," she told Esta. "If he never returns, our lives will be hard, but in the end, they'll be better. A man like that can't be saved from himself. A man like that leaves only destruction in his wake."

"I'm sorry," Esta said, speaking truly. She had a feeling that the woman was on the cusp of some revelation, and she needed the right combination to unlock her willingness. "But this man, the one you were so good to tend to and comfort, even when it could have put you in danger? He *is* an honorable man. You must know something more."

Patience knew something about the artifacts, there was no question of that fact. Without her help, Harte would die. But even with the cuff, even if she could take him forward to a time where medicine might save him, Esta knew that it still might not be enough.

"Please," she said. She had never begged before. She had never felt desperate enough to beg, not even when she'd been tied to a chair at the mercy of a madman. *"Please,"* Esta repeated.

Because she could not imagine a world where Harte Darrigan didn't exist.

The woman's mouth pressed into a tight line, and Esta knew that everything was lost—Harte, the artifacts, herself. . . .

But then Patience relented.

"When my husband brought the pieces home, I sensed them, even before he showed them to me." She paused.

Esta waited silently, because it felt like something as simple as breathing might shatter the moment. But she immediately understood the implication of what Patience Lowe had just told her.

"I knew that my husband couldn't have obtained such pieces honestly, because I knew that they were too important for someone like *him* to have. When their true owner came for them, I didn't want to be empty-handed." She went to the bed and lifted the mattress, propping it on her shoulder so she could pull something from within the frame. Then Patience brought a small package wrapped in white linen and knelt next to the hole in the floor.

Esta's eyes were locked on the package that rested in the woman's lap. But she was afraid to lean too much into the hope that already made her feel light-headed.

"My husband never knew what I was or what I could do. He was too fond of talking about righteousness and abomination, and I knew from the beginning that it would be dangerous to reveal myself to him," Patience told Esta, her expression sour. "He thought these pieces were merely expensive, but I knew better."

"You knew they were powerful," Esta said. *Because Patience is Mageus.*

Patience unwrapped the package, and Esta almost sobbed in relief the second she saw the glint of silver and felt the power of the cuff's dark stone call out to her.

"You may be right about this one being a good man. He saved my boy when my husband would have sacrificed his only child for a bit of gold. If you truly believe you can save your friend, then I can't keep these from you." Patience held out the parcel, the necklace and cuff gleaming against the soft linen.

"Thank you," Esta said, taking them. The artifacts were delicate pieces, but they were heavy with the weight of magic, and when Esta touched them, she could feel their power calling to her. She slid on the cuff immediately and tucked the necklace into the leather pouch with Maggie's concoctions.

Esta had no sooner secured them and turned her energy to figuring

LISA MAXWELL

out how she would get Harte up from the hole in the floor than bells began chiming. It was almost like the heavens themselves were celebrating, except that there was nothing celestial about the sound. It was a tinny, jagged noise that sounded every bit like a warning.

"Mama," the boy said, coming into the room with a look of panic.

The color had drained from the woman's face. "There's someone in the tunnel," Patience said, glancing back over her shoulder. She spoke to the boy in urgent, rapid German.

"Were you followed?"

"No. I was careful."

"Then how could they find us?"

She turned to Esta. "We must go. It is not safe here—"

"Not without him," Esta refused. She could save him. She *would*.

"No one should be in that tunnel. My husband built it as a way to escape from the enemies he made. If someone is there, they followed you. If they followed you through those tunnels, they are not friends."

"Help me carry him," Esta begged. "I know you have done so much already, but please, I need to get him outside."

Patience was shaking her head, backing away with her arms around the child. "I can't. If they find us here with you—" She shook her head again, then took her son's hand and disappeared through the door. They were gone before Esta could stop them.

THE WORLD CRUMBLES

1904—San Francisco

Esta couldn't blame Patience for running with her child. Not when she'd kept Harte alive long enough for Esta to find him, and especially not when she'd relinquished the cuff that could save them both. Esta had no idea what it must be like to have a child, the constant, urgent need to protect that small life, even at the cost of your own. She didn't really even know what it felt like to have a family. But she knew what she felt for Harte. She wouldn't let him go. She would not give up, not now.

If I can get him outside . . .

Esta didn't know San Francisco. She had no idea what she might find when she slipped ahead through the layers of time. She understood it would be dangerous with Seshat lurking beneath Harte's skin, but desperation made her reckless.

"Come on," she said, barely noticing how bad Harte smelled as she took him under the arms and started to pull him up out of the hole.

Harte had lost so much weight in the days since she'd seen him that he felt almost skeletal in her arms. With every tug, a terrible keening erupted from his throat. It sounded awful, painful—not quite human. Still Esta didn't stop. With the cuff on her arm and the necklace in the pouch tucked close to her body, she kept going. As she pulled him little by little through the apartment, the jangling bells became more insistent, and then she heard new sounds coming from the storeroom. Someone was pounding on the trapdoor in the floor.

Esta ignored that threat as well. If she could only get Harte outside the building, it would be safer to use Ishtar's Key. On she went, steadily tugging him along, until they were in the narrow alleyway outside the small apartment.

Night had not yet descended, but the alley was tucked far enough back from the larger street that it lay deep in shadows. Only the faintest hum from the city beyond reached her there. Exhausted, Esta lowered Harte to the ground and saw that he was looking at her. His mouth was moving again, and this time she recognized the whisper of her name hissing from his lips.

"See you," he whispered, each word a rattling breath. "Once more . . ." And then he reached for her, but before he could touch her, his eyes fluttered closed and his hand went limp, falling away.

Esta leaned over him and for a long, terrible moment, she thought it was too late. "Damn you, Darrigan," she said, her words choked with her tears. She gave him a not-so-gentle shake until his chest rose and fell again. "Don't you dare die on me until I make you pay for leaving me on that train. Do you hear me?"

He lay silent, his breath ragged.

They needed to get somewhere with more space, somewhere that might still be open in—*how many years?* She wasn't sure. The street would be safer. A park if she could get that far.

"You hold on a little while longer, and I'm going get us out of here," she said, talking to him and to herself at the same time. She was trembling with the fear of what would happen if he died as she considered which way they should go.

"No . . ." The word came out as barely a whisper. Harte's eyes opened halfway. "Too late."

He was right and he wasn't. Maybe in 1904 it was too late for him, but now that Esta had Ishtar's Key, Harte had a chance.

"It's not even close to too late," she told him, pulling him up so his head could rest on her lap.

Harte groaned at the movement, his face crumpling in pain. "Seshat . . . gone . . ."

"She's gone?" Esta asked.

"Not yet." Harte's eyes seemed unfocused as he stared up at the starless sky. "But when I die—"

"You're not going to die."

His eyes found hers then, the stormy gray so familiar and so intent as they finally focused on her. "Thoth is coming. . . . Go. Leave—"

Esta choked back tears she could not stop from falling. "When have I ever taken orders from you?"

She felt the vibrations of what might have been a laugh shuddering through his chest. But then he gasped and looked up at her again. "I die . . . Seshat dies."

The realization of what Harte was saying made Esta go cold. If she was being honest with herself, she'd known that this had always been one answer. Originally, before she'd returned to the past and changed everything, Harte had died on the Brooklyn Bridge. Originally, the Book had been lost, and Seshat had never been a threat. Harte wasn't wrong. If he died now, the ancient goddess would be finished. The world would be safe. She had her cuff. She could go back, set things right before Nibsy could collect the artifacts. With them, Esta could possibly even find Jack and take back the Book.

And Harte would be gone.

It was an impossible choice—a single person for the world itself.

But Esta had the Quellant now, and she had her cuff. She knew how to get the artifacts back and she knew how to subdue Seshat. There was still a chance to save Harte *and* go back and set things right. She would not choose if there was still a possibility that she could do both.

From within the house, Esta heard a crash that told her time was running out. She gripped Harte around the midsection and pulled her affinity close, concentrating on the seconds and then beyond them, to the layers of years that were and would be. Searching.

A man appeared in the doorway, a satisfied smile drawing his thin

LISA MAXWELL

mouth into a cruel curve. "Esta Filosik," he said, apparently not realizing what she was doing.

She didn't even bother to look up. All of her concentration was on searching for the right year. Too close and there might not be medicine advanced enough to save him. Too far, and Esta risked any number of things—including crossing the stones with one of her many previous trips through time.

"Mr. Grew sent us for you," the man said.

Maybe she should have cared that this man could take her to the Book. Maybe she should have allowed him to lead her directly to Jack, but Esta knew Harte wouldn't make it if she did.

"You can tell Jack Grew that he can go to hell," Esta growled, finally finding the place she wanted—a clearing, a flash of chrome, and the whirling brightness of neon lights—and she closed her eyes and focused all her affinity on that time and place. On the *possibility* that waited there.

The man lunged for her, but she rolled them both away, through the layers of time to the city that waited beyond. As she slipped through, Esta felt the darkness rise in her. Around her. *Consuming* her. Seshat's power felt weaker than before, but it was still more than Esta could control. The ground began to shake, tossing the man back as it cracked beneath his feet.

Power slammed through Esta, hot and potent and *so* satisfying, and suddenly she lost hold of the layers of time. The ground was still shaking beneath her, more violently now. She heard someone scream, a crash.

She knew it was Seshat, but she could not give up. Not when Harte's life was at stake.

With all of the strength she had, Esta shoved Seshat's power back as she pulled on her own affinity again. She felt Ishtar's Key heat dangerously against her arm as she pushed through the layers. Another power was sliding alongside her own. The ground continued to tremble, and as a chasm opened beneath them, Esta found herself falling, not into the gap in the earth but through time once more as darkness swelled and the world began to crumble around her.

A NEW ALLIANCE

1902—New York

Viola sat with Jianyu at the edge of the small room at the rear of the house, listening to Abel Johnson explain the situation they were facing to his friends. The back room was crowded with people, like too many sardines in a can. The air was hot and close, and tempers were beginning to fray. Though Viola remained quiet in the corner, she did not miss how some of Abel's friends often turned, giving her sideways glances without hiding their unease. She tried hard not to care.

She and Jianyu, along with Theo, Cela, and to some extent, Abel, had spent the last few weeks waiting and planning, but things had changed, and now everything was moving too quickly. Thanks to Theo, they knew that in a matter of days the Order would bring the Delphi's Tear back into the city and install it within the inner chambers of their new head-quarters. If that was allowed to happen, the chances of ever retrieving the ring would become much more unlikely—maybe impossible. With the shortened timeline, it had become obvious that they needed help.

Abel had finished his explanations, but he hadn't quite come to his point. Viola could read the mood in the room, though. Already she sensed that things would not go so easily as Cela and Abel had assured her.

When Cela glanced back at the two of them, her expression was guarded. Cela had been cordial ever since Jianyu had woken, but Viola knew that Cela had still not forgiven her for attacking Jianyu. *For attacking* her.

Cela's constant suspicion grated, but Viola accepted it as her due. It was no more than she was used to, after all. Hadn't she lived with looks just as sharp for as long as she could remember—from her own family, and later from those in the Devil's Own who did not understand why Dolph should put so much trust in a woman? If a lifetime of judgment had not broken her, neither would Cela Johnson's. No matter how deserved that judgment might be.

"The bottom line is that this isn't our fight, Abel," the one called Joshua said with a frustrated sigh. He was a stout man, whose shirt stretched tight across his stomach whenever he moved. He was maybe a year or two older than Abel and had a quietness about him that Viola had appreciated when they'd first met more than a week ago. This quietness gave his words more weight somehow. "We have pressure coming at us from all sides with the strike looming in Philadelphia, and now you're asking us to go stirring up trouble with the Order? If we do that, we'll be putting a mark on the back of every Negro in this city."

"We're already wearing that mark," Abel said.

"Well, I damn sure don't need to make the one on my back any bigger," another man argued. He was older still, and his face wore the kind of weariness of someone who worked too much and for too little. His hair was tightly curled about his head and had a reddish cast when the light hit it.

"I understand, Saul," Abel said. "But maybe by working together, we can make those targets a little smaller. Maybe we don't have to fight alone."

"Or maybe helping these folks does the opposite," another said. "We have families of our own to protect."

Saul's wife, a woman with skin as dark and smooth as ebony, placed her hand on Saul's knee. Her hair had been pulled back from her narrow face in a serviceable braid, but the humidity of the day had it curling around her temples, not much different from what Viola's own hair was doing at that moment. "We got children, Abe. Are you really asking us to put them at risk for a fight that isn't even ours? I'm sorry, but Joshua and my husband are right. We can't get involved." She sounded sorry for it, but unwilling to be moved.

Joshua leaned forward again. His deep-set eyes looked like they had already seen too much. "Look, Abe, I know that you and your sister like these folks, and I'm sure that you want to help, but we have *real* issues to solve right now. We have the meeting with the steel workers next week. If we can't get them to open their labor union to our men, it's going to set us back at least ten years. You should be focused on those problems, not some treasure hunt."

"It's not a treasure hunt," Cela told them, speaking for the first time since they'd gathered.

"You're right," Aaron said. "What you're talking about is robbery."

"Cela, honey, we'd like to help, but not like this," said another woman from the end of the table. She was older than the others, with a broad face and a bosom to match. "You know what they would do to us if we were caught helping with this crazy plan of yours, don't you? More than a hundred people—*our own people*—were murdered last year in cold blood for doing nothing but trying to live. We're barely through May, and this year's numbers look every bit as bad. This here city is *still* simmering with unsettled anger from what happened less than two years ago after that plainclothes officer got himself killed."

"Because we aren't even allowed to protect our own women when a white man attacks them," Aaron added.

The woman nodded in agreement. "*You* know what we lost during those days." She pursed her narrow mouth. "Can you really ask us to risk starting all that up again?"

Cela kept her tone even, her gaze steady. "Hattie, I know exactly what *we* lost," she told the other woman, emphasizing the word in a way that made it seem almost personal, and Viola couldn't help but wonder what Cela and Abel *had* lost.

"Then you should know better to start trouble where there wasn't none before," the older woman told her, sitting back in her chair with her arms crossed, like the point was irrefutable.

Viola remembered the unrest two years before. A plainclothes police officer had been killed, and his death had started a chain reaction of violence. The trouble had been mostly kept to the Tenderloin, though, because the police's violence had been focused on the colored people who lived there. It hadn't really touched the Bowery, and it certainly hadn't touched her. And anyway, Viola'd had her own troubles at the time.

Cela's brother, Abel, had been listening quietly to the conversation without saying much, but he spoke now. "I can't ask any of you to step up and put your lives at risk for a cause you don't believe in," he said quietly. "But for better or worse, Cela and I are committed. If you aren't, I'll understand, and we won't hold that decision against you one bit. But if you don't want to be involved, I think it's best if you go now."

Uneasy silence descended over the room as Abel's friends suddenly seemed unwilling to look at one another. Aaron and his wife were the first to stand and go, taking their leave without apology or explanation. Three others followed, until it was only Cela, her brother, and Joshua. A moment later, though, Joshua stood as well, his cap in his hands.

"I'm sorry, Abel. I'd like to help, but . . ." He didn't finish. Simply turned and left with the rest.

The three of them seemed stuck in the silence, until the sound of a carriage pulling up broke through their stunned disappointment.

"That'll be Theo," Viola murmured as the reality of what they'd failed to accomplish struck her. They would be alone against the Order, and they weren't ready.

Cela went to let Theo in, and when she returned with him, he looked more troubled than usual. "Tell me you have good news," he said.

"I'm afraid not," Abel told him. There was still a bit of tension there between the two, Viola noticed. Abel held himself a little straighter, kept his voice a little more formal when Theo was around. He clearly hadn't forgotten the first time they'd met, on the corner in the Bowery, even with Theo's willingness to act as their spy.

"They're all cowards," Cela said. Her voice seemed to echo in the now-empty room. "Every one of them."

Abel sighed and looked at his sister. "They're not cowards, Cela, and you know it. Those are some of the bravest men I know, but I can't blame them one bit for not wanting to put their necks on the line for this," he told her. "And you shouldn't either."

"Of course I should," Cela started, but Jianyu placed his hand on her knee to steady her.

"Why?" Abel asked, his brows raised. "What exactly has any Mageus ever done for us except get you wrapped up in their messes?"

"We are grateful for your help," Jianyu said. "We understand that your friends have lives to protect."

Abel nodded, looking even more exhausted. "They're good people," he told Jianyu. "I think they wanted to help, but Negroes all across this country have a hard enough time these days without inviting more trouble."

"As though they're the only ones who suffer," Viola huffed, her words coming before she could think better of it. Once they were spoken, she felt immediately shocked that she had said them at all. They were words she had heard a hundred times before—her mother's words and her brother's. They were her family's sentiments, but they'd surprised her by coming from her own mouth.

"Viola—" Jianyu's voice was a warning now.

She felt every pair of eyes in the room upon her, especially Cela's and Abel's. Their understanding—their judgment of her—was clear. More, she knew it was *deserved*.

"I didn't mean—" But Viola wasn't sure that there was anything she could possibly say to retract the words. She *had* meant them, even after all the Johnsons had done for her and for Jianyu, and suddenly her cheeks felt warm with that knowledge. Irritation and shame all mixed together.

"Oh, I think we all know *exactly* what you meant," Cela said, sounding even cooler than before.

"Cela . . ." Abel looked even more tired now.

"Don't *Cela* me, Abel Johnson," Cela said. "You put your reputation on the line to ask for help. The least this one here could do is be a little grateful for it."

"We *are* grateful," Jianyu said, stepping in before Viola could respond. He cut Viola a quelling look. "It does not stop our disappointment, though."

Abel leaned back into his chair, as though he was too exhausted to stay upright any longer. "You have to understand their perspective. . . . What happens if this goes badly? Who pays the price?"

"It's not a risk any of us takes lightly," Jianyu acknowledged.

"But we don't all take that risk equally," Abel reminded him. "The Order will come for all of us if we fail, yes, but Hattie wasn't wrong when she spoke of the lynchings."

"My countrymen are hated as well," Viola argued. "When I was a girl, eleven were hanged in New Orleans." Her family had prayed for weeks, for the men who had died and for their own safety.

"This conversation isn't about *you*, though," Cela said. "We aren't talking about how your countrymen have suffered. We're talking about what's at stake right now if my brother's friends offer their help."

"You're not wrong," Abel told Viola. "But what you need to understand is that the decision that my friends and I make to help you is a decision that impacts more than our small circle. More than a *hundred* of my brothers were lynched last year alone. *Citizens* of this country were killed in broad daylight, and the authorities looked the other way—or they helped—usually over some white woman." He eyed Viola pointedly. "Mrs. Wells exposed the truth about that particular kind of violence a decade ago in the very paper owned by the man whose house you're now standing in, and it *still* happens with impunity."

"There's little point in comparing suffering," Theo said, his tone verging on dismissive. "Terrible things happen every day to many different people."

"Spoken by a boy born with a silver spoon," Abel said. "Don't you see? It's all related. All of us are implicated. You included, Barclay."

"What is that supposed to mean?" Theo asked.

"You don't think I saw the way you looked at me when we first met?

Or don't you remember?" Abel asked. His voice was soft, pleasant even, but there was no mistaking the steel in it. "I knew exactly what was going through your mind when you saw Viola getting into my carriage."

"I didn't . . . That is to say, I didn't mean anything." Theo looked momentarily stunned.

Abel shook his head. "In the end, the numbers don't matter. One or one hundred, each is a life stolen—a promise wasted—all because of ignorance and hate. That, and that *alone*, is why I haven't put a stop to Cela's determination to help you."

Cela cut a sharp look at her brother, but she didn't say anything against him.

Silence swelled in the room again. Tension thick and palpable threatened to overwhelm, but it was Theo who surprised Viola by breaking it.

"I do believe I owe you an apology," he told Abel.

Abel straightened his shoulders, pulling himself up to his full height. Waiting. They were all waiting to see if this fragile alliance would crack or crumble beneath the pressure of their differences.

"You're right," Theo admitted, rubbing at the back of his neck. "When we first met, I behaved rather badly, I'm afraid. And for no reason at all. There was no reason for me to regard you with any suspicion. You're right to point that out now."

"I appreciate you saying that, but it doesn't change the facts. You reacted like you did, and others will react the same. They always do." Abel looked to Viola. "The bottom line is that a lot of people in the Bowery can hide what they are—they can tuck their magic away and lie low until the winds change. My friends can't. There's no hiding the color of our skin, and we wouldn't want to anyway. They have every right to say no to what we're asking of them, even without those reasons."

Theo's apology hadn't eased the tension in the room. If anything, there was even more now than there had been before. They all seemed to be looking to Viola, expecting something from her. Her instinct was to push back against that expectation and against their *judgment*.

But then, Viola's instinct was *always* to push back. She'd pushed back against the weight of her family's expectations since she was young, hadn't she? It was as natural to her as breathing. She'd rejected their hatred of her magic. She'd rejected their control over her. Their hatred and judgment had driven her from home and led her to the Devil's Own.

A thought settled over Viola then, one that left her more than a little shaken. How was her family's hatred toward her affinity any different from their other hatreds? The words that she had just spoken, the thoughts that had just overwhelmed her, those were her *family's* thoughts—her mother's and her brother's. They judged anyone who didn't fit into the small view of the world as they knew and understood it. They found anyone wanting who wasn't like them. It wasn't only her magic they rejected. They looked down upon the whole world outside their narrow community and their singular way of life. And she had accepted those views like mother's milk.

How had she not seen this about herself before? How had she, who had believed so much in what Dolph hoped and worked for, somehow still managed to carry her family's narrow-mindedness deep within her. Unexamined. She'd somehow missed that the seeds of something too close to hate grew already deep in her heart.

Had Dolph known that about her all along? Perhaps he'd been right not to trust her completely, not to take her into his complete confidence, as he apparently had Jianyu. Her words, still hanging in the air, shamed Viola more than her family had ever been able to, and suddenly she felt the fight drain out of her, leaving her hollowed out. Empty.

"I'm sorry," she said, feeling her cheeks burn and her throat go tight. "After all you've done, after all we've asked of you . . ." No. That wasn't it. "Even if you'd done nothing at all to help us, my words—my thoughts—they shame me."

Cela frowned, as though confused, but the anger in her expression eased a little.

"I would understand if you want to walk away from this now," Viola told Cela. "If either of you wanted to."

"We don't have any plans to back out now," Cela said. Her expression had softened a little, but she was still frowning. "Right, Abel?"

"My sister's right. We promised our help already," Abel agreed. "We'll keep that promise."

"But you said—" Viola started.

"Everything I said is true," Abel told her. "But our family doesn't go back on our word once it's given. What's more, I wouldn't want to. Even with the danger we might face, I can see that there's something bigger going on here than our differences." He glanced at his sister. "Cela was right when she made the commitment to help Jianyu. Maybe we can't change everything, but Cela and me, we're gonna try to help you change this *one* thing. Neither of us is walking away."

WAKING

1952—San Francisco

Harte Darrigan couldn't recall much about what had happened to him since the night he'd escaped from the Committee and made his way to his father's house for the second time. He remembered standing across from the door he'd knocked on that first day he'd arrived in San Francisco, before everything had gone wrong. And he remembered waiting to see if anyone was home so he could get Esta's cuff and the necklace back. Everything after that felt like a dream—or perhaps, more like a nightmare. All of it seemed too impossible and too awful to be real.

Now that he was beginning to wake, Harte realized he wasn't dreaming. And he certainly wasn't dead—he was in too much pain for that. It felt like he'd been beaten and bruised from head to toe, pummeled over and over until the agony had turned to monotony. But the pain seemed far too pedestrian for damnation, so Harte figured that he'd survived. He had the vague recollection that Esta had something to do with it.

Esta.

He remembered more then—she'd come for him, as Seshat had predicted. She'd done something. . . . Harte couldn't remember what had happened next. If he was still alive, he knew that it must have been Esta who'd saved him, like she had too many times before. But the memory of Seshat's promise was clear in his mind.

She will come for you, and when she does . . . she will be mine.

Harte lurched upright in a panic—or he tried to. His muscles screamed as he lifted his head from the pillow, and he found himself too weak to actually move. There was something covering his face, but he managed to tear it away, and then he saw her.

Close to his bed, Esta was sleeping in a straight-backed chair, alive and whole and seemingly untouched by Seshat's power. Harte was almost afraid to move. If he did, the moment might shatter and reveal itself as a dream. She looked impossibly perfect with her dark lashes resting on her cheeks. Her chest rose and fell in a slow, steady rhythm, and Harte couldn't remember having ever seen her so still or relaxed. She looked almost peaceful.

No, he realized. She looked *exhausted*. Maybe it was the shadows that the garish light was casting over the planes of her face, but her skin looked too pale, and there were dark circles beneath her eyes.

She was no longer dressed in the men's clothing she'd taken to wearing in St. Louis. Her hair now curled about her face in a way that looked unbearably feminine, even with its short length, and her wide mouth had been painted a soft coral pink that made her lips look like petals against her tawny skin. If she weren't so far away from him, Harte would have taken her hand in his, just to feel the warmth of her. Just to be sure that this wasn't another hallucination.

At that thought, Harte sensed Seshat rumble within him, and he knew that whatever had happened, the ancient power hadn't given up. He knew, too, that Esta saving him had been a mistake, but somehow he couldn't quite bring himself to be sorry about it.

Harte shifted a little, trying to sit up, and the movement was enough to alert Esta. Her eyes flew open as she woke with a start, but it took a second for her to realize where she was. The emotions that crashed through her expression made him blurt out a laugh.

Damn. It *hurt* to laugh.

"I can't imagine what you could possibly find funny," she said, trying hard to scowl at him as she moved closer to his bedside.

Esta didn't sound angry, though. She sounded like she was about to cry, which was impossible, because his girl was tough as nails.

He tried to casually shrug off her question, but it hurt too damn much to move even a little. Instead, Harte allowed his head to loll back against the pillow. He took his time memorizing every inch of her face, as Esta brushed a lock of sweat-damp hair away from his forehead. Then he remembered the rest of what had happened—ever single one of his failures—with a terrible rush of certainty.

"I lost your cuff," he told her.

She was adjusting his covers, even though they were perfectly fine. "Yes, you did."

"You should have let me die for that fact alone," Harte told her, unable to meet her eyes.

Esta tilted her head to the side and considered him. "Probably . . ."

But she didn't sound even a *fraction* as furious as he'd imagined she would be. "You aren't angry?"

"Oh no," she told him with a tired sigh. "I'm absolutely livid. Furious, even."

She didn't sound furious. Harte wasn't sure *what* emotion was coloring her voice, but he didn't think he'd ever heard it there before.

"I should never have taken it," he told her.

"No, you absolutely should not have." Her mouth turned down a little, but she looked more sad than angry. "You *definitely* shouldn't have left without discussing it with me first. I thought we'd moved past all that. I thought we were partners."

"I know." He sighed. Then he swallowed what little pride a man could have while wearing a gown without any drawers beneath and completely at the mercy of a woman he'd wronged so badly. A woman he *loved*. "I was scared."

"I can handle Seshat," she told him.

He didn't know that she was right about that. Harte had the feeling that the ancient goddess hadn't even begun to show them what she was capable of, but he wasn't talking about Seshat. "I didn't leave because of Seshat," he admitted. "She was an excuse."

Esta was silent, her steady gaze urging him on.

"It was what I had to do here—what I had to face. About my past. About *myself*." The rush of words must have taken more oxygen than he'd expected, because suddenly Harte felt dizzy. He closed his eyes and tried to draw in a steadying breath, but that hurt as well.

"*Did* you face it?" she asked.

Harte considered that. "Maybe," he told her, feeling incredibly tired.

Nothing had gone right, but he understood something now that he hadn't before. Seeing his father through older, more experienced eyes had changed him. Maybe not completely, but something inside of him had shifted nonetheless. Meeting his brother had changed him even more.

When he opened his eyes again, Esta was staring at him. "You'll tell me about it later." It was a command and a threat all at once.

"I didn't get the Dragon's Eye," he told her. Another failing. Another regret.

"I didn't get the Pharaoh's Heart," she said with a shrug. "I had the Book in my hands and I lost that, too."

"You had the Book?" Harte started to sit up again, but a wave of dizziness overtook him.

"It doesn't matter," Esta said as though their entire existence hadn't been focused on this one goal. "We'll get it. We'll get all of the artifacts. And we'll go back and fix our mistakes." Worry darkened her eyes once more. "But first you have to get well."

"So you *don't* want to murder me?" he asked carefully.

Esta let out a sigh that sounded like nothing more than simple weariness and exhaustion as she took his hand, rubbing her thumb in gentle circles. He felt so awful that the friction was almost painful, and Seshat's power still rustled softly, somewhere down in the depths. Perhaps he should have pulled away, but Seshat still felt very far off and every bit as weak as he was, and Esta was touching him—and she wasn't even strangling him.

"It's not exactly satisfying to kill someone who's already half-dead," Esta told him. A small smile curved at the corner of her full mouth, but her golden eyes still seemed far too sad. "I've decided to wait a while, until you're a little stronger. I want to make sure it's *really* worth the effort."

It wasn't the reaction Harte had expected, and he wondered if this was another dream—a feverish delusion brought on by desire and hope and desperation. "I'll deserve whatever you have planned for me."

He meant every word.

A noise from the hallway had Esta sitting up a little straighter.

"Someone's coming." She pulled her hand away from his, leaving the spot she'd been touching cold. "There's so much I haven't explained to you. . . . Don't tell them anything you don't need to. In fact, it might be easier if you pretend you can't remember what happened. I'll be back once they're gone."

Esta was gone before he could stop her—not that he actually could have stopped her. He wasn't exactly moving that quickly. Or at all.

A moment later, the curtain around his bed drew back to reveal a clean-shaven man in a white overcoat wearing thick, dark-rimmed spectacles. He was flanked by another man in a dark-green suit coat and a woman dressed in a light-blue gown with a white apron and a white, winged cap on the crown of her head. Her attire reminded him a little of something a nurse might wear, but he didn't think that could possibly be right, considering that her skirts were nearly up to her knees.

"I see you've decided to return to the living, Mr. Jones," the man in the white coat said in a kind of jocular tone. "I'm Dr. Calderone, and this is Mr. Fisk and Nurse Bagley. She's taken good care of you these past few weeks. Mr. Fisk here is a government man, but I suppose we won't hold that against him, will we?"

Harte wasn't sure what he was supposed to say to that, so he didn't respond.

The doctor looked over a clipboard that held a stack of papers, conferring with the other man as he flipped through them, while the nurse busied herself by tending to Harte. He tried to shoo her away, but he'd grown so weak that there wasn't much he could do besides suffer the indignity of having himself lifted and rolled as the sheets were changed out beneath him.

After a few long minutes, the doctor peered at Harte through his thick lenses. "You're a lucky man to still be here, you know."

"I can't say I feel particularly lucky," Harte grumbled, wishing the doctor would leave so that he could figure out where Esta had disappeared to. *She promised to come back,* he reminded himself. Seshat had not taken her, and he hadn't lost her. That thought alone would have to get him through the next few minutes.

"I suspect you feel like something dragged out of the bay," the doctor told him with a smile that didn't match the sentiment of his words. "Considering how close you were to death, I'd say that's to be expected. For a while there, I had my doubts you'd pull through. The whole thing was a crapshoot, trying to figure out how to treat you. Of course we read about certain diseases in medical school, but I'm not ashamed to admit that you're the first case of plague I've ever treated. Actually, I believe yours is the first case we've seen in the city for decades."

"Forty-six years," specified Mr. Fisk. "The Committee eradicated that particular disease in 1906."

Forty-six years.

Harte had to have misheard. . . .

Since he'd opened his eyes, his thoughts had been so focused on Esta and on the pain that he felt that he hadn't noticed his surroundings. Now the strangeness of everything started to sink in—the cut of the man's suit, the transparent tubes that hung around him, and the steady whirring of some electric machine next to his bed that looked like one of the futuristic exhibits at the world's fair.

The doctor was still prattling on about something, but Harte couldn't hear anything the man was saying. His mind was racing, an urgent jumbled mess of memories tumbling through it as he tried to remember, but the one thought that came to him again and again was *What did Esta do?*

BLOOD IN THE VEIN

After the unsettling discovery of her own craven weaknesses, Viola remained quiet for the rest of the day. She sat and she listened, but she didn't interject much as the others planned for the few remaining days ahead. What was there to say that could make anything better? They would get the ring because they had to. It would be harder without the help of Abel's friends, but if they positioned themselves just right, it might still be possible to sidestep Nibsy, and Paolo as well. To *win*.

It was late—far too late—by the time Viola realized how many hours had passed. The streets were already mostly empty of carriages and people, and night was beginning to fall. If she didn't hurry, her brother would miss her. He might have questions that she couldn't answer without ruining the tenuous grasp they had on the possibility of victory.

"I have to go," she told the others, gathering herself to leave.

"I'll take you," Theo said, also standing.

"No," she told him. "Stay. You should finish things here. You're needed."

"Take my carriage at least?"

Viola didn't want to. Every time she stepped into the soft interior of Theo's carriage, she thought of Ruby, and for now—while things were still so fragile—she couldn't be distracted. Still . . . without the carriage, she would certainly be late. "Thank you," she told him.

"I'll walk you out," Theo said.

"Let me," Cela told him. "You stay here and finish."

The two women had built a fragile truce between them in the weeks before this, but their argument earlier had shaken something loose in Viola, something that she couldn't put back in the place it had once been. Now that she was faced with the prospect of speaking with Cela alone, Viola felt suddenly nervous.

Cela led the way toward the front of the house in silence, and Viola wished she could find an excuse to avoid the conversation that was about to happen.

"You were awful quiet today," Cela said when they reached the small vestibule before the front door. "I mean, after we had words."

"It seemed better to listen," Viola said truthfully. *And to think . . .*

Cela nodded, as though agreeing. Then she let out a long sigh. "I don't know that I like you, exactly," Cela told her, "but I want you to know that I don't bear you any ill will. Jianyu trusts you, so I'm willing to trust you too. I'm willing to start again, if you are."

It was a bit of grace that Viola did not feel she deserved.

"I owe you an apology," she told Cela softly.

Cela simply stared at her, quiet and waiting, not giving so much as an inch.

When Viola had aimed Libitina back in Morgan's ballroom, she'd thought she was doing the right thing. Later, she'd told herself that she hadn't known who Cela was. How could she have known that Jianyu would be working with a brown-skinned girl? But now she wondered how she could have been so shortsighted. Now she wondered why she had aimed to kill. Had it been from desperation or the heat of the moment? Or had Viola taken one look at Cela in the rumpled servant's uniform and seen only the other girl's brown skin and curling hair? Had Viola heard her mother's voice in her ears, as she had earlier today?

She couldn't know for sure, but if Jianyu had not stepped in front of her blade, Viola might never have thought anything of what she'd done. If she had not heard Abel speak a little while before, she might never have wondered why she'd made that particular choice. And she would have been worse off for it.

"I can't take back the things I've done," Viola said finally.

In response, Cela's brows rose and her lips quirked as though to say, *That's not much of an apology.*

Viola bit back an answering smile at the other girl's backbone. Cela was right. "I *am* sorry for what I did," Viola told her. "For what I assumed about you, and for the ugliness in my heart that day. You and your brother," she said. "Your kindness and your bravery . . . it humbles me. I will work to be worthy of it."

"It's not about working for it," Cela said with a frown. "Everybody's worthy from the moment they're born, and maybe if more people understood that, we'd have a lot less ugliness in this world."

The words struck an odd chord in Viola, one that vibrated through her in ways she wasn't ready to hear.

Before Viola could respond, Cela frowned. "I'm betting everything I have on the two of you, you know. I'm trusting you to keep Abel safe."

"I will do anything in my power to see that you and your brother come to no harm," Viola said.

"I'm going to hold you to that." Cela gave Viola a small nod before she went back to join the others, a sign that maybe the future between the two of them didn't have to be so fraught with tension.

By the time Theo's driver finally dropped Viola off back in the Bowery that night, it was much later than she'd intended it to be, far later than was acceptable or easily explainable, and she could only hope that her brother was too busy to notice. Her hopes were dashed, though, when she stepped through the back kitchen entrance and saw her brother waiting. With him were Johnny the Fox and another of his lackeys, Razor Riley.

"So nice of you to finally join us, Viola," Paolo said. "I imagine you have a reasonable explanation for where you disappeared to for so long."

She lifted her chin, defiant. "I went out."

"Out . . ." Paolo's tone was dangerously amused. "I'm afraid you'll have to do better than that, little sister."

Torrio smirked at her. "She was probably with her friends on 127th Street."

Viola couldn't stop her eyes from widening. She'd thought she'd been careful, but the Fox was wearing a triumphant look on his ugly face. She'd thought she had everything under control—Nibsy and Paolo and the danger the Order posed. But if her brother knew about Cela and Abel . . .

"Ah yes, the eggplants you've been visiting." Paolo flicked his cigarette to the ground, then snuffed it out with the sole of his polished shoe. "When, *exactly*, were you planning to tell me about them?"

She took an instinctive step back.

It was such a stupid thing to say. *Eggplants.* It had been a joke in her family, a bit of absurdity that they'd used between themselves to pretend they were only having a bit of fun. It wasn't hatred. It wasn't the sort of evil you had to confess to Father McGean before you went to mass. It was a *joke*.

But it wasn't. It never had been.

It turned Viola's stomach now to realize how easily she'd been a part of that ugliness, how easily she'd allowed herself to use their hatred as a way to belong. When her family had arrived in this country, they'd had so many troubles—and for no reason at all. They'd been hated by the pale Germans who had long ago made themselves into members of the community, and by the freckled Irish who already spoke English when they stepped from the boat. They were too strange with their rosary beads, too dark, too unwanted, and so her family had reveled in the small knowledge that it could be worse. That at least they were better than some.

Viola had never thought anything of that reasoning, because when her mother and her brother were talking about others, they weren't focused on her. They weren't focused on *her* faults or the whispers that followed *her* through the streets, strange, unnatural girl that she was.

She'd been wrong to go along with their ugly joking. Viola saw that now so clearly, but there was nothing she could do. It wasn't the time to correct Paolo, because the word he used was nothing compared to the threat behind it—the knowledge it implied and the sure danger it meant for Cela and Abel.

"I don't know what you're talking about, Paolo. And anyway, you listen to this one now?" she asked, jerking her chin at Torrio in a show of defiance. Hoping that he didn't scent her terror. "I thought it was the other way around?"

Torrio's eyes glinted in a way she didn't like. *He knows too much.*

Paul ignored the slight. "Now, now, mia sorella, the time for lies is at its end. I've given you too much room to run free, I think, and now it's time we talk about how you're going to repay me."

"What is it you want from me?" Viola asked, fighting to keep her composure, even as her mind was already spinning.

"I want the thing that everyone wants, Viola. I want the ring James Lorcan is so keen to have." Paolo shrugged. "I also want to make Lorcan sorry for trying to double-cross me with that blaze in Tammany's fire-house, and I want the Order to pay for what they tried to do to me at the gala. I want their precious treasures, and I want their power, and unless you want your friends uptown to find their way into the river, you're going to help me get it."

Viola had been trying to protect her brother from Nibsy Lorcan because she'd still been holding on to what she'd been raised to think about family. Blood wasn't water. Blood was *important.* Family was all that a person could rely on when the world would rather see you dead. . . .

Except, that sentiment wasn't exactly true. Viola was more than the blood in her veins—she *would* be more. Perhaps she had been too late to save Dolph, but she would not let Paolo touch Cela or Abel. She would not let her brother touch Theo or Jianyu. Even if it broke her mother's heart in two, even if it severed any connection to her family or her past, Viola vowed that she would destroy Paolo herself.

NOT NEGOTIABLE

1952—San Francisco

Nearly fifty years. Esta had cost Harte almost half a century. It seemed an impossible amount of time to lose. Harte knew people who didn't even get to count that many years in a single lifetime.

"Mr. Jones?" The doctor was frowning down at him. "I asked whether you have any other questions for me."

Harte had a million questions, but none that this particular man could answer. He shook his head and closed his eyes, wishing they would leave him be. He needed to see Esta. He needed to understand. Eventually, the ruse worked. The two men left, but unfortunately, the *click-clack* of the nurse's heeled shoes remained.

"We'll have you fixed up in no time," she clucked. "More fluids and plenty of rest, and you'll be out of here before you know it."

Harte wanted to be out of there *now*.

Allowing his eyes to open a crack, he watched the nurse as she fluffed his pillow and checked on a tube that seemed to be attached to his arm. He hadn't noticed that before either. Now he could almost feel the ache from where a gleaming silver needle had been inserted into his bruised skin. It connected to translucent tubing that wound up to a glass bottle hanging above him.

"Would you like me to fetch your wife?" the nurse asked before she went.

"My *wha*—" Harte caught himself before he finished. "My *wife* . . ." The

448

word felt strange in his mouth, especially when it was connected to Esta. And yet the *rightness* of it rocked through him. Considering what he was, what his affinity could do, the idea of ever being married had not seemed realistic. It *still* wasn't realistic, but somehow he couldn't stop the idea from taking root.

"Well, it's not visiting hours for a little while yet, but the poor lamb has been so worried about you that I think we could make an exception."

"Yes," Harte said, trying to keep his voice measured. "Please. I'd very much like to see my . . . my *wife.*"

"Only for a few minutes, mind you," the nurse tutted, waggling her finger at him playfully. "Dr. Calderone has ordered plenty of rest, and we can't go against the doctor's orders."

It didn't take long for the nurse to return with Esta, but it might as well have been hours.

"Just a little while, now," Nurse Bagley reminded them as she escorted Esta to Harte's bedside.

Now that Esta was standing and Harte had the time to look, he allowed himself to really take in what she was wearing—her full skirt was a soft lavender blue that came only to midcalf, and her cream-colored blouse was capped by a soft-looking woolen cardigan that skimmed the curves of her body. It cut in at her waist and accentuated her figure better than any corset he'd ever seen her in. It was enough to make him completely lose his train of thought.

"Thank you," Esta told the nurse, her hands clasped demurely before her as she looked at him. But the tightness in her eyes didn't match her words.

Harte waited until he heard the *click* of the door closing behind Nurse Bagley before he trusted himself to speak. "You look—"

"We have to go," Esta said, launching into action. She was at his bedside in an instant.

"What's going on?" he asked. The warmth that had been curling inside of him went suddenly cold with the understanding that something was clearly wrong.

"I don't know, but something," she told him. "Three carloads of men in suits just arrived. I saw them pull up while the doctor was in here, and I don't think they're coming for visiting hours." She pulled back the covers for him and helped him sit up. "Do you think you can walk?"

"Honestly? I'm not certain." His weakness galled him, but Esta was gone before Harte could so much as complain, and before he could blink, she was back with a wheelchair. He tried to stand, but instead swayed on unsteady legs and ended up back where he started on the bed.

"Let me help you," she said, even as he tried to bat her away. She didn't leave him much choice, though. Before Harte could argue, Esta secured him under his arm like he was some sort of invalid, which he supposed he was. But the truth of the matter didn't make that fact any easier to swallow as she helped him into the chair.

Within him, he felt Seshat starting to rouse, stretching like a cat that had woken from a long nap. She felt like a shadow of herself, but Harte flinched away from Esta all the same.

"She's still there?" Esta asked.

Harte nodded as he pulled the needle from his arm. To his relief, it didn't bleed much, but it wasn't enough of a distraction. Within his skin, he felt Seshat growing ever more aware of Esta's presence, and Harte understood that nothing had changed. She might be weakened, as he was, but she wasn't gone. And she wouldn't stay weak for long.

"You should go," Harte told her, knowing that there was no way he could get out of the hospital under his own power and no way he could allow Esta to help him now that Seshat was waking.

Esta ignored him. She'd already taken a leather pouch from her handbag and was busy looking through it for something. Finally, she seemed to find it, and she withdrew a small white tablet that reminded him of the quinine he'd taken as a boy to ward off fever. She offered it to him. "This should help."

"What is that?" he asked, eyeing the tablet.

"You're not going to like it if I tell you, so maybe it's better if I don't," she said.

Harte narrowed his eyes at her—or he tried to. He suspected that he was currently too pathetic-looking to intimidate anyone, not that he'd ever managed to intimidate Esta anyway. "Why would I take something I'm not going to like?"

"Because you trust me."

He couldn't help but wonder if her earlier quip about waiting until he was well before she killed him had any merit to it.

She let out an impatient breath, clearly frustrated at his hesitation. "It's a type of Quellant."

That was a surprise. "Isn't that what the Antistasi used in St. Louis?"

"Yes," she told him. "But Maggie improved the formulation. This version won't knock you unconscious, but it will still block your affinity—and it should block Seshat's power as well."

Harte didn't like the idea of willingly giving up his affinity—however much a bother it had been for him—but the idea that the Quellant might mute Seshat's power? He tried to remember back to St. Louis. . . . He couldn't be sure, but it did seem like Seshat had gone silent when the Antistasi had doused him with the Quellant. If Esta was right, taking the tablet might protect her from Seshat. That alone would be worth the risk.

His instincts screamed against taking the tablet, but he ignored them and swallowed it down before he could allow himself to second-guess the idea. The effect was immediate and awful. It wasn't only the bitterness that filled his mouth but the cold numbness that flooded through him, drawing his affinity away until he felt hollowed out. But in that emptiness, he sensed . . . nothing. No stirring of power. No rasping, ancient laughter. It was almost a relief.

"Well?" Esta asked.

"It might have worked," Harte told her, afraid to be too sure in case he was wrong.

"There's one way to find out." Esta offered him her hand.

Harte hesitated. Every time he touched Esta, he was giving Seshat another opportunity to make good on her threat.

"Harte?" Esta asked, frowning.

"If we're wrong, I won't be able to hold her back," he admitted, hating himself for his weakness. "She wants you, Esta. She's not going to stop trying, and I can't—"

"It will be okay," Esta said, offering her hand again. "Trust me, Harte."

He wanted nothing more than to do just that—to reach for her, to take her hand. It seemed such a small thing, such a normal, inconsequential action, but for Harte Darrigan, touching someone had always been complicated. The goddess living within his skin made everything even more dangerous. Especially for Esta. He couldn't risk her life. He couldn't chance losing her—not now.

"You should go on without me," he said, still staring at her offered hand. Her fingers were long and graceful, the fingers of a pickpocket who'd never been caught. "It isn't worth the risk."

"You've already taken the Quellant," she said. "If it's not going to work, better to know now."

Before he could stop her, Esta grabbed his hand. Her skin felt warm and soft as her fingers closed around his, and then the sound of the room drained away, leaving the world silent, and then . . . nothing. Seshat didn't so much as shift inside of him. The emptiness grated against his already weak body, but for the first time in *ages*, he felt only himself.

"It worked," Harte whispered, barely able to believe it could be possible. It had been so long since he had touched *anyone* without holding back, but it had been especially too long since he'd touched Esta. He tightened his fingers around hers, afraid to let himself wonder what this new development meant for him. Maybe, *just maybe*, this was actually an answer. Maybe it could buy him a little more time, because now that he wasn't dead and gone, Harte Darrigan realized again how much he wanted to live.

Esta let out a shaking breath that made him suspect she'd been every bit as nervous and unsure. "You know what this means?" she asked.

It meant that he could kiss her again. . . .

　　　　　　　LISA MAXWELL

"I can take you back to 1902," Esta said, apparently thinking of something else entirely. "We can stop the Thief and the Antistasi and the Defense Against Magic Act. We can set everything back the way it's supposed to be. We can make things *right.*"

Harte tried to ignore the pang of disappointment he felt at her words. But Esta was right. They should be focusing on what they'd set out to do, not on what it would feel like to press his mouth against hers. But then another thought occurred to him.

"Esta, you know we can't cross the stones," he told her.

"If we can get the Book back from Jack, we won't have to," she told him. "We can use it to—"

"How are we even supposed to *find* Jack? It's been nearly fifty years!"

"You know about that," Esta said, looking suddenly uneasy.

"I know," Harte agreed. "But I don't understand why."

"I didn't have a choice," she explained. "You were so sick, and you needed antibiotics—penicillin. It's a type of drug that can cure infections, even really awful infections, like the one you had." Esta pressed her lips together before she spoke again, more determined now. "It was the only way, Harte."

"You could have left me there," he told her. "You *should* have. If I died, Seshat would have disappeared right along with me. It would have been so much easier—"

"Don't," Esta told him, her voice sharp now. "Don't you dare say that I should have just sat there and watched you die. You are *not* negotiable. Not for me."

He stared at her, shocked by the emotion in her voice, and fought the urge to argue that she was wrong. But he couldn't bring himself to do it. Greedy bastard that he was, Harte wanted her to feel for him even a small bit of what he felt for her. He wanted her to need him, wanted to *be needed.* Not for the cuff he'd taken, but for himself.

The truth was that no one had ever needed *him*—not his mother or Paul Kelly. Not even Dolph Saunders. They'd each needed his power.

They'd needed what he could do for them. He understood now that he'd taken Esta's cuff because he'd been worried that he, alone, wouldn't be enough to draw her back. But her words erased that worry. She hadn't come back for the cuff. She'd come back for *him*.

Harte wished that he could freeze this moment, or bottle the feeling bubbling up inside of him. Even for a little while. Because he knew it couldn't possibly last.

"That goes both ways, you know," he said when he finally trusted himself to speak without betraying everything he felt.

He thought that he'd succeeded in hiding the true depth of his emotions. His voice had been steady, easy even, but suddenly Esta's cheeks went pink and her eyes went soft.

"We'll figure it out," she told him. She was already pulling away from him, as though the terrible rawness of the moment had been too much for her. "Seshat and the Book and the artifacts—we'll figure out all of it. But first we need to get out of here."

Still holding his hand, Esta pushed the chair into the hallway and then through the hospital's corridors. Their gleaming white floors were filled with nurses in skirts so short that not even madams would have worn them in public. Esta released time long enough to take the elevator down, and Harte couldn't help but notice that there wasn't an operator in the empty car. Esta simply pressed one of the buttons that lined a panel near the door, and the machine began to move.

The nurses, the machinery, they were all indications of how much the world had changed in the years he'd lost. *In the years I've gained,* he thought ruefully. Forty-eight years. A lifetime.

As the doors opened at the bottom floor, the world went quiet again, and Esta pushed Harte through the still, silent lobby, dodging around people frozen in time. Harte didn't miss the men Esta had noticed arriving earlier. They were unmistakable with their dark suits. Familiar silver medallions gleamed on their lapels, and at the sight of them, Esta moved faster.

"Did you see them?" she asked, as she continued on toward the hospital's exit.

"You were right. They look like trouble."

"But did you see what they were *wearing*?" she asked. "Those medallions on their coats?"

"Like the Jefferson Guard," Harte realized. "Do you think it's the Society? It's been so long. . . ."

"Maybe, but it could be any one of the other Brotherhoods," Esta said. "What we did in St. Louis brought them together back in 1904. It doesn't look like much has changed in nearly fifty years," she told him, grimacing.

Then she pushed his chair out into the night air.

If Harte had thought he was ready for what waited for him beyond the hospital, he'd been wrong. The scene outside was like something that not even the inventors and scientists at the world's fair could have imagined. The streets were smooth ribbons of black, completely devoid of horses and packed instead with machines painted in every color imaginable. They were nothing like the motorcars he'd gawked at back in St. Louis at the Palace of Transportation. Those machines were as square and boxy as a wagon, but these machines? They seemed more like sculptures than vehicles, impossible art forged from metal as smooth as water and crystalline glass.

They *gleamed*. Bright silver glinted off each curve of them, and their bodies shone like the paint was still wet. And the buildings. In New York there had been one or two buildings that scraped at the sky, but they'd stood apart, like sentinels above the rest of the city—not like this. In the years that had passed, San Francisco had become enormous. The hospital itself was a massive brick structure that rose at least ten stories above him. *And the lights.* Broadway had glowed at night, but everywhere Harte looked, electric lights flashed and twinkled even more brightly.

It all felt like too much, and yet . . . it was *perfect*. All Harte could do was stare in wonder and horror and awe. The world around him was new and unknown and *perfect*. It was right there—so close to being *his*. So was Esta.

But only for a little while.

Harte reached back and put his hand over hers as he looked up at her, and Esta's expression flickered to concern as she inquired whether he was okay. He nodded but couldn't figure out how to put all the things he wanted to say in words that would make any sort of sense. Esta seemed to understand, though. Wordlessly, she paused to let their fingers intertwine as the city continued to spin around them. For a moment the world was distilled down to the two of them. Harte felt only the warmth of her skin, the strength beneath, and not any of the rumbling power that had dogged him since he'd touched the Ars Arcana in the Order's vaults.

Then something shifted in Esta's expression. Her eyes had softened and gone glassy, but now she blinked resolutely as her entire posture seemed to stiffen with resolve. He could feel her pulling away from him, even while their hands remained clasped. "We'll need to find somewhere to lie low," Esta told him. "Maybe a hotel or—"

"Esta." Harte squeezed her hand gently, and she went silent and stopped walking. "Thank you."

He felt her relax a bit. Her golden eyes softened, and she gave him a small nod. All the things that Harte wanted to say hung in the silence between them, but before he could figure out where to begin, the moment had passed.

"We should go," she said, blinking again as though to will away any hint of tears. "If those men back at the hospital were there for us, they'll have figured out that we've left by now, and the Quellant won't last forever." She released his hand and started pushing the chair again.

As they began to move again, Harte felt a wave of exhaustion sweep over him. Esta was right. Her words were a reminder that freedom wasn't possible anymore—not for him. Maybe it never had been. The men with medallions glinting on their lapels were sure signs that the wonders of the world around him would always remain out of reach. So, too, would

Esta. The Quellant she'd given him would soon wear off, and Seshat still prowled within his skin.

Now more than ever, perhaps, Harte knew that he would not allow the goddess to touch Esta. The time would come when they would run out of the Quellant, and if that happened before they managed to control Seshat, Harte would do whatever he had to in order to keep Esta safe and whole. He would give his life, and gladly, if it meant that Esta would be able to go on without the threat of Seshat's power. But as he watched the lights shine and listened to the automobiles slide along, as he caught the clean, floral scent of Esta's soap in the air, Harte Darrigan wondered how he would ever bear to let it all go.

INESCAPABLE

Jack Grew slammed the phone onto its receiver so hard that the bell within vibrated at the impact. The news he'd just received had anger curling hot and furious in his blood.

They'd managed to lose Darrigan and Esta. *Again.*

All the resources Jack had bestowed upon the various Brotherhoods— the Committee especially—all the investment he'd made in waiting so patiently for so long, and the idiots in California had managed to let Esta and the Magician escape. The patient in question had been admitted to the hospital weeks ago, but no one had noticed that the man matched Darrigan's description until earlier that day. Jack should have left immediately, but from all accounts, the patient was in no shape to go anywhere. Instead, he'd trusted the Committee's watchmen to do the work he'd been destined to do, and they'd let Darrigan escape. Again.

Jack walked across his office to the broad table that contained a map of the entire country. He studied the shoreline of California, tracing it with a single fingertip as though he could touch Darrigan from afar. It was too bad he couldn't transport himself there, through the power of his thoughts alone.

They were still there, he knew, looking at the curve of the bay as it cut into the California coastline. *Right there.* Somewhere in the hills of that city—waiting for him to discover them. He returned to his desk and made a quick call. The plane would be ready within the hour, and by evening, he would be in San Francisco taking care of things personally, once and for all.

Jack Grew had always known Darrigan and Esta would resurface. Even when his advisers had wanted to pull back from the project, even when the various chairmen of the various Brotherhoods had wondered if his ongoing surveillance program had persisted long enough, Jack understood what Esta Filosik was capable of, and he knew that the work he was doing would pay off. He hadn't expected to wait nearly fifty years, of course. But the sureness within him, the voice that guided his every victory, had counseled patience . . . and once again it had proven correct.

He walked around the large model, examining all that he had accomplished in the lifetime he'd lived so far. The country spread out before him, the hills and valleys, rivers and streams all in perfectly rendered relief, and among them a series of pins dotting the landscape in an inescapable net. His life's work. His final victory. Each pinpoint of blue was a tower already built and ready to be armed. Each pinpoint of red was a tower nearing completion. When they were finally connected, their power would create an impermeable net across the entire country, collecting feral magic better than the Brink ever could and destroying any maggots who still managed to hide themselves away from the righteousness of the law.

A knock came at the door, and Hendricks ducked his head through the opening. "The car is here for you, Mr. President."

"Good," Jack said, still relishing the way the title sounded after all these years. "I'll be there in a minute."

When Hendricks was gone, Jack turned back one last time to examine the map. Perhaps it was time, finally, to bring his great creation to life. Darrigan could try to run, but he would never escape. Wherever Seshat was hiding, her power would finally, *finally* be his.

PART

IV

THE CHANGED CITY

1952—San Francisco

After they escaped from the hospital, Esta managed to find them a safe room at a decent hotel fairly quickly. It was easy enough to use her affinity to dodge behind the counter, lift a key, and adjust the paper ledgers to make it seem like they'd paid.

The next day, she searched the local paper for news of their escape from the hospital, but she found no mention of it. If the Brotherhoods knew that Esta and Harte were in the city, they hadn't publicized that knowledge. That fact didn't make Esta feel any better, though. The Society and the Syndicate had allowed the public to continue believing that the Thief was dead, even while they were searching for her at the Curtis Brothers' Show. Still, as long as the entire city wasn't searching for them, they had some time for Harte to recuperate. And he needed it.

For the next few weeks, they stuck close to the hotel as Harte grew stronger. As stir-crazy as she might have felt, Esta didn't go out for much more than food or supplies. At first, she'd been afraid to leave Harte for more than a couple of minutes because he'd still been so weak, and then later because there was a part of her that worried he would disappear again if she looked away. But as the days passed, their routine grew more familiar, and the room became a kind of den, a safe nest away from the dangers that had been dogging them for so long. Even Seshat had remained quiet. The goddess seemed to understand that her fate was tied to Harte's and that Harte needed to heal. In the peace of those long days, Esta found it too easy to imagine that the whole world was contained in that small room, and there were moments when she could almost forget what still lay ahead for them—and for her, especially.

Then, about three weeks later, everything changed.

She and Harte had been sitting together on the couch in an easy, companionable silence, when Esta woke from an unintended nap and discovered that it was later than she'd realized. Harte had dozed off too. She started to lift herself from the couch carefully, so as not to wake him, but his eyes fluttered open.

"I should get going," she told him. "We need dinner, and I—"

"Later," he said softly, tracing his finger across the back of her hand.

It was barely anything, the lightest fluttering of skin, warm and sure, against hers. But it was the first time he'd made a move to touch her on purpose since they'd settled in the hotel, and the shock of his skin made Esta's breath catch.

"Stay a while longer," he said, his gray eyes calm as the morning fog.

"The deli on the corner will close soon," she explained.

"I'm not really hungry."

"You will be, and even if you aren't, you'll need to eat," she told him. "I know you're feeling better, but you have a ways to go. You're still so thin."

"I'm not sick anymore, Esta," Harte murmured.

But Esta noticed the angles of his cheekbones and the way his collarbones jutted sharply beneath the soft cotton of his shirt, and she could only see how close she'd come to losing him.

"I'm okay," he told her gently. "You don't have to keep worrying about me."

"Fine." She tried to pull away, confused and embarrassed by the rush of emotions she felt, but he pinned her hand more firmly with his. He was right. She knew that. Harte didn't need her to take care of him anymore, not like he had in those early days. "Let me go, Harte," she said, her voice barely a whisper.

"Not yet," he said. He lifted his hand to cup her cheek. He might have said he wasn't hungry, but his eyes told a different story.

"Darrigan . . . ," she warned, but the catch in her voice betrayed her.

His face came closer, and Esta couldn't move. Didn't want to. In the days that had followed their escape, she'd barely thought about anything but making sure he stayed well, grew stronger. She'd cared for him like a nurse for a patient, never letting herself see him as a man—as himself. But now something essential seemed to have changed between them.

He paused, waiting for her consent, and she knew that if she let him come any closer, if she allowed him to press his lips against hers, there would be no turning back.

"We can't stay here forever," she told him, still not pulling away.

"But we can stay right now. We can for a little while longer," he replied, his breath warm against her lips.

"Can we?" she asked, and she found she really didn't know the answer. They had so much ahead of them to accomplish. And Esta had not forgotten what happened in Denver, the too-clear warnings time had issued.

In answer, Harte pressed his mouth against hers, soft and firm all at once, and every cell in her body seemed to sigh. It felt like she'd been swimming underwater, without air, for *so long*, and now she'd finally surfaced.

Esta could not stop herself from letting Harte pull her into the kiss. Her mouth opened slightly, and their breath intermingled, warm and sweet and so right that she thought she might shatter. She felt the warm slide of his tongue against her lips, and then, as she opened farther for him, it was over. He pulled away, his eyes wide with something that might have been pain or might have been fear.

"She's back," Esta said, knowing immediately what had put that expression on Harte's face. Seshat had been quiet, so they'd been saving the Quellant, but they should have known better. It had been too much to hope that Seshat's absence could have been permanent.

He scooted away from her, and then he stood and went to the window as he ran a shaking hand through his already rumpled hair. His eyes were stormy now. "I shouldn't have touched you. I should have known better."

"We both should have . . ." She never should have allowed it. They couldn't risk everything for something as silly as kissing—even if in that moment kissing felt more essential than anything.

The heat in Harte's eyes made Esta's throat go tight, and she knew they'd reached a turning point that couldn't be ignored. They couldn't stay there, in that room—in that time—avoiding their responsibilities any longer. Nibsy could still be out there searching for the stones. Jack certainly still had the Book. And hiding from the world wouldn't protect them . . . not when the greatest danger lived inside Harte's skin.

"Dinner," she told him, as if a simple errand could ever be enough to distract her.

The next morning, Esta stood at the window, watching the city wake as she contemplated her options. Below, a monochrome sea of gray and black suits made their way along the crowded sidewalks while trolleys and buses plodded through the streets. For the last few weeks, she'd been completely focused on Harte—on making sure he grew stronger every day. Now she looked at the world outside their room and wondered what their actions in 1904 might have done to this time, to *this* present. It was long past time to find out.

Harte was watching a variety show on the television, laughing at a comedian with a puppet, when Esta walked over and switched off the set.

He looked up at her, clearly annoyed.

She settled on the bed next to his feet, keeping far enough away that she wouldn't be tempted to touch him. "I think it's time we start figuring out what our next move should be. We need information. I'm thinking about going out. I could find the library or—"

"I have a better idea," Harte told her, already lifting himself from the bed.

Esta couldn't dissuade him, and within the hour, he was bathed and dressed in the clothes she'd stolen for him. The pants and shirt hung a little more than they should have from his thin frame, but with the way he'd been improving over the last couple of days, she knew it wouldn't be long before he filled them out.

With his dark hair slicked back, his face cleanly shaven again, and the modern cut of his pants and jacket, Harte almost looked like he'd stepped out of an episode of one of the old-fashioned shows he'd been watching. His color was better, and he couldn't hide his anticipation at the idea of leaving the hotel. As much as Esta wished she could convince him to stay and rest a little more, she couldn't really refuse.

Once they were out of the hotel and into the briskness of the late-fall day, Harte paused for a second to look around, his expression filled with something akin to wonder. He'd been watching the city from the windows of their fourth-floor room, but now that he was out in it, Esta wished she knew what he was thinking. She'd grown up in a world even louder and faster and more modern than this one, but since Harte had spent his life with gaslights and horse-drawn carriages, the cityscape before him must have felt like stepping onto another planet.

Harte didn't seem thrown off by it, though. Actually, Esta thought he was handling everything surprisingly well, considering. As he'd convalesced in the hotel room, he seemed to take the changes around him in stride.

They took a bus over to Grant Avenue, and from there they cut through the streets of Chinatown to reach the neighborhood known as Jackson Square. Chinatown was bustling with tourists and denizens alike. They walked along beneath buildings topped with pagoda-like roofs, while red lanterns hung on wires that crossed the streets and ornate dragons curled around streetlamps painted bright seafoam green. Harte stopped.

"What is it?" Esta asked, panic sliding through her. "Are you feeling okay?"

"What happened to this place?" Harte said with a hushed awe in his voice.

She hadn't noticed at first, but now that she really looked around, she understood what he was referring to. Grant Avenue was a wide street, filled with distinctive architecture and ornate flourishes. It was the Chinatown of movies and postcards, but it wouldn't have been there fifty years before. It certainly wasn't the Chinatown that Esta had seen from a distance, trapped behind a barbed-wire barricade.

"I'm not sure," she told him. "Time passes, I guess. Things change." It wasn't a good answer, but it was the only one she had to give.

Together, they walked up Grant Avenue, and Harte's worry eased into curiosity. Esta tried not to be too obviously amused at the way Harte marveled at the changed world. They turned onto Washington Street and then wandered north on Montgomery, until Harte came to a stop in front of a two-story brick building at the corner of Montgomery and Jackson Street. According to the historical marker out front, it had once been a bank built by William Tecumseh Sherman, the Civil War general. It wasn't a bank any longer. It seemed to house offices of some kind.

Harte stared up at it, frowning thoughtfully. "This was where the Committee's headquarters used to be," he said. "At least, I think it was. I thought the building was bigger."

"It might have been at one time," she told him. "At some point, there was an earthquake. It might have knocked part of this building down."

"Maybe . . ." He frowned, staring up at the building. "I'm sure this is it. I had the Dragon's Eye in my hands, and I was almost home free." His expression faltered.

"You did the right thing, Harte." She wanted to reach for him, but since the day before, he'd been careful to keep a certain amount of distance between them.

"I let it go." He turned to her, his expression bleak.

"You saved your brother's life," she said softly. "But, Harte, even if this is the same building, the crown can't still be here."

Harte looked like he wanted to argue, but Esta explained how she'd stolen the Dragon's Eye from the Chinatown in New York in the 1940s— nearly a decade before.

Harte listened, but she could sense his stubborn determination. "You said that St. Louis was different because of the train derailment we caused, right?"

"I'm not sure what that has to do with—"

He shrugged. "Maybe something has already changed the path of the Dragon's Eye."

"I guess it's possible," Esta admitted, even if she didn't think it was likely.

"I know you think I'm wrong," Harte told her. "But the fact is, we don't really know how this all works, do we?"

"How what works?" Esta asked.

"Time," he said. "We don't know how our actions affect the course of history. We've seen that they do, but we can't predict the effect of the things we've done—or might still do. Not *really*. Even trying to undo what happened in St. Louis . . . We don't know if it's actually even possible. You're just guessing and hoping you're right."

"I'm not *just* guessing," Esta told him, hating that he was closer to the truth than she wanted to admit.

"I didn't mean to start an argument." Harte let out a ragged breath. "But you have to admit . . . When I came here in 1904, I did something that hadn't been done before. It's possible that changed something. It's possible that the Dragon's Eye could still be here."

"It's been fifty years, Harte."

"If it's not here, then we haven't lost anything but time, and with the Quellant, you can always steal us more of that. But I think we should go in and take a look," he said, pointing to a sandwich-board sign sitting on the sidewalk that advertised an exhibition within. The offices seemed to be for some kind of historical society that had a museum open to the public.

Esta couldn't argue that it sounded promising.

"Even if the headpiece isn't in there, maybe the exhibition inside will have some clue about what happened to it," Harte said.

"Maybe," Esta said, still feeling uneasy. But Harte was already moving toward the arched front door, and she didn't have any choice but to follow.

THE DRAGON'S EYE

1952—San Francisco

Once Harte was inside the building, he realized he'd been bracing himself for an attack. Instead, he was met with nothing but
silence in the cool marble lobby. He could see the echo of the
bank it had once been, but now the room held a few large displays. The
caged bank windows had been replaced by an open counter, where an
older man sat. Harte sensed Esta entering behind him. When he turned
to her, he was once again surprised by how pretty she looked in the
strange clothing of this time, with her hair curling around her face and
her lips painted a soft pink that made his mouth go dry. Within him,
Seshat pressed at her cage, reminding Harte that he couldn't slip again,
not like he had the day before.

Seshat had been so quiet as Harte recuperated that he'd started to
believe she might have given up—maybe she was content with his
promise to destroy Thoth and would not insist on using Esta to take her
revenge on the world itself. The day before, Harte had woken from a nap
and, for a moment, he'd forgotten the danger. All he'd seen was Esta, and
he couldn't stop himself from touching her, from kissing her. But when
his lips had touched Esta's, he'd let his guard down and Seshat had surged
and reminded Harte of all that was at stake.

"Welcome," the man said. "I assume you're here for the exhibit?" He
glanced between the two of them, and then, after taking their admission
fees, pointed them in the direction of the rest of the exhibition.

The main displays were on the second floor of the building. They started at the mouth of the staircase, and trailed through a series of small galleries that told the story of San Francisco from the beginning. Large, printed signs described the city's history, or at least the history that started with Spanish priests establishing missions, through to Mexico's surrender of the land to the United States. Along the way, various artifacts were spotlighted from above, their glass cases forming a winding path toward the back of the building.

As Harte and Esta went through the archway, they passed a young guard in a dark, ill-fitting suit. Harte sensed Esta tense as they passed him, but she continued on. When they were finally out of the guard's sight, Esta leaned so close that Harte felt Seshat lurch.

"Did you see the medallion on his lapel?" she whispered.

Harte frowned. He hadn't noticed, but he trusted Esta's instincts. "There must be something here they're trying to protect."

Together they wandered through the displays, and Harte didn't have to pretend that he was interested in the artifacts, especially the ones pertaining to the Vigilance Committee. It had apparently been started back in 1851 as a way to fight the lawlessness and corruption in the city. An etching depicted a building with two men hanging from nooses. There was a display with medallions that reminded Harte of the open-eyed ring his father wore, and a model of Lady Justice staring with her eyes wide open.

When they came to a display about earthquakes that had happened early in the century, they paused. Beneath a wall of photos was a model of the city, most of the streets destroyed by the quake. Chinatown had been flattened, as had most of the area around it. But the building they were currently in had remained standing . . . for the most part. It explained the missing top floor.

The level of sheer devastation made Harte pause. "The whole city was destroyed," he realized. *Twice.* He'd never seen anything like it. No wonder Chinatown seemed so changed from the streets that he'd walked only a few weeks before.

Esta was frowning. "I knew there was a big earthquake sometime early in the century, but I don't remember there being two. . . ."

"That's what it says," he read, running his finger along the words etched into the placard. "The first one was in July of 1904, and then there was another two years later, in April of 1906. It destroyed most of what had been rebuilt and burned the rest of the city to the ground."

Her brows were furrowed. "July?" Esta stepped closer and read the placard again. "That's when we were there, Harte. Look at this—the map. Look at where they think the epicenter was."

He leaned forward, but he knew already what he would find. On the other side of Chinatown, the small dead-end Dawson Place was marked with a red bull's-eye.

"I knew that Seshat was powerful, but I didn't realize—" She looked at the map again as though it might tell her some other story if she stared at it hard enough. "I did this." She lifted her hand and touched the spot on the map.

"You don't know that," Harte told her, wishing there was something more he could say.

"I do." She looked at him, her whiskey-colored eyes filled with certainty. "I felt her. When I slipped you forward. I thought I could hold her back, but I—"

The guard entered the room behind them, and Harte went on high alert. "Later," he told Esta as he nudged her along, ignoring the way Seshat rattled within.

As they rounded a corner and entered the next gallery, Harte noticed a glass case that glowed golden from within at the same time Esta grabbed for his arm. Seshat's power rustled at her closeness, but Harte barely noticed, because he'd already seen what had made Esta gasp. *The Dragon's Eye.* Miraculously, it was still there, every bit as ornate and fanciful as the day Harte had found it deep within the Order's vaults.

This time the crown wasn't sitting out in the open, but behind a thick case of glass that reminded Harte of the one that had contained the

Djinni's Star back in St. Louis. There was no hint of opium, as there had been at the fair, but he circled the case carefully, pretending to read over the information about the crown as he tried to figure out what security they would have to get through.

He looked up to find Esta staring at the headpiece, mouth pulled into a frown and her brows furrowed, like she was confused. He sidled up next to her. "The security seems minimal," he whispered. "We could try to take it now. . . ."

Esta shook her head ever so slightly. If he hadn't been looking for her answer, he wouldn't have realized she was telling him no. She glanced up at him, and he watched indecipherable emotions play across her features. She was about to say something, when the guard from before entered the room. This time he wasn't alone.

"Do you know, I think I've had enough touring for one day," Esta said. Her voice had a false brightness to it that couldn't mask her nerves. "I'm positively famished, though. Maybe we could find a place to eat?"

"Of course," he told her, playing along. He didn't allow himself to make eye contact with the guards, who were clearly following them.

Harte braced himself for an attack as they worked their way out of the exhibit and took the stairs back down to the lobby. They nodded to the man at the front desk, then let themselves out into the noise of the streets. Once they were outside, Esta picked up her pace, but a few blocks away, Harte tugged her to a stop. He leaned against one of the ornate lampposts.

"We need to keep moving," Esta told him. "I think we're being followed."

Before he could argue, she threaded her arm through his and began tugging him along. Even with the layers of clothing between them, Seshat pressed at Harte, writhing within him to get to Esta.

Soon, she whispered. *Soon the girl will be mine.*

No, he thought, shoving Seshat back into the farthest depths of what he was. *I will destroy us both before I ever let you touch her.*

Harte thought he could feel Seshat's mocking amusement, but he turned his attention back to Esta. "They were waiting for us. I should have expected it. I never should have brought you there—but it's been *fifty years*."

"Thoth's been waiting for centuries to get control of Seshat," Esta reminded him. "What's fifty years in the grand scheme of things?"

When they reached California Street, a cable car was stopped in the center of the intersection, blocking the flow of traffic. Just as the driver had finished collecting his fares and was returning his hand to the large hand brake in the center of the car, Esta tugged Harte into the street and urged him on. He didn't hesitate. Ignoring how exhausted and drained he felt, he sprinted alongside Esta to reach the trolley. They barely managed to hop on as it started moving—too late for anyone to follow. While Esta paid their fares, Harte collapsed into one of the empty seats. He didn't miss the two men standing at the corner, where they had been, watching the cable car pull away. Their frustration was clear, and on their lapels, silvery medallions gleamed.

Once the trolley car was underway, Esta settled into the seat next to Harte.

"We'll go back," he promised. "Tonight. We'll make a plan and then—"

She leaned in close, and suddenly Harte couldn't speak. She spoke low, so no one else could hear. "Are you sure that the headpiece you tried to steal was the real thing?"

Seshat prowled within his skin, and Harte pulled back, preserving the careful distance between himself and Esta.

"Of course . . ."

"You felt the power in the stone?"

"Yes—" But thinking back, Harte couldn't *actually* remember if he'd felt anything. He'd been so sick, and everything that day had happened so fast. "Honestly, I don't know," he admitted. Then he realized . . . "I didn't feel anything back there."

Esta glanced at him. "That wasn't the real Dragon's Eye. It was a replica—a damn good one, but a replica all the same," she told him. Strangely, she didn't seem upset by this news. "I wonder if they know?"

"What are you thinking?" he asked, trying to figure out her new mood.

"I'm thinking there's a good chance that you didn't lose the Dragon's Eye," she said, her golden eyes brightening. "I'm thinking that maybe the Committee never had the original to start with."

"Of course they did," Harte said, wishing it were otherwise. "My father told me that he sold it to them. He *gloated* about it. If he'd sold them a fake, he would have bragged about that, too."

Esta glanced at him. "But what if your father was wrong?"

Harte frowned. "What do you mean?"

"What if he only *thought* he sold the real Dragon's Eye to the Committee?" Esta asked. "What if they only *thought* they bought the real thing?"

Harte rubbed his hand over his face, tired in mind and body from trying to follow her and her logic. "You're not making a lot of sense."

"Remember how I told you that your stepmother, Patience, must have given your father's creditors replicas of the cuff and the necklace when they came to collect your father's debts—replicas that she'd probably used her affinity to make?" Esta asked.

Harte still remembered how shocked he'd been to learn that his father had been married to a woman who was Mageus without ever knowing it. "You think she made a replica of the Dragon's Eye, too?"

Esta nodded. "If Patience could sense the power in the cuff and the necklace, it stands to reason that she would have sensed the power in the Dragon's Eye as well."

Harte was glad he was already sitting down. "But she didn't tell you anything about the crown."

"Why would she? She didn't know me, and I didn't tell her I was looking for it," Esta said. "But I think it's absolutely possible that your father sold a fake crown to the Committee."

"It would have put him at risk if he'd been found out," Harte said, thinking through the implications. "You really think she would have done that to her husband?"

Esta shrugged. "From what she told me, she wasn't exactly fond of him. She seemed glad that he was gone."

"He wasn't the type of man *anyone* would be fond of," Harte said.

"It's likely that they *didn't* figure it out," Esta said. "If they had, they would have reacted long before you ever showed up to take the crown."

"But Jack would have realized—Thoth would have known," Harte said. "It's clear he's working with the Committee."

"Which only proves my theory. Think about it, Harte. If Jack discovered that the Committee had a real artifact, he would have taken it from them. There's no way it would still be on display nearly fifty years later. It's more likely he let them believe it was real because it served his purposes."

Harte couldn't argue with that logic. "So what do we do now?"

"Patience helped us once before," Esta said. "Maybe she would be willing to help us again. Even if she doesn't still have the crown, she might know where it is."

Hope warmed Harte as the cable car rattled along down California, cutting through a canyon of buildings. He was still a little short of breath, and his legs felt like he'd run for miles, but the cool, damp air brushed against his face, reviving him a little as they traveled along. With everything that had happened, could the Dragon's Eye truly still be within reach?

Then another thought occurred to him. "It's been nearly fifty years. I doubt she's still alive."

"What about your brother?" Esta asked. "He might know something. He might even have it."

"Sammie would be close to sixty by now himself." So much time had passed, Harte wasn't even sure that the boy would remember him. "He might be gone by now as well." The thought made his mood sink.

"It's possible," Esta agreed, but still, she seemed more determined than disheartened. "But we might as well look into it. If we can't find them, we'll be no worse off than we already are."

Harte felt every second of the day's excursion. "If Sammie is alive, I don't know where we'd even start to look for him. . . ."

Esta still didn't seem worried. Her mouth curled into a small smile. "Luckily, I do."

THE ARS ARCANA

1902—New York

Jack Grew was exhausted from the evening of arguing minutia with old men. It was later than he'd intended to stay at the Chandlers' dinner party, but he still ordered his driver to take him south instead of in the direction of his comfortable town house on the edge of Washington Square. It had been a long day of maneuvering and positioning and *pretending*, but his plans were progressing . . . and the evening was still ahead of him.

As the hack carried him through the city, he took a cube of morphine, then tipped his head back against the carriage's plush interior, closed his eyes, and enjoyed the familiar warmth spreading within his blood. His senses came alive, and he could feel within him that sureness that always grew sharper with the languid, dreamlike warmth of the drug. By the time the carriage arrived at the docks, Jack was relaxed and more than ready to begin the night of work ahead of him.

He unlocked the door of the warehouse and let himself inside its dark, musty interior. Lighting a lamp, he made quick work of securing the door to ensure he wouldn't be disturbed, then lit the other lamps he'd stationed at various points around the large room. The entire room smelled of axle grease and dust, and in the softly glowing light, he took account of his progress so far. A new machine was rising from the bits of bent metal and broken glass. Without an assistant, progress had been slower than Jack might have liked, but he had time. The Conclave was still months away.

On the far side of the room, a long table held his plans. After the mess at Khafre Hall, he'd found the entire warehouse ransacked. The table had been overturned, and little had been left of the blueprints and models but ash and dust. He'd managed to reproduce what had been lost, just as he would reproduce his machine. Jack smoothed out one of the few documents that had survived the carnage, a half-burned scrap of an illustration depicting the Philosopher's Hand. In the palm, a fish lay burning in mercurial flames, uniting the elements. It was the symbol for quintessence. Great alchemists understood the importance of this most powerful of all elements. Aether, it was often called, the substance that aligned all other elements. With quintessence, one could turn iron into gold. With quintessence, one could transmute matter—or magic.

Quintessence was the ingredient Jack had been missing before, when his first attempt at building the machine had failed so completely. His desperate desire to solve that problem had blinded him to Esta's and Darrigan's treachery, but in the end he'd discovered the solution despite them. Thanks to the Book of Mysteries, Jack now understood exactly what he needed to complete his machine—he needed an object infused with feral energy. As above, so below. Like to like. Not even the purest uncut diamond was durable enough to contain the dangerous power his machine would collect. He needed feral magic to capture feral magic, and he would have exactly what he needed once he obtained the ring he'd been so close to retrieving at the gala.

Jack took the Book from its place near his heart and set it on the table next to the Philosopher's Hand. With the morphine thick in his blood, he allowed his mind to wander free as he turned the pages. Sometime later, he realized he was staring at a page he'd never seen before, one written in English rather than the strange, unknown languages that filled so many of the other pages.

This wasn't a new experience. In the weeks since Jack had taken possession of the Ars Arcana, he'd discovered that it was rarely the same book twice. He had not yet come to understand how or why it revealed certain things to him but was grateful that it continued to do so. It had to be a signal of his continued worthiness, a sign that he was destined to prevail.

The writing on these new pages had been done in a cramped, sloping hand. The varying weight of the ink and the discoloration of the thick vellum told Jack that the page had likely been created long ago, before the smooth consistency of fountain pens was even an idea. He flipped through the next few pages, all in the same matching hand. His excitement only grew when he noticed a small notation at the bottom of one of the pages—*Is. Newton* had been inscribed there, in the same cramped style as the rest. With only a cursory glance, Jack understood *immediately* what this was. There on those pages, Newton had detailed his creation of the artifacts.

Righting a stool that had been knocked over in the destruction, Jack took another cube of morphine between his teeth and settled himself to read. On those pages, Newton had inscribed detailed illustrations of five precious gemstones, and alongside each drawing were notes about the gemstone's origin and the properties of the stone itself. Apparently, the old alchemist had carefully selected only the most perfect of materials, gemstones prized for their purity and historical importance. The individual stones had been drawn from the five ancient mystical dynasties, and each was famed for the power that it held. Then Newton had used a ritual involving the Ars Arcana itself to imbue the stones with the feral magic of the most powerful Mageus he could find—each aligning with one of the five elements.

But something had changed. As the notes continued, Newton's hand grew more erratic and uneven. Later illustrations had been hastily scribbled onto the parchment, and still others had been blotted out. The content of the words matched their appearance. The clear English notes shifted into a confusing and often unintelligible series of arcane phrases. They were most likely coded alchemical recipes, metaphor layered upon metaphor, but Jack couldn't be sure of the meaning other than to understand that something had scared the old magician. Something had brought Newton to the brink of sanity before he'd managed to pull himself back.

Jack turned another page and found a diagram that looked very much like a copy of the symbol that was carved into the front of the Ars Arcana. The writing here was still erratic and clouded in metaphor, but the illustrations were clearer. The series of diagrams in the following pages seemed to depict the creation of what looked to be silver discs, each inscribed with the same strange design that graced the cover of the Ars Arcana, but when Jack turned the page, the information ceased. The next page was completely blank, as though the Book had decided to withhold its secrets. He couldn't tell what the purpose of the discs had been, or why Newton seemed so keen to create them.

Jack flipped back through the pages and examined Newton's notes once more, marveling at how close Newton had come to unlocking the true power within the Book, only to fail. The weight of what he'd been attempting had nearly driven him to madness. In the end, Newton had turned from the occult sciences and back to a safer and far more pedestrian path. Apparently, he had been too weak to handle the enormous potential of what he'd discovered. Instead, he'd given the Ars Arcana to the Order, along with the stones, for safekeeping.

As Jack closed the Book, his mind was still clouded with the haze of morphine. He considered the symbol carved into the cover, and as he meditated on it, he traced its intricate lines with the barest touch of his finger. In and out and around, following the figure as it doubled into itself over and out again, infinite. Impossible. Beyond his reach. Jack understood there was some larger secret here, but the Ars Arcana was not ready to reveal it.

It would soon enough. Jack had utter confidence that once he proved himself worthy, the Book would reveal everything. Until then he would focus on his machine and the destiny before him. Once he had the power contained within the Delphi's Tear, he would finally finish his great machine and show the world what could be achieved when power and science coalesced. Luckily, the old men of the Inner Circle had put Jack in the perfect position to make all of that possible.

THE DRAGON'S PEARL

1952—San Francisco

As the taxi glided through the streets of San Francisco, Harte tried to focus on the bright lights of the city instead of the gown Esta was wearing beneath the folds of the soft strip of cashmere she'd wrapped artfully around herself. All his life, Harte had wanted to see the world, to escape from Manhattan and explore the land beyond the Brink, but nothing could have prepared him for the amazement he felt seeing the sleek motorcars speed along. They flashed like schools of impossible fish beneath the city's lights. Nothing could have prepared him for the astounding wonder of it all. But somehow, nothing seemed half so astounding as the dress Esta was wearing.

From the front, the neckline of the frock skimmed her collarbones and was demure as anything she might have worn in his own time, but the back . . . Esta had asked him to pull the most ingenious little sliding fastener up to secure the dress, but even fastened, the back dipped nearly down to her waist, exposing an expanse of her smooth skin. The sight had been enough to rob him of words and make his palms sweat.

Her mouth had quirked a bit when she'd noticed his reaction, but Esta hadn't said anything as she'd tucked the leather pouch with Maggie's concoctions into her beaded evening bag. *Just to be safe,* she'd told him. Harte didn't argue with her logic. After they'd been followed earlier, it made sense not to take any chances. They might be followed again, and if that happened, they wouldn't be able to risk returning to the hotel.

Esta had used up most of the Quellant in those early days to be sure that Seshat would remain quiet while she'd taken care of Harte. Now there was only one tablet left, and they knew they had to save it until they were ready to return to 1902. Without the Quellant to leash her, though, Seshat prowled freely again beneath Harte's skin. She'd been mostly quiet, but he could tell that she was only waiting for an opportunity. He wasn't about to give her one, not when he was so close to protecting Esta for good.

Once they had the real crown and after they'd located the Book, they would use the last of the Quellant to go back to 1902 and retrieve the ring from Cela Johnson. Once Esta had all five of the artifacts, Harte would take care of Seshat so Esta wouldn't have to. She would be left with the Book and the power within it, and with that, she could defeat Nibsy Lorcan. She would be safe. For good.

And until then? Harte would be content with being an arm's length away from her, caught up in the sweetness of her perfume as they floated along in the plush comfort of this strange, quiet machine.

Without even thinking, Harte lifted his fingers to rub at his lips, but he could no longer resurrect the memory of the kiss they'd shared two days before. It felt like it had happened in another lifetime. He let his hand fall back into his lap and studied the passing streets as they rode on in silence until the taxi stopped at the address Esta had given the driver.

It had been far easier than Harte had expected to find his brother. Esta had located a telephone directory once they'd returned to the hotel the day before, and from there it had been a matter of sorting through the various entries to find Sammie. That had taken a while, but eventually they found a person who might be Harte's brother—a Sam Lowe, who owned a nightclub just outside of Chinatown.

Once out of the car, Harte felt the crisp snap of autumn's chill in the air. He could hear the sounds of an orchestra filter through the heavy golden doors each time they opened to admit another couple. On the enormous marquee above, the nightclub's name glimmered: THE DRAGON'S PEARL.

"It's too perfect not to have some connection." Esta glanced at Harte. "The crown is here. It *has* to be."

"Let's not get ahead of ourselves," Harte said, wanting her to be right and also not wanting to be disappointed. "First we need to see if the Sam Lowe who owns this place is really my brother."

Esta linked her arm through his and paused, as though to confirm that this was okay—that Seshat was calm.

"It's fine," he told her. "I can handle this." The power inside him was rumbling at Esta's closeness, but with the layers of fabric between their skin, Harte was able to push the ancient power back easily enough.

For now, Seshat whispered softly.

Harte grimaced in reply.

"I wish we had more of the Quellant," Esta said, noticing his discomfort.

"I'm fine." *At least for now.*

Besides, he hated the idea that he needed Maggie's formulation even to stand next to Esta. Even more, he hated the way the Quellant made him feel: cold and empty and incomplete. That aching hollowness was almost enough to have him yearning for something to take the pain away. He wondered if it was anything like what his mother felt after she'd ventured too close to the Brink. If so, Harte understood a little better why Molly O'Doherty had reached for the numbing lull of opium.

Together, Harte and Esta followed the crowd of people through the golden double doors and into the nightclub. Once they entered, they were surrounded by the sounds of the orchestra's music, crystal clinking, and couples speaking across linen-covered tabletops. The whole place was decorated in dark gleaming wood and gold accents. In the center of the room was a wide-open dance floor, which was anchored by a five-piece band that was playing a soft ballad. This wasn't the raucous Haymarket, with its painted ladies and packs of hungry young men roving for a night on the town. The clientele here was mostly couples—mostly older and mostly white, but the waitstaff and other workers all seemed to be Chinese people. Jewels glittered around every woman's neck as couples glided across the dance floor in smooth, looping circles or sat leaning close across tabletops, their quiet murmuring like the rustling of money.

The hostess was a Chinese woman wearing a red satin gown. Her dark hair had been cut nearly as short as Esta's and was curled and fluffed about her face in the style that seemed to be popular everywhere in the city. She led them to a table in the back corner of the club, away from the lights and bustle of the open dance floor, as they'd requested. Esta looked over the menu, which was divided into both American and Chinese offerings, but Harte could hardly concentrate on food. Instead, he scanned the room and the dance floor for any sign of the man who could be his brother.

"Are you sure he'll be here tonight?" Harte asked after they'd placed their order. He didn't know why, but he'd almost expected Sammie to be waiting for him at the door.

"That's what I was told by the person who answered the phone earlier," Esta said, looking around the room. "From what I understand, he's here every night."

"We should have come yesterday," he told her, frustrated at his own weakness.

"You needed to rest yesterday," Esta told him, her golden eyes flashing with something that looked too much like pity for Harte's liking.

He'd seen that look too many times since he'd woken in that damned hospital bed. As he'd recovered in the hotel, she'd been there by his side, watching over him as though he might disappear if she looked away. Harte didn't even want to think about the ways she had helped him. He would have been incinerated by the shame of his own weakness had he been well enough or strong enough to care at the time. And always, fear and pity had been stark in her expression—like he'd been some kind of wounded animal to save . . . except for that afternoon when he'd woken from an unintended nap and, not thinking about the consequences, had kissed her. It hadn't been pity in her eyes then. It had been hunger and hope as deep and unspeakable as his own.

Harte knew he should tell her how grateful he was. He could at least tell her how beautiful she looked that night, but he couldn't figure out where to start. He opened his mouth again and again—he probably looked like a fish—but the words wouldn't come.

Esta turned to him, and her expression shifted to concern. "Are you okay?"

"Fine," Harte mumbled, feeling stupid. Before he could pull himself together and try again, though, the orchestra trilled and the house lights began to dim. The dance floor was suddenly bathed in cool blues and pinks.

A line of chorus girls with their legs bare to the hip sashayed onto the floor. Their shoes clickety-clacked in rhythm as they came, and the scraps of their costumes threatened to come undone with every bounce and shimmy. Their act was followed by a Chinese couple. The woman was dressed in a diaphanous gown of silk and feathers that made her look like a bird of paradise, and the man, tall and slender in a topcoat and tails, spun her around the floor in a dreamlike waltz as easily as if she weighed no more than the feathers on her gown.

Their meals arrived, but Harte wasn't hungry. He picked haphazardly at the food on his plate as one act after another took the stage. Esta must have been as nervous as he was, because she didn't eat much either. By the time the waiter carried away their barely touched plates, the show was winding down, and there had been no sign of Sammie.

With the ringing of the piano, the entire club went dark, and a single beam of light flickered on to illuminate a girl in the center of the dance floor. She had hair the color of fire and was holding an enormous translucent sphere, like a giant soap bubble. The orchestra hummed softly, and she began to dance.

"She's not wearing anything at all," Harte murmured, feeling his cheeks heat in embarrassment. He'd seen plenty of bare arms and legs during his days onstage, but nothing like this.

Esta glanced at him, and Harte could tell she was trying not to laugh.

"I believe that's the point." But her expression shifted when the girl started dancing, and suddenly Harte felt the unmistakable warmth of magic—*natural* magic. "Did you feel that?" Esta whispered.

He nodded. "It can't be a coincidence."

In the center of the stage, the girl turned and dipped, holding the sphere so that it somehow never managed to reveal anything overly pertinent. But as lovely as the girl was with her willowy figure and softly waved dark hair falling around her shoulders, even the promise of seeing her entire body couldn't hold Harte's attention. It was nothing compared to the sight of the gentle slope of Esta's exposed back, the delicate pearls of her spine traveling down into the low dip of her dress.

When the floor show was over, he would ask her to dance. He would take the risk and hold her close. He could almost imagine what it would be like to rest his hand on the curve of her lower back, skin to skin . . .

Yes, Seshat purred.

No. Harte fisted his hands beneath the table to be sure that he did not reach for her. He couldn't allow himself to indulge in fantasies about being close to her again. He *wouldn't.*

He forced himself to look away from the smooth expanse of Esta's skin, ignoring the heat in his blood, and focused on studying the crowd instead. The people in the audience looked less titillated than vaguely interested in the girl on the floor, but Harte noticed one person watching the crowd instead of the floor show—an older man standing on the side of the dance floor with a scar that marred the corner of his mouth.

In a sharply cut black suit with satin lapels and a crimson tie, the man was dressed better than any of the other waitstaff. He held a set of menus in his arms, but he watched the room with the alertness of someone clearly in charge. He was older—*so much older*—but Harte would have recognized Sammie anywhere. Despite the man's lighter hair, Harte could see their father in Sammie's features, but Harte's brother wore them with a quiet dignity that Samuel Lowe had never quite managed.

Harte nudged Esta's arm, careful to limit their contact. "I think that's him." He nodded to where Sammie still watched over the room.

"It could be. . . ." She didn't sound as sure, but Harte knew.

The music was building, and before they could discuss it any further, the bubble burst and the girl pranced offstage to thunderous applause, exposing the pale globes of her bottom as she went. Sammie waited a second longer, but when a group of women in evening gowns emerged from the curtain behind him to begin circulating through the club, Harte's brother ducked into a back hallway.

"I'm going to follow him," Harte said, already on his feet.

"I'll come with you." Esta started to stand, but Harte was already shaking his head.

"I think it's better if I do this on my own."

Part of him didn't want to let Esta out of his sight, but with the dress she was wearing and the way Seshat seemed to sense his weakness, Harte knew it would be safer for everyone if he went alone.

Coward, Seshat mocked.

Harte didn't disagree. He *was* a coward. A braver man wouldn't have been afraid to keep Esta close, and a stronger one could have easily resisted touching her. But Harte Darrigan had never been anything but a bastard and a con, and now he was a desperate one at that. The Dragon's Eye *had* to be there. With the threat to his health behind him, he could already feel Seshat growing impatient. The sooner they had the crown, the sooner they could find the other artifacts, and the sooner he could put an end to the threat Seshat posed.

And until then? Harte wasn't so careless as to put everything at risk—especially not Esta—for something as insignificant as his pride.

WHAT CAME AFTER

1952—San Francisco

W hen Harte ducked through the curtain to follow Sammie, he found himself in a hallway that ran behind the stage. For a moment he was overwhelmed by the memories of another life: the feeling he'd get waiting in the darkened wings for the cue to enter the spotlight, his nerves jangling as the scent of greasepaint and powder filled his senses. But those days were long behind him.

Harte shook off his regret. If he didn't keep moving, someone was bound to notice that he didn't belong backstage. When a chorus girl's expression bunched with a question, he only nodded to her and kept walking like he was supposed to be there. Luckily, no one stopped him.

He passed by the dressing rooms and then turned into a long hallway that ran behind the stage. At the end of it, light spilled from an open doorway. Harte approached carefully and saw that it was an office. Behind a broad, cluttered desk, his brother was too focused on a stack of paper to notice him. Easing into the room, Harte pulled the door closed behind him. At the sound of it closing, Sammie finally looked up, irritated at the interruption. The irritation quickly turned to confusion, though . . . and then the color drained from his brother's face.

Harte felt suddenly, unaccountably embarrassed. He tucked his hands into his pockets and tried to force himself to appear at ease. "Hello, Sammie."

The man at the desk didn't respond at first. He only stared at Harte, shaking his head as his mouth moved without any sound coming out. Finally, Sammie seemed to find his voice. "It's not possible."

"It shouldn't be." Harte tried to ignore the nervousness he felt. He'd known Sammie only as a boy, after all, and then for only a very short time. They'd never discussed who they were to one another, and after everything Harte had put the kid through, he hadn't been sure what kind of reception he'd receive showing up so many years later.

Sammie stood and came around the desk, his hand reaching for Harte. "You look exactly like I remember you. Like a ghost—"

"I'm not a ghost," Harte told him, stepping back before his brother could poke him.

"Then how—" Sammie shook his head. "You haven't aged a day."

The weariness in Harte's body said otherwise. "It's a long story, and honestly, it's one you'd probably be better off not hearing." Harte hesitated, trying to figure out the best way to go about what he had to do, but in the end he found that he didn't have the stomach for anything but sincerity. He softened his voice. "How have you been, Sammie?"

At first his brother simply stared at him—in shock or disgust or sheer confusion, Harte couldn't tell. His stomach sank as he realized that maybe he'd miscalculated. He'd hoped that his brother would welcome seeing him, but now he wondered if he should have been more careful.

But then his brother seemed to come to terms with the situation he'd found himself a part of. "It's been a *long* time," Sammie said, giving Harte an expectant look. "A *lifetime* . . ." Then, when it was clear that Harte wasn't going to volunteer any real explanation, his brother shrugged. "You know how lifetimes go—there's good and there's bad mixed together. I'm lucky. I've had more good than bad."

"I'm glad to hear that," Harte told him, and he meant it.

"I have you to thank for it," his brother said, leaning against his desk.

Harte frowned. "I doubt that." He'd caused Sammie more trouble than anything else.

His brother's brows went up. "You don't think I remember that you saved my life that day?"

Harte shifted under the intensity of his brother's gaze. He wasn't any hero, and the last thing he wanted now was praise. *Especially* when he knew the danger he might be dragging Sammie back into. So he deflected. "Your father wouldn't have really let them—"

"Yes, he certainly would have," his brother interrupted. "You knew it, and I knew it too, even as young as I was back then. Our father would have let those men kill me if it meant saving himself and his precious reputation." Sammie lifted a single brow. "If you hadn't done what you did, I doubt I would have lived past that day."

At first Harte thought he must have misheard. "*Our* father?"

"She told me who you were," Sammie told him. "My mother, I mean. She said she knew the second you showed up at our home that you were his son. He'd never talked about having another child or another family, but Mother knew what kind of man she'd married."

Harte hadn't realized how still he'd been holding himself, fearing what Sammie might think or do. Now he felt only relief. It made his legs unsteady enough that he lowered himself to the leather sofa that stood against the wall. "I didn't realize she knew."

"She recognized him in you. She told me that it scared her at first— that *you* scared her with your intensity and your demands—but she realized that you weren't anything like him when you saved me that day. It's why she took care of you instead of returning you to the Committee." Sammie let out a breath, like he was letting go of part of the past he'd been carrying for too long. "He never came back, you know. Wherever he sailed off to, he stayed gone."

"I'm sorry . . ."

"Don't be," Sammie said, waving his hand in dismissal. "Our father was a weak and unhappy man, made all the worse because he thought he was being guided by some higher power. His disappearance was the beginning of my life, not the end of it."

LISA MAXWELL

Sammie's words were an unexpected balm. Even in the midst of the fever that had almost killed him, Harte had worried what his actions might have done to the boy and his father's wife. He'd worried about how they might have suffered for his impulsiveness, as his own mother had.

"It must be some life you've lived," Harte said softly. "You have quite the place here."

When Esta had discovered that Sammie owned a nightclub, Harte hadn't expected anything half as opulent as the Dragon's Pearl. How his brother had gone from the shy, skinny little kid to the man now sitting behind the desk, a golden bracelet glinting on his wrist, Harte couldn't imagine.

Or maybe he could. After all, hadn't he done the same for himself?

Sammie's expression turned a little smug. "I built it all myself."

"Really?" Harte asked, wondering if it had been built from the profit from a priceless lost artifact. "That must have been . . . difficult."

"No more difficult than anything else I've lived through," Sammie said. "Mother died when I was very young—not long after we met, actually. I was just a kid, and it was a struggle to stay alive for a long while."

"Was it one of the earthquakes that took her?" Harte asked, thinking of the exhibit they'd seen the day before.

"They were hard—terrible to live through—but no. Mother died because of what came after." Sammie got up from where he was leaning against the desk, went to a sideboard, and poured some amber-colored liquor into two crystal glasses. Then he handed one to Harte before downing his own in a single swallow.

"What came after?" Harte asked, not bothering to lift the cup to his lips. Instead, he watched the emotions play across Sammie's expression.

Sammie was old—older than Harte had ever imagined himself being. His dark-blond hair had already turned an ashy gray, and there were deep creases at the corners of his eyes that spoke of a lifetime filled with laughter. Even as old as he was, Sammie looked fit and healthy. He was about the same height as Harte, but he had a presence to him, a confidence and sense of self-possession that Harte had noticed from across the nightclub. With his hair slicked back and the sharp cut of his perfectly tailored suit, Sammie could have stood next to the richest and most powerful men in the country and not looked one bit out of place.

Sammie quirked a brow in Harte's direction as he poured himself another glass. "You know what came after. . . ." He gave Harte a pointed look.

"I've been away," Harte said, giving up nothing.

"Must have been a hell of a long time," Sammie said, again questioning without really asking.

"It was," Harte admitted. It was all that he would admit to. Slipping through time was Esta's to speak of, not his.

His brother's eyes narrowed a little, clearly trying to figure out another way to interrogate Harte, but finally Sammie seemed to relent. "If you know about the quakes, you must know that the Vigilance Committee determined that the first earthquake wasn't natural. They said it was some kind of attack by the Devil's Thief." He leaned against the desk again as he sipped the second glass of whiskey, this time more slowly than he had the first. "For the two years that followed, life in the city was nothing but raids and roundups. It was for our protection, the Committee said. They reasoned if the Devil's Thief had been hiding in the city, then there must be others with the illegal magic as well. They weren't wrong," he admitted with a shrug. "Back then, a lot of people had the old magic."

"Like your mother," Harte prodded. He wanted to see how much Sammie knew, or at least how much he was willing to admit.

Sammie nodded. "Yeah, like my mother. The period after the first quake was bad, but we survived it. The Committee took the opportunity the quake provided to focus their blame on the Chinese people for hiding the Devil's Thief—kind of a two-for-one. Chinatown dealt with the worst of it, so Mother was able to rebuild the shop without much trouble. We mostly managed to avoid the Committee's notice. But when the second quake came two years later, things got worse. That one was bigger, and it burned most of the city to the ground. Everyone was desperate to blame someone. The Committee took advantage of the devastation and blamed the Devil's Thief again."

"Did they have proof?"

"Who needs proof, when you run the city?" Sammie finished the last of the whiskey in his glass. "Anyway, after the second quake in '06, that's when the Committee built their tower."

Harte felt suddenly apprehensive. There was another tower once, another machine and another plan that was meant to attack the old magic. "What tower?"

"The one in Portsmouth Square. The Committee told the public that the tower would only *detect* magic," Sammie said. "It was supposed to serve as a warning in case someone like Miss Esta ever attacked again, and it was only supposed to target Chinatown. People were happy to go along with it, but a lot of us knew it was a lie. Stories of the Brink in New York had made their way across the country years before. No one really believed the Committee would be happy with simple *detection*.

"They built the thing right in the center of Portsmouth Square, and by 1908 it was ready—even before a lot of the other buildings were. I was still a kid then, but I knew things were bad. I should have done more to convince my mother to get out. . . ." Sammie paused, staring down at his empty glass. "The tower killed more people than either earthquake—people far outside Chinatown," he said. "It killed people—Mageus—all over the city."

"I'm sorry," Harte said. He didn't need Sammie to explain what had happened. He'd seen Jack's first machine for himself, and he understood too well what it was like to lose a mother. There was nothing he could say that would come close to making Sammie's loss any easier, even if it had happened years ago. But then Harte had another unpleasant thought. "This tower, it's not still operational, is it?"

"No," Sammie told him, blinking a little, as though clearing the memories from his mind. "Once Roosevelt heard what had happened—especially when news started spreading about exactly how many people died—he had the tower dismantled. But it was too late for too many, my mother included. I left San Francisco not long after that. I couldn't stomach staying. For a long time, I traveled around, looking for work where I could, busking on street corners for coins and begging when that didn't work.

"When we got dragged into the First World War, I signed up and served."

"The *first* world war?" Harte asked, suddenly struck by how much must have happened in the time he'd skipped over—and how much he didn't know.

Sammie nodded. "Somehow I didn't end up dead, so I came back to the States and started working in Chicago. It's where I met Mina. She was a Chinese woman who grew up here in San Francisco, but she toured all around as a singer on the Chop Suey Circuit. But traveling was starting to lose its shine for her." He shook his head with a tired-sounding laugh. "Mina was tired of dealing with backwater towns filled with people who'd never seen a Chinese person before, so we got married in Illinois, since it wasn't legal here in California. Still isn't. But San Francisco was always home to Mina. She wanted to come back here, where she'd grown up, and I loved her more than I feared my memories, so I agreed.

"I took all my savings and everything I had to start this place, but I did it for her. There were already a couple of Chinese clubs opening up in the city, but we wanted the Pearl to be a place where any performer could feel at home—Chinese or Mageus alike. That was around 1938. Mina died eight years ago, but I couldn't bear to get rid of the Pearl." Sammie smiled softly, and Harte didn't miss the sadness in his eyes. "The club reminds me of the good times we had, every single night." He set the glass on the desk and met Harte's eyes. "But you didn't really come back here to find out about my life, did you?" Sammie asked.

"No, I didn't," Harte admitted. "But I'm glad to hear it, nonetheless."

"I know why you're here," Sammie said, his expression never flickering. "My mother told me that someone might come for the crown one day. I've been ready for that eventuality for most of my life, but I never once imagined it would be you."

The surprise of Sammie's admission blindsided Harte, but somehow he choked out the question he needed to ask. "Do you still have it?"

Sammie shook his head. "I'm afraid you're a decade or so too late."

Harte was about to ask what had happened to the crown when Esta burst through the door. "We have a problem," she told Harte, already digging in her evening bag.

Sam gasped. "Miss Esta?"

She froze at the sound of her name, and then her expression brightened. "Hi, Sammie. It's good to see you again." Then the smile fell from her face as she looked to Harte. "I think they've found us."

"Who found you?" Sam asked.

"I'm not sure," Esta admitted. "But I'd bet money that they're with one of the Brotherhoods. A half-dozen men in dark suits came in a minute ago. They're standing at the back of the club, and I don't think they're here for the floor show."

She'd barely gotten the words out when a red light above the door began flashing. Sam looked up at it, and his expression turned flinty.

"That's trouble all right," he said, nodding toward the flashing light. "There are watchmen in the club."

THE RETICULUM

1952—San Francisco

Y ou're sure they're watchmen?" Esta asked, frowning.

Sam nodded as he picked up the phone on his desk and lifted the receiver to his ear. "My people know how to pick out the Committee's men, even when they're trying to hide." He turned his attention to the phone. "Yeah . . . Li, send Gracie back, would you? And Paul and Dottie as well."

Sammie barked a few more orders into the phone, and once he'd ended the conversation and replaced the receiver, he turned to them. "You need to go. Maybe the watchmen followed you or maybe this is one of their usual checks. Either way, if the Committee finds you here, I could lose everything."

On the other side of the office, a large bookcase was built into the wall. Sam went over to it and ran his hand along the underside of the second shelf until an audible snap could be heard, and the bookcase hinged from the wall. Behind it was a heavy steel door secured by a series of combination locks.

Before Esta could gather her thoughts, the office door opened, and three people entered. One was the girl with the bubble. She was dressed now, but barely. The glimmering silver evening gown that clung to her lean body revealed almost as much as it covered. Up close, she looked older than she had onstage, where the footlights had washed out the fine lines around her mouth and eyes, but she was still strikingly pretty. Her dark-red hair was pinned up into a softly waved chignon, and her lips were painted a matching scarlet. Her beauty aside, there was a sharp perceptiveness in her wide-set eyes that hadn't been apparent during her act.

The other two were the Chinese dance team—Paul Wing and Dorothy Toy. They'd changed from their tails and evening gown and were dressed in street clothes. The husband was tall and slim, with a narrow face and eyes as sharp as his cheekbones, while the wife was willowy and petite. Her heart-shaped face was anchored by a narrow nose and a wide, generous mouth. When she performed earlier, her dreamy smile had betrayed a slight overbite, but she wasn't smiling now.

"What's the deal, Sam?" Paul asked.

"Watchmen," Sam said as he finished with the final lock and opened the heavy door to reveal a passageway.

"Any idea who they're looking for?" Dorothy asked, fear clear in her expression.

Sam glanced at Harte. "I don't know," he said, "but it'll be safer if you get out of here now. Better to be sure."

The bubble girl, Gracie, folded herself into Sam's arm, and Esta realized they were together. They made an odd couple, with him being so much older, but they still looked right somehow. Gracie appeared to have a backbone to match Sam's clear confidence.

Sam placed a soft kiss on her forehead. "Gracie, Paul, Dottie, this is Harte and Esta—they're old friends of mine. You all have a lot in common, if you catch my meaning."

Paul eyed Harte and Esta with a new appreciation. "I see . . ."

"Could you take them on over to the safe house, while I deal with the problem out front?"

"Of course, Sam," Paul said. "Thanks for the warning, as always." He'd already taken his wife's hand, and together they were ducking through the passageway.

Sam turned to Harte. "They'll show you the way. You'll be safe there until I get rid of the watchmen out front."

"But, Sam, honey, I'm not even dressed," Gracie told him.

"No time for that, sweetheart." Sam took off his tuxedo jacket and draped it around her shoulders. "Better safe than warm."

"You built your nightclub with an escape route?" Harte asked, frowning at the dark tunnel ahead of him.

"I didn't, but it serves my purposes. The building was modified by bootleggers during the early days of Prohibition," Sam explained. "But it was definitely one of the selling points for me when I decided to open the Pearl. A lot of the best performers have the old magic, and if I wanted the best, I needed to give them a way out in case we were raided."

Harte gave Esta a blank look, and she realized he wouldn't have any idea what Sam was talking about.

"The government outlawed alcohol in 1920," she explained to Harte.

"But you serve drinks here," Harte pointed out.

"Oh, Prohibition didn't last *that* long," Sammie said. "President Grew repealed the Volsted Act almost as soon as he took office after Harding died, back in '23."

Esta's heart practically stopped. "President Grew" was a phrase that felt as impossible as it was absurd. "I'm sorry, but did you just say *President Grew?*"

Sammie frowned. "Yeah. Why?"

"You don't mean *Jack* Grew?" Esta asked, feeling light-headed.

Sam was looking at her more strangely now than he had when she'd stepped into his office, appearing after fifty years and looking no older than the last time he'd seen her. "What other President Grew would I be talking about?"

"I don't know," Esta said weakly. "I'm just having trouble believing that Jack Grew was president."

"Still is," Sammie said with a confused frown.

"But that would mean he's been president since the twenties."

Sam sighed. "Unfortunately, there's no law against that. With the Brotherhoods on his side, it's been basically impossible for anyone to beat him."

Esta was having a hard time processing what Sammie had just told her. Jack Grew had somehow managed to become president. Worse, apparently Jack had been president for nearly thirty years . . . which meant that history had probably been rewritten in ways too overwhelming—too *terrible*—to comprehend.

"Figures that Jack would make sure liquor is still legal," Harte said, but his attempt at humor fell flat. He couldn't know how wrong this bit of news was, but he looked every bit as unsettled as Esta felt.

"Of course, Nitewein is still outlawed," Sam said. "Anything that pertains to old magic is. That part of Prohibition never really went away, which is why you all have to get going. I can't have the Committee discovering that I employ unregistered Mageus here in the club. Just listen to Gracie and the others, and I'll meet up with you later."

"Be careful," Gracie told Sam, giving him a kiss squarely on the lips and then straightening his tie. A second later, she ducked through the opening in the wall herself.

"We're not done talking about the crown," Harte told Sam.

"It's here?" Esta asked, eyeing the office, wondering if she might be able to pull time slow and take a look. . . .

"No," Sam told her, but his eyes cut to Harte. "I'll explain everything later. I promise. Right now I need you to get out of here."

Harte frowned like he wanted to argue, but Esta could see the worry and nervousness strung tight through Sam's entire body. He wasn't lying about the danger, and besides, it was clear what his relationship with Gracie was. As long as they were with her, Sam wasn't going anywhere.

Once they were both through the opening, Gracie handed Harte a heavy metal flashlight. He examined it with a puzzled expression as the safe door behind them sealed them into the darkness. Esta tried not to let her amusement show as she took it from him and demonstrated how to click on the beam of light.

They were all silent as they traveled through the series of corridors that stretched behind the wall of the nightclub and then down to a short tunnel that apparently connected it to the building at the rear. It opened into the storage room of a busy restaurant kitchen, which was filled with steam and the noise of clattering pans and orders barked in a blend of languages—Chinese, English, and Spanish all mixed together. Once they were outside, they followed an alley for two blocks, until they came to a set of steps that led to the door of a small studio apartment. The glass in the windows had been papered over to keep the light from escaping, and while Paul locked the door, Dottie made sure the coverings were secure before giving Gracie the okay to turn on the lights.

"How long has Sammie had this place?" Harte asked.

"Since he had to hide me during the war," Dottie explained as Gracie went over to the small kitchenette that was tucked into a corner and ran some water for the teapot that had been sitting on the stove. "There's a room behind the back wall, where I lived for about three years."

"You lived behind the wall?" Harte asked.

"I was doing a solo act at Sam's club back in '39—before I met Paul. But after Pearl Harbor, things changed fast. Once the authorities found out another one of the other girls was actually Japanese, they took her away. Took her right off the dance floor one night, and I think it really shook him up, you know?"

Esta could tell by the blank confusion in Harte's eyes that he didn't understand, but Dottie didn't seem to notice.

"I'd been pretty good friends with Mina before she passed, and Sammie already knew what I was . . . I mean, other than Japanese."

"Japanese?" Esta asked, her stomach sinking. She understood the implications of Dottie being Japanese during the Second World War. "I didn't realize . . ."

"Occidentals don't usually know the difference," Dottie said with a shrug. "A lot of the girls in the Chinese clubs aren't Chinese. Toy is just a stage name. My given name's Takahashi, but I haven't used it in a while."

When Esta had discovered that Sam owned the Dragon's Pearl, she also learned that it was only one of many clubs spread throughout the city that featured Chinese performers. Most of the other clubs, like the Forbidden City, were owned by Chinese proprietors and had completely Chinese casts, but Sammie's seemed to employ a mix of performers. The clubs all catered to white audiences, including the Dragon's Pearl.

"Anyhow," Dottie said, "Sam figured it was only a matter of time before the authorities found me, too. But he knew the stakes were a lot higher for me."

"Because you're Mageus," Esta realized.

Dottie nodded. "There's no way I could have hidden what I was in one of those camps. He bought this place and outfitted it. They never did find me. Now he keeps it in case someone needs to lie low for a while."

"It's too bad Ellie Wong didn't use it," Gracie said. "Did you hear that she disappeared last week?"

"No," Dottie said, her mouth falling open in uneasy surprise. "Was it the Committee?"

Paul grimaced. "From what I heard, there was a raid on the Forbidden City. Everybody split, like they do, but after, no one could find her. She hasn't been seen since."

"Maybe she's hiding somewhere, waiting things out," Dottie said, a faint hope tingeing her voice. "Or maybe she got the papers she needed to leave. A lot of people have been going north."

"Maybe . . ." Gracie didn't sound all that convinced. "But that's not what most people over at the Forbidden City think. Ellie hadn't been talking about leaving, and they're all nervous."

"They'd be stupid not to be," Paul said. "Every time things get too quiet, the watchmen get bored and people start disappearing. I don't know what the Committee is going to do when the Reticulum is finally finished. There won't be anyone left to harass."

"Oh, I doubt that'll ever happen," Gracie said dismissively as she returned her attention to the tea she'd been preparing. "If they were ever going to finish it, they would have by now."

But Esta didn't miss the nervous tremor to her voice, and from the look Harte gave her, neither did he.

"What's the Reticulum?" she asked, almost afraid to know the answer.

Suddenly an uneasy silence descended over the room that had the hair on Esta's neck rising as three pairs of eyes swiveled to her.

"The *Reticulum*," Dottie said, like Esta should already know this.

But when Esta simply shook her head to indicate she didn't understand, Gracie's brows drew together. "Who did you say you were again?"

"Friends of Sam's," Harte supplied. "*Old* friends. We've been away for a while."

Gracie's expression was doubtful, clearly suspicious. "You must've been on the moon," she said, but neither Esta nor Harte responded to the implied question. Gracie frowned as she glanced at the two dancers, who both gave a kind of shrug, but in the end they must have decided they trusted Sammie enough to let the impossibility go. "The Reticulum is President Grew's number one priority. Has been for years."

"He's used the promise of finishing it to keep himself in office," Paul said darkly.

"But what is it?" Esta pressed.

The three exchanged glances, almost like they were nervous even to talk about it. Finally, Dottie spoke. "It's a kind of magical net they're building over the entire country—from sea to shining sea, as they say. If they ever manage to finish the network, they'll be able to eliminate the old magic once and for all."

PAST FEARS MADE PRESENT

1952—San Francisco

As Gracie described the Reticulum in greater detail, Harte listened with a kind of horrified detachment. All at once he was both there in that tiny, cramped studio apartment and also back in a warehouse in Manhattan where Jack Grew had boasted to him about a machine that would eliminate magic better than the Brink ever could.

Harte had done what he could to destroy that machine before he'd left the city, but he should have expected that something like this would be possible, especially since he'd been stupid enough to literally hand Jack the Book. Even with all he'd experienced, though, Harte was having trouble imagining something on the scale of what Sammie's friends were describing.

"You're saying that the Reticulum could kill every Mageus in this country," he said, his voice sounding as hollow as he suddenly felt.

"I'm sure there will be places where a person could go," Paul said. "Remote, out-of-the-way places, but who can go live in the wilderness? Who would want to?"

"The Brotherhoods would probably just build another tower there once they found out about it, anyway," Gracie said dourly.

"The rest of the country has really *accepted* this?" Esta asked, sounding every bit as horrified as Harte felt.

"They haven't told people the truth," Paul explained. "According to all the official statements, the mechanisms in the towers simply detect and neutralize unregistered magic. If those who have the old magic turn themselves in and give up their power willingly, they wouldn't be affected at all."

"After what happened in San Francisco, people must know that's a lie," Harte said, thinking of Sammie and the mother he'd lost.

"Individual people might know," Gracie said. "But people in general? Crowds don't care about the details."

"Oh, people know," Dottie said bitterly. "People *always* know. But they don't care enough to stop it. The internments of American citizens during the last war certainly didn't concern them. Why should this? For most people, it's easier to look away. Even good people can convince themselves that something so terrible could only happen if the victims deserved it. 'If they had simply turned themselves in,' they'll say. 'If they had only given up their magic,' they'll say."

"It doesn't help that the Brotherhoods know how to keep the country scared," Paul agreed. "Anytime people in a community start questioning the need for the Reticulum, the Brotherhoods simply do a raid and show exactly how many unregistereds there are hiding in plain sight. They round them up and cart them off, and the community settles down."

"It's enough to keep everyone quiet," Dottie said.

By now the tea Gracie had been preparing had long since been forgotten. The discussion of the Reticulum and the danger they were all in had been enough to make the already-somber mood in the apartment practically funereal.

"There has to be something that can be done," Harte said.

"Oh, plenty *is* being done," Paul told him. "The Antistasi dismantle the towers almost as fast as the government can build them."

"They're still around?" Esta asked, sounding almost breathless.

Gracie nodded. "Of course. There's also the Quellant, if you can manage to get ahold of some. If there is a raid, it makes your affinity impossible to detect."

Harte glanced at Esta. Her lipstick had worn away, and she looked more tired than he'd first noticed. But her eyes had a new brightness, a hopefulness that he understood. After all, if they had more of the Quellant, he could protect Esta from Seshat. He could buy himself more time.

"How hard is it to find?" Harte asked.

"You can only get it on the Nitemarket," Paul said. "Though it's damn expensive these days, from what I've heard."

"It was a little easier to come by during the war," Dottie explained. "Sammie always made sure we all had a good supply of it, just in case."

"Do you still have some?" Esta asked, but the three performers shook their heads almost in unison.

"Sammie might," Gracie said. "I can ask when he gets here. . . . It sure is taking him a while, isn't it? He usually comes fairly quickly."

They all seemed to look at the clock on the wall at once, and suddenly it did feel like it had been a long time. Not long after, though, Sammie finally arrived, looking more than a little harried.

"I think I lost them," he said as he locked the door behind him, making sure to secure the extra latches.

"You always do." Gracie welcomed him back with a kiss, but Sam's posture didn't relax at all with the greeting.

"It wasn't as easy as it usually is," he told her. Then he turned to Dottie and Paul. "It should be safe enough now, but maybe take the long route home?"

"Will do," Paul said. "It's been . . . interesting," he told Harte and Esta with a quizzical smile. Then he turned to Sam. "You want us to drop Gracie off too?"

"Sam can take me home later," Gracie said, curling into Sam's side.

He gave her a quick squeeze but then released her. "I think it's better if you go with Paul and Dottie tonight, sweetheart."

"I thought you said you lost them?" Her nervousness was apparent, even to Harte. "What's going on, Sam?"

"Nothing I can't handle, but better not to take chances, right?" Sam chucked her affectionately on the chin. "You have two shows tomorrow, anyway."

Gracie frowned up at him. "But you're still coming by later?"

"I can't promise anything. Not tonight," Sam said, his expression faltering a little as he glanced in Harte and Esta's direction again. "I have a couple of things that need to be taken care of first."

Harte didn't like the sound of that at all. Neither, it seemed, did Gracie, but she didn't argue any further. A few minutes later, they finished saying their good-byes. Once the others were gone and the door was locked behind them, Sam located a bottle of whiskey in the cupboard above the stove and took a couple of long swallows before offering it to Harte.

Harte shook his head. "What happened after we left?"

Sam's expression was bleak, like he'd been wrung out and put up to dry. "The watchmen were on a tear, all right. They questioned me for a long time, and not particularly nicely." He took another long swallow straight from the bottle before pinning Harte with a knowing gaze. "They specifically wanted to know about you two."

Harte could feel the exhaustion of the day creeping over him, but he willed himself upright. "What did you tell them?"

"Nothing," Sam told Harte, lighting a cigarette and loosening his cuffs as he talked. "People always think that giving up information will save their sorry asses, but I've been around too long to make that kind of mistake. If you tell the Committee anything, they usually make sure you don't talk again."

Harte felt some of the tension drain from him. "Thank you," he said, trying to infuse his voice with all the sincerity he could.

"Don't thank me yet," Sammie said. "They're still looking for the two of you. They know you're in town, and they're not going to stop until they find you. As good as it is to see you again, the faster you get out of town, the easier it's going to be on everyone."

"We can't leave without the Dragon's Eye," Harte said.

"That's the thing. . . ." Sam took a long drag on the cigarette before expelling the smoke in a slow, steady stream. "Like I told you, I don't have it. I sold the crown at the Nitemarket years ago—back in '38. I needed the funds to start the Pearl."

"Who did you sell it to?" Harte pressed, thinking that maybe they could find the buyer.

"Who knows," Sam said. "No one uses real names when they're buying or selling at the Nitemarket. It's safer for everyone that way."

"But you know *when* you sold it." Esta gave Harte a look that made his stomach sink. He knew exactly what she was thinking.

"No, Esta . . ."

"Think about it, Harte. We know where Jack will be now. If we go back to 1920, we could get the Dragon's Eye, *and* we could take back the Pharaoh's Heart and the Book as well. We could stop Jack from taking office, and we could make it so this Reticulum nightmare never existed."

"You're talking like you have some kind of time machine," Sammie said, trying to laugh off the idea, but he grew serious when they didn't join him. "You're not *actually* talking about a time machine?"

"I think that the less you know, the safer you'll be," Esta said, choosing her words carefully.

The amusement drained from Sammie's expression. "You're not going to explain?"

"Esta's right," Harte agreed. "You've dealt with enough tonight. You've already put your business—your whole life here—in danger because of us."

"I'm more than strong enough to withstand whatever the Committee dishes out," Sam said, indignant. "I managed well enough during the last war. Dottie's still here, isn't she? Plenty of others, too."

"Yes, and we're going to make sure that you stay here too," Harte told him. Then he turned to Esta. "Say we do go back. Even if we can get the Book and the dagger from Jack, we only have one tablet of Quellant left," he reminded her. They would need that to get back to 1902.

"Maybe that doesn't have to be a problem," Esta said, glancing at Harte's brother. "Not if Sammie could find us some more."

"These days, the Nitemarket can be a little dodgy," Sammie hedged. "But if it's important—"

"No," Harte said. "You've done enough for us. I'm not having you take any more risks for our sake."

"He's not supposed to be president," Esta said softly. "This Reticulum they were talking about? It's not supposed to exist. None of this was supposed to happen."

"You're sure?" Harte asked, even though he knew already that Esta wouldn't have said it if she wasn't.

"Jack Grew isn't supposed to be *anyone* important. You said he's been in office since Prohibition?" she asked Sam, who was looking more than a little confused at their conversation.

"He was Harding's vice president," Sam explained. "He took office after Harding died, but he's won every election since."

"So much should have happened since then," Esta murmured. "Wars and a depression and presidents who changed the country and the world."

"Oh, we've had wars all right," Sam said, stubbing out the cigarette on the edge of the sink. "A depression, too. But President Grew has been at the helm the whole time, for better or for worse. A lot of the time, it's been worse."

"This Reticulum he's building," Harte asked Sammie. "How much of a reality is it?"

"It's getting close to completion, even with all the Antistasi have done to delay its progress," Sam said. "It's close enough that I keep telling Gracie to go—a lot of Mageus have already gotten false papers and left. I got her some too, but she won't leave without me, and I have too many people here depending on me."

"Harte, we can stop this," Esta said softly. "Jack. The Reticulum. All of it."

"How are *you* possibly going to stop it when an entire network of Antistasi hasn't been able to?" Sam wondered. "There are towers in every state and in every major town, and with television stations needing places

LISA MAXWELL

to broadcast, they've only grown faster. There's no way you can dismantle the network now—I don't care how powerful you think you are."

"We can if the network was never built in the first place. . . ." Harte let out an unsteady breath, then turned back to Esta. "Just so you're aware, I hate this idea."

"I know," she told him. "But it could work. We could get the Book, the artifacts, *and* make sure Jack Grew never has the power to hurt anyone again."

TRAPPED IN TIME

1952—San Francisco

The next morning, Esta woke to the sound of rain. She pulled the window coverings back far enough to see that the sky was an impenetrable gray. The heaviness of the rain and overall gloom of the day might have seemed like some sort of premonition if Esta had been the type to believe in signs. She wasn't, but the weather cast a pall over her mood nonetheless.

Harte began stirring on the couch, where he'd insisted on sleeping. He needed the rest more than she did, but he'd refused to take the bed out of some kind of misplaced sense of chivalry, *the idiot*. His dark hair was sticking up in all directions like a disheveled chicken, and though Esta couldn't help but smile at the sight, she didn't miss the circles beneath his eyes.

They'd stayed up late into the night planning for what needed to be done. From what Esta could see, there was one place where they knew for sure they could find Jack in the past: the Republican National Convention of 1920. If Esta and Harte could get to the convention, they might be able to stop Jack and steal both the Book and the Pharaoh's Heart, all at the same time.

From what Sam explained, the event had been a turning point—the First World War had recently ended, and everyone had their opinion about what kind of nation the country should become. That year, Jack hadn't really been seen as a serious candidate, but the Antistasi had launched an attack on the convention, and Jack had seized the opportunity to activate a tower in retaliation. People weren't as horrified as they had been with his first tower in San Francisco. Instead, the success of that little exhibition allowed the Brotherhoods to rally the party and push Jack's nomination through for the vice presidency. Once Harding died unexpectedly in 1923, Jack took over.

They knew it would be difficult to steal the Book and the dagger from Jack in the middle of the convention, but if they could find him before the attack galvanized the public against those with the old magic, it might be possible to get close to him. It might be possible to *stop* him and save countless lives.

Harte still hated the idea, but Esta had held firm. History was long, and the country wide. They couldn't pass on this opportunity, not when it was the surest bet they'd had so far. And if they couldn't get more Quellant? If they could never return to 1902? They could at least take Jack Grew out of the equation. Even if they couldn't get the Book or the Pharaoh's Heart, they had to stop the threat of the Reticulum from ever materializing. And if they *did* manage to get both the Book and the Dagger? It was the best possible scenario. It was a risk they had to take.

Harte was pacing the floor by the time Sam finally arrived nearly twenty minutes late, looking tired and harried.

"The Nitemarket wasn't exactly hopping last night," he said. "There's rumors that the two of you have surfaced, and it seems that everyone's nervous about the Committee and what the Brotherhoods might do. I could only find a few more Quellant. Not as many as I'd hoped."

"Thank you," Esta said as she accepted the small wax envelope and glanced inside at the familiar tablets. *Only four.* Which was four more than they'd had before, she reminded herself as she tucked the packet into her leather pouch. It was enough to accomplish what they had to do. "They're exactly what we need."

"The bank opens in about forty minutes," Sam told them, handing over a parcel that contained a change of clothes for each of them. "The sooner we get this over with, the better, as far as I'm concerned."

Sam's car was waiting one block over—a red Mercedes with fenders that had more sleek curves than one of his chorus girls. Even with the umbrellas he'd brought, they were all sopping wet by the time they reached it. The bank where he'd kept the crown before he'd sold it was across the bay, in Oakland. They'd gone over the plan more than enough the night before. Maybe it was nerves or maybe there wasn't anything more to say, but they rode in silence in the plush, leather-lined interior as Sam navigated through the rain-splattered streets and across the massive steel bridge that connected the two cities.

Harte was sitting in the front with Sam, and he watched out the window, his eyes alert as they sped through a changed world. Esta could tell he was taking everything in, but she was more concerned with watching for signs that they were being followed. She didn't see any, but she wouldn't relax until the Dragon's Eye was safely in their possession.

Sam pulled the Mercedes into a spot about half a block from the bank. He cut the ignition and turned to Esta, draping one arm over the seat. "You're sure you don't need my help for this?"

Esta nodded. "We'll need your safety-deposit box number and the key."

He frowned as he held it up. "I'll get it back?"

"Of course," she lied, taking it from him and palming it. They hadn't explained everything. As far as Sam knew, they were only popping back long enough to get the crown. He thought they planned to return. "We're going to pay you back tenfold, I promise."

Sam gave her a doubtful look. "I can't help thinking I should be going in there with you," he told them. "It would be nothing at all for me to let you into the vault myself."

And then he'd have to explain how the people he'd been with had disappeared.

"It's really not necessary," Esta told him. "You have so much more to lose than we do if anything goes wrong."

"Just because I've got some years on you now doesn't mean I can't still handle myself," Sam said sourly.

"I don't doubt it. But you've already done more than anyone could have asked of you," Harte told him, speaking to Sam as if he were still a young boy and not the old man he'd become. "Remember, if we're not out in five minutes, you leave. Just go. Don't look back and don't worry about us. Whatever you do, *don't* come in after us."

Sam frowned, but he didn't fight them about the issue anymore.

Harte came around the car with the umbrella for Esta, and they started walking toward the entrance to the bank. She'd already removed her gloves. "Are you ready?" she asked, handing him one of the remaining tablets of Quellant.

"Not really." But he placed it into his mouth anyway and couldn't suppress a shudder. "That's terrible."

"I know." Esta remembered too well what it had been like to take Maggie's Quellant—to feel that essential part of herself sliding away. "Everything okay?" she asked when a strange look came over his face.

"I think so. . . ." Harte's brows were drawn together, like he was trying to figure something out. Then his expression relaxed a little. "The only positive thing about this whole situation is that I get to do this," he said, slipping his hand into hers.

His palm was warm, and Esta felt a shiver of awareness when his skin touched hers. She waited, her breath tight with something that felt too close to longing, but she didn't sense the vining warning of Seshat's energy. All she felt were the calluses on Harte's palms as their fingers intertwined. In that moment they were simply two people—a girl and a boy—walking together in the rain. For a moment, Esta allowed herself to imagine a life like this, where they could be . . . normal—whatever that meant. Safe, if there could be any such thing.

And if that life could not be? Could maybe *never* be? Esta would relish this stolen calm before the storm they were about to create.

The bank was housed in an unremarkable brick building with a large clock above the heavy double doors. "Ready?" Esta asked when Harte hesitated at the bottom of the steps leading up to the entrance.

He glanced over without bothering to hide his nerves. "What if we make things worse?"

Esta had the same worry, but she squeezed his hand gently. "If we don't try, they can never get better." Then she tilted her face up to him, and before she could allow herself to think through all the reasons why she shouldn't, she pressed her mouth against his.

Harte's lips felt cool against hers, soft with surprise, but he reacted almost immediately, deepening the kiss. His fingers closed around hers, and when she finally pulled away, the tightness around his jawline had softened and his stormy eyes looked hungry.

"Why did you do that?" Harte asked, still sounding a little breathless.

"Because you looked like you needed it," Esta told him. "And because I wanted to." She couldn't stop the smile that curved her lips. Before he could ruin the moment—before he started telling her all the ways that it had been a bad idea—she pulled him toward the bank. She tried not to let herself worry too much about the darkness she thought she noticed lurking in the depths of his eyes, a darkness that seemed to be waiting.

Inside the bank's vestibule, the steady patter of the rain went silent. People spoke in the hushed whispers usually reserved for funeral homes or churches or for being in the presence of large quantities of money. Esta didn't ask if Harte was ready, but instead simply pulled the seconds slow, until the soft sounds of the bank receded and the world went still.

They made their way into the cavernous marble and wood lobby. It was early enough that there were very few people around. Dodging behind the service counter, Esta carefully lifted a key ring from the belt of one of the tellers, and together they found the vault where the safety-deposit boxes waited. Luckily, the vault itself had already been opened for the day.

The vault was lined floor to ceiling with small, bronze-colored doors. The safety-deposit boxes would contain any number of things—important papers or keepsakes, but also gold and coins, cash and jewelry. Maybe it would have been safer to keep time completely still, but each box required two locks to be simultaneously unlocked—one with the master key they'd stolen from the teller and one that they needed to pick on their own. She couldn't do that *and* hold on to Harte, so Esta released time and started on the first lock. Beyond the entrance to the vault, she could hear the sounds of the bank coming back to life.

"I don't like this," Harte whispered.

"Me neither, but the faster we get to work, the faster we can get out of here," Esta said as she finished popping the lock she'd been working on.

Inside she found gold coins and a few pieces of jewelry, which she pocketed before moving on to the next and then the next. She couldn't let herself think about the people she was stealing from, or what these small treasures might mean to them, and in a matter of minutes she had quite a haul—cash and jewels, antique coins, and some old stock certificates as well. None of it would be traceable, because she was taking it all with them, back where no one would be looking for it.

Harte started working as well. His years of training for his act had made him a deft lockpick, and he worked almost as fast as she did with the master key. They replaced the boxes as they went, so that at first glance no one would notice anything had been taken. They were working so efficiently that in a matter of minutes they'd cleared enough to make Sam a very rich man.

Esta was finishing up when they heard footsteps approaching. She barely had time to lunge for Harte, who was on the other side of the vault, but before she could pull the seconds still, Sammie appeared in the doorway.

"The watchmen." His eyes were wide, and he was panting.

Esta understood immediately and reached for Sammie, but shots erupted and he shuddered, jerking violently—one, two, three, four times—and staggered out of her reach, falling sideways into Harte's arms.

Esta sprang into action, slamming the vault door closed and pulling the seconds slow all at once. The world went starkly, deafeningly silent.

At first all she could do was stand there, her heart pounding in her ears as she looked at the scene in front of her—the shocked anguish on

Harte's face, his arms outstretched to catch his brother, and the blood that had splattered the bronze doors from where Sam had been hit squarely in the back.

Esta was frozen with indecision. If she released time, the people who had shot Sammie would have the door to the vault opened in a matter of minutes—maybe even seconds. But she understood that she couldn't simply pull Harte and Sammie into the net of time with her. If she brought the two back into the regular march of seconds, Sammie's wounds would bleed and Harte's brother would die. All Esta could do was stand there between the seconds that separated life from death. Between the past that had been and the future she could remake, knowing that she couldn't stay there, trapped in time within an airless vault forever, but neither could she let go.

UNEXPECTED

1902—New York

Jack Grew was sitting in the back parlor of the Vanderbilt home with a group of other men, doing his level best to avoid the preening debutantes on the dance floor. The fact that the whiskey he was drinking seemed to be mostly water did nothing to help his growing irritation. It wasn't enough that the Order had decided he was worthy of trust. *No.* Jack's family had decided that he was in need of something more— namely, a wife. They had collectively decided that he should spend more time out in society and were determined that he suffer through every summer soiree since the gala.

It would be good for his reputation, his mother insisted. The more the important families of the city saw him, the less they would think of that girl's unfortunate death, his aunt had agreed. Marriage, the women had decided, would serve to help rehabilitate his image.

Rehabilitate. That was the actual word they'd used, as though Jack were some invalid convalescing with tuberculosis. Morgan, of course, was no help. Jack's uncle was clearly in the minority of opinions in the Inner Circle and was perfectly happy to allow the women of the family to arrange Jack's life. Morgan made it no secret that he would have preferred his nephew not be involved with the plans for their new headquarters, and he reminded Jack of this every time their paths crossed.

That night was like every other dinner party he'd been forced to attend. He made his required appearance to appease the cackling hens in his family, but that was Jack's limit. Instead of the crush of the ballroom, he found his usual spot with the men in the back parlor, far from the mothers with their sharp eyes and unwed daughters in tow. The last thing he needed was to be tied to one of those bits of muslin, not when he had more important things to accomplish.

Jack was playing a hand of rummy with a few of the older fellows, since they, at least, tended not to put much stock in gossip or marriage marts, when he noticed a familiar face—one he hadn't seen for weeks. Theo Barclay was walking through the parlor with the High Princept and two other men from the Inner Circle.

There was something about the group that bothered Jack. Maybe it was simply Barclay's appearance, or the ease with which Theo seemed to be conversing with the older men. Something was wrong with the portrait they made as the men cut through the back parlor, and Jack's instincts were prickling. He folded his hand and excused himself from the table, then made his way toward the trio.

"Barclay?" Jack called out. When Theo Barclay turned, a question—or was that a bit of panic—in his eyes, Jack pretended delight. "I thought that was you. But I thought I'd heard you were headed for the Continent with your lovely bride?"

Theo gave Jack a stiff excuse for a smile as the High Princept simply lifted his brows at the interruption.

"Ruby already departed, but I'm not set to leave quite yet, I'm afraid," Theo said, suddenly looking even more uncomfortable.

"But you *are* to be married?" Jack asked, wondering if the rumors he'd heard had any merit to them. He wouldn't be surprised, really. Reynolds, pretty as she might be, was nothing but a hoyden, and Barclay was hardly the type capable of bringing her to heel.

"Yes," Barclay said. "The wedding won't be until autumn, though. Ruby had her heart set on the colors of the season. Who was I to deny her?"

"Who indeed . . . other than her fiancé," Jack said, still considering Barclay's unexpected appearance that evening. "I hadn't realized that you knew each other." He motioned between Theo and the High Princept.

"Mr. Barclay is a new initiate," the old man said.

"Is he?" Jack stared at Theo, who was turning quite the shade of pink. "I hadn't realized you had any interest in the occult sciences, Barclay."

Theo blinked. "I, ah . . . Well, that is to say . . ." He was doing an absurdly bad job at covering his discomfort, which only proved to Jack that something was *certainly* amiss.

"Young Barclay here is quite an accomplished student of ancient art," the High Princept said. "He did your uncle a great service recently, returning one of the pieces lost in the robbery at the Metropolitan."

"Did he?" Jack's instincts were on alert, and in his jacket pocket, the Book's weight felt like an anchor. "How very . . . unexpected."

"Oh, not really," Theo said, looking distinctly uneasy. "I often frequent the auction houses looking for interesting pieces, and when I saw this *particular* piece come up, I knew immediately what it must be."

"Indeed?" Jack said, still eyeing him. "Can I inquire about which piece you returned?"

"An amulet," Theo told him. "From ancient Babylon, I believe."

Jack knew exactly what Theo was referring to—a bit of unpolished ruby carved into a seal. It had been one of the pieces Jack had been *particularly* interested in examining before the fiasco of the robbery had taken his opportunity. "My uncle must have been grateful for its return."

"He was," the Princept said. "Morgan himself recommended the boy's immediate initiation."

It was all too convenient and more than a little suspect, considering that Jack had never heard of Barclay's interest in the Order before this.

"Did he?" Jack said, considering Barclay anew.

Theo gave him a wobbly, unsettled smile. "Your uncle has been most gracious, but I was simply happy to be of service. He's quite well known as a collector in many art circles. Simply speaking with him about his holdings was an honor."

"I'm sure it was," Jack said dryly.

His uncle collected antiquities, rare art from the ancient world, including an array of pieces that were related to the occult sciences. Tablets and seals, amulets and figures carved with runelike markings. An entire portion of the collection had gone missing some months before, but there hadn't been any sign or clue since. Strange that Barclay, who was eminently *forgettable*, should be the one to return an item when any number of private investigators had been unable to do the same.

"Morgan was quite impressed with the extent of Barclay's knowledge and expertise when it came to certain pieces in the collection," the Princept said, turning to Theo. "It seems your art degrees weren't the frivolous waste that many of us originally believed them to be."

It was something closer to anger that flushed Theo's cheeks this time. "It seems not," he said evenly.

"Your family must be quite proud," Jack said.

"I'm sure yours feels the same after your resounding triumph at the gala," Theo replied, though his tone did not match his words. "I was there, you know."

"Oh, I'm aware," Jack drawled. "I had the pleasure of directing your lovely bride in her tableau, after all. She's turned out to be quite the beauty, hasn't she? Quite the hellion, too, from what I hear. She'll need a firm hand to rein her in. Are you sure you're up for such a job?"

Barclay's jaw had gone tight. "Unlike *some*, I'm not so insecure as to feel the need to treat my beloved like a broodmare."

Jack's fists clenched at the not-so-veiled insult, but the High Princept cleared his throat before he could so much as respond. "Yes, well. We have people waiting for us, Jack. I was going to introduce young Barclay here to some of our other members."

"Of course," Jack said, bowing his head slightly but keeping his eyes pinned to Theo Barclay.

It was no accident that the collection of ancient Ottoman art that his uncle had intended to display at the Metropolitan was stolen a few weeks before Khafre Hall was destroyed, Jack was sure of it. Just as he was certain that Theo Barclay had not found this piece from his uncle's collection by pure chance.

"Congratulations on your good fortune, Barclay." Jack extended his hand. "I'm sure you'll make a fine addition to our membership."

After a moment's hesitation, Theo took it, and they shook like gentlemen. But Jack held his grip for a heartbeat longer than necessary, relishing the way Theo's eyes widened ever so slightly.

Barclay was up to something—that much was certain. Jack had only to discover how he could best use that knowledge to his advantage.

TIME HELD ITS BREATH

1952—San Francisco

Harte stumbled under the weight of Sam's body. His brother was heavier than he looked, and as Sammie fell into him, Harte was barely able to break his fall. They both ended up on the cold metal floor of the vault. The next thing he knew, the vault door was being slammed closed, and Esta was standing over them with a look of quiet horror in her eyes.

"Sam?" Harte tried to maneuver to see if his brother was conscious. He could already feel blood soaking into his own clothing, but he refused to acknowledge the truth of it.

Sammie didn't respond. His face was slack and his eyes partially closed, but Harte couldn't process what had just happened. He looked up to find Esta with her hand clasped over her mouth. She was shaking her head, and Harte knew then, without her even saying a word. But he still didn't want to accept the truth of it.

"No," he told her, moving so that he could gently lay his brother out on the floor of the vault and try to shake him awake. He couldn't be the cause of another innocent life being snuffed out. Not again. Sammie couldn't die because of him.

Harte was still holding his brother, tapping gently at the face that now wore the years of an old man. Those years didn't seem to matter, though. All Harte could see was the boy beneath, the child he'd once given up everything to rescue and who'd then found Esta and rescued him in turn.

It can't end like this.

Their attackers were still outside, though. Dimly, Harte realized someone was already working the heavy tumbler of the vault door, and soon enough, the door would open once again and they would be trapped.

"He's gone, Harte," Esta said softly. Her voice trembled, even as the hand on his shoulder was firm as she tried to pull him away.

Harte ignored her and concentrated on Sam's face. *If he would only wake up* . . .

Esta tugged at him again. "We have to go," she said. "That lock will only keep them out for a couple more seconds."

"I'm not leaving him here," Harte told her. "I can't."

She crouched down and took his hand, but Harte refused to look at her. He couldn't leave his brother here to be found by their enemies. He *wouldn't*. "We're going to take him." As long as Harte had ahold of Sam, Esta couldn't leave him there.

"We can't," she told him. Her voice was soft, but the words still felt like a slap. "If Sammie disappears, they'll know for sure what happened here."

"I don't care about that," Harte told her.

"What happens when we get back to 1920, Harte?" Esta asked. "We can't stop guns that have already fired. We can't change what just happened by taking Sammie with us, but if we go now, it doesn't have to be like this." Her voice was more urgent now. "We can fix this, Harte, but we have to go. *Now.* You have to let Sammie go, because if they catch us here, this is how your brother's life ends. The Brotherhoods aren't going to let us get away again."

Harte was still shaking his head. He'd tried to save Sammie once before, and in the end it had come to this. "What if we can't change anything?" He looked up at her then. "What if we make it all *worse*?"

"I don't know," she told him. "But if we don't go now, everything ends right here. Including Sammie's life. Let go of him, Harte. Give me your hand."

Esta was right. Harte *knew* she was absolutely right about everything, but it felt impossible to let go of his brother. To leave him like this, alone on the cold floor of a darkened vault.

The turning of the lock on the vault had stopped, and Harte could hear the lever being depressed.

"Harte, please . . ." Esta's voice was gentle.

Before the door could open, she grabbed Harte's shoulder, and the sound drained from the vault as they were caught in the power of her magic. Finally, Harte made himself release his brother and left him there on the floor, outside of Esta's hold on time. Harte's legs seemed to move of their own accord, as he forced himself to his feet. Without another word, he took Esta's hand. She was trembling, he realized, the same as himself. But his legs were strangely solid beneath him.

Harte did not take his eyes from his brother's face. His body was cold, his brain numb, and every bit of himself felt as distant and dead as the Quellant had made Seshat's power. On the bloodstained floor of the vault, Sam stared up at them, sightless and silent.

"Let me . . ." Still holding Esta's hand, Harte bent down to close his brother's eyes. "This *has* to work," he told her.

Esta's face was dappled in shadow. "It will," she told him, her voice as determined as her expression. She wrapped her arms around him, pulling Harte into the warmth of her embrace. The vault was silent, and time seemed to be holding its breath. All at once the world felt like it was contracting around him, ripping itself apart in a great roaring, and then, suddenly, all was quiet again, and Harte found himself spinning through the endless darkness.

No . . . not *endless* darkness, and it was only his own head that was spinning. The floor was solid beneath him as Esta let go of his hand and the world righted itself. Nearby he could hear her breathing, soft and steady, as though the world itself hadn't been turned inside out.

Esta clicked on the flashlight that Sam had given them, and a beam illuminated the vault. Harte didn't need the light to know that Sammie was no longer there on the floor. He could only hope that Esta was right and that they could change the past so his brother would *never* be there.

Esta had already launched into action and had located Sammie's box. A moment later she opened the small metal door.

Harte felt the wash of power before Esta even lifted the golden crown from within Sammie's box and replaced it with everything they'd stolen from the other security boxes. He wondered how he hadn't recognized the fake Dragon's Eye for what it was. Still, standing there with the memory of his brother's body clear in his mind's eye, he didn't feel any relief. How could he, when obtaining the crown meant that he was one step closer to his inevitable end?

LOST

1920—A Train Heading East

Esta didn't know how she managed to guide Harte out of the bank vault and get him to the station in Oakland without anyone noticing the bloodstains on his clothes or his general state of shock, but she did. She bought two overnight tickets for a train to Chicago that left within the hour and sat silently by his side as they waited for the boarding call. Since the Quellant was still suppressing Seshat's power, she took the risk of taking his hand in hers, but he didn't respond. It was clear he was still reeling from the loss of his brother.

Esta thought she might almost understand what loss like that felt like. She'd lost too many people in her life—had herself been the cause of deaths and disappearances. There was the hollow shock of discovering too late that Dolph Saunders had been her true father and the pain of learning that her friend Mari had disappeared, erased from existence because of some change Esta had made in a seemingly unconnected past. Then there was Dakari. Esta still felt a numbing grief when she thought of her friend and mentor, and every time she did, the memory of him being murdered that night in Professor Lachlan's study rose in her mind.

Even once they were underway, safely ensconced inside the cramped quiet of the train berth, Harte remained distant and far too quiet. They barely talked through dinner, and Esta felt like she was looking at him through the wrong end of a spyglass. Harte was right there, an arm's length across the narrow table from her, and yet he felt too far away.

Worse, the air between them seemed to be charged with an

awkwardness that had *never* been there before. Esta felt like she was dining with a stranger instead of the one person who had always seemed to see her better than anyone ever had—even when they'd still been enemies. It felt like all of the intimacy they'd shared in the previous weeks, the long days and nights of his recovery—first at the hospital and especially at the hotel in San Francisco—had evaporated into nothing in the presence of his grief.

Or perhaps, the truth of that intimacy had finally come to the surface. Perhaps it had stripped bare each of their vulnerabilities far more than either of them had ever planned, exposing the soft, white underbellies they'd taken such pains to cover and protect for so long.

Still, Esta wanted to say something—*anything*—that could close the distance between them again. "It wasn't your fault, Harte," she whispered, finally breaking a silence that had grown too oppressive for her to bear.

He glanced up at her, his expression so dark that she knew it had been the wrong thing to say. "Sammie's dead, Esta."

"But you weren't the one who killed him."

His mouth went tight, and he stared down at his barely touched plate of food. "Is that how you feel about your friend Dakari?" he asked. His voice was gentle, but the question still felt like a slap.

"That's not the same," Esta argued, but she couldn't stop the guilt and shame from rising up within her, right alongside the memory of that night in Professor Lachlan's library.

"Isn't it?" Harte asked.

"Of course not," she said. Still, Esta couldn't blink away the image of Dakari's face when Professor Lachlan had aimed the gun at his chest. She would never forget the shock of betrayal and confusion that had flashed through Dakari's dark eyes as the bullet tore through him, nor the sound of his body hitting the floor. All because Professor Lachlan had been trying to bend Esta to his will.

"Sammie would never have been shot today if not for me dragging him into our troubles, Esta. He'd still be running his club and helping

Mageus like Gracie and Paul, and he could have lived to a ripe old age. I never should have walked into his life again. I should've learned after what happened with Julian. So please don't try to tell me this isn't my fault. It's as much my fault as if I'd pulled the trigger myself."

"Should I blame myself for Dakari's death, then?" Esta asked, feeling unbearably brittle.

"Of course not," he told her.

"It doesn't work both ways, Harte. If you caused Sammie's death, then I'm every bit as guilty of Dakari's," Esta said, letting the truth of that settle over her. "Dolph's too, for that matter."

"That's not what I'm saying." Harte raked a hand through his hair.

"But it is," she told him gently, tears burning in her eyes. "It's *exactly* what you're saying."

"No—" He reached for her hand.

She looked down at their fingers intertwined. "You're not wrong, though. Not really. Dakari did die because of me; that fact is irrefutable. So did Dolph. So did my mother and who knows how many other people."

Harte's voice was soft when he spoke again. Far gentler than she deserved. "You didn't kill any of them, Esta."

"That's my point," she whispered, feeling strangely lighter. "You're right . . . I *didn't* kill Dakari. It was Professor Lachlan who pulled the trigger." She felt something loosen within her and gave Harte's hand a gentle squeeze. "*You* didn't kill your brother, Harte. You saved him when he was just a boy. You gave him a long life, and you'll give him another one if everything goes as we hope it will."

"But we don't know for sure." Harte tried to pull away, but Esta didn't allow him to retreat.

"You're right," she admitted. "We can't know for sure right now. But we *have* to believe it. We have to keep going."

Harte pulled away from her then, and this time she let him. Before she could figure out how to make things better, though, the porter interrupted to clear away their plates and prepare the sleeping quarters. Harte wouldn't quite look at her as he announced that he would take the top bunk and climbed into it without another word.

Left with the choice between sitting up by herself or trying to sleep, Esta undressed, stripping down to the nylon slip she was wearing beneath the simple flared skirt, and climbed into her own bunk. She didn't know what the next few days would hold. If they were lucky, they would have the Book and four of the artifacts. If everything worked out, they would be one step closer to returning to the past and controlling Seshat once and for all. Even that promise didn't lift her spirits, though, not when her possible end was inching closer, and not when the distance that had sprung up between the two of them made her feel like she'd lost something essential.

Esta had spent her whole life holding people back, pushing them away. Because it was what she'd been taught. Because it was *safer*. Even now she understood that she'd never really thanked Dakari, never told him what his friendship had meant to her, because she'd been scared. Scared that he would reject her, as she'd once thought her own parents had. Scared to admit that she needed someone to depend on, other than herself.

As the train hurtled eastward, carrying them toward whatever fate or time or luck held in store, Esta realized she was so *tired* of being alone. She was tired of being solitary and strong. Most of all, she was tired of holding herself away from *Harte*.

If the Book offered no other answers for controlling Seshat's power, Esta would have to give her affinity—her very *self*—to stop Seshat. That was fine. She could accept that end as her destiny. But she could not accept going to her death without Harte knowing what he meant to her. After all, Esta had never been one for regrets.

Easing herself out of the warmth of her own bed, she shivered as the cool air of the cabin made gooseflesh rise along her arms. She didn't let herself hesitate or second-guess but instead climbed directly up into the bunk above. Harte startled when she slid in beside him, but she ignored the way he tried to pull away from her. Instead, she curled around him, enjoying the warmth of his body and not allowing him to go. She was done hiding, finished with the endless push-pull between them.

You are not negotiable. She still felt her cheeks burn every time she thought about how the words had tumbled from her in the hospital before she could stop them.

That goes both ways, you know, he'd replied.

They hadn't talked about the exchange since, but Esta had convinced herself that Harte understood. His words proved it, didn't they? But then he'd pulled back, away from her.

"Esta—" Harte's voice was strained, a whispered plea between them, but she couldn't tell what he was asking for.

"You took the Quellant," she said simply. "We have a little time. . . ."

"I can't," he told her, even as she tucked her face into the place where his shoulder met his neck and pressed a kiss there.

"You could try," she whispered into the crook of his neck, breathing in the smell of him. Because, god, she just needed to feel something other than grief and pain and hopelessness.

No. Not *something.* She needed *him.*

"Esta . . ."

"Please, Harte," she whispered, not really knowing what she was asking for. All Esta knew was that she needed this, Harte's arms around her and the feel of their bodies pressed together.

He seemed to relent, and she felt his body relax little by little as they lay there. The train rocked and swayed beneath them as it carried them onward. Eventually, Harte turned to her, his face so close that she could smell on his breath the sweetness of the wine he'd sipped at dinner. "I have nothing to offer you," he whispered, his voice a hollow version if itself. "No past, no future."

I don't need a future. I might not even have one.

"You have right now," Esta said, the words coming without planning or any artifice. The moment they were free of her, she felt the truth of them. "I can steal all the time in the world, but right now is all that we've ever had."

"It's not enough." Harte's face turned away from her again, and he stared up at the ceiling. "You deserve more than that."

"Maybe . . . but I'm not asking for more." Esta placed a small, soft kiss on the underside of his jaw, just beneath his ear where his skin was smooth and smelled of whatever tonic he'd put on after shaving earlier that day. It was different from the scent he'd worn in New York, but it still seemed completely perfect for him. Warm with a hint of some spice, it was a scent that felt closer to home than any place she'd ever been.

A long stretch of minutes passed between them with nothing but the shuffling of the rails, the steady rocking of the car, and in the silence, Esta felt a quiet sureness that *this* was where she belonged, whatever might happen. She knew Harte would turn away from her again. She felt it coming, the shift in his body that would break the connection she needed so desperately, a connection that confirmed that she was still real and whole and alive, when everything else felt like it was crumbling around her.

Harte turned to her instead, surprising her. "I shouldn't," he said, his voice as raw as the look in his eyes.

Before Esta could prepare herself, before she could even feel the relief that shuttled through her when she realized what his words meant, his lips were on hers. And she was lost.

THE NIGHT-DARK COUNTRY

1920—A Train Heading East

Harte could no more have stopped himself from kissing Esta in that moment than he could have stopped his heart from beating. Ever since he'd left her on the train, he'd imagined what it would have been like to stay. To remain curled beside her in that narrow bunk and see her wake in the morning, her face soft with sleep and her eyes wanting him. Now he seemed to be handed a second chance, a gift he did not—*could not*—possibly deserve.

While he lay writhing in feverish pain back in San Francisco, the thought of Esta had been Harte's only comfort. The knowledge that he *had* to continue on, if only to make sure he made things right for her, had kept him fighting against the fever that had ravaged his body. How many hours had he spent in that limbo between life and death, holding on only because dying meant never seeing her again? In those dark, painful hours, how many times had he imagined this? Hoped beyond hope to be *worthy* of it.

Of *her*.

And then, after she'd saved him, he'd spent all of those days so close to her without ever touching her—not really—even though his fingers burned to feel her skin. To pull her close. He'd held back, because he knew he couldn't risk it. Because Harte understood too well the danger he was putting her in simply by existing. Because of Seshat.

But thanks to the terrible emptiness caused by the Quellant, Harte didn't have to worry about Seshat—not for a little while longer, at least.

The time would come when the goddess would rouse herself, push past the fog of the drug, and make her presence known. That he didn't doubt. But for now Seshat was silent. Absent. It was only himself and Esta, alone in the middle of the night-dark country, and the space between them brimmed with possibility.

He'd dreamed often of kissing her, of course. Even as he'd burned with the shame of all that she had to do for him as he had healed, each time Harte had collapsed into sleep, his traitorous brain had conjured Esta in his dreams. But with Seshat within him, he'd given up the possibility of ever having a moment like this.

You are not negotiable, not for me.

Had he been standing at the time, the words she'd spoken to him would have brought him to his knees, but once they were safely out of the hospital, neither of them had approached the issue again. In the hours and days since, he had not allowed himself to hope for the feel of Esta's hands cupping his face, the weight of her body pressing down on him, as it was now, as she moved over him and deepened the kiss, her legs on either side of his as she caged him in. But now he didn't have to hope. Now she was there in truth, over him. *With* him.

He wanted to tell Esta to wait, to slow down, because he wanted to remember every brush of her skin and taste on her lips. But her mouth was ravenous, her hands tugging at his shirt and pushing it up over his head, like she was driven by something more than need. Harte thought it felt too close to desperation, but then her cool palms ran across the bare skin of his chest, and he forgot about slow. He forgot about anything but the scent of her, softly clean and barely floral, and the feel of her, smooth and strong and *his*.

This time there was no echoing laughter. This time Seshat was locked away and could not mock or threaten.

Esta broke their kiss long enough to pull off the scrap of material she was wearing, and as she lifted her arms over her head to remove it, the moonlight sliced across her bare torso, illuminating the curves of her body. But she didn't give him nearly enough time to look or revel in the moment. She was kissing him again, hungry and insistent, pressing herself against him, the soft roundness of her body against the hard planes of his own.

Her hands were everywhere, like fire burning along his skin, and Harte was aware suddenly of what his illness had taken from him. His leanness was all bone and sinew without the strength he'd once had. But Esta didn't give him time to be self-conscious.

"Esta—" Her name was a prayer on his lips, and he could not have answered, even to himself, whether he meant for her to stop or to go on.

"I like the way it sounds when you say my name like that," she whispered against his neck, a smile in her voice as she nipped at his shoulder.

"Wait," he panted, as her lips explored the planes of his chest, farther down his torso.

Esta paused only long enough to look up at him, her golden eyes glinting in the darkness, as bright as the stone in the Dragon's Eye. "I want this, Harte. Tell me you want this too."

"Of course I do, but . . ." She moved again, and his words fell away, along with his reluctance.

What was the point of being chivalrous when her touch was turning his skin to flame? The heat of her mouth left a trail of fire across his skin. And when she rose up over him, burning as brightly as a phoenix, Harte knew for certain what he had perhaps always known, even from that first moment in the Haymarket, when he'd seen her across the ballroom and had felt instantly drawn to her. No one would ever match him so well. No one would ever fit with him as she did.

However much time they might have left, however much time Esta might steal for them—days or years or eternities—it would never be enough. There would never be anyone else for him but Esta. Not ever again.

The train lurched around a curve, and Esta lost her balance, falling onto him, her bare body like a brand against his. Somewhere in the distant recesses of his mind, Harte knew that it was too much, too fast. But he didn't stop. *Couldn't.* He shifted so they were side by side, equals as they'd ever been, hands roaming, mouths ravenous. An ecstatic fumbling need drove them onward toward some conclusion that they did not quite understand until it crashed over them, turning them both to ash.

When Harte finally came back to himself, his arms and legs were so tangled with Esta's that he could no longer tell where his body ended and where hers began. All he could do was lie there feeling slightly apart from everything. Finally, the sound of Esta's soft laughter brought Harte back to himself. He felt something dangerously close to happiness, and his mouth began to curve in answer. Then, all at once, he remembered everything that had happened. Sammie was dead. His brother was dead, and *this* was how he mourned him?

The memory of Sammie's body, bloodied and broken, rose in Harte's mind, and the shame of feeling anything close to happiness flooded through him. It was followed swiftly by a bolt of sheer panic as he realized what had just happened. What he'd *allowed* to happen.

He pulled away then, untangling himself from the warmth of Esta's arms so he could lie as far from her as possible in the narrow bunk. If she touched him now, he wouldn't be able to help himself.

"What is it?" Esta's eyes were soft and sleepy as she smiled at him. She looked utterly open, utterly *vulnerable.* Because she *was* vulnerable. Harte had allowed his control to slip, and his selfishness had put her in danger.

"I don't know what that was," he said, staring up at the ceiling of the berth. His voice sounded stiff and stilted, even to him. "But it can't happen again."

He could practically *feel* the smile slide from her lips as Esta propped herself up on her side to look down at him. "You don't know what *that* was?" she asked, her voice filled with humor, but it was tinged with wariness as well.

"Of course I know what *that* was," Harte said, feeling his cheeks burn. Her brows were drawn together and the emotion in her eyes was quickly giving way to something more alert. "We shouldn't have . . ." But Harte couldn't finish, because he was enough of a bastard to not want to take any of it back. Even though he knew he should.

Esta's voice was still soft, but there was a prickliness to her tone when she spoke again. "You said that you wanted—"

"I *did*," he admitted. Maybe he shouldn't have wanted her, and he definitely shouldn't have allowed himself to have her, but he wouldn't lie about the truth of the matter now.

"Then what's the problem?" Esta's words were clipped as she pulled away from him and sat up completely. She pulled the thin cotton sheet up along with her, as though she suddenly realized how bare she was and felt too exposed.

Harte couldn't bring himself to look at her. Even with the sheet covering her, he now knew every inch of the body hidden beneath. He wanted to know it better—wanted to trace his thumb over the scar on her shoulder that he hadn't noticed before. He wanted to press his lips there and take away the memory of whatever had caused it. He wanted to trace the silvery line at the base of her throat where Nibsy had cut her, until there was nothing in the world but the two of them again.

But it all felt too intimate . . . too *dangerous*. It was safer to let her establish this distance. Safer, too, if they were honest with each other about what this had been—what it could ever be. He thought of the nurse back at the hospital, the way the woman had called Esta his wife and how that had made him feel: terrified and awed and desperate all at once. With his body still warm and his mind still buzzing with pleasure, Harte wanted . . . He wasn't sure what he wanted other than Esta. But he was still a man without a future, without anything to offer her. He'd forgotten that for a moment, and he'd let himself take too much.

"It was a mistake."

"*Excuse me?*" Esta's voice had turned into a blade every bit as dangerous as Viola's.

Harte winced inwardly at the sharpness of her tone—the *hurt* in it as well—but there was something he had to say. He was going about this all wrong, but he was still so light-headed and overwhelmed, and he had to make her understand. "I never should have allowed it to happen."

"Allowed?" Esta's full mouth parted slightly.

Harte braced himself for her to finish, but where he'd prepared for fire, Esta gave him only ice. There was a long beat of silence, with the train car rocking and swaying beneath them, as though it were trying to convince them to return to the minutes before, when there had been only the rhythm of their bodies and mouths.

"You know, Darrigan, you are a complete and absolute *ass.*" Esta's voice was devoid of all feeling or warmth.

Harte had the sudden and unpleasant premonition that he'd made a terrible mistake.

A sliver of moonlight cut through the space where the curtains had slid open, casting its glow over Esta's face—the soft mouth that had just been on his body, the sharp nose that he'd once thought made her striking more than classically pretty.

How had he ever thought that? Now he saw her, *all* of her. Not only her body, but the woman she was. He saw her strength *and* her vulnerability, her bravery *and* her fear. And when he saw her golden eyes glassy with unshed tears, he realized his utter stupidity. He'd spoken poorly, and because of that, she'd misunderstood.

But it was too late for him to take back his words or to repair the rift he'd created between them. A second later Esta slid out of his bunk without another word, leaving him with only the steady sound of the train beneath them and the empty comfort of his pride.

COMPLICATIONS

1920—A Train Heading East

Esta lay awake for the rest of the night. She could not silence the memory of Harte's words. They ran through her mind again and again, steady and constant as the train consuming the tracks beneath her.

It was a mistake.

I never should have allowed it to happen.

She could hear Harte's faint breathing above her, the soft not-quite snores he made as he slept the sleep of the righteous. She had thought he'd understood. When he'd laid his mouth on hers, when he'd pulled them both under, breaking through the casual stoicism they each wore like armor, she'd thought he was in agreement. Apparently, she'd been wrong.

She'd spent so much of her life trying—*trying*—so hard to be what she was supposed to be. The perfect thief. Loyal to her provider and mentor, loyal to her team. The perfect weapon. Honed and sharpened. Cast from steel. It didn't matter that Esta was *good* at all of those things. It didn't matter that her heart beat in time with the seconds when she lifted a wallet or found the final number in the tumbler of a lock. What mattered was that *none* of it had been a choice. Her life, her profession, her talent and drive . . . it had all been handed to her—*forced* upon her—and Esta had accepted each as her due. They had been nothing more and nothing less than the cost of belonging.

But Harte? He'd been a *choice*. From the first time she'd encountered him at the Haymarket, to when she'd saved him from the end he should have met at the Brooklyn Bridge, to a few moments ago, when she'd let go of all propriety and control, Harte Darrigan was a choice Esta made again and again. Often against her better judgment. With him, she had never been anything more or anything less than who she truly was meant to be. And that *couldn't* be a mistake. Could it?

Esta wasn't sure what she was supposed to feel other than a biting disappointment and the sharp cut of something that she couldn't help but admit was hurt. Was she supposed to feel *different* somehow because of what had happened between them? Was she supposed to feel transformed?

She felt neither.

By the next morning, though, Esta managed to pull herself together. It wasn't like she had any other choice. She would not give the night before any more importance than Harte had. She would do what she'd always done—she would press onward, pretending confidence and hoping that she could spin its magic around her once more.

She would try.

They sat, too quiet and too awkward, barely picking at their break-fasts. Esta watched the land passing outside the train window so that she wouldn't have to look at him. Harte fidgeted with some dry toast, and she could tell he wanted to say something, but she didn't want to deal with any more excuses. Not now. Not in the bright light of morning, when everything about the night before made her feel like an utter fool. Harte apparently didn't understand that her silence meant that there was no need to discuss it.

"About what happened last night," he started.

Esta turned to him, ready. She gave him what she hoped was a calm and dignified smile. "I'd rather put it behind us."

"You can really do that?" Harte eyed her, his jaw suspiciously tight.

"Of course," she lied. She made a show of spearing a bit of potato and pretended to enjoy it, forcing herself to swallow it down.

"Just like that?" he asked, frowning. "You can act like last night never happened? Even after we—"

Esta slammed her fork down a bit more forcefully than she had intended, but at least it shut him up. She needed Harte to understand what she was about to say, and she needed him to understand it *now*. Because she didn't think she could handle it if he kept reminding her of what might have been . . . but what clearly wasn't.

"I will figure out a way to put last night behind me because I *have* to," she told him. "So do you. Whatever *mistakes* were made last night no longer matter. When we get to Chicago, we'll have *one* chance to steal the Book and the dagger from Jack. You know what the future holds, and we cannot allow the Reticulum or Jack Grew's presidency to become a reality. Last night was . . ." Her throat went tight. She suddenly had no idea how to finish that sentence.

"It was what?" Harte asked, and Esta wanted to believe that there was a note of longing in his voice that matched her own.

"It doesn't matter," she said, shoving aside the sentiment. "Last night can't figure into what happens next. We can't let it distract us."

Harte was silent, and Esta allowed herself to relax a bit, believing that everything was settled.

"And if there are . . . consequences?" Harte asked softly.

Consequences? It took a second, but then it hit her what he meant. "You mean . . ." She'd been so stupid. She hadn't even considered—

"There won't be," she told him, as though saying the words made it a fact.

Harte's dark brows drew together. "You can't know that for sure."

"I know that it doesn't matter," she told him, trying not to think about a future that could never be.

"How can it possibly not matter?" Harte was angry now, she could tell. But Esta was angry too. Or maybe she was hurt, and the two emotions felt close to the same when everything was so mixed up and desperate.

"Because it doesn't." She leaned over the plate of food that she no longer had any interest in. "Did you forget how this might well end?" she asked him. "There's only one way we know of to control the power of the Book—Seshat's power." She thought carefully about her words before she spoke again. She needed him to understand. "You know what Professor Lachlan tried to do to me when I returned to my own time. My affinity can unite the stones. We can use it to control Seshat's power. I've already accepted that I might not get to walk away from this, Harte."

As she'd spoken, Harte's face had gone pale. He was shaking his head like he didn't want to listen, or maybe like he didn't believe her. "The Book will have another answer," he said.

"It might not." The pain in his expression made Esta soften her voice. "Once we have the Book, we'll be able to get the stones back to 1902. The Quellant should hold off Seshat for the time being, at least. But we have only so much Quellant left, and you can't live with her inside your skin indefinitely, Harte. She has to be removed, and her power has to be controlled, and—right now, at least—there's only one way we know of to do that."

"Esta—"

"Maybe the Book *will* have some other answer. I hope it does. But if it doesn't, or if we can't *get* the Book, then I won't have any choice. I'll use my affinity to unite the stones, the same as Professor Lachlan would have. There's a good chance I'm not going to survive that, Harte."

"So last night," Harte said, swallowing hard. "It only happened because you felt like you had nothing to lose."

Esta stared at him in disbelief. How could he possibly be so blind? So *stupid*. "Last night happened because I have *everything* to lose."

"I should have thrown myself from the train leaving St. Louis," he said flatly.

She glared at him. "Martyrdom isn't a good look on you."

"But it works for you?" Harte asked, anger tingeing his voice. His hands were shaking a little, and he still looked practically colorless.

"It's not martyrdom. It's reality," Esta told him. "We have to find a way to control Seshat, and so far there is only one way we know of. I *can* do it, and I *will* if I have to. It's a reality we both need to accept."

"I *won't* accept that." Harte tossed his napkin onto the table. "There's no reason you have to give up your life to stop Seshat, not when there's an easier way."

"You don't get it, do you?" Esta asked. She shook her head, fighting back tears that she would *not* allow. "You weren't some itch I had to scratch last night, Harte. I have no interest in being some kind of hero. I don't want to die to save the world. But I'd happily give my life to save *you*."

Harte stared at her, and Esta immediately realized her mistake. With her words, she'd exposed far too much of her tender, beating heart, and the silence that filled the berth somehow felt more dangerous than any enemy she'd ever faced. She hadn't ever felt so exposed before.

Then Harte took her hand, and some of the panic receded. Her stomach flipped as his long, strong fingers intertwined with her own. His gray eyes were soft as he looked at her, and when he spoke, his voice was barely more than a whisper. "What makes you so certain I don't feel the exact same way?"

Esta couldn't move. She was afraid that if she did, the entire world around them would shatter and fall away. That *she* would shatter as well.

How had she not considered this? Last night, she'd been so angry at herself for thinking he hadn't understood, but now? She realized she'd been wrong. He *had* understood—*did* understand—and somehow that made it even worse. There was a raw openness in Harte's expression that was terrifying.

A realization settled over Esta that stole her breath, plucked it straight from her chest with fingers as nimble as her own. If Harte felt for her even half of what she felt for him, he would never allow her to do what she intended. If they could not find another way to stop Seshat—one that did not involve her using her affinity and giving up her life—Harte would take himself out of the equation to protect her, and his death would destroy her just the same.

PART

V

TRAFFIC AND LUCK

1902—New York

Cela Johnson decided that maybe she wasn't actually made for a life of crime right about the time that everyone else decided that *she* should be the one to sit on the rooftop of the tallest building on Thirteenth Avenue to watch for the Order's ship. She'd spent her share of evenings sitting on fire escapes, like everyone else born in a city that sizzled with the summer heat, but this was something different somehow.

To Cela's back, Manhattan's streets sprawled in all directions, an impossible stretch of humanity. Abel was out there somewhere, waiting like everyone else, for the signal she would send. In front of her, the Hudson River glinted, a chain of gold in the early-evening sun. Somewhere out beyond the river, the Order was making ready to move their goods, was maybe already moving them.

Cela lifted her spyglass to study the boats dotting the river, hoping that the sign she was looking for would come sooner rather than later. One of those boats held the ring that Darrigan had given her, the ring that had turned her life upside down. Soon a boat would start to inch its way toward one of the many busy docks that lined the western side of the island, and then the game would begin.

Noting the sun's low position in the sky, Cela checked her watch again. It was already 7:26. Not quite time, since nothing would happen until the sun was exactly at the right angle, nearly sitting on the horizon. But it was getting close.

The minutes felt like they were crawling by, but Cela didn't dare so much as look away or blink. The boat they were looking for would dock no earlier, and also probably no later, than 7:46, when the sun was exactly six degrees above the horizon. It was the beginning of a period the Order called the Golden Hour, when the sun was supposedly at its most powerful.

It wasn't when the sun was at its brightest, mind you, which would have been what any rational person might have assumed. Instead, it had something to do with astronomy. The Golden Hour, according to Theo's information, was marked by the sun's path, from six degrees above the horizon to six degrees below on this particular day—the Manhattan Solstice. Six because it was a powerful number. A sacred number, even, according to the men in the Order.

Maybe there was something to their beliefs, Cela thought as she watched the ships drifting in the distance. Six days for the good Lord to make the world, six points on the Star of David, and the devil himself loved the number so well he took it three times over.

The Order was depending upon the power of this false solstice, when the alignment of the sun would give their evil charms more power. Until the sun dipped below the horizon, the cargo would be untouchable. Literally untouchable, from what Theo told them.

Still, Cela thought this so-called Golden Hour was poorly named, especially since it wouldn't even last a whole hour. Fifty-two minutes was all the time the Order would have to take advantage of. In that time, the boat had to dock, and their treasures had to travel through the city streets and arrive at the Order's new quarters in the Flatiron Building. For those fifty-two minutes, some kind of strange magic would ensure their treasures would be safe. But if the wagons happened to be delayed, if they didn't reach their destination before the end of those fifty-two minutes, the shipment would be vulnerable.

It was essential that those wagons were delayed.

In a city that had more traffic snarls than pigeons most days, it seemed an easy enough thing to accomplish. If a train happened to be late, if it happened to find itself held up on Death Avenue—maybe by an over-turned cart, for instance—the wagon bearing the Order's goods wouldn't be able to take a direct route, straight across the island to reach the Flatiron Building. The wagons would have to be diverted around the chain of train cars and backed-up wagons, maybe for blocks in either direction.

With a little planning, the cluttered streets in the lower part of Manhattan would work in their favor. With a little luck, they would use Paul Kelly's men and Nibsy Lorcan's boys to divert the wagons and funnel them *away* from the Flatiron. If they could keep those wagons running until it was too late for the sun to provide its protection, it would be pos-sible for Jianyu to relieve the Order of their treasures before either Paul Kelly or Nibsy Lorcan could get to them. The ring could be retrieved.

If they managed to cut the Order's legs out from beneath them, maybe people would see that it *was* possible to rise up and topple the rich and the powerful. Maybe more things could change as well, and not only for Mageus.

Maybe. But Cela wasn't counting any chickens, especially not before they'd even gathered the eggs. There were too many things that could go wrong. For one, they still didn't know for sure where the ship would dock. For another, they were depending too much upon the capricious-ness of traffic and luck.

It didn't help that their planning had gone sideways a couple of days before. Somehow, Viola's brother had found out about his sister's trips to Harlem. He'd made demands, and then he'd made threats. Thank god, Viola had managed to warn them. It was a risk the Italian girl had taken, and one that Cela appreciated. She understood *exactly* how bad it was that Paul Kelly knew who she and Abel were. His Five Pointers had been causing trouble in the city for years, dangerous trouble. The kind of trouble that made people end up dead.

Cela might have understood why Viola and Jianyu had decided to use this Nibsy Lorcan fellow and try to play the two dangers off each other, but she still didn't like it. Everything she'd heard about Nibsy made Cela think he wasn't someone who could be easily duped or led. There was too much that could go wrong. For starters, Cela wasn't sure whether Viola had actually been able to convince Nibsy that she was on his side—not when Viola's eyes flashed with hate every time she heard his name. Cela also wasn't sure that a fifteen-year-old orphan could neutralize the threat of Paul Kelly, as Jianyu was hoping he would, even if the boy had managed to betray an entire gang and kill their leader to take power.

She only hoped that with Nibsy and Paul Kelly involved, there would be others to take the blame if things went wrong. Because if she or Abel were caught by the Order? Even the threat of the Five Pointers didn't worry Cela quite as much as what might happen if things went *that* wrong.

It was more than Cela's and Abel's lives at stake. Maybe Abel's friends had decided to sit this one out, but Cela knew that nothing was ever that easy. If word got out that the two of them had been involved and public sentiment turned against them, it could also turn against every Negro in the city—exactly like it had two years before, during the riots that killed her father.

Cela saw something then, far off on the Hudson. A small steamer ship that had been sitting in the middle of the river started to turn toward the shore, and when she checked her watch again, she had a sense that this was the ship she was looking for. She couldn't have been more certain if the ship had flown a banner declaring itself, but she watched a minute longer to be sure of the direction and the approximate location of the landing. When it was clear she'd been right, she tucked the spyglass under her arm and picked up the mirror.

Once the signal was given, it would be relayed along the rooftops, and their plan would be set in motion. Where the boat docked mattered, and the direction the wagon headed mattered even more. If the train was stopped too early, the Order would be able to avoid it. If they stopped it on the wrong part of Eleventh Avenue, the blockage would be useless.

Careful not to drop the mirror, she raised the spyglass again, prepared to send the first signal. Then something on the river drew her attention, and she stopped short. There were at least three ships moving now, each making a steady, even progression toward Manhattan. Each heading toward a dock evenly spaced along the island's edge.

Scanning the water, Cela looked for some indication of which ship was the right one, when realization struck. There wasn't a single ship, as they'd expected. The Order had sent *three* ships. And they were heading to three different docks. It was an eventuality that none of them had considered or prepared for.

Cela lifted the mirror and let it catch the light, sending a series of bright flashes. She hoped that the others would understand. *If they don't . . .* She pushed that thought aside and sent the message once again, to be sure. Even with this unexpected twist, their plans *had* to work. Too many lives hung in the balance.

NO REASON TO CHOOSE

1902—New York

James Lorcan had spent too many nights sleeping on the roof of the Bella Strega to let a little thing like the height of the building make him nervous, but he could tell that Paul Kelly didn't feel the same. The broad-faced gangster looked positively green and was doing his level best to stay as far from the edge as possible. James, on the other hand, had one foot perched on the cornice as he surveyed the streets below and the river beyond.

The sun was dropping quickly, falling ever steadily toward the horizon. Soon, the Order's boat would dock and the game would begin. Anticipation sizzled along his skin, brushed up by the frisson of energy stirring the Aether around him. Change was in the air, and the outcome would be his to command.

With Kelly was Viola, who still looked like she was ready to murder someone—mostly her brother. James suspected the only thing stopping her was the threat Kelly had made against the lives of her friends in Harlem. If Kelly ended up dead, orders had been given to end Cela Johnson and her brother, Abel, as well. It was a situation that had successfully positioned Viola right where James wanted her.

He ignored the tension radiating between the siblings and focused instead on the view through the spyglass. The river was crowded with boats, but he was too far inland to see much of the shoreline. Instead, he watched a dark figure on a rooftop about four blocks west.

"Can you see anything at all?" Kelly asked, clearly impatient for his own turn at the spyglass. Though why he hadn't thought to bring his own, James didn't know. "Is she where she's supposed to be?"

"She's there," Viola told her brother.

James watched a bit longer, until he could sense that Kelly was at the end of his patience, and then he waited a few seconds longer still before handing over the glass.

"She'd better *stay* there," Paul muttered, holding the glass to his eye.

Viola caught Nibsy's eye while Kelly was studying the skyline, her brows rising slightly in a question. He gave her a small nod, nothing noticeable, but enough to keep her leash loose. Viola had no guarantee that James would uphold his end of their bargain, but she had threatened to kill him—and happily—if he went back on his word. It was a promise she reminded him of now with a slight narrowing of her violet eyes.

Too bad that it was a promise she wouldn't live long enough to keep.

Paul Kelly, Viola, and the Order. Each posed a threat to James' plans. Kelly, because he wanted the Strega; Viola, because she wanted to avenge Dolph; and the Order, because they would destroy magic if they could. None would get their wish. If all went as James planned, the biggest threats to his control over the Devil's Own—and over the Bowery— would be taken care of by the end of the day.

He gave Viola an easy smile, glancing up over his glasses, but Viola only glared at him before she turned away.

When she'd come to him three days ago, James hadn't been surprised, of course. He'd ensured that Viola *had* to turn to him when he told Torrio to reveal Viola's jaunts to Harlem. James had known implicitly that Paul Kelly would not have been able to stand for his sister aligning herself with the people she'd chosen. Kelly might act the part of a gentleman, he might be all spit and polish, but at his heart, he was the same as anyone else—easily led by his hatred and fear.

How Viola had found Cela and Abel Johnson, James still didn't know. He didn't actually care as long as they remained useful for keeping Viola in line. After all, she might pretend to be the cold, calculating assassin, but James knew better. He'd seen her with Tilly, and he'd seen her with Dolph. Her fear for her friends was a weakness.

The Aether wasn't a scrying bowl or a crystal ball, but it had guided James nevertheless. He'd known that he needed Viola's help, even if he wasn't sure *why*, and once her involvement was secured, the vibrations in the Aether had changed—they'd become nearly *certain* of his victory.

"I think something is happening," Paul said, excitement coloring his voice. "One . . . two . . . three . . ." He counted the pattern, short and long, but then he frowned, pausing.

"What is it?" Viola asked, the nervous energy in her voice giving away her fear.

Kelly didn't respond at first. His lips moved in a silent count, but then he did finally turn on her. His face was red with temper, but his voice held a deadly calm. "Your friend is a dead woman."

"What are you talking about?" Viola asked, trying to take the spyglass from him. "Cela wouldn't do anything—"

"It's nothing but nonsense," Kelly snapped.

"Give me that," Viola said, finally taking the spyglass from her brother and lifting it to her eye. She was silent as she watched, her frown deepening. "I don't understand. Cela wouldn't risk such a thing. Something has happened."

James agreed. Against his skin, the Aether shifted, swirled, opened new possibilities. Something *was* happening, indeed.

"May I?" he asked, and reluctantly Viola handed over the glass.

Sure enough, James could clearly see the flash of Cela's mirror. He watched, counting the flashes—long and short—and then James started to laugh from the sheer absurdity.

"I can't imagine what you find funny, Lorcan," Kelly growled.

"I expect that you wouldn't, considering that it's *your* information that was wrong," Nibsy told him, lowering the spyglass. They'd depended on Kelly's sources to make their plan. One boat was supposed to dock at the specified time, and then the wagon carrying the Order's treasures would cut one clear path through the city before sundown. But apparently Kelly's sources had been wrong. "That girl isn't playing any game. She's using Morse code. She's doing exactly what she's supposed to be doing."

"Which dock will it be, then?" Kelly demanded. "Where will the boat land?"

"It's not a single boat as we expected," James said. "It appears that there are three."

"Three?" Viola asked. "You're sure?"

James raised the spyglass again. "Positive," he said, and he handed the spyglass back so Kelly could see for himself.

Kelly's jaw clenched as the seconds ticked by. When he'd seen enough, he lowered the glass. "Why would there be three?"

"Clearly, the Order must have been expecting an attack," James said. "They've made a move you didn't predict, and now we have to play their game."

"I'm not interested in any games," Kelly snarled.

"Don't worry," James said as he reveled in the way the Aether bunched. "We're not going to let them win." He took the mirror to signal back to the girl on the roof that they understood her message. "The Order believes themselves to be clever, but they've made a tactical error. We'll still win in the end."

"How?" Kelly demanded. "Any one of those ships could be carrying the goods."

"Or they all could," Viola said, suddenly sounding unsure.

"I don't think they'd take that risk," Nibsy said, letting the possibilities unfurl around him. "Multiple ships mean more to guard and additional chances that some of their treasures might go missing. They lost far too much when Khafre Hall burned. They won't want to sacrifice anything more." He paused, letting the Aether vibrate through him, listening. "No," he told them, feeling surer than ever. He understood then what he had to do to ensure his own victory. "The other ships are nothing but a distraction. The Order will keep the shipment together. One of those ships holds what we're after."

"But which one?" Viola asked, squinting toward the river. "What do we tell the others?"

"The train can't block enough of Eleventh Avenue to account for multiple routes," Kelly said, frowning. "If we choose the wrong place to stop it, the wagon we want could get through."

"There's three of us and three boats," Nibsy said. "There's no reason to choose."

THE DEVIL'S MARK

1902—New York

Viola gave Nibsy a cutting look. She'd been against Jianyu's idea that they go back to Nibsy for help. She'd come up with every possible reason why it was a terrible idea to trust Nibsy—Dolph's murderer—to neutralize the threat that her brother posed to Cela and Abel, because she'd known that he would turn against them—they both had. But at the time, there had been no other solution.

"You want us to go separately?" she asked Nibsy, suddenly more than suspicious.

"We could each follow one of the wagons," Nibsy said easily. "It's the only way to be sure."

But a single glance at the guileless expression on Nibsy's face told Viola that he was lying about something. Not about the ships. No, that particular trick made sense. Theo had warned them that the Order was nervous and that they should expect the unexpected. This new complication with so many ships certainly counted. But Nibsy's idea of each of them going a separate way? Viola didn't like it. It was too convenient that Nibsy would want to be away from the threat of her knife and her affinity.

"You seem far too eager to be off on your own," she said coldly as she narrowed her eyes at him.

"We'll have very little time once the boats land," Nibsy reminded them both. "We won't have room for hesitation or indecision. If the wagon, whichever boat it may be on, reaches the new headquarters before sundown, we won't be able to touch it. Splitting up makes the most sense. At least one of us is sure to reach the Order's goods."

Paolo had been silent for too long, a fact that made Viola wary. "And then what?" he asked now, his voice cold and calculating. "What assurance do I have that you won't go back on your word and take more than your share?"

"You think I would dare to cross *you*, Paul?" Nibsy said with a surprised blink.

More lies. More deception. Of course Nibsy would cross Paolo. It had been his plan from the start, and both Viola and her brother knew it. Why else would Paolo have been so willing to accept Viola's plan to go to Nibsy pretending friendship, if not for the fact that Paul thought he could use her to keep Nibsy Lorcan in line?

Both wanted the other out of the way. That fact seemed the only thing about the situation that worked to Viola's benefit. Let them have their little pissing contest. She had no intention of getting caught in the crossfire. Viola cared only about retrieving the ring and stopping the Order from regaining so much as a foothold in the city. She cared, too, about making sure that Cela and Abel were not harmed by their decision to commit themselves to this cause. Everything else—her brother and Nibsy, too, for that matter—could go to the devil as far as Viola was concerned.

"Of *course* you would try to cross me," Paolo said. "But you won't live for long after if you try."

"Enough," Viola told them. They didn't have time for this bickering. To the west, the boats churned toward shore. To the east, the tower waited, poised to solidify the Order's power once again. "We don't need to chase wagons," she told them. That had never been the plan anyway. "We know where they're going. We'll meet them there."

Nibsy's gaze slid to her. "And when they arrive?"

"We'll stop them from going any farther," she told them, wishing she felt surer than she sounded. "Together."

"We should still send the signals," Nibsy told Paul. "Any delays might help."

"No," Paul told him. "I want my people on Fifth Avenue waiting for the wagons, not running around the city like chickens after a fat worm."

"The Order is expecting an attack. It would be a shame to disappoint them," Nibsy argued. "If they don't run into any problems, they may start to believe that their plan to distract us hasn't worked. They might try something else we're not expecting."

Paul frowned. "Fine." But the tension strung between the two was enough to put Viola's teeth on edge.

Men. They were exhausting. And they were wasting time.

"What of the train?" Viola asked, drawing their attention back.

"Right across Twenty-Third," Paul said as though taking control of the situation. "We'll block their straightest route. If your people are ready to the south, mine will take the north," he told Nibsy. "And the three of us will take the building."

Nibsy took the mirror to send the signals as Paul inched closer to the edge of the roof, making sure not to get too close, and gave a sharp whistle. He listened, and then a moment later, he whistled again. "Where the hell is he?"

"Who?" Viola asked.

"Johnny. He's supposed to be waiting downstairs."

"We'll catch him on our way out," Nibsy told him, tucking the mirror away. He started for the rooftop door, but Paul grabbed his arm.

"Not so fast," her brother said. "I don't need you taking off and getting ahead of us."

"As if I could outrun you," Nibsy said. He gave a small flourish of his hand.

As Paul charged into the stairwell, Nibsy slid a glance to Viola. She couldn't tell what emotion was behind it. Satisfaction, maybe? Or perhaps amusement?

"After you," Nibsy said, and when Viola began to argue, he shrugged.

"I'd prefer to keep that knife of yours where I can see it, if you don't mind."

"I don't need a knife to stop your heart," she muttered as they began to descend the stairs, but she'd barely taken another step when the skin on her back felt suddenly cold. It was as though someone had slipped a piece of ice down her collar. Beneath her shift and her blouse, Viola felt the strange sensation of the mark she wore—*Dolph's* mark—trembling.

The feeling—the very *thought* of the mark coming to life—made her stumble, and she nearly missed the next step.

"Have a care, Viola," Nibsy said, but his voice was flat, without any hint of true concern.

It can't be. Viola glanced back up at him, but she couldn't read his expression. The glass of his spectacles flashed in the dim light, obscuring his eyes, but his mouth was soft. He seemed relaxed. Calm. But his hand gripped the cane that had once been Dolph's, and there was something possessive in the way his thumb traced the coils of the gorgon's serpentine hair. It made her shiver. It made her *wonder.*

"Is anything wrong?" Nibsy asked, his brows lifting above the wire rims of his glasses. "Something you wanted to say to me?"

"No," she said, shaking off her misgivings. She continued her descent, stepping more carefully now, even as she fought the urge to scratch at the ink in her skin.

Even in life, Dolph had never threatened her with the mark she wore. Not like he threatened others. He'd never needed to. Viola's loyalty had been absolute because Dolph had been, before all else, a trusted friend. But she'd heard stories about what happened to those who dared betray him or the Devil's Own. The fantastical stories about the curse of the serpents that were inscribed in their skin and the way Dolph Saunders could use those marks to unmake their bearers by taking their magic.

Viola hadn't wanted to believe those tales. They'd seemed too ridiculous to be true, but then, she hadn't known the man who'd written the journal entries about taking Leena's power. She hadn't known the version of Dolph Saunders who'd studied strange sigils to control demons and then hid his work behind unreadable markings. Viola had wondered many times in the days after Nibsy had shown her the sheets torn from Dolph's journal, notes written in Dolph's own hand, whether she had truly known Dolph Saunders at all.

But now, to think that Nibsy might be able to control the power Dolph had once claimed for himself, terrible and unnatural as it was? *Impossible.* Or so Viola hoped. She couldn't begin to contemplate what he might do with such power. She didn't want to.

She'd barely reached the next landing when a noise sounded from below. Gunshots rang out, and shouts echoed up the stairwell. On instinct, Viola started toward the sound, but Nibsy caught her by the wrist. "It would be more prudent to wait a minute or two," he said, completely unruffled by the commotion.

He wasn't at all surprised by the noise, she realized. "What have you done?"

"I've taken care of your brother . . . or rather, John Torrio has taken care of Paul for me," he told her. "That's what you wanted, wasn't it? To stop him from harming your friends?"

She frowned at him, but she was too smart to say anything.

"It's a funny thing, Viola. . . . The authorities were more than willing to turn a blind eye when your brother limited himself to simply terrorizing the poor urchins of the Bowery, but when he attacked the city's wealthiest men and their wives?" Nibsy shrugged. "They've been looking for Kelly for weeks now, and a certain sly Fox told them *exactly* where your brother could be found today."

"What of his Five Pointers?" she asked. "You know what will happen to Cela and her brother when Paolo doesn't call them off."

"They'll do whatever John Torrio tells them to do," Nibsy said. "Which will be what *I* tell him to do." He gave her a small, satisfied smile.

"And what is it that you'll tell him?" Viola asked, her fingers itching for her knife. She wished she could end this farce, but as long as Cela's and Abel's lives hung in the balance, she held her tongue.

"That all depends on how closely you stick to our agreement," Nibsy said easily.

"If anything happens to Cela or Abel Johnson, I *will* kill you," Viola promised. After all, if Paul was truly out of the way, she didn't need Nibsy. She certainly didn't need his threats. And if Jianyu would have counseled patience? Jianyu was nearly a mile away.

"I have no interest in harming your friends, Viola." Nibsy regarded her seriously through the thick lenses of his glasses. "Torrio, on the other hand, may not be so generous. Once we have the ring, I'll release them. But remember, if I die, so will they."

She could still kill him. She could kill Torrio, too, but Viola could not save Cela and her brother *and* help Jianyu get the ring. She could not be everywhere in the city at once. She would have to play Nibsy's game—for now, at least. She vowed, though, that she would not let him win.

"As long as they remain unharmed, you have nothing to fear," she said easily, refusing to allow herself to betray even a glimmer of the worry she felt churning in her stomach. "If you can't keep Torrio on his leash—"

"Torrio knows better than to cross me." Nibsy adjusted his grip on Dolph's cane. "But we should be going. After all, the Order's shipments won't wait."

It doesn't matter. Viola tried to tell herself as she continued down the stairs with Nibsy at her back. Even with this unexpected twist, things would work out. Hadn't they expected trouble from all sides? She would take back the ring, and then she would take her revenge on Nibsy Lorcan. She would stop his scheming before John Torrio could do anything to Cela or Abel. She *had* to. And if she couldn't?

She'd argued against Theo's involvement from the start. She'd tried to persuade him to be on a ship already sailing for the Continent by now, but she found herself suddenly grateful that he'd refused to budge in his determination to help them. If all else failed, Theo was positioned with the Order, there inside the new building, a last resort that they might very well need.

MINOR GODS

1902—New York

J ack Grew stood at the stone railing of the balcony on the eighteenth
floor of the Flatiron Building, gazing out across the city. *His* city.
Below, people scurried along like ants, unaware that he watched them
like a god from above. The sun was low in the sky. Already it scraped at
the tops of the buildings. Already the light was shifting into a golden haze,
and soon the streets would glow with the power of the sun's rays, as they
did only twice a year.

The ancients understood the solstice's importance. Each of the five
mystical dynasties knew that the power could be harnessed simply by
studying the movement of the stars. Pyramids and standing stones, towers
and obelisks, each of the dynasties had their monuments to the sun, so
why shouldn't this, the world's greatest city, have one as well?

But the men who built Manhattan had not been content to be directed
by the stars. They had sought, instead, to bend the heavens to their will.
The city's grid was only one example of the Order's influence on the
island. The grid had been positioned, not along the arms of the compass
rose, but with a careful attention to ley lines and numerology. This alignment of the city's streets was a tool to increase the Brink's power, but it
meant that on the traditional solstice, the streets of Manhattan would
remain as shadowed as ever. But on the *Manhattan* Solstice, dates known
only to those in the Order—dates discernible only through careful study
and mastery of the occult sciences—the streets would shine like gold,
electric with the power of the sun.

On those days, the average citizen would wander on, eyes down and focused on the muck of their own life, as they always did. Most would never look up and notice the phenomenon, much less understand the potential. But Jack understood. When the Order had asked for his assistance, the Book had been only too willing to oblige by revealing even more of its secrets. Thanks to the Book, he knew how to tap into that power—to *direct* it. It was yet another sign that soon the old men who thought they ruled over him would be completely irrelevant.

Someone cleared their throat behind him, and Jack turned to find Theo Barclay standing with his hands clasped. Anticipation sizzled through Jack's veins.

"The High Princept said you had some use for me?" Barclay said, amiable as ever, though there was a tightness around his eyes as he stepped into the chamber. He carried into the room a wariness that Jack found more than satisfactory.

There was something about Barclay's face that always gave Jack the urge to lay a fist into it, to rearrange the other man's classically handsome features. Now, though, he held himself back. It wasn't the time. *Not yet.*

"Actually, yes. I do." Jack gave Barclay an easy smile, anticipation already building. He stepped back inside, leaving the door ajar so the summer winds could stir the warm air. "Well, what do you think?"

Theo looked around the chamber, his eyes widening a little as he looked around. "It's quite a lot to take in," Barclay murmured, running his finger along one of the carvings in the wall. "The detail is astounding."

Jack understood the awe that colored Barclay's expression. He'd felt it too, the first time he saw the walls of intricately carved sandstone blocks, inlaid as they were with gilding and marble and onyx. Now the walls glittered in the evening light that poured through the open balcony door. An elaborate golden staircase, delicate and intricately wrought, wound itself upward in the center of the room to a large, circular medallion carved with the Philosopher's Hand. Beyond that portal, an even more fabulous chamber waited.

All around the triangular chamber, burnished walnut shelves stood in rows precisely arranged to take advantage of the power derived from sacred geometry. Presently, those shelves were empty and waiting to be filled with the Order's remaining books and scrolls, which would be brought into this room as soon as the danger had passed. In the center of the room stood an altar that had been rescued from the charred remains of Khafre Hall.

"This room is actually modeled on one in an ancient Egyptian temple, you know."

"Is it?" Theo turned, his expression betraying his open interest as he dropped his guard.

"The Temple of Thoth had one of the greatest libraries in the world," Jack told him. The Book throbbed against Jack's chest—a reminder and a promise. "Some called it the Library of Life. It's said that writing was invented there, along with the same rituals we still practice today."

"Thoth?" Theo pursed his lips, his brow furrowing. "One of the more minor gods, wasn't he?"

"On the contrary," Jack said, forcing his voice to remain even. "To those who understand the history of the occult sciences, he is absolutely *peerless.*"

"Well, this room is certainly impressive, as is the entire arrangement, Jack. Five floors of the highest and most exclusive real estate in Manhattan," Barclay said. He gave Jack a half smile that looked tense. He was scared and clearly nervous but trying to play it off. "Everything is beautifully appointed. No one could doubt the Order's influence once they see this."

"It *is* rather impressive, but we had quite the bar to meet after what Khafre Hall had been," Jack told him, pretending not to notice how on edge Barclay was. "Though *you* were never invited, were you?"

"No," Barclay said with a shake of his head. "I never had the honor."

"It was a beautiful old building. Inside and out, Khafre Hall stood as a monument to the majesty of our civilization and to the wonder of the occult arts," Jack told him, feeling a wave of regret for his own hand in its demise. The regret, though, swiftly turned to anger.

Because I was tricked. Because Darrigan and that bitch of a girl made me look like a fool. But Jack wouldn't allow himself to be deceived again. Barclay would learn that soon enough.

"Khafre Hall was a marvel," Jack continued, running his fingers over the granite top of the tall, square altar that anchored the room. "We believed it to be impenetrable, with all of the various wards and protections placed around the building."

"It's a shame what happened to it," Theo said, still looking gratifyingly uneasy. "So much history and art . . . lost to a band of thieves."

"Lost to *maggots*," Jack corrected, allowing the fury to infuse his words before reining himself in once more. "But not *all* was lost. So much of this chamber was taken whole from the levels far beneath the city streets. This very altar once stood in the center of the old Mysterium."

"It's a beautiful piece. Fourth century, I believe?" Theo asked. He glanced up at Jack. "It's amazing any of it survived the fire."

"Not really so amazing. The Mysterium itself was warded with protections that other parts of Khafre Hall did not have." Protections that had kept Jack out, but he would be kept out no longer. He smiled at Barclay. "The old Mysterium was also far below ground level, carved into the very bedrock of the city and protected by the many rivers that still run beneath these streets. Of course, those rivers provided a means of escape for the maggots who attacked the Order this past spring. The new Mysterium won't have that particular weakness."

Theo looked around, far too interested for Jack's liking. "It does look well secured."

"This is simply an antechamber," Jack corrected, amused at the surprise in Barclay's expression. "The new Mysterium is above." He lifted his eyes to where the spiraling stairs disappeared into the ceiling. "The chamber above us is even more secure than this one, and far more so than its predecessor. Only the highest level of the Order has the privilege of entrance. If the alarms are triggered by an unworthy soul, the seal will engage, the air will drain from the space, and only the blood of the High Princept himself will be able to open it," Jack said.

Or at least, that's what the Inner Circle believes.

"But enough about that," Jack said, changing the topic to keep Barclay off-balance. He was enjoying the way Barclay's nerves were growing more frayed by the second. "Come, have a look at this view." He opened the glass door and stepped out onto the balcony, and when Barclay hesitated, he taunted him. "Don't tell me you're afraid?" He leapt up upon the wide stone railing so he could stand, a god above the men below. "It's incredible, this city. Come, see Manhattan as you've never seen it before."

"Come down from there, Jack," Barclay said, stepping out onto the small stone terrace. "There's no sense taking chances."

"What chances?" Jack laughed. "Don't you see? As above, so below. *We're* now the ones above, Barclay. *Far* above. We're practically in the clouds. Closer to heaven and the angels themselves. Closer, as well, to the power those divine beings will inevitably bestow upon those who are worthy." He could not stop himself from smiling as he felt the wind cutting against him, the Book anchoring him. "And those who are not worthy . . ." He withdrew the red blossom from his lapel and crushed it in his palm as he leaned out, holding his arm far over the edge.

"Jack . . . ," Theo warned, his eyes growing wider.

"We've designed these chambers with every attention to security. Walls within walls, chambers within chambers, each with fail-safes. If an intruder manages to get into the Mysterium this time?" Jack let the petals drop from his finger. "Unlike the defensive weakness of Khafre Hall, from here there's only one escape."

The wind gusted, taking the bits of the red petals into the air. Some swirled back onto the balcony and landed, like drops of blood, at Theo Barclay's feet. Jack hopped down from the railing. He kept his gaze steady as he enjoyed the play of nerves and indecision flashing through Barclay's expression. *Weak.* But he knew that already.

"*Was* there something that you needed from me, Jack?" Barclay asked, his voice noticeably tighter than it had been when he finally spoke again. "I was on my way out when the Princept said you wanted to see me."

"You aren't staying for the ceremony?" Jack asked, frowning. It was impossible that he'd been wrong about Barclay. . . .

"My ship leaves this evening," Theo told him.

"Ah yes. You're off to retrieve your bride." Jack smiled pleasantly as he began to circle to the left. Barclay, nervous as ever, matched his movement, never giving Jack his back.

"I'm only going for a visit for now. I'll be back next month, but Ruby won't be back until fall, closer to the wedding date."

"Still, it's a shame you can't attend this evening's events, especially after all you've done to help."

"I've been happy to be of service, and I appreciate the chance to see this. . . ." Theo nodded toward the view of the city as he tucked his hands in his pockets, still nervous. Still gratifyingly uneasy. "I wish you all the best of luck on the ceremony, though."

"Oh, we won't need luck," Jack said, coming up next to Theo. "Not when we have power on our side. Look there, you can see the Hudson River, more than a mile away."

"So you can," Theo said, glancing at Jack instead of in the direction of the river.

"The boats have probably already landed, and even now the wagons are making their way through the city," Jack told him with a smile, enjoying the moment when realization rippled through Barclay's features.

Barclay turned then, frowning deeply. "Was there to be more than one?"

"Oh," Jack said, feigning innocence. "Were you not told? The Inner Circle decided on a change in plans."

"A change." Barclay turned back to the view, suddenly looking rather unwell.

"The Order expected an attack, and there was concern that someone among our ranks wasn't as devoted to our cause as he should be," Jack

LISA MAXWELL

said, never blinking. "Other arrangements were made. Three boats, each holding a single wagon. A diversion, if you will, for any who would try to stop our purpose."

"To give the one carrying the cargo a chance," Theo said. "Brilliant. Just . . ." He cleared his throat. "Brilliant."

"It is, rather." Jack took a moment to gloat. "The maggots who were planning to attack the shipment won't know which to follow. They thought to delay us, but instead, we'll keep them running . . . right into our trap." He took a step away from Theo. "Do you know the most brilliant part of all, though?" He waited until Theo had turned fully toward him, because Jack wanted to see the emotions that played across his face when he found out. "There's nothing in *any* of those wagons."

"Nothing?" Barclay's voice had a hollowness to it, like knocking on a tomb. It delighted Jack. "But we went to the trouble of warding them?"

"They're still warded, as we'd planned, but there's absolutely nothing inside."

Barclay blinked. "I don't understand."

"The story you were given about the boats was nothing but a test—a trap, if you will. The delivery isn't coming from the Hudson. It never was. The boat landed on the East River earlier today. The Order's most valuable treasures are already here, stowed in the Mysterium. Safe and protected from all dangers." Jack let his mouth curve. "Or that's what the rest of the Order believes. They're all downstairs, congratulating themselves on their superiority, unaware that the artifact they've attached all their hopes and dreams to is about to go missing."

By now Jack had maneuvered so that he stood between Barclay and any escape. He withdrew the pistol from his coat and leveled it at Theo.

"Jack?" Theo's hands went up without hesitation, but the confusion in his expression was priceless.

"This is where we say good-bye, I'm afraid, Barclay."

"What is all this, Jack?"

"It's the proper end for a thief," Jack said easily.

"I'm no thief." Theo took a step forward but stopped when Jack eased back the trigger. "I didn't take any artifact."

"You and I know that's only *barely* true," Jack said. "But the truth doesn't matter—especially not if your friends attack those wagons, as I expect they will. By the time tonight is finished, your treachery will be an established fact."

Theo let out a nervous, tittering laugh. It was the kind of involuntary noise people make when they realize they're in real danger and understand there's no way out. "I don't know what's going on here, Jack, but I assure you that this is all a misunderstanding. Whatever it is you think I've done—" He licked his lips. "Certainly, this is a mistake."

"No mistake, Barclay. Right now your friends are out there in the streets, chasing their own tails." Jack smiled. "By the time they realize that the wagons are empty, it will be too late. The sun will have set, and the Order will learn that they're under attack. When their precious artifact goes missing and they find you where you are not supposed to be, they'll assume that you are the cause."

"There will be no evidence," Barclay said.

Jack only laughed. "When has evidence ever mattered to embarrassed and fearful men? They will look for someone to blame. They'll *need* someone to hate, to *punish*. And when they find your body, broken and smashed on the walk below, they will point to you."

Barclay's expression was a mask of confusion. The fear in his eyes was *delicious*. "You can't make me jump, Jack."

"No?" Jack smiled pleasantly. He gave a shrug. "Perhaps not. But you'll fall one way or the other by the time the night's over, Barclay. Enjoy the view."

Jack was already back inside before Barclay could realize what was happening. He closed the door and locked it before Theo had even started to move, barring it with the combination of the heavy leaden locks and the runes the Book had given him for this very purpose. On the other side, Barclay pounded on the glass, his screaming made silent by the barrier between them. Jack watched with some amusement as Barclay tried jerking on the door, but when he grabbed the handle, he recoiled as pale-yellow smoke started pouring from the place he'd touched. A rather convenient little charm, Jack thought.

Desperate, Barclay slammed his fists against the pane of glass again and again, as though he would willingly slice his wrists to shreds if it meant escaping. But Jack knew that nothing Barclay tried would work. The glass and the door together were built to withhold any blow, and they were warded with the same magic that had once protected the Mysterium.

Jack turned toward the stairs in the center of the room, toward the next steps in the plan he'd devised to retrieve the Delphi's Tear. He left Theo Barclay to take care of himself.

With the enchantment layered into the smoke, Barclay was doomed anyway. The longer he stayed on that balcony, the better the ledge would begin to look. The wide-open expanse of sky would call to him, and by the time the sun had set, he would be so delirious that a different kind of exit would begin to look reasonable. Barclay would jump, and he would die, and in the chaos stirred by the events to come, Jack would walk away with the ring.

IN FOR A PENNY

1920—Chicago

Harte and Esta didn't discuss anything more about what had happened between them on the train, especially not once the Quellant faded and Seshat began to stir again. Instead, Harte couldn't stop thinking about what had happened—what he wanted it to mean—but he allowed the matter to drop, and they seemed to enter into an unspoken agreement, a fragile truce that was both a relief and a frustration.

What more was there to say about the matter? Wishing for a future or a long life with Esta wouldn't make it so.

Harte knew exactly how headstrong Esta was, and he knew it would be pointless to argue with her about using her affinity if it cost her life. He knew how he felt as well. He would do everything he could to retrieve the Book, but if the Ars Arcana didn't hold any answer to their dilemma—if it didn't show them a way to control Seshat while keeping Esta alive and whole—Harte still knew of one sure way to end the threat Seshat posed without harming Esta. He didn't need to argue with her about it. He would only need to *act*.

The truth of the matter was that Harte would not allow anyone else to lose their life for him or *because* of him. Not like Sammie had. He had been the one who had tried to steal the Book of Mysteries from the Order's vaults, and *he* would be the one to accept the consequences for the mistake of letting Seshat loose into the world. Not Esta.

And if she carries your child? Seshat whispered, a dark amusement curling in her voice.

The goddess felt stronger than she had before—more like she had back in St. Louis—except now Harte knew she was furious with being muzzled and chained by the effects of the Quellant. It was clearer than ever that taking Maggie's formulation had destroyed any hope of a truce, even with his continued promise to end Thoth.

Would you be so quick to sacrifice yourself and seek the easy escape of death? Seshat taunted. *Would you leave them unprotected and make your child a bastard, as you are? If you do, Thoth will destroy them both.*

Harte tried to push away Seshat's words. He knew what she was doing—trying to weaken him, trying to make him waver—but by the time they arrived in Chicago, he was exhausted from trying to ignore the unresolved issue between them. The train slowed into the station, all steam and grinding of brakes. Esta was looking out the window of their small Pullman berth, her expression a study of concentration, and Harte wondered if she was considering the same thing he was.

"Esta, when would you . . . ?" Harte hesitated, feeling unbearably, stupidly embarrassed.

"What?" Her dark brows drew together as she turned to him. "Are you okay? Is Seshat—"

"I'm fine," he said, cutting her off. The last thing he wanted to do was talk about Seshat. But Esta only gave him a questioning look. "I mean, she's still there, but that isn't what I wanted to discuss. We need to talk about what happened between us."

Esta grew wary. "What about it?"

"When might you know?" Harte asked, feeling his cheeks flame, and when she didn't understand, he was forced to spell it out for her. "If there were any . . . *complications.*"

"Complications," she repeated. Her expression had gone strangely, carefully blank. "Are we back to this, then?"

"You know I would never allow—"

"You wouldn't *allow*?" The wariness shifted to impatience now.

"That's not what I meant," he tried to say. "Only that if there *is* a child—"

"We are *not* talking about this right now, Harte," Esta snapped.

"I could marry you," he blurted.

Her mouth fell open, and for a moment, she looked as shocked as he felt from saying those words out loud. But then anger replaced shock. "Could you?"

Harte knew he was on precarious ground. It had come out all wrong.

"Esta—" He tried to collect his thoughts—tried to figure out how to say everything he felt—as she waited, dangerously quiet.

"Forget it, Harte," she said after a moment. "I think I'll pass on your generous offer to make an honest woman of me. I'm fine. We are getting off this train, and we are going to focus on finding Jack and the Book. We have enough to worry about without you inventing more problems."

She turned from him then to collect her bag with a cold determination, while Harte stood there wondering how he'd screwed everything up so absolutely. Again. Esta was already opening the door and heading out into the corridor before he could even begin to consider how to repair the fragile peace he'd broken, and then they were disembarking and the time for conversation had passed.

The station was packed and filled with an energy like something about to begin. It was because of the convention, Harte realized. Somewhere in the city, Antistasi were planning the attack that would set history on a different course, and somewhere in the city, Jack Grew was waiting with the Book. Still, even with so much at stake, Harte was painfully aware of Esta next to him—especially the anger that radiated from her stiffened spine and tight jaw. She refused to look at him.

With Esta resolutely ignoring him, Harte tried to push aside his hurt and his embarrassment. He needed to keep himself alert as they made their way through the station, watching for any sign of trouble. He didn't remember much about leaving the bank or catching the train in Oakland.

He'd been reeling still from the death of his brother, but now he saw that the world had changed once more. Chicago was all flash and energy, with boxy motorcars and bustling sidewalks and buildings that towered overhead. The air was thick with the scents of exhaust and bitter cigarettes and the noise of street vendors with their wares. Men in light-colored, slightly wrinkled-looking suits and groups of young women walking arm in arm without escorts filled the sidewalks. The women wore dresses that fit loose, with low waists that obscured the shape of their bodies and hemlines that exposed their ankles, and many wore hair cut bluntly at their chin, every bit as short as Esta's.

It didn't take them long to find lodging in a small hotel. Esta lifted a few wallets so they could purchase some new clothes, and eventually her icy demeanor began to thaw and she started to talk to him again. But they never regained the warm easiness of the truce they'd come to on the train. She was purposely holding herself back from him now, and Harte knew it was his fault.

Three days later, not much between them had improved, especially with Seshat pacing impatiently beneath his skin. But they'd uncovered a promising lead—whispers of a nightclub where Mageus were rumored to go. It wasn't much, but it was a start toward locating the Antistasi in the city, and so that evening Harte found himself standing beneath the brightly lit marquee of the Green Mill wearing one of his new ready-made suits and trying not to stare too hungrily at Esta. Her dress was ready-made as well, but it fit her like it had been tailored specifically for the long lines of her body. The fabric skimmed over her curves, a shimmering column that ended only slightly below the knee. It looked like it was made from dark, liquid gold, and Harte wanted nothing more than to reach out and touch the material—and the girl beneath.

He didn't have to worry about Seshat that night, because they'd decided to risk using one of the remaining Quellant tablets. For the first time in days, the goddess's mocking laughter and threatening whispers weren't echoing in Harte's mind, but he barely noticed. All his concentration was on Esta and the dress she was wearing, and the fact that she was still holding herself away from him. He might have so little time left, and he wanted to fix things between them before it was too late. He wanted to bring her back to him—to make sure she was safe and protected—but Harte understood that they had a job to do. He tucked his hands into his pockets and kept them—and his thoughts—to himself.

The convention had started the day before, and so far the ballots had been inconclusive, but they both knew it was only a matter of time until the presidential nominee would be decided. Once that happened, the Antistasi would attack, unless he and Esta got to them first and convinced them to abandon their plan.

Esta had described the Green Mill as a saloon, but that was underselling it a bit. The establishment took up nearly an entire city block. But unlike some of the German-run beer halls back in Manhattan, the Green Mill's many rooms and gardens were all polish and shine.

They passed through the crowded saloon in the front of the building, ignoring the mahogany bar that served a menu of seltzers and juice, then continued on to the sunken gardens that stood at the center of the complex. Open to the warm summer night air, the gardens were filled with people dancing and laughing. Harte still didn't quite understand the whole concept of Prohibition. He couldn't figure out why anyone thought it would be necessary—or even possible—to make alcohol illegal. From all appearances, his instincts were right—the people bouncing around the dance floor, their arms and legs flying in all directions, looked far less sober than the so-called dry gardens should have allowed.

"The entrance to the speakeasy is over there," Esta said, frowning at the crowded dance floor.

Her lips were a dark, deep red, and she'd done something to accent the peaked bow in the center, so her frowning only served to draw Harte's eyes to her mouth. Which only served to remind him how her lips had felt against his a few days before. Which reminded him how her whole body had felt against his. And that made him damn uncomfortable in a lot of different ways. It made him remember just how badly he wanted things that he could not have.

Harte realized suddenly that Esta was looking at him expectantly—he'd missed whatever she'd just said. "What?"

She let out a frustrated breath. "I said that we'll have to go around the dance floor. Do you have a preference which direction?"

In for a penny . . .

Harte took Esta's hand and, though she jumped at his touch, he didn't let her pull away as he led her toward the swirl of dancers. For the last few minutes, the couples crowding the dance floor had been doing some sort of dance that involved kicking and hopping, but now the music had shifted into something slower.

"What are you doing?" Esta asked as Harte swept her into a formal embrace and then whirled her onto the floor and into the crush of other couples.

"I'm dancing with you," he murmured.

"Clearly," she said dryly.

He felt sure she would pull away from him. She had every reason to, with how badly he'd mucked up everything a few days before. But when she didn't immediately, Harte moved a little closer.

"This isn't really the time or place," Esta told him, but she followed his lead, her feet tracing the easy loping circles of the waltz they were caught up in.

Harte leaned back and raised a single brow as he looked at her. "I'm not sure I could think of a much better one." Then he lifted his arm and pushed Esta gently into a twirling spin before closing the frame of their position again. "It reminds me a little of the night we met."

She gave him a smile that was all teeth. "I must remember things differently. How long did it take for your tongue to heal, anyway?"

He bit back a laugh at her tartness, glad to have something other than ice from her. "Nearly a week," he told her, remembering his surprise when their first kiss—a ruse he'd forced upon her to stop her from using magic where she shouldn't—had turned dangerous. At least for him. "I should have never let you go," he whispered, repeating the words he'd said that night.

"What?" Her steps faltered, but Harte kept her upright and continued their waltz.

"It's what I said to you that night. Back at the Haymarket. You were dancing with some old goat, and I was trying to get you away from him and warn you about how dangerous it was to use your magic with Corey's men watching. I had to distract you somehow. It worked well enough then." He looked into her eyes. "Is it working now?"

"Don't, Harte," she whispered, her words coming to him on the back of the melody that surrounded them.

But he wasn't listening. Or rather, he was, but he needed Esta to understand. "I thought it *was* all nothing but a ruse, you know." He twirled her again. They were near the middle of the floor now, making their way across to the far side of the gardens. "My ridiculous words. That kiss."

"We need to focus," Esta reminded him, but her voice caught as she spoke.

"You're right." He took a moment to really look at her, a golden flame among peacocks, an Amazonian *goddess* among bits of fluff. It was more than her beauty; there was a strength emanating from within her that was unmistakable. That was *irresistible*. It always had been.

"That's not what I meant," she said.

"I'd like to kiss you now," he told her. They'd stopped dancing for some reason, probably because he'd stopped, but the rest of the dancers continued to move around them.

Esta's brows drew together. "I'm not sure that's a good idea."

"It's probably a terrible idea," Harte told her. "But it's all I've been able to think about for *days*."

"Are you sure you weren't really thinking about *complications*?"

"I'd like to kiss you," he repeated, because there wasn't room for lies

LISA MAXWELL

between them any longer, especially not there, embracing as they were on the swirling dance floor.

Her pink tongue darted out, licking her crimson lips, a clear sign she was every bit as nervous as he was. Her eyes, the same liquid gold as her dress, were serious as they studied him. Unreadable. Finally, as the song was winding down, she spoke. "I can't promise I won't bite you again."

"I think it's well worth the risk." He pulled her closer, his hand at her waist, skimming over the silky softness of her dress, and drew her toward him.

He took his time about it, because he wanted her to understand that what was between them—what had *always* been between them—was something rare. It wasn't perfect, not by a long shot, but it was real and alive and maybe it was even a little dangerous as well.

Leaning toward her, Harte paused before his mouth touched hers, letting himself enjoy this stolen moment. Letting Esta want it as much as he did. He could detect the faintly floral scent of her soap. Then, with his free hand, he gently tipped her chin up, reveling in the shiver of anticipation he felt course through her, and pressed his mouth against hers.

Once again, they were on a dance floor, surrounded by music and moving bodies, but this was nothing like their first kiss. That had been a taking, and a surprise for both of them. That first kiss—and so many others, including the ones on the train—had been a battle of wills. Harte wanted this one to be different, so he started as soft as a question. He didn't linger too long. He didn't part her lips with his tongue or force himself upon her. He held himself back as he drank in the truth of their connection and the small moan that escaped from her lips. Then he released her.

As kisses went, it was positively chaste, and yet when he pulled back, Esta had a dazed look in her whiskey-colored eyes that he rather liked. He was fairly certain he was wearing one to match.

"That was—"

She didn't get to finish her sentence before they were interrupted.

"Mr. Darrigan?" Two large men were suddenly beside them. Bouncers, probably. But how could they possibly know his name?

Harte turned to them and gave the two men his best confused look. "I'm sorry, but you have the wrong fellow."

They took a step closer, and the larger of the two spoke again. "I don't think we do, Mr. Darrigan. You can come easylike, or we can make this hard. Either way, Mr. Torrio wants a word with you."

Harte's stomach dropped clear to his feet. "Mr. Torrio?" It couldn't be. It wasn't possible.

The only Torrio Harte knew was John Torrio—Johnny the Fox— who'd worked for Paul Kelly. It couldn't be that his past had found him, not there, in that strange future. Not when he'd been so close to everything he'd never realized he needed.

"If you don't remember him, I'm sure we can find a way to remind you," the smaller of the two said with a leering smirk. "If you'd come this way . . . Your doll should come along too."

"Oh, she's not mine," Harte said, glancing at Esta. "I only took a turn with her on the dance floor. I'm sure she'll want to get back to the good time she came for."

"Still . . ." The big man inched up behind Esta, making it clear that she wasn't getting out of this meeting. "Mr. Torrio would like to meet you both."

THE CHICAGO OUTFIT

1920—Chicago

E sta kept her expression aloof as Harte argued with the two men who'd cornered them. He was clearly trying to give her an out, but it wasn't working. She didn't have any plans to go, anyway. If these two goons wanted her to play the role of some flighty arm candy, she'd give them what they expected, at least until a better opportunity presented itself.

Looping her arm through Harte's, Esta slid closer. "I don't mind saying a quick hello to your friend," she said with a vacant, airy smile. "But then I want to dance again."

The larger of the two gave her a once-over. As his cold eyes traced her body from head to toe, Esta's skin crawled. It was possible she'd gone a *little* overboard on her look for the night—her bobbed hair lay in finger waves around her face, her lips had been lacquered in a deep red, and her eyes were ringed with kohl. Maybe the dress *was* a little much, but looking in the mirror earlier, Esta had been more than satisfied that Harte would swallow his own tongue when he saw her.

Luckily, the guy's perusal didn't last long, and he didn't show any real interest. He was more concerned with taking them to Torrio—whoever he was.

Even with the two men shoving them along, Esta was having a hard time shaking the memory of Harte's lips upon hers. For the last three days, she and Harte had existed in a kind of limbo. They'd plotted and planned and, all the while, they'd made sure to keep at least an arm's distance between each other. They had not spoken any more about the train—not about Harte's question about *consequences* or his terrible forced proposal, if you could even call it that. And they definitely didn't talk about the fact that neither of them were willing to let the other sacrifice themselves. It seemed that they'd come to an agreement—they would do everything in their power to get the Book back from Jack, and they would hope against hope that it held some solution. And if it didn't? Or if they couldn't manage to retrieve it? Well, those were scenarios that they didn't need to argue about. *Not yet.*

Still, hours and days of Harte being just out of reach had been the worst kind of torture. Esta might have wanted to get his attention with her outfit that night, but the kiss had still been a surprise, and the effect of it even more so. She'd seen the hunger in his expression, and so she hadn't expected softness, but somehow, the teasing of his lips was exactly what she'd needed. It had felt like a balm against the frustration from the past couple of days. But the appearance of the two brutish-looking bouncers had quickly changed things.

It didn't help that the men looked like every gangster from every bad mafia movie she'd ever seen. They were big, broad guys dressed in sharp suits with noses that had been broken at some point. Their dark hair was slicked back from faces too rough to ever be considered handsome, but they moved through the Green Mill like they owned it.

"Who's Torrio?" Esta asked Harte, making sure to keep her voice too soft for the bruisers to hear her.

"He was one of Paul Kelly's guys back in New York."

"Paul Kelly? As in, the head of the Five Pointers?" Esta asked, frowning. Harte nodded.

Esta hadn't met Kelly, but she knew about him. The Five Pointers were one of the most famous gangs in the city. Once they'd even been backed by Tammany Hall. "I don't think Kelly's behind this," she told him, trying to remember any other details from the history that had been drilled into her by Professor Lachlan. "Paul Kelly's power faded when the bootleggers took over."

"You make it sound like that's bad news." Harte glanced at her, a question in his eyes.

"The thing is, what's interesting about the Five Pointers isn't the Five Pointers themselves. It's what came after. They recruited and trained gangsters who grew to become even more powerful and vicious than Paul Kelly ever was. People like Al Capone."

Harte shook his head. Of course he wouldn't know the name. In 1902, Capone was still two decades away from being a player. But now?

"Capone's probably the most famous bootlegger and gangster of the twentieth century . . . and he was based in Chicago."

By then they'd been escorted inside, through the darkened bar to the back corner, where a table of men sat in a plush velvet booth that had clearly been selected so they had a view of the entire room. Esta recognized only one of the three—a man with hooded eyes, swarthy skin, a wide nose and mouth, and three long horizontal scars that cut across the left side of his face. *Al Capone.* He was younger than most pictures she'd ever seen of him—maybe around twenty. Even this young, he wasn't a handsome man. His face hadn't quite filled out the way it would in his later years, and his dark hair hadn't receded yet from his round face. From his position at the table, he was clearly not the one in charge. Not yet.

The person who *was* in charge was seated at the center of the table, his back to a corner. He was an older man in his midforties. It had to be John Torrio.

Unlike Capone, Torrio didn't have the deep olive skin of the Sicilian mobsters who would take over in the popular imagination. He was smaller, or he seemed to be next to his young protégé, with a narrow face and small eyes that turned down at the corners. There was something about Torrio that reminded Esta of a rat or some other member of the rodent family. Everything about him, but especially his confidence, seemed dangerous.

When she hesitated to approach the table, one of the bouncers escorting them took her by the arm. She tried to pull away from him—she probably could have, if she'd wanted to make a scene—but his grip was too secure.

The other bouncer pushed Harte forward, until he was squarely in front of the booth that held the trio of men.

"Harte Darrigan," the man in the middle of the booth said, his eyes narrowing even more as he took them in. "I've heard of putting people on ice, but Jesus Christ, you haven't aged a day."

QUITE A PREDICAMENT

1920—Chicago

Harte could almost see the teenager he'd once run with in the older man sitting at the table in front of him. Same square face, same beady little eyes. But the skin of Torrio's neck had grown loose, and his hair had turned a dull gray. If he hadn't been expecting Torrio, Harte would have likely looked right past this older man—clearly, he *had* walked right past him without noticing already.

Still, when Torrio spoke, Harte was struck by how he hadn't really changed all that much. Worse, Torrio was pointing out a significant issue—Harte hadn't aged a day in comparison.

The larger guy next to Torrio, the one with the scars on his cheek, looked more interested in his drink than the newcomers his boss was talking to. "You really knew this guy back in the old days, Johnny?"

Torrio's gaze slid to the scar-faced guy next to him before returning to Harte. "Oh yeah. Darrigan and I go *way* back."

"It's been a long time, Johnny," Harte said, without so much as blinking. He wasn't about to let Torrio see exactly how nervous he was. He needed to get Esta out of there, and preferably as quickly as possible. "You still working for Paul Kelly?"

"I took care of Kelly years ago," Torrio said with a satisfied smirk. "Left New York for greener pastures not long after. This here is my club, and Chicago's my city." His expression turned even sharper. "Anything happens in my city, I know about it. So I gotta ask—what are you doing here, Darrigan?"

"I'm only here to take in the sights," Harte said easily, even as his skin crawled with apprehension. "I'd appreciate it if your guy there took his hands off the girl."

Torrio nudged the guy next to him. "You hear him? He's talking like he's in some kind of position to issue orders." The two guys gave Torrio questioning looks, but then Torrio's amusement drained away. "You think I'm dumb enough to believe that story? I ain't some easy mark, Darrigan. Like I don't know that you showing up here looking like some kind of ghost don't mean problems." His eyes narrowed. "You got one chance to tell me the truth—Why did Lorcan send you?"

"Lorcan?" Harte was too thrown off to hide the confusion he felt at hearing Nibsy's last name come from John Torrio's mouth. He only barely managed to pull himself together in the next breath. "I don't know any Lorcan," Harte lied. He didn't risk glancing at Esta, but he knew she must have noticed the name as well.

"Bullshit," Torrio spat. "You think I don't know what's what? You show up here, not even aged a day, and try to tell me it's not some kind of hocus-pocus from Lorcan? What does he want this time? A bigger cut? Well, he's sure as shit not getting any more from me. He sits safe in his little fortress back in New York and issues orders like I don't know when he's trying to pull my strings. James Lorcan might think that just because he's given me some good tips, he can keep me on a leash like some kind of pet, but you can tell him those days are done, you hear? You tell him I don't need his information anymore. I've been doing fine on my own. Or maybe I'll tell him myself," he said, his beady eyes narrowing, "once I get rid of you."

"Johnny, you got it all wrong," Harte said, holding up his hands in surrender. "I don't know any Lorcan, and I certainly don't work for him. I'm not here to cause you any trouble."

"I don't believe that for a second." Torrio studied Harte as though he could read the lie simply by looking at him. "But maybe we should find out for sure." He glanced at the two large security guys who'd ushered Harte and Esta to his table. "Take these two down to the tunnels and keep an eye on them. And have Mikey bring me the house phone. I have a call to make."

Harte heard Esta's gasp and turned to see the bruiser who had her by the arm already dragging her away. She was struggling against the guy, but he seemed to be able to counter every move she made.

"Enough," the other one said, pulling a dark pistol on Harte. "Tell the hellcat there to stop, or you both get it," he told Harte.

Esta froze at the bouncer's threat, and her kohl-rimmed eyes went wide when she saw the gun pointing at Harte.

"It's fine," Harte told her, trying to keep it together. But his blood felt hot from seeing the other man's hands digging into the bare skin of Esta's arm. He hated knowing that there was no way he could fight these men—not in the shape he was in, weak as he still felt, and definitely not with a gun pointing directly at his gut. "This is nothing but a big misunderstanding. Johnny here is going to make a call, and he'll see that we don't know any Lorcan."

Esta's jaw had gone tight, and he could see the fury that shimmered in her eyes—*and* the fear that shadowed them. If Torrio made that call, Nibsy would know exactly where—and *when*—they were.

"Let's go." The bruiser who had Harte shoved him toward the bar. "You too, doll. And don't try nothing."

If Harte hadn't taken the Quellant, maybe they could have escaped. A simple touch, a silent command, and they would have been free. It would have been worth the risk Seshat posed to get Esta away from John Torrio and his men. As it was, though, Harte's affinity lay far beyond his reach. Still, even with the mess they had fallen into, he couldn't really bring himself to regret taking it. Not when he still remembered how Esta had softened against him when he'd kissed her a few minutes before.

Maybe she had been right, back on the train. Maybe all they'd ever had was the moment in front of them. Harte had used that moment on the dance floor well, and now he would deal with the one they currently faced. Somehow.

When they reached the bar, the bartender gave them a small nod, and the guys led them around a corner into what looked like a storeroom. There was a heavy metal door in the back wall and, beyond it, a staircase. The guy who had ahold of Esta was already dragging her down the steps, while the one with the gun kept watch on Harte up top.

Harte had barely started descending the steps himself, when a commotion erupted in the room behind them. Men were shouting, and then came a series of loud crashes that sounded like bottles breaking. The bouncer who had Esta glanced back, but he seemed barely concerned as he dragged her.

The one who had Harte nudged him forward with the butt of the gun. "Let's go, unless you want to deal with the Feds."

At the bottom of the steps, the hall stretched into a dark tunnel that ran the length of the building. Esta had already been shoved through a narrow door as the other bouncer pushed Harte forward until he could see that they were being placed in a closet-size cell, with a dirt floor and damp brick walls. The door was heavy and looked to be made out of metal rather than wood. With the gun pressed close to his spine, Harte didn't have any choice but to join Esta inside.

He eyed the lock as he went and was relieved to see it wasn't anything complicated enough to keep them for long. Still, the sound of the heavy door closing shuddered through him as the two bouncers locked him and Esta into the dark, windowless prison.

Harte felt Esta slide closer, her hand finding his in the pitch-darkness.

"Are you okay?" she asked.

"Fine. You?"

"I'll be better when we get out of here," Esta told him. She released his hand, and then he heard her begin to rustle through her beaded evening bag.

"You don't happen to have a hairpin or something in there, do you?" he asked. "For the lock?"

"I have something better." A second later the *skritch* of a match sounded, and Esta held the flame up to show Harte the slim bronze pick they'd used in the bank vault. "Do you want to do the honors, or should I?"

"You're a wonder, you know that?" he mused, taking the pick from her as the flame of the match reached her fingertips.

Esta cursed and dropped the match to the ground, where it went dark. "I'd be more of a wonder if I had a flashlight," she grumbled.

He couldn't see her, but he could hear the frustration—and the nervousness—in her voice. Esta hated dark, tight places, probably the result of being locked in a closet by Nibsy when she was a toddler.

Luckily, it had been a long time since Harte had needed light to pick a lock. Years of practice in boxes and safes and cases of water had made him an expert in breaking any lock blind. This one was no exception. He could sense Esta close by him as he worked the pick into the lock, feeling for the pins inside the mechanism to give way. She wasn't crowding him, but in the darkness, that didn't matter. She could have been ten feet away; the lightless space made it feel like she was right there, next to him. The scent of her was a distraction, and the warmth of her both steadied him and made his nerves jangle.

"Esta . . ." He paused, not exactly knowing what he wanted to say. If he wanted her to be closer or to step back so that he could think.

She went very still.

"On the train . . ." He paused, feeling more than ridiculous, but it needed to be said. She had to understand. "You have to know—"

"It's fine," Esta told him, her clipped voice coming to him through the pitch-blackness.

"It absolutely isn't," he said. He stopped what he was doing and reached for her hand, feeling how it shook slightly—from the cold of the room or from nerves, he didn't know. "I was an idiot."

"You were," she said, and without being able to see her face, he could not sense what she was thinking. "But that isn't exactly a new development."

Harte barked out a surprised, grateful laugh, and as he moved closer,

Esta went suddenly still, as though she was waiting to see what would happen next. He paused, giving her room and time and an escape, if she needed one.

She was *so* close, and even without Seshat's constant prowling, Harte felt unsteady. He knew that if he kissed her, he would not want to stop.

"Are you going to take care of the lock, or do you need me to do it?" Esta asked finally. Her voice was breathy, and Harte understood he hadn't been alone in his desire, but it was also enough to shake him back to the moment at hand and to force him to focus.

"I can handle it," he said evenly, trying not to feel too disappointed. He worked carefully, letting the vibrations and the tension on the pick guide him, wishing Esta's feelings were as easy to unlock as the bit of metal beneath his hand.

He hadn't quite managed to release the lock when an explosion sounded on the other side of the door. Even with the thickness of the metal, Harte could hear the blast and feel the vibrations. It was enough to make him lose his concentration, and all the progress he'd made on the lock. Then a barrage of gunfire erupted, a muted *rat-a-tat-tat* that seemed impossibly fast, followed by more shouting. And then . . . silence.

Esta grabbed his arm. "What's going on out there?"

"I'm not sure, but maybe if we're lucky, it'll have taken care of Torrio for us," he told her, knowing that they couldn't possibly be *that* lucky. More likely, whatever was on the other side of the door would be another problem . . . and most likely a well-armed one.

For what seemed like an endless stretch of time, they stood together, Esta's hand on his arm, and they waited. Listening. They were concentrating so hard on trying to hear the danger that might be coming for them that they both jumped when a narrow window slid open in the door. The scent of gunpowder drifted in through the bright slash in the darkness. Then a set of mismatched eyes—one brown, one green—appeared in the window.

"Well, well . . . looks like the two of you have found yourselves in quite the predicament," a familiar voice said right before the lock clicked and the door swung open. On the other side, the hallway of the tunnel was filled with an unnatural fog that glowed with a bright lavender-and-yellow swirl, and Jericho Northwood stood grinning at the two of them, looking a few decades older and every bit as ornery as he ever had.

THE CITY'S SHADOWS

T he sounds of bells and sirens were already echoing through the city, fueling the anticipation and heating the blood in James Lorcan's veins. The Order knew for sure now that they were under attack, but James' plan was only beginning to unfold.

In the back of the open horse cart, Viola still looked a little stunned from what had happened a few minutes before. She'd watched her brother be carted off in a Black Maria, but James knew that she understood that she *still* wasn't free—not if she crossed James when he held the lives of her friends in his hands. She was clinging to the side of the cart's bed, trying to stay upright as they careered through the city. Off-balance, literally and figuratively, just as James preferred her.

In the distance, James heard the keening whine of a locomotive's whistle and the noise of a city stirring to find itself awash in confusion. *Finally*, it was beginning. As Werner urged the poor, bedraggled mare to move faster, only James himself knew how it was all destined to end.

Mooch and a few others from the Devil's Own rode cramped in the bed of the cart along with Viola. James had selected them each by hand—some for their particular abilities, and some, like Mooch, that he preferred to keep close. When the redhead exchanged an uneasy glance with Viola, his pale skin flushed so quickly and easily that James knew his suspicions had been right. There was something between the two—a connection had likely facilitated Viola's little bout of larceny and the disappearance of Dolph's journal. James figured that if the two were so happy to work together, they could die together as well.

The ride down Twenty-Third Street took only a handful of minutes, but with the sun ever lower in the sky, it might as well have been hours. Then, as the sun drew closer to the horizon, something odd began to happen. As the sky shifted closer to twilight, the streets began to light with a strange, almost ethereal glow. The drab red brick of buildings brightened in the odd light, and the puddles of water and troughs along the road turned to molten pots of gold. The city's shadows all stretched east, like nature itself was pointing their way. Urging them on.

It was a startling thing to see the road before them bathed in such a light, especially in a city where the streets were usually at least partially shaded by the ever-growing buildings that lined them. But for James, it was a sign that he'd been right. His plan would work. The Aether vibrated, dancing around him, and the sun warmed his skin as it lit their wagon in the eerie light.

"The Golden Hour," Viola murmured, lifting her hand as though she could catch the sunbeams and the power they supposedly held. Her drab, olive-toned skin suddenly looked almost bronze in the sun.

"It's beginning," James agreed. He looked back to see the sun descending right down the center of Twenty-Third Street. The fiery haze of the shimmering orb was framed perfectly by the buildings as it sank toward the river. It was an odd sight, and it might have even been beautiful if James had the time to appreciate beauty. As it was, they were racing the sun, and every minute was one fewer they had to stop the Order from securing the artifact. Because if the Order's delivery arrived before they did . . .

Block after block, the cart rattled over trolley tracks and uneven cobbles until finally the street emptied into the wide area in front of the wedge-shaped tower, but when they finally arrived, something was already happening. Police wagons stood in the plow-shaped plaza in front of the building. They were surrounding another plain wagon, and some of the dark-suited officers were trading fire with someone in the building on the other side of Fifth Avenue, while others were already tussling with men on the ground.

"Those are Five Pointers," Viola told him. "My brother's men."

"I'm aware," James said, satisfied with the way the Aether swirled around him. "It looks like Johnny the Fox hasn't turned into a rat. He's kept his promises."

"You knew the wagon would be here?" Viola asked, confusion swimming in her violet eyes.

"You've played three-card monte, haven't you, Viola?" Nibsy asked, faintly amused by her shock. "The shuffling of the cards is never anything more than a distraction. The money card is always already in the dealer's hand. The second we knew about the extra ships, I knew the goods wouldn't be on them."

"But if you knew there was nothing in the other wagons . . ." Viola frowned, finally piecing things together.

Too late, James thought. *Always too late.*

"Do you mean that Cela's brother and the rest, they are risking themselves for *nothing?*"

Nibsy shrugged, unbothered by her sudden worry. "They're doing what they're supposed to be doing—providing a necessary diversion so the Order doesn't realize we've caught on to their little game."

"And what of the Devil's Own?" she asked, clearly bristling. "Have you risked their lives as well?"

Nibsy turned to her then. He made sure that his gaze was unyielding. "The Devil's Own belong to me now, Viola. They do what *I* say."

"And if they're caught by the police, what then?" Viola pressed. "If they're killed?"

"Life and death." Nibsy tilted his head, trying to conceal his amusement as he considered her dismay. "Isn't that what our dear friend Dolph used to say? *Life and death.* Two sides of the same coin. It's what they all signed up for when they took his mark." Then he allowed his mouth to curve as Viola blanched, the color draining magnificently from her face.

"I never expected you, of all people, to be so squeamish about something so banal as a few deaths. People die every day in the Bowery. You *know* that. You've taken more than a few of those lives yourself."

One of the Five Pointers broke through the ranks of police suddenly, drawing everyone's attention. The man charged toward the back of the plain, waiting wagon, but the instant he grabbed hold of the rear door, strange markings on the wagon were illuminated, as though by electricity, and the man began to scream. The Aether trembled as the Five Pointer's face contorted in agony, but the man didn't release his hold.

Werner and Mooch, even Viola, turned away, repulsed by the sight, but Nibsy watched with a cool detachment.

"What the hell's happening to him?" Mooch asked, fear strangling his words.

"I told you the wagons would be protected," James said.

"But you never said they would do *that*," Werner argued.

"Didn't I?" James asked, masking his amusement.

"Any one of us could've been killed," Werner said, frowning.

"Not unless you had disobeyed my orders," James told him. He watched with some satisfaction as the Five Pointer continued to writhe and scream.

If Torrio had thought to cut James out, he'd thought wrong.

"You kept this information from me as well," Viola huffed, still visibly shaken by the sight.

He turned to her. "No one was supposed to touch the wagons, only to redirect them. Anyone who tried to change our agreed-upon plan and attempted to board one of the wagons would have deserved whatever happened to them," he said, making his voice cold as he eyed her. "But then, I'm confident in the loyalty of the Devil's Own. It's the other parties involved that I didn't trust."

"You still should have told me," she charged.

He shrugged. "There was no reason to."

Temper flashed in Viola's eyes. "You said we were partners."

"No," James told her. "I said you should come back to the Devil's

Own, that you should join *me*. I *never* said we would be equals."

Growing bored with Viola's display of temper—and with the conversation—James directed Werner to pull the cart into the park across from the building, far enough from the skirmish to be out of range and out of sight.

He turned his attention to Logan. "Is it there?"

"The wagon's already empty," the boy told him.

"How can he know this?" Viola demanded, as though she had any right to an answer.

"It's his job to know," James told her as he considered the building. "The Delphi's Tear will already be inside, then." *Unfortunate, but not catastrophic.* Not when he had yet another ace to play.

"Then it's impossible," Viola said, sounding far less devastated than she perhaps should have. But then, did she really believe he wouldn't see through her duplicity?

James glanced at her over his spectacles, and this time he did not bother to affect any look of innocence. "I will consider sparing the lives of your friends if you tell me everything you know about what waits for us inside that building. *Everything* Theo Barclay learned about the layout of the Order's new headquarters and what we might find inside."

Viola stared at him, disbelief coloring her cheeks. Fear, too, if he wasn't mistaken.

"Did you truly think I wouldn't find out that you had someone on the inside, Viola?" he asked, bored with her continued act. "Did you really think I wasn't aware you were trying to set your brother and me at odds with each other? You were never actually interested in coming back to the Devil's Own or pledging any *real* loyalty to me. I knew that for sure when I discovered that Dolph's journal had gone missing from my rooms a few weeks ago."

"You mean *Dolph's* rooms," she told him, confusion turning to anger. "You stole them from him, just as you stole his cane. As you stole his *life*."

"It was your brother's Five Pointers who took Dolph's life," James lied.

LISA MAXWELL

"I simply stepped in to lead the Devil's Own when no one else would, including *you*."

"Lies," Viola seethed, and James felt a pain course through his chest. "I know what you did. It was *you* who murdered Dolph, not any Five Pointer. I should kill you now."

James ignored Werner's and Mooch's sudden interest. "Where did you get that information, Viola?" He tilted his head to one side, watching the emotions flicker across her face. "Let me guess. You believed tales whispered to you by Jianyu—though why you would trust him, I can't imagine. Not after what he did to Tilly."

"You have no business speaking her name," Viola snarled.

The tightness in his chest increased, and James couldn't repress his grimace. Logan was already moving to attack, but even with the pain near his heart, James held a hand up to stay him. Let Viola dig herself a deeper grave.

As the boys in the cart paused, waiting for his order, James clenched the head of the cane and tried to gather his strength. He felt the power beneath it. In the past weeks he'd grown so close to touching the promise of that power, and now he focused all that he was into it. He was gratified to hear Viola suck in a sharp breath, and he glanced up to see the confusion—the fear—in her eyes. He knew what had caused it, because he felt it himself, the echo of power in the mark he wore on his own skin. From the way the others shifted uneasily, he could tell they felt it as well. Which was fine. It would serve as a warning to all—that he was more than he seemed. That he should not be crossed.

"Have a *care*, Viola," James said, repeating his warning from a little while before through gritted teeth. "Your friends' lives still hang in the balance, and Torrio knows *exactly* how underhanded you can be. If I don't send the order to stop him, your friends will die."

He felt the pressure in his chest recede.

"Much better," he said, adjusting his grip on Dolph's cane. He held his focus on the marks for a few seconds longer, to show her he could, before he released them. "I only ever agreed to take you back because I knew you could provide additional information about what was inside that building. It seems my premonition was correct. You'll give me that information, and you'll give it now."

"It won't do you any good," Viola told him. "If the artifact is already inside, it will be impossible to take it back out."

Nibsy gave her a pitying look. "Come now, Viola. Nothing's ever impossible, especially not when your friends' lives are on the line." He saw her realization when it struck. She had made a play, and now she understood her loss. "I'm sure you'll figure out some way to retrieve the artifact. After all, sunset won't wait. And neither will my ring."

AN EXPECTED INTERRUPTION

After finishing with Theo Barclay, Jack Grew took the stairs down from the Library of Life room to the chambers below, whistling as he went. It was a strange little tune, and he realized as he reached the sixteenth floor that he couldn't recall where he'd heard it. Actually, he couldn't recall having *ever* heard it, except maybe in dreams, but Jack dismissed that idea at once. It didn't matter where he'd picked up the song. Things were going his way, and by the time night dropped her veil over the city, the Delphi's Tear would be his, and Theo Barclay would be no more.

The Order's ceremony to consecrate the top five floors of the Flatiron Building as their new headquarters was to be held in the more public chambers on the sixteenth floor. Here, a larger portion of the membership could be in attendance, as the upper floors were reserved for the wealthiest and most powerful members.

Like the library above, the more public sanctuary was also located at the front of the building so the members could take in the grandeur of the city. To enter, members were required to navigate a series of antechambers, each fortified with their own protections. Between each, narrow winding turns had been designed to disorient and confuse, so that by the time the member stepped into the space, he would immediately be overtaken by the view. Centered in front of the bank of windows was an angular altar. It had been carved from a single enormous piece of lapis lazuli, and the setting sun illuminated it, turning the altar as brilliant as the summer sky.

Jack entered behind a few of the other members, appreciating the warm glow of the phosphorus lamps that hung from gilded chains around the edges of the room and the ornate designs etched into the walls. With its windows, the entire space was bathed in the ethereal light of the Golden Hour. To the west, the sun had nearly reached the water. It would be only a little while longer now. Until the sun dipped below the horizon, Jack would enjoy the pageantry that was to come. And after . . . he would make his move.

Before the altar stood five women clad only in silken sarongs. Their bare skin had been painted in gold from head to toe, which made their bodies glisten in the strange light. Around each of their necks, a single large crystal dangled from a golden chain. Each pendant had been cut to symbolize one digit of the Philosopher's Hand: the key, the crown, the lantern, the star, and the moon. The elements necessary to transmute existence. The women were living statues; they barely blinked, even when the members inched forward to take a closer look. They'd been one of Jack's better ideas for the ceremony, but his best was yet to come.

While the other members swooned over the new surroundings, Jack felt nothing but satisfaction. Soon the Delphi's Tear would be his, and with it the ability to finally complete his machine. He would show the Order how wrong they had been to deny him for so long. He would show the Inner Circle the path down which their destiny must lead.

Jack took a seat close to the edge of the room as the lights went dim and the ceremony began. In the back of the chamber, a door opened that had not seemed to be there a moment before. It was a brilliant bit of illusion, and the men around Jack murmured appreciatively as four members of the Inner Circle made their way toward the altar. When they reached the front, they formed a line, and then one stepped forward and began to speak about the illustrious history of the Order of Ortus Aurea.

Jack barely paid attention to the old man's droning. What did he care about the past, when the future stretched in all its brilliant possibilities on the far horizon? On and on the speech went, and all the while Jack pictured what would come next and prepared himself. The old man prattled on for what seemed like an eternity, until finally bells could be heard from somewhere within the walls and the door at the back of the room opened once more.

This time it was the High Princept who appeared. He was flanked by two other men, each draped in white linen and wearing masks that obscured their identities. When the three reached the blue altar, the two masked men unrolled a scroll and held the wide swath of it upright, so the Princept could read an incantation. He invoked the gods and the angels, and he beseeched them to protect this place that would be a sanctuary for years to come. When he was finished, the masked men withdrew the scroll, and as one, the members in attendance stood and applauded.

Jack played his part, rising and clapping along with the rest. He would let them enjoy their moment, because he knew that his own plan was already unfolding.

In the preceding weeks, he'd worked long and hard to prepare for this night. He'd been forced to humble himself, bowing and pretending subservience, when he knew that the old men of the Inner Circle were nothing more than a past that hadn't realized it was over. In the end they'd trusted Jack enough to use him, but they hadn't allowed him to attend the ceremony to install the artifact into the Mysterium earlier that day. They said it was because he wasn't officially part of the Inner Circle—not yet. But Jack understood an excuse when he heard one. They were still holding him at arm's length.

No longer. The High Princept's arrival signaled that the time was finally at hand. He checked his watch and saw there were still a few minutes until the sun dipped farther than six degrees below the horizon, minutes during which the Order still would believe themselves to be protected by the power of the Golden Hour. But in those remaining minutes, they would find out how vulnerable they truly were.

An alarm sounded in the outer chamber, and Jack frowned down at his watch. It was a few minutes earlier than he'd planned, perhaps, but close enough. As the members began murmuring at the sudden interruption, the High Princept stood to reassure them.

"Gentlemen, we expected no less than an attack this evening, but please. Settle yourselves. Every precaution has been taken," he assured the room. "Every measure of possible protection has been put into place for this very eventuality, and the maggots who would try to disturb us this evening will find themselves sorry. As we sit here, safe in the sanctuary of our own making, the building is turning itself on our intruders."

As if on command, heavy shutters rolled down over the windows, leaving the entire sanctuary bathed only in the glow of the phosphorus lamps. It was exactly as Jack had hoped: The lamps cast enough light to throw the flickering shadows that would allow him to move through the crowd without being noticed.

"All of the chambers beyond this one will lock, making entrance or exit impossible," the Princept continued. "Even now security measures are being activated that will snuff out the threat any intruders might pose as easily as a candle."

The Princept didn't bother to tell the rest of the members that it had been Jack who had set up the entire system, which was, he supposed, probably for the best. It was unlikely any of the members would realize that the protections Jack had designed also contained an extra feature for this particular night: It would release a series of alchemical reactions that would appear to be an attack. The effect would doubtlessly cause enough confusion to keep the members of the Order distracted. In the end, it would seem that Jack's security system had worked and the building had been defended. In reality, the attack would be nothing more than smoke and mirrors. He'd learned that bit from Darrigan, back when he'd believed the magician had some real connection to the powers of the occult. The attack was nothing but misdirection—a diversion intended to keep the Order from realizing what was *actually* happening.

"As long as everyone is accounted for," the Princept called, "we are all safe here until the danger passes."

Jack waited, keeping his expression even as the men around him began looking over one another, counting among their ranks. He waited long enough to be sure that the room was already buzzing with confusion, and then he called out. "Barclay's missing! He was right here . . . but now he's gone."

It didn't matter that Barclay had never been there to begin with. The men around him reacted exactly as Jack had predicted they would. With confusion and then suspicion . . . and then, predictably, with *anger*.

Smiling to himself as the mood of the room shifted, Jack ducked behind a tapestry, depressed a lever hidden there, and let himself out into the hallway. The rest of the members would whip themselves into a fit while Jack retrieved the ring. In a matter of minutes, he would return to the sanctuary below, undetected, and when the Order discovered that the artifact was missing, Barclay would look like the culprit. The poor, desperate, *dead* culprit.

TIMES CHANGE

1920—Chicago

J ericho Northwood and his crew had only come to the Green Mill that night for the Nitewein that John Torrio and his lot sold to lure Mageus into the establishment. He hadn't expected to find a couple of familiar faces in addition. Now he had to figure out what he was going to do with them.

In truth, North had never expected to see hide nor hair of Esta Filosik, much less Harte Darrigan, again. He'd only expected that one day, when he was least expecting it, the life he had would simply disappear. He'd turned in each night thanking his lucky stars for the gift of one more day to be the man he was, living the life he had, and each morning he'd wake up with the grateful wonder that it was all still there, his life still intact and his family still whole and real in his arms. But now Esta was back, and with her, the threat she posed to him—to his life and to everything he'd built and everyone he loved.

He knew what Maggie would say. *Some things are destined,* his wife would tell him with that soft smile she always wore when she was somewhere between amused and exasperated. *There's no way around the two of us,* she'd say as she braided their youngest girl's hair. His Maggie had an absolute faith in the inevitability of the two of them and the little family they'd built for themselves, a belief that nothing—not time, nor magic—could shake. *Some things are meant to be.*

North didn't know that he quite agreed. He knew exactly how possible it was to change the course of things. Maggie could keep her faith, but North wasn't willing to chance everything he was and everything they'd built to the whimsy of fate. Not that he had any clue how to fight against something as slippery as destiny or as unyielding as time.

It didn't help any that the fear of what Esta could do to his life had only grown with each addition to his family. Their children were a spot of light in North's life, and he didn't trust fate to keep their lights aglow. But then, he had to admit that fate—fickle though she might be—had somehow seemed to smile on him far more than he'd ever deserved. He'd lost everything and then found Maggie. They'd made terrible mistakes with the Antistasi, and somehow still managed to make it through to the other side. Their life together, their children—if those were all gifts of fate, Jericho Northwood was damn lucky. Now, it seemed, fate had delivered Esta Filosik to him once more, but he wasn't sure what that meant.

"This way," North directed, leading the way through the eerie fog that filled the tunnel. "It'd be an awful big help if the two of you would each grab a case." He pointed to the stack of wooden crates that his guys were already carting out of the tunnels. "We don't have much time before the real agents show up."

Thankfully, Esta and Harte didn't argue or give him any trouble. Even dressed in some kind of slippery-looking scrap of a thing, Esta grabbed a crate and followed the line of men to the truck they'd parked out back. Once the crates of Nitewein were loaded up, North noticed Esta and Harte trading meaningful glances. Sirens were already singing in the distance.

North knew exactly what they were thinking, but he wasn't about to let them go so fast, not when he was still considering what he should do about them. "Why don't you hop on in? We can give you a lift."

"Oh, I think we can find our own way back," Harte said, and then offered his hand along with his thanks.

North didn't take the outstretched hand. "I wasn't really asking." He narrowed his eyes a bit, still considering his options if they didn't comply. There wasn't any way he was letting these two get away from him, not without figuring out what they were up to. "I think we ought to catch up a bit, don't you?" He let his gaze linger on Esta, a clear, if unspoken, challenge.

After a couple of seconds, she relented. "We *are* old friends, after all," she told Harte without even so much as blinking.

Old friends . . . North couldn't help but laugh, especially since they both looked like a couple of kids. Hell, it was hard to believe he'd ever been that young himself, even if he hadn't been all that much older the last time he'd seen the two of them. But their appearance—the smooth skin of their faces, devoid of the lines that already mapped his own life's joys and frustrations—was confirmation that Esta could do exactly what she'd threatened years ago in Denver. The question was whether North would give her that chance.

Reluctantly, Harte helped Esta up into the back of the truck, and then he hopped up himself. North followed, closing the rolling door behind them, then made his way between the crates that had been stacked along each side of the truck's bed and knocked a couple of times on the front wall. A second later, a window opened.

"Are we all set?" the driver, Floyd, asked.

"Let's get going," North told him, barely getting the words out before the truck was lurching into gear. "You okay up there, Rett?" North asked the passenger, who turned to look at him with familiar mismatched eyes. Floyd was one of the local guys who was helping out on the run, but Everett was his and Maggie's oldest boy.

Maggie had about wanted to skin North alive for taking Everett on this particular job. She still saw the boy as the fat, freckled toddler he'd once been, never mind that Everett was taller than North these days. He supposed it was a mother's prerogative to see the babe she'd once held in her arms, but a father understood when his boy was becoming a man. And he understood that men needed something more than their mother's apron strings. Everett spent too much time sitting in corners reading until his eyes crossed or tinkering at Maggie's side, and not enough time out in the world, as far as North was concerned.

Not that Maggie was wrong to have her worries. The jobs they did were always dangerous—always had been—and they usually did come with some complication or another. Right then, Chicago was riskier than usual, what with the Republican Convention in town. But of all the complications he could have worried about or prepared for, North hadn't expected this one.

Esta was studying the two of them, and North could practically feel her thinking. "He's yours," she said softly.

"He is," North said, beaming at his son with a pride he never bothered to repress. The boy shook his head in response, rolling his eyes a little like he was tired of the attention.

"Then Maggie . . ." Esta didn't finish, and North suspected that he understood why. Every time he thought of that night in Denver, his throat got a little tight, and he felt the fear of losing his girl all over again. It didn't matter that she was as hale and hearty now as she ever had been.

"Maggie came through okay," he told Esta. "The doctor George took us to saved her life."

"I'm glad to hear that," Esta told him, and North thought she might have even meant it. "I've been thinking about her these last few weeks . . . wondering."

Weeks? It was almost impossible to comprehend, considering that it had been years upon years for North.

"Cordelia was such a good shot," Esta said.

"Thankfully, the doctor was better. But you're right. Cordelia was good—too good. Maggie uses a chair now to get around." He couldn't stop the smile that came when he thought of his wife. "Not that it's slowed her down one bit."

"Then you've been happy?" Esta asked with a hopeful note.

"As much as anyone can be, I suspect," he told her. "I take it you never made it back?" He kept his words vague, but from the tightening of her lips, North knew Esta understood. He didn't miss the way Harte tensed at the question either.

Esta shook her head a little. "No. Not yet."

"But you will."

She didn't immediately respond.

"We have four kids," North told her. "Everett here's the oldest, then we got the twins, and little Ruthie is the youngest." He met her eyes, daring her to look away. Daring her to face what it meant if she carried through with her plan and took those lives from him.

"This lady knows Mama?" Everett asked, unaware of the tension in the back of the truck.

"I met your mother back in St. Louis," Esta confirmed. "Your father, too. We worked together for a while."

"That was years ago," North said. The last thing he needed was Everett getting some idea in his head that Esta was harmless. "Back before Denver."

From the way Everett's mouth went tight, North knew the boy understood his meaning.

"I'm glad to see that the two of you made a good life for yourselves," Esta said.

"We do okay," North said. "But that's mostly to do with Maggie. Once she healed up, she was a woman on a mission. News traveled fast about what happened, and it didn't take all that long for Maggie to wrestle control away from that Professor fellow. Especially since he was trapped behind the Brink."

"Maggie leads the Antistasi now?" Esta asked, and there was a note of something North couldn't decipher in her voice.

"No one person leads them anymore," North corrected. "Maggie saw what happened with Ruth and with the Professor. Even if she could have stepped up, she didn't think any one person should have that much power. Still doesn't. The Antistasi have gone back to being what they always were supposed to be—a loosely organized group of like-minded individuals. We still take action when it's warranted. Like tonight at the Green Mill."

"Because Torrio is working with the Professor?" Esta asked.

North was suddenly glad for the darkness of the truck. They'd been trying to figure out what Torrio and the rest of the Chicago Outfit had wanted with Mageus in the city for some time, but now that the words were out of Esta's mouth, the pieces came together. It was another of the Professor's ploys to wrestle back control.

"Actually, we were there for the Nitewein," he explained. "The Chicago Outfit tends to use more opium in theirs, which gets people hooked a lot faster. In the last few months, they've started using it to blackmail any Mageus who are unlucky enough to get caught up with them. We weren't aware of Torrio's connections," he admitted. "But that makes a helluva lot of sense, especially considering what the Outfit has forced people to do with their affinities."

"*Good* people," Everett added. "And they end up taking the fall when things go sideways, like they always do."

"What will you do with the Nitewein you've taken?" Harte asked.

"Probably we should destroy it," North admitted. "But I'm not one of the teetotalers who want to tell other people how to live their lives. It ain't exactly fair that Sundren get to buy their bootleg liquor and drown their troubles in relative safety but we don't. There're plenty who use the Nitewein to help them handle the effects of affinities they can't otherwise use." He paused, wondering how much the two of them knew . . . how much they'd missed. "It's gotten a lot worse, you know. The Defense Against Magic Act has only been strengthened these past years with Prohibition."

"It's going to get even worse still," Esta told him with a quiet certainty that made North feel more than a little uneasy.

"I'll have to take your word for it," he said. "Right now, though? There are plenty who need a bit of something to take off the edge, so we'll dilute the mixture and then unload it on the Nitemarket."

The truck rumbled to a stop, and North knew he had to make a choice about what to do with this new development. The back door lifted, and he jumped out, considering his options. "Why did you say you were in Chicago?" he asked, looking up at them.

"We didn't," Harte said, hopping out of the truck. He was dressed to the nines, sleek charcoal suit and crisp collar and cuffs—or it had been before the little dustup they'd found themselves in that night. Esta stood above them, looking like she was auditioning to be a hood ornament in that gold dress of hers. Harte helped her down.

By now a few others had come out of the warehouse to help them unload the Nitewein. North gave them a subtle nod, and they surrounded the truck. One of his guys stepped closer to Esta and took her by the arm, to keep her from shifting out before they could stop her.

"Maybe it would be best if you start explaining," North told them.

Harte seemed to suddenly realize they'd gone from being rescued to being trapped once again. He eyed the one who had ahold of Esta, looking like he wanted to kill the man himself. "Maybe you should call off your men."

North shook his head. "Not quite yet. Just because we might have worked together before doesn't mean I'm amenable to renewing our partnership. Especially when I know what it might eventually lead to." He focused on Esta, a reminder that he knew what her plans were.

"I know what you think of me," she said, her voice surprisingly calm considering her position. "And I know that if it weren't for Maggie, you probably wouldn't have let me leave Denver. But you trusted me once before, and I'm asking you to trust me again. Because we need your help."

"For what?" North asked.

"We need to find the Antistasi in Chicago. A group of them are planning some kind of attack on the convention, and we need to stop that from happening," she told him. "If they go through with the attack, it's going to change things in ways you can't even begin to comprehend."

North knew he shouldn't even ask. Every time these two had turned up, his life got flipped on its head. But he couldn't stop himself. "What is it that you think is going to happen?"

"If the Antistasi do what they're planning, the Brotherhoods are going to retaliate by activating some kind of a tower."

Everett had come up next to them and was listening. "Like the one on top of the Coliseum?"

"What's this you're talking about?" North turned to look at his oldest.

"It's a great big thing," Everett said. "Didn't you see it? We drove right by it last night."

North had been to Chicago enough times that he hadn't really been paying attention, but Everett was new to the city and had been taking everything in like the rube he was.

"If you remember, I was busy doing the driving," North told Everett, annoyed with himself for missing something like that.

"I'm not sure how you could've missed it," Everett said. "It was way up on top of the building's roof, and it was all lit up like a Christmas tree, with a great big American Steel sign and the Stars and Stripes spotlighted from below. I figured it was some sort of advertisement."

"That's J. P. Morgan's company," Esta said darkly as she traded another meaningful glance with Harte. "That tower isn't an advertisement. It's a weapon."

"What do you mean?" North asked.

"Just what I said. That tower isn't some decoration. It's a weapon, similar to the one that the Vigilance Committee used in California years ago," she told him. "You know about what happened there?"

"Of course." *Everyone* had heard about that. "It was a damn tragedy. The number of people who died . . ." North shook his head. "But it isn't possible that they'd build another. Roosevelt promised that the government wouldn't build anything like it, ever again. People wouldn't accept such a thing."

"American Steel isn't the government," Harte reminded North. Then he glanced briefly at Esta. "And as for people standing for it . . . times change."

North made his expression carefully blank. "You're saying you know for sure this will happen?"

Esta nodded. "If the Antistasi attack the convention, Jack Grew and the Brotherhoods are going to activate that tower. If that happens——"

"People will die," North said. "A lot of people. *Innocent* people."

"Didn't you know?" Harte said darkly. "There *are* no innocent Mageus. According to Jack and the Order and all of the Brotherhoods, there never were, and if they have their way, there never will be."

"Even if there are Antistasi here in the city planning some sort of deed . . . Even if the Brotherhoods retaliate, it won't work. Something like that, I can't believe the public will stand for it. They might not care if Mageus are rounded up and quietly deported or imprisoned. It's easy enough for people to ignore the things that they don't have to look straight at, but you're talking about a lot of people dying. Children and old people and everyone in between. You're talking about outright *murder*. If the Brotherhoods start up that tower, it'll backfire on them, same as it did in California."

"This time will be different," Esta said. Her face was partially shadowed, but even concealed by the darkness, her eyes were serious and filled with a sadness that even North couldn't possibly ignore. "The public will not only stand for it, but they'll reward Jack Grew—the person responsible for the tower and its effects—at the convention."

"Well, see, that's where you're wrong," North said, feeling a bit of relief. "They just decided on that Harding fella as the presidential nominee."

"When?" Esta demanded.

"Earlier this evening," he said, frowning at her tone. "An hour or so before we found you at the Green Mill. Seems to me your predictions are a little off this time."

"There's still the vice presidential nomination," Harte said.

"And then when Harding dies . . ." Esta didn't finish.

"How could you possibly know all that?" Everett asked Esta. "You're talking like you can prognosticate the future."

"It's not prognostication if you've seen it for yourself," North told his son, wishing it were otherwise.

"The bottom line is that if they voted to nominate Harding tonight, we're running shorter on time than we thought," Esta said. "We need to know what the Antistasi's plans are. We need to stop them."

"How do I know you're not just trying to scare me into cooperating?" North asked.

"I *am* trying to scare you," Esta told him. "Unless we do something, the attack *will* happen. The tower will be activated, and Jack Grew will become president. Once he's in power, Roosevelt's promises will be moot. Jack will build more towers—a whole network of them. Enough to wipe out every bit of the old magic in this country."

"We're going to figure this out with or without your help," Harte told him.

"With your help, we can maybe save even more lives, though. Including your own," Esta said. "Because if you stay here in the city, you're both going to die."

North wanted to argue that what they were saying was ridiculous. There was no way the events would unfold like that. But he knew better than to doubt Esta.

"It's like I said, the Antistasi aren't exactly organized these days," he said. "I've been in Chicago for nearly a week, and I haven't heard any rumors about anything happening at the convention. Whoever's planning it is keeping things quiet."

"But you *are* still involved with them. You could help us find out who's planning it," Esta said.

North hesitated. "Possibly," he admitted reluctantly. "I know someone who might know what's going on. We can find him at the Nitemarket."

THE GOLDEN HOUR

1902—New York

Jianyu Lee was stuck. He had positioned himself out of sight behind a cart parked on the outskirts of Madison Square, not quite a block away from where he'd intended to be, but he could not venture any closer. Not without being seen. *Especially* not with boys he recognized from the Devil's Own, boys who certainly would recognize him as well, prowling through the park. Jianyu had the sense that they were searching for something—possibly even for him—and so he stayed back, unable to do more than wait.

Everything had been going to plan until, quite suddenly, it was not.

Jianyu's first indication that something was amiss had been when the wagon, flanked by police on horseback, had arrived from the east nearly an hour before. He had known immediately what the wagon carried, even though it had been too early. *Far* too early, considering that sunset had still been minutes away. *All* of their information had indicated that the Order's boat would not even *land* until the Golden Hour began.

They had expected the Order to be prepared for an attack—Theo had warned them of the nervous energy among the old men of the Inner Circle—but they had not expected this.

Jianyu's reaction had been immediate. Without even hesitating, he had reached for the light, as he always did—then everything had changed. As the daylight took on a golden cast, the usual warmth of his affinity had transformed into a searing heat. The light had flashed around him, bright and impossibly *hot*. It had felt as though the sun itself had come down

612

from the sky and had been attempting to consume him, and Jianyu could do nothing but release his affinity, even as the sunlight was still searing the surface of his skin. The truth was an unexpected blow. Something about the strange light on this strange day, during this strange hour, had changed the rules of his affinity.

They had expected the Order to use certain protections. They had known that the Order would use something about the power of this false solstice to keep what was left of their treasures safe, but they had all believed the protection would be only on the wagon carrying the goods. Perhaps even on the ring itself. Jianyu had not imagined—none of them had imagined—that the protections the Order used could also affect their affinities.

Or maybe it was only his that had been affected. Maybe because his magic aligned most closely with the light, Jianyu was more susceptible.

Whatever the case, his skin still stung, and though he wanted to pull the light around him and take the packages the men were beginning to unload from the wagon, he could not. He understood from the way the daylight had gone almost amber that there was no point even in trying. Apparently, the Golden Hour was more than a quaint description. It was a powerful type of ritual magic. All he could do was stand and watch as a group of men opened the wagon, removed a heavy crate, and took it, under armed guard, into the building.

It galled Jianyu to know how close he had been to the artifact. The ring had been *right there*, but as long as he could not wrap the light around himself, as long as he could not use his affinity, he could do nothing. He was far too conspicuous, especially in this part of town, far from the community of Chinese people who lived around Mott Street. Without his affinity to hide him, he would be immediately noticed. Immediately *targeted*.

Jianyu simmered with the frustration of being able to do *nothing* but wait, but then sirens had started to call through the city streets, and he had known it was truly beginning. He had known there was no way to warn Viola that all their careful scheming had been for nothing. He couldn't reach Cela or Abel to tell them that their plan was crumbling like ash.

Though it felt like he was stuck, drowning in a dragon's pool, in the end Jianyu had decided to stay where he was and to wait. He could only hope that whatever strange power was at work, it was only temporary. Certainly, as soon as the sun set and the Golden Hour waned, he would have access to his magic once again. *Certainly.* With his affinity, he could still hope to find the stone, even if it was behind thick iron walls or layers of protections.

It had been no easy task to remain unseen as the minutes crept on, especially once some of Dolph's boys had entered the park. Twice Jianyu had nearly been seen by one of the Devil's Own. Then, suddenly, things had changed once more. Two carts filled with Five Pointers had arrived and launched an attack on the now-empty wagon. Shots had been fired from buildings across the street as the plaza in front of the new skyscraper had erupted into a battle.

A few minutes later, Nibsy had arrived with a wagon of people. Viola had been there in the back, along with Mooch, Werner, and a light-haired boy who was not one of Dolph's, but Jianyu recognized him. The blond boy had been in Evelyn DeMure's apartment that night weeks before, when they'd almost retrieved the Delphi's Tear. They had failed that night. They could not fail again.

Jianyu moved closer to the wagon. If he could signal Viola, per-haps they could figure out a new direction. But there were too many people around, and the park itself was too open, with young trees and wide walkways that left nowhere for him to hide. Viola and Nibsy were arguing, and Viola turned to the park—Jianyu thought perhaps she saw him—but then she climbed down from the wagon and followed Nibsy's boys around the side of the building.

He had to stop her. He could not allow her to go into such danger alone.

Again Jianyu reached for his affinity, but before he could even grasp the light completely, he again felt the sun's power sear his skin, and once more, he was forced to release his affinity and the light with it.

By then it was too late. Viola was gone.

Nibsy turned, his head swiveling around toward the park. The lenses of his spectacles flashed golden in the setting sun, and Jianyu pulled back behind another carriage before he could be seen. When he chanced another look, Nibsy was still studying the park, his brow furrowed thoughtfully. Watching.

Frustrated with himself and the entire situation, Jianyu began walking away from Madison Square. He would take the long way around the building, cutting down a block or two east, far from the police and Nibsy. He would position himself to enter the building once the strange golden light eased. What else could he do? He only hoped that when the sun sank below the horizon, he would be able to touch his affinity. Until then, he could not simply stand there and wait.

THE TRUTH OF HISTORY

1920—Chicago

Esta couldn't help but study North and Everett as she and Harte followed the two toward the entrance of the Nitemarket. The father and son were of similar height and build, though Everett hadn't quite filled into his shoulders yet, and they moved alike with an easy, loping grace. In the yellowish glow of the streetlamps, North's reddish hair and Everett's ashy brown didn't look any different.

She understood from the way North glared at her that he hadn't forgotten her intention to go back and change the past. Now that he had not only Maggie to think of, but also Everett and his other children, the threat she posed was that much more dangerous. Esta couldn't fault him for worrying about that, but she also couldn't put everything aside for his fears . . . not when the truth of history lay before her, dangerous and demanding of her attentions.

Still . . . meeting Everett made things more real. Knowing what effects her actions might have now was different from thinking about some unknown future North and Maggie *might* have created. Everett was real and whole and every bit as vulnerable as any of the people Esta was trying to save by stopping Jack. Her returning to 1902 might negate his very existence. She would have to deal with that reality eventually, but not tonight. Not when the crescent moon hung like a scythe over the second city, a reminder of the reaping that would come if they couldn't stop the events that were about to unfold.

They took the L west until the tall buildings of the central part of

Chicago began to flatten out, and eventually they arrived at a station some-where near Cicero. A few blocks from the stop, North led them to a lonely house in the center of an otherwise empty lot. It looked to be condemned.

"Once we're in the Nitemarket, it would be best if you leave the talking to me," he instructed. "That goes for you, too, Rett. Don't do anything stupid."

"It was only that one time—" the boy started.

"That *one time* was more than enough," North told him, sounding every bit like the father he was. "Your mother'll skin me alive if anything happens to you."

Esta bit back a smile at the two. In some ways, North still looked like the boy he'd once been, even beneath the lines of his face. He and Everett could have been mirror images, separated only by the passing of years.

The four of them went around the back of the building, where the lot was strewn with trash and old cigarette butts, and North led the way up the decaying steps to the back door. Inside, the house didn't reveal anything more. Plaster crumbled from the walls, and the floor was weak and rotted out in more than one spot, but once the door was closed, the noise of the outside world went suddenly silent—a lot more silent than the rickety old walls should have warranted.

"What kind of a game are you trying to play?" Harte growled.

North didn't answer, but a second later, a door on the other side of the room opened, and a small man emerged wearing enormous spectacles, with lenses so thick they made the eyes behind them look unnaturally small. Esta glanced at Harte, who looked every bit as unnerved as she felt by the guy's unexpected appearance.

"The weather doesn't look promising," the small man told them.

North stepped forward. "When the moon shines red, it's a nice enough night for a stroll."

The man eyed them before he finally nodded. Then he stepped aside so they could pass through the doorway that waited behind him.

Harte glanced at Esta, but she only shrugged in answer. It *could* be a trap, but considering that North knew what he had to lose if anything happened to her, she doubted it was.

North went first, moving toward the open doorway without hesitation, and Everett followed just as quickly. Esta gave Harte another small shrug and followed as well.

As she passed through the door, though, she felt the brush of magic—warm and cool all at once. Natural *and* ritual mixed together in a dizzying swirl of energy, and the world seemed to contract, pressing in on them. Moving forward felt like pushing through some impossibly thick substance, and then all at once the sound of the world came roaring back and Esta winced against the brightness of a brilliantly blinding light.

When she opened her eyes again, she found herself in a warehouse. It was a long, narrow building with a peaked metal roof, and the sound of rain pattering above caused a kind of quiet roar to surround them. Strings of flickering bulbs were draped overhead, providing the only light, and the long space was filled with various stalls, each displaying an assortment of ordinary-looking objects. It looked like some kind of flea market or junk sale, except the vendors eyed each of the shoppers with sharp suspicion and everyone spoke in low, hushed voices.

"This is the Nitemarket?" she asked, feeling unaccountably disappointed by how normal it seemed.

North nodded as he started to lead them through the aisles. "Keep your eyes down and your mouths closed."

"It's raining," Harte said, looking up at the ceiling.

In Chicago, the sky had been cloudless.

"I don't think we're in Kansas anymore," Esta murmured.

North glared at her with confused frustration. "Chicago never was in Kansas."

"It's just an expression," Esta told him as she shrugged off her mistake. "So what are we looking for? There's not a lot of anything but junk here."

"Junk that people would kill and die for," North said in a low whisper. "Pretty much everything sold here is illegal in about twenty different ways, but the one thing it all has in common is that it's infused with the old magic."

Esta glanced over at him. "Like your watch."

"Exactly." North's jaw was tight, and she realized he was nervous.

"Did you ever replace it?" she wondered, looking at the table they were passing. It looked like a collection of tools—hammers and awls, saws and vise clamps, each rusted and ordinary-looking.

"I thought about it for a while, but once I learned what it took to make a piece like that?" North shook his head. "I don't need that kind of power. No one does." His eyes cut in her direction, the judgment clear in them.

Esta found that she couldn't disagree.

Harte was examining a table covered with a display of knives and brass knuckles. "Someone must sure want that kind of power. A lot of some-ones, from the look of this place."

North pulled him away before he could pick up a pair of cuff links. "Doesn't mean they're right to. Come on," he told them. "I think I see Dominic over yonder."

Esta followed them down the narrow aisles. "Where did all of this come from?" She marveled at the sheer number of objects for sale. The variety as well. She'd assumed that magic-infused objects were rarer.

"From the same place as any magical object," North said. "Someone gave up their affinity to make each item you see here."

"Willingly?" Harte wondered.

"Does it matter?" North asked. "I imagine giving up even a part of your affinity would take a toll bigger than anyone could predict before they agreed. I don't want to think about what something like that would do to a body, even if they *had* been willing."

Esta didn't have to imagine. She *knew*. When Professor Lachlan had trapped her in New York and tried to use her affinity to unite the stones, she had felt the very beginnings of her magic being ripped away from her. She already knew the terror of feeling herself about to fly apart far too keenly. But now she wondered if that was also what Leena had experienced when Dolph Saunders had taken part of her affinity for his cane. Esta thought maybe she understood a little better Leena's decision to tell Dolph that their baby had died and to hide Esta away from him after she was born. Suddenly, the hall of goods around her seemed more sinister.

"Most of these are nothing but trinkets . . ." North was still talking, unaware of the direction of Esta's thoughts. "Nothing like the stones in the Order's artifacts. But even if someone thought they were making the decision freely, there's a lot of complications that could come up— whether they really understood what they were agreeing to, whether they were under duress. And that's if they were *actually* willing. Most of the time, the arrangements weren't as equitable as the sellers here would have everyone believe." He shook his head. "Once I realized what it took to make my watch, I found I didn't have any interest in finding another piece like it. I don't need that kind of weight on my conscience."

The stone in the cuff on Esta's arm felt somehow heavier than ever. Unlike the stones Seshat had made in her attempt to preserve the heart of magic—objects that she created willingly from her *own* power—the Order's artifacts drew their power from the affinities of Mageus that Newton had sacrificed in his attempt to control the Book.

From what Harte had witnessed, the lives of other innocent Mageus had been taken more recently to recharge the stones. He'd described for her the bodies of the missing Mageus he'd found in the Mysterium. They'd each been suspended in a web of dark, unnatural magic. All to preserve the Brink and the Order's power.

The origin of the Order's artifacts wasn't news to Esta. Someone had died, and because of that lost life, she could use the stone to slip through time. That was a fact. Every time Esta used the Key, she used that stolen power. Another fact. She'd tried to ignore those facts for a long time now. She'd told herself that she was using the stones for an honorable pur- pose, but standing there amid the swirling eddies of magic—natural and corrupt, hot and cold power alike—Esta wondered if she'd been conning herself all along. What did it mean that she was still willing to use power that wasn't rightfully hers? How did that make her any different from Thoth?

"It's not the same thing," Harte whispered, easily guessing the direction of Esta's thoughts. Her surprise must have shown, because he slid his palm against hers, tangling their fingers in a moment of stolen comfort.

She didn't even pretend to deny that he was right. "How is my using Ishtar's Key any different?"

"I don't know," he admitted. "Maybe it's not, but the world isn't black or white, good or evil. Ever since the day you came back for me, every choice you've made—right or wrong—has been because you believed it would help in some way."

"Not always. Not in St. Louis . . ."

"In St. Louis you made mistakes. We both did. We're trying to right those now." He squeezed her hand gently. "It's all we can do."

"I don't know if that's enough." Esta started to pull her hand away. She didn't deserve his comfort or his understanding.

But Harte caught her hand again and laid a kiss on her palm. "No one is blameless, Esta. Even saints had their sins. It isn't possible to live a perfect life, and even if you could, it wouldn't be very interesting." He released her hand then, and when he spoke again, his words came slowly. "You make mistakes. You learn. We all do. Sometimes it takes a little bad to cause an enormous amount of good. Dolph Saunders understood that. Would you blame him for the life he chose? For the sins he committed?"

Esta thought about the father she hadn't really known. She wasn't sure what to do with the goodness he'd shown to her and to the people in the Bowery, or with the terrible things he'd done as well—especially what he'd done to her mother. Finally, she shook her head. "I honestly don't know."

"That's fair enough," Harte said. "But it's like you told me back on the train—it's not your fault. Having the cuff, using it. You didn't create any of this. All you can do is figure out how you want to live in it."

He was right. The stone in her cuff had been made through the worst possible means. The mistakes she'd made in St. Louis had been terrible. But Esta wasn't walking away from her responsibilities. Not now. Not *ever*.

"Maybe you're right," she admitted. "But look at all of this, Harte. These are *Mageus* buying and selling power that isn't theirs to trade. How is this any different from what the Order does? It's all the same—people forgetting that the affinities we hold inside of us aren't separate from who we are. Maybe I didn't create any of this, but it'll be my fault if I allow it to remain."

Harte's mouth curved a little, and his eyes held promises that she wasn't sure he could keep. "Then by all means, let me be the one to help you tear the whole damn thing to the ground."

THE NITEMARKET

1920—Chicago

North didn't realize he'd lost Harte and Esta until Everett tapped on his arm.

"Your friends are still back there," his son said, giving North a look that reminded him of Maggie in its directness. And its impatience.

He knew Everett was itching to know more about the two strangers they'd picked up at the Green Mill, but the Nitemarket wasn't the time or the place to explain things—especially not to speak the name of the Thief. She was still something of a legend both loved and hated, depending on who you were talking to.

Since he didn't want to draw any more attention to their group than they already might have attracted, North retraced his steps rather than shouting for the two to pick up the pace. They were about twenty yards back, their heads close together as they spoke in voices too low for him to hear. Whatever they were talking about, their expressions were too serious for his liking.

"You two coming or what?"

Esta seemed startled by the interruption, but in a blink her expression transformed itself from surprise to her usual calm composure. She gave him a look so blandly disinterested that if North hadn't known better, he never would have thought she'd been lagging behind the group to start with. The problem was, he *did* know better.

Finally moving again, the four made their way deeper into the Nitemarket, looking for North's contact. They didn't talk much, and

Everett—thank heavens—did what North had told him: He kept his eyes down and his hands tucked into his pockets.

North had never been a fan of visiting the market, even if it did provide their family with a good living. Between Maggie's formulations—at least the ones she was willing to part with—and the goods North was able to liberate—like the Nitewein from that very night—the Nitemarket provided the Northwoods a steady stream of income, which helped augment whatever breeding horses on their ranch outside Kansas City brought in. *And* the market kept them connected to the Antistasi. Neither North nor Maggie had any desire to be drawn all the way back into the Antistasi, but if they kept one foot in the game, North hoped they could maybe see danger coming long before it arrived.

Like he'd told Esta and Harte, the Nitemarket wasn't a safe place. A person who knew where to look could usually find one of the many entrances in any good-size town—well, any town except New York City—but the market itself never seemed to be in the same location twice. It moved from place to place each night, presumably to avoid detection, but the market didn't limit entrance to Mageus, which made it even more dangerous in North's estimation. There were any number of Sundren who had managed to find their way into the cramped aisles of vendors and goods over the years. Usually, the outsiders were well-intentioned folk interested in family lore, or sympathetic souls looking for the thrill of brushing up against the old magic. Occasionally, though, there were Sundren who found the market specifically to cause problems. You never knew when you might run afoul of the occasional raid or groups of Sundren vigilantes playing at being heroes.

North probably shouldn't have brought Everett. Maggie certainly wouldn't have let the boy come if she'd been there to have a say. But with Esta's warnings about the tower—however unlikely they seemed—North felt better having his son by his side, even in a place as dangerous as the Nitemarket.

In one of the last stalls at the back of the long, cavernous hall, North finally found the contact he'd been looking for. Dominic Fusilli was an older man with a middle like pudding and hardly a white hair left to cover the mottled scalp of his head. They'd met about five years before, but North still didn't exactly trust Dom. Still, the older man had his uses.

"Northwood," Dom said, seeing the four of them approach. "I see you brought Junior."

"This is my oldest, Everett," North said, reluctantly making the introductions.

"He's the spitting image of you, isn't he?" Then Dom realized that Harte and Esta were also with them, and his eyes narrowed. "And a couple of others as well?"

North stepped in front of Esta, blocking the peddler from examining her too closely. It had been years since the Devil's Thief had disappeared, but it wasn't worth taking the chance that Dom might recognize Esta. The old guy pretended not to know what was going on, but North hadn't been green enough to buy that act five years ago. There wasn't any sense underestimating Dom now.

"Just some friends visiting from out of town," North said, dismissing the pair as he tried to change the subject to something safer. "I got a shipment recently that you might be interested in."

Dom was still trying to see around North without being too obvious about it, but the mention of more goods served as enough of a distraction to draw his attention back to their conversation. "That so?"

North nodded. "Nitewein. Prime vintage from what I can tell."

"Interesting." Dom scratched at the day-old stubble on his chin. "Word is the Chicago Outfit got raided earlier tonight. A lot of the product went missing. Turns out, though, it wasn't actually the Feds."

"Oh, I wouldn't know anything about that," North said easily, hooking his thumbs through the loops of his jeans. "I doubt the shipment I'm looking to unload is anything as powerful as the stuff from the Green Mill."

Dom's expression turned wry. "Especially not after you dilute it."

Since there wasn't any heat in his words, North took it to mean Dom was interested and that he didn't particularly care about the source. "I'll put you down for a case or two."

"Best make it three," Dom said. "Demand has been up lately. I assume we can discuss the price when you deliver? Or did you want to settle that now?" His gaze again traveled to the others with North.

"Later is fine," North said, trying to draw Dominic's attention back. They made a few quick arrangements for the delivery, and then North held out his hand and Dom took it, sealing the deal between them. "There is one other thing. . . ."

Dom's bushy brows rose a little. "Oh?"

"Everyone at the market knows that if there's something happening, you're the first to know," North said, laying it on thick. He could sense Esta and Harte growing impatient behind him, but he ignored the two of them and focused on Dom. North knew the old man well enough to handle him.

"I can't deny that I tend to know a thing or two," Dom preened.

"It's just that, well . . . usually I wouldn't pay rumors any mind, but since I brought my boy with me, I feel like maybe I should be a little more careful. Maggie'll be none too happy if I let anything happen to him. You know how she is."

"*Your* Maggie?" The old man shook his head, probably remembering the one run-in he'd had with North's wife. "I sure do."

That's what Dom got for trying to swindle his girl, though. Maggie had torn the old man up one side and down the other when she realized he'd been trying to get out of paying her for a delivery of some Quellant. After that, Dom wouldn't have anything to do with Maggie, and she didn't want North to have anything to do with him either. But Dom was too good a contact to cut out completely, so North dealt with the old man alone.

"Anyway, I've been hearing some whispers in Chicago about something big happening. I don't suppose you know what's in the works?" North asked.

Dom frowned, the bushy brows drawing together like woolly bears creeping over his eyes. "I haven't heard anything about anything. Things have been quiet all around."

"Are you sure?" Esta asked, breaking in like she was part of the conversation.

North stepped in front of her again. "She's not used to big cities," he explained when Dom looked suddenly wary from her interruption. "Gets nervous about things." He lowered his voice a little. "You know how women can be."

That seemed to mollify Dom a little, even if North could practically feel the heat of Esta's fuming behind him.

"So you haven't heard of any deeds in the works?" North asked again. "Because I'd hate to get in the middle of something unexpectedly, especially with my boy here."

"If anything is happening, it's not part of the usual network. No one would be stupid enough to start trouble with the convention in town— too much security and too much risk for anyone with any sense."

"That's what I suspected," North said, his mind churning at the implications. Esta had plenty of reasons to lie about the attack. She knew how he felt about her wanting to go back to change the past, and he had a sinking feeling this was another one of those *misdirections* of hers. "I appreciate your confirmation, anyway."

"Anytime," Dom told him, still trying to get a peek at the strangers with North. "Give Maggie my best."

"Will do," North said with a tip of his hat.

He wouldn't, of course. Maggie would have him by the short hairs if she knew he was dealing with Dom again. *Especially* if she knew he'd introduced the man to Everett.

With a jerk of his head, he got Everett and the other two moving, but all the while he could feel a headache building. North wasn't sure what Esta and Harte's game was, but he didn't plan to be a pawn in it, not this time.

He led them back toward the entrance of the market but ducked into

THE SERPENT'S CURSE

627

a side aisle that was empty once they were well out of Dom's view. He closed the distance between himself and Esta, snagging her wrist so she couldn't get away from him.

"You got about two minutes to tell me what you're playing at," North hissed at Esta, using every inch of his height to tower over her.

"Back off," Harte said, the words coming out like a growl from low in his throat as he stepped toward them, but Everett had read the situation and was already between them, pistol drawn. Harte took another step forward, apparently not caring that he didn't have any chance against a gun.

"You might not want to mess with that," North warned Harte. "The boy has a way of tinkering with things to make them more effective."

"All of you, stop it," Esta said, not bothering to hide her frustration. North felt her tug at his wrist, but she didn't do more than test his grip. "I'm not playing at anything." Her voice was as calm and even as the liar she was born to be. "What I told you before was the truth. I can't help it if your contact hasn't heard anything."

"Dom's been with the Antistasi for a long time, and he knows things before anyone else. If the Antistasi had something planned—especially something as big as you're saying it'll be—he would know."

"The attack *will* happen," Esta insisted, not backing down one bit.

"Then it won't be done by the Antistasi," North told her.

Esta froze. For a second she looked like one of the hares that go stock-still when they get caught unaware out in the fields at the ranch, like not moving could save them from danger. "Then it's *not* the Antistasi." Her voice sounded unsteady, like she was shaken by this realization. She looked at Harte. "It's a setup," she told him.

"What?" Harte shook his head, clearly not following any better than North.

"It's a *setup*," she repeated, turning her attention back to North. "The whole attack . . . You could be right. Maybe the Antistasi *don't* have anything planned, but whoever *is* going to do the attack will set them up to take the fall for it."

"Nice try," North said. "But I'm not buying what you're selling, and I think we're finished—" There was a commotion at the other end of the hall, coming from the direction of the exit to Chicago. "What the—" But the string of curses that came out of North's mouth were lost in the noise of an explosion.

The Nitemarket was under attack.

ADESSO

1902—New York

Viola wasn't quite sure how everything had turned upside down so quickly.

She should have been smarter. She should have realized that the same boy who had betrayed Dolph—who had *killed* Dolph—would not be so easily defeated. A boy like that could do practically anything. But Viola hadn't imagined that skinny little Nibsy Lorcan could convince the Fox himself to move against her brother. It was unthinkable, but it had happened all the same.

Viola chanced a glance back at the park, wondering if Jianyu was nearby. The plan had been for Jianyu to wait near the building, a backup that neither Nibsy nor Paolo would know about, but that was before, when they believed that they could stop the wagon from arriving until after the Golden Hour's protection waned. But nothing else had gone to plan, and Viola could only hope that Jianyu was close. She hoped, too, that he'd heard Nibsy's threat and would understand that he must go to help Cela and Abel before John Torrio could harm them. She risked another look back toward the open spaces of Madison Square Park, but she could find no sign of Jianyu there or anywhere else.

"You're not thinking of running now, are you?" Nibsy asked, eyeing Viola and then glancing to the park.

"Of course not," she told him, cursing herself for being so careless. She had to focus. She couldn't make any more wrong steps, not when so much was at stake.

A few minutes later, Viola had little choice but to follow Mooch and Werner, along with the one called Logan, around the side of the building. With the Five Pointers occupying the police out front, it wasn't difficult to slip in through the back, not when Werner was quick to suffocate the few men who were waiting in the lobby. They'd fallen unconscious before they could so much as draw their guns.

Of course Nibsy himself didn't come along with them, the snake. He'd made excuses about his leg—he would only slow them down—but Viola saw the truth in his eyes. Nibsy Lorcan had never intended to put himself in danger, not when he had the lives of the Devil's Own to offer instead.

The new boy, Logan, was sent to lead them. Nibsy seemed to trust him above the others, but Viola couldn't understand why—she could tell that Mooch and Werner felt the same. Logan Sullivan had a look of fear in his eyes that made Viola nervous. She knew that fear could make people do stupid things, and she wasn't interested in dying—not today.

Beyond the entrance, the lobby's marble floors and walls shone in the evening's strange golden light. The ceiling was arched as gracefully as any church's and every bit as ornate. This wasn't the world of dirty tenements and crowded barrooms that all of them were used to. It was far grander than the cluttered shops and businesses they frequented south of Houston. They all seemed caught by the wonder of the sight—all except Logan.

"We need to get moving before the Order realizes we're in the building," Logan directed. He was jittery, this one, with shifty eyes and a tightness around his mouth that Viola didn't like. He was also carrying a lopsided satchel slung over his shoulder. *For the goods we find,* he'd explained when Viola had asked. But he glanced away, and she sensed there was something more about his plans that he wasn't revealing.

"Stairs or elevator?" Mooch asked.

"Stairs," Viola said immediately, but Logan disagreed.

"We'll be too exposed in a stairwell," he said. "The elevator gives us our best chance. It's faster, and we won't exhaust ourselves with the climb."

Viola had heard about elevators, but the tenements of the Bowery didn't have any need for them, so she'd never been in one herself. She stepped carefully across the threshold and into the glittering mirrored box, wary of every creak and groan. It felt too much like allowing herself to be trapped, but she didn't fully appreciate how terrible it would be until Logan pulled a gate over the entrance, caging them in like animals. With a push of a lever, the room suddenly lurched, and Viola grabbed for the gilded railing as they began to rumble upward.

The shining mirrors reflected her face back at her, and she saw that the weeks had not been kind. Dark smudges of exhaustion lay thick beneath her eyes. Her hair was pulled back from her face, but the heat and humidity of the day had it fuzzing up around her face. She looked *so* much like her mother, she realized—worn and tired. She wore the same expression as the women who worked morning until night to care for their families because it was their duty and their lot in life. Because they had no other choice.

Watching herself in the mirror, Viola could not help but think of Ruby, who always looked fresh and polished. Ruby, who would no doubt be completely at home in such a shining, beautiful place as this. It was more confirmation of what Viola already knew, of how impossible Ruby's words—her *kiss*—had been.

Viola's eyes met Werner's in the reflection of the mirror, and she saw that she wasn't alone in her apprehension about the elevator. Mooch, too, looked nervous. Only Logan seemed at ease.

"We're like fish waiting in a barrel," Viola muttered, looking away from the mirrored wall so she did not have to see her own fear. She cursed softly, trying to keep herself steady as the contraption jerked, but she could not force herself to relax as the elevator rattled onward, rising to whatever waited for them above. "As soon as these doors open, they'll be waiting. And then what will we do?"

"Fish don't have any weapons at their disposal," Logan said, unbothered. His eyes were focused on the dial over the door.

"I have only one knife," Viola told him. "Libitina, she's deadly, but she cuts one at a time, no more."

"You have more than a knife," Werner said, leveling a knowing look at her through the mirrored wall. "Same as me."

Viola could only stare at him. Here was a boy who could take the breath from a person's lungs. She'd seen how easily Werner had disposed of the men in the lobby. "It doesn't bother you?"

"Why should it?" Werner shrugged. "When we get to the top, whatever is waiting for us on the other side of this door won't hesitate to kill me. I don't know about you, but I'd prefer not to die." He grimaced, the nerves clear in his expression. "Not for a little while, at least."

The elevator rumbled to a halt on the eighteenth floor, and Logan turned to them. It was only the four of them standing there in uneasy silence, hearts in their throats, but the moment the cage doors opened, there would certainly be more.

"Ready?" Logan asked.

"Do we have a choice?" Sweat was glistening at Mooch's temples, and his hands were shaking.

"No," Logan admitted. They all held their collective breath as he pulled back the inner cage before depressing the lever that opened the outer door.

They had expected an ambush, but only an empty hall greeted them. They stepped into the gleaming silence, but there were no men with guns waiting—and no indication that any would come. There was only a polished grandeur that made the elevator look nearly shabby in comparison.

Viola had been inside Khafre Hall. She had seen the Mysterium for herself, but this one hallway surpassed anything she'd seen in that older building by far. Granite as deeply green as the trees in Central Park lined the walls. Golden sconces hung at even intervals along the walls, glowing with a warm, ethereal light. Inlaid gold glinted everywhere.

"Where is everyone?" Werner whispered as they eased their way down the hall.

"It's nearly sunset," Logan told them. "If our information was right, the members of the Order should be in their ceremonial chamber starting the consecration. They'll stay there, under the Golden Hour's protection, until the sun sets. We have to get moving. We won't have much time to take the ring once the sun is down and the power of the Golden Hour ends. This way."

Still on alert, they started down the hall, in the direction of the front of the building, where it pointed toward Madison Square Park. The Mysterium would be there somewhere, and with any luck, it would already hold the ring. It didn't matter that these other boys wanted the artifact. They had pledged themselves to Nibsy Lorcan, and Viola would not allow them to have it. She would wait until the time was right, and then she would take what she needed and be gone.

They were only halfway down the hall, though, when an alarm sounded.

"They know we're here," Werner said, licking his lips.

"We knew they would," Logan reminded him. "Let's go."

They'd taken a few steps more when the glowing lanterns suddenly went out. The windowless hallway went completely dark except for the square of daylight that shone through an open doorway at the end of the hall.

"Go!" Logan shouted, but no one needed to be told.

They tumbled through the entrance of the room as a steel door began to slide closed to cover the opening. Viola heard Mooch yelp and turned to find him caught by the door. With a flick of her blade, his jacket fell away. After the heavy door sealed them in, they could no longer hear the screams of the sirens.

The chamber they found themselves in was silent as a church. It was a large room lined with empty shelves. Its walls seemed to glimmer in the fading daylight, and Viola realized it was because there were veins of gold and precious stones set into the sandstone panels. The boys were studying the steel doors that had barricaded them in, but Viola was drawn to the center of the room, where a familiar table-like altar waited.

"I've seen this before," she said, her pulse racing.

This same table had been in the Mysterium, she was sure of it. When she and Darrigan had completed the puzzle of a lock in the vault far below the main levels of Khafre Hall, this very table had risen from the floor to expose the cabinet that had held the Ars Arcana. It had held a single bowl filled with a strange liquid. Now the bowl was gone. In its place was a box carved from some brilliant blue stone that had been polished to gleaming.

Viola reached carefully for the box, not really sure if she should touch the small chest, but when she ran her fingers across it, she sensed the cold of false magic . . . but nothing else.

"What's this?" Mooch asked, eyeing the box.

"I'm not sure." She used the tip of Libitina to flip open the golden latch and then the lid of the box itself. Nothing happened.

Werner had come up next to them as well. "Looks like junk," he said, clearly disappointed with the tarnished circlets of metal they found inside.

The two boys turned away, clearly unimpressed, but Viola paused at the sight of them. She remembered now—this very table had been sitting atop these same silver discs in the Mysterium those many weeks ago. But it wasn't only the *objects* that were familiar. They had been carved with a design that Viola had seen before—first on the book depicted in the painting of Newton that was hanging in Dolph Saunders' old rooms, and then later, with the unreadable notes in Dolph's journal.

Certainly, the marks inscribed into the surface of the metal discs were the same emblem, the *sigil*, as Theo had called it. She lifted the first disc and saw that there were more of the same beneath—four, in fact. There had been four in the Mysterium as well. It was too much a coincidence that she should find this symbol here, in the possession of the Order, when Dolph Saunders had thought to protect what he'd known about it.

Logan had already stepped beyond the altar and was looking up to where a golden staircase spiraled up to the ceiling. He scrambled up the steps and reached his hand toward the carving on the medallion in the ceiling where the staircase ended, tracing his finger along the lines inscribed there.

"It's up there," he told them. "The ring. I can feel it beyond this door." He pounded on the ceiling, but nothing happened.

Viola hesitated, but then she took one of the discs and examined it more closely. It was about the size of her palm and far heavier than she had expected from the nearly paper-thin bit of metal, but the cold energy felt like ice in her hands. It reminded her too much of the power of the Brink, but she tucked the four discs into her skirts. She imagined that Theo would be interested to examine them; perhaps he would have some idea of what the objects were. More than that, the etchings on these pieces reminded her of the drawings in Dolph's notebook. If Dolph had thought to conceal his notes about what they were, Viola had the sense that they must be important, even if she could not see why or how.

Werner had already lost interest and wandered away. He was staring at the wall of windows. "Who is that?"

Viola turned, following the direction of Werner's gaze, and for a moment it was as though he'd stolen her air. A man was standing on the balcony's ledge, silhouetted by the setting sun.

Not a man. *Theo.*

His arms were spread wide, but Viola couldn't tell if he was bracing himself on the enormous stone pillars or preparing to release them. She raced to the end of the room and grabbed the handle to the balcony door. It was stuck and impossible to open. She jerked at it, so desperate to open it that, at first, she did not feel the cold energy radiating from the latch. Withdrawing Libitina, she positioned the thin blade into the keyhole and pressed, letting the knife slice through the metal until the door swung open.

"Theo!" she said, stepping onto the balcony. "Come down from there! *Adesso!*" Her voice was shaking, and so was she as she moved toward him, trying to wave him down. At first he ignored her. "What are you doing up there? Sei pazzo? Theo!"

Theo turned finally at the sound of his name, but his eyes were blank.

It was as though he didn't know her. *No.* It was as though he didn't even *see* her.

"Do you feel that?" Mooch asked, coming up beside her. He shuddered.

Viola did feel it, the cold that seemed to have settled on the small balcony.

"He's under some kind of spell," Werner said.

"We have to get him down," Viola told them. Her heart pounded in her chest. They were so high up. There wasn't a single building in the Bowery even half so tall.

"We're not here for him," Logan said. "We're here for the ring. It's up there, and we have to find a way to get to it."

"The ring can wait," Viola said, turning back to Theo. She inched closer, careful not to disturb him. Considering the dazed and empty look in his eyes, Viola was afraid that anything she said or did might make him move in the wrong direction. "Theo, please. You have to listen to me."

"Look, if we get the ring, we can break whatever spell they put on him, right?" Logan asked, his voice betraying an urgency that Viola herself understood. She realized that perhaps his participation was no more voluntary than her own.

Werner frowned at Logan. "We can't leave him like that. He could jump any second now."

His words sent a bolt of panic through Viola that she had, until that moment, been keeping at bay. "Shut up," she told him sharply. "He's not going to jump." *He can't jump.*

"We don't have time for this," Logan told them. His voice was tighter now, more anxious. But Viola could tell that his worry was not for Theo. "The sun is already setting, and any minute now, someone is going to come. We have to figure out how to get that door open." He swallowed hard, the apple of his throat bobbing. "You know what will happen if we don't get the Delphi's Tear for James."

"You should know what will happen to you anyway if you follow a viper like Nibsy Lorcan," Viola told him.

"You don't know anything about James Lorcan," Logan said. His jaw was tight now, his voice angry.

"I know he'll put the knife in your back himself if it serves his purposes," Viola told him. "Ask this one." She gestured to Mooch, who only looked away. *The coward.*

"We're not leaving him up there. There's time for both," Werner said to Logan. Then he turned to Viola. "What should we do?"

"I don't know," she admitted. "I'm afraid that if we touch him, he might jump."

"Can you put him to sleep?" Werner asked. "I could try to take his breath, but that might make him panic. If you could—I don't know—relax him a bit?"

Viola frowned. "I think maybe, yes. That would work."

"When he collapses, we'll have to grab him before he tumbles," Werner told Mooch, who also inched closer.

"This is insane," Logan said. "You're wasting our time over a member of the *Order*?"

Viola ignored him. "If you're ready," she told the other two, aware that Logan was retreating into the empty library.

She closed her eyes and sent a quick prayer to any angel or saint who might be listening, and then she sent her affinity out. There was Theo's heartbeat, steady and true, and because Viola knew that it belonged to Ruby, she vowed that it would not stop. Then she tugged softly, slowing his pulse until finally he wobbled and started to go limp.

Theo didn't simply collapse, though. He bobbled, not backward, as she'd expected, but forward, toward the ground below.

A COLD ENERGY

Esta turned and saw that the source of the attack on the Nitemarket was a group of men dressed in long leather coats. They were covered from head to toe and were wearing masks and dark glasses that obscured their faces. There were only a handful of them, but three had machines that shot streams of green-tinged fire as they walked. One by one the booths went up in strange, crackling flames. Some of the vendors stayed and tried to rescue their goods, but the masked men ignored them. They continued working their way through the hall, and as they did, they began blocking the various entrances and exits. If they blocked the one to Chicago, Esta wasn't sure how she and the others would get back.

The heat of the flames and the icy coldness that came from the magic within them was thick in the air as Esta reached for North and Everett—Harte had already grabbed her arm—and yanked time to a screeching halt. The net of Aether that held the world in its grasp tugged uncharacteristically against her grip on it as she struggled to keep hold of three separate people and their affinities. Then she felt something else—an electric warmth that felt too much like Seshat's power—beginning to brush up her arm.

Esta looked to Harte, whose teeth were gritted, like he was struggling against himself.

"Those flames are doing something to the Quellant," he told her, confirming her fears. "It feels like it's being drained away."

Everett had startled from the sudden silence of the world, but now he looked at her with curiosity and interest. Esta wondered if she'd made a miscalculation in revealing the truth of her affinity to him, but North already knew anyway. And she didn't really have a choice, unless she was willing to leave North and his son behind to face the masked attackers alone.

Whoever the masked men were, it was clear that the attack was strategic and well organized. From the way they'd positioned themselves to cut the warehouse in two—and had immediately started herding the patrons like sheep—these men knew the market. The flames coming from their weapons burned with a cold energy that spoke of the type of ritualized magic used by the Brotherhoods. With their dark coats and masked faces, they looked like something out of an old sci-fi movie, but Esta knew that the creeping energy already vining itself up her arm was maybe even more of a threat. If the flames were eating away at the Quellant, she needed to get the four of them out of the Nitemarket now, before Seshat could do any real damage.

"We need to go," she told North and Everett. "*Now.* Whatever you do, don't let go."

"But the others," Everett argued. His expression was every bit as stubborn and mulish as North's had ever been, but it also bore the trace of Maggie's keen intelligence. And her kindness.

"We don't have time," Esta told him.

Everett was shaking his head, starting to pull away from her. "If we leave them here, they'll die."

Esta gripped him tighter, but she could already see darkness forming in the corner of her vision, and the ground was beginning to vibrate beneath them. She spoke to North, knowing he would understand without the explanation Everett seemed to require. "I won't be able to hold this much longer if we don't go now."

North's jaw went tight, and she knew he understood. "Let's go, son," he said, giving Everett a stern look.

"But, Pa—"

"It's not up for debate. You can't really expect me to explain to your mother what happened if you get hurt, can you? You know exactly what losing you would do to her." North's expression was stern, but his voice came out as barely a whisper.

"But all these people," Everett said, clearly torn.

"We can't save everyone," North told him, laying his free hand on his son's shoulder. "We never could."

Everett clearly didn't agree, but apparently he didn't have it in him to argue with his father—or maybe he didn't have it in him to break his mother's heart. He came, reluctantly, but he came.

The exit was still there, unmarked and seemingly undisturbed, but they all hesitated together before they went through.

"Do you think there's trouble waiting for us on the other side?" Everett asked.

"We'd be foolish not to expect it," North told him.

"It doesn't matter," Esta said, forming the words around clenched teeth. She could feel Seshat's power building, and already darkness was beginning to bleed into the world. Already she could feel the ground beneath her feet beginning to tremble. They had to go—*now*.

As they launched themselves through the doorway that led back to the shack in Cicero, Esta felt the same strange pressure of the passage, and as soon as they were through the doorway, she felt the fabric of time tearing from her fingers and from itself. She did the only thing she could do—she let go. Of Harte and the other two. Of time. Of *everything*. Together they tumbled through the doorway, into the dark dankness of the run-down shack.

And into the sights of three men with guns drawn.

The second Esta shook herself free of Harte, Seshat's darkness drained away. Immediately, she pulled the seconds slow again at the same instant that the waiting men fired at them. Time went still once more, but the bullet was already out of the gun and careening toward Everett. She pushed North's son out of the way, pulling him into the net of time with her only long enough for him to gasp in surprise before he hit the floor. Then Esta got back to her feet and ripped the guns from the men. When they were disarmed, she leveled the two pistols at the men and released time.

North had his own gun drawn a second later.

In the distance, sirens screamed. So many sirens. Something was happening, and from the sound of things even this far out from the city, it was something big.

"Who are you?" she demanded, shoving the dark nose of the pistol toward the men. "Who sent you?"

They weren't masked. They were maybe in their early twenties, dough-faced men who were barely more than boys, and they had the bland, pasty sameness of the midlevel businessmen who flooded the subways in New York twice a day in her own time. Esta doubted she would have been able to pick any one of them out of a lineup. The only thing remarkable about them at all was the silvery medallion that each wore on their lapel, medallions that were glowing a familiar eerie blue.

"We don't answer to maggots," the one on the left sneered. "And it's too late for you anyway. There's no stopping what the Brotherhoods have already set into motion." He gave her a cold smile, exposing a small black capsule held between his teeth. When he bit down, Esta heard a crackling snap, and blackness flooded the man's pupils.

Before she realized what was happening, there were two more snaps, as the others broke whatever they were holding between their teeth and joined the first. North moved for the men, but Harte pulled him back. It took only a few seconds for the darkness in their pupils to begin transforming the men, pulling them inward until suddenly they were gone with only a burst of numbing cold left behind in their wake.

"What the hell—" Harte swore as he scrubbed at his mouth. His eyes were wide with disbelief. "They're gone."

"I don't think those were the authorities," Everett said.

"I don't either," Esta agreed. "You saw their badges. . . ." She glanced at North and knew he'd recognized them as well.

"They were definitely from the Brotherhoods," North said. His face was caught in the shadows of the room, but Esta could tell that the truth of the situation was starting to become more real for him.

"Something's happened," she told them, her stomach sinking. "Those sirens—"

But North's attention was on Everett, who'd been moving toward the door that led back into the Nitemarket. He snagged his son by the collar. "Where do you think you're going?"

"If those men were from the Brotherhoods, the ones inside probably are too. If we don't go back, people are going to die in there," Everett told him, straightening so that he was taller than his father.

"And you think I'm going to let you go die with them?" North asked.

"I can stop this," Everett said, his face a mask of stubborn determination. "You know I can." He pulled a couple of small metal devices from his pocket.

"Maybe you can, and maybe you can't. But that's not a chance I'm willing to let you take," North told him. "Right now we're not going anywhere but back to the warehouse, where you'll be safe. Before anything else happens."

But Esta had a strong suspicion that North already knew his idea of safety was an illusion, especially if the attack had already happened.

"I can't leave now, not knowing I could've helped." Everett tried to pull away from his father, but North was still the stronger of the two. "You can't ask me to live with that."

"As long as you're alive, I can ask anything I want of you," North told him.

"What are those?" Esta asked, nodding toward the small objects Everett had in his hands. They didn't look like much—quarter-size bits of metal and wire that were clearly homemade.

"One of his inventions," North growled. "He's always tinkering with something or another."

"They're neutralizers," Everett told them. "They could stop those men and their weapons. Easily."

"It doesn't matter what they can do. You're not going back in there, and that's an order," North said, sounding every bit the old man he'd become.

Esta ignored North's blustering and studied Everett. The objects in his hand weren't the vials or concoctions Maggie had created. They looked much more advanced, well beyond the technology that should have existed in the twenties. "You really think those are enough to stop what's happening in there?"

"I *know* they are," he said.

"We don't have time for this," Harte argued. "I'm with North on this one. We need to go. Now."

Esta shook her head. "I think Everett's right. We have to go back. Especially if those sirens mean what I think they might."

"Like hell," North growled, stepping between Esta and his son. The action was sweet, but Everett was so far from being a boy that it was also a bit ridiculous.

"Think about it," she pressed. "If we allow the Brotherhoods to destroy the Nitemarket and get rid of everyone inside of it, who will be left to question the attack that's maybe already underway?"

"That might be, but if you're thinking of going back in there, you can do it without Everett," North said. "He's not—"

"What I'm *not* is a child," Everett cut in, his expression earnest and determined. "I know you think I'm too soft. I know you see me reading and tinkering and working by Mama's side, and that you want me to be more like you. But I already am, or I wouldn't care about this so much. I can do this. I *need* to do this."

"I can keep him safe," Esta told North.

"No." Now it was apparently Harte's turn to play the hero. "I'm not letting you go in there alone."

It took everything Esta had not to roll her eyes at him. As much as she was warmed by his concern, she knew they couldn't risk him going back in there. "Seshat isn't going to be any help if you come with me," she reminded him. "You stay here with North and keep watch in case anyone else does happen to show up. Everett and I will take care of the men in the Nitemarket."

Esta handed Harte the other pistol she'd been holding. With time pulled slow, she wouldn't need it. Then she held out her hand for Everett.

"I still don't like this," North said, stepping forward.

"That's because you got old," she told him dryly. "You've lost all your sense of adventure." But there was an emotion in his eyes—a fear that Esta knew she might never understand—and it made her soften a little. There wasn't really a version of her story that she could see ending with the sort of *consequences* that North and Maggie had to watch over. "I'll take care of him, North. I promise."

It felt like an odd promise to make since Everett was no child. He was a couple of years younger than Esta herself, but he was more than tall enough to feel like her equal.

"Ready?" she asked, and when Everett gave her a determined nod, she reached for her affinity and left the others suspended in time.

"It's quite a trick you can do there," Everett said, clearly trying to cover his unease with a little bravado.

"Yeah, well . . ." She shrugged off the unspoken question. "I'm more interested in seeing what sort of tricks *you* can do."

Once they were back inside the market, Esta saw that the destruction had progressed. More of the stalls were being consumed by the strange flames that filled the space both with the heat of fire's normal oxidation and the icy energy that was the mark of unnatural magic. It felt the same as standing too close to the Brink, and considering what the explosion had done to the Quellant that should have still been in Harte's system, she didn't have any desire to get close enough to the flames to test them.

Esta gave Everett a small jerk of her head, indicating that she'd follow his lead. Together they went to the first of the masked men, and she watched as he examined the weapon. He reached out to touch it, but she pulled him back.

"Don't," she warned. "We don't need company."

He gave her a small nod, like he understood, but paused to study the piece before carefully placing one of the small devices on the metal tank strapped to the first man's back. "I don't want to activate it now," he told her. "Not unless we want to get caught up in them going off—I mean, they won't hurt us, but they might make it more complicated. It would be best to set them off all at once and then get the hell out of the way."

"Sounds like a plan," she told him.

She studied the room as Everett led the way to the next masked figure. The flames were still undulating, slow and steady as they continued to burn, and all around, the Nitemarket was being consumed. People had started to flee almost immediately, or else they'd started to gather their merchandise in a feeble attempt to save what they could, but one person caught her eye.

Esta hadn't noticed him at first, but she recognized Dom standing not far from where the four of them had been when the attack originally broke out. He had a look of sheer fury on his face, and in his hand he held a bottle that looked like a Molotov cocktail. Apparently, he thought he could fight all five men with a single homemade bomb.

"How much does your dad like Dom?" Esta asked as Everett finished laying the last device. She pointed to where the rotund old man was standing, a portrait of rage and vengeance.

Everett shrugged. "From what I understand, he doesn't necessarily trust him, but Dom's a pretty dependable buyer. They go back quite a few years. My mom, on the other hand . . . she hates him."

Esta could see why. Something about Dom gnawed at her. She had the sense that he knew more than he was letting on, but she also had the feeling that leaving him behind would be a mistake. "Let's bring him with us."

She made sure to take the bottle from him before pulling him into the net of her affinity, which turned out to be a smart move, since he startled when she touched him. Thankfully, Dom didn't pester her with questions. His eyes narrowed as he took in his situation—her and Everett, the bomb now in her hands, and the world around them, silent and still—and seemed to accept it at once.

"I thought you looked familiar," he told her.

Esta shrugged off his comment. "I have a very ordinary face."

"You have a very *famous* face," Dom countered. But he didn't press. "I take it this is a rescue?"

"Of sorts," she agreed. "Follow along, and we'll be out of here in a second."

The three of them moved together—awkwardly at first and then increasingly with more coordination—until they reached the masked men. Once they were past them, Everett took another small device from his pocket—an object that looked like nothing more than an ordinary lighter.

"Is there a way to release time and get things moving again?" he asked.

"I promised your father I'd keep you safe," she reminded him.

"It'll only take a second. I want to be sure that the devices work," he added when she hesitated to answer.

She didn't love the idea. With the rest of the world frozen in the net of time, they were safe, but Everett had a point. It had been enough of a risk to come back that it made sense to make sure the risk had been worth it.

"Fine, but only for a second," Esta said, hoping that she didn't come to regret it. "Keep ahold of me, just in case."

Everett nodded, and carefully, Esta released the seconds. Confusion swarmed around them again, but neither Everett nor Dom so much as flinched. With a flick of his thumb, Everett struck the flint wheel of the lighter and a flame appeared. It took less than a second for the devices that he'd placed on the masked men to spark, and a second later the devices were crackling as blue-white smoke began to flow from them, billowing around them until they were almost obscured.

The masked men immediately realized that something had happened and turned, trying to find the source of the smoke, but before they could do more than twist, the smoke surrounding them began to solidify, and within seconds, they were each encased, head to toe, within a shell of hardened foam. The flames from their weapons died almost immediately, but not the flames that were still consuming the market itself.

"Will it kill them?" Esta asked, frowning at the ingeniousness—and deviousness—of the invention.

"No," Everett said, returning the lighter to the safety of his inside jacket pocket. "There's plenty of oxygen in there for them. But it'll drain any unnatural magic from the immediate area, and it'll hold them until someone else can deal with them."

Everett started back toward the men, but Esta held tight to him. "We need to go."

"I'm coming," he said, trying to pull away. "But I want one of those."

"No—"

"We need to know what we're up against," he told her.

The fire was still churning around them, and Esta knew that North would kill her for sure if anything happened to Everett, but she also saw his point. "Only if you can do it quickly."

It took him barely any time to break one of the flamethrowers from the pile of foam it protruded out of. "Got it," he told her, returning with a cocky smile and his eyes alight with interest as he looked at his new acquisition.

Beside her, Dom seemed far too quiet.

"Are you ready?" she asked, making her voice gentle. When he didn't answer at first, she asked if he was okay.

He looked around, taking in the extent of the destruction. "I can't believe it's gone," he said, his voice strangely hollow. "Everything I built."

"Everything *you* built?" Esta asked, eyeing him.

"You're not the only one with secrets," Dom said, finally glancing at her. He suddenly seemed somehow younger than his appearance would otherwise suggest, and Esta wondered whether the face Dom presented to the world was anything more than a mask. But that feeling lasted only a second, before her attention was drawn back to the danger around them.

The building that housed the Nitemarket was still burning. The fire had gone on long enough that it was clear there was no saving the building, but without the men and their flamethrowers, at least the people could escape. Everywhere she looked, the patrons and vendors alike were streaming toward other exits and returning to wherever they'd come from.

"I think I can put it out," Everett said, digging through his pockets.

"We need to go," Esta told him.

"But the market—"

Dom let out a long, tired-sounding breath. But then he shrugged. "It's fine."

"It's not fine," Everett argued, still trying to find something in the seemingly endless number of pockets he had tucked inside his jacket. He had to stop to cough, though, an indication that the smoke was getting to be too much.

"Now, Everett," Esta said, tugging on him.

"He built this. We can save it."

"I'll build it again," Dom told him, clapping his hand on Everett's shoulder. "*I'm* the market, boy. This is only a building. And buildings can always be rebuilt."

IMPOSSIBLE CHOICES

1902—New York

L ogan Sullivan dreamed of air-conditioning and flush toilets. He dreamed of street sweepers and automobiles, and especially, he dreamed of his smartphone, an object more powerful than the Mageus in this time, even with the surprising strength of their affinities, could imagine. He wanted to go home, back to *his* city and his own time, and the only way he was getting there was through Professor Lachlan.

Or rather, the way back was through the kid the Professor had once been, a kid named James Lorcan, with thick glasses and too much swagger for his wiry frame.

Logan knew that he had to keep James happy, or he was going to be out on his ass. Without the ring, Logan wasn't going anywhere. He'd be doomed to live out the rest of his—probably short—existence trapped in a past where people died of things like constipation. The way he saw it, there wasn't any choice. The Delphi's Tear was Logan's ticket out. With it, James assured him they could lure Esta back to the city, and once she was back, Esta could get Logan the hell out of there. Without it? Well . . . the ring was the only thing keeping James Lorcan interested in Logan, and James was the only thing between Logan and the many, *many* dangers of the city.

It didn't help that Logan should have already nabbed the stupid piece of jewelry weeks ago. James hadn't even bothered to hide his anger when Logan had let the Delphi's Tear slip away at Morgan's gala. Logan knew exactly how angry James had been because the kid had the exact same twitch near his right eye as Professor Lachlan. Logan had been on the wrong side of that anger enough times to know that it wasn't anything to mess with, but somehow the older Professor Lachlan seemed more reserved and polished—softer even—than this kid. James Lorcan looked like nothing, but he was all claws and teeth, and he had a whole gang to back him up. If Logan failed again, he doubted James would be so forgiving a second time.

Clearly, the ring was the only thing that should have mattered, but anyone could see that the dude on the balcony was in trouble. *Serious trouble.* A fall from that height? Without a parachute? Nobody could survive that. Logan tried to tell himself that the guy wasn't his problem. He tried to tell himself that he couldn't save everyone, but that he could help a hell of a lot of people if he got that artifact. If only he could figure out a way to get that door in the ceiling open so he could get to the ring. It was *right* there. . . .

Then he heard the girl scream.

From the first time Logan had met Viola, she'd seemed like a real ball-breaker. She was the last person he would have expected to make a sound like *that.* The scream was a high-pitched and utterly *female* noise, and it was so full of terror that he turned back. The three were leaning far over the railing, apparently holding on to the man, who had just jumped.

They have him. But Logan couldn't bring himself to turn away, not even when he saw the sun touching the water of the Hudson. Not even when it was clear that soon he would need to act.

Cursing himself and Esta and Professor Lachlan all at once, Logan ran to the balcony's edge. Whatever false magic the guy had been under had, apparently, broken. Now he was looking up in sheer terror at the people holding on to his arms.

"Help me," the guy screamed, his voice cracking with fear. His feet flailed so wildly to find some purchase on the medallion carved into the side of the building that Viola almost lost her grip on him.

Logan pushed her aside and took hold himself, cursing his stupidity all the while. Mooch glanced over at him, looking every bit as confused by Logan's involvement as he always looked, but Logan didn't care. He knew what they all thought of him. Every single one of the Devil's Own treated him like something that had crawled out of the latrines behind the Bella Strega. They'd been suspicious at first, and now that James kept putting him in charge of things, they hated him on sheer principle.

It wasn't a new experience, exactly. When he'd first been sent to New York to work under Professor Lachlan, Logan had suspected—at least at first—that Esta had hated him too. Luckily, she'd wanted the Professor's approval too much to let anyone know how she felt, and eventually she'd gotten over it. His situation now wasn't much different. To the Devil's Own, Logan was an outsider. An uninvited interloper who had moved up the ranks too quickly. He probably would've felt the same way in their position.

"If you let him go . . . ," Mooch warned, straining under the effort it was taking to hold tight.

"Don't let go of me," the guy pleaded.

"On three," Werner instructed. "We're all going to pull at the same time."

But the guy was freaking out so much that they were barely able to get his fingertips to the ledge.

"More," Mooch said. "We have to pull harder."

"He's gotta settle the hell down," Logan said. Sweat had broken out on his back and forehead, and with the gusting breeze, his skin felt clammy and slick beneath his clothes.

"Theo," Viola called. "You have to stop."

But Theo—apparently that was his name—wasn't listening to reason. The guy had already convinced himself he was a goner. "Please, you have to tell Ruby—"

"Tell her yourself," Viola snapped, sounding more like herself now.

Logan felt a burst of warmth filtering through the air. A moment later Theo's eyes drooped a little and the fight seemed to have drained out of him. He was deadweight now, but at least he wasn't actively fighting against them.

It had been a few weeks, but it was still unnerving how much stronger affinities were in this time. Logan had noticed it immediately, the way the old magic seemed to hang in the air, like cobwebs he was constantly surprised to walk into. Now he felt the telltale sign of Viola's power, and it lifted the hair on the back of his neck.

"One more time," Werner commanded, and started the count.

They pulled again, and this time they got Theo up and over the railing. He collapsed on the ground, conscious now, but visibly shaking. He might have been crying a little . . . or a lot, actually. He was gasping, and if he kept it up, he was going to pass out.

"Can't you do that thing to calm him down again?" Logan asked.

Viola glared at him. "Would you be so calm?"

Logan couldn't exactly say that he would be, so he didn't say anything else about the guy's whimpering. It didn't matter that he'd put everything on hold to help them save the guy. None of them had softened toward him.

"Fine," Logan said. "You're welcome, by the way."

It's not like I belong here, he reminded himself. He didn't need to worry about these people *or* what they thought of him. He only had to focus on what he'd been sent to do—the ring was still beyond his reach. He needed to figure out how to get that door in the ceiling open.

He'd barely stepped back into the library room and was about to head up the winding staircase again to take another look when he heard a grinding noise. The steel door that had trapped them was beginning to move. Slowly, it was retracting back into the wall, and Logan could already see a pair of legs waiting to enter on the other side.

Logan rushed back outside. "Someone's coming," he told the others, urging them to get out of view.

"We're trapped," Mooch said, his eyes wide.

"Shut up and get down," Logan ordered, pulling back to hide behind the half wall that ran beneath the windows as he closed the balcony door. Viola was on the other side, holding on to Theo, but he still looked like a mess.

Logan raised his fingers to his lips, and then he eased his head up, just enough to peer back into the library chamber. "There's only one," he told them. It was a younger guy with sandy hair, the guy from the gala—Jack Grew.

Jack had been facing toward the balcony the first time Logan looked, but now Logan chanced another peek and saw that Jack was already climbing the steps. He watched as Jack reached the top of the steps, took a pin from his lapel, and pricked his index finger. After he smeared the blood across the tips of his other fingers, Jack pressed his hand against the image of the Philosopher's Hand that was inscribed on the medallion. It wasn't even a second later when the heavy metal seal began to move, retracting into the ceiling and leaving an opening. Jack continued up the steps and disappeared into the chamber above.

Logan closed his eyes for a second and sent his affinity out to confirm . . . yes, the ring was there.

"He's gone," Logan said, standing now. He kept one eye on the opening in the ceiling, in case Jack Grew started to descend.

"We need to get Theo out of here," Viola told him. "Now, while we have a chance."

"No," Logan said. "We need to get the Delphi's Tear. That's what we were sent here to do, and that's what we're going to do. It's still up there." The round doorway was still gaping open like a portal, and the ring was *right there*. It was so close that Logan could not walk away from it—none of them could. Not when it would be so easy to climb the steps to overtake Jack Grew.

He could get the damn artifact, and he could go *home*.

Viola froze, and her dark brows drew together like she didn't believe him. "You can't know that for sure," she said.

"It's what I do," he explained. "If I want to find something, I can find it, especially if there's any trace of magic to it."

Werner let out a low, soft whistle. "No wonder Nibs keeps you around," he told Logan, giving him a newly appraising look.

"It takes some concentration," Logan admitted, shrugging off their sudden interest. "And I can only focus on one object at a time. But I know the ring is there. Even with all the other energy in the air right now, I can feel it, clear as day. We can't leave. Not when we can go up there right now and take it."

At first, though, none of them moved to agree. They all stood there stupidly, like the answer to so many of their problems wasn't sitting *right there*, like a fruit ripe for the picking. Logan wasn't sure what to make of their hesitation. It wasn't anything he'd ever experienced. Esta certainly wouldn't have hesitated. She would've closed her eyes and pulled time slow and the ring would have been theirs.

But Esta was gone, Logan reminded himself. She'd double-crossed him and left him alone in an unfriendly city with a pack of Lost Boy wannabes for company. Never mind that at the time this all happened, he'd technically been holding her hostage. But she'd betrayed Professor Lachlan and their whole mission first, hadn't she? Every bit of this situation was Esta's fault.

Logan looked at the two guys James had sent with him—the kid with the dirty-blond hair called Werner and the redhead, Mooch. They looked like they would cut someone without thinking twice, but now they were staring longingly at the freedom offered by the now-opened doorway. He didn't blame them, exactly. Now that the Order knew they were under attack, it would be a lot harder to get out of the building than it had been to get in. It would be a hell of a lot easier to walk away now, while they all still could.

Too bad walking away wasn't an option for Logan.

"You know how important this is to James," he told the two of them. "There's only one man up there. *One.* There are four of us, and I know what you all can do."

"You can't," Theo said. There was a little more color in his cheeks now, but his light eyes were still unfocused from the spell that had encouraged him to climb up on the ledge. "That chamber's protected."

Logan looked to the west, across the city that would someday climb far beyond the height of this building. The sun was sinking below the water now, its circle of orange beginning to melt into the Hudson. "The sun's already going down. Any minute now their protections will be worthless."

"You don't understand." Theo had managed to pull himself together a little, but he still looked dazed. "If that door closes while you're in there . . ." His voice was unsteady, like he was still trying to catch his breath. "No way out, except one."

No way out except one sounded about right to Logan. It was the ring or nothing. Whatever protections the Order might have in store, Logan was ready, and he was more than willing to risk them.

"It's right there, Viola," Logan said, willing her to understand. "We can't give up now. You could take out the guy upstairs without even *touching* him. So could you," he said to Werner. "Besides, you can't really be thinking about listening to this guy. He's one of them. *Of course* he doesn't want you to go up there."

"Theo's with us," Viola said. "But the ring . . . This one, he's right, Theo. We came for the ring. We have to *try*."

"Not worth it." Theo was shaking his head now. "If you're locked in, you'll be trapped."

"Theo—"

"I know how important this is to you, Viola, and if there were any way to get the ring, I would help you in a heartbeat. But it's not possible. Jack told me everything. If you go up there, you won't be coming back down." Theo took Viola's hand. "I have to go, and so do you. I need to get out of here before Jack realizes I didn't jump like he planned." He seemed to be leaning on Viola more now, and her violet eyes were wide with indecision.

"Jack Grew?" Logan asked, his instincts buzzing at the sound of that name. "He's the one who opened the door up there. We can take him."

"You could help us," Viola told Theo. "If you did, we could be sure to win."

"I can't." Theo looked at Viola now, and there was a new desperation in his expression. "I can't risk being trapped up there. Don't you understand? Jack set all of this up because he wanted me to take the fall for the theft of the ring. When he discovers I didn't die, he'll do everything he can to pin the blame on me . . . and then he'll go after Ruby. You *know* he will. If I don't go now, there won't be anyone to protect her."

Something shifted in Viola's expression. An emotion lit her eyes that Logan didn't like the look of one bit.

"*Viola*," Logan cautioned. He'd been waiting for something like this to happen. He'd been *warned*. "You know what will happen if we don't get that ring," he told her. "Your friends, the ones that Torrio guy is holding—what's going to happen to them if you walk away now? If you leave now without the ring, you'll never get across town in time to save them."

THE PROBLEM OF THE RING

1902—New York

Viola let Logan's threat roll off her back. She was too busy trying to keep Theo on his feet to worry about some too-soft boy with too-pretty eyes reminding her of what was at stake. She knew *exactly* what was at stake—the ring, to start. If they didn't retrieve it now, while the doorway in the ceiling was open, they likely never would. Or worse, *this* boy would, and if he survived, he would give it to Nibsy.

Somehow, though, the problem of the ring seemed suddenly small compared to her other problems. Viola had Theo to worry about, for one. Considering the way he was leaning on her, he wasn't going to walk out of the building on his own. If he didn't make it out of the building, if he didn't make it onto the ship that would carry him across the seas, who would be there to protect Ruby from Jack Grew? Certainly not Viola herself. She couldn't even leave the city, and Jack Grew could go anywhere.

And then there were Cela and Abel. . . .

Viola had treated them so poorly, and still they had risked so much. They had risked *everything*—all for a cause that was not even theirs. Logan was likely correct—she couldn't hope to reach Cela and Abel in time if she walked away now, but another question worried her.

"What happens if Theo is right and we do get trapped up there?" Viola asked Logan. "Yes, we can dispense with Jack Grew easily enough. He's a fly to be swatted. But if that door closes, if it locks us on the other side, what happens then?"

Logan eyed the opening in the ceiling, but he didn't answer.

"I'll tell you what happens," she told him, hating the truth of it. "No one will stop Johnny the Fox from hurting my friends. At least if I go now, I have a chance to save them, however slim it may be."

"I can't believe you're going to give up on the Delphi's Tear when it's *right there*," Logan said with clear disbelief. "If you walk away now, the Order will win. They will finish consecrating this chamber, and they will begin building their power, and they will never stop working to destroy magic. Someday, years from now, the old magic will be hardly anything but a myth, and it will be your fault."

Logan was not wrong. The ring was one of the artifacts Dolph Saunders had been willing to die for. Could Viola really walk away, knowing she was so close?

But she understood that Theo had not been lying, and she trusted him—perhaps as well as she trusted anyone. If Theo Barclay, who had risked his reputation and his life, said that there was no way out of the room above if that seal closed, she believed him.

"If we're trapped up there, the Order still wins," she told Logan.

"The halls are dark," Theo said. "It means the members are still secured in their sanctuary below. We can go now, before they've realized what happened here. We can leave now, and we can all live long enough to try again some other day."

Viola turned to Logan, not quite believing that everything had come to this, about to tell him that she had to go—that they *all* must go—when a familiar voice spoke close to her ear.

"We cannot leave the ring."

Viola turned to find Jianyu standing there. He'd appeared suddenly in the room, like an apparition.

Logan cursed from the surprise of Jianyu's appearance, and even the others jumped.

"What are you doing here?" Viola asked, her voice rising.

Jianyu gave her a bemused look at her spark of temper. "I saw you go into the building, and so I followed when I could," he said simply. "You would prefer I left you to accomplish this on your own?"

It wasn't that, but Viola understood that if Jianyu was there, then he had not heard Nibsy's threats as she'd hoped. If he was standing there, high above the city in the Order's most guarded rooms, no one was protecting Cela and Abel.

She shook her head. This wasn't the plan, but then, the plan had gone wrong nearly from the start. "Where were you before?" she demanded, even though it no longer mattered. Not when so much else had gone wrong.

"Delayed," Jianyu told her, and from the frustration in his expression, she suspected that something had happened—something they had not planned for. "That does not change what must happen next."

"If we're trapped up there, Cela and Abel will die," she told him. "Once Nibsy realizes we aren't coming out, he'll let Torrio kill them."

"Then go," Jianyu said. His expression was determined. "There will be some time before Nibsy knows for sure what has happened here. I will retrieve the artifact, as we planned, and you will go to protect our friends."

Viola hesitated. "But if Theo is correct and you're trapped when the door closes . . ."

"I will not be seen when it is opened again," Jianyu reassured her.

It was possible, she supposed, for Jianyu to make himself undetectable if he were locked into the room above. It was maybe possible that he could do what she could not. Perhaps they could still manage to succeed despite everything that had gone wrong during this terrible mess of a night.

"Go. Get to Cela and Abel," Jianyu told her again. "You are far better suited to handle that particular problem."

Jianyu was right. With her knife and with her affinity, she could neutralize Torrio's threat—as long as she arrived in time.

Viola gave Jianyu a nod. It was, it seemed, the only way. Then she turned to the others. "I'm going with Theo. Come with us?"

"You have your orders," Logan reminded Mooch and Werner. "We all do." He was glaring at Viola.

"He's right," Werner said. "Nibsy won't be happy if we come back without the ring."

"Will he be happier if you don't come back at all?" Viola asked him. "Will he even care?" When Werner didn't respond at first, she threw up her hands. "Nibsy can't expect so much of you if death is certain. Dolph never would have asked such a thing of you. He would not have asked it of *any* of us," she told them.

The invocation of Dolph's name sent an uneasiness through the group. It was Mooch who finally broke the momentary silence.

"Viola's right," Mooch agreed, stepping away from Logan. "I've already been to the Tombs once this month, and I don't have any plans to go back. I ain't interested in dying here either. Not for Nibsy Lorcan."

Viola gave him a nod of thanks.

Werner looked between Logan and Mooch. "I dunno, Mooch. Nibs gave us a job. . . ."

"It can't be done," Mooch argued. "Besides, you know what happened the last time he gave me a job to do."

Werner considered the issue.

"You can't walk away from this," Logan argued, but it was clear he'd lost control of the situation.

Werner ducked his head a little, meeting Logan's eyes. "I'm going with them," he said. "I'll take my chances with Nibsy. He ain't that tough, anyway."

"Come with us," Viola told Logan. "Jianyu can retrieve the artifact. There's no need to die here. Not for Nibsy."

"I don't have any plans to die," Logan told her, backing toward the staircase. His expression had hardened now, and his voice was stiff. "And I'm not about to let him walk off with the ring. If you're going, then go. But I'm staying." He glared at Jianyu.

Viola turned to Jianyu. "Are you sure about this?"

"I will get the ring," he told her, as though anything that day had been so easy as that. *I will keep it from this one.* He didn't say the words, but it was there in the silent sureness of his expression. "Go. Make certain that Cela is safe."

Viola didn't want to leave Jianyu, but they were out of time. Theo was already pulling at her hand, dragging her back into the library. She looked back only once, and Jianyu gave her a small nod. A silent promise. *Go,* his expression seemed to say. *Time is running out.*

He was not wrong. If Viola could make it back to the building where Cela was stationed before John Torrio made a move, she would be more than lucky. But she would try. *Madonna,* she would try.

"We should take the back staircase," Theo told them, leading the way to the other end of the building.

"The elevator worked last time," Mooch argued.

Viola hated the idea, but one look at Theo told her that Mooch was right. "Do you know how to work it?" she asked.

"I watched Logan," Werner said. "How hard could it be?"

In the end, it was Theo who depressed the lever to control their descent. They could still hear alarm bells ringing as the elevator vibrated around them. The small clocklike device above the door counted down to what might be an ambush.

When the doors opened, they were ready, but so, too, were the Order. When they stepped from the small cage, three men were waiting. Viola's knife was already drawn, but Mooch stepped in front of her. He closed his eyes, and flames erupted from the marble floors, first behind the men, who turned to see what had happened. Then the flames began to encircle them, holding them in place. The men drew guns, but the flames contracted suddenly, causing the men to press together, dropping their arms so they wouldn't be singed.

Mooch opened his eyes and gave Theo a smug, satisfied smile. "That should hold them."

Theo looked momentarily taken aback. "If it doesn't bring the whole building down."

"It won't," Mooch said, lifting his hand to show a small flame dancing at his fingertips. He let it weave between his fingers like a snake, but it didn't so much as singe his skin. "They do what I say." Then he closed his fist, extinguishing the flame.

Theo appeared briefly uneasy, but he blinked, and a look of utter concentration came over his face. "This way. We're close."

The four of them escaped through a service door. As they exited, Nibsy's boys started to leave, but Viola snagged Mooch by the arm.

"Nibsy can't know what happened in there," she told him. "Not yet. You have to buy me some time."

He pulled away. "I don't have to do nothing for you."

"You'd still be rotting in the Tombs if not for me," Viola reminded Mooch, but he was already walking away from her.

"We need to go," Theo urged. "I have to get to the ship if I want any chance of stopping the rumors that Jack has surely already started about me. He'll try to frame me when the ring disappears—especially if he's not the one who gets it. I can't be seen here. And *you* have to get to Cela and Abel before the Five Pointers can."

Viola looked up at the impossible building jutting like a blade against the deepening twilight of the evening sky. She sent up a prayer for Jianyu's safety, and then she and Theo melted into the crowd.

THE MYSTERIUM

1902—New York

J ack Grew stood in the center of the new Mysterium and paused long
enough to take in the wonder of his surroundings. The walls of the
room were lined with gilded sigils, the names of angels and demons
who lent their power to those worthy enough to carry out their will.

As above, so below.

Now Jack Grew was higher than any other—quite literally. The rest of
the men in attendance shivered and quaked in fear two floors below him,
and the rest of the city was lower still.

It had been almost too easy to reach this point. The old men in the
Inner Circle had been so taken with his demonstrations at the gala that
they had been more than willing to allow him the privacy to work on the
measures he'd proposed to seal the Mysterium—blood magic, as ancient
as the Nile itself. Guaranteed not to be corruptible or breakable. They
had been so excited about the enchantment, they'd never questioned his
truthfulness. Why would they, when they never doubted his desire to join
them? Who, after all, *wouldn't* want to become one of the chosen?

Only the man who had already surpassed them all.

The Inner Circle—the High Princept, especially—never considered
that membership in the Inner Circle meant nothing at all to Jack, so the
High Princept never suspected that Jack had also given *himself* a way into
the new Mysterium. A spare key, of sorts, that he had built into the very
enchantment he'd devised.

On instinct, Jack patted the place where the Book usually sat in his jacket pocket. His pulse jumped to find the pocket empty, but he reminded himself that this was for the best. He'd left the Ars Arcana back in his rooms, under lock and key in a heavily warded safe. It had been a hard decision—the temptation to keep it always with him was enormous—but Jack couldn't chance losing the Book, and he knew he couldn't be sure that the Inner Circle wouldn't have some surprise in store. He understood that some members still didn't completely trust him, so he had to be prepared in case they'd layered in some other protection that he was unaware of.

He could not allow anyone to discover that he had the Order's most prized and important artifact. Not now. Not when he was so close to retrieving the ring, and with it, to finally finishing his great machine. Still, the absence of the Book bothered him. Jack could almost feel the weight of it still there, a phantom limb.

So far everything was going to plan. It had been easy enough to duck out of the sanctuary without being seen, and when he'd arrived at the antechamber, the door opened easily, exactly as he'd planned. He'd found the balcony empty, as he'd hoped it would be.

Jack could have looked. There was part of him that wanted to. Seeing Barclay's broken body splayed on the pavement below would have given him *enormous* satisfaction, but he wouldn't be greedy. He would save that particular moment for after, when he would have the time to savor it.

Instead, he'd gone directly to the stairs, directly to the Mysterium above. There, the wall of windows at the end of the room made the streets of the city glow in an electrified gold, like an illuminated map through the crystalline glass. The windows had been specially designed and bespelled by the Inner Circle to reveal the truth of the Order's power. Through them, the men of the Inner Circle could be reminded that the city—every *inch* of the island—had been touched by the Order's power. The winding paths in Madison Square pulsed with a deep scarlet, and beyond the edge of the island, the Brink itself shimmered with ribbons of astounding colors, the only protection against the uncivilized threat of feral magic.

The strange threads of color looked different than they had earlier, though—the ribbons seemed more erratic, and now there was a shadowy darkness woven through their spaces. Jack wasn't sure what could be causing such an effect. He'd heard the worries the old men in the Order had about the Brink, concerns that it was waning in its power, but it was more likely that the difference was simply an effect of the solstice's power.

Either way, it didn't truly matter. The Brink was already becoming irrelevant. The Order might have been emboldened by retrieving the Delphi's Tear, but Jack knew that soon there would be more bridges and trains leading out of the city, maybe even a tunnel under the river. The Brink was a vestige of the past. It had served its purpose, but it would not be enough to stop the onslaught of maggots that insisted on coming to these shores. The Order must change to address that threat, or they, too, would fall into irrelevance, and their great nation—their *peerless civilization*—would fall to ruin.

Jack Grew would not allow that to happen.

In the center of the Mysterium was a replica of the Tree of Life wrought from iron and gold. Within the maze of its spindly branches were five open spaces, and in one of those spaces, the Delphi's Tear floated, suspended in the Aether. The entire piece seemed to glow from within. For the time being, it had an extra layer of protection upon it, charged as it was by the power of the Golden Hour. If the Order had been able to complete their ceremony, this protection could have been extended in time, recharged at each subsequent solstice.

If the Order had been able to complete the ceremony . . .

The air around the ring shimmered as Jack circled the sculpture and examined the artifact, waiting. With the Delphi's Tear, he would show the Order—no, the *country*—that there was a better way, a more modern and powerful approach to dealing with the threat of feral magic. He would show everyone how the occult sciences could change the world. He had only to wait for the golden light to dim, and with the confusion in the sanctuary below, the protections of the Golden Hour would fade. Jack would be able to take the ring and forge a new path toward a new future.

Once the sun had dipped below the horizon, Jack watched as the electrified streets began to dim. Far off, the Brink still lit the river with its strange colors, but the sculptural tree began to dim. Its protections began to wane. The Golden Hour had come to an end.

It was time.

Jack reached for the ring, certain of his victory, but he had not yet touched it when a pain erupted in the back of his head, sharp and *absolute*. His legs went out from under him at the impact, and he barely caught himself as he crumpled to the floor, his vision already blurring.

As Jack tried to gather his wits and focus through the pain, a masked figure stepped up behind him. Barely holding on to consciousness, Jack could only *just* make out the shape of a man. He realized then what had happened. Someone was there with him in the Mysterium. Someone had broken through every protection he'd created, throwing his plans into chaos.

No. This couldn't be happening. *Not again.*

Before Jack could even bring himself to his knees, the thief had already grabbed the ring, dislodging it from the Aether, and then turned to retreat. But the instant the thief's unworthy hands had touched the artifact, the protections Jack had put in place awoke. The medallion at the entrance of the Mysterium began to slide back into place, blocking the exit before the thief could reach it.

Jack couldn't help but laugh at the absurdity of the situation he found himself in as the thief darted around the room, looking for some other option. But there was no escape from a doorless room high above the city streets except one. Jack tried again to stand, but his head spun, and he collapsed again, unable to do more than simply lie there with the room swirling around him.

If he could make it to the doorway . . . perhaps he could pull himself across the floor and perform the ritual to open it—except that he knew that plan was pointless. Even if Jack could get *himself* out of this chamber, he was in no shape to stop the masked figure from also escaping. Better to be trapped there together. At least this way the bastard who'd hit him wouldn't be able to take the ring. At least this way Jack could make it appear that he was protecting the Order's treasures, and the old men would never know the truth.

Jack thought that he had planned so carefully. He'd been sure that he'd accounted for every possibility, and *still* this had happened. Soon the sanctuary below would open. Soon the Inner Circle would rush up to the Mysterium to check on the artifact, and the High Princept would use his blood to open the door. Soon they would find Jack here, and there would be questions.

It doesn't matter. Jack would have answers. When they finally discovered him, the perpetrator would already be disposed of. Perhaps he wouldn't get the ring that night, as he'd hoped, but Jack would be hailed a hero.

The thief pounded on the bronze seal on the floor, but after a few minutes, the thief seemed to understand that he was trapped. He ran to the end of the room and tore at the doorway that led to the balcony. The warm summer air gusted into the room, helping to clear Jack's head. His vision was still unsteady, but the pain was beginning to recede.

"There's no other way out, I'm afraid," Jack said, carefully pulling himself upright. He reached into his jacket and took out a pistol, aiming it at the intruder. "You're welcome to jump, but if you hand over the Delphi's Tear now, there's no need. I might even allow you to live."

The thief stepped out onto the balcony instead. Then, before Jack understood what he was doing, the figure threw himself off the ledge and disappeared into the wind.

STUBBORN TO A FAULT

1920—Chicago

Jericho Northwood took one look at the weapon his son was carrying when Everett returned from the Nitemarket with Esta and knew that things had gone too far. Esta might have kept her word by keeping Everett safe, but she'd clearly let the boy take too many risks. North had every mind to tell her so, except he didn't know how to without exploding or saying something that might embarrass Everett . . . or revealing something he'd regret, especially since they'd brought Dominic Fusilli with them. The last thing he needed was Dom any more entangled in the Northwood family's business, so North kept his mouth shut tight as they all tromped back to their warehouse.

As the elevated train rattled into the city, North tried to organize his thoughts. Everything seemed so much more complicated than he'd expected when he'd decided to bring Everett along for a quick bootlegging run. He'd only wanted to help toughen the boy up a little, not get him killed in the process. But with the sirens filling the city air, it was becoming more apparent that Esta might be right about the tower. It was an idea that made North's blood run cold.

He hadn't been much more than a kid himself when the tower in California had been activated, but he remembered the aftermath. The idea that something like that might happen again seemed completely impossible, but if Esta was right about the attacks, she was probably also right about the rest. The way North figured it, there was only one thing to do.

Once they were back at the warehouse, they were greeted by the man who'd driven the truck earlier. "There's been an attack," Floyd told him.

"We figured when we heard the sirens," North said. "What's the word?"

"It's the convention. According to what they're saying on the wireless, the delegates were in the middle of taking a vote on the vice presidential candidate—that easterner, Coolidge, was set to win—when everything went haywire. They're talking about monsters, and they're blaming the Antistasi."

"Monsters?" North asked.

Floyd nodded. "Great beasts, according to the descriptions of the people who made it out. This one guy, he was saying the creatures looked like they were made from shadow. They killed a bunch of people already, and as far as I can tell, the attack is still going on—there are still people trapped in the Coliseum."

North glanced at Esta, who gave him a dark look in return. *I told you,* she seemed to say.

"I want to hear for myself," North told Floyd.

"We have the wireless set up in the main room."

Together they went into the warehouse, where the other Antistasi North had hired were already gathered around the receiver, listening intently to the nonstop bulletins. They listened for a long time, trying to get a sense of what had happened. The attack had been violent. Already, they were starting to count the dead. But when the reports grew repetitive, North knew there was nothing more to learn, and he clicked off the receiver. In the end, fifty-three had been killed by some kind of magical beasts, and because the attacks were similar to what had happened at the Conclave back in 1902, they were already blaming the old magic.

Back then, the government had used the attacks on the Conclave to pass the Defense Against Magic Act. But that had been an attack on a private group of wealthy men. The convention was public, and the death toll was already horrifying. There was no telling what the Brotherhoods would do, no telling how much more they could turn the public against Mageus . . . except North already knew what came next. Esta had already told him what would happen.

At first no one moved or spoke. The group kept staring at the now-silent receiver, and then they began exchanging uneasy looks with one another.

"I know that they blamed the old magic for attacks like this before, but I've sure never heard of any Mageus with an affinity like *that*," one of the men said, finally breaking the silence.

"Because it wasn't Mageus," Esta told him. She looked to North. "It was a setup. And it worked. Coolidge should've been nominated tonight, but now . . ." She didn't finish. She didn't need to.

North launched into action. "The shipment I was telling you about is in the back," he told Dom. "We're going to be leaving town tonight. I'll give you whatever you want for a good price, if you help me get it off my hands."

Dom's eyes lit. "Mind if I take a look now, seeing as I'm here and all?"

"Be my guest," North said.

"You're leaving?" Esta asked once Dom had disappeared to find the promised crates of Nitewein.

"As soon as we can pack everything up and Dom hands over enough cash for me to pay the guys I hired for the job," he told her.

"You can't run from this," Harte said, stepping forward with fury in his eyes. "We told you what was going to happen."

Which was exactly why he was leaving. "I have my boy to consider," North said, refusing to feel even the smallest bit of guilt. "I'm not going to stay here and let him die."

"So that's it? You're not going to help us?" Harte asked, stepping even closer, as though he wanted to go toe-to-toe.

North lifted his chin. "I'm going to protect what's mine for as long as I can."

"I don't blame you," Esta told him, placing a hand on Harte's arm. She cut a warning look at him, before turning her attention back to North. "But I wish you'd reconsider. We could use the help."

North shook his head. "Not this time."

"The tower could go off as early as tomorrow night," Harte pressed. "You'd walk away from that, knowing how many people will be hurt?"

"If it meant my family was safe?" North glanced at Everett, the boy with his eyes and Maggie's heart. The boy who had made them a family. "I most certainly would."

"Safe." Esta gave him a sad shake of her head. "You say that like it's possible for people like us to be safe."

"For the last fifteen years or so, safe is *exactly* what I've been," North told her.

"Have you?" Her tone was unreadable.

"I have my ranch, my family," he told her. "I don't need this mess you're stirring up."

"We're not the ones doing the stirring," Harte told him.

"Mark my words," Esta added. "If that tower goes off, it won't only be Mageus in Chicago who will be harmed. When Jack Grew becomes president—*when*, not if—nothing is going to stop him from making life for those with the old magic worse than it's ever been. Even Mageus like you, who think they can run off to safety. They're going to build more towers. Eventually, they're going to come for your family, too."

"Eventually isn't today." North understood what was at stake. He wasn't an idiot, was he? Hadn't he lived through more deeds and fought long and hard for the promise of a future for his children and their children's children? But that future was still a ways off, and Everett was right here, real and whole. He couldn't set the boy's life aside for some distant possibility.

"We didn't stop the attack, but we can still stop Jack and the terrible future he's planning," Esta told him. "We can stop 'eventually' from ever arriving if we destroy that tower. Tonight. *Before* he sets it off. We can save the Mageus in the city *and* those who have no idea what's coming. Help us destroy the tower, and we can save your family."

"You can't destroy the tower tonight," Everett argued. "An attack like that wouldn't help your cause at all. You'd just be giving the Brotherhoods another reason to rally everyone against the old magic."

"Leave it be, Everett. This is none of our business," North told his son.

"The kid has a point," Harte said to Esta.

"No," North told them, stepping between his son and the other two. "He doesn't. He's not getting involved. Get your stuff," he told Everett, who had the weapon he'd brought back with him from the market on his lap. He was already starting to take it apart. "We're leaving as soon as we're packed."

Everett set the metal body of the flamethrower aside. "You can go if you want, but I'm not ready just yet."

Looking at his son, the boy's face a portrait of stubborn determination, North was struck immediately by how young Everett still was. It didn't matter that North himself had been even younger when his own father had died or that he'd been about Everett's age when he'd been jumping from place to place, getting into all sorts of trouble.

"I didn't ask if you were ready," North said.

"But I can help," Everett insisted. "I understand machines. I've studied everything I could about the California towers—at least in theory." Everett turned to Esta and Harte. "I can help," he repeated.

"Maybe you can," North told his son, "but you're not going to."

Everett frowned at him, and North saw the flicker of temper flash in his boy's eyes. That little show of backbone was what he'd wanted from his son all along, but North found himself now wishing he'd never started down this path.

"Son—"

But Everett stepped around North, ignoring the warning he'd infused in that single word, and spoke directly to Esta. "If you're going to go after that tower, you need to be smart about it," Everett said. "It's not enough to destroy it tonight. That would be another attack, and another reason for the Brotherhoods to retaliate. They might even be able to repair the tower in time to set it off like they're planning to, and you wouldn't have stopped anything. It would be better if we let the whole thing play out, but if we could disable the mechanism so no one realized . . . Or maybe if the machine didn't work like they expected . . . With a couple of adjustments to the tower, we could turn their whole plan into an enormous, embarrassing catastrophe. We could save the people in this city who have the old magic *and* make Jack Grew and the Brotherhoods look like incompetent, dangerous fools all at once."

"You don't by any chance have an idea for how to do that?" Esta asked, exchanging a silent look with Harte that North didn't like one bit.

"Yes," Everett told them.

"No," North said at the same time. "I told you—he is *not* getting involved. We're leaving tonight."

Everett met North's eyes. "I can help with this, Pa."

"What do you expect me to tell your mother if I have to go home without you?" North demanded.

"Tell her the truth," Everett said. "If I can help these people stop the Brotherhoods from succeeding with the massacre they have planned, then I'm gonna. I think she'll understand."

Esta's expression was unreadable as she studied Everett. Then her gaze lifted to North, and when her eyes met his, North put everything he could into the silent plea he sent her. *Leave me my son.*

"Your father's right," Esta said gently. "I can't ask you to risk your life. Your parents have done too much for us already for me to let you get caught up in this."

"I'm *already* caught up in it," Everett said, his jaw going tight. Then the boy turned to North. "I was born caught up in this. You can leave if you want. I wouldn't blame you, but I'm staying."

"Like hell you are," North growled, fear finally snapping his temper in two. "You're going to get your ass moving so I can get you back to your mother in one piece. One way or another we're pulling out of this city within the hour. If that means leaving all those books you brought with you behind, so be it."

"I'd like to see you make me go," Everett said. He squared his shoulders, like he wanted to remind North that soft as he might be, he was still already grown.

"You heard what I said," North ordered, ignoring his son's posturing. "Bring that contraption along if you'd like, but you're not staying here. You're coming back to the ranch with me. Tonight."

Everett met North's stare, and he didn't back down. "I am not going to leave every Mageus in this city to die because you're afraid."

The accusation rankled, but North saw that it wasn't the stubborn petulance of a child shining in his son's eyes. Everett looked every inch the man North had hoped his son would one day become, and he was struck suddenly with the irony of it all. He'd thought to toughen his son up, to transform him somehow, but the boy was already there. And North hadn't been smart enough to see it.

"Every Mageus in the city isn't your concern," North told him, but he knew already that this was a battle he was destined to lose.

"Of *course* they are," Everett said. "Isn't that what you and Ma have been going on about since I can remember? Helping others. Protecting those who can't protect themselves."

As much as the boy took after Maggie, he had too much of North's own stubbornness. How had North missed that before? Had he never really *seen* his own son? "I'm sure these two can take care of it well enough," North said, but there wasn't any real conviction in his words now. The truth was, he would have done the same years ago, back before he discovered what losing something really meant.

"You don't think I know why you brought me along this week?" his son asked. The Adam's apple in Everett's throat bobbed as he swallowed down the emotion that was swimming in his eyes. "You don't think I understand that you want me to be a little rougher and a little tougher—a little more like you?"

The look on Everett's face had North's heart clenching. "Son—"

Everett held up a hand to stop his father's protest. "Well, I'm *not* like you. I'm probably always going to choose a book over a horse and learning over brute strength, but there are times when a little book learning can come in handy, and this might be one of them."

Esta had been listening to everything Everett said, but her eyes were on North. In them was a question that North understood—it was up to him to answer.

"You know you're as bad as your mother sometimes, don't you?" he said, shaking his head at his son. "Always trying to save the world instead of your own tail."

Everett's smile was immediate and nearly incandescent in its hopefulness.

North chucked his arm around his boy, his heart aching with the helplessness he felt. He couldn't protect his child without destroying him in the process, and North wouldn't be the one to do that. "Your mother's going to murder me."

"I hate to interrupt such a lovely family moment . . ." Dom was back, and who knew how long the slippery old man had been listening. "But I'd like to get on with my night. If you're ready to sell, I'll take the lot. Nine fifty a case work for you?"

"Nine fifty?" That price was less than a third of what they usually took, but it would be enough to pay his men and send some back to Maggie and the kids as well. "That's basically robbery."

"If you have another buyer . . ." Dom shrugged with a knowing look, and North understood that there wouldn't be any other buyers—not if Dom had his way. He'd put word out that the goods were tainted, or worse, he'd tell people where they'd come from.

"Make it ten, and you have a deal," North threw back, because he knew that taking the first offer would only serve to make Dom suspicious. But his heart wasn't really in the negotiation.

"Done." Dom pulled out a thick stack of cash and counted out the amount before handing it over.

North tucked the money away without looking twice. Being short-changed was the least of his worries.

LISA MAXWELL

"I'll have some of my guys come by to pick up the goods by the end of the week," Dom said, offering North his hand.

"I won't be here," North told him as they shook, and he hoped it was because he was home with Maggie instead of dead and gone. "But I'll make sure the crates are waiting for you."

"Then I guess this is good-bye for now," Dom said. "It was an informative evening, Northwood." He eyed Harte and Esta, who had managed to keep quiet through the conversation. "I'll say one thing: You certainly do keep some interesting company."

"You're welcome to them," North grumbled.

Esta had come over by that time. "I'm hoping you can keep our little meeting between us," she said.

Dom tilted his head. "I make it a policy to never make promises I can't keep," he told her.

She didn't seem bothered by his refusal. "I understand . . . though it might make it harder for you to reestablish your business if anyone found out who really was in charge of running the Nitemarket."

"A threat?" Dom said, rubbing at his stubbled chin. "And not a very creative one at that. I expected better of you, Miss Filosik." He appeared to be suppressing a smile.

Esta's eyes narrowed a little. "You're a frustrating man, Mr. Fusilli."

"And a helpful one," Dom said with a slight twist of his mouth. "I couldn't help but overhear your discussion. I might have something that could help."

Esta didn't betray even an ounce of surprise. "Do you?"

Dom made a small flourish of his hand. "Walk me out, and maybe I can be persuaded to divulge it."

Esta glanced at Harte, who didn't look happy about the situation, but she only gave him a shrug before following Dom out.

"Do you really think you can disarm the machine in the tower without anyone realizing?" Harte asked Everett, part of his attention still on Esta and Dom as they left.

"I know how the California tower worked. I think we could do something even better than disarming it," Everett told Harte. Then his gaze shifted to North. "But I could probably use some help."

North knew when he was defeated. "It's not like I'm about to let you go climbing up there alone."

"Look on the bright side," Everett told him. "If we fail, you won't have to worry about Ma killing you."

North stared at his son. "You don't know your mother very well if you think she wouldn't drag me back from the dead just for the sake of killing me a second time."

ALREADY FALLING

1920—Chicago

The following evening, the June heat was thick and sticky as Harte stood next to Esta in the line of people waiting to enter the Chicago Coliseum. He felt the sweat already dampening the cotton of his shirt and the hair at his temples, but he was too exhausted to care. No one had slept much following the events at the Nitemarket. They all realized how little time they had to stop a deadly future from unfurling. Even with the short nap Esta had forced on him before they left, Harte felt every bit as old as North looked. Seshat might have been silenced by another tablet of the Quellant, but in his muscles and in his bones, Harte felt every second of every minute that he'd been awake.

The mood of the enormous crowd congregating around the building was boisterous. A group of women in white dresses held signs and shouted at every man passing, demanding women's suffrage. Other groups held signs supporting candidates, men whose names Harte didn't know and didn't particularly care to. Occasionally, a shout would go up—*America first!*—and in unison, the rest of the crowd would respond with raucous shouts and chants of *Harding! Harding!* There was an energy in the air despite the heat, an excitement that even Harte, who'd never cared for the often dirty dealings of the political machine in New York, could feel.

There was another emotion running through the crowd as well—fear. Or maybe it was anger. From the hushed whispers and anxious expressions many of the attendees wore, it was clear that the attack on the convention the night before was fresh in their minds. Many of the people in line to enter wore black armbands in solidarity with the fifty-three men who had been killed during the previous night's attack. Others held signs of support and shouted for an end to the threat of feral magic. None of them had any idea that the attack had been staged, and Harte wondered if they would care even if they *did* know—or if the attack had simply given them permission to put their truest and ugliest beliefs on display.

"It's exactly like Sammie described," he murmured to Esta. He realized then that he hadn't *quite* believed his brother's story. Not completely. Deep down, he'd hoped that Sammie had been exaggerating or had misremembered past events, but now Harte saw how naive that hope had been.

He understood fear, of course. He was well acquainted with the quiet, often unexamined hatred it inspired, and he knew as well what that hatred could do when channeled and directed. But he'd never imagined that it could unite *so* many people so quickly and absolutely. Short of standing in Khafre Hall that night so many weeks ago, Harte had never really seen the hatred against what he was—*who* he was—made quite so obvious.

"They've added security," Esta whispered. She nodded up toward the roofline, where men holding rifles lined the top of the building. "And that banner's new too."

The Coliseum was an enormous structure with a facade that reminded Harte of a castle with its multiple medieval-looking towers and arched entrances. The whole building was decorated with patriotic bunting and flags that hung limp and still in the windless air. In the center of the roofline, a tower rose, its steel frame a dark outline silhouetted by the setting sun. The tower bore a placard with the logo of American Steel at its apex, and hanging from that was an enormous silken banner. On it was an image Harte recognized: the Philosopher's Hand.

Harte had seen copies of this familiar alchemical formula many times before in his studies. He'd seen it in the warehouse where Jack Grew had built his first machine, and he'd seen it again in the bowels of Khafre Hall. But this version was different. The emblem on the banner reminded Harte a little of the moving picture box that had been in the San Francisco hotel room, because the image seemed almost *alive*. It had clearly been charmed in some way. The five elemental icons floated above the disembodied hand's fingers—crown, key, lantern, moon, and star—each rotating slowly, glowing with their own unique phosphorescence. The palm held the fish in a flame-bound sea with softly undulating waves. It was the symbolic representation of quintessence—Aether. But though the flames churned, the banner did not burn.

"Jack showed me a similar image back in New York," Harte told Esta. "This one appearing now can't be a coincidence."

"It's happening tonight." She sounded more worried than she had earlier. All day, she'd worn her usual air of confidence as they'd gone over the plans and preparations, until everything was excruciatingly clear and everyone was ready. Now she looked nervous.

Harte couldn't say anything to bolster her, though, because they'd finally reached the entrance. Esta fell silent as Harte handed over the tickets Dom had procured for them, and a man wearing a too-familiar silvery medallion on his lapel waved the two of them through.

"They're everywhere," Harte whispered, noticing that every few yards there was someone else wearing one of the medallions that served to detect illegal magic. Many wore badges bearing the enchanted image of the Philosopher's Hand as well.

"Of course they're everywhere. The Brotherhoods will be the reason Jack gets the nomination," Esta reminded him. "Unless we stop him."

Once inside the building, they allowed themselves to be carried with the crush of other attendees toward the main hall. Harte pulled the pocket watch Everett had given him from the inside pocket of his vest, but he was disappointed to see nothing but the time displayed by the hands. The watch was one of Everett's contraptions—not magic, because that would have been too dangerous in a hall filled with members from the Brotherhoods. Instead, the piece worked with some kind of radio signal. Apparently, where Maggie was adept with mixing formulas, her son had the same touch with machinery. When Everett and North were done with the tower, the watch would vibrate and its hands would begin to spin. So far they were holding maddeningly steady.

"I hope we weren't wrong to trust North and Everett," Harte said as he watched the steady ticking of the seconds, waiting for something to change.

"Rett was determined to help us," Esta reminded Harte, even as she scanned the crowded hall.

"He's not the one I'm worried about."

She glanced at him. "You think North would get in the way?"

"You and I both know that North has a family full of reasons to walk away from all this and to take his oldest son with him." Harte had seen the fear in the cowboy's eyes. His own father might never have looked at him with that same kind of concern, but after losing Sammie, Harte had at least a little understanding of what North might be feeling. "One good dose of one of Maggie's concoctions, and Everett wouldn't have much choice."

Esta's mouth went tight. "I don't think North would do that to Everett. Besides, if North was going to run, he would have last night."

"Maybe . . ." Harte hadn't forgotten the cowboy's reluctance to allow Everett to stay. "But if they left instead of heading to the tower, we'd never know. We're just assuming they're up there." He jerked his head toward the ceiling.

"If you were this worried, you should have let me go with Everett," Esta reminded him.

"We already went through this," Harte told her. "You can't be in two places at once."

"With my affinity, it would have been easy to—"

"Not with all these medallions. Besides, it's more important that we focus on getting the Book and the dagger from Jack," Harte said, cutting off the discussion. It hardly mattered that with her affinity, Esta practically *could* be in two places at once. He wanted her with him, though, because at least when she was near him, he knew she was safe. "Whatever happens with the tower, getting the Book and the dagger is more important anyway."

Esta frowned as though maybe she didn't agree.

"We cannot allow Jack or Thoth to keep that Book, Esta." Harte took her hand, tangling their fingers. He hated the Quellant and how empty it made him feel, but at least it allowed him to touch Esta while he still could. The Book was the best chance he had of saving Esta from herself—of maybe even saving them both—but if they couldn't get it back, he'd take whatever time he had left with her. "We need the secrets contained in those pages."

"You're right," Esta admitted. "I think we can trust North and Everett, though. This is going to work, Harte. It has to." She gave his hand a soft squeeze and then lowered her voice. "How is she?"

"Quiet," he said, knowing that Esta was talking about Seshat.

So far the power inside of him felt as absent and empty as his own. Still, he couldn't forget what had happened at the Nitemarket. Whatever those men had done during the attack had made the effects of the Quellant all but evaporate. Harte knew that he had to prepare for the possibility that it might happen again. As long as Seshat's power still lived inside him, he would continue to be a liability.

"Esta . . ." He wasn't exactly sure how he could make her understand.

She turned to him with a question in her eyes, her expression serious and guarded. There was so much he wanted to tell her, so much he wanted from her—with her—but he settled for the only thing he could do *for* her.

"If anything goes wrong tonight and you have a chance to escape, even if it's without me, I want you to promise that you will," he told her.

"We've been over this, Harte." Her eyes flashed with impatience, and she started to pull her hand away from him, but he caught it before she could pull away completely.

"Too many times," he admitted. Her fingers felt delicate entwined with his, but he knew they were strong and capable—just like Esta herself. "I still want your promise. If something happens, and it becomes too dangerous for you to take me with you, I need to know you won't hesitate. I *need* you to go on without me."

"And what about stopping Seshat?" Esta asked.

"I'll take care of her." He couldn't meet her eyes. "I've told you where you can find the ring—"

"No. Absolutely not," Esta told him with a determined tightness in her jaw.

"Think about what happened at the Nitemarket, Esta."

"I can fight off Seshat. I have before," she argued.

Harte hated everything about the conversation. "Maybe . . . But at what cost? The earthquakes we caused were all Jack needed to build the first tower. We can't risk something like that happening again, especially not here, where everyone is already scared and angry. Even if we are able to get away, the mess we leave behind could be devastating."

She shook her head, stubborn as she'd ever been. "I'm not going through all of this again with you, Harte. We will find Jack. We will get the Book. We will leave. *Together.* That's the plan, and that's what we're going to do."

Harte could feel himself clenching his teeth. He'd thought long and hard about this through the small hours of the night as they'd plotted and planned. If push came to shove, he'd do whatever he had to in order to give her a chance to go on—to survive.

"And what if there's no way to leave together?" Harte asked. "What if the choice is you going or both of us dying?"

Esta only stared at him. "It won't be."

"You don't know that," he said, wishing it were otherwise. "And it might not be only your life at risk. . . . What if what happened on the train—"

"*Nothing* happened on the train," Esta said, her words clipped and her cheeks an angry pink.

"You mean—"

"There were no *consequences,*" Esta hissed. Her jaw was tight and her golden eyes flashed with anger. And with hurt. "Don't worry. There's no need for you to make an honest woman of me."

"That's not what I . . ." He paused, not knowing what he was supposed to say. Not knowing why he felt a twinge of disappointment mixed

LISA MAXWELL

in with the relief. There was nothing to stop him now from doing whatever he had to in order to keep Esta safe.

"Promise me, Darrigan," she told him, eyes narrowing as though she'd sensed the direction of his thoughts. "We leave together. Promise me that you won't do something stupid."

Harte didn't want to make any promises that he couldn't keep. He certainly didn't want to waste any more time arguing with her when he knew already what he was willing to do.

"You know, you look lovely tonight," he said instead.

Esta frowned at him, and it looked like she wanted to continue their argument, but then she seemed to sense that it was pointless. "I look like a boring old lady," she told him with a droll twist of her lips. They weren't painted the dark crimson of the night before, but that didn't make them any less distracting. "Just like every other boring old lady here."

She was right about the crowd—there were quite a few women in attendance, and they were definitely older for the most part—but Esta was utterly wrong about her appearance. True, her dress might have been a bit more sedate than the shimmering column of gold she'd worn to the Green Mill. Made from a dark olive linen, the color might have looked dowdy or utterly forgettable on anyone else. But not on Esta. The otherwise drab green somehow warmed the deep golds in her skin and made her whiskey-colored eyes look even brighter than usual.

The boxy frock had a low-set waist that obscured Esta's shape, but it didn't matter. With her height, the fit of the dress made her look willowy and graceful, and somehow its straight lines only drew more attention by hinting at the body hiding beneath it.

"Lovely," Harte repeated, lifting their joined hands and placing a soft kiss on the back of hers. He paused, their eyes locked, before he allowed his lips to brush across her knuckles again.

Esta's cheeks pinkened a little more, but this time it wasn't anger that colored them. "We need to focus on finding Jack," she whispered, gently pulling her hand away.

"I can focus on multiple things at once," he said, drawing his mouth into a wry grin, glad that however mad at him she might be, there was still something undeniable there between them. But the sadness in her eyes made Harte's smile falter. He wanted to know what had put that emotion there. "Esta—"

"We don't have to talk about this, Harte. We need to focus on the one thing that's important right now," she told him, brushing off the moment. "The rest can wait."

Harte wanted to argue. He wished they had a little more time and that he was a little less of a coward. There was so much he wanted to say— there were things he needed to tell her. He felt as though they were on the precipice of something he did not fully understand. It was somehow even more dangerous than the threat of the machine or the possibility of an unthinkable future. Whatever was between them felt bigger than the Order or the Brotherhoods and more powerful than the ancient being that waited deep within him.

It didn't seem to matter that Harte had escaped from death so many times—in chains and in water and in a feverish delirium. *This* moment felt infinitely more fraught. Like that step from the bridge he'd been willing to take so many months ago, Harte knew that with Esta, there would be no going back. He could retreat. He could take this exit that she was offering.

Except . . . it was already too late. He'd already jumped, was already falling, without any chance of returning to where he'd once been. Depthless water below, endless sky above, and all that mattered was the gold of Esta's eyes.

"What if I don't want to wait?" Harte asked softly, taking her hand again.

She gave him the smallest of shrugs and untangled her fingers from his. "That isn't your choice to make," she told him, and then she turned and began to lead him through the crowds to the enormous hall that waited beyond.

AN AWAKENING

1920—Chicago

Esta's knuckles still burned from where Harte had kissed them, and her cheeks felt like they were on fire. She didn't know why she'd just lied to Harte. It would be a week or more yet until she had to worry about whether what they'd done on the train—

No. She wasn't even going to think about *that*. Especially not there, surrounded by so many people wearing the Brotherhoods' medallions and a crowd who would happily cheer on their destruction. Not when Jack—the Book and the dagger as well—were so very close. She would figure all that out later, if there was even anything to figure out at all. Until then, Esta would do what she always did. She would pull the hard shell of self-discipline and focus around herself as she plunged onward toward the job ahead of her. And she would not let herself wonder whether Harte would have felt the same about a future together if the threat of *complications* hadn't been hanging over them.

The main hall of the Coliseum was an enormous arena with a vaulted ceiling running the length of the room and stadium seating ringing the main floor. Red, white, and blue buntings lined each level of the balconies, and flags were hanging in rows across the ceiling. Large signs with bold block letters demarcated the seating for the various states' delegates, and in the middle of the arena stood a main stage decorated in the colors of the flag. On it, a small woman had been speaking ever since they'd entered the arena. Her voice boomed out through the cavernous space, and periodically the crowd would erupt into cries and cheers when she made another point they agreed with.

"How is she doing that?" Harte asked Esta.

"It's a microphone," she told him.

"Magic?"

"Technology," she corrected. "It's electrified."

Heat swirled in the air, sultry and close, as the woman spoke. Her voice rose and fell, her words carefully crafted to condemn the women who would distract the men gathered there—*important men*—from the essential work of governing with inauspiciously timed demands for suffrage. Suffrage could wait, she cried, when the nation was whole and safe. When America put America first and took care of its own.

Women still couldn't vote, Esta realized. Perhaps suffrage would be granted soon—she didn't know *exactly* when that would happen or whether something they'd done might have changed that, too—but for now the women in the hall were nothing more than decorations on the arms of their men, without power or voice. And *this* woman was asking them to remain that way.

"I would remind you of Mr. Harding's words. Last night, in this very room among this very body of delegates, he accepted our party's nomination and reminded us all of our duty. In his great words, it is an 'inspiration to patriotic devotion—to safeguard America first . . . to stabilize America first . . . to prosper America first . . . to think of America first . . . to exalt America first . . . to live for and revere America first,'" she shouted, pausing so that the crowd could cheer after each beat of the speech. "So I say to my sisters, we must put our country before our own meager desires. The attack on our convention has illustrated that now is not the time to press the question of votes for women. Now is the time to focus only on the sanctity of our greatest institutions. The safety of our children and our very lives depends upon strong men who will enact strong policies to keep our families safe from the threat of those who would try to turn our country against the ideals of its founders."

The crowd's cheers grew overwhelming, and as the volume rose in a fevered pitch, the woman stepped back from the podium, clearly pleased with herself. Esta felt only disgust.

"We can change this," Harte murmured, like he'd read her thoughts. He brushed his hand against the back of hers, and Esta allowed the small intimacy of the contact. "We *will* change this. The world doesn't have to be this way."

"Doesn't it?" Esta asked, glancing at him.

Maybe they could stop the Reticulum, maybe they could even go back to where they'd started and try to set history back on its intended course. But what would it matter? Esta remembered what Thoth had told her back in Denver: Time and magic could not coexist. If he was telling the truth, it meant that no matter what she and Harte did, no matter how much they changed, the old magic would eventually die. It was also what Seshat had feared and was the reason she'd created the Book in the first place. The only question, it seemed, was how it would happen. And when.

"No," Harte said, his expression determined. "It *doesn't*."

Then Esta gave herself a shake. Maybe magic *would* die. Maybe one day it would fade away, but *how* the old magic met its final end mattered, she reminded herself. Maybe she couldn't stop the march of history. Maybe she couldn't stop the march of time, either, but she could stop this massacre. She could stop *this* future from unfolding. What they were doing there mattered—*it had to*—even with a sea of angry people around them that seemed to say otherwise.

The arena was sweltering, the temperature and mood both roiling and hot, as patriotism and excitement and anger all mixed together. The woman ended her speech with a rousing call for the nomination of Jack Grew, and a portion of the arena surged to their feet, cheering in response. But not all of the men in the crowd cheered, Esta noticed with a little relief. Large sections of the arena remained seated and unmoved, even as the announcer called for another ballot.

The time had not yet arrived, but with each new ballot, the moment when Jack would activate the tower drew closer. They needed to get the Book before that happened, but it would be far easier to take the Book when he was alone rather than in front of this crowd. To do that, they needed to find him.

"I think the speakers are coming from over there," Harte told her, pointing toward a small gap in the crowd where a man was approaching the stage.

"It's as good a place as any to start," Esta said, stepping away from him, so that she could focus.

They'd barely started making their way around the edge of the arena, toward the area where the speakers seemed to be entering and exiting the stage, when a man with dusty-blond hair and wearing a crooked boater hat trimmed in red and blue stepped into their path, blocking their way. Harte moved in front of Esta, to shield her from whatever might be coming.

But as Esta pushed Harte aside and took her place next to him, where she belonged, she realized the guy wasn't a threat—or at least not an immediate one. He was wearing a ridiculous smile and an even more ridiculous hat, which looked like the Fourth of July had thrown up on it. On his arm, he wore a black band emblazoned with the Philosopher's Hand, and his eyes were bright as he held out a pair of small silver pins.

"A vote for Grew is a vote to grow," he crowed.

It was a damn stupid slogan, as far as Esta was concerned. It didn't even make sense. "No thanks," she told the guy. "We're here for Coolidge."

"Mr. Grew offers these with his compliments, wherever your loyalties lie. We're all in this fight together," the guy said, practically glowing with righteousness and pride.

Esta was about to tell him where he could put the medallions when Harte took them instead. "Thank you," he said, tucking the pins into his pocket.

"Mr. Grew will be speaking later tonight, and I hope you'll give him a listen. He has a real plan for protecting our future," the guy said, even as Harte was pulling Esta along through the crowd, away from him.

"I can't believe you risked taking those," she told him, making sure to keep her voice low enough so as not to be overheard.

"Not much of a risk. Not with the Quellant I took. Anyway, I figured it would be worse to raise his suspicions," Harte said, shrugging off her worries. "Besides, if North and his kid manage to come through like they promised, Everett might want to take a look at how these work. Maybe it would help if the Antistasi knew what they're up against."

Esta couldn't fault that logic, even if she didn't like the idea of having the medallions so close.

They made their way around the arena's perimeter and were nearly in line with the stage, when another round of balloting began. The states were called one by one, and one by one representatives came to the floor of the hall to call out their votes. She and Harte paused to watch and listen, but in the end the voting was inconclusive. Jack had a good portion of the delegates, but not enough for the majority he needed. Not yet.

Harte checked the pocket watch Everett had given him.

"Anything?" Esta asked.

He shook his head and then tucked the watch away. "No. Nothing."

Esta could tell exactly what Harte was thinking—North and Everett were taking too long. She'd expected Everett's watch to have given some signal by now too. "We don't even know where Jack is," she told Harte, trying to stay positive. "Maybe he hasn't arrived yet. There's still time. . . ." She only wished that she knew how much.

Harte's eyes were serious as he searched the arena. Realizing the night wasn't over, the crowd was growing more unsettled, and a disconcerted rustling sifted through the arena as tempers rose to match the temperatures. "This crowd isn't going to hold," he said. "Not with this heat."

A little while later, the mood of the entire arena seemed to shift. An alertness went through the crowd like a wave crashing over the shore.

"There," Harte murmured as Jack Grew began to climb the steps to the stage. Harte had already pulled Everett's pocket watch out to check it again, but as he was opening it, Esta felt a cool energy course through the air.

"Did you feel that?"

Harte's eyes had gone a little wide as he stepped even farther away from her. "I did. And so did Seshat."

OUT OF TIME

1920—Chicago

D eep beneath Harte's skin, between what he was and what he
could only ever hope to become, Seshat began to shift and
move, awoken by whatever terrible magic had suddenly snaked
through the air and drained the Quellant from his blood. The ancient
goddess swelled, pushing at the boundary between them as she recognized the threat in their midst.

Thoth.

The sound of the name came to Harte as clearly as if Seshat had been
standing right next to him and whispered it directly into his ear. All at once
the arena fell away and Harte saw himself standing under a star-scattered
sky, and the humid heat of the room turned into the dryness of the desert
stretching all around him. A second later, though, the vision was gone.
Once again Harte was back in the crowded Chicago arena, standing in the
middle of the sweaty, sweltering crowd with Jack Grew holding the stage
above.

Jack stepped up to the podium and accepted the cheers that greeted
him. He let the crowd's applause grow and basked in their approval for
a long while, before finally lifting his arms to quiet the crowd. After the
arena went silent, he stepped closer to the podium and began to speak.

"Our convention occurs at a moment of crisis for our nation," Jack
said, his familiar voice echoing through the cavernous room. "The recent
attacks on this fine city—on this hallowed convention—are yet more
evidence of the threats to our great nation's very way of life. There has

been much talk about our party's chosen platform, our moral obligation to place our nation before the needs of an Old World, torn by a war that was not our creation. But the threat to our well-being lies not only outside our borders. As the events of last night showed us, the threat is already within our borders. It waits within our cities and towns, and any politician who does not grasp this danger is not fit to lead."

Much of the crowd roared again, and Jack accepted their approval, his chin tilted up to take it all in as a satisfied smile crept across his lips.

"Anything?" Esta asked.

Harte checked the watch and found nothing but the steady ticking progress of the second hand. "Not yet," he told her.

"They should be done by now," she murmured, echoing his own thoughts.

"We can't worry about that right now," Harte told her. If North and his look-alike son had abandoned them, it was too late to worry about it. If they were in trouble? "We need the Book. That's what we're here for."

Seshat chose that moment to lurch, and Harte couldn't stop himself from grimacing at the feel of her power beginning to grow.

"Seshat?" Esta asked, frowning.

He nodded.

Jack had started to speak again, his voice clear and his words painfully direct. "Those with feral magic are a blight on our great land. A disease that threatens the very fiber of our nation. For too long they have freely roamed our streets, threatening peaceful citizens. And now the opposition party would have us prostrate ourselves to foreign powers? The Democrats would have us join a so-called League of Nations and open our coffers to rebuild *other* lands, with no regard for the impact on public safety or the resources of our own great nation. Those are resources meant for the protection of our *own* people. Those are resources that should be used to fight the threat that already exists among us.

"Lenroot does not understand this threat. Allen does not understand this threat, and Coolidge *certainly* does not understand it. *None* of the other men who would ask for your vote understand the true danger. None have worked tirelessly to address the feral power that would have us kneel before it, that would destroy our very way of life . . . But *I* have."

As Jack droned on about his many accomplishments, it was clear where the other candidates' supporters were. The delegates from states that had not yet decided to throw their support behind Jack's candidacy sat quietly listening, barely clapping even at his more vociferous points, but the longer he spoke, the more delegates there were that began applauding.

"We all know the tragedy that befell this very convention hours ago," Jack said, his voice going low and sorrowful. "We have seen too many times the death and destruction that illegal power can generate. Too often, innocents have fallen victim to its terrible truth. But where is the other party's response to such a devastating attack? Where is Coolidge's?" Jack paused while the crowd shouted and booed. "You're right. They remain silent. They do *nothing.*"

The crowd roared again, a mixture of anger and hissing disapproval for the other candidates' platforms and actions.

"And what has been done about those who perpetrated such a terrible crime upon the innocent? Upon the *just*? *Nothing.* They've been allowed to crawl back into the shadows, hidden and protected by those who would ask for your votes. Tonight, those with illegal, unregistered magic sleep soundly in their beds, unworried about their future, while the families of the fine men killed last night mourn and this city cowers in fear. Among our candidates, who will stand for those good, true Americans who want only to preserve our way of life?" He paused, letting the crowd swell. "*I* will. This is my promise. And I will make good on that promise this very night."

The crowd erupted again, some cheering while other sections rumbled with confused shouts, but it was clear that Jack had them in the palm of his hand.

Esta leaned her head toward Harte a little. "We're out of time. Are you sure there's no sign yet?"

He checked the watch again, but . . . *nothing*. It only read the time: nearly half past eight. He couldn't help but wonder if the world would make it to nine before everything changed.

Once, Harte had stopped Esta from killing Jack. He had believed that the benefit would not outweigh the price she would pay for the weight of Jack's life on her soul. But with all he'd gone through, all he knew about what was to come, Harte thought that it was possible he'd been wrong. For the right cause, perhaps it might even be worth the price.

You would kill the one but leave the rest? Seshat's voice curled in his mind again. *Look at them, so eager for blood to be spilled. So eager to prove themselves more powerful than they should ever hope to be. They are no better than Thoth. Yet you would absolve their sins? Why? With the girl, we could punish them all and rebuild the world anew.*

Harte watched the crowd, the anger in their faces. The righteousness in their expressions—and the excitement. They were like a pack of dogs drawn to an injured animal, ready to attack. He could not deny the truth of what Seshat said. . . . But he pushed away the temptation of her words.

"You would kill them all for the sake of the one who betrayed you," Harte said softly, speaking directly to Seshat.

"What?" Esta asked, turning to him, but Harte's focus was on Seshat, and especially on her power roiling and swelling within him.

They deserve *to be destroyed,* Seshat responded. *Their hearts are rot and ash, unworthy of the wonders this world could be if magic lived free once more.*

"It wasn't the world that betrayed you," Harte said.

Was it not?

"It was only one man," Harte argued. "A weak man, at that."

"Harte?" Esta's voice broke through the fog that Seshat's presence had created, and he realized that he'd been speaking aloud. She was trying to tell him something. "We have to go. *Now.* It's our only chance."

Seshat purred her encouragement, but Harte pressed her back, fighting against her power and the pull of her temptation.

"The second you use your affinity, every person wearing one of Jack's medallions will know what's happening," Harte argued. "And we don't have any idea if the machine is disabled."

"If I use my affinity, no one will be able to catch us. We can slip in, get the Book, and be gone in a blink, before they even know what's happening."

But Harte could feel Seshat prowling inside of him, ready to pounce. "I can't go with you."

Esta glared at him. "We've been through this."

"The Quellant is gone. We can't risk what Seshat might do." Esta was shaking her head, opening her mouth to argue, as she usually did, so Harte softened his voice. "If you're right, if everything goes well, you'll be back before I can even blink."

"No, Harte . . ."

"I'll be right here," he promised. "I'm not going anywhere."

Jack was still droning on, but above them the ceiling of the arena was moving, the large panels drawing back as the mechanism moving them groaned and creaked. The crowd was entranced as the night sky appeared above them, and topping the roof was the tower. It was capped with a small platform, but there was no sign of North or Everett, no sign that the job they'd been sent to do had been done.

"You have to go," Harte urged. "Jack has the Book, Esta. He's right *there*, and it's ripe for the picking. If we don't take it now, we might never have another chance."

She looked like she wanted to argue.

"We need the Ars Arcana, Esta. It's our best chance of finding a way to stop Seshat without destroying you."

Something in Esta's expression eased a little.

"You have to go. *Now.* And remember, if something goes wrong—if it's between getting the Book or coming back for me—you have to *keep* going."

"I am *not* leaving you behind." Esta lifted her chin and pressed her mouth against his. Her lips were firm, but Harte could feel her trembling, and in that moment it didn't take Esta's affinity to make time stand still, only the feel of her lips, warm and sweet and *his*.

Suddenly they were standing in a star-swept desert, the heat of the night brushing against them as a different heat built within. He heard a woman's laugh, low and throaty, and he pulled away, gasping. Suddenly it wasn't Esta in his arms, but another woman, one with hair braided like snakes, eyes ringed dark with kohl, and a hint of madness in her expression.

Then, all at once, the desert fell away and Esta was there, her eyes wide and her cheeks flushed. "I heard Seshat," she whispered. "Just now. I felt her." She shuddered.

"We need the Book, Esta." He grimaced as Seshat pressed against the boundary between them. "Go," he told her as the ceiling above came to a grinding halt.

Finally, she nodded. Fear was stark in her eyes as she pulled away from him, and Harte had to clench his hands into fists at his sides to keep from reaching for her. But he'd barely blinked, and Esta was gone.

BRITTLE BONES

1920—Chicago

Time hung still and silent around Esta, and she hardly felt the tug of the Aether as she allowed herself a moment to look at Harte. Every emotion—surprise and desire and *fear*—were all mixed together in his storm-colored eyes. The memory of his kiss was still on her lips, but the echo of Seshat's laughter rang in her ears.

Harte was right to urge her to do this without him. Esta knew that, and yet stepping away from him felt wrong. There was a part of her that worried that if she turned away now, he'd be gone. But she knew that fear was nothing more than the ghostly pain of a wound that had long since healed. Harte wasn't going anywhere. He wouldn't leave her behind again.

All around her, the arena had paused in a sultry silence, swamped with the humid heat of the summer night and caught in the net of her affinity. How long had Esta been nervous each time she'd reached for the seconds? Probably ever since they'd blown up a train leaving New York. Now, though, she felt the strength of her power, felt the way that Aether connected time and space, ordered the world.

I could tear this all apart.

The thought came to her stark and pure and clear. *If North and Everett failed . . . If the machine goes off, so many people will die. And no one here would mourn the loss.* Esta felt all of the hate and all of the fear, thick as the summer's heat that surrounded her. If North and Everett had not succeeded, she could bring down this entire arena to destroy the tower and the machine it held. And if it also destroyed the thousands of people who cheered on the destruction of innocents? *So be it.* She could eliminate the threat of Jack Grew once and for all. Esta felt the temptation stirring within her, felt herself pulling the strands of time a little more. . . .

She stopped, suddenly appalled at the direction of her thoughts. She was shaken by how tempting they had been, even though she didn't know where those thoughts had come from. Destroying the Coliseum wouldn't help. She *knew* that. Tearing this place in two might stop the machine, but it wouldn't stop the hate.

Esta realized she was hesitating, which was something she'd been doing too much of recently. Or maybe it was an improvement, since her impulsiveness had caused her so many problems before. But the memory of Denver was still fresh. Somehow, Thoth was not bound by her affinity, and Esta knew that what she was about to attempt might not be easy. But she would not fail again. This time she would be ready. She took one last look at Harte, and then she began moving toward the stage, where Jack Grew waited beneath the night sky.

When Esta finally made it to the center of the arena, she climbed the steps to the stage, careful to sense any possible disturbances in the Aether. Ready for whatever might happen.

Jack stood before her with his hand raised and his mouth open, caught in the middle of his ranting. Esta hadn't seen him since Denver. It had been only a matter of weeks for her, but for Jack it had been much, much longer. The years hadn't been kind to him. He looked even older now than the very first time she'd encountered him, back in Schwab's mansion in New York. His already-soft face now sagged with age, and his skin gleamed with sweat, pink and sallow all at once. If he'd ever been an attractive man, the years—and the drinking—had stolen his looks as deftly as any thief. Jack's eyes were the same, though. Watery blue, they still burned with righteousness and hatred, and looking at him, Esta knew that she would not be sorry for whatever happened to him tonight— whatever she had to do.

She took one final look around the room to see the world as Jack saw it. Patriotic bunting decorated the balconies and draped from rafters overhead, men wore boaters trimmed with red, and the crowd was entirely focused on the stage, so many of them with a feverish look in their eyes. *Because they believe in this.* Because their own lives were so narrow and pinched and *fearful* that Jack Grew was enough to represent a hope for something more—or at least, something different.

Slowly, Esta inched closer to Jack. His raised arm made what she had to do even easier, not that she really needed the assistance. She'd been lifting wallets and diamonds for as long as she could remember, and dipping her fingers into the concealed pocket within Jack's coat felt as natural as breathing to her.

The Ars Arcana was there, waiting for her, like she knew it would be. Her finger brushed against the crackled leather, and she swore that she felt a light frisson of energy, warm and cold mixed together. This time she would not lose it. This time there was no chance of her being pulled into the darkness of the void, not while the cuff was on her arm, ready and waiting.

Carefully, her fingers gripped the Book, and she started to pull. Little by little, inching it out from where it had been concealed, waiting for something to happen. Nothing did. When the Book was nearly free, she reached for it with her other hand, to steady the weighty mass of it.

Suddenly Jack's hand latched onto her wrist like an iron manacle, just like before. This time, though, Esta wasn't surprised, not like she'd been back in Denver. She acted immediately, using all of her weight and strength to wrench herself free. But it was impossible. Jack was so much stronger than he'd been before. No matter how she twisted or writhed, Esta couldn't break his grip. It was like wrestling with a marble statue, cold and completely unyielding. *Unnatural.* But she still had the Ars Arcana gripped tightly in her hand, and she vowed to herself that only death's fingers would pry it free.

The room was still frozen in time as Jack jerked Esta back to him, and when he opened his mouth, it was not Jack's voice she heard.

"Where is she?" Jack asked in a voice that reminded Esta of brittle bones and broken stone. He shook her, his strength impossible. "I know she's here. I can sense her power." His nostrils flared like he was scenting the air. "Seshat . . ." The name came out like a whispering hiss, long and soft, but the sound of it was like nails on glass to Esta. Then Jack turned on her, his eyes bleeding into blackness as the pupils grew and obliterated the watery blue, and the world slammed back into motion around her.

UNEXPECTED

1902—New York

Cela listened to the alarm bells bouncing off the sides of the city's building as the sun traveled toward the horizon. Soon it would set, and New Jersey would begin to grow dark with the first minutes of twilight. The evening creep would find its way to Manhattan's streets, and she would know—one way or the other—if their plan had worked.

After Cela packed up the spyglass and made sure there wasn't any evidence of her being up on that rooftop, she took one last look at the towering building to the east. It was something to see, even from that distance. The world was an impossible place sometimes—hate and love, science and magic, all wrapped up into one. It changed so fast, often in the blink of an eye, and yet . . . some things never changed at all.

She took the steps down to the street quickly. She'd be glad to have her feet on solid earth, where feet belonged, but when she came through the stairwell door into the bar that occupied the bottom floor of the building, the saloon was empty except for two men. It didn't take a genius to look at their broad, flat foreheads and swarthy skin to know that the Italians hadn't shown up at this particular bar for a random drink. Even if they hadn't reached for their guns as soon as she came through the door, Cela would've known they were Paul Kelly's men.

At first she thought maybe she could pretend she didn't understand why they were there, but she hadn't taken more than two steps before they closed ranks.

"Why don't you go ahead and have a seat?" the one said, kicking a chair so it slid across the floor in her direction.

She glanced up at the bartender, a West Indian man who was polishing a glass and who glanced away as soon as their eyes met.

No help at all.

It was clear—he didn't want any trouble, and she didn't blame him, exactly. Businesses like this depended on their owners making nice with all types. He didn't know her and didn't owe her a thing.

Straightening her spine, Cela faced the two Five Pointers. "Is there something you gentlemen needed?" she asked, pretending innocence.

The one with the scar across his eyebrow smirked. "Sit."

Reluctantly, she took the chair and did what he said. They'd expected problems, she told herself, but for the Five Pointers to have come after her so soon likely meant that something had gone very wrong.

Cela had known this would be a possibility the second she'd realized the Order had sent three ships instead of one, but she trusted Jianyu and Viola. She only had to wait this out, and they would come through for her. She *had* to believe that.

It wasn't like she had much choice.

A few minutes later, things got even worse when Abel was pushed through the door of the saloon by another pair of Five Pointers. He should've been clear on the other side of town, so the fact that he was there made Cela's stomach sink. It meant that things were worse than bad. It meant that things might even be beyond fixing.

She stood to go to Abel, but the one with the scar—and a gun—stepped between them. "Save the reunions for later," he said, waving his sidearm to instruct two of the others to lead Abel to a chair across the way.

"You okay, Rabbit?" Abel asked. "They didn't touch you?"

"I'm fine," she told him, which was a flat-out lie. There wasn't anything at all fine about this situation.

The minutes dragged on, one after another, until the city was shaded by night and the streetlights came on. The saloon was filled with the kind of uneasy silence that you find in funeral homes or hospital waiting rooms, where the news coming is sure to be bad.

"Johnny should've sent someone by now," one of the men said, his flat Bowery accent twisting the words.

"You know what he told us, Razor. These things take time. We're supposed to sit tight until we hear—no matter how long that takes."

The one called Razor—like that was any kind of name—thumbed at his nose. "I don't like it. If Paul finds out—"

"Paul ain't gonna find nothing out," the other guy said. "He got picked up earlier by the coppers. Saw it myself. He was all trussed up and carried off in a police wagon. The way I see it, he'll be in the Tombs for weeks. That is, if they don't transport him to Blackwell's Island for a longer stay."

Abel caught Cela's eyes from across the open space. Paul Kelly arrested? That answered one question but raised others—including why they were being held here by Kelly's men, especially if Kelly himself wasn't calling the shots anymore.

The doors of the saloon flew open, and a large, boisterous group of men burst through the door. They were clearly day laborers, probably from the docks nearby, and they'd clearly already been drinking. There were a couple of Negro men in their number, but Cela didn't recognize them.

Kelly's guys were on their feet in an instant, but the newcomers were already at the bar and causing all sorts of commotion. Out of nowhere, someone threw a punch, and their drunken noise transformed to an impromptu brawl. The barroom was suddenly a mess of confusion. Men were everywhere, wrestling and shoving one another, knocking over tables and chairs. There was nothing Kelly's guys could do but back up and try not to get caught up in it.

Abel was at Cela's side in a second. "You okay?"

"I told you I was," she said, flinching at the sound of a glass breaking. She glanced at Razor, but he was stuck behind a trio of men who were tussling in the corner.

"You all about ready to go?"

Cela looked up and realized it was Joshua standing there. "What—"

"Quick, now, before they realize," Joshua said.

Together they picked their way through the chaos. They were nearly at the door . . . and then they were there, and all they had to do was open it, and—

When the door swung open, another Five Pointer was there. He wasn't overly tall, but he had shoulders like a brick wall, and he had a gun pointed in their direction.

Abel started to step forward, but Cela caught his arm. She wasn't about to lose her only brother like that. From behind, she sensed movement, and when she turned, Razor and the other man were there, boxing them in.

"Where do you think you're going?" the guy at the door said with a smirk.

Her brother gave Joshua a look that Cela didn't like one bit. "Abel Johnson," she whispered. "Don't you do anything stupid."

"You should listen to the girl," the Five Pointer with the gun said, but the words were barely out of his mouth when his whole body jerked. He barked out a surprised yelp as his eyes went wide, and then he lunged for them.

Except he wasn't lunging . . . he was *falling*. A second later, he was laid out, face-first, on the ground, with a knife sticking out of his back. The too-familiar silver handle glinted in the light spilling out of the saloon's open door, and in the street beyond, Viola was there, looking ready for murder.

From behind her, Cela heard a strangled gasping noise, and when she turned, she saw the Five Pointers' faces contorted with pain. Razor crumpled to the floor, lifeless, and a second later, his friend followed.

Viola was already pulling her knife from the dead man's back. "Hurry," she told them, her eyes scanning for other dangers.

Cela didn't fight her brother when he grabbed her by the wrist and dragged her out into the night, with Joshua close behind. Her mind was still reeling. Outside, they picked up their pace, keeping to the shadows in case anyone else was watching. When they were a few blocks away from the saloon and it was clear that they hadn't been followed, they finally slowed to a stop.

"Thanks for the help," Abel said, taking Joshua by the hand and then pulling him in for a rough, brotherly embrace. "I hope the guys won't be in too much trouble for it."

"Seymour's gonna have a bill for you if they bust up too much of his stuff, but it'll be okay," Joshua assured Abel. "Another few minutes and they'll break it up."

"I don't understand," Cela said, looking between the two of them. "You planned this?"

"Not specifically," Joshua told her, glancing at Abel. "And it's not like I did all that much. We all would've been in hot water, if not for your friend there."

Cela followed Joshua's gaze to where Viola stood, her shoulders hunched and her usual defenses clearly in place. She looked away when Cela met her eyes.

"You said you didn't want to help," she said to Joshua, still not understanding. "No one wanted to help."

Joshua shrugged. "I didn't. I'm still not willing to get mixed up with any sort of magic, but you didn't really expect I'd leave my man here hanging, did you?"

Her brother was looking too smug for his own good.

"I didn't—" Cela didn't know what to say. "Thank you," she finished finally. It was all that seemed appropriate, and still it wasn't nearly enough.

"Come on, Rabbit," Abel said, once Joshua had gone off on his own way. "We need to get going. It's not going to take too long before Kelly's boys realize what happened."

Cela looked to Viola. The Italian girl had been standing apart from them, and now her arms were wrapped around herself, like she'd caught

LISA MAXWELL

a chill despite the warm summer air. There was a lot that needed to be said, but Cela wasn't sure where to start, so she settled for the thing that seemed most important. "Thank you," she said softly, stepping closer to Viola. "We owe you our lives."

Viola's cheeks flushed, and she looked away. "It was nothing."

"That's not at all true," Cela said, laying a hand on Viola's arm. Jianyu had told her a little about how Viola felt using her affinity to kill. She had some sense of what the choice to take out the Five Pointers might have cost her. "You kept my brother safe. You came back for us. If you hadn't, we'd probably be dead."

Viola looked up finally. "I made a promise to you before."

Cela paused, remembering that night . . . the conversation they'd had in the darkened doorway of Mr. Fortune's house. Then, she hadn't been ready to give an inch, not after how ugly Viola had acted. Now? She wasn't sure what to think or where this put them, but she had the sense that they were somewhere new. "Thank you for keeping that promise." She let her hand fall away. "Where's Jianyu?"

"He'll come soon," Viola told Cela, but then her gaze rose.

When Cela turned, she could see the Flatiron Building rising above the city, slicing into the twilight sky.

She was about to turn back to Viola when she saw it—a man falling from the topmost point. He was no more than a speck plummeting to the ground, his arms spread like a bird's, as if he were about to take flight.

RIOTOUS FURY

1920—Chicago

The Chicago Coliseum had become a riot of noise and confusion. Harte had barely blinked, and suddenly Esta had appeared on the stage in the center of the room. She was holding the Book in her hand, but Jack Grew had her by the wrist. Seshat railed at the sight, but Harte barely noticed. All he was focused on was the way Jack was gripping Esta's arm and the fact that she hadn't already been able to wrestle away from him. Jack held on tightly to Esta despite her writhing, and within seconds he'd taken the Ars Arcana from her and shoved it back inside his jacket.

The Book hardly seemed to matter anymore, though, not when Harte saw the fear that was stark in Esta's expression. For once he understood Seshat's point. At that instant, he would have gladly destroyed everything just for the opportunity to kill the bastard.

Harte was already pushing his way through the riotous crowd to get to Esta when he felt another blast of cold energy shuttle through the room. Suddenly the doors to the arena clanged shut, and as the cold settled over him, Harte realized that he couldn't move. Struggle as he might, he could not take even one more step toward Esta. He was trapped in the eerie unnatural energy, locked in place and powerless.

"Help me," Harte said to Seshat, not caring who heard him. "If I can get to Jack, I will destroy Thoth."

I remember too well what happened the last time you made that promise. I gave you every chance, and you wasted it on an urchin.

This is different.

Is it? Seshat mused. *You had a chance already to kill him, or don't you remember? In the train station, weeks ago, the girl would have ended him. You stopped her then. Why should I trust you now? Why should I risk everything I am—everything the old magic could ever be—when you've allowed weakness to rule your actions again and again?*

It wasn't weakness to save my brother, and it wasn't weakness to spare Esta the horror of taking a life, Harte argued.

No?

No. This time is different, Harte promised. *This time, I will kill him with my own two hands.*

You have no chance, Seshat told him, her voice hollow. *Maybe before, you could have fought him. Perhaps you could have destroyed him years ago, when you stopped the girl from taking his life. Perhaps then . . . But now? Look around. Thoth has had far too long to reveal the secrets of the Book to the body that carries him. You should have let me have the girl. I would have ended Thoth and all of the hatred he has inspired before his power could grow. Look at what he has become. Look what your weakness has done.*

Harte did look—the entire hall was in an uproar. Those who had been sitting without making any judgment were now on their feet with the rest. Confusion swirled in the air, and stirring it was fear and hatred so thick that Harte could practically taste it, bitter on his tongue.

"So you're giving up?" he demanded. "You would let Thoth win?"

Seshat was silent, and Harte had the sense that she was waiting for something. But he couldn't understand her hesitation, not now when the danger—and the opportunity—were so clear.

Jack ignored the noise of the crowd and stepped to the microphone, dragging Esta along with him. His hand still locked around her wrist, he shouted, "As above!"

There were those in the crowd who answered, "So below!"

He shouted the phrase again and again, and each time he did so, Harte felt the cold energy swirl. Each time, more of the crowd answered back, until the discontent and confusion joined into a unified whole. "So below," the crowd responded. "So below."

"You need not fear feral magic," Jack thundered when he finally had most of the crowd on his side. "Not here in this place. Not when *I* stand before you." Esta was still struggling to get free, but Jack jerked her toward him and then took her by the chin with his free hand. "Do you recognize this woman?"

The crowd rustled and rumbled, until a cry split the steady noise. "The Thief! He has the Devil's Thief!"

"Impossible!" came shouts from delegates around the room.

"Not impossible," Jack crooned into the microphone. "Not when feral magic runs in her veins. Look at her! She appears to be nothing more than a girl, but many of you remember too well the terror she once inspired in the dark days before the Brotherhoods were united—before *I* worked to unite them. Look at her!" he shouted again, and Harte could hear the mania in his voice. "Look at how her face remains ageless. *Unnatural.* It is a mark against the very laws of nature and the known universe."

The crowd roared again. Jack had brought more of them under his thrall. With the cold energy radiating through the arena, its icy tendrils cutting through the sultry air, Harte wondered if Jack had actually put them under some spell. All around him, the medallions that had been distributed by the Brotherhoods were glowing a cold bright blue. Harte pulled the pair of medallions out of his own pocket and saw that they were also aglow, their eerie light caught like lightning in the palm of his hand.

On the stage, Jack had released Esta's throat so he could raise his hand to quiet the crowd. "But this abomination is not the only danger here tonight," he murmured. "There are others among us, others who refused the protection the Brotherhoods offered today. They pretend to be with us, pretend to have the care of our great nation in their hearts, but in truth they are enemies." Jack paused, his mouth curving with delight as the crowd began turning and searching for the traitors in their midst.

Then suddenly cold energy crackled around Harte, and all sound drained from the room. It was like being caught in time with Esta, only no one was frozen. All around him, the people rioted, but Harte could hear only a single voice that carried to him over the silence.

"I know you're here, Darrigan," Jack said, his voice amplified without the help of any electronic augmentation. "You can end all of this if you'd only come forward."

All around Harte, people pointed and faces contorted with suspicion as men and women searched for those without the Brotherhoods' medallions. They called them out and began to pull them from their seats.

"Give yourself up," Jack said as he scanned the room from the safety of the stage. "Do you know how simple it would be for me to kill her right now? I could twist her delicate neck as easily as a bird's." His hand moved back to Esta's throat, but he didn't yet squeeze. "Maybe that's too easy, though. After all this time, I deserve more for my effort, don't you think?"

Harte's vision flickered then, and the sky began to fall through the opening in the ceiling. Stars tumbled into the arena, filling the entire space and transforming the world around Harte into a desert night. Suddenly Jack was a different man, one with his head shaved clean and his broad shoulders draped with white linen.

Seshat raged at the sight of Thoth, but Harte now sensed something more than fury—he felt her fear as well. She wanted to destroy Thoth, but she was *afraid* of him too. Harte realized then that it wasn't any spell of Jack's that was holding him in place. It was Seshat's doing.

She was *terrified*, and hers was a fear thick and cold enough to make Harte shudder.

As quickly as the vision appeared, the desert drained away, leaving simply Jack on the stage. "It will be such a joy to watch the power be stripped from her," he said. "I wonder what it will feel like when it happens. I wonder if I'll sense her suffering or only the thrill of what she gives me." Jack paused, searching the room again for Harte. "But it doesn't have to be this way. You *know* that Esta is not the one I want, Darrigan. You, on the other hand . . . I would gladly let her go free for the pleasure of watching *you* suffer as I destroy the evil inside of you. Bring me Seshat, and I'll let your precious little thief go. You can save her. But only if you show yourself."

Harte knew it was a lie. But even if he'd wanted to hand himself over, his feet were glued in place and his head was filled with the riotous fury of the angry goddess.

"Suit yourself," Jack murmured. "Seshat . . ." This time it was not Jack's voice, but a voice far more ancient and terrible that echoed through Harte's mind. "You think to escape my power?" Jack laughed, a cackling that sounded like the cracking of dry bones. "The boy cannot save you now. When my tower comes alive, you will have nowhere to hide. One way or another, before this night ends, your power will finally be mine."

The energy in the room crackled again, and suddenly the noise of the crowd returned. But Jack was lifting his arm to silence them. "There is no need to fear those who hide among us," he told the crowd. "Not any longer. Those who have attacked our city, those here in our noble ranks pretending goodwill when only evil lurks within their dark hearts, cannot escape our notice any longer. It begins here, with the final defeat of the Thief. Tonight, when we protect our cities and our people from the threat of feral magic once and for all."

The crowd was cheering, screaming its frenzied assent. They were with Jack now in the way only a crowd can be with someone—pushed on by an inertia impossible to harness or control.

"Years ago, we set about to protect our way of life. The tower in California demonstrated what might be done with enough fortitude, but Roosevelt bowed to the weakness of his party. Our own party will not bow. We *will* have our justice for those innocents brought low by the terrible danger of feral magic. Innocents like our brothers who were slain last evening." He ripped back a drape from what had appeared to be a table on the stage and revealed a lever-like mechanism. "And we will have our justice *now*."

The electricity that ran through the crowd had nothing to do with

LISA MAXWELL

magic. It was a miasma of hate and anticipation, righteousness and cowardice churning as one.

"The other candidates have not answered the question of how they will bring the illegal magic to heel once and for all, but I will answer that question for myself. *Tonight.* With your support, we will put an end to the danger feral magic presents to Chicago once and for all." Jack paused as the crowd cheered wildly, and then he leaned close to the microphone. "Are you with me?" he shouted. "Shall we put into action the promise of the great men who came before us?"

He had most of the room on his side as he held his hand to his ear, urging their cheers to grow, but not all. There were those who looked unsure. Others were already moving toward the still-locked doors. Either they didn't want to be part of this moment or they were afraid for their own lives.

It wasn't a surprise. Harte knew too well that there would always be those who would choose to side with the Order and the Brotherhoods even if the old magic flowed within them. But the illusion of safety was only that—an illusion—and as people reached the doors, they found them locked and guarded. Impassable.

Harte wanted to check the watch, but he couldn't move. He was frozen as solidly as if Esta had trapped him in time. Seshat held him still as she raged within him, pressing at the walls.

I can stop this, Harte begged her, fighting against her with all of the strength he had. *Let me go, and I'll kill Jack here and now. I will end Jack's life and Thoth's with him.*

Seshat remained silently pacing beneath his skin.

You know *what that tower is capable of,* Harte pressed. *You've seen my memories, and you've seen my fears. If Jack activates his machine, Thoth will win. He will take everything you are, everything you ever hoped to be, and you will be powerless against his control. Unless you let me go. It's our only chance. It's your only chance.*

The voice inside of him wailed, but suddenly Harte found that he could move. With his legs under his control once more, he sprinted toward the stage, shoving aside anyone he had to in order to reach Esta before Jack threw the lever. He was nearly to the steps of the stage—

"Tonight, it ends," Jack shouted, and Harte understood that he would be too late.

Before he could even reach the edge of the arena's floor, Jack pressed the lever, and the tower above began to crackle to life.

The crowd surged to their feet, stomping and whistling, and Jack's face was glowing with satisfaction. The lights in the arena hummed and flickered as the machine at the tower's apex started to glow.

CAUGHT BETWEEN

1920—Chicago

If North could have dragged Everett away from the mess of the convention, he would have. He would've risked most anything—drugging Everett into submission, tying him up, carrying him back to his mother . . . *anything*. He would have even risked Everett's hatred if he could have been sure that the boy would be safe. But North had been around a long time. He'd seen power come and go, and the one thing he'd learned through it all was that there were no guarantees of safety in this life, not when a meddling thief could slip back through time and unwind your whole existence in the blink of an eye.

In the last sixteen years, North had learned that all he could depend on was the present as it stood in front of him, in all its beauty and all its terror. The past and the future were nothing but stories people told themselves to feel like they had some control over their lives. So when he thought about taking away Everett's free will, even though he had the means, North found that he couldn't bring himself to do it. His boy had stood there with his shoulders back and asked North to treat him like the man he was becoming, and it would have been the gravest betrayal of that trust for North to do anything but agree.

Which is how North came to be standing on the roof of the Coliseum and discovering for maybe the first time exactly how much he hated being up high. Everett had taken to it like one of those little trained monkeys he'd seen once when the circus had come through Kansas City.

It was like the boy didn't realize how easy it would be to fall or how fragile his body actually was.

It took a lot longer to gain access to the roof than they'd been planning, even with the combination of Maggie's formulations and Everett's gadgets that they had on hand. They were running behind schedule, and by the time they made it up to the roof, the ceiling of the arena had already been drawn back. Above, the sky had turned dark, and all around them, as far as he could see, the city was lit up for the evening, like a million stars had fallen down from the heavens just for this occasion. North felt a sudden ache looking at it all, a yearning for his little house out on the lonesome prairie—for his wife and his children, too—all hundreds of miles away. There the sky was always spangled with stardust thick as milkweed in December.

"Ready?" Everett asked when a cheer erupted from the people assembled below. He looked up at the steel-framed structure that loomed over them, stretching stories into the night. He adjusted his pack of tools and other gear on his shoulder.

"Not really," North admitted, but he followed Everett across the roof and to the base of the tower anyway.

He let Everett go first and watched as the boy began to scale the steel frame with a graceful ease. He was about to start climbing himself when something stopped him. He had the oddest sense that he should wait a minute longer . . . and that sense made his skin prickle in warning.

Turning, he scanned the expanse of the rooftop for whatever it was he was waiting for, because he knew well enough to trust that sense he'd been born with. Even with his watch long since ground into trash, North wasn't helpless. The old magic that flowed through him had gotten him out of too many scrapes for him to ignore it now.

It wasn't even two minutes later when the threat appeared, like he'd suspected it would. A man stepped from the shadows wearing a medallion that flashed in the dim light. He was a great big bear of a guy, and he was wearing a long, dark duster jacket that reminded North of the uniform worn by the Jefferson Guard years ago in St. Louis.

"You're not supposed to be here," the man said, already reaching for the weapon holstered beneath his long coat like some kind of cowboy from the Old West. But he'd barely had it out when something drew his attention. Instead of aiming the gun at North, he pointed it upward. *Toward Everett.*

North looked up to see that Everett had nearly reached the top of the tower. He was high enough that he was completely unaware of what was happening below, but not out of the range of that gun. His boy had a little farther to go before he would reach the safety of the platform at the top, where he could duck out of the line of fire. And Everett had no idea he was a target.

Without even considering the consequences, North ran for the man, slamming into him as the gun went off. The shot echoed through the nearby buildings. North felt a sharp burning in his side, but he ignored it and used all of his strength to shove the Guard to the ground. Right about when the Guard flipped him onto his back, North realized he was outmanned.

"Pa!" Everett called from above.

North looked up to see Everett starting to descend. "No!" he shouted. "I'll take care of this!"

It was a lie born of hopeful bravado and desperation. The Guard was stronger than he looked, and North doubted that he'd be able to do much more than buy Everett a little time, but if that was all he could do, that was what he would do. "Go on! You're almost—"

His words were cut short by the impact of the man's fist across his face.

North's vision doubled and blurred, but he held on to consciousness even as he tasted blood filling his mouth. North used his weight to shove the Guard off, rolling until they were nearly at the edge of the opening of the roof. Above, Everett was still hesitating, clearly torn and unsure about what to do, but the tower was beginning to crackle to life.

"You gotta go!" he shouted to his son, even as he struggled to keep the Guard from choking the life out of him. "You got once chance before this is all for nothing."

Still, Everett didn't move, and then, to North's horror, he began to descend.

No. If that tower came to life, they were all goners—every single one of them—and everything North had done, everything Everett had risked, would be wasted.

North could feel his body starting to fail him, could feel the years that he'd lived in every aching bone, in every shuddering beat of his heart. And he could feel the pain in his side, sharp and strangely familiar, even though he'd never been shot before. There would be no magic capable of bringing him back, and his death would be pointless if Everett didn't complete the job they'd come to do. No one would be safe if this tower activated—not Everett or Maggie or any of their kids waiting for him back at home. This had to be stopped here and now, and his boy was the only one who could do it.

North ignored the screaming pain in his side and wrenched himself free of the man's fists. It wasn't for long, but it was long enough. After all, he hadn't come so far or taken so many risks to let his son die from indecision—so he'd take the choice from him.

He looked up at Everett. "Give your mother a kiss for me."

North grabbed hold of the Guard and jerked to the right, throwing them both off-balance, and they tumbled through the opening together, falling away from the sound of Everett's screams and into the void of light and noise below.

FALLING INTO DARKNESS

1920—Chicago

Esta watched the crowd in the arena surge to its feet in response to Jack throwing the lever. They stomped and whistled their encouragement as the lights of the arena flickered overhead. She looked up to see bolts of energy circling around the apex of the tower like strange lightning pulsing in the night sky—a beacon and a warning all at once to anyone within sight of the Coliseum.

Suddenly, two figures were falling through the split in the ceiling, caught in a strange embrace as they plummeted to the ground. At first Esta couldn't understand what she was seeing—a stunt or a dummy? It had to be—but no. They were men. One had red hair—Esta was *sure* she saw red hair. *North,* she thought, her hope falling right along with him. Then the sound of their bodies hitting the ground seemed louder than anything. It was a dull, sickening thud that left the crowd gasping and Esta hollowed out by grief.

For North. For Everett. For them all.

Too late. Too late to run, too late to save themselves unless they stopped this. She *had* to find a way to stop it.

"You don't have to do this, Jack," Esta said, trying to speak to Jack instead of the demon that had possessed him.

Jack turned to Esta, and she saw that the watery blue had pushed aside the black. "Don't I?" he asked, his voice somewhere between Jack and Thoth.

"You can fight him," she pleaded. "Think of the people you're about to kill. Think of what he's turning you into."

There was more blue in his eyes now than black, more of Jack in his voice when he spoke. "That's *exactly* what I'm thinking of," he said, and he pushed the lever even farther, causing the power to surge once more.

In that instant, the darkness swelled again in Jack's eyes as well, overtaking the blue until only a deep blankness looked back at her. "Did you honestly think that anything he's done has been against his will?" Thoth asked, laughing. "I forced nothing upon him."

"You turned him into a monster," Esta said, still trying to pull away. If she could only reach the lever . . .

"You're telling yourself stories, girl. He dreamed of a machine that could create beautiful chaos—one that could destroy those who taunted him with their power—long before my servant in Greece found him. I didn't create his hatred or his fear. I simply used them to my advantage. They provided me an entrance to his mind and a willing body to bring my vision to light, and in return I bestowed upon him the power to make every one of his dreams come true."

A scream from the crowd suddenly tore through the room, punctuating Thoth's words. Jack threw his head back and laughed as another scream split through the noise of the hall, and another. "You thought you could defeat me?" Thoth laughed at her. "You thought you could escape me, and instead you ran straight into my arms. And now it's too late. There is no escape for you now. I will have your power—your life—at my disposal." The tower was glowing and crackling with energy above them. "And then I will take Seshat's power as well, and with it I will finally be able to control the beating heart of magic. I will become *infinite*."

He was right. Thoth, Jack, it didn't matter who was speaking to her now. It was too late to run, too late to stop the bright bolts of light streaming from the tip of the tower, searing like lightning into the night sky. But as the panic grew in the arena around her, Esta didn't feel the cold power she'd expected to come over her. Something else was happening instead in the crowd of delegates and spectators.

At first Esta couldn't make sense of what she was seeing, but then she understood: The medallions the Brotherhoods had given out were starting to burst into flames. It wasn't the old magic that was being affected by the tower but the *corrupted* magic of the Brotherhood, and Esta could not repress her laugh at Everett's cunning. He'd explained to her how they could give the Brotherhoods a taste of their own poison, and his idea had *worked*.

As each medallion burst, the flames began to spread at an incendiary pace, and in a matter of seconds, the arena erupted in pandemonium. Flames from the medallions consumed the coats and shirts and dresses where they'd been pinned, and the people who'd willingly taken them were screaming, tearing their own garments from their bodies to escape.

They did it. The relief flashed through her bright and hot and complete, but it was short-lived. She still needed to get the Book away from Jack—and somewhere caught in the now-riotous crowd was Harte.

Everywhere, people were trying to escape from their burning garments and from the hall itself. The whole crowd was moving almost as one, pushing and climbing over one another as they tried desperately to reach the still-locked doors.

Slowly, Jack—or the thing inside of him—seemed to realize something had gone wrong. When the medallion Jack himself was wearing burst into flames, he released Esta to tear it from his coat. But even once the medallion was gone, smoke still poured from beneath his collar and cuffs. Jack pulled at the buttons of his shirt, tearing it open to reveal rows of strange symbols that glowed like embers on his skin. He seemed to scream more in rage than pain at first, but as he clawed at his skin, the markings only glowed brighter.

Esta was beginning to back away when Jack suddenly went strangely still. His head whipped around to look toward the steps that led up to the stage.

"Seshat," Thoth's voice hissed from Jack's mouth, its weathered rasp as old as time itself, and a serpent's smile crept across his face. His chest was still smoldering, but now Jack did not seem to be feeling the pain of the flames. "I thought you might join us."

The smell of burnt skin and sulfurous smoke was thick in the air as Esta turned to see Harte climbing the steps to the stage, his stormy eyes steady on her.

"No!" she screamed. But Jack had already leapt for Harte. It happened so fast—Jack lunged across the stage, pushing Harte back down the steps, until they were both on the ground, wrestling for control. In a blink, Jack had the advantage. His hands were around Harte's neck, strangling him.

Two of the men who had been onstage with them lunged for Esta, grabbing her by the arms to hold her in place. She twisted, catching one off guard as she kicked out viciously at the other's knee. In a fluid movement born from years of training under Dakari's watchful eye, Esta twisted again and again, meeting the men blow for blow until they were down and she had freed herself.

The men had been easy enough to dispatch, but she'd wasted precious time. Harte was no longer fighting, and Jack was looming over him, with his knee on Harte's chest. The Pharaoh's Heart was in his hand. Jack was already bringing the dagger down, directly toward Harte's chest, when Esta pulled time slow. Without hesitating, she was down the stairs, using all of her weight and all of her strength to knock Jack away from Harte.

Jack fell to the ground. His chest still glowed where the ritual magic he'd tattooed onto his skin continued to smolder, but the dagger clattered away and his coat lay open, revealing the Book. It was so close. Everything they'd fought for was right there, within reach, but Esta's eyes turned to Harte—

She wasn't thinking about Seshat or the danger of touching him when she made her choice. She wasn't thinking about anything other than how his lips had already gone blue, how his eyes already looked glassy and unfocused. She wouldn't lose him. Not now. Not after everything.

She pulled herself up and was at his side in an instant. "Harte," she said, cupping his face with her hands, drawing him into the net of her affinity.

He didn't move, but a shuddering breath was released from his lungs. "Harte, you have to wake up," she said, bringing her face close to his to listen. "We have to go." But Harte lay as quiet and unmoving as if he was still frozen in time. He wasn't breathing.

Not knowing what else to do, she placed her mouth over his and filled his lungs with her own breath, but before she could pull back, his hands were on her arms, pinning her in place, and she felt herself falling into darkness.

THE SERPENT'S CURSE

1920—Chicago

Night fell from above, obscuring the confusion around her, and stars swirled around Esta until she found herself standing in an open chamber with stone-carved walls the color of sand. If she focused hard enough, she could almost look through the illusion and see the world as it was—the people still frozen in her hold of time and Jack lying nearby—but only just. And it was *so* difficult to focus beyond the illusion for very long. It was far easier to give in to it.

Above, the sky glimmered with an endless swath of stars, and along the edges of the room, flames climbed from great curved cauldrons of iron. Standing before Esta, a woman with hair coiled like snakes around her face and eyes like obsidian waited. *Seshat.*

"You came to me," Seshat whispered, anticipation thick in her papery voice. "You came to me *again.* As I knew you would."

Esta took a step back. She felt panic climbing inside her as she looked around the room, trying to see through the illusion Seshat had created, to find Harte. Even now he could be dying.

"I didn't come for you," she told Seshat. "I came for *him.*"

Seshat reached out for Esta, as though she hadn't heard. "Take my hand, and together we will awaken the *true* heart of power, unleash the possibilities of chaos, and begin again. Together, we can unmake this world—all of its meagerness and hatred—and realize our fate."

Esta shook her head. "I don't want any of that. And neither do you."

"You think you know my heart?" Fires flashed in the depths of

Seshat's eyes as her hand dropped to her side in a fist. Suddenly she looked nearly inhuman in her rage. Esta had seen visions before; she'd seen Seshat in the throes of hope, but now the ancient goddess looked broken and twisted.

"Look what he's done to you," Esta whispered, unable to keep the horror and sorrow from her voice. "Look at what Thoth's made you into—"

"He's done *nothing* to make me. All I am I've claimed for myself."

"No," Esta protested, desperate to reach Harte. "You've *allowed* him to twist you and your plans into something else. You want to take your revenge on Thoth, fine. Take it. Death—worse than death—it's only what he deserves. Jack as well. But the whole world?" Esta's voice broke at the thought of it. She thought of Maggie, who would be waiting for North, not knowing what had happened. She thought of Everett, who'd been willing to risk everything and had lost even more. She thought of Viola and Jianyu—of all the Mageus in the city and across the land who would be destroyed by Seshat's anger. And the Sundren as well—deserving of such a fate or not. They were not hers—or Seshat's—to judge. To *condemn*. "The world doesn't deserve your wrath."

"Does it not? Once I felt as you do now. But can you not hear the cries of the people around you?" Seshat asked, her eyes narrowing. "You must see their hate here in this place, clear as the night above us. Do you not feel their loathing, hot and thick in this room, as they demand your end? And *still* you would save them?" There was a note in her voice, Esta realized. Anger, yes, but also something more. Something that sounded strangely like confusion. Maybe even curiosity. "They would kill you—each and every one of them would gladly take your life if given the chance." There was a question hanging in the air between them.

"Maybe they would," Esta admitted, still trying to sense Harte beneath the nearly impenetrable illusion Seshat had spun. "But this one room isn't the entire world. There are those who would stand by me, those who would give their lives to fight next to me—to protect me. North did. Just tonight he gave himself so others might live. He gave up *everything* for a chance at a different future. If you rip the world apart, his sacrifice was for nothing."

"What do I care of the sacrifice of one *man?*" she sneered.

"Why did you do it, then?" Esta asked, pleading. "I've seen your heart as well. I know that you were trying to save magic. Why do *any* of that if you only meant to tear the world apart in the end?"

"Because I did not understand until it was too late. There *is* no saving magic," Seshat said, her eyes flashing dark and eternal. "I thought to preserve the promise of the old magic through writing. By stabilizing its power, I thought to protect it from time's devouring jaws, but I only succeeded in weakening the old magic further—*faster*—instead. Magic was always destined to die away, but by taking a part of it, I made everything worse. Just as taking the affinity of a Mageus to create an object of power can destroy a person, taking a part of magic's own heart only served to hasten the end of *everything*—chaos and order, magic and reality alike."

"But you made the Book," Esta pressed, refusing to believe that this could be true. "You used your affinity to create an object outside of time to *protect* the beating heart of magic."

Seshat's eyes glinted, and something like sadness—maybe even regret— shadowed her expression. "But it did not work. Because of Thoth, I could not finish what I had started—I could not complete the ritual, could not reinsert the protected piece of magic back into the whole of creation, and those failures left the last piece of pure magic even more vulnerable. To time. To weak and craven souls who would use the power for their own. Maybe long ago, I could have corrected my mistakes. Now it is too late. Now there is only one answer. To preserve magic, we must destroy time. It is the only way."

But destroying time meant destroying reality itself. "Maybe it's magic that should die," Esta realized, her heart clenching at the thought. "Maybe it *should* simply fade away, and the world could keep spinning."

"Do you really think it's so easy?" Seshat scoffed. "You have seen the image of the serpent devouring its own tail. . . ."

"The ouroboros," Esta said. It was the symbol Dolph had taken, and the Antistasi as well.

"*Yes.* It's a representation of *balance*, but such balance comes at a price. It is the serpent's curse to continue on for infinity, devouring itself and holding all that is—and all that is not—in perfect equilibrium. Now it is my burden as well. You see, I disrupted that balance when I created writing, and in doing so, gave time a victory over the power of magic. My actions caused the old magic to die even faster. I created the Book because I thought I could replicate the balance of the ouroboros. I believed that if I took a piece of pure magic outside of time's grasp, then magic *could not* die."

"The Book," Esta realized. "Thoth showed me what it could do, the way it could hold the dagger. He said that the dagger existed and yet didn't all at once—that it was outside of time and reality."

"Yes," Seshat said. "I thought I could hold back time's fanged jaws with the creation of the Book, because I knew even then how essential the old magic was to the very existence of the world. *Everything* in the world—the sun and the stars and *even time itself*—it all begins and ends with magic. I knew that if the old magic dies, time is doomed as well, and the world with it. And it will not be an easy death. It will be a slow and terrible unmaking that will spare no one and nothing."

Esta thought she might understand what Seshat meant. Hadn't she herself felt the horror of being pulled out of time? Of nearly being unmade by time? But what Seshat was describing would be far larger, far more terrible. "But you stopped it by creating the Book. You did preserve that piece of pure magic. Why destroy *everything*, when we could destroy Thoth instead?"

"You still don't understand, do you, child?" Seshat's expression darkened, her eyes shuttered. "My creation of the Book was a mistake. By taking a piece of pure magic, I weakened the whole, and when Thoth stopped me from completing the ritual—when he destroyed the stones I had created to hold my fractured power—he made it impossible for me to return the heart of power to the whole. If I could have completed the ritual, I would have been able to protect magic without destroying time. If I had completed the ritual, time would no longer have had the power to touch magic, and all would have been preserved. Instead, both time and magic are at risk. If Thoth brings that piece of magic back into time's reach, it *will* die . . . and so will the whole. So, too, will time, and it will take the world with it."

It was like the Brink, then—they'd discovered not long ago that it couldn't be destroyed because it contained the affinities of all the Mageus it had killed. Bringing down the Brink would destroy magic itself—and if Seshat's words were true, then it would destroy the world as well. *But maybe it's never been about destroying the Brink.* Maybe they should have been trying to *fix* it instead.

"Do you see now?" Seshat pressed. "It would be a *mercy* to end this world compared to what will happen if time has its way—or if Thoth does. With my power, he would be able to use the beating heart of magic without risking time's wrath. Whatever power he gains over the part, he will have over the whole, and all I have done—all I have sacrificed—will have been for naught." Seshat leaned her face close so that Esta could feel the warmth of her breath, could smell her perfume, a scent like jasmine and old parchment and ancient books. "But if we destroy time . . . perhaps magic can begin again. Perhaps *everything* can begin again."

"There has to be another way, another solution," Esta said. "You can't actually *want* this?"

"I do not deny that I will take joy in Thoth's destruction—and the destruction of this ugly, meager world along with it. But what I *want* hasn't been of any consequence for eons. I will not be sad to give these last pieces of what I am to see this world unmade, and all the terrible souls it contains along with it—especially if it means that Thoth can never prevail."

"If you allow Thoth to make you into a monster, then he's already won." Esta was breathing hard, and her eyes were burning with tears she refused to shed. "He's twisted you into something worse than even himself. Your vengeance must have blinded you or you wouldn't be so willing to give up everything you were meant to be and become nothing more than a pawn to Thoth."

"Your life must be worth very little that you would insult me so," Seshat hissed. In a blink she'd latched onto Esta's already sore wrist. "You came to me. You chose *me*."

Esta could feel herself breaking apart. There was a moment when she considered how easy it would be to give in, to let go and allow Seshat's power to take her—especially if Harte was gone. But she didn't give in. Gathering all the strength she had left, she tore herself away from Seshat.

"No!" Esta snarled.

"You can't win, child," Seshat purred. "I saw your heart, your very soul. You understand what would happen if Thoth controlled my power. You know what he would do with the heart of magic trapped inside the Book. You want this as much as I—"

"No!" Esta roared again, and this time she focused her affinity, reached for the spaces between the seconds, and pulled, only a little, until the illusion began to waver like an earthquake rumbling beneath their feet. "There has to be another way. I will not sacrifice myself for your vengeance. I will fight you every second of every day, until time devours us both." Her chest was heaving, her heart pounding in her ears like a steady tattoo, urging her on. "But give me Harte, and I will tear Thoth from this world. I will *become* your vengeance." Esta struggled to hold her affinity steady, unsure of what Seshat would choose and unsure of what power she really had to stand against the goddess. "Give me Harte," she said again, softer this time. "Give me Harte, and once Thoth is no longer a danger, I will finish what you've started. The world deserves that chance. Give me Harte, and I will do what you could not. I will use what I am to finish what you started and save the old magic from the ravages of time and right the balance between them. I will take on the burden of the serpent's curse. But only for Harte's life. He's the one I came for. He's *always* the one I will come back for. *Not you.*"

Seshat's expression was unreadable as she stared at Esta. Seconds passed—or they could have been minutes or hours, since suddenly time seemed an empty promise. Finally she cocked her head a bit to the side, a painfully human gesture. "I wonder, child," Seshat whispered. "Would he do the same for you?"

Esta believed she knew the answer to that question, but she wasn't foolish enough to play Seshat's games.

"Fine," Seshat said. "But I will hold you to your promise. Destroy Thoth if you can. But if you cannot figure out a way to finish what I began—a way to bring magic and time back into balance—you *will* give yourself over to me. You will fight me no longer. And we will do what we must."

Suddenly the fires went out, and the room went completely dark, the only light coming from the stars above. Seshat sank back into the darkness. And then the illusion of the chamber faded, leaving only the arena—the chaos and smoke and hot fury in the air.

Beneath Esta's hands, Harte gasped, his lungs pulling in air and his eyes fluttering open, the stormy gray of his irises still unfocused.

"Destroy Thoth, as you've promised," Seshat whispered. It sounded like the goddess was there in the flesh. Esta could practically feel Seshat's warm breath close to her ear, but when Esta turned to look, she saw nothing but Jack lying on the floor nearby, his body still smoldering. "Fail and I will not be so merciful again."

"Esta?" Harte's voice rasped when he spoke, and his hands came to the bruised skin of his neck.

"I'm here," she said, her throat closing with an emotion she was not ready to face. And then she released him, leaving him back in the stillness of time.

The arena hung in silence around her as Esta stood, taking a moment to steady herself—to look at Harte, his eyes filled with a heartbreaking softness—and then she walked to where Jack lay on the ground, frozen in time.

Jack's eyes were wide, and his face was contorted in rage. The lapels of his jacket had flopped open, and the top edge of the Book was visibly peeking from its inside pocket. She knew that the second she touched the Book, Thoth would awaken—unless she took care of him first. She needed to act, before Thoth had a chance to understand what was happening. She would have to kill them both before Jack could fight back.

Esta's hands were surprisingly steady as she picked up the dagger from where it had fallen to the floor. Its weight was familiar, and when she held it in her hand, she thought she felt the answering call of the stones in the cuff and the necklace she wore beneath her clothes. But whether the echo of their power was a warning or encouragement, she didn't know. She ignored their warmth against her skin and took the dagger to where Jack lay.

He'd hurt so many, Esta reminded herself, even as her hands shook. Jack had taken life after life, and worse, he'd inspired the hate of so many. He hadn't created that hate—neither had Thoth—but together they had urged it on, given it purchase and light to grow, and because of him, so many had suffered. So many would suffer still.

Jack Grew was a vapid, insecure little man, and his death wouldn't be a loss for the world . . . not really.

It would be worth it—the dark stain she would claim for her own soul—to take his life. To save so many more. It was a weight Esta knew she could carry, one that she would happily bear, just as her father, Dolph, must have borne so many of his own sins. . . . And it didn't matter whether Harte would do the same for her. It did *not*.

Esta lifted the dagger and felt the power of the Pharaoh's Heart coursing through the air as she knelt by Jack, and then, before she could second-guess herself, she brought the dagger down, straight toward his heart.

The tip of the dagger hit bone, but then Esta felt the energy of the Pharaoh's Heart flare, and the dagger sank to the hilt in Jack's chest. Almost immediately, she felt Thoth's power rise up, awful and absolute, as it reached for her. But she held tight to the hilt of the dagger and pushed all of her affinity, all of herself toward Thoth.

She could feel Jack beneath her, but she could also feel something more pulling at the net of time—something less clear and less distinct lurking within him. Esta pushed her affinity toward Jack again, searching for the spaces between where he ended and Thoth began, and when she found the demigod, she used everything she was and everything she would ever be to tear at the shape of Thoth. To rip him from Jack, to tear him from that moment in time, until the darkness in the spaces between the world flooded through him.

A scream echoed from Jack's mouth—part human and part something that might once have been human long ago. As he screamed, a shadowy flood of dark energy poured out of his mouth and began to swarm in weaving tendrils through the room. It came together above them, a thick coil of inky black, and then all at once it burst open into a shower of ash like a terrible firework exploding above.

The power reverberating through the Aether knocked Esta back, and when she hit the floor, she lost her hold on the seconds. The world slammed back into motion, and the noise of the arena assaulted her as she watched the bits of darkness fall, descending onto the people in the arena. When they landed upon her skin, they felt like shards of ice that had the same cold energy and power as the Brink.

Esta brushed them away as she climbed to her feet and lunged for Jack. He was still writhing in agony as she took the Book from the inside of his coat, and when she looked into his eyes, she saw only watery blue. And fear.

She felt no victory as she took the Book from the pocket of his jacket.

He'd hurt so many people, but that didn't seem to matter as she watched him, weak and pathetic, with blood dribbling from the corner of his mouth. His hand was grasping for the knife that now protruded from his chest, but his fingers couldn't seem to take hold of it. Jack looked up at her again, pleading, and Esta felt an overwhelming sense of revulsion as the truth of what she'd done washed over her.

"Please . . ." Jack reached for her, his voice no more than a whisper as his eyes found the Book she held in her hand.

There wasn't time, though. Even if Esta had wanted to help him, police were already on their way through the frenzied crowd, which had finally managed to pry open the arena doors and was pushing to escape. She scrambled to her feet and reached for the hilt of the dagger. There was a sickening feel of bone grinding against metal and the wet suck of blood and muscle as she pulled the dagger from his chest.

The second the blade was free, Jack's arm went limp, falling to the floor next to him. His eyes were open and unseeing, a cloudy blue with no trace of black.

Esta turned back to Harte, who was still trying to right himself. She tried to pull the seconds slow, but her affinity slipped from her fingers as her legs wobbled beneath her. She'd given every bit of her energy to fighting Seshat and destroying Thoth, and now she was too exhausted to hold time for more than a second. Before she could reach Harte, they were surrounded by men in police uniforms, and Esta's arms were being wrenched behind her back.

Unable to do anything with her arms pinned, Esta watched as the men picked Harte up. Then they were moving, her barely able to keep on her feet and Harte half carried by the officers who'd surrounded them. Before the crowd could realize what had happened or could turn on them, they were whisked by the police down the back of the stage and then out through a hidden exit near the side of the arena.

Esta was too exhausted to struggle free of the police officers' hold on her. Instead of fighting, she let herself go limp and allowed them to carry her along. She hoped that she could collect enough strength to escape once they were no longer touching her, but the officers didn't release her as they led her and Harte outside to a waiting police van. Another officer with a face like a knife waited there, rifle at the ready. Deep-green eyes over a sharp nose met hers, and Esta had the oddest sense that she'd seen him before. She probably had, patrolling in the arena.

"Get them in the back," he growled as they approached.

When the van doors opened, Esta saw that Everett was already there, sitting on one of the benches with his head in his hands. Unceremoniously, she was hoisted up and shoved into the van, landing at his feet.

Harte was tossed in next, and immediately he reached for her. As he grabbed her hand, Esta realized that all she felt was the coolness of his skin. *No sign of Seshat.* But even with that knowledge, she still remembered Jack's watery eyes pleading with her, his lips foaming with blood. She'd killed him. Thoth was gone. But she would have to live with the memory of Jack's death—the memory of blade on bone and blood—for however long she had left.

The green-eyed officer jumped into the back with them, and Esta scrambled to her feet. Ready for whatever might come.

"Settle down," the officer ordered as the van doors closed, plunging them all into darkness.

Exhausted and weary as she was, Esta reached for Everett and prepared to slow time, but before she could grasp her affinity, she felt an odd push-pull that reminded her of the chamber they'd used to enter the Nitemarket.

The truck lurched into motion, and Esta stumbled backward, nearly falling. But a pair of arms caught her, and she realized that the darkness of the van was transforming itself. Suddenly, like she had with the entrance to the Nitemarket, she found herself somewhere else entirely.

The police officer who had climbed into the back with them started to laugh. He brushed at the mustache on his upper lip until it seemed to melt into his face. "You should see the looks on your faces," he said, slapping Harte on the back without any heat or malice. "You'd think you'd never seen a simple makeup powder before."

Harte looked too dazed to respond. Esta felt the same.

"What's going on?" she demanded.

The officer pushed his cap back on his head and crossed his leg like he was on some kind of pleasure tour. "I do believe this is what they call a rescue," the officer said.

"Why would you rescue us?" Harte asked, eyeing the officer's uniform. It looked damned authentic with its double row of buttons and the worn brass star on his chest. "You don't even know us."

"Don't I?" the officer asked, staring at Esta now. "I see the tickets I gave you worked."

Esta's mouth fell open a little. "Dom?"

"That isn't really my name, of course," he said. "But I guess it's as good as any of the others, if you need to call me something."

Harte didn't quite understand. "But you were—"

"Old? Fat?" The man dressed in the police uniform—Dom, if he was to be believed—shrugged. "And you dismissed me easily because of it, didn't you?"

"Why would you help us?" Esta asked. She had the sense that Dominic Fusilli never did anything unless he thought he could benefit from it.

"You saved my life," Dom said, rubbing at his chin. "I figured it's only right that I return the favor." When Esta stared at him in clear disbelief, he leveled an unreadable look in her direction. "And you might say I have a vested interest in your mission."

"How could you possibly know what my mission is?" Esta asked, not bothering to hide her suspicion.

"You want to destroy the Order, don't you? Bring down the Brink? Once New York is open and free, I can expand the Nitemarket." He gave her an impish smile. "I figured it was only good business to help you out however I could."

It was an answer, but she didn't think it was the entire answer.

"Are you going to tell us where we're going?" Harte asked.

"Isn't it obvious?" Dom pushed back a sliding panel in the wall of the truck, and warm air streamed through the opening.

Beyond, Esta saw the gleaming lights of an enormous city. Buildings climbed to impossible heights, even more than they had in either Chicago or San Francisco. At first she was too disoriented to recognize where she was, but then Esta saw the soaring stone towers of the Brooklyn Bridge.

ALL THAT MATTERS

1902—New York

When Jianyu came to, alarm bells were still clanging, and he understood exactly what had happened. He should have expected such a betrayal, and even now, with his head aching, he wondered how he had not. He should have suspected something was amiss when the one called Logan—Nibsy Lorcan's newest acquisition—waved him on and allowed him to lead the way up the narrow, winding steps to the Mysterium. He should never have turned his back on the other boy. He understood his mistake the moment Logan had attacked. Jianyu's legs had been taken out from beneath him. Pain had exploded through his head, and his vision had gone black.

From the look of things, he had been dragged behind one of the bookcases, but Jianyu refused to be grateful for the small mercy Logan had shown him. The doorway in the ceiling above had disappeared. In its place was the bronze seal that had been forged to depict a mystical hand. Jianyu had no way to tell whether Logan was still up there—whether he was trapped with the artifact he had sought or whether he had managed to escape with the ring before the chamber had been sealed.

The back of Jianyu's head continued to ache, and he felt more than a little unsteady as he pulled himself to his feet. He had no idea how long it had been, no sense of the time that had passed. What he did know was that he had to leave, *now*, before the Order was released from their sanctuary below. Before anything else could go wrong.

He also knew that he had failed again.

The sound of footsteps and shouting came to him suddenly from the hall beyond, and Jianyu understood something more—he was trapped. Without hesitation, he opened the light and managed to wrap it around himself before a group of robed white men entered the room. He recognized some of the men from the gala and, before the gala, from Khafre Hall and the Metropolitan. Then their numbers parted, and a white-haired man stepped through. It was the same man who had taken the stage that night in Khafre Hall, the same one who had trapped Esta. *The High Princept.*

The fact that they could not see him did not stop Jianyu from drawing farther back into the corner of the room. Outside, the night was already growing deeper. He no longer felt the heat of the strange ritual magic that had seared his skin during the Golden Hour, but his skin still felt raw. He should go—he should escape now, while the door was open and the way was clear—but something stayed him. He could not leave without the ring.

The Princept hurried up the steps and began some complicated ritual to open the portal overhead, as the others waited. Once the door was open, they climbed, one by one, disappearing into the chamber above. Again, Jianyu considered his options, and then he began to move toward the ladder himself. If Logan was still trapped with Jack Grew, there remained a chance to retrieve the Delphi's Tear. He would not leave such a chance untaken.

He climbed the staircase soundlessly, but when he entered the Mysterium, he saw no sign of Logan. The men were all red-faced and shouting.

"I don't know how the maggot managed to get the seal open!" Jack railed. Two of the robed men were flanking him and had taken him by the arms. "My designs were perfect. I accounted for every possibility." He tried to jerk away from the hold the men had on him.

"Clearly not *every* possibility," the Princept said. "The artifact is gone. We gave you our trust. You knew what regaining the Delphi's Tear meant to the Order—knew how essential it was for rejuvenating the Brink. Without the artifacts, we cannot perform the ritual at the Conclave. Without the ritual—"

"The ring couldn't have gone far," Jack said, cutting the Princept off. He nodded toward the open door of the balcony. "Even if the protections I placed failed, there was only one way for the maggot to escape. You should be able to collect the artifact easily enough from a dead man."

The Princept gave a small nod, and two of the men went out onto the open balcony to check. The other men all waited for their report.

"There's no one below," one of the robed men said, glaring.

"That's impossible," Jack said, still struggling against the other men's hold on him. "I saw the thief jump."

"Search him," the Princept demanded.

But Jack tore away from the men and shoved past the Princept to the balcony, where he leaned far over the stone railing. As the men followed, cornering Jack, Jianyu inched closer to examine the large golden tree that seemed to be growing in the center of the room. In its tangled gilded branches were five open spaces, likely for the five artifacts. He stepped out of range as the men dragged Jack back inside and began to search him for the missing ring. Jianyu waited, silent and ready to take the artifact the moment he could. He wished he could rush the men himself, wished that for once he could let the anger that burned within him spill out . . . but no. He would wait and he would remain patient, because he understood it was more important to *win*. It was as he had told Cela. Anger could wait. It would have to.

"It's not here," another of the robed men said finally, leaving Jack disheveled and panting.

Jack tore himself away from their grip. "I *told* you—"

But Jianyu did not wait to hear any more of their talk. If the ring was not there to be taken, if Logan's body was not below for all to see, then it was pointless to stay. He began to move back toward the staircase. He would go while he could. He would find Viola and Cela, and they would figure out what to do next. But he had barely reached the opening in the floor when another of the Order's robed men began to climb the stairs.

When the man entered the chamber, the others turned for the news.

"Did you find the maggots responsible?" the High Princept demanded.

"No . . ." The robed man's jaw clenched. "But we have another problem. Newton's sigils are gone."

By the time Jianyu extricated himself from the building, night had arrived. With the glare of the streetlights in this part of the city, it was simple now to keep the light open around him, but his feet could not seem to carry him fast enough. Once he found himself on the broad stretch of Fifth Avenue, though, he turned immediately west and began to run toward the building where Cela had been positioned. He did not allow himself to think about what might have happened to Cela or Abel if Viola had not made it in time. But if Paul Kelly's men had harmed his friends . . .

He was barely two blocks away when he saw them, standing on the corner of Twenty-Third Street. Viola, Abel, and Cela were all staring up at the building he had escaped from minutes before. Cela's deep-brown skin had taken on an almost silvery glow in the light thrown by the streetlamps, and Jianyu was struck suddenly by her beauty—the curve of her smooth cheek and the way her hair was curling around her temples, the strength in her narrow shoulders and the graceful, nimble fingers she had lifted to her mouth.

The direction of his thoughts made him nearly stumble and lose hold of the light.

Cela Johnson was not for him. He could offer her nothing—not safety, nor home, nor the promise of a future. He had his path set before him, and he would follow it through until the end. And if that thought made him feel suddenly more tired than he ever had been before? It did not matter. It *could* not matter.

Jianyu waited until he was closer to release his hold on the light. He did not let himself acknowledge—or revel in—the relief he saw in Cela's eyes. But he could not stop his heart from racing when she threw her arms around him, tucking her face close to his neck.

"I thought we'd lost you again," she whispered, hugging him a moment longer before she finally released him and stepped back.

Jianyu could still smell her perfume or her soap—a warm, sweet fragrance that made him suddenly unsteady. He glanced at Cela's brother, but if Abel thought anything of his sister's actions, he did not show it.

"We saw the man jumping from the building, and we thought . . ." Cela didn't finish.

"That was Logan," Jianyu said.

"What happened?" Viola asked. "Did you get the ring?"

Jianyu shook his head. There would be time later—to explain how Logan had attacked him and fled, to figure out what had happened to the boy and the artifact he had taken. "Did either of you take something from the Order's chambers?"

Viola frowned, but she took a package from her skirts no broader in diameter than a bowl of rice. She offered it to Jianyu, and when he peeled back the handkerchief she'd wrapped around it, cold energy filtered through the air.

He could not stop the smile that split his face. "We may not have the Delphi's Tear, but neither does the Order. Without the ring, they will not be able to reestablish their power. They need the artifacts to fortify the Brink, but even if they might retrieve them, without these sigils, they will no longer be able to control it."

NEARLY HOME

1920—Brooklyn

Esta watched the lights of the city—*her city*—grow closer and brighter as Dominic Fusilli's truck cut through the streets of Brooklyn. A moment before, she'd been in the heart of Chicago, but now, through whatever magic Dom used to create the entrances of the Nitemarket, she was home . . . or nearly home. She hadn't expected her heart to twist at the thought of returning. She hadn't realized how much she'd missed it, her city, with its tangled streets that never slept. For Esta, it had been only a matter of weeks since she'd left, but suddenly those weeks away felt so much longer.

Across the Hudson River, the Manhattan skyline wasn't *quite* the one she'd grown up with. There was no Chrysler Building with its Art Deco spire, no Empire State Building anchoring Midtown, and no Freedom Tower at the tip of the island. Those iconic landmarks wouldn't be built for years to come, but in this version of the skyline she could begin to see the promise of what the city would one day become. These streets glowed so much brighter than anyone could have imagined back in 1902, and the light the skyline threw off, the way it illuminated the atmosphere like a halo around the city, settled something in her chest.

She would not let herself think of the memory of the dagger plunging into Jack's chest, past bone and sinew, or of the memory of Jack's eyes—suddenly too human—pleading with her. She would not let herself wonder how she would go on living with blood on her hands, even if it had been necessary, even if Jack had deserved to die right alongside

Thoth. There would be time enough to think of that—to live with that—later.

Esta felt the tension vibrating from Harte, and she realized he was holding himself away from her. She didn't let go of her hold on the Book as she took one of their remaining Quellants and offered it to him.

"She's quiet," he said, hesitating.

"Take it anyway." She placed it in his hand. "Just in case."

He took the small white pill with shaking hands and placed it in his mouth. His eyes closed as he bit down, shuddering again as his throat worked to swallow. Little by little, the tension in his body eased, and eventually he opened his eyes. He stared at her as though testing himself.

"Better?" she asked after a long moment.

Harte nodded, though from his grimace—and from experience—Esta knew it was also worse.

"We won't need it for much longer," she assured him. "We're going to find a way to get her out of you. We're going to find a way to control her once and for all." *We have to.*

Harte didn't immediately agree. He leaned closer now, and there was something unsettling and almost resigned in his expression as he lifted his hand, tentative at first, to brush a lock of her hair back from where it had fallen into her eyes. Apparently he'd decided it was safe, because he cupped her face gently and tilted his own forward so he could rest his forehead against hers. "I saw Jack holding on to you up on the stage, and I thought I'd lost you."

"Not a chance," Esta said, feeling suddenly weak in the knees at the memory of Jack about to drive the dagger into Harte's chest.

But she couldn't let herself think about that, so she kissed him instead.

For a moment, the entire world narrowed to the feeling of her lips against his. For a moment, nothing else mattered. The dark blood that stained her dress, the way Everett rocked quietly in grief, even the difficult road that still lay ahead of them—it all melted away. There was only

Harte. His hands framing her face, his breath intermingling with hers. For a moment, she could forget. For a moment, she could hope.

Too soon, he broke the kiss with a sigh. But he didn't move away.

"I won't lose you," he told her softly.

She pulled back a little. "What makes you so certain I don't feel the exact same way?" she asked, giving his words back to him.

Esta knew they were standing at a crossroads, and the moment before them was far bigger than any single person, bigger even than she and Harte together. There was no way to save any one of them without saving the whole of magic, but they would be working against the snapping jaws of time itself. Still . . . they now had four of the lost artifacts. And they had the Book as well. The Ars Arcana was theirs again, and with the towers of the bridge awaiting them in the distance, and the promise of the city beyond, Esta would do whatever was necessary. She would find a way to to keep the promise she had made to Seshat. She would find a way to save them *all*.

WHAT WAS TO COME

James Lorcan waited in the shadows of Madison Square Park, watching the uppermost floors of the skyscraper for some sign of what had happened within. At the building's base, police clashed with Five Pointers. No one else was looking up, and so no one saw the figure that seemed no larger than a bird leap from the top floors. No one saw him tumble downward for less than a heartbeat, before a parachute emerged and carried him on the wind.

It had worked. James had barely believed it could be possible when Logan had suggested jumping to escape the top floor of the building. It seemed like a suicide mission to trust your life to a bit of silk, but the Aether had told James to go along with the other boy's idea, and so he had. Logan would either fly or fall, he'd figured. Either way, the ring would be his.

He watched for a long moment while Logan floated over Twenty-Third Street, and then he lost sight of him beyond the trees of the park. James waited a little longer before he snapped the reins and urged the horses onward down Madison Avenue. When he reached the corner of Twenty-Sixth Street, he stopped the wagon there and waited to see what would happen next. If Logan tried to run with the ring, he wouldn't get far. James had made sure that his own people lined the neighborhood around the Flatiron, just in case.

But Logan didn't try to run, as he might have. As perhaps he *should* have if he'd been a bit smarter. Instead, he emerged from the park a few minutes later. He'd already disposed of the parachute and the pack that had carried it. When he saw James in the wagon, relief flashed through his expression, and a moment later he was climbing inside.

"You have it?" James asked.

The boy's mouth kicked up on one side as he pulled something from his pocket and then dropped an enormous golden ring into James' outstretched hand. The setting held a stone as clear as a teardrop. *The Delphi's Tear.*

It was everything James had expected it to be and even more than he'd hoped. Almost immediately, he could sense the pull of the artifact calling to him. Whispering to him of its power, cool and steady and absolute. He felt the power within the cane vibrate, as though it knew what was to come.

"I found that for you once before," Logan said, his eagerness giving way to a cocky pride. But then his expression faltered, confusion replacing the confidence. "Or I will . . . someday. But maybe I won't have to if you hold on to it this time."

James didn't bother to respond. The future was nothing more than a story that was his to write—or to *rewrite*, as it were. The ring was heavy, and the gold of the setting had the deep burnished color of metal that was older and purer than the fashion of the day. It felt strangely warm in his hand, and for a moment he let himself marvel at it.

At the power it held within it—the kind of power that required a life sacrifice.

At the possibilities now before him.

Silently, he slid the ring onto his smallest finger, and he felt the Aether around him lurch again. It felt kinetic, exhilarating.

Right.

AUTHOR'S NOTE

⁓

The Last Magician series is, at heart, fantasy, but it is also a work of historical fiction. From the very beginning, I wanted to make it clear that this world is set in the real past, and that conceit has brought with it a host of complications beyond the usual worldbuilding of a fantasy series. Specifically, history is not pretty or sanitized, and historical fiction cannot be either, not if it is to be *true* in any sense of the word.

Looking back at our history, studying and recovering it, often brings to light a wealth of problematic incidents and issues—many of which are hurtful and offensive to modern readers. It is the job of the writer to make choices about what to include and what to leave out, and how to represent truthfully the often terrible events that have created our present. Writing fiction meant for entertainment, however, has allowed me freedom that the academic historian doesn't have. Fiction offers more flexibility in the choices I've made to position characters and events, and even in the language I use to represent the very real past.

Language has real power. If it didn't, ethnic slurs wouldn't be able to inflict such pain and violence, and people wouldn't use them to dehumanize others. But slurs aren't the only type of language that has power. The labels we place on each other and claim for ourselves also have power, but often labels that were once used in the past are later recognized as or become offensive to modern ears. One of those words is the label "Negro."

In previous books in the series, I've resisted using antiquated labels for groups. For example, historically, it would have been more accurate for the book to refer to Chinese Americans as "Oriental," a term that is now recognized as being offensive. Even in the 1950s, Sammie's friends in San Francisco would likely have referred to themselves with this term, just as they refer to the white patrons as "Occidentals." In the end, I decided against using that term, not only because it is offensive to modern readers, but also because it didn't add anything to the text other than historical accuracy. Because of the breadth of people and nations covered by the term, it wouldn't have helped me to describe more clearly any single, specific community. More importantly, using the term would not have contributed to Sammie's friends' agency in any way.

The term "Negro," and my use of it in this book, however, is somewhat different. Though the term may sound uncomfortable and problematic to modern ears, historically it was used by the African American community to claim an identity for themselves. In the late nineteenth century, "colored" would have been the common term, but by the early twentieth century, there had been a movement, led in part by Booker T. Washington and W. E. B. Du Bois, to replace "colored" with the term "Negro." Some historians see the increased use of "Negro" as a way that Black communities distinguished themselves from other immigrant groups and people of color. Other historians have suggested that the increased immigration during this period might have motivated the Black community to establish a group name, in the way the Italians or Polish immigrants had group names and corresponding identities.

Whatever the reasons the term began to grow in use and popularity, perhaps it is more important to recognize that by the early twentieth century, the term "Negro" came to stand for a new way of thinking—it signified the hopes for racial progress and aspirations of the Black community. During the first half of the twentieth century, "Negro" was the preferred term used to describe Black Americans. In 1928, Du Bois wrote that "etymologically and phonetically it is much better and more logical than 'African' or 'colored' or any of the various hyphenated circumlocutions."[1] According to one survey, before 1940, 74 percent of respondents self-identified as preferring the label "Negro" and 21 percent preferred the term "colored." Only 4 percent self-identified as "Black."[2] The label "Black" would not come into more common use until the 1960s, and "African American" even later—in the late 1980s.

My decision to have Cela and Abel claim the term "Negro" was intentional. Unlike "Oriental," which obscures individual ethnic identity, Cela's and Abel's use of the term "Negro" in this book does the opposite. The use of the label allows the Johnsons to align themselves with a historically specific identity and to claim agency as part of a larger community, just as their historical counterparts were doing at the time.

1. W. E. B. Du Bois, "The Name 'Negro,'" *The Crisis: 70th Anniversary Edition: Part I*, vol. 87, no. 9 (1980): 420-421.

2. Tom W. Smith, "Changing Racial Labels: From 'Colored' to 'Negro' to 'Black' to 'African American,'" *The Public Opinion Quarterly*, vol. 56, no. 4 (1992): 496–514.

ACKNOWLEDGMENTS

This book was not an easy one to write. Anyone who's been follow-ing me on social media knows that. If you've been waiting for the next installment of Esta and Harte's story, thanks for sticking around. You've been more than patient, and your support has buoyed me and humbled me. Thank you to each and every reader who sent me notes of encour-agement, who told me that it was okay not to work myself sick, and who told me that you were willing to wait for it. I hope that *The Serpent's Curse* is everything that you hoped it would be. Thank you for sticking with me and these characters. I couldn't do any of this without you.

Thanks, too, to my long-suffering editor, Sarah McCabe, who dealt with more delays and missed deadlines than anyone should. From the very beginning, her keen insights have made this series immeasur-ably better. I am so lucky to be working with someone as supportive and patient as she is. Thank you to everyone at Simon & Schuster: Justin Chanda, Karen Wojtyla, Sarah Creech, Katherine Devendorf, Chelsea Morgan, Sara Berko, Penina Lopez, Valerie Shea, Jen Strada, Lauren Forte, Lauren Hoffman, Caitlin Sweeny, Chrissy Noh, Alissa Nigro, Anna Jarzab, Emily Ritter, Christina Pecorale and the rest of the S&S sales team, Michelle Leo and her education/library team, Nicole Russo, Cassie Malmo, and Ian Reilly. Thank you to Craig Howell for another incredible cover and Drew Willis for the gorgeous map designs. Thank you to Risikat Okedeyi and Shenwei Chang for their thoughtful readings and astute comments on earlier drafts of this book. Their insights made me a better writer, and any failings in this book are completely my own.

I owe an enormous debt of gratitude to my first home at S&S and the entire team at Simon Pulse. I feel fortunate to have had the opportunity to work with Mara Anastas and Liesa Abrams. Mara, especially, supported me and my books from the very beginning, and I will always be grateful to her for the career she helped me build. Thanks as well to my new home at McElderry, who have been awesomely welcoming and supportive as I've finished this book.

A million times a million thanks to the awesome readers of The Devil's Own street team, especially to Amanda Fink, Augustina Zanelli, Daria Covington, Davianna Nieto, Emily Howald, Julieta Ninno, Kayleigh Bowman, Kim McCarty, Sammira Rais-Rohani, and Alessandra Pelligrino. You are all rock stars.

Many thanks to my agent and friend Kathleen Rushall. I am so grateful to have you in my corner. Thank you for keeping me sane and always having my back, even when I don't have my own. Thank you especially for your patience as I figured out that I can't work like a machine—I got there eventually. Mostly. Your support and understanding mean everything. Thanks for being a better advocate for me than I am for myself.

To my writer friends who keep me sane in this bizarre business. To the Fiery Bitches: Jaye Robin Brown, Kristen Lippert-Martin, Angele McQuade, Shanna Beasely, Shannon Doleski, Sara Raasch, Olivia Hinebaugh, Danielle Stinson, Mary Thompson, and Anne Blankman. I hate this stupid virus for ruining our time together this spring, but I admire and miss the hell out of you ladies. Next year, or bust. To Helene Dunbar, Christina June, Scarlet Rose, Abbie Fine, Peternelle van Arsdale, Anna Brightly, Vivi Barnes, Flavia Brunetti, Lev C. Rosen, Jenny Pernovich, Kendal Kulper, and the whole community of kind, talented writers—in person and online—who make me better every day. Thank you to the booksellers and teachers and bloggers who have championed this series. I owe my every success to you.

Finally, to my guys. Jason, Max, and Harry. I'm sorry you had to live with this book right along with me for the last two years. You are patience and love and light, and I'm so glad you're mine. None of this would be worth anything without you.

LISA MAXWELL is the author of the Last Magician series and *Unhooked*. She grew up in Akron, Ohio, and has a PhD in English. She's worked as a teacher, scholar, bookseller, editor, and writer. When she's not writing books, she's a professor at a local college. She now lives in Virginia with her husband and two sons. You can follow her on Twitter and Instagram @LisaMaxwellYA or learn more about her upcoming books at Lisa-Maxwell.com.